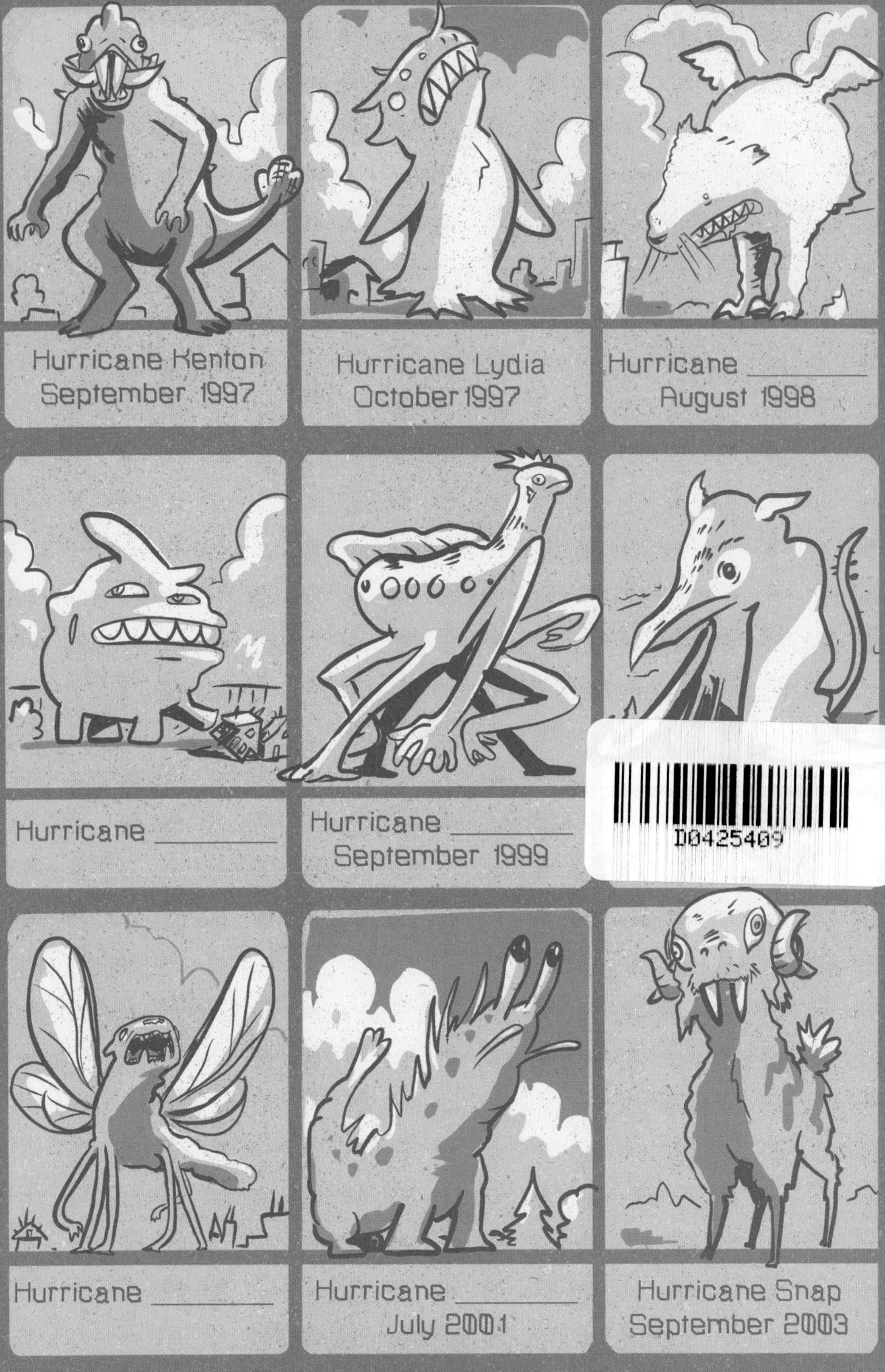
Hurricane Kenton
September 1997
Hurricane Lydia
October 1997
Hurricane ________
August 1998
Hurricane ________
Hurricane ________
September 1999
Hurricane ________
Hurricane ________
July 2001
Hurricane Snap
September 2003

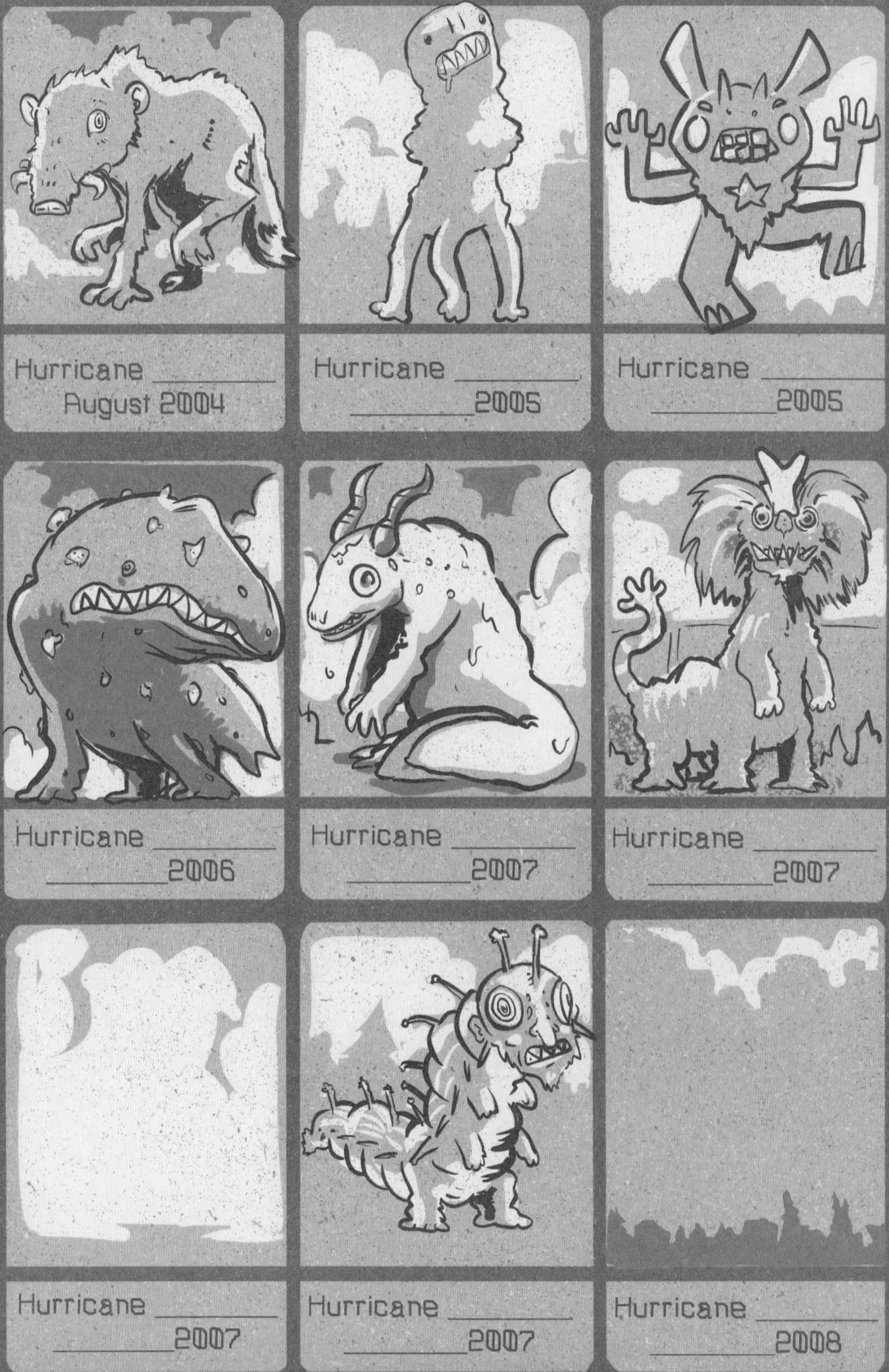

Hurricane ________
August 2004
Hurricane ________
________ 2005
Hurricane ________
________ 2005
Hurricane ________
________ 2006
Hurricane ________
________ 2007
Hurricane ________
________ 2007
Hurricane ________
________ 2007
Hurricane ________
________ 2007
Hurricane ________
________ 2008

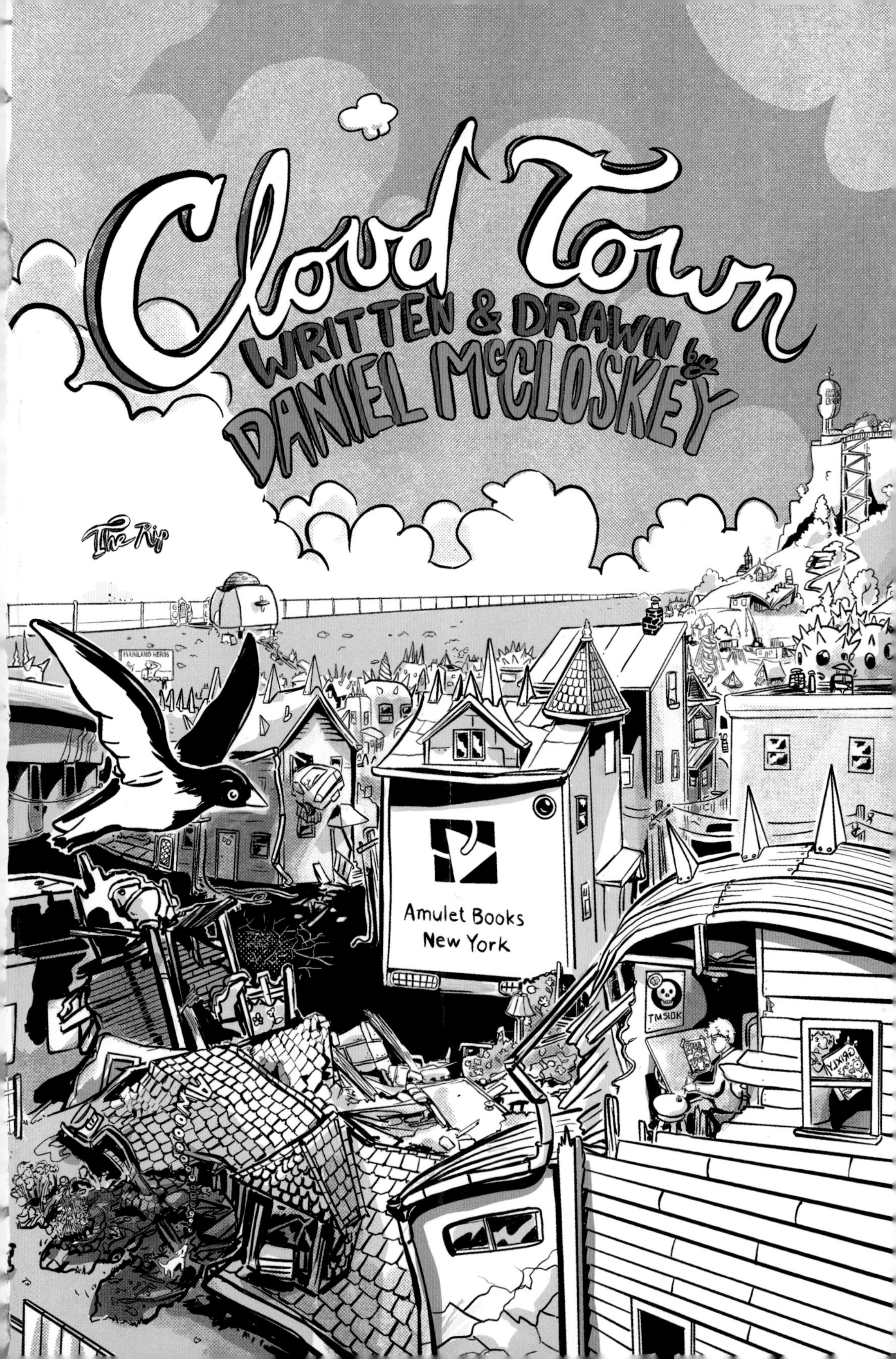
Cloud Town
WRITTEN & DRAWN by
DANIEL McCLOSKEY
The Rip
Amulet Books
New York

PUBLISHER'S NOTE: This is a work of fiction. Names, characters, places, and incidents are either the product of the author's imagination or used fictitiously, and any resemblance to actual persons, living or dead, business establishments, events, or locales is entirely coincidental.

Library of Congress Control Number for the hardcover edition: 2020939758

Hardcover ISBN 978-1-4197-5311-4
Paperback ISBN 978-1-4197-4964-3

Printed and bound in China

Amulet Books are available at special discounts when purchased in quantity for premiums and promotions as well as fundraising or educational use. Special editions can also be created to specification. For details, contact specialsales@abramsbooks.com or the address below.

ABRAMS The Art of Books
195 Broadway, New York NY 10007
abramsbooks.com

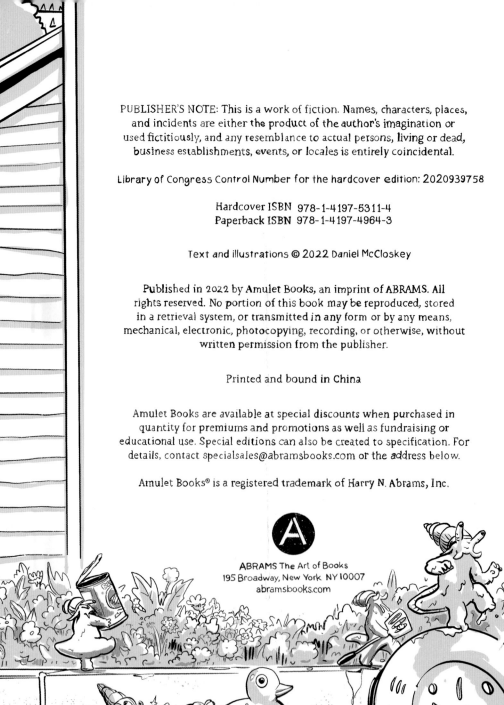

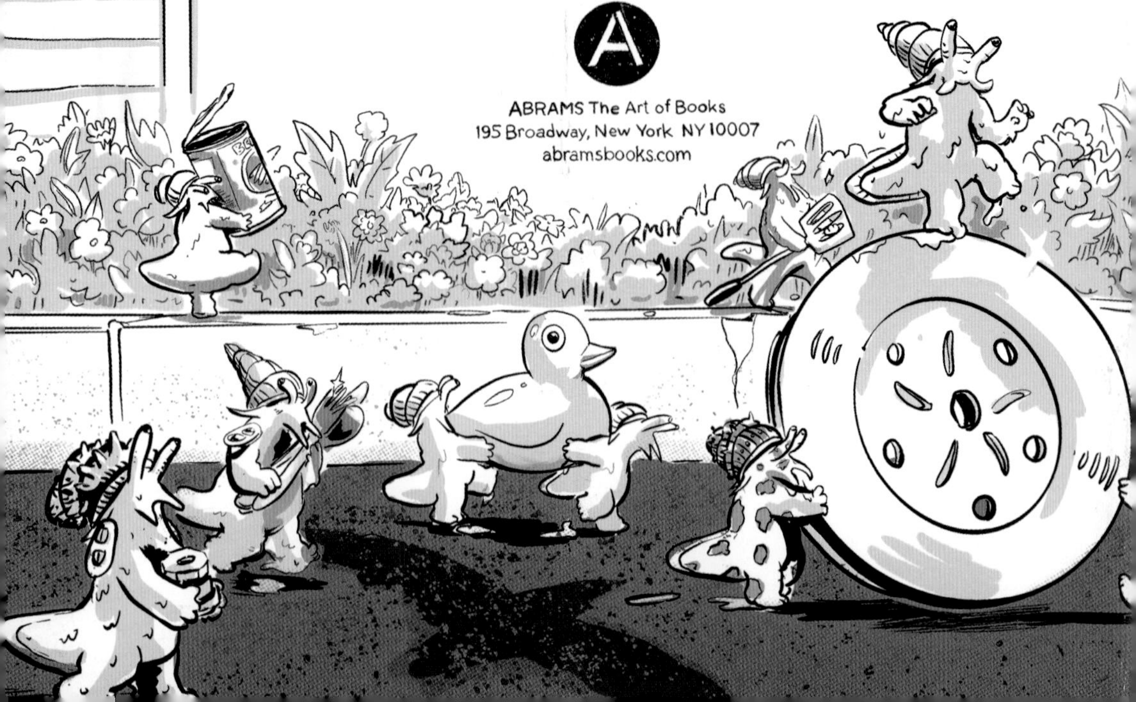

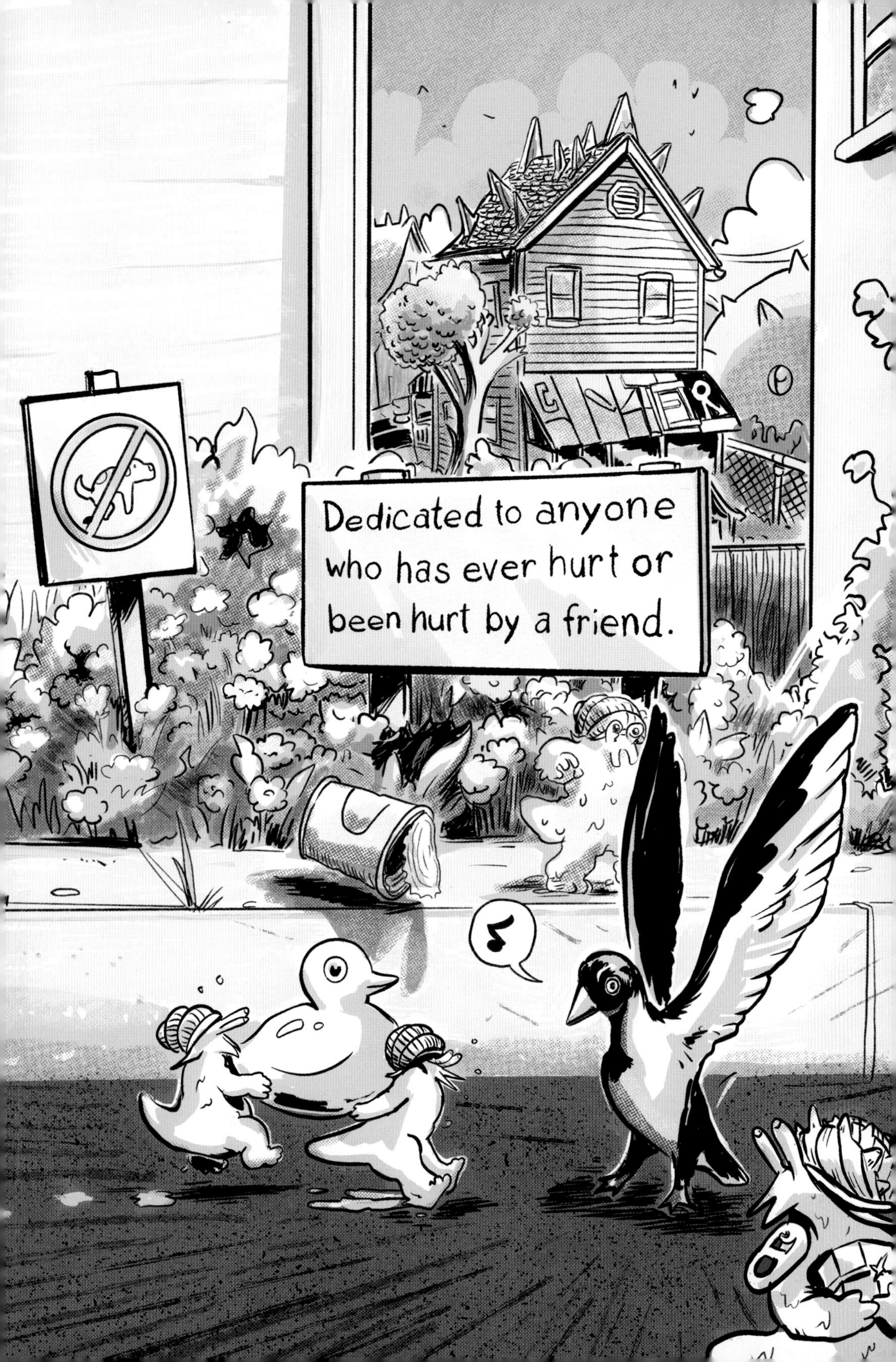
Dedicated to anyone who has ever hurt or been hurt by a friend.

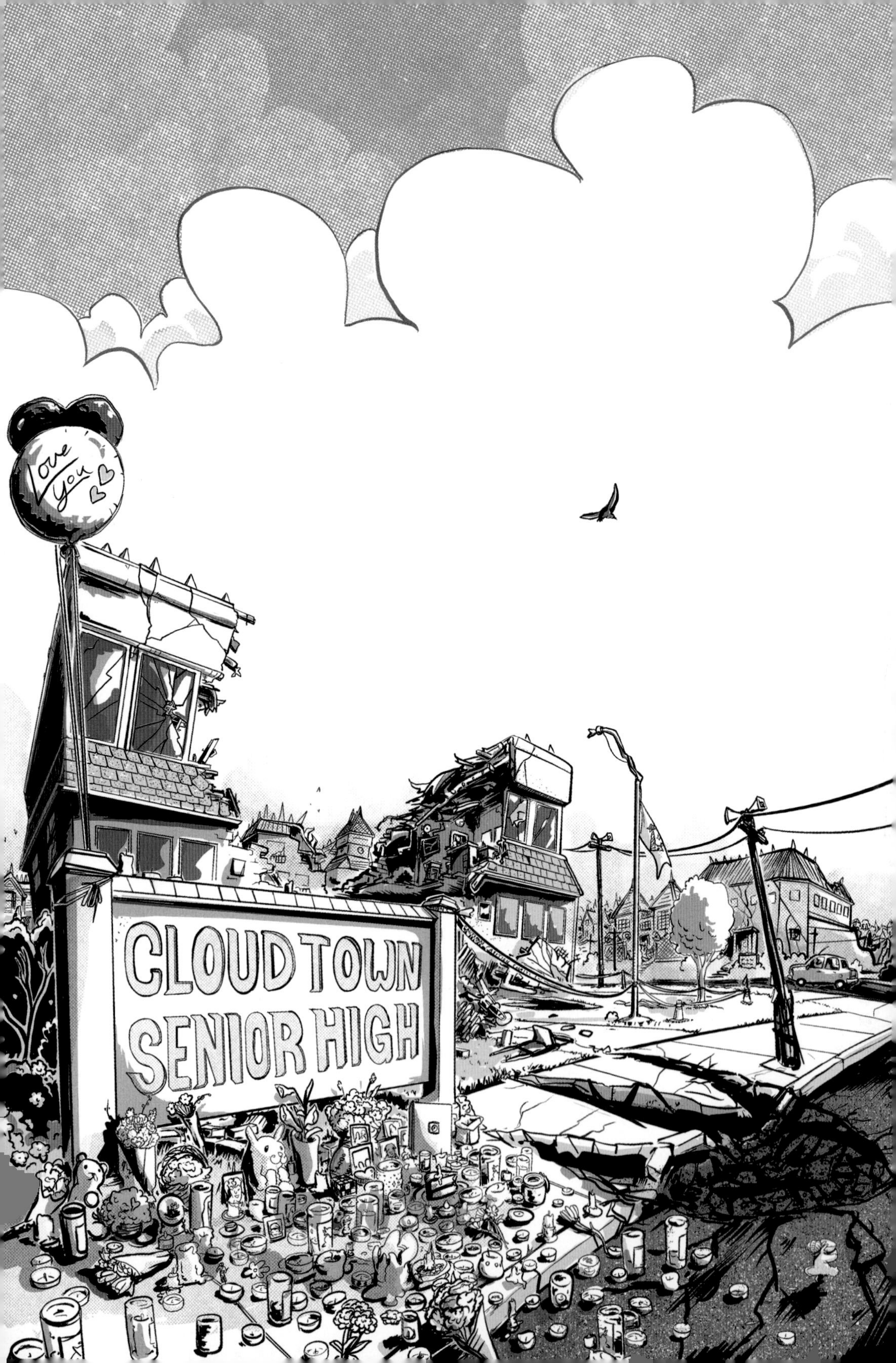
Love you
CLOUD TOWN
SENIOR HIGH

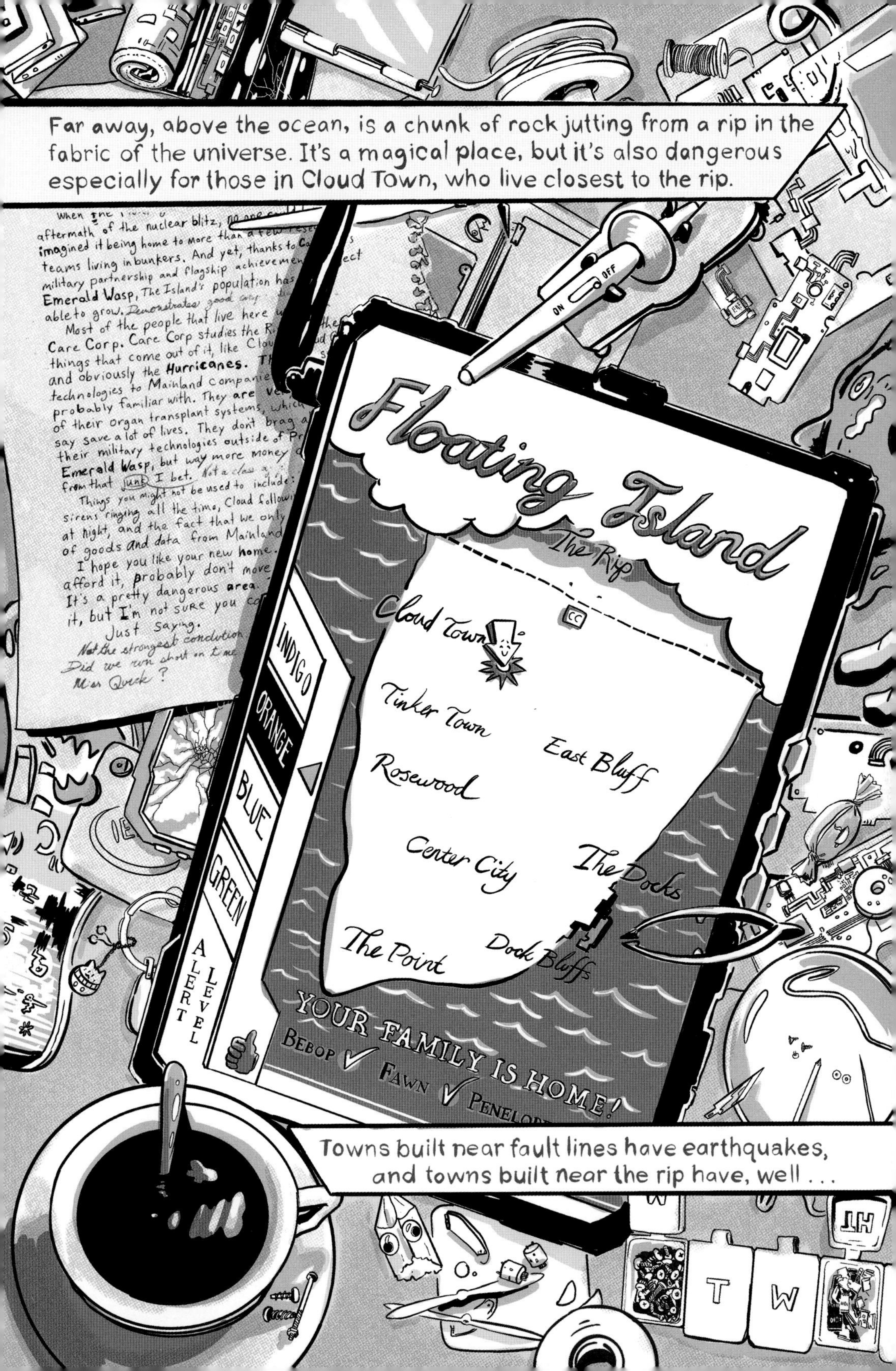

Far away, above the ocean, is a chunk of rock jutting from a rip in the fabric of the universe. It's a magical place, but it's also dangerous especially for those in Cloud Town, who live closest to the rip.
aftermath of the nuclear blitz,
imagined it being home to more than
teams living in bunkers. And yet, thanks to
military partnership and flagship achievemen
Emerald Wasp, The Island's population has
able to grow.
Most of the people that live here
Care Corp. Care Corp studies the
things that come out of it, like
and obviously the Hurricanes.
technologies to Mainland compan
probably familiar with. They are
of their organ transplant systems,
say save a lot of lives. They don't brag
their military technologies outside of
Emerald Wasp, but way more money
from that junk I bet.
Things you might not be used to include:
sirens ringing all the time, Cloud followi
at night, and the fact that we only
of goods and data from Mainland
I hope you like your new home.
afford it, probably don't move
It's a pretty dangerous area.
it, but I'm not sure you c
Just saying.
Did we run short on time
M's Quick ?
Floating Island
The Rip
CC
Cloud Town
Tinker Town
East Bluff
Rosewood
Center City
The Docks
The Point
Dock Bluffs
INDIGO
ORANGE
BLUE
GREEN
ALERT LEVEL
YOUR FAMILY IS HOME!
Bebop ✓ Fawn ✓ Penelo
ON
OFF
Towns built near fault lines have earthquakes, and towns built near the rip have, well . . .
T
W

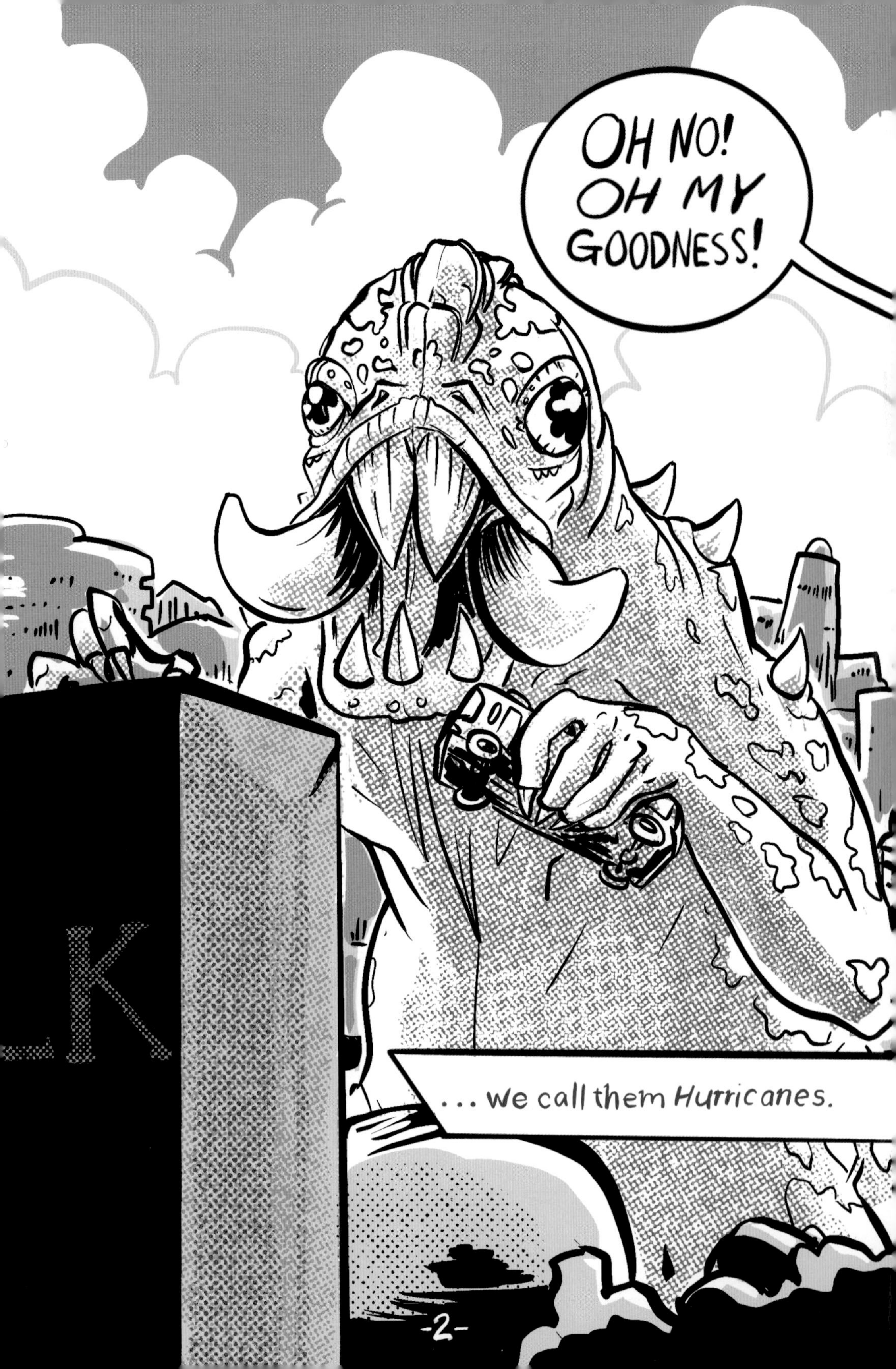
OH NO! OH MY GOODNESS!
... we call them Hurricanes.
LK

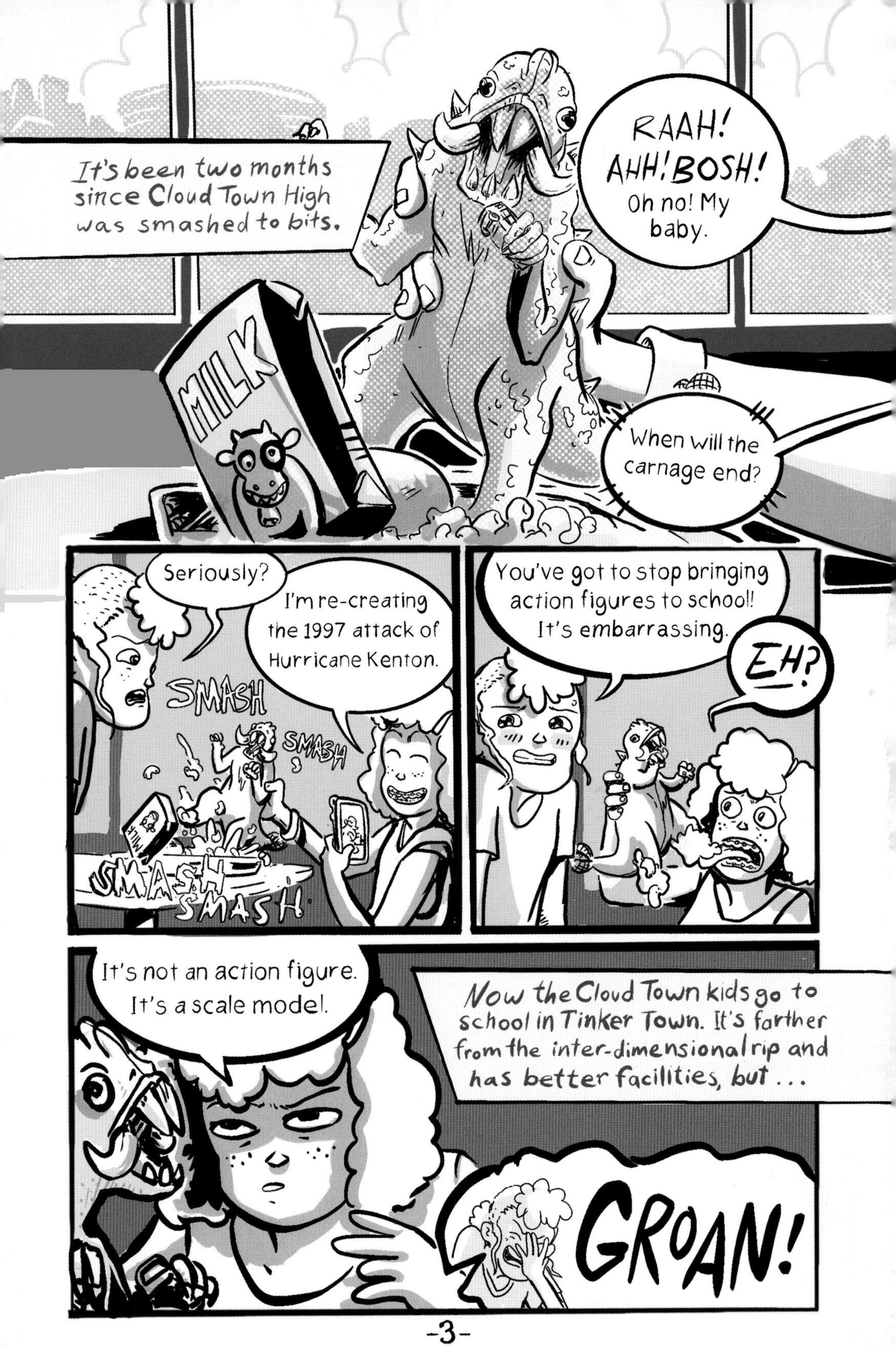
It's been two months since Cloud Town High was smashed to bits.
RAAH! AHH! BOSH! Oh no! My baby.
MILK
When will the carnage end?
Seriously?
I'm re-creating the 1997 attack of Hurricane Kenton.
SMASH
SMASH
SMASH
SMASH
MILK
You've got to stop bringing action figures to school! It's embarrassing.
EH?
It's not an action figure. It's a scale model.
Now the Cloud Town kids go to school in Tinker Town. It's farther from the inter-dimensional rip and has better facilities, but . . .
GROAN!

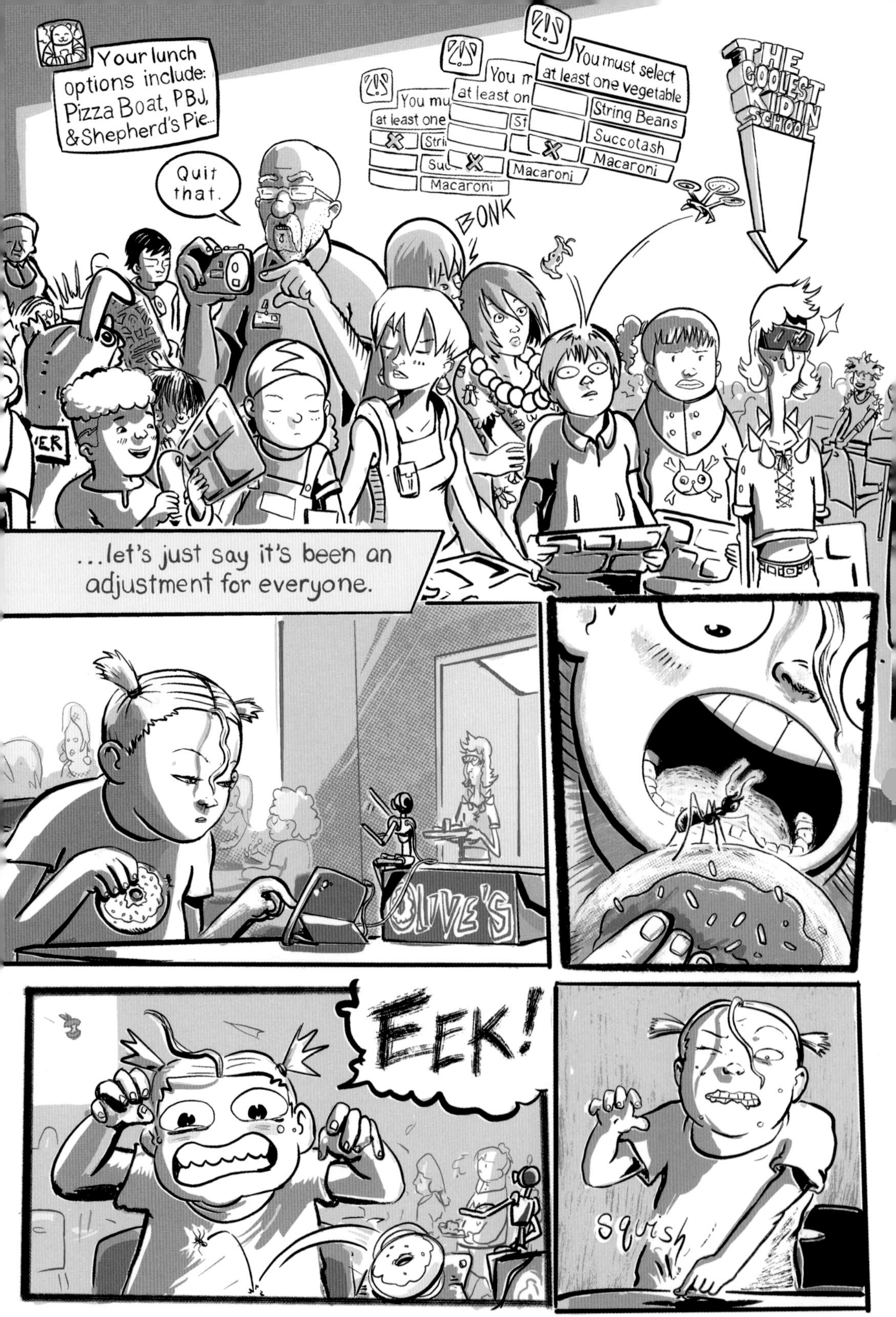
Your lunch options include: Pizza Boat, PBJ, & Shepherd's Pie...
Quit that.
You mu
at least one
Stri
Suc
Macaroni
You m
at least on
St
Macaroni
You must select at least one vegetable
String Beans
Succotash
Macaroni
BONK
THE COOLEST KID IN SCHOOL
...let's just say it's been an adjustment for everyone.
OLIVE'S
EEK!
squish

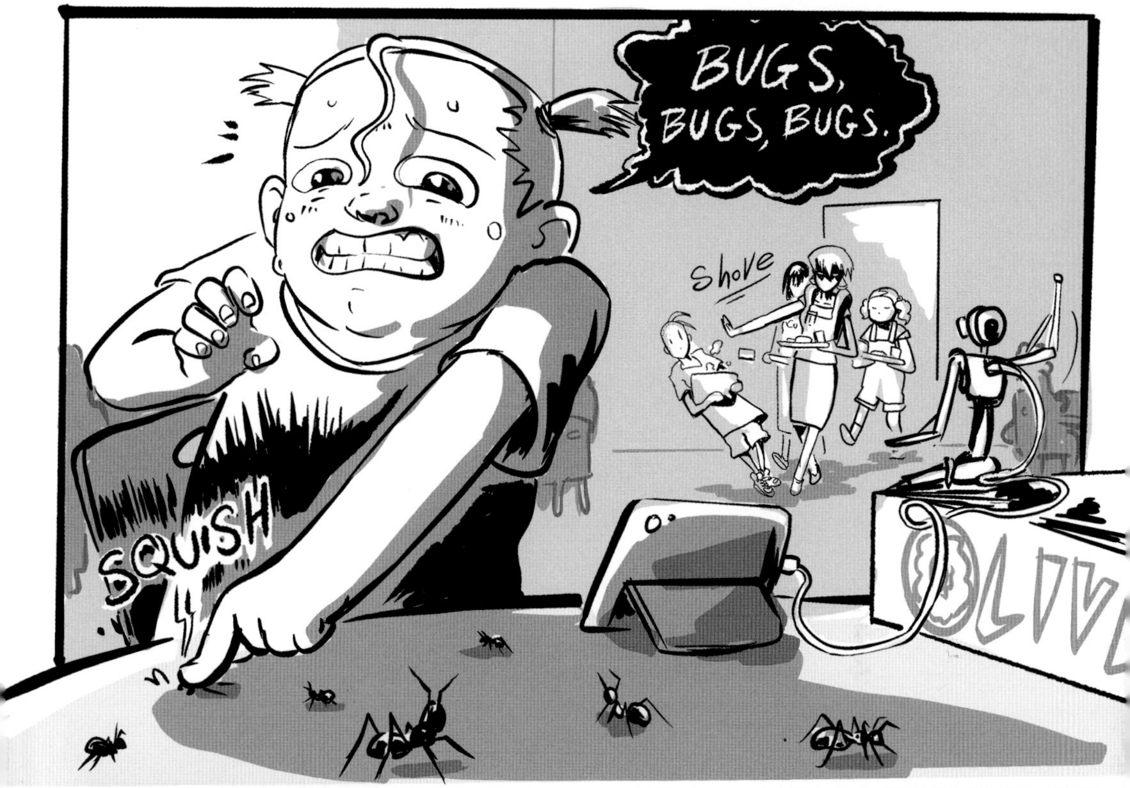
BUGS, BUGS, BUGS.
Shove
SQUISH

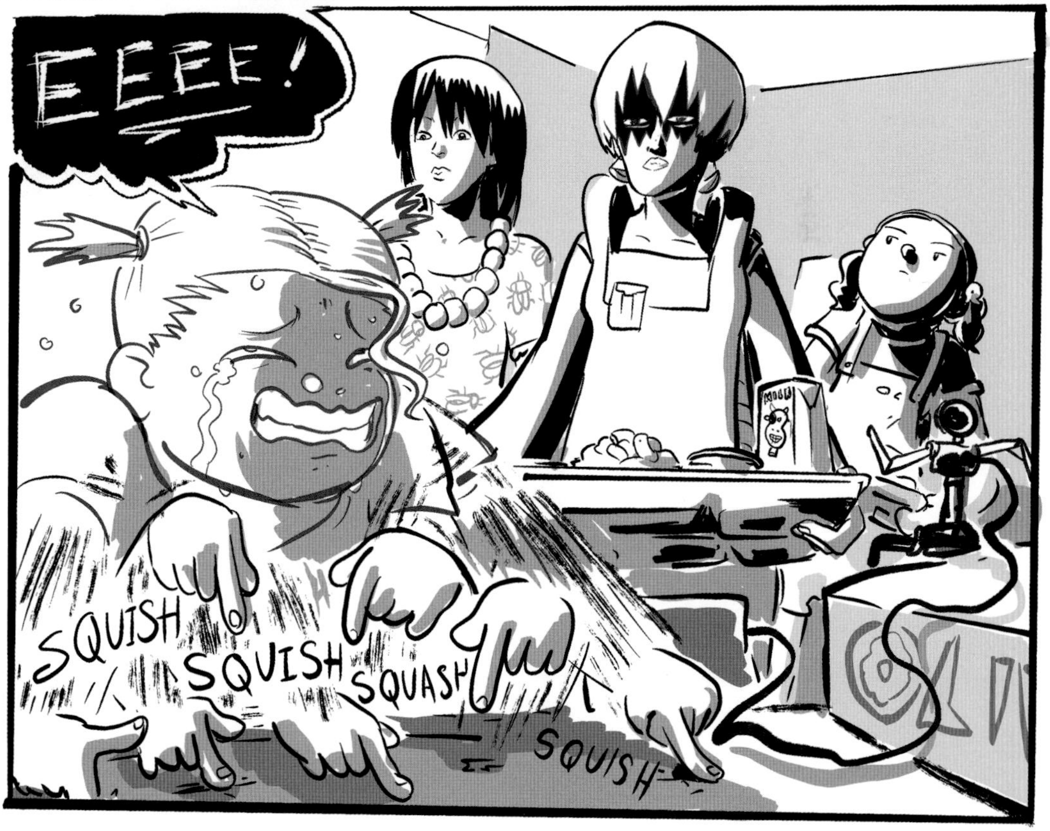
EEEE!
SQUISH
SQUISH
SQUASH
SQUISH

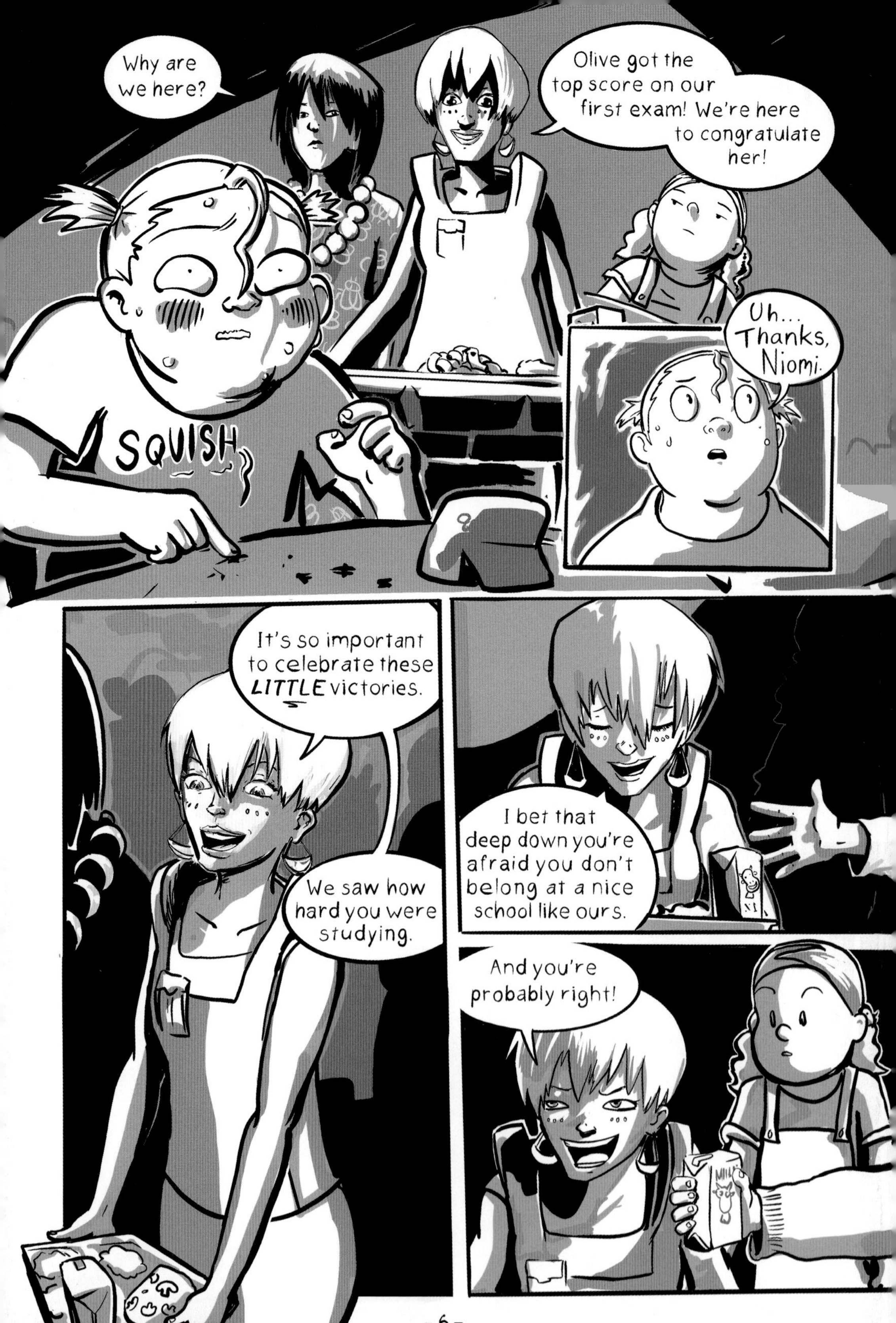

Why are we here?
Olive got the top score on our first exam! We're here to congratulate her!
SQUISH
Uh... Thanks, Niomi.
It's so important to celebrate these LITTLE victories.
We saw how hard you were studying.
I bet that deep down you're afraid you don't belong at a nice school like ours.
And you're probably right!

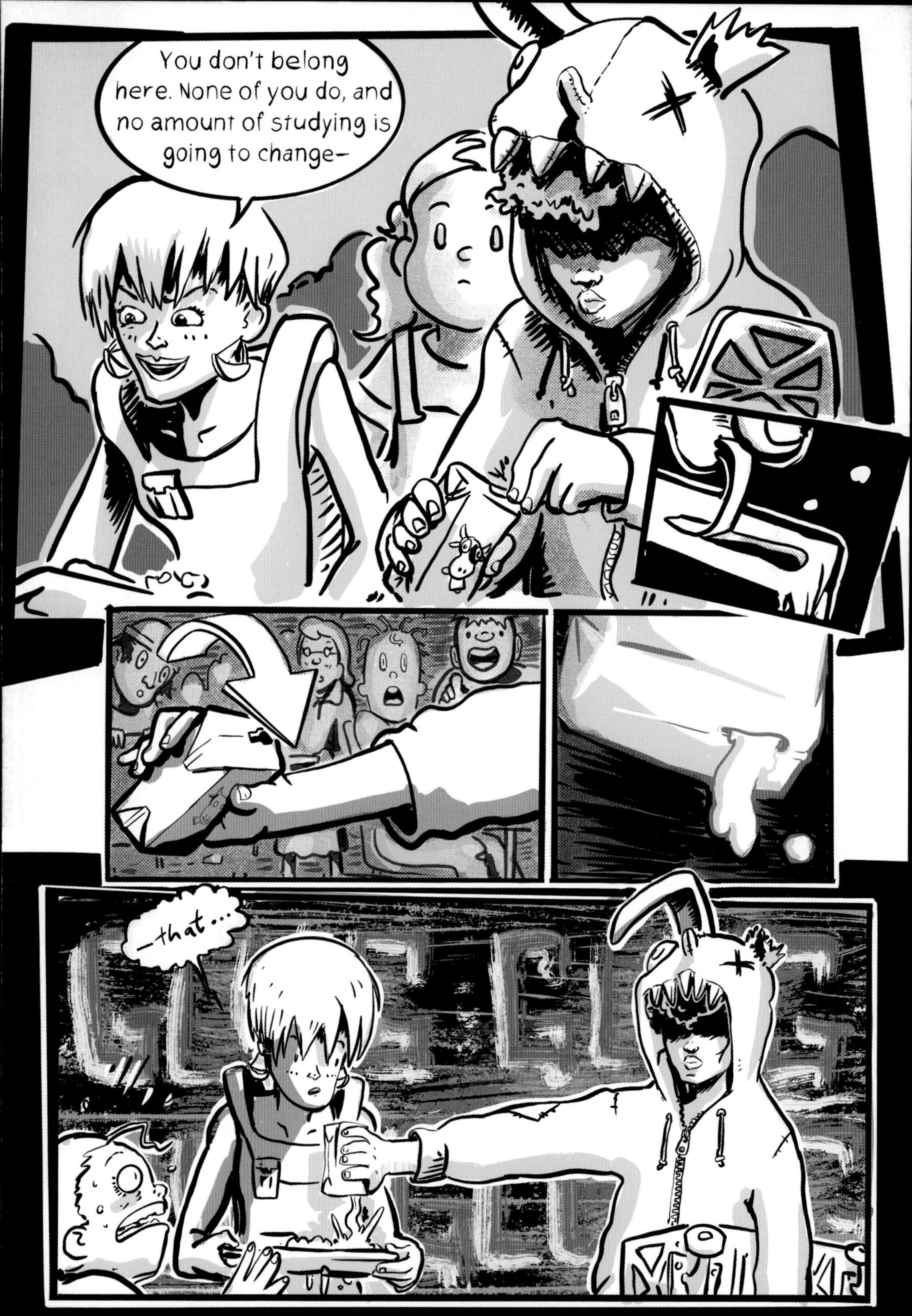
You don't belong here. None of you do, and no amount of studying is going to change-
-that...

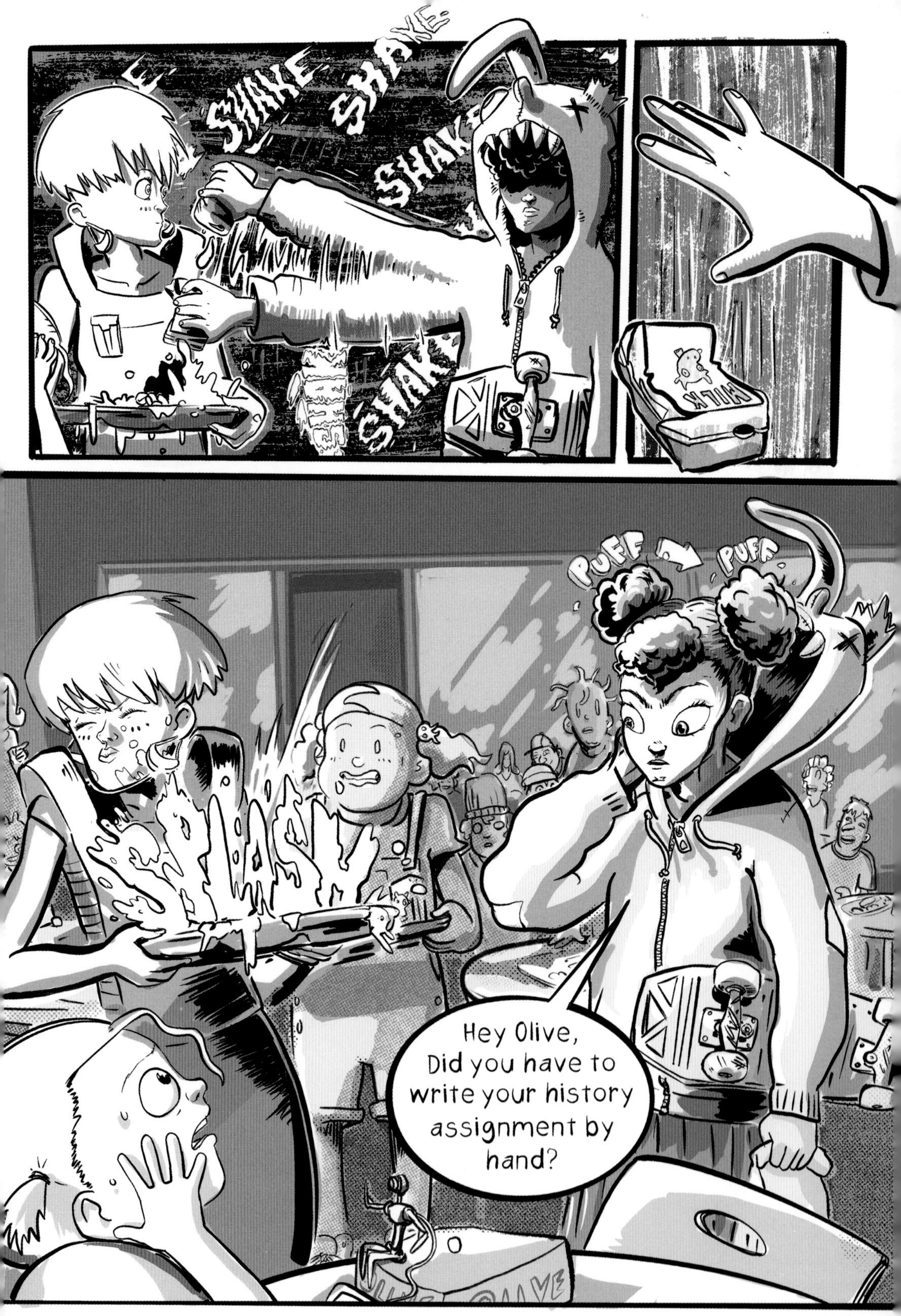
SHAKE
SHAKE
SHAKE
SHAKE
PUFF
PUFF
Hey Olive,
Did you have to
write your history
assignment by
hand?

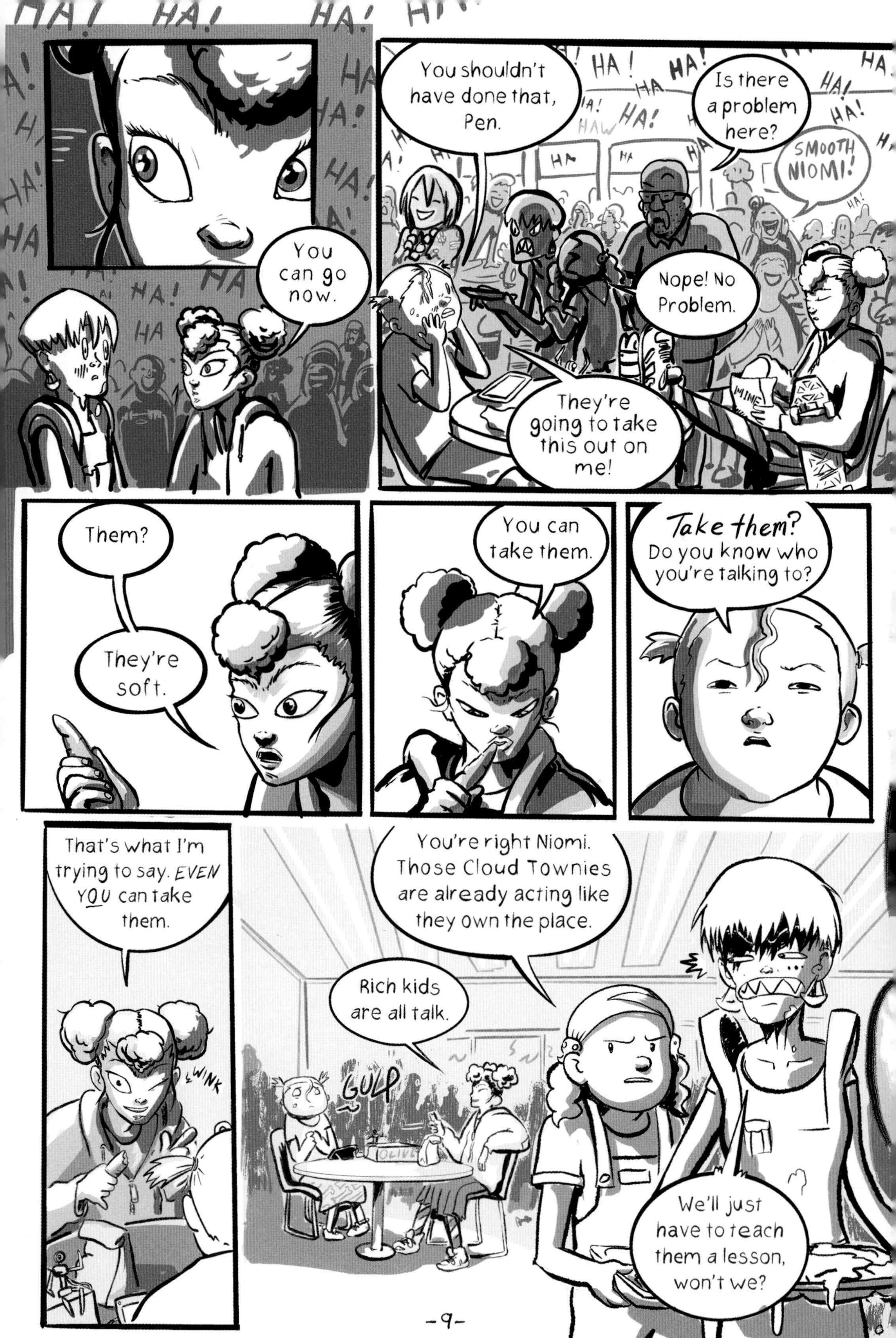
HA! HA! HA!
You can go now.
You shouldn't have done that, Pen.
HA! HA!
Is there a problem here?
SMOOTH NIOMI!
Nope! No Problem.
They're going to take this out on me!
MINE
Them?
They're soft.
You can take them.
Take them? Do you know who you're talking to?
That's what I'm trying to say. EVEN YOU can take them.
WINK
You're right Niomi. Those Cloud Townies are already acting like they own the place.
Rich kids are all talk.
GULP
OLIVE
We'll just have to teach them a lesson, won't we?

Hardly anyone would live on Floating Island if it weren't for Care Corp. Care Corp studies the rip and uses what they learn to build things.

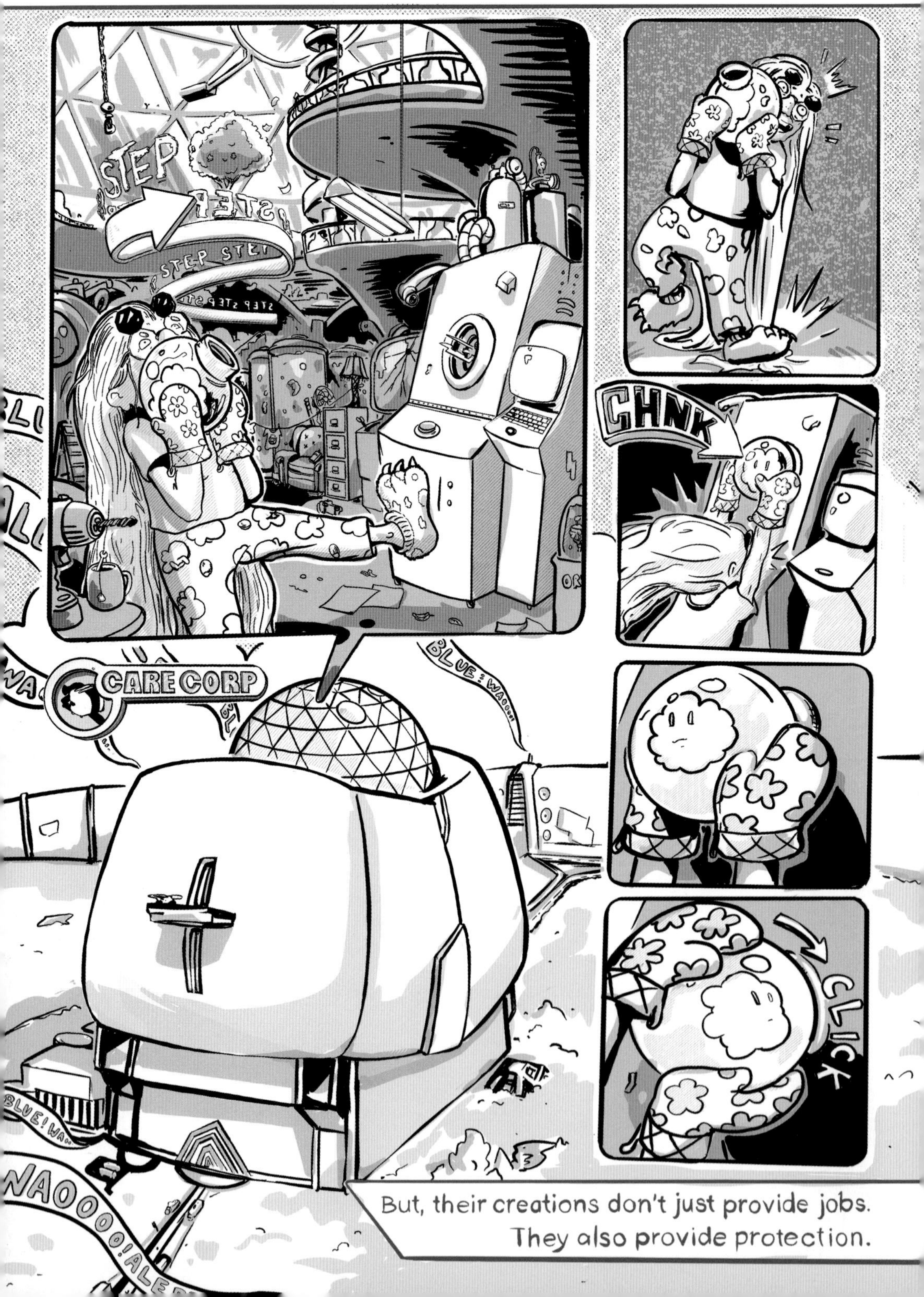
STEP
STEP STEP
CHNK
CARE CORP
CLICK
But, their creations don't just provide jobs.
They also provide protection.

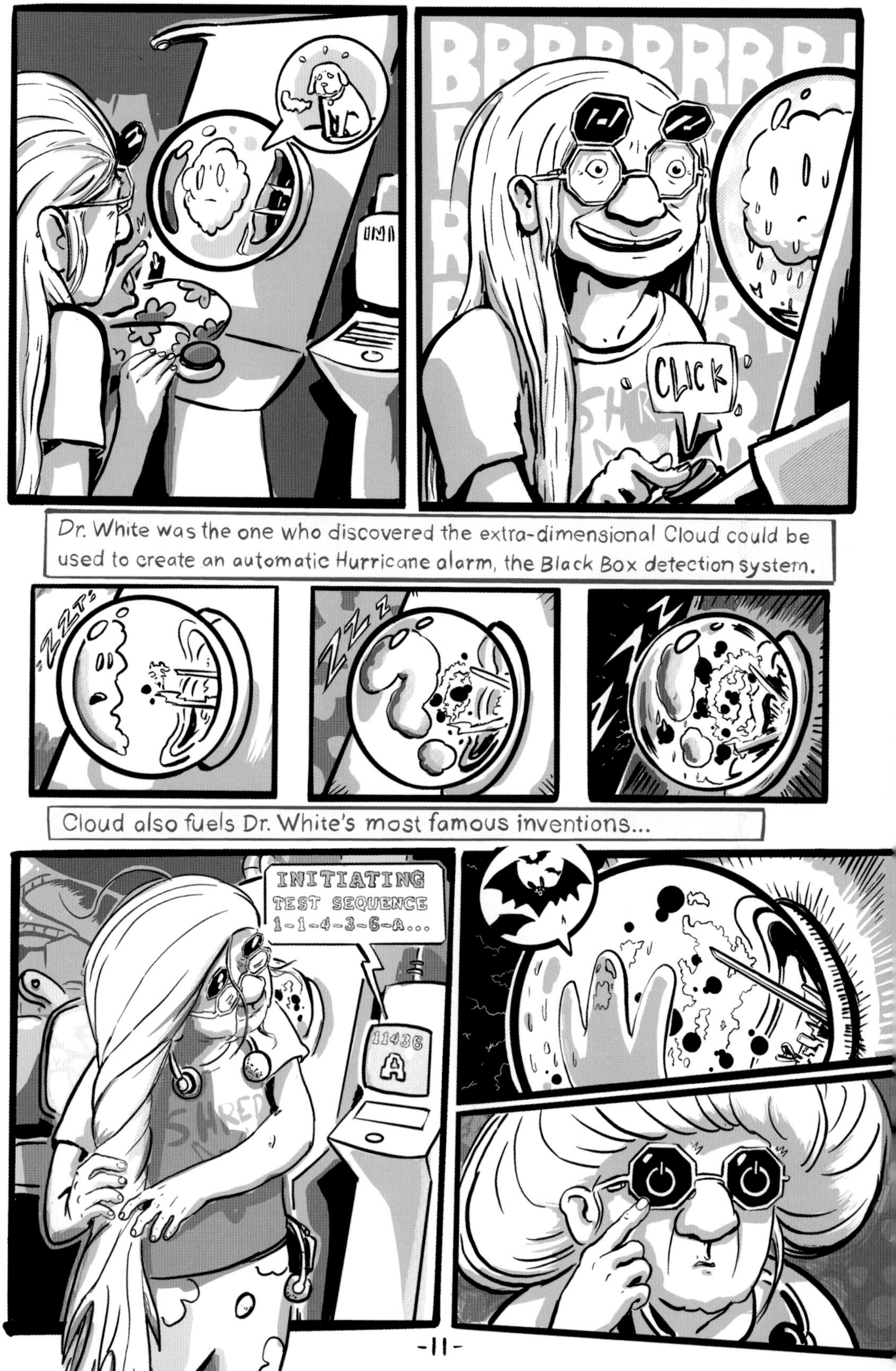
BRRRRRRR
CLICK
Dr. White was the one who discovered the extra-dimensional Cloud could be used to create an automatic Hurricane alarm, the Black Box detection system.
ZZZT
ZZZ
Z
Cloud also fuels Dr. White's most famous inventions...
INITIATING TEST SEQUENCE 1-1-4-3-6-A...
11436
A
SHRED

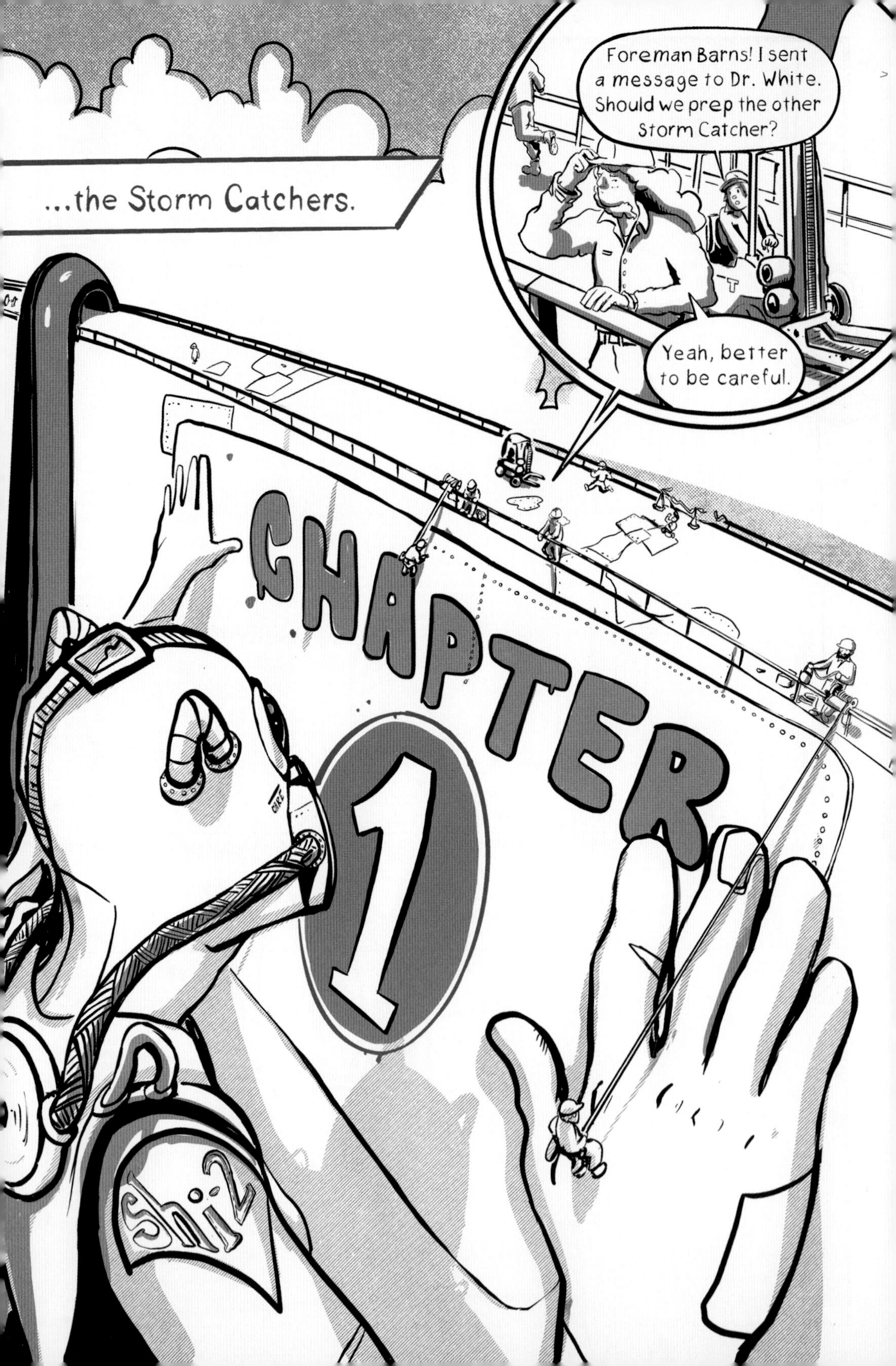
...the Storm Catchers.
Foreman Barns! I sent a message to Dr. White. Should we prep the other Storm Catcher?
Yeah, better to be careful.
CHAPTER
1

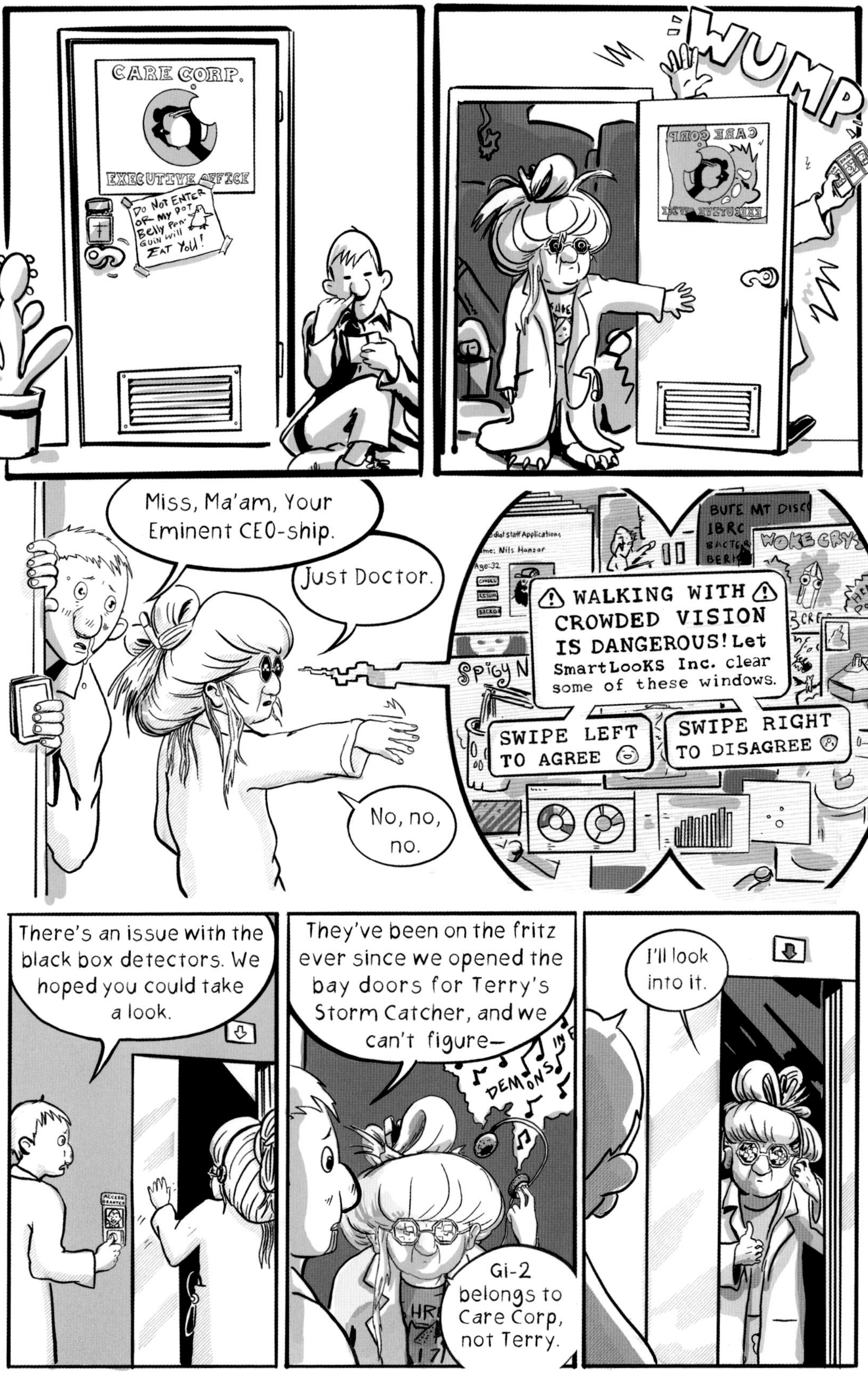
CARE CORP.
EXECUTIVE OFFICE
Do Not ENTER OR My POT Belly Pen-Guin will EAT YOU!
WUMP
Miss, Ma'am, Your Eminent CEO-ship.
Just Doctor.
WALKING WITH CROWDED VISION IS DANGEROUS! Let SmartLooKS Inc. clear some of these windows.
SWIPE LEFT TO AGREE
SWIPE RIGHT TO DISAGREE
No, no, no.
There's an issue with the black box detectors. We hoped you could take a look.
They've been on the fritz ever since we opened the bay doors for Terry's Storm Catcher, and we can't figure—
DEMONS IN
Gi-2 belongs to Care Corp, not Terry.
I'll look into it.

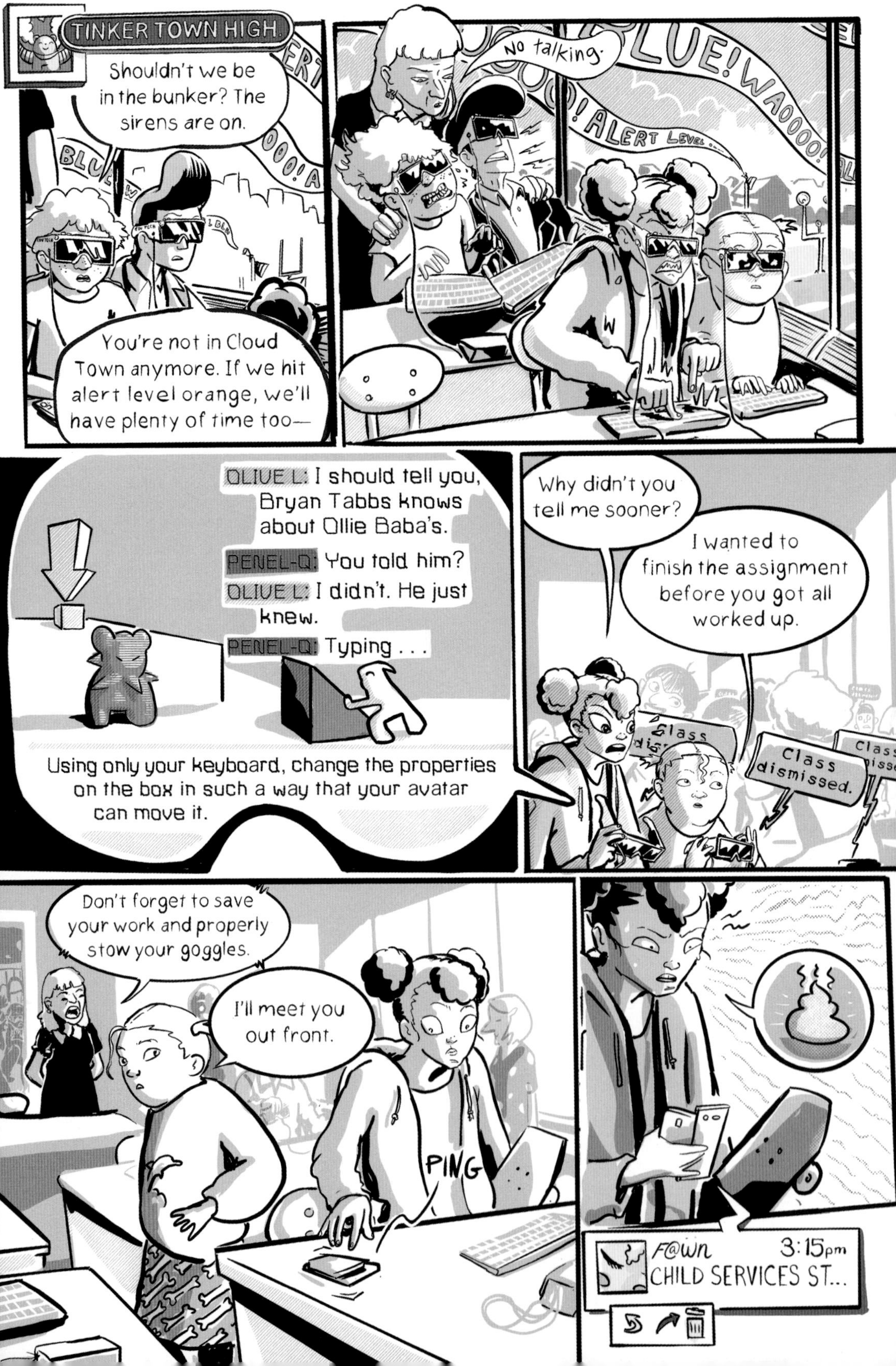
TINKER TOWN HIGH.
Shouldn't we be in the bunker? The sirens are on.
You're not in Cloud Town anymore. If we hit alert level orange, we'll have plenty of time too—
No talking.
BLUE! WAOOOO! ALERT LEVEL...
OLIVE L: I should tell you, Bryan Tabbs knows about Ollie Baba's.
PENEL-Q: You told him?
OLIVE L: I didn't. He just knew.
PENEL-Q: Typing . . .
Using only your keyboard, change the properties on the box in such a way that your avatar can move it.
Why didn't you tell me sooner?
I wanted to finish the assignment before you got all worked up.
Class dismissed.
Don't forget to save your work and properly stow your goggles.
I'll meet you out front.
PING
F@wn 3:15pm
CHILD SERVICES ST...

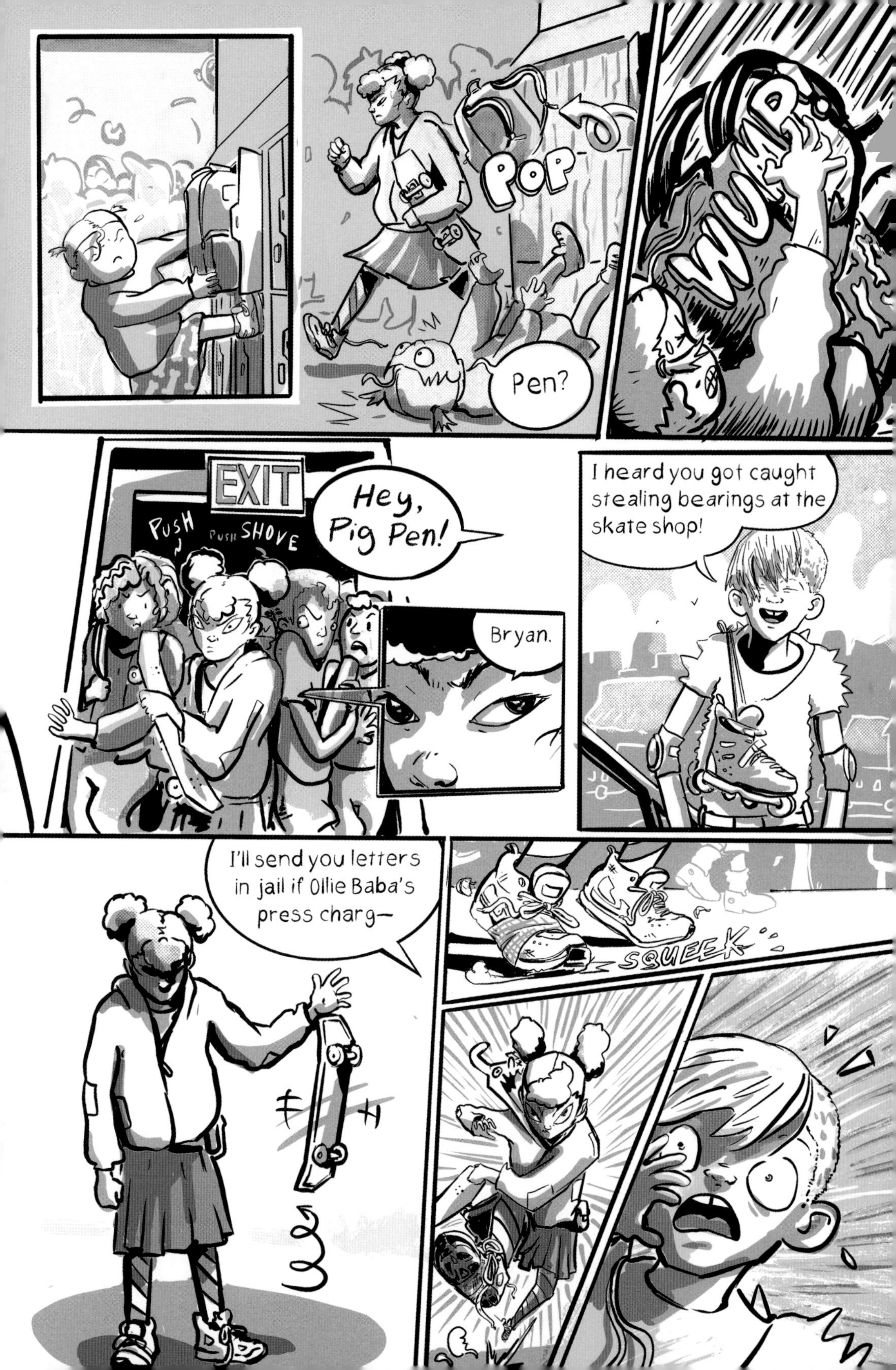
POP
Pen?
WUMP
EXIT
PUSH
PUSH SHOVE
Hey, Pig Pen!
Bryan.
I heard you got caught stealing bearings at the skate shop!
I'll send you letters in jail if Ollie Baba's press charg—
SQUEEK

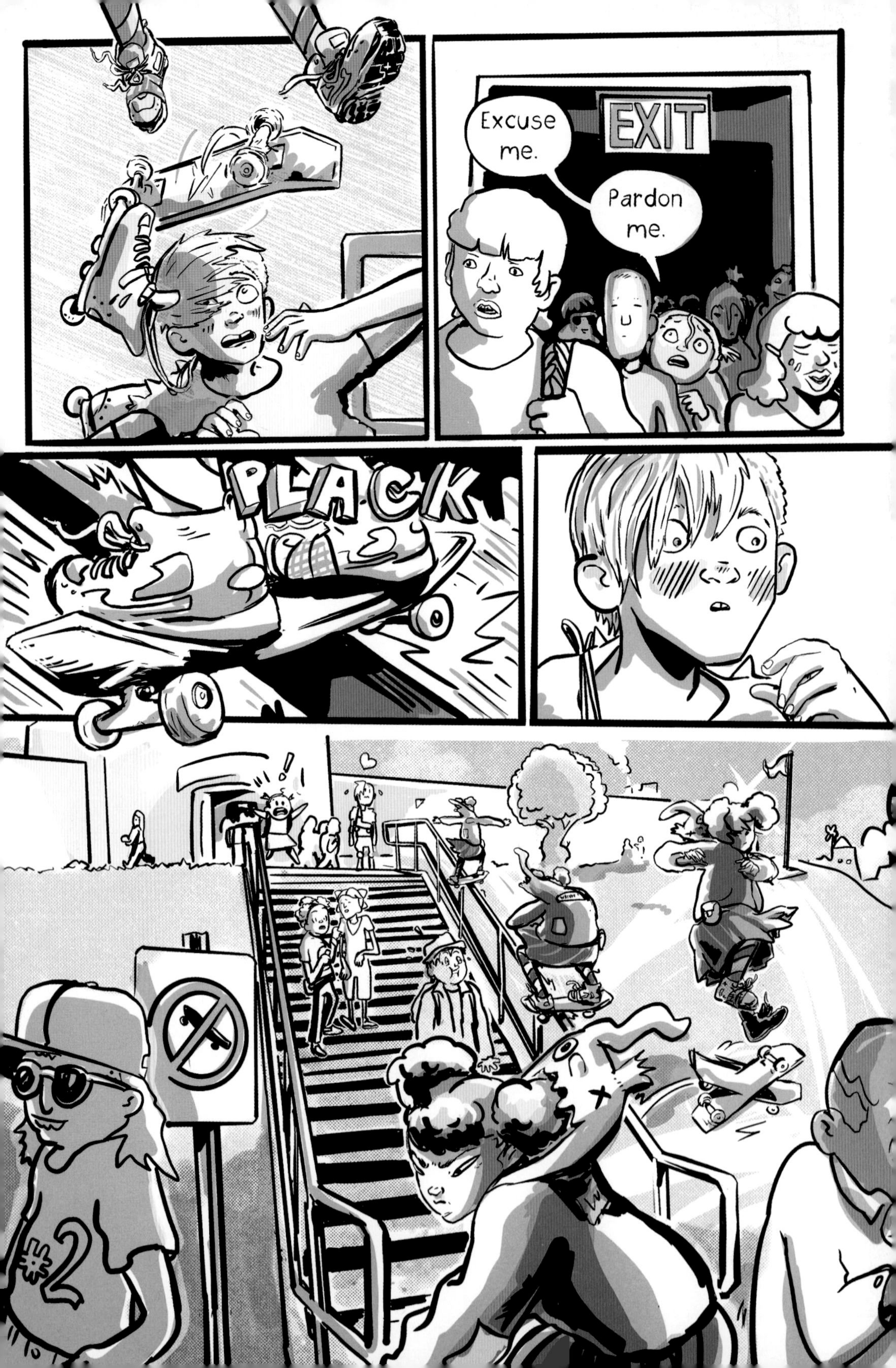

EXIT
Excuse me.
Pardon me.
PLACK
#2

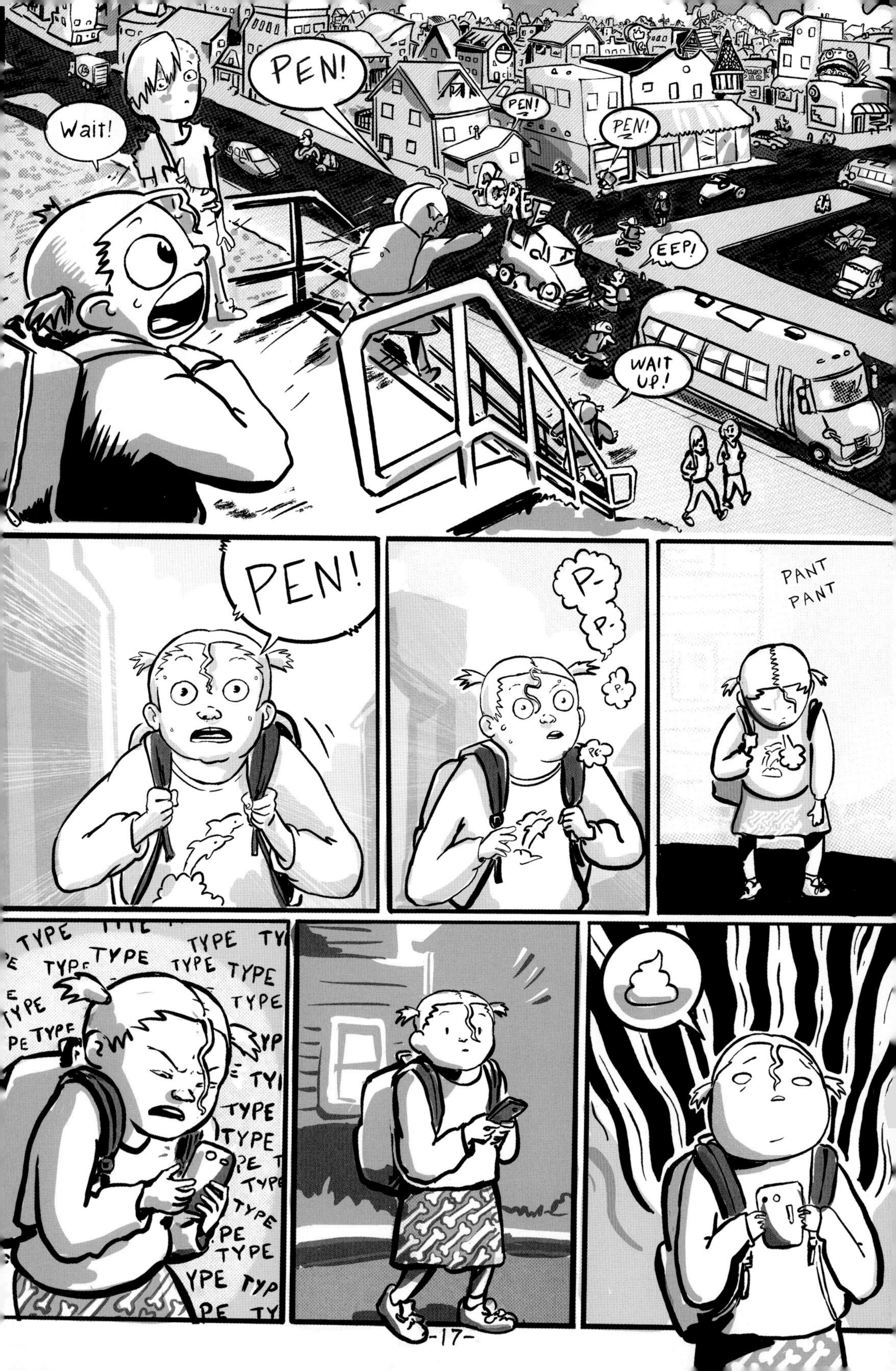
Wait!
PEN!
PEN!
PEN!
EEP!
WAIT UP!
PEN!
P-
P-
PANT
PANT
TYPE
TYPE
TYPE
TYPE
TYPE
TYPE
TYPE
TYPE
TYPE
TYPE

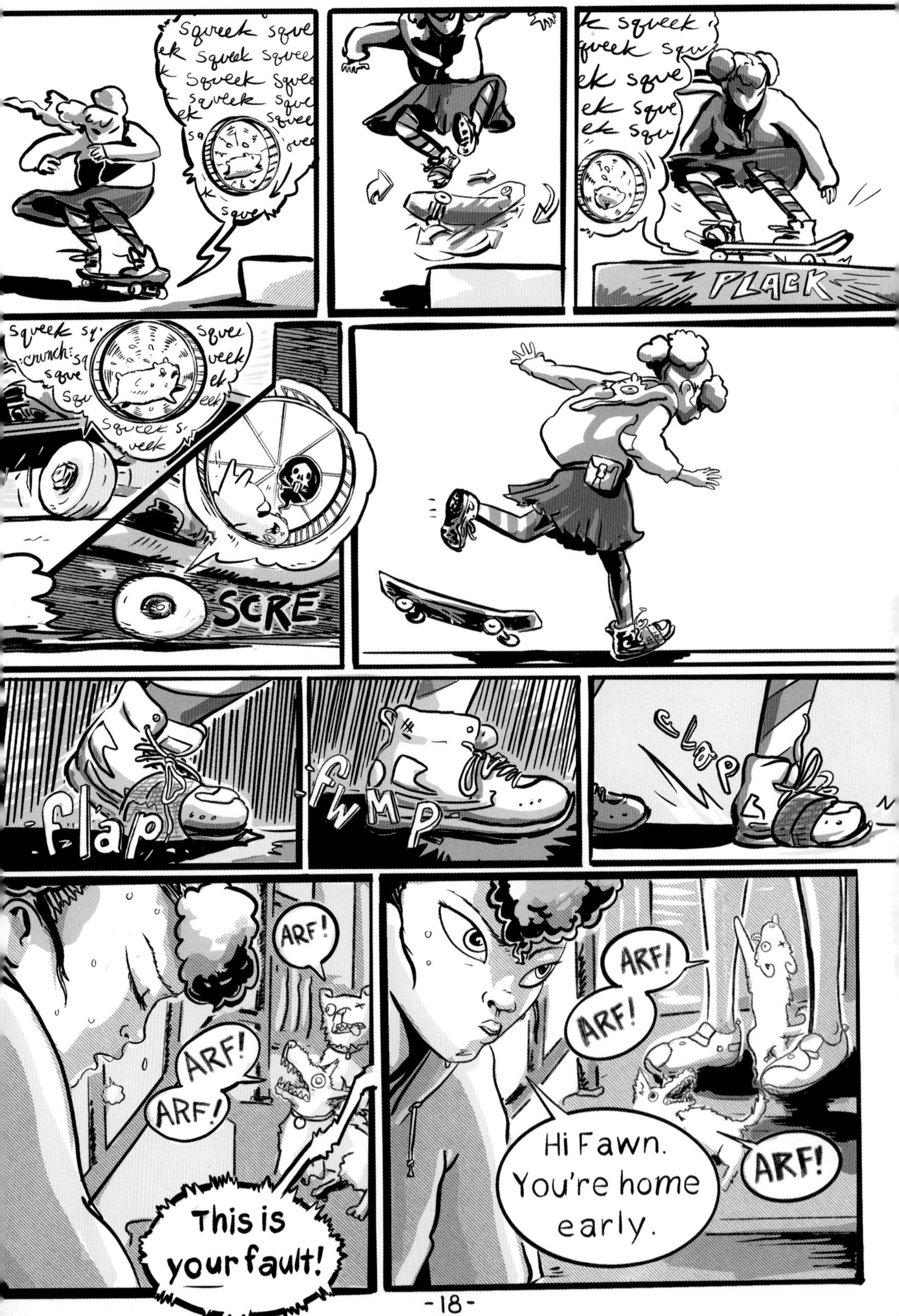
squeek squeek squeek squeek squeek squeek squeek squeek squeek squeek
squeek squeek squeek squeek squeek
PLACK
squeek :crunch: squeek squeek squeek squeek squeek squeek
SCRE
flap
fwmp
clop
ARF!
ARF!
ARF!
This is your fault!
ARF!
ARF!
Hi Fawn. You're home early.
ARF!

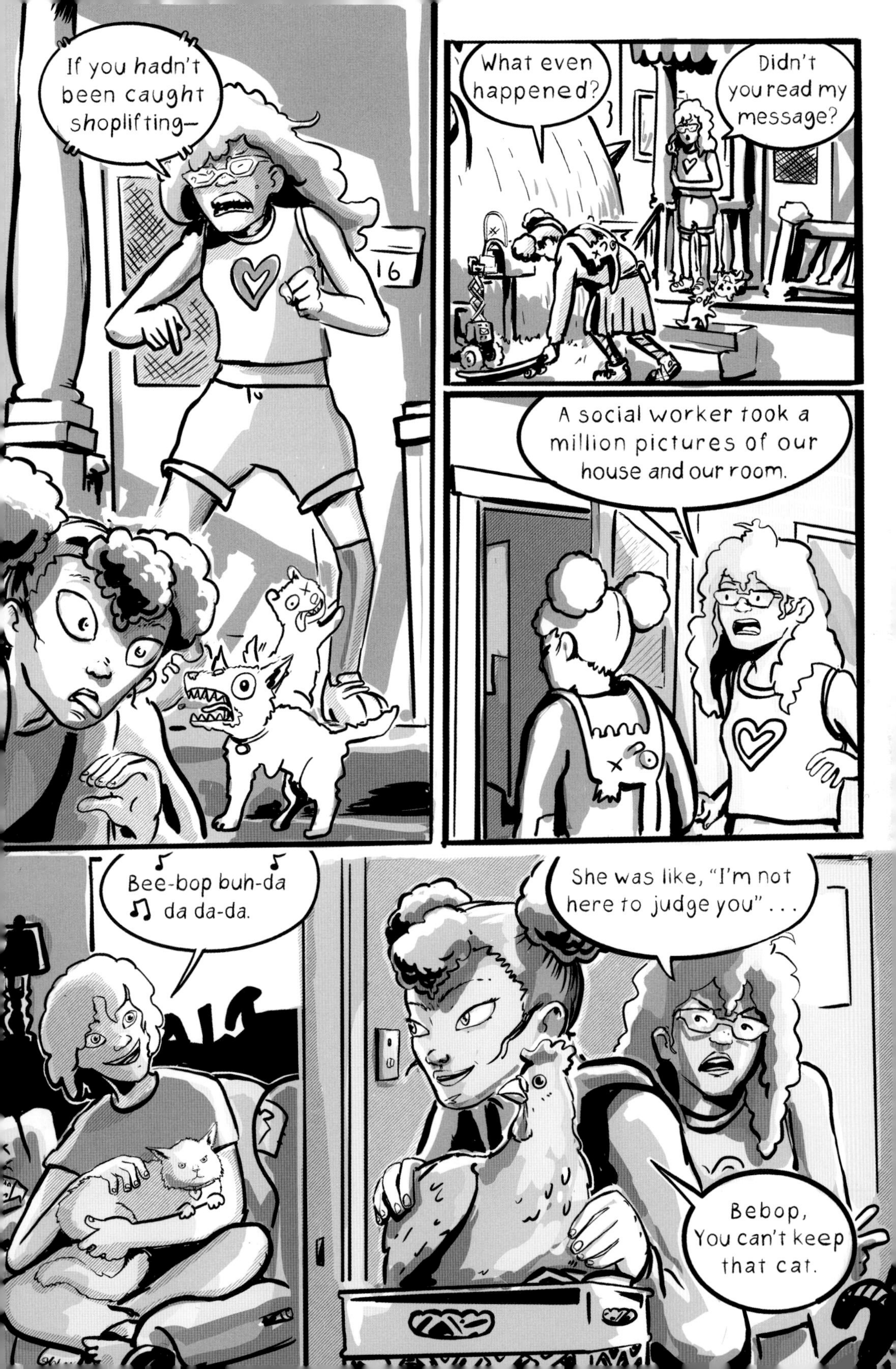
If you hadn't been caught shoplifting—
What even happened?
Didn't you read my message?
A social worker took a million pictures of our house and our room.
Bee-bop buh-da da da-da.
She was like, "I'm not here to judge you" . . .
Bebop, You can't keep that cat.

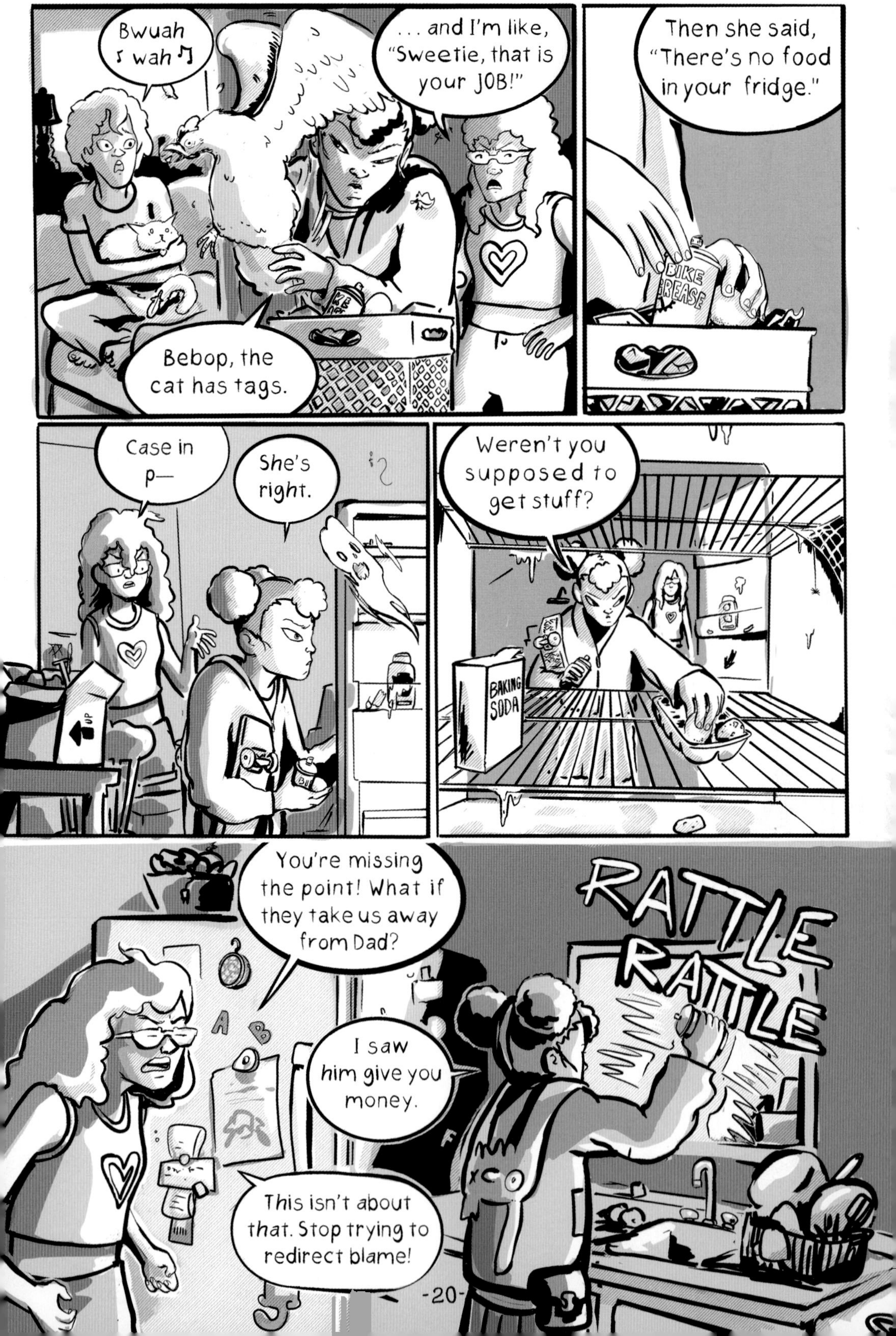
Bwuah ♪ wah ♫
... and I'm like, "Sweetie, that is your JOB!"
Bebop, the cat has tags.
Then she said, "There's no food in your fridge."
BIKE GREASE
Case in p—
She's right.
UP
Weren't you supposed to get stuff?
BAKING SODA
You're missing the point! What if they take us away from Dad?
RATTLE RATTLE
I saw him give you money.
This isn't about that. Stop trying to redirect blame!

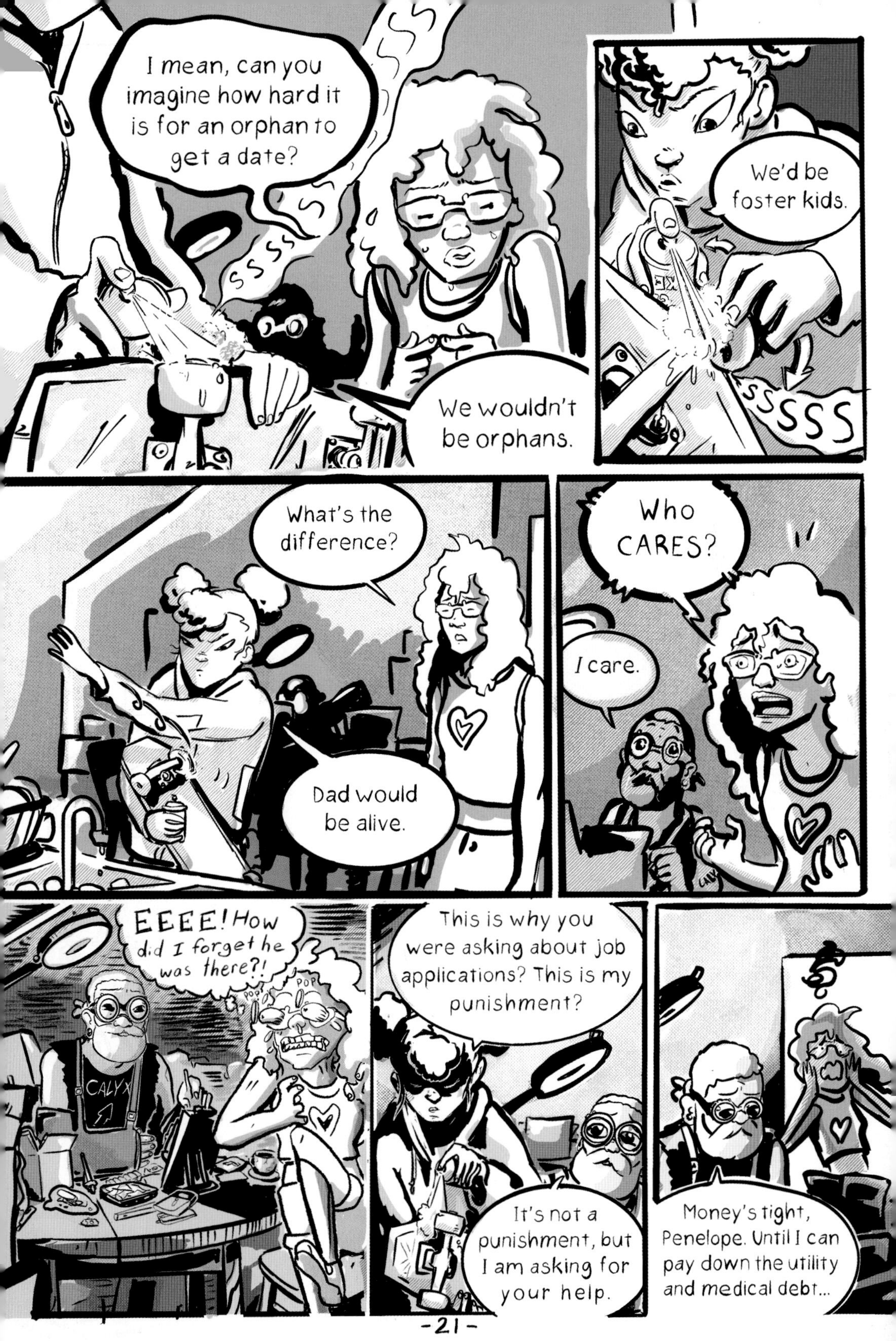
I mean, can you imagine how hard it is for an orphan to get a date?
SSSSS
We wouldn't be orphans.
We'd be foster kids.
SSSSS
What's the difference?
Dad would be alive.
Who CARES?
I care.
EEEE! How did I forget he was there?!
POP POP POP
CALYX
This is why you were asking about job applications? This is my punishment?
It's not a punishment, but I am asking for your help.
Money's tight, Penelope. Until I can pay down the utility and medical debt...

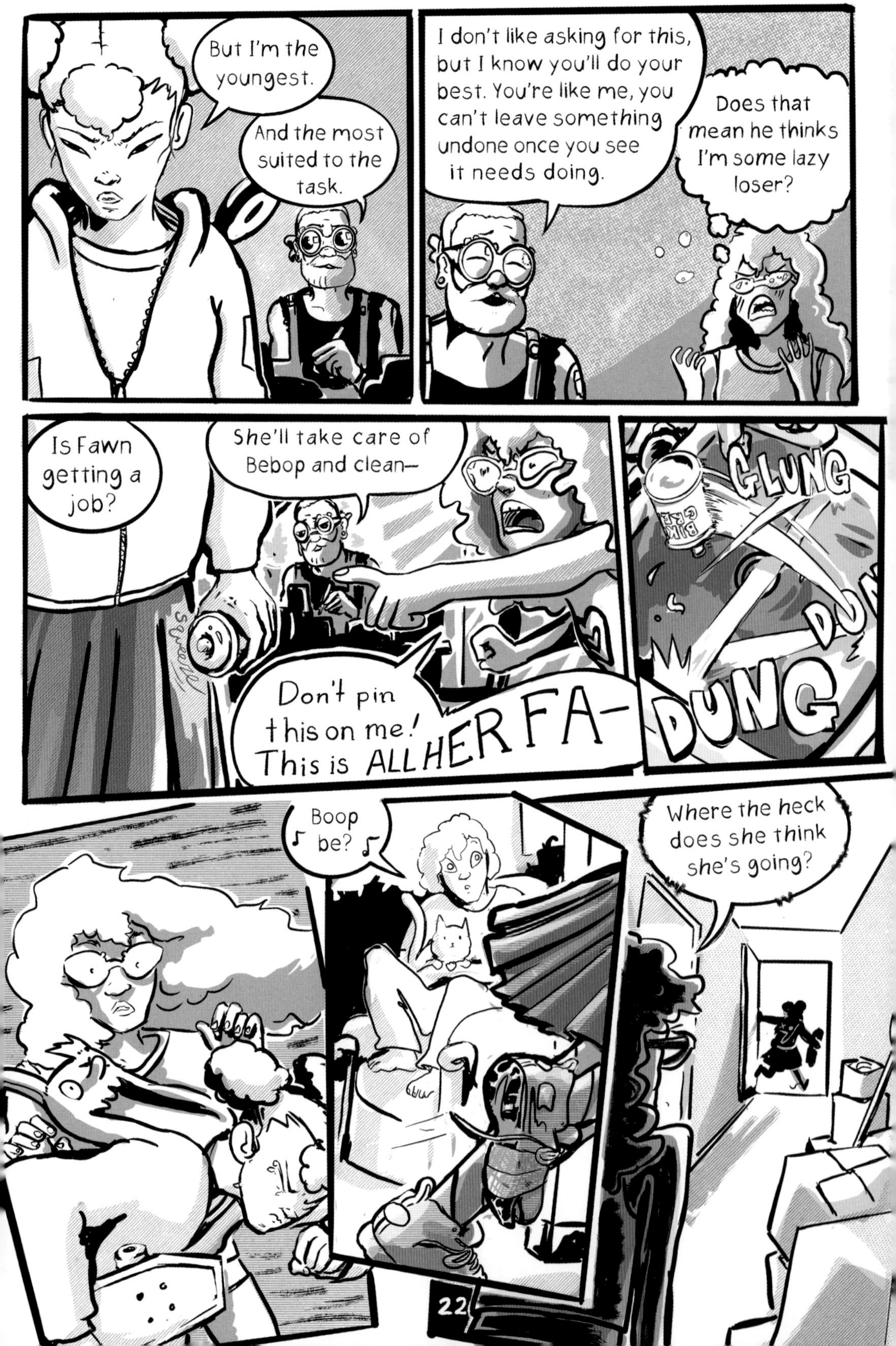

But I'm the youngest.
And the most suited to the task.
I don't like asking for this, but I know you'll do your best. You're like me, you can't leave something undone once you see it needs doing.
Does that mean he thinks I'm some lazy loser?
Is Fawn getting a job?
She'll take care of Bebop and clean—
Don't pin this on me! This is ALL HER FA—
GLUNG
DUNG
Boop be?
Where the heck does she think she's going?

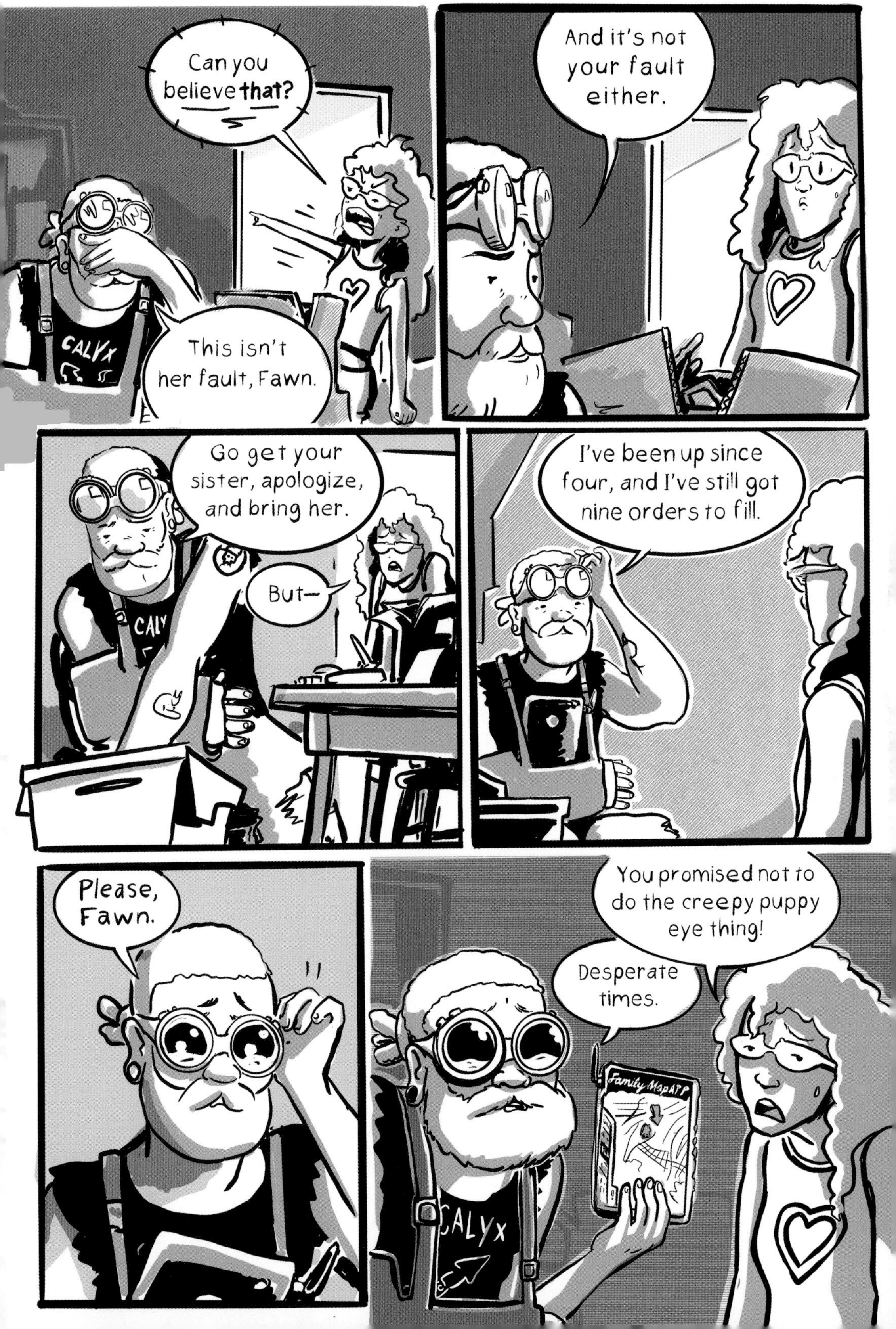

Can you believe that?
This isn't her fault, Fawn.
CALYX
And it's not your fault either.
Go get your sister, apologize, and bring her.
But—
CALY
I've been up since four, and I've still got nine orders to fill.
Please, Fawn.
You promised not to do the creepy puppy eye thing!
Desperate times.
Family Map APP
CALYX

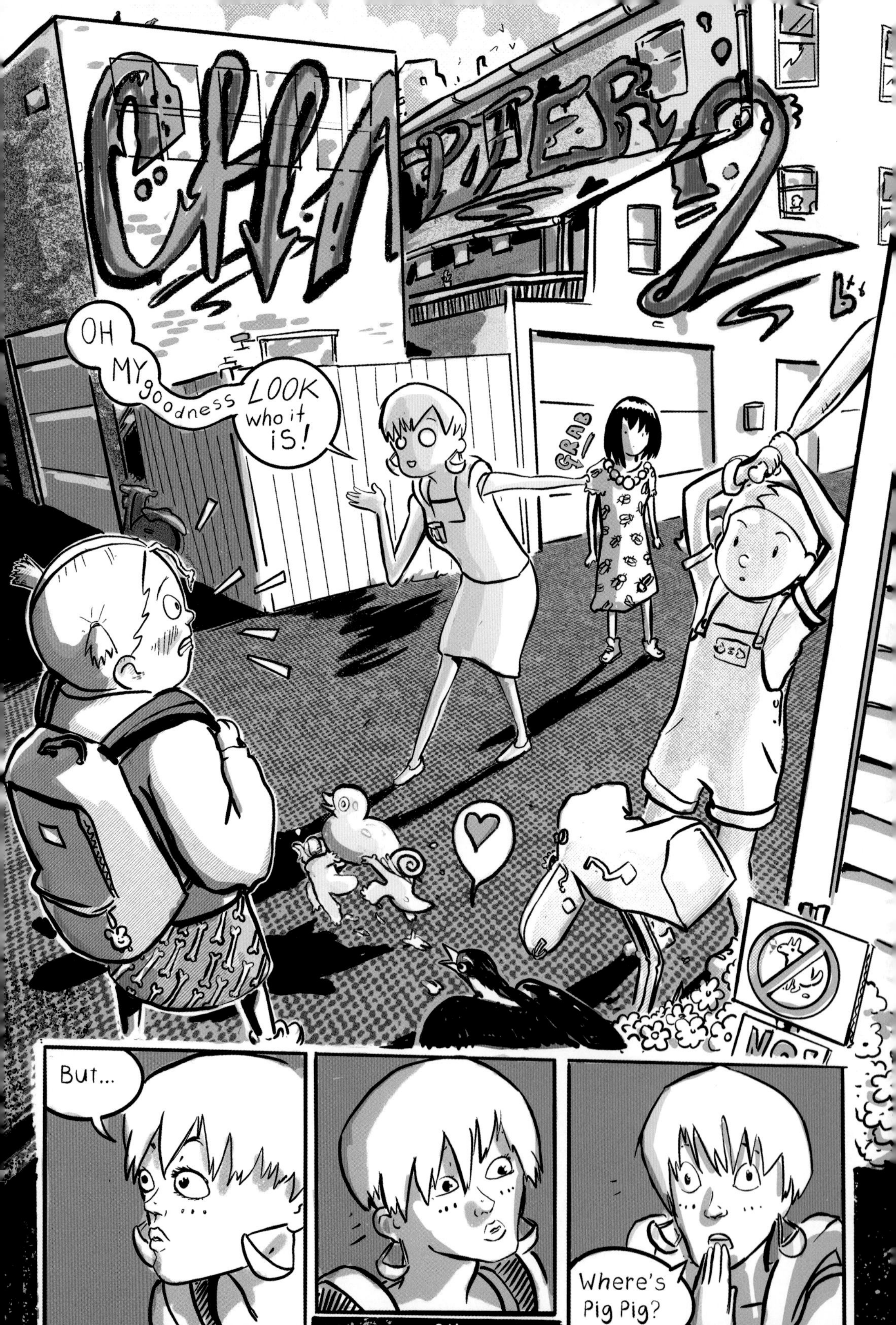
CHAPTER 2
OH MY goodness
LOOK who it IS!
GRAB
But...
Where's Pig Pig?

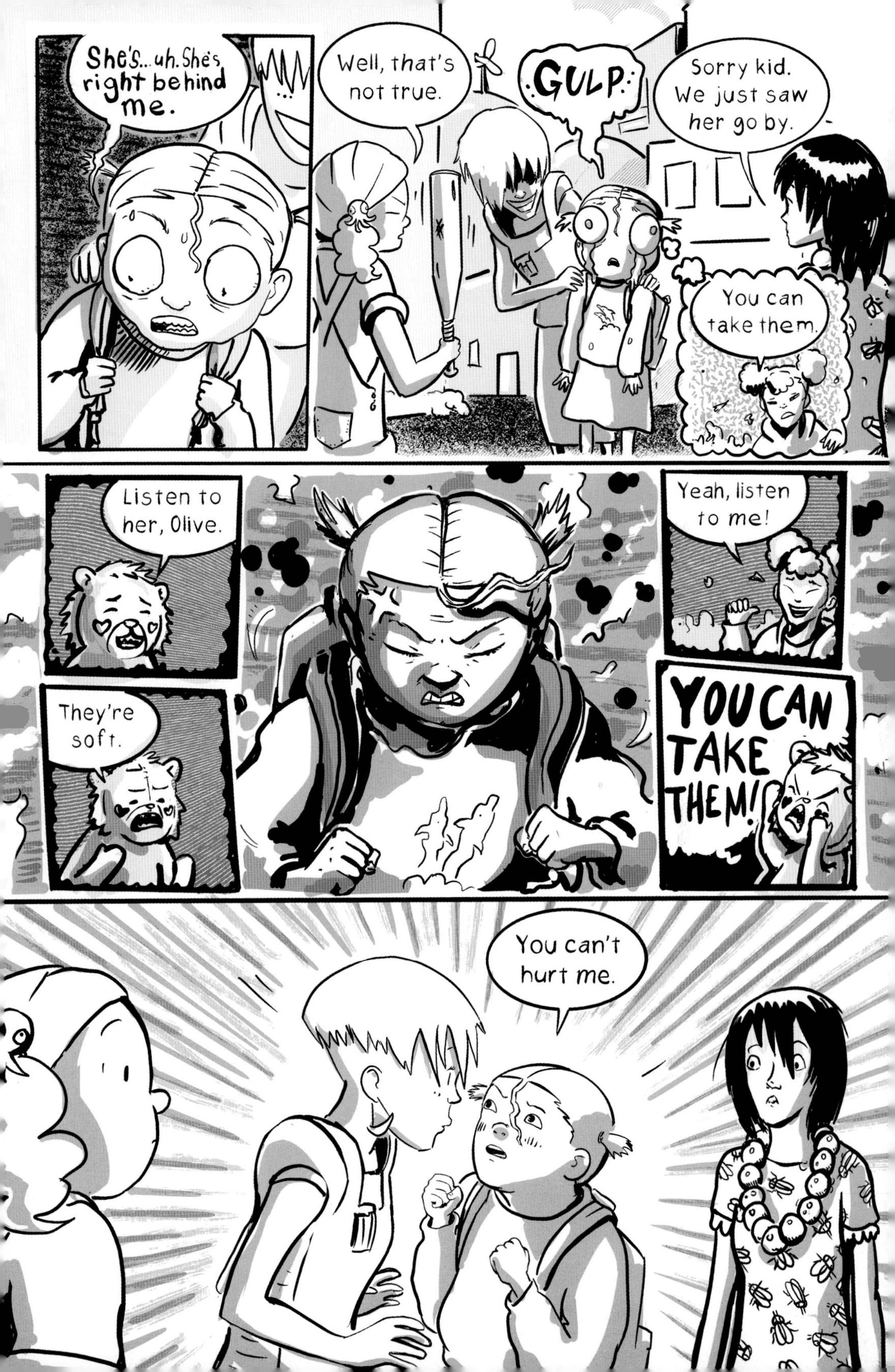

She's... uh. She's right behind me.
...
Well, that's not true.
GULP
Sorry kid. We just saw her go by.
You can take them.
Listen to her, Olive.
They're soft.
Yeah, listen to me!
YOU CAN TAKE THEM!
You can't hurt me.

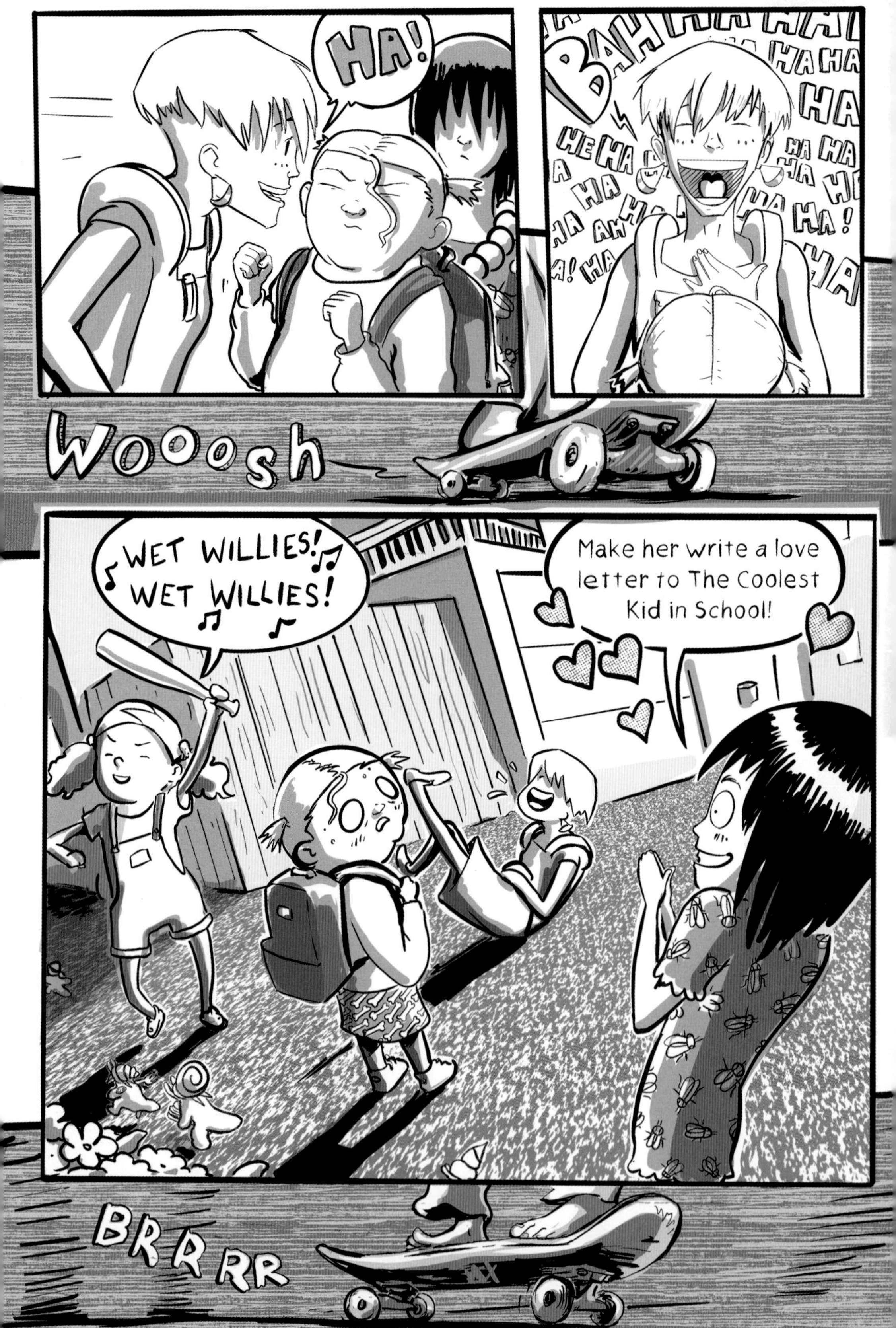
HA!
BAHAHAHA
HAHA
HA
HEHA
HA HA
HA!
WOOOSH
WET WILLIES! WET WILLIES!
Make her write a love letter to The Coolest Kid in School!
BRRRRR

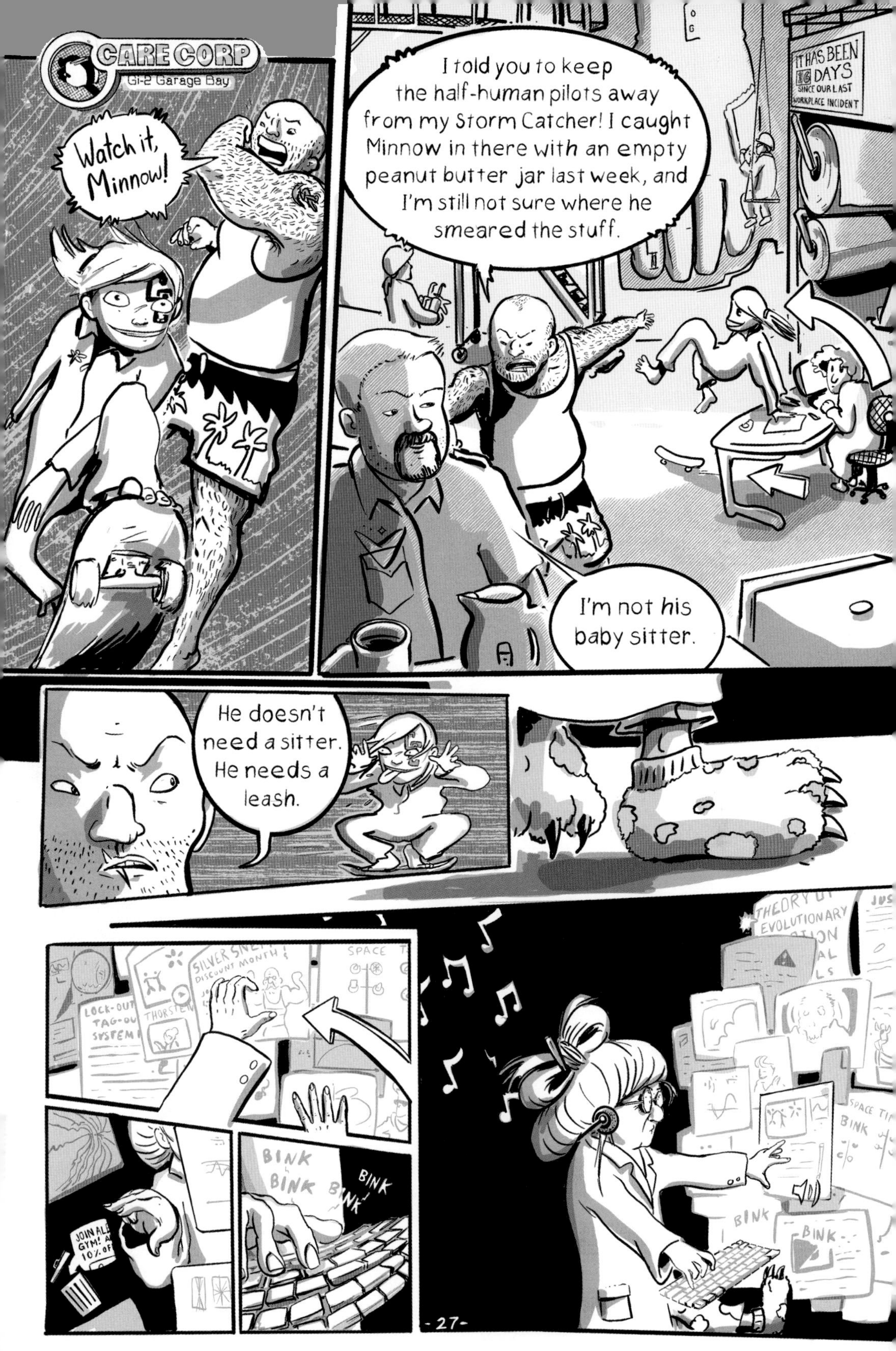
CARE CORP
Gi-2 Garage Bay
Watch it, Minnow!
I told you to keep the half-human pilots away from my Storm Catcher! I caught Minnow in there with an empty peanut butter jar last week, and I'm still not sure where he smeared the stuff.
IT HAS BEEN 16 DAYS SINCE OUR LAST WORKPLACE INCIDENT
I'm not his baby sitter.
He doesn't need a sitter. He needs a leash.
THEORY OF EVOLUTIONARY
SILVER SNE
DISCOUNT MONTH!
SPACE
LOCK-OUT TAG-OUT SYSTEM
THORSTEN
BINK
BINK
BINK
BINK
JOIN AL GYM! 10% OFF
BINK
BINK
SPACE TI
BINK

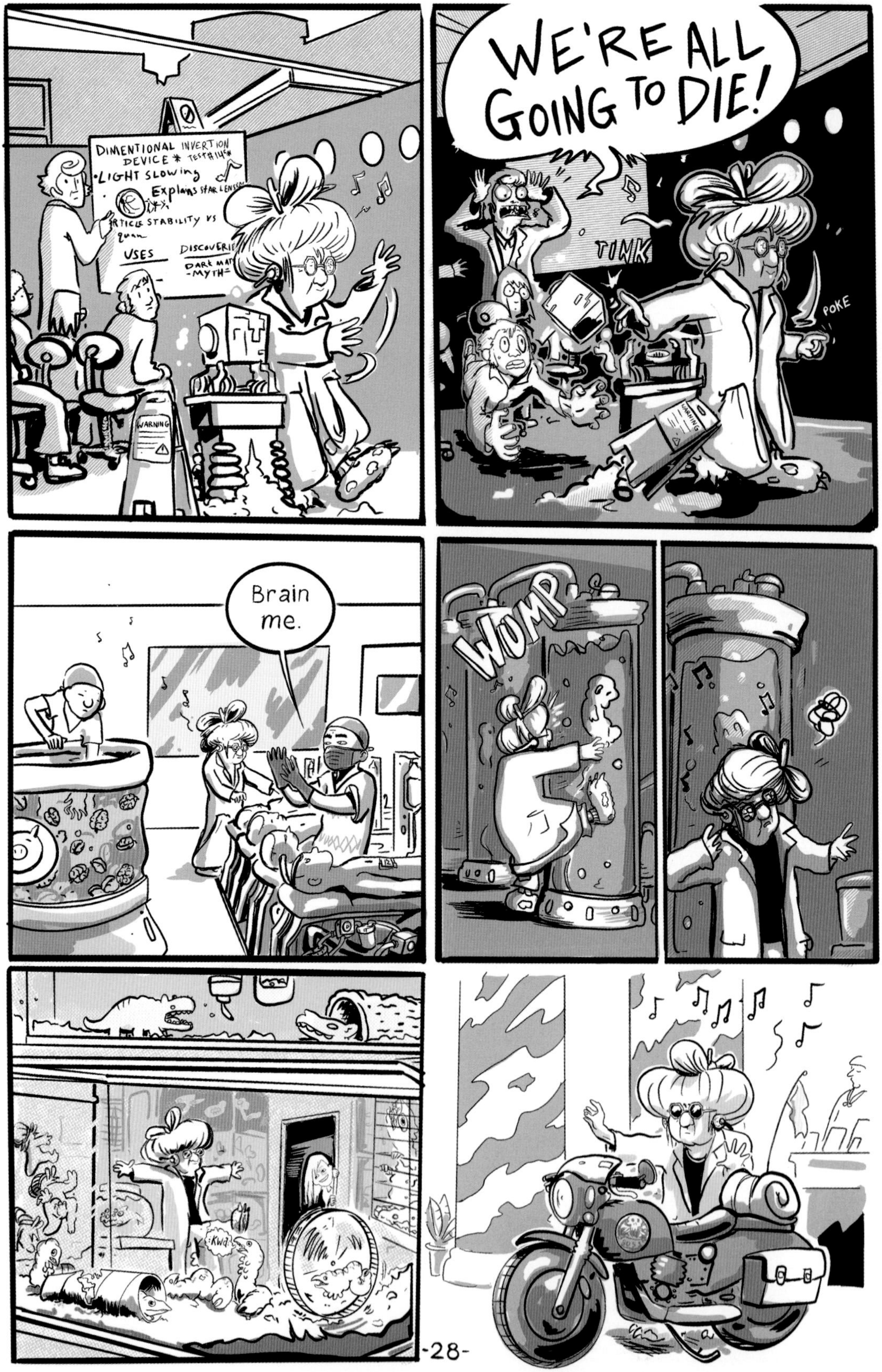
DIMENTIONAL INVERTION
DEVICE * TEST#14*
•LIGHT SLOWING
USES
WARNING
WE'RE ALL GOING TO DIE!
TINK
POKE
WARNING
Brain me.
WOMP
KWA?

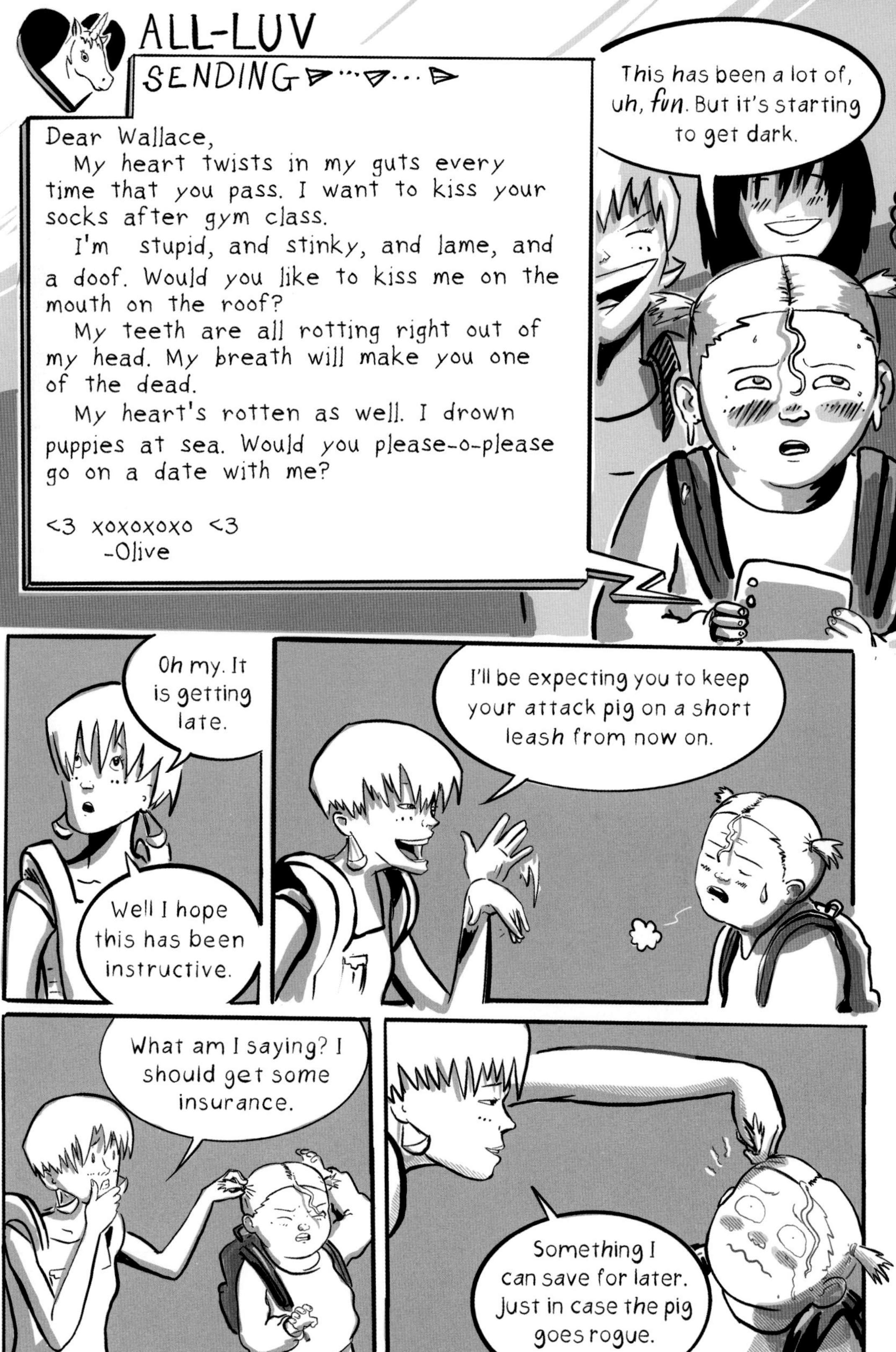
ALL-LUV
SENDING
Dear Wallace,
My heart twists in my guts every time that you pass. I want to kiss your socks after gym class.
I'm stupid, and stinky, and lame, and a doof. Would you like to kiss me on the mouth on the roof?
My teeth are all rotting right out of my head. My breath will make you one of the dead.
My heart's rotten as well. I drown puppies at sea. Would you please-o-please go on a date with me?
<3 xoxoxoxo <3
-Olive
This has been a lot of, uh, *fun*. But it's starting to get dark.
Oh my. It is getting late.
Well I hope this has been instructive.
I'll be expecting you to keep your attack pig on a short leash from now on.
What am I saying? I should get some insurance.
Something I can save for later. Just in case the pig goes rogue.

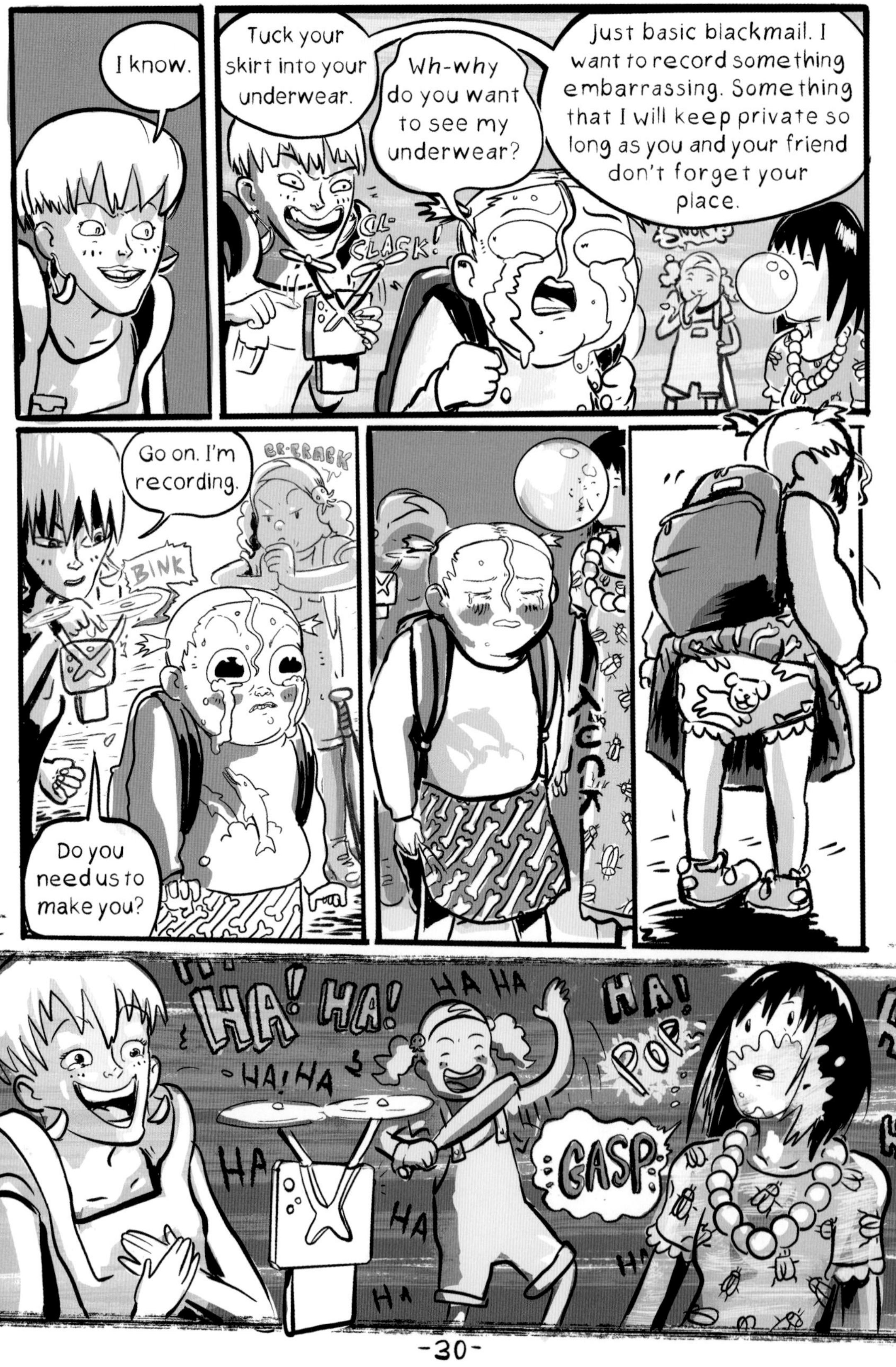
I know.
Tuck your skirt into your underwear.
Wh-why do you want to see my underwear?
Just basic blackmail. I want to record something embarrassing. Something that I will keep private so long as you and your friend don't forget your place.
CL-CLACK!
Go on. I'm recording.
CR-CRACK
BINK
Do you need us to make you?
YUCK
HA! HA!
HA HA
HA!
HA!HA
HA
HA
HA
POP
GASP

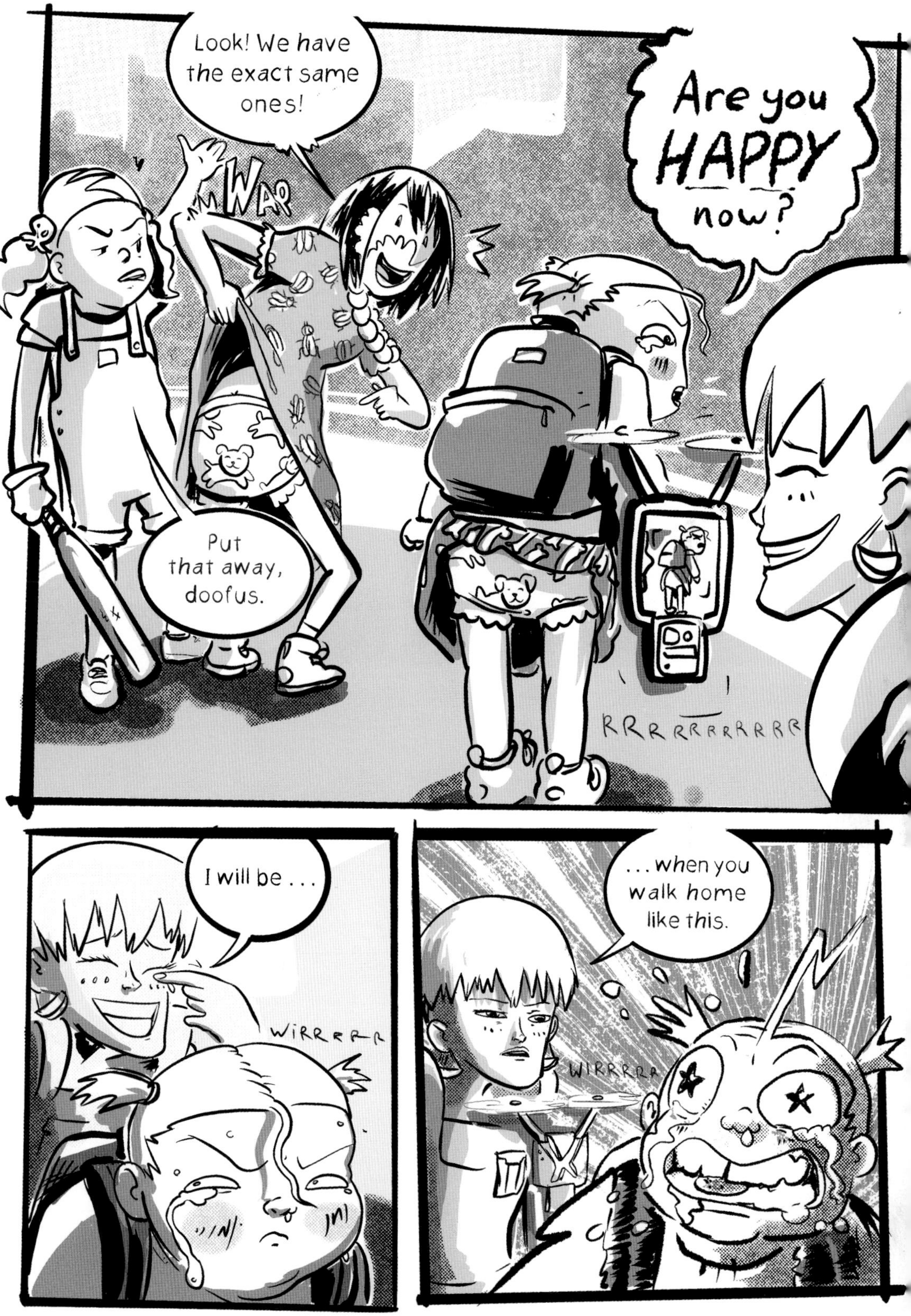
Look! We have the exact same ones!
WAP
Are you HAPPY now?
Put that away, doofus.
RRRRRRRRRRRR
I will be . . .
WIRRRRR
. . . when you walk home like this.
WIRRRRR

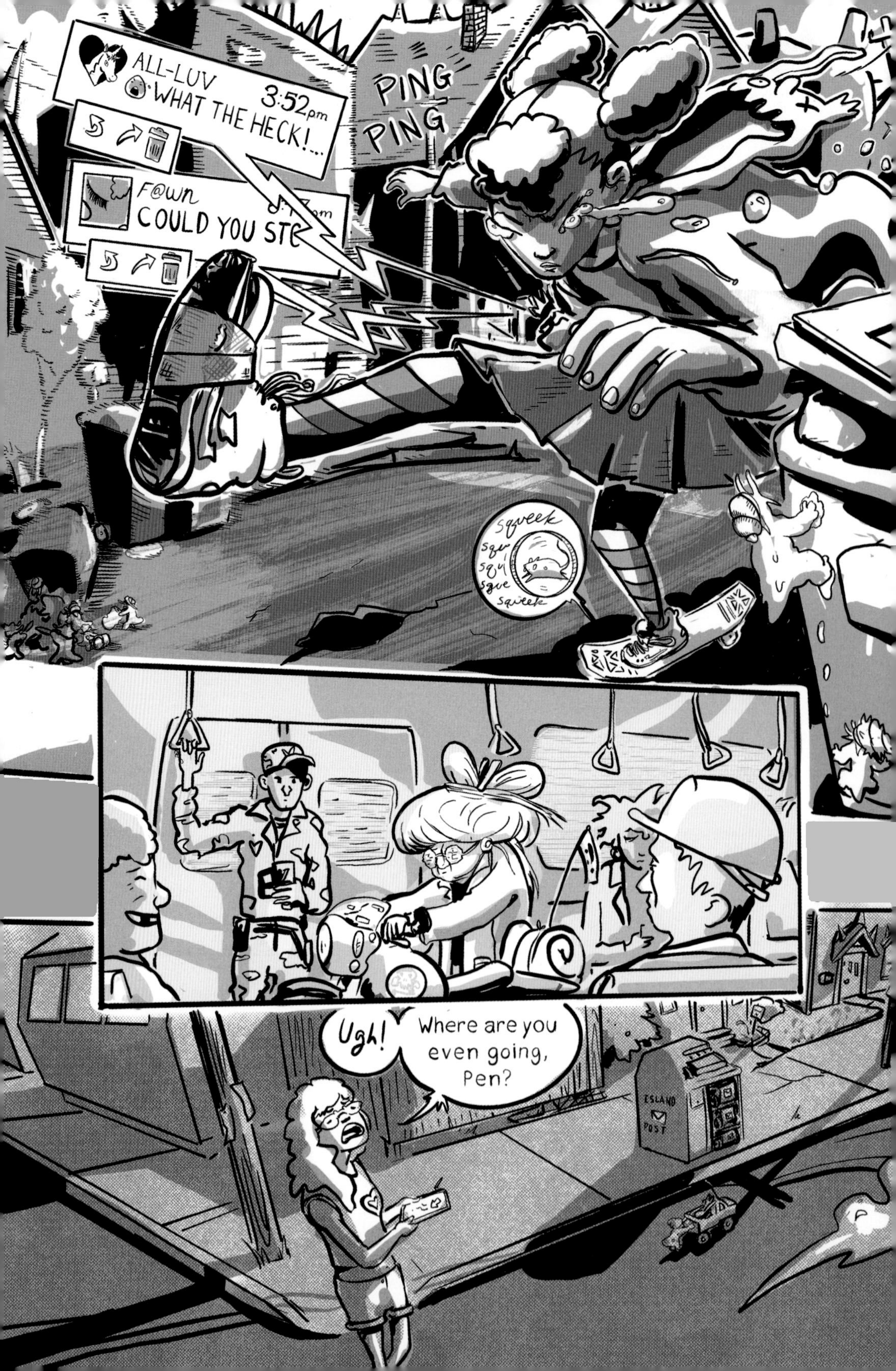
ALL-LUV
WHAT THE HECK!...
3:52pm
F@wn
COULD YOU STO
PING
PING
sqveek
squeek
Ugh!
Where are you even going, Pen?
ISLAND POST

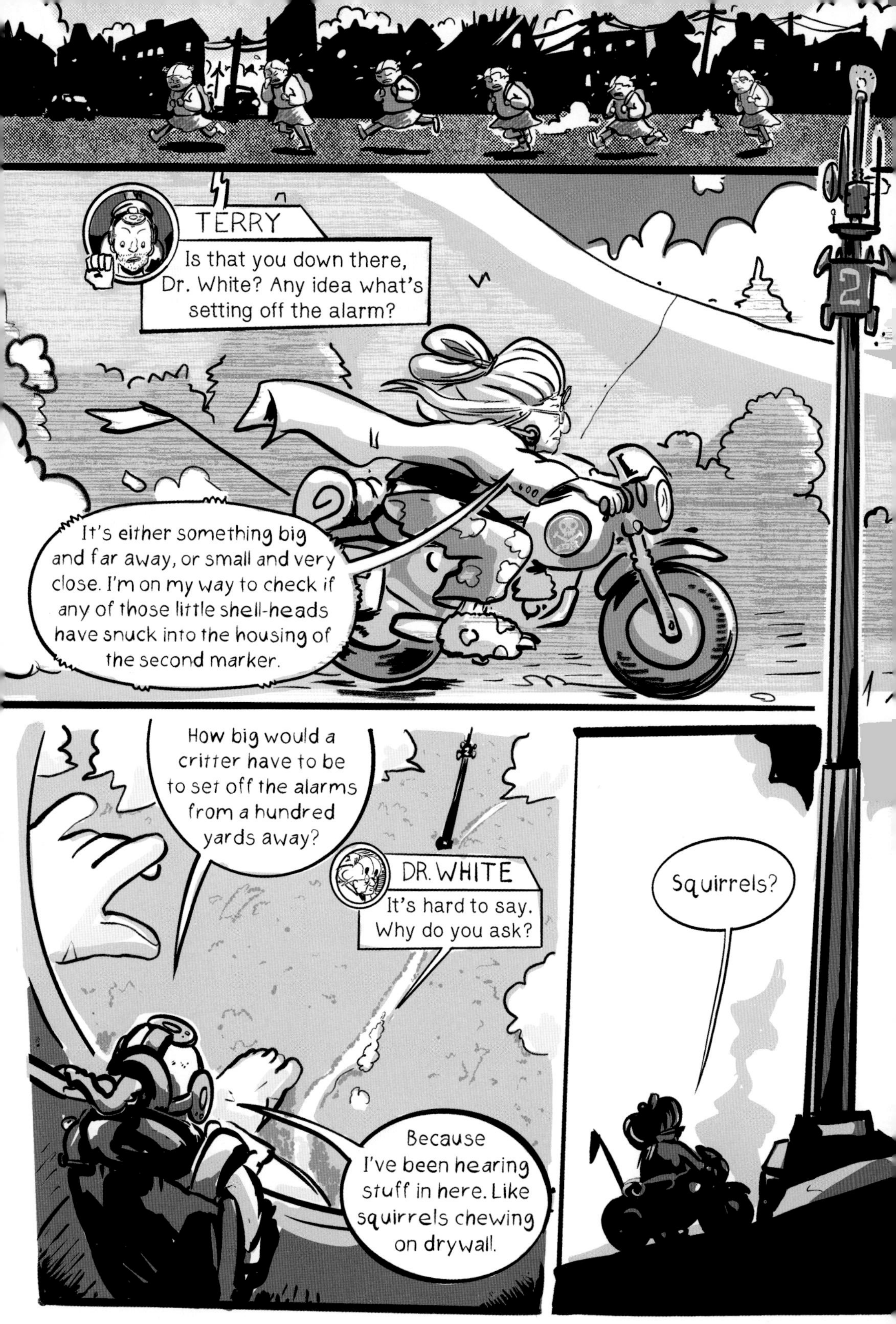
TERRY
Is that you down there, Dr. White? Any idea what's setting off the alarm?
It's either something big and far away, or small and very close. I'm on my way to check if any of those little shell-heads have snuck into the housing of the second marker.
2
How big would a critter have to be to set off the alarms from a hundred yards away?
DR. WHITE
It's hard to say. Why do you ask?
Because I've been hearing stuff in here. Like squirrels chewing on drywall.
Squirrels?

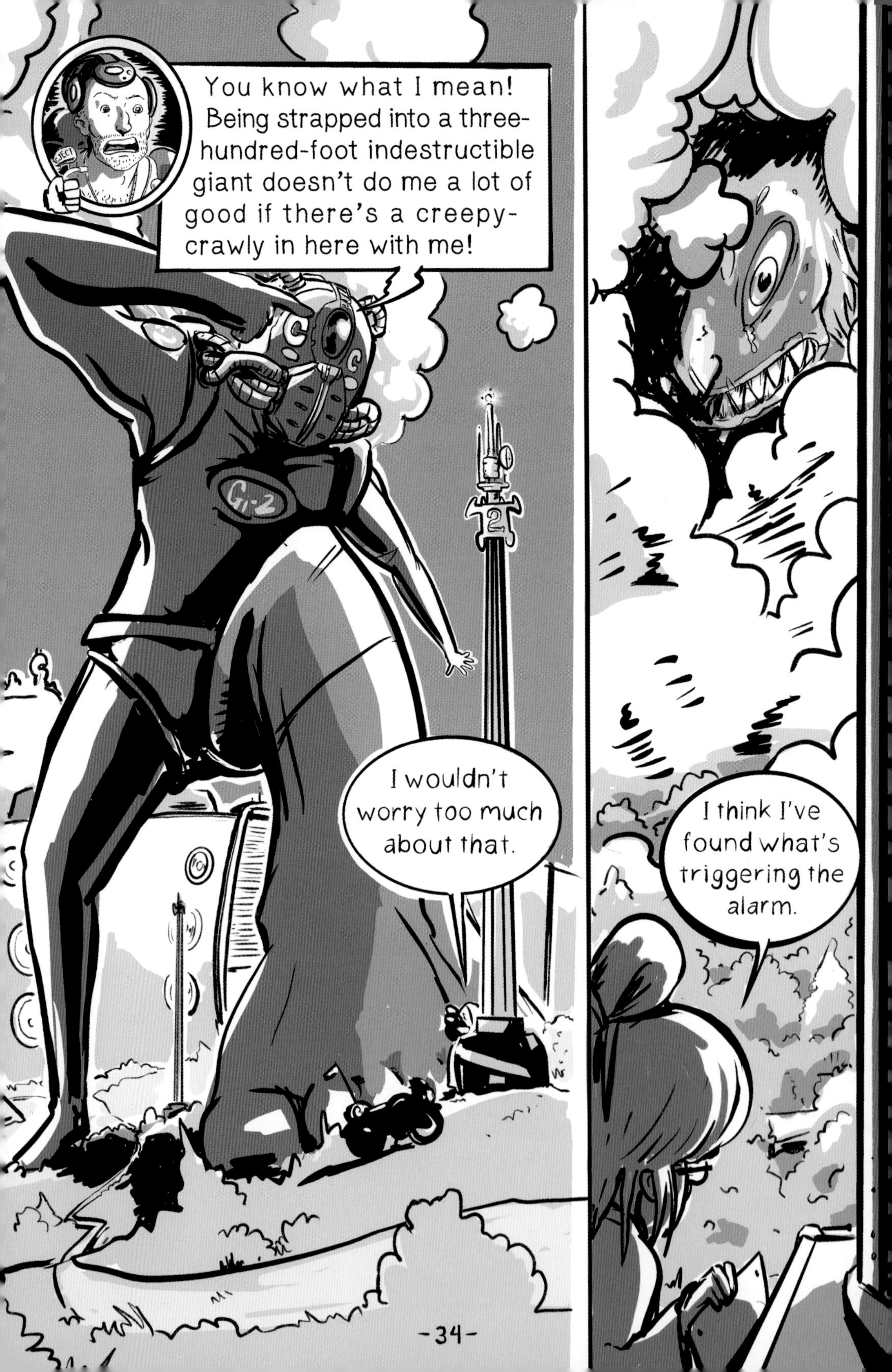
EJECT
You know what I mean! Being strapped into a three-hundred-foot indestructible giant doesn't do me a lot of good if there's a creepy-crawly in here with me!
Gi-2
2
I wouldn't worry too much about that.
I think I've found what's triggering the alarm.

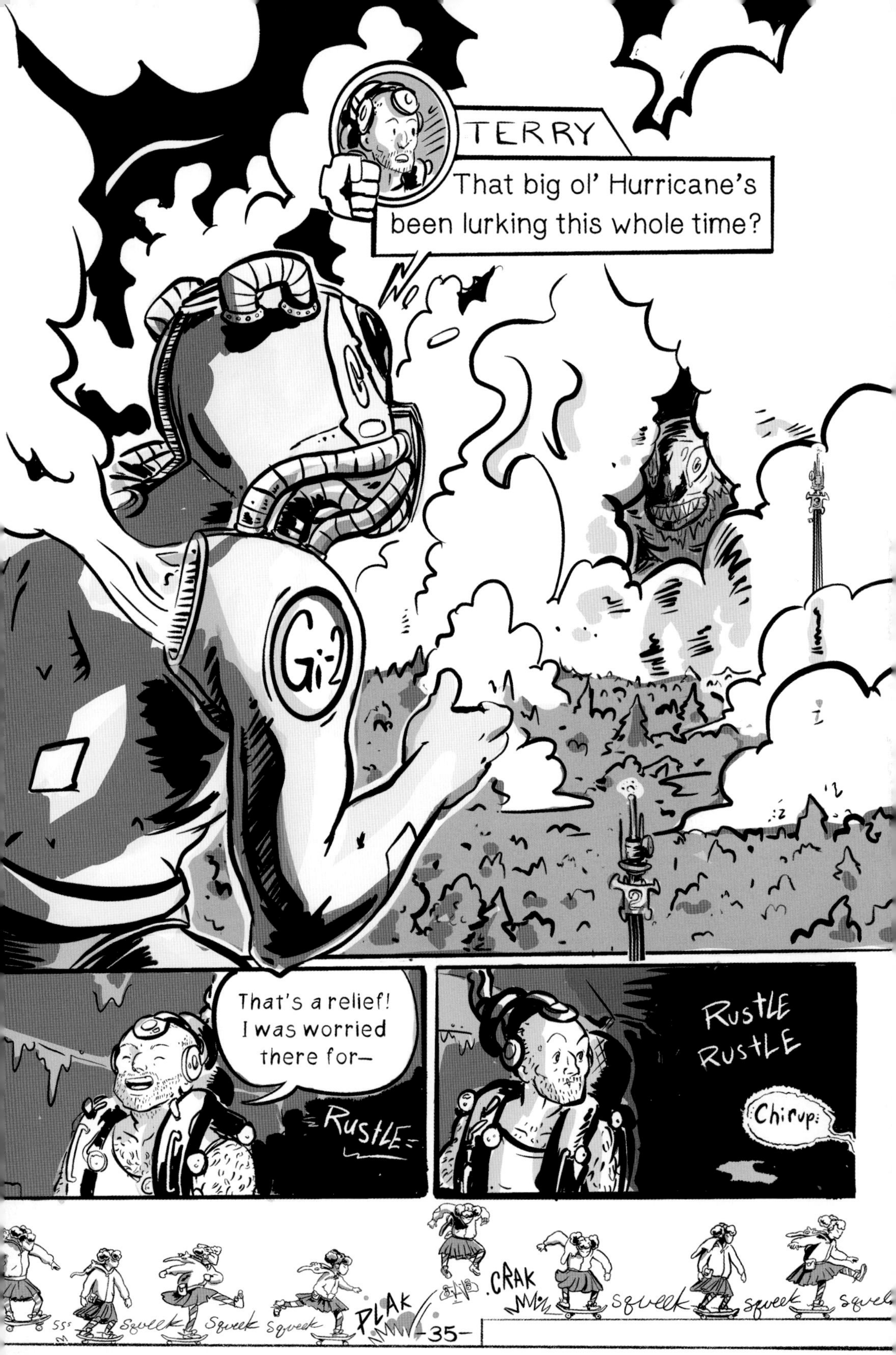
TERRY
That big ol' Hurricane's been lurking this whole time?
That's a relief! I was worried there for—
RUSTLE
RUSTLE RUSTLE
Chirup
SSS
Squeek
Squeek
Squeek
PLAK
CRAK
Squeek
squeek

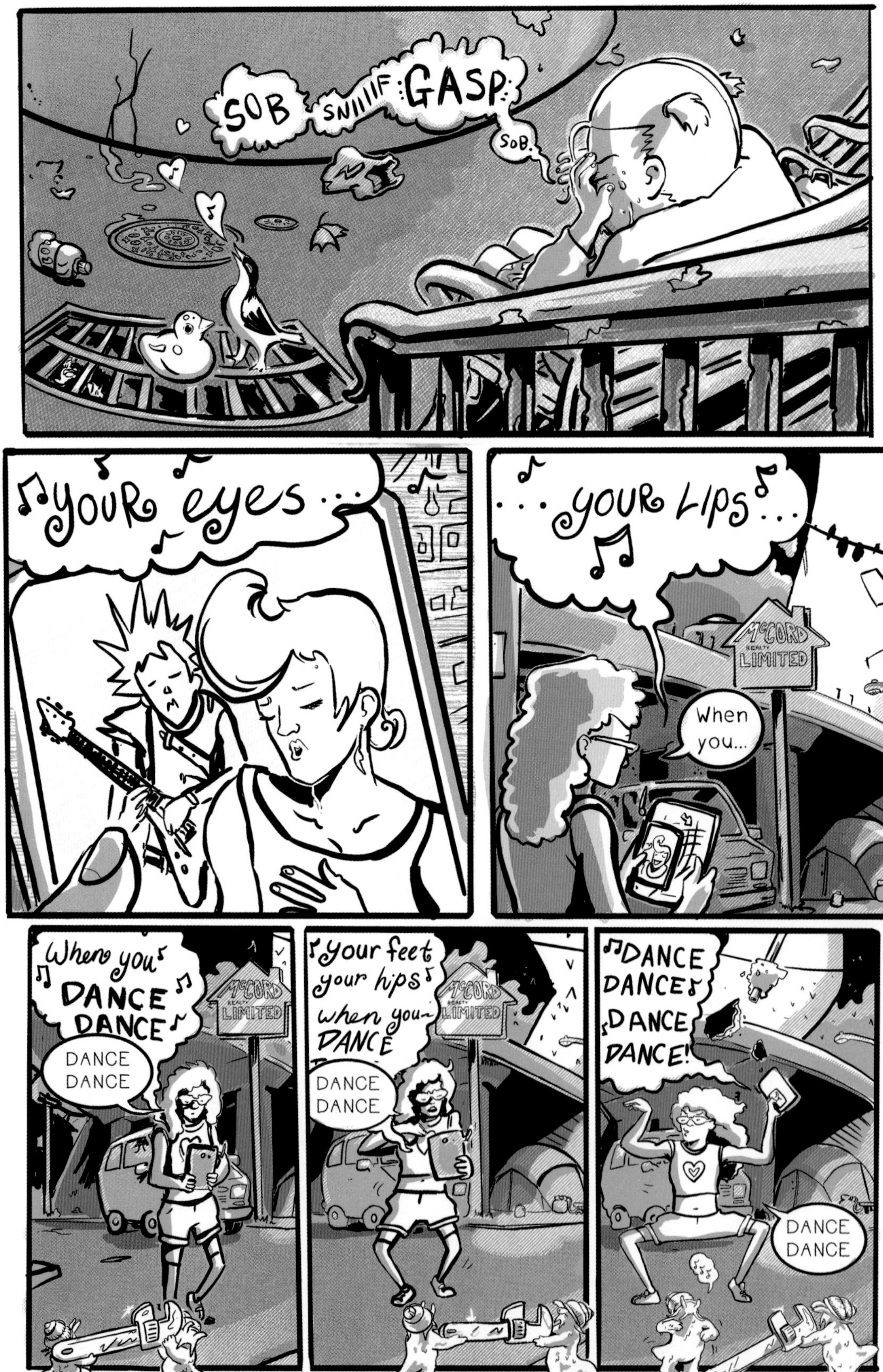
SOB SNIIIF GASP
SOB.
YOUR EYES...
...YOUR LIPS...
McCORD REALTY LIMITED
When you...
When you DANCE DANCE
DANCE DANCE
Your feet your hips when you-DANCE
DANCE DANCE
DANCE DANCE DANCE DANCE!
DANCE DANCE

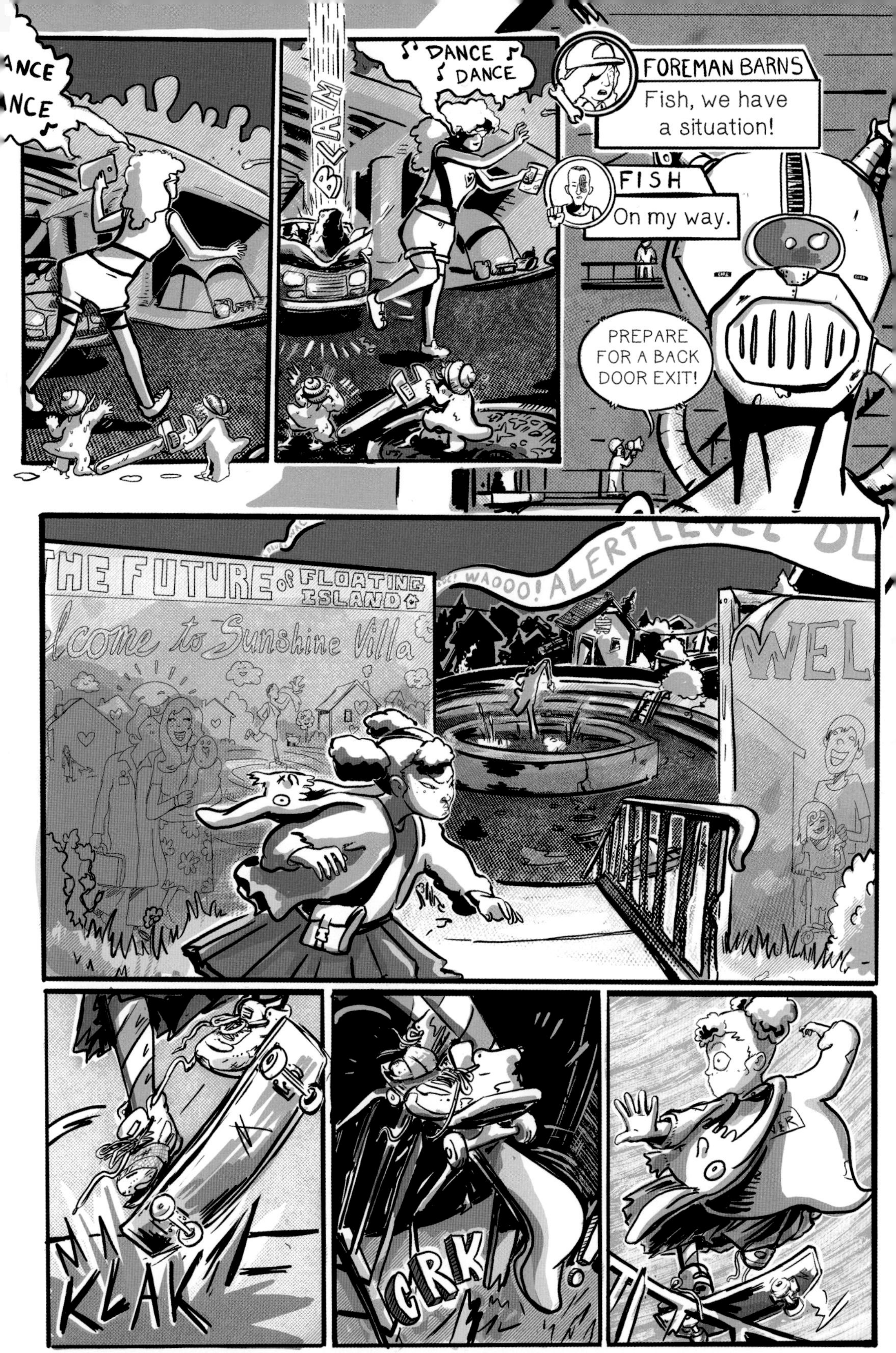

ANCE
ANCE
BLAM
DANCE DANCE
FOREMAN BARNS
Fish, we have a situation!
FISH
On my way.
PREPARE FOR A BACK DOOR EXIT!
THE FUTURE of FLOATING ISLAND
lcome to Sunshine Villa
WAOOO! ALERT LEVEL
WEL
KLAK
CRK

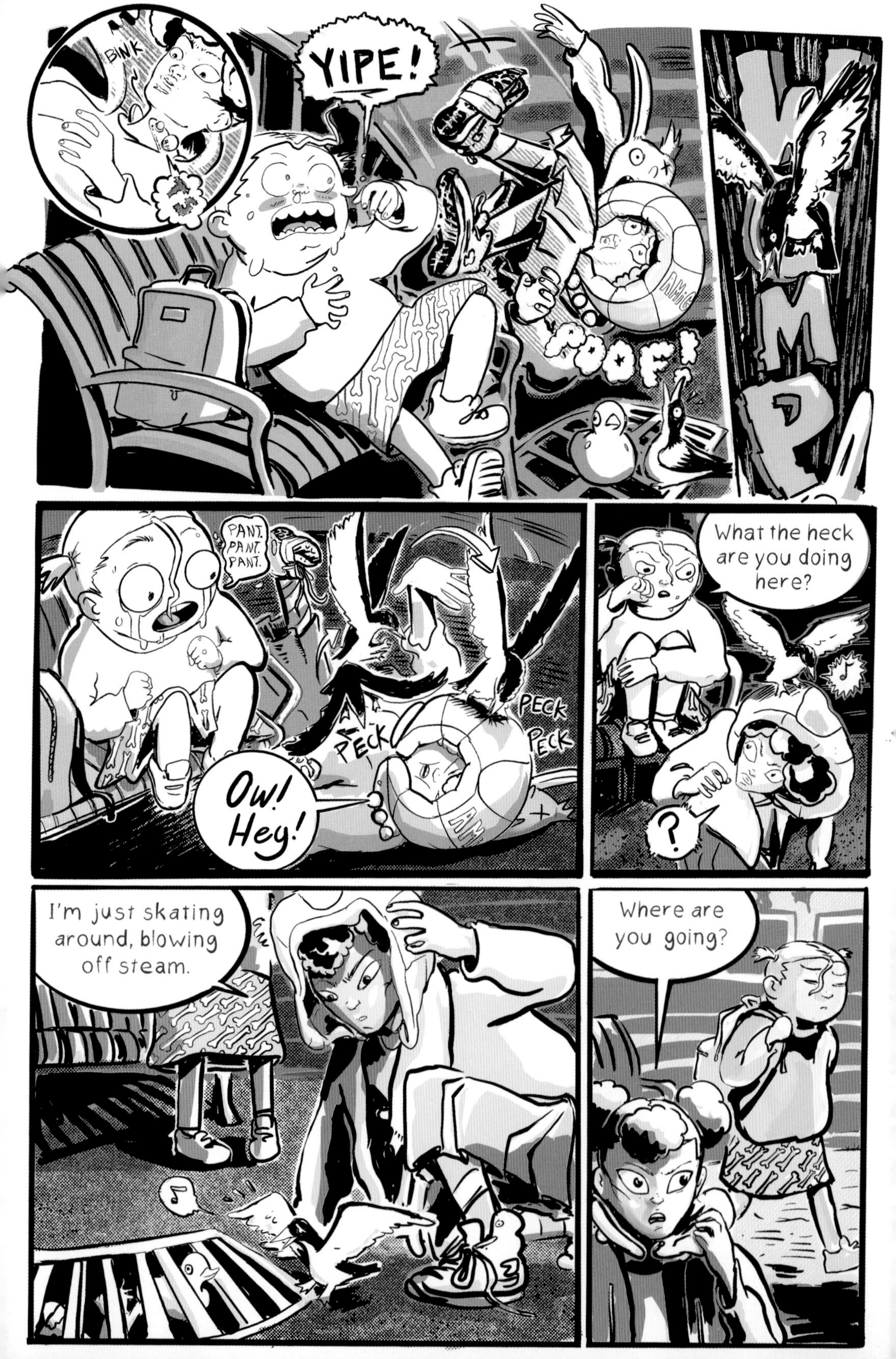

BINK
YIPE!
POOF!
PANT.
PANT.
PANT.
PECK
PECK
PECK
Ow!
Hey!
What the heck
are you doing
here?
?
I'm just skating
around, blowing
off steam.
Where are
you going?

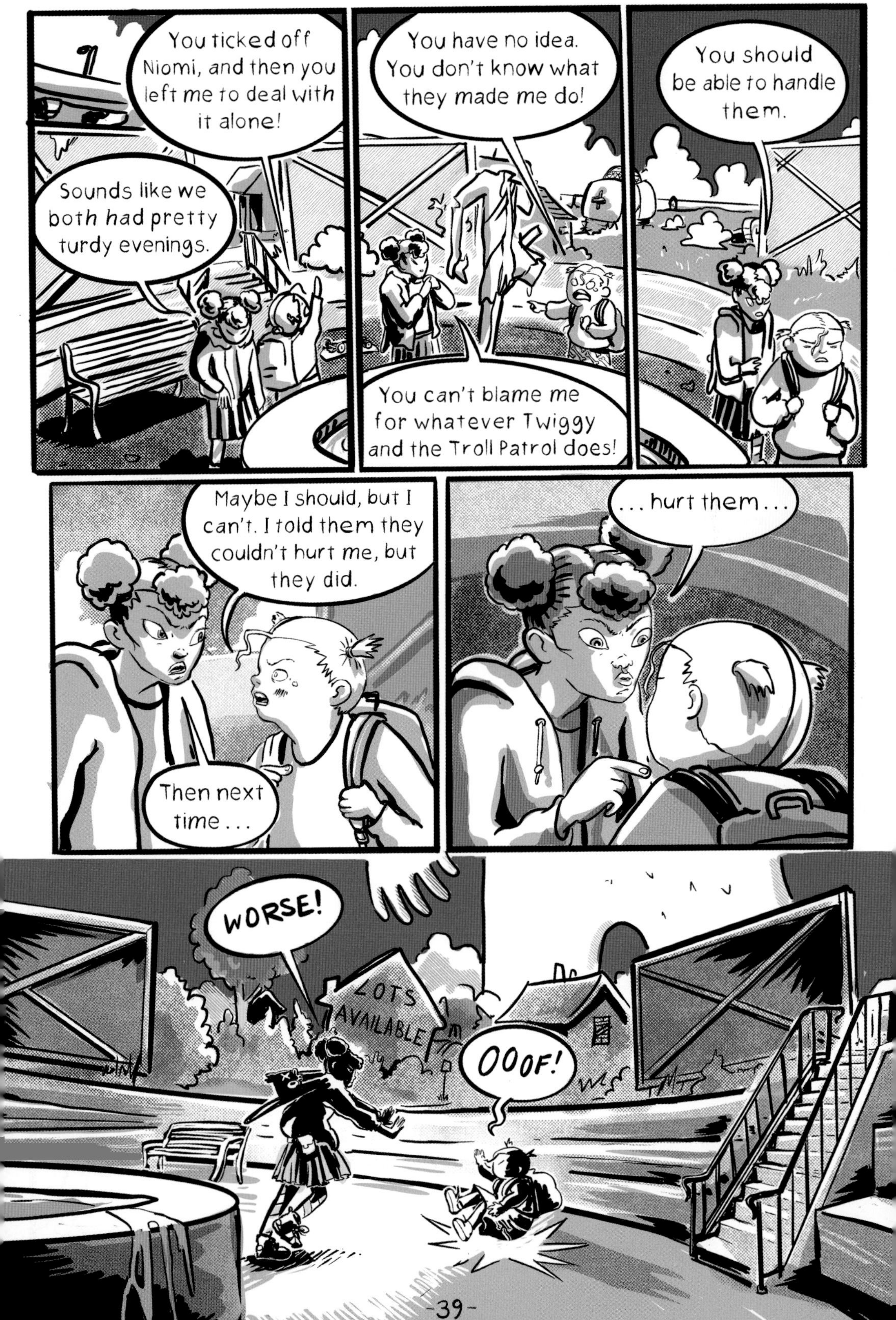
You ticked off Niomi, and then you left me to deal with it alone!
Sounds like we both had pretty turdy evenings.
You have no idea. You don't know what they made me do!
You can't blame me for whatever Twiggy and the Troll Patrol does!
You should be able to handle them.
Maybe I should, but I can't. I told them they couldn't hurt me, but they did.
Then next time . . .
. . . hurt them . . .
WORSE!
LOTS AVAILABLE
OOOF!

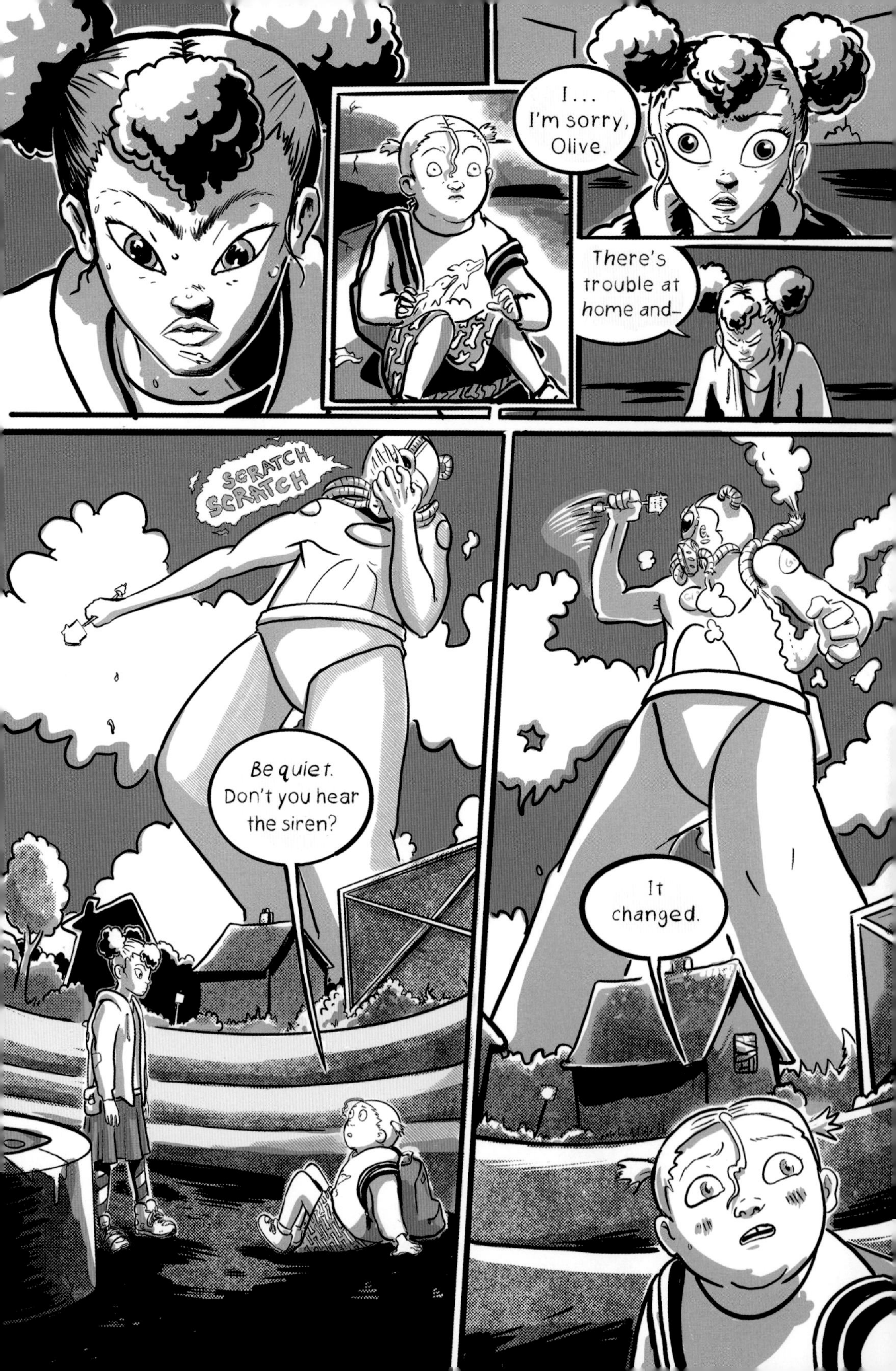
I... I'm sorry, Olive.
There's trouble at home and-
SCRATCH SCRATCH
Be quiet. Don't you hear the siren?
It changed.

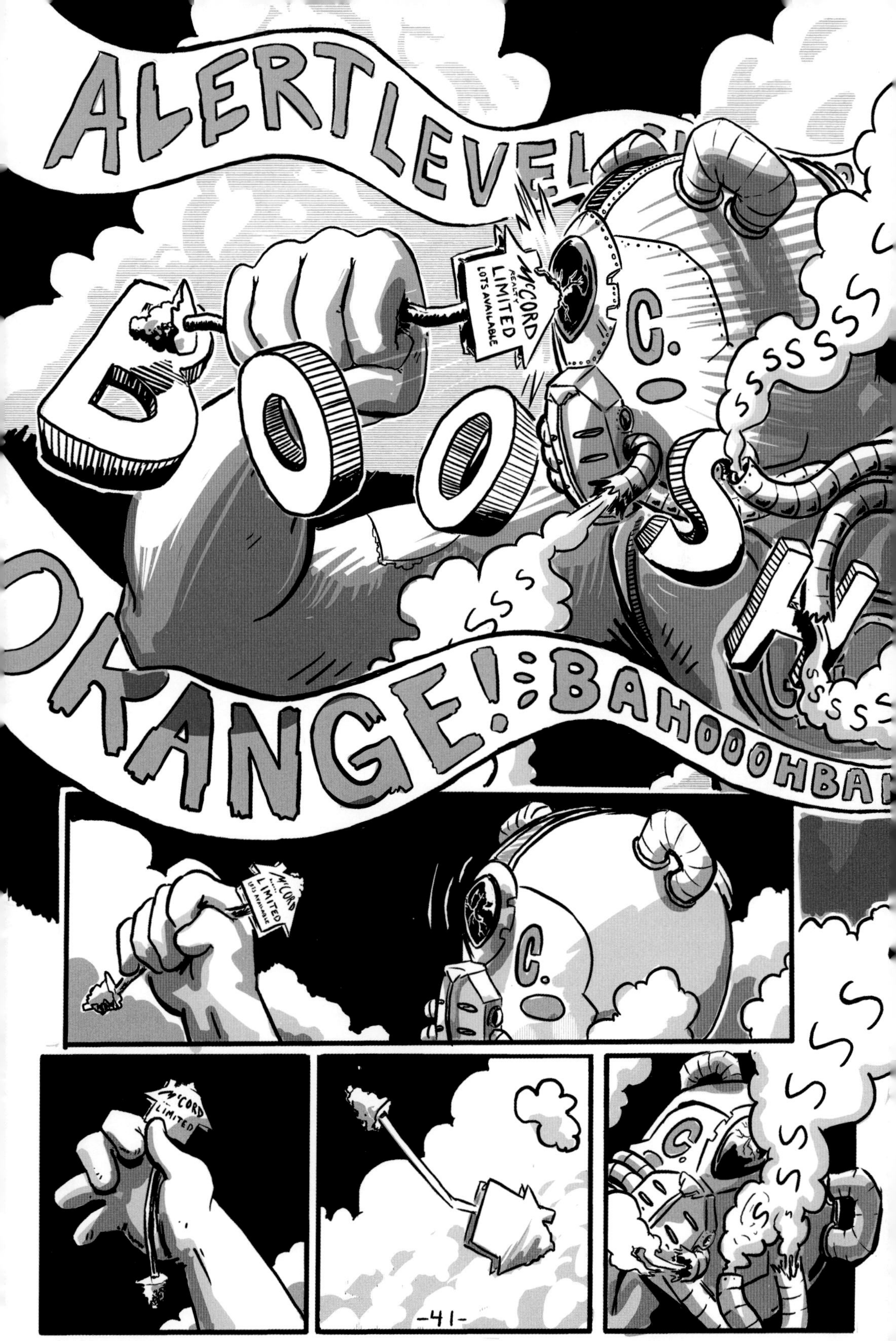
ALERT LEVEL
ORANGE!
BAHOOOOHBA
DOOSH
SSSSSSSSS
SSS
SSSS
McCORD REALTY LIMITED LOTS AVAILABLE
C.
McCORD LIMITED LOTS AVAILABLE
McCORD LIMITED
SSSS

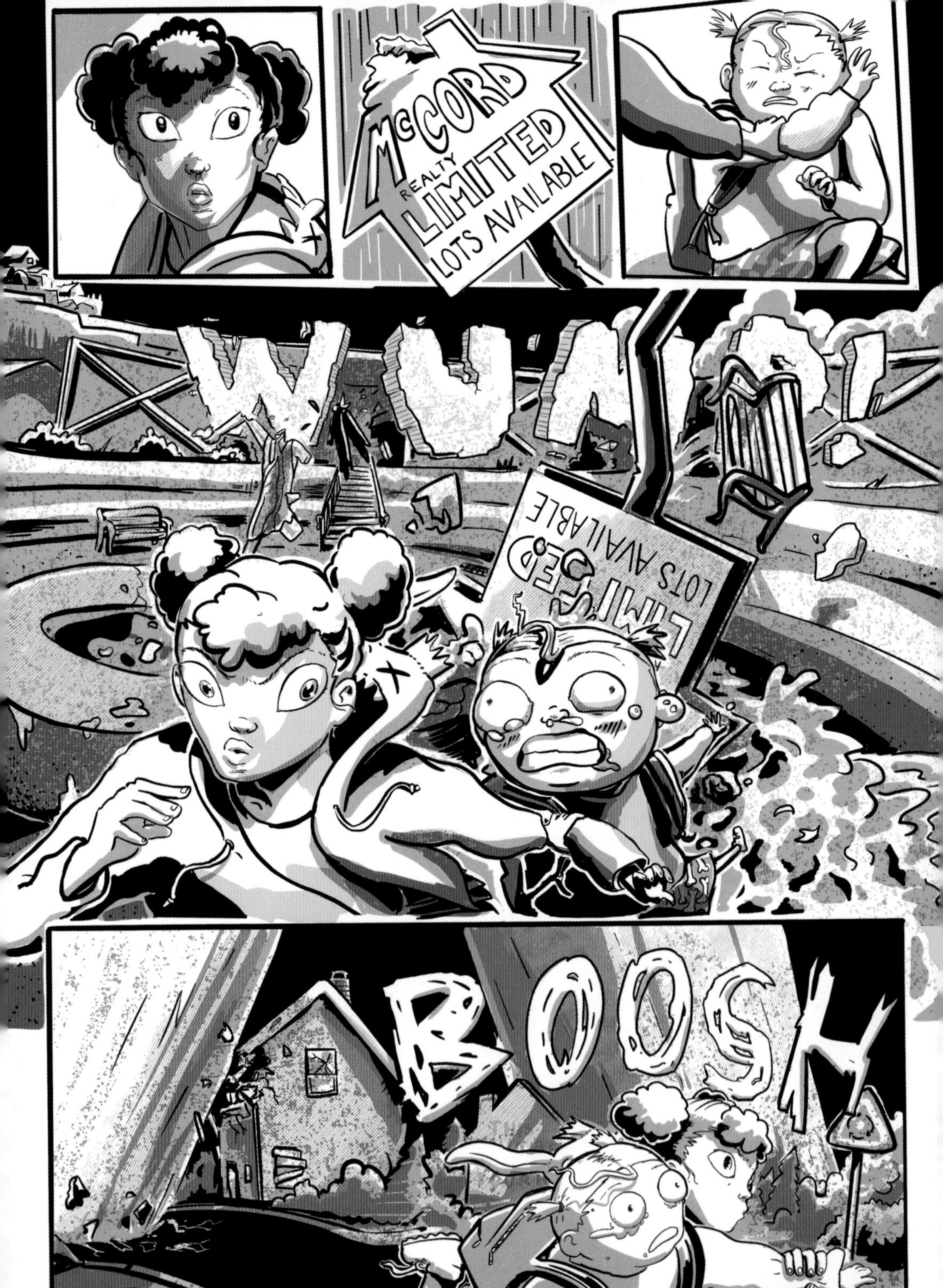
McCORD REALTY LIMITED LOTS AVAILABLE
WUMP!
BOOSH!

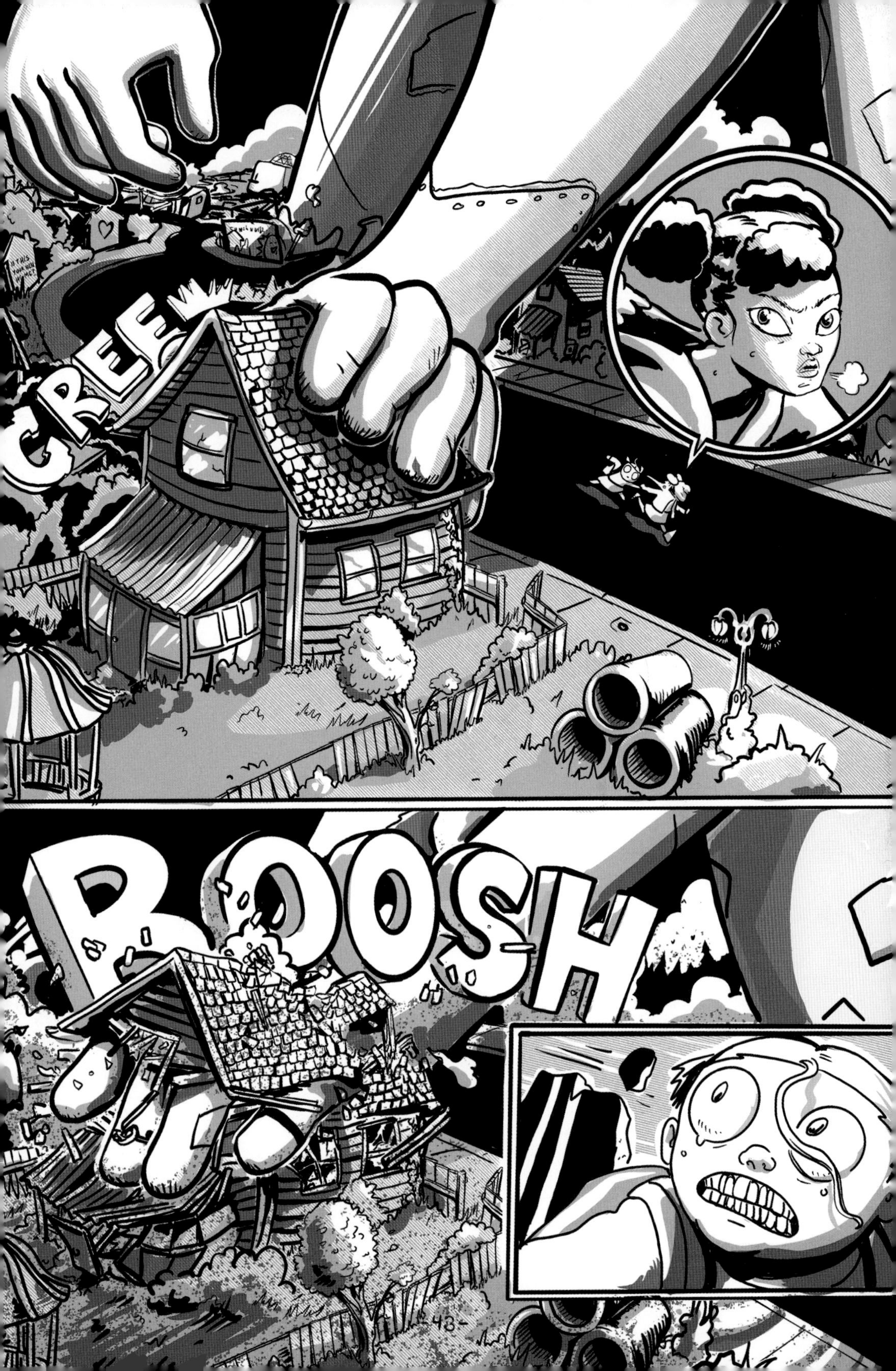
IS THIS YOUR NEW HOME?
CREE
BOOSH

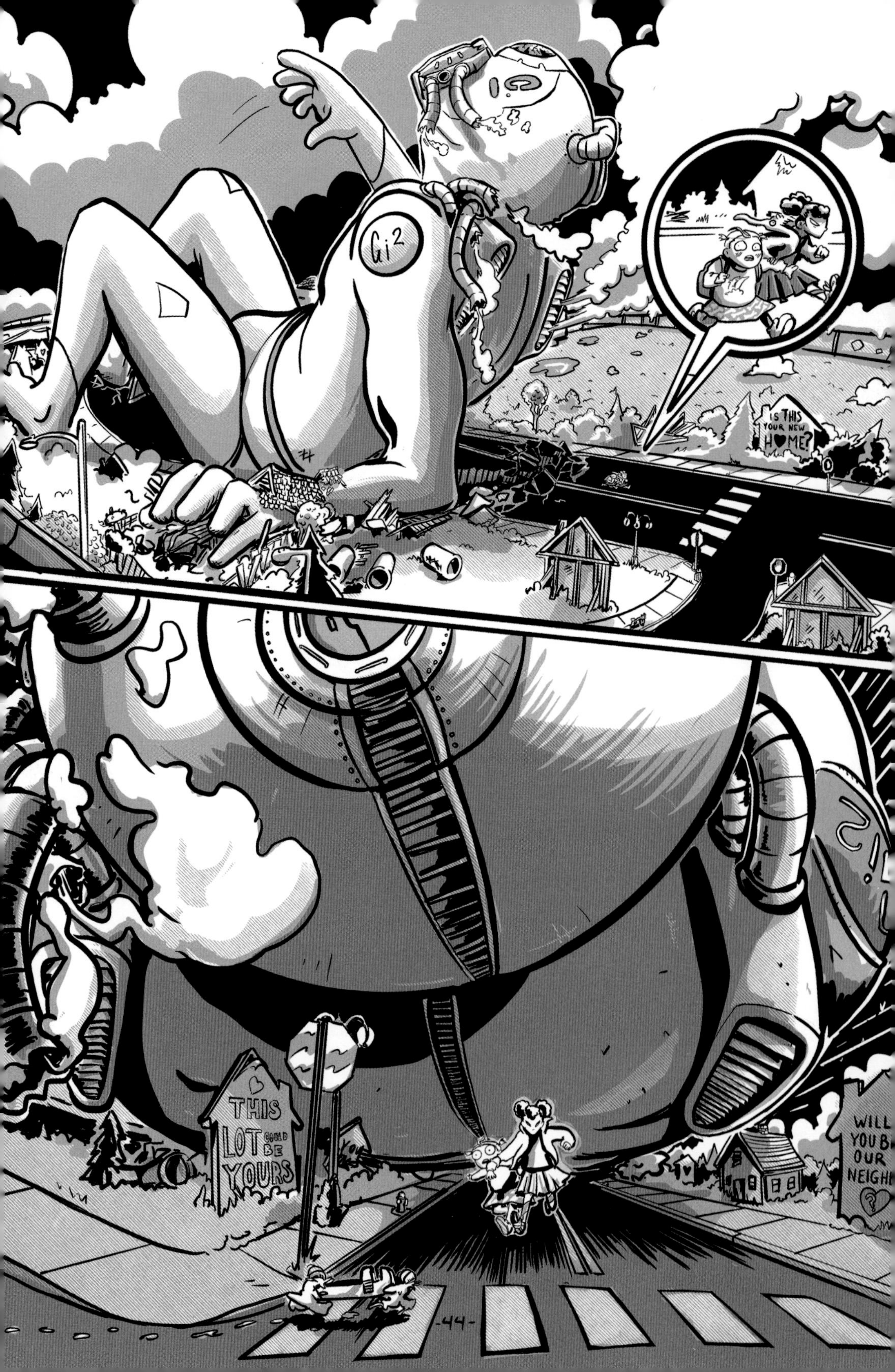
Gi2
IS THIS YOUR NEW HOME?
THIS LOT COULD BE YOURS
WILL YOU B OUR NEIGH

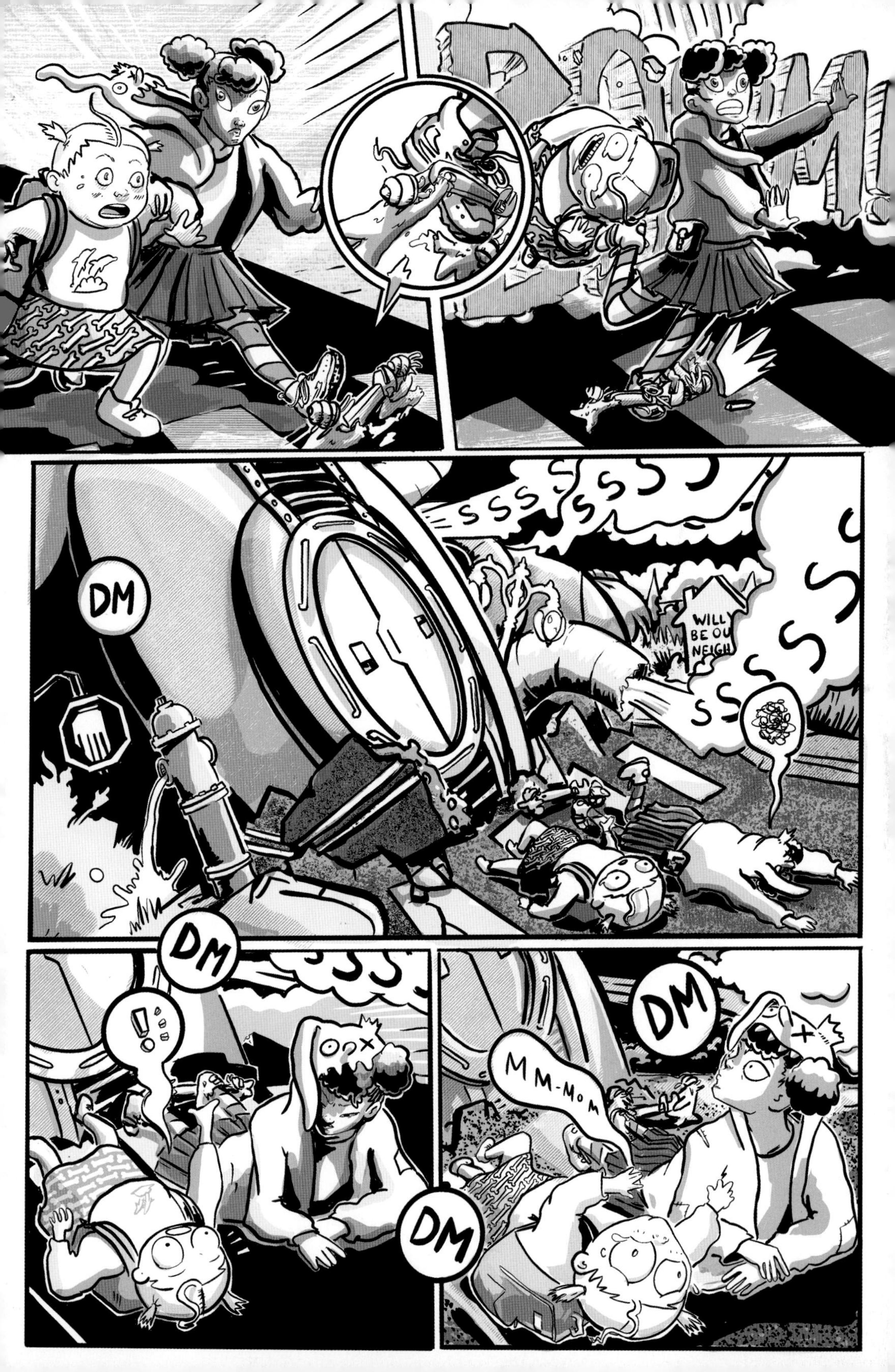

BOOM!
SSS
SSSS
DM
WILL BE OU NEIGH
SSSSS
SS
DM
!
DM
MM-MOM
DM

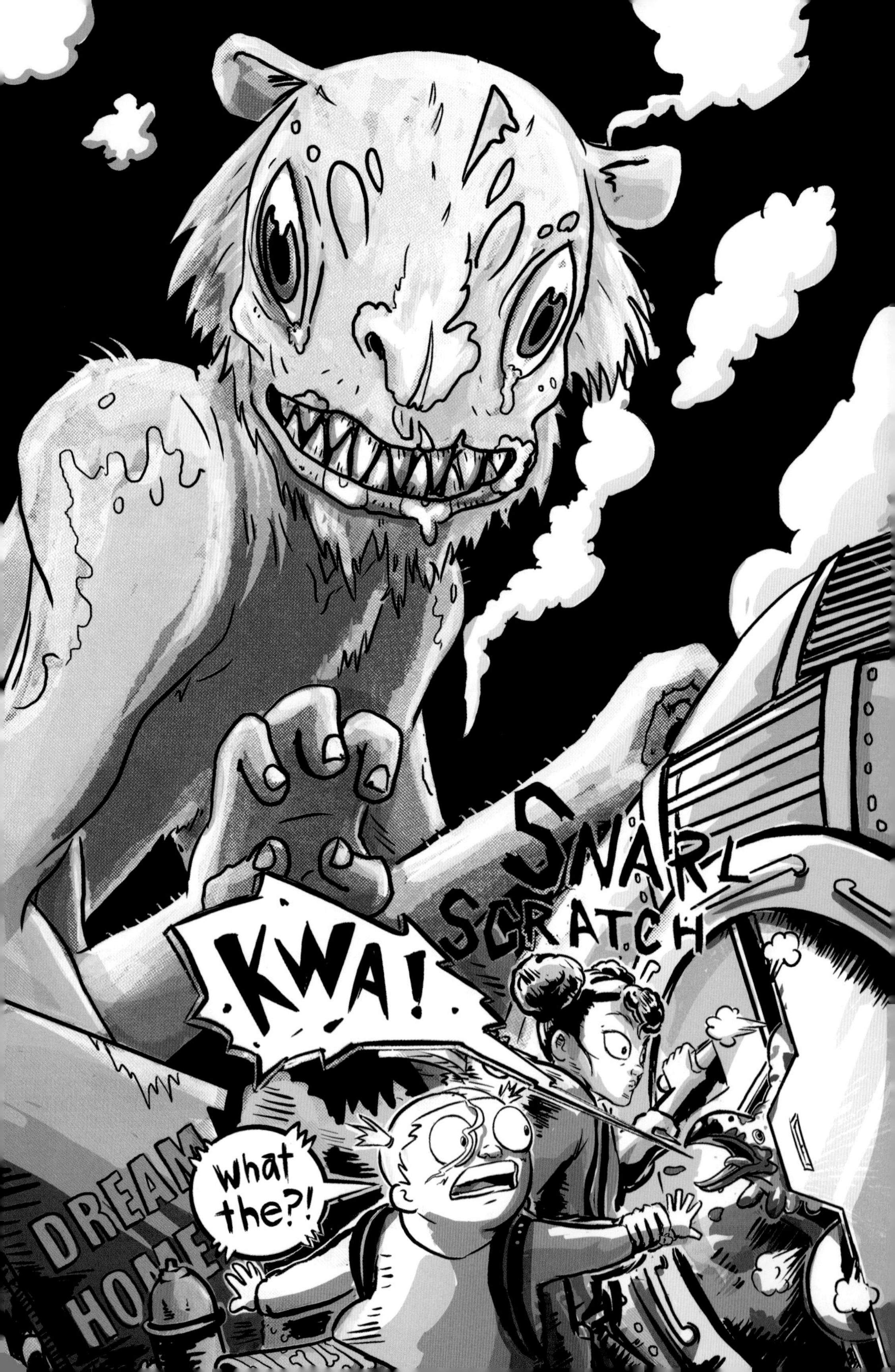
SNARL
SCRATCH
KWA!
what the?!
DREAM HOME

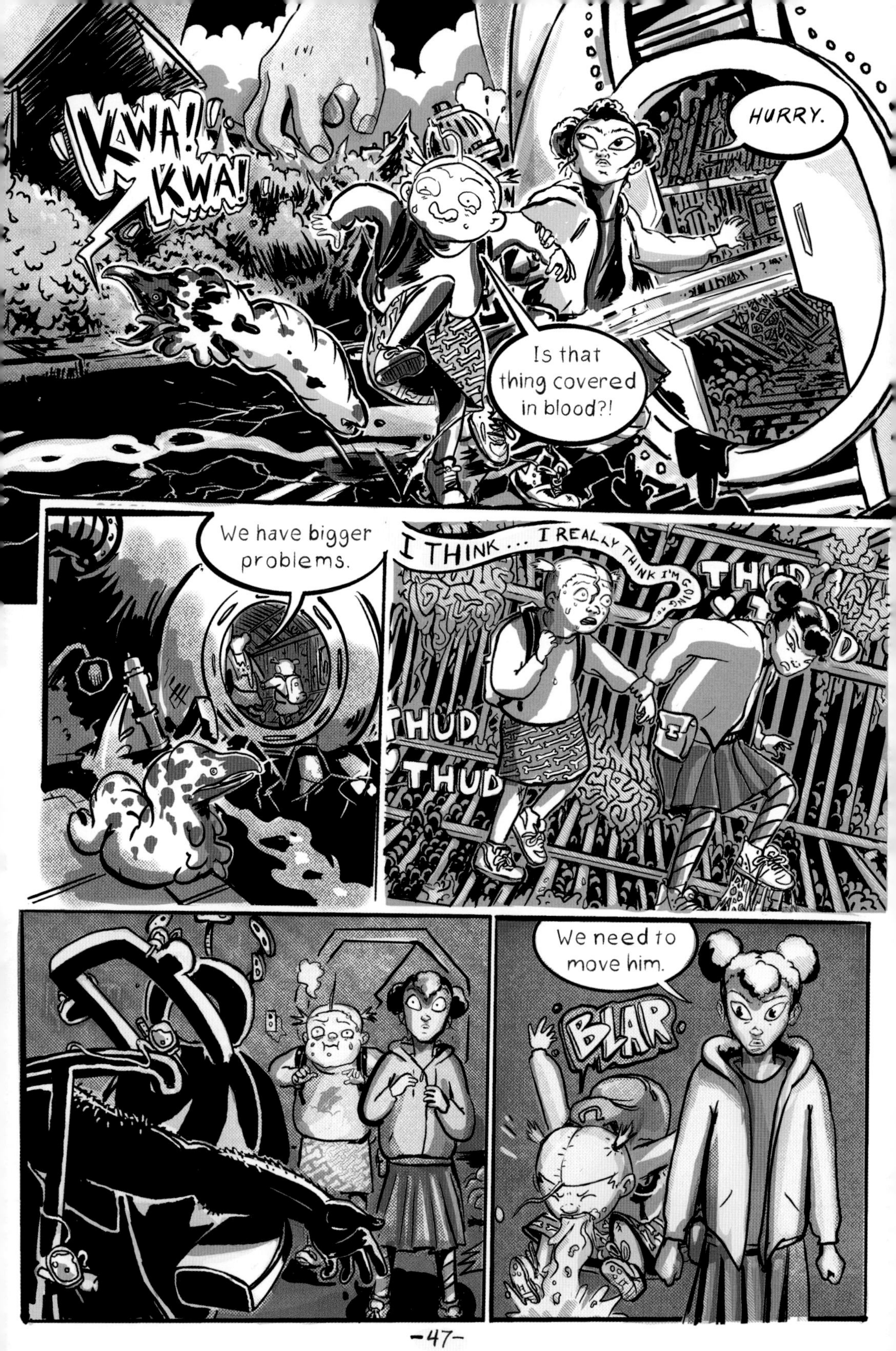
KWA! KWA!
HURRY.
Is that thing covered in blood?!
We have bigger problems.
I THINK... I REALLY THINK I'M GOING TO
THUD
THUD
THUD
THUD
We need to move him.
BLAR

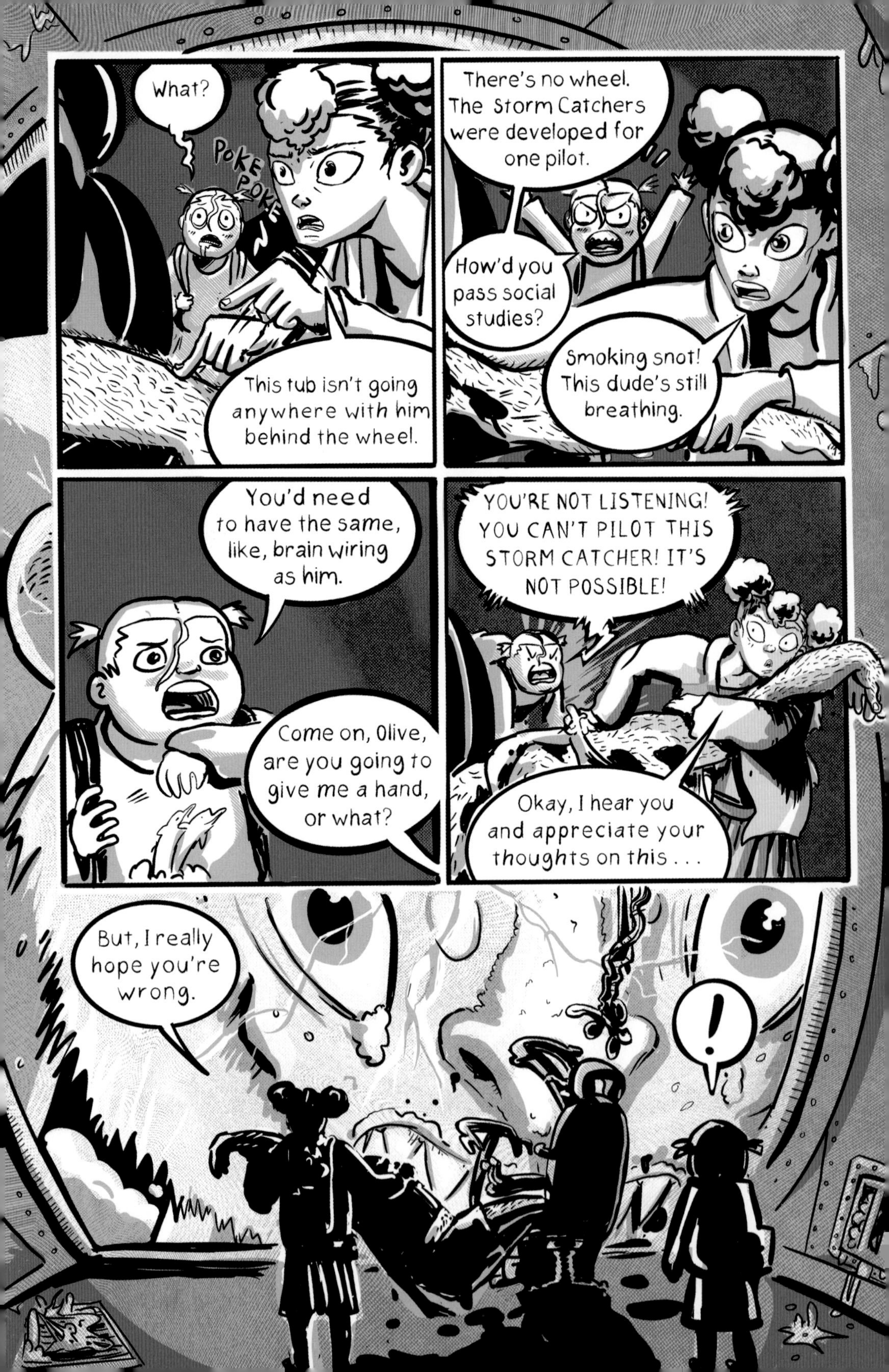
What?
POKE POKE
This tub isn't going anywhere with him behind the wheel.
There's no wheel. The Storm Catchers were developed for one pilot.
How'd you pass social studies?
Smoking snot! This dude's still breathing.
You'd need to have the same, like, brain wiring as him.
Come on, Olive, are you going to give me a hand, or what?
YOU'RE NOT LISTENING! YOU CAN'T PILOT THIS STORM CATCHER! IT'S NOT POSSIBLE!
Okay, I hear you and appreciate your thoughts on this . . .
But, I really hope you're wrong.
!

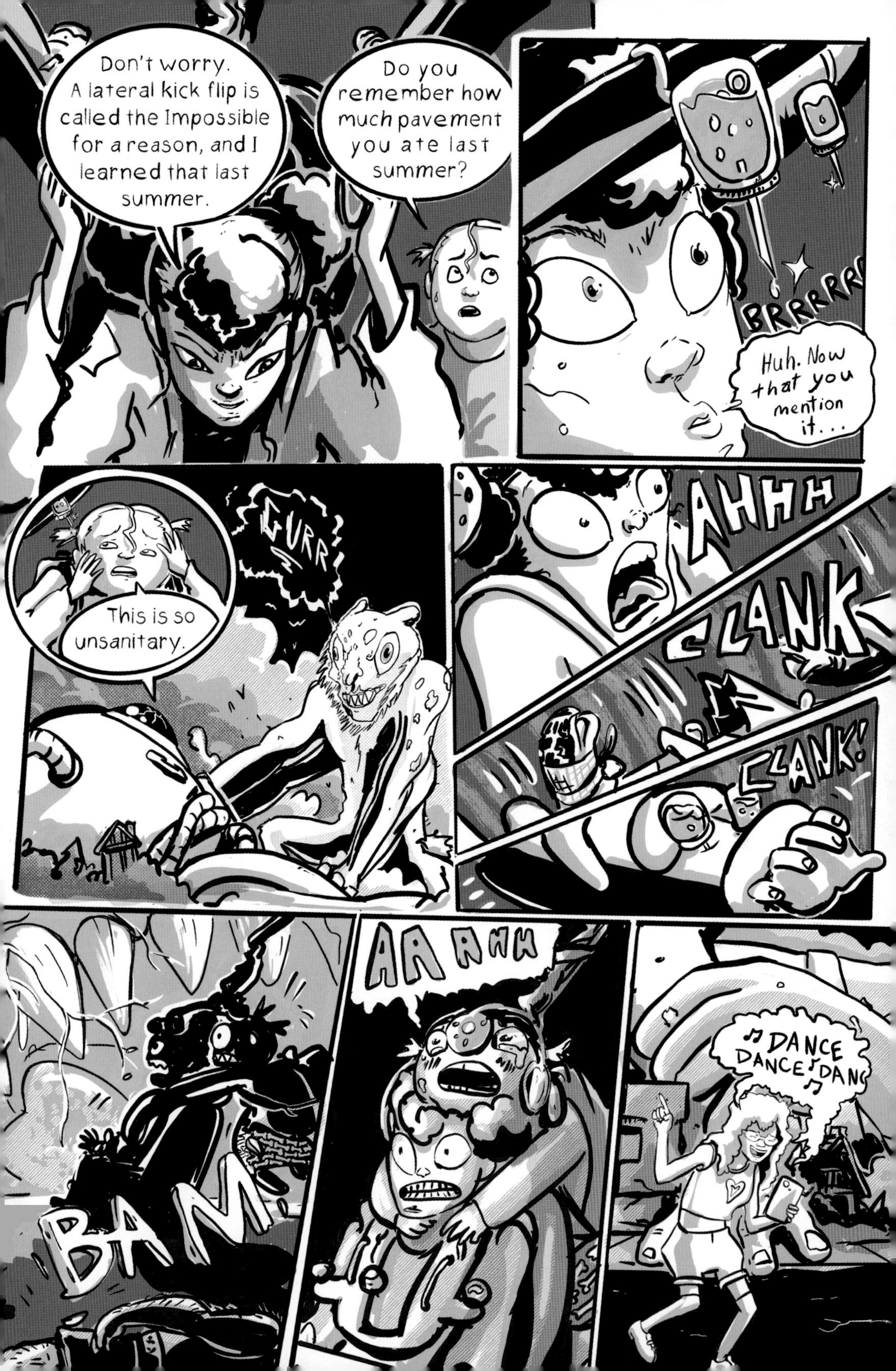
Don't worry. A lateral kick flip is called the Impossible for a reason, and I learned that last summer.
Do you remember how much pavement you ate last summer?
BRRRRRR
Huh. Now that you mention it . . .
This is so unsanitary.
GURR
AHHH
CLANK
CLANK!
BAM
AAAHH
DANCE DANCE DANC

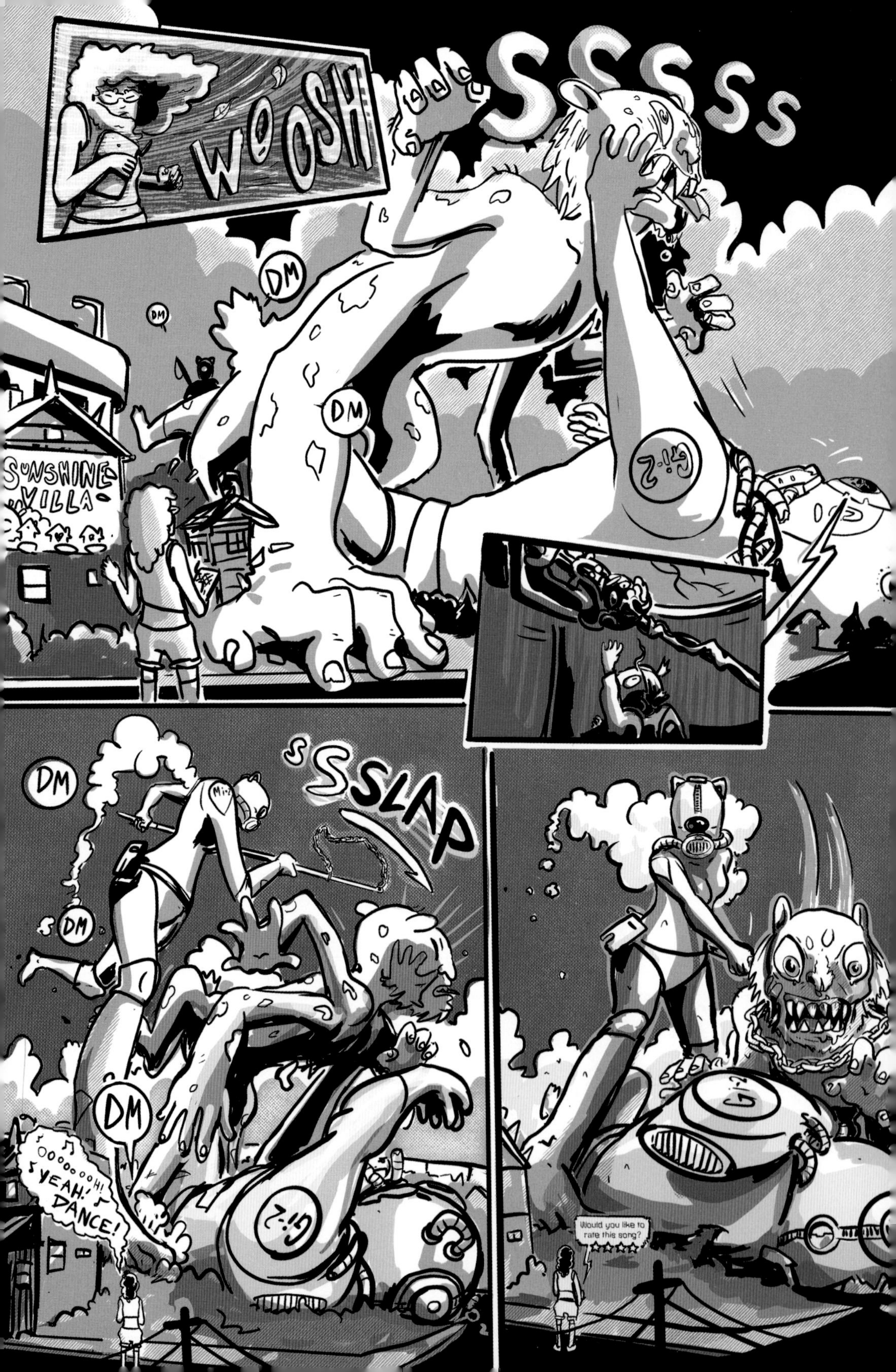
WOOSH
SSSSs
DM
DM
SUNSHINE VILLA
DM
Gi-Z
DM
sSSLAP
DM
DM
OOOOOOOH! YEAH! DANCE!
Gi-Z
Gi-Z
Would you like to rate this song?

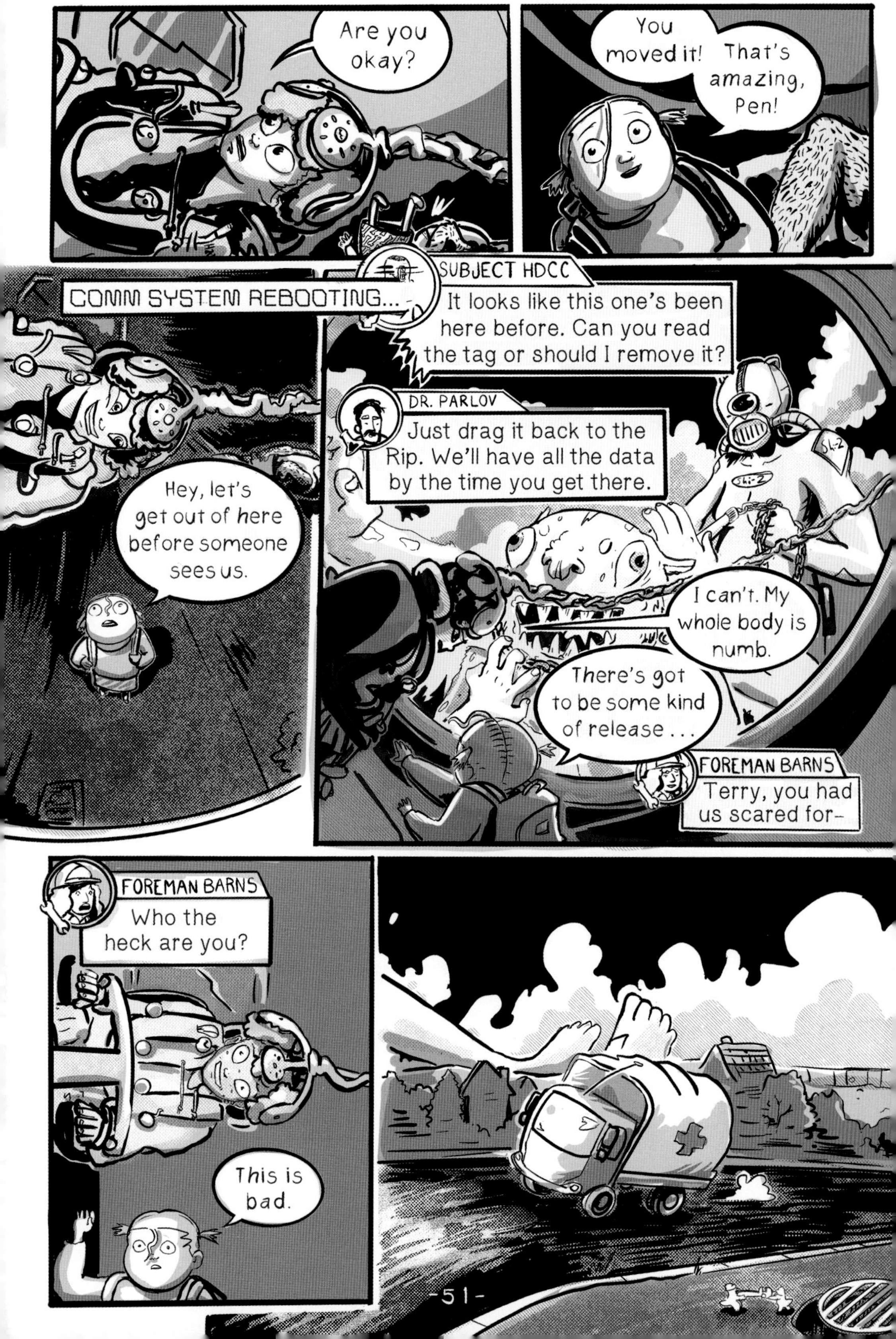
Are you okay?
You moved it!
That's amazing, Pen!
COMM SYSTEM REBOOTING...
SUBJECT HDCC
It looks like this one's been here before. Can you read the tag or should I remove it?
DR. PARLOV
Just drag it back to the Rip. We'll have all the data by the time you get there.
Hey, let's get out of here before someone sees us.
I can't. My whole body is numb.
There's got to be some kind of release . . .
FOREMAN BARNS
Terry, you had us scared for–
FOREMAN BARNS
Who the heck are you?
This is bad.

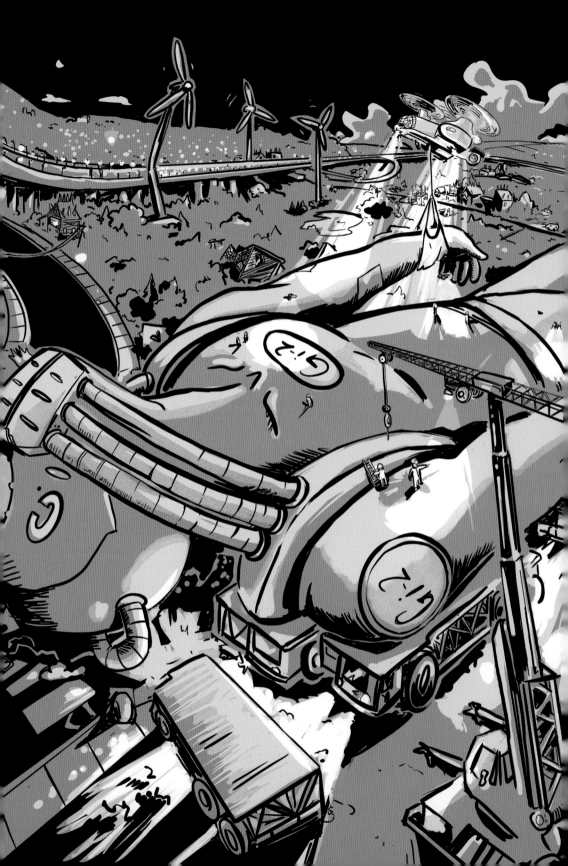

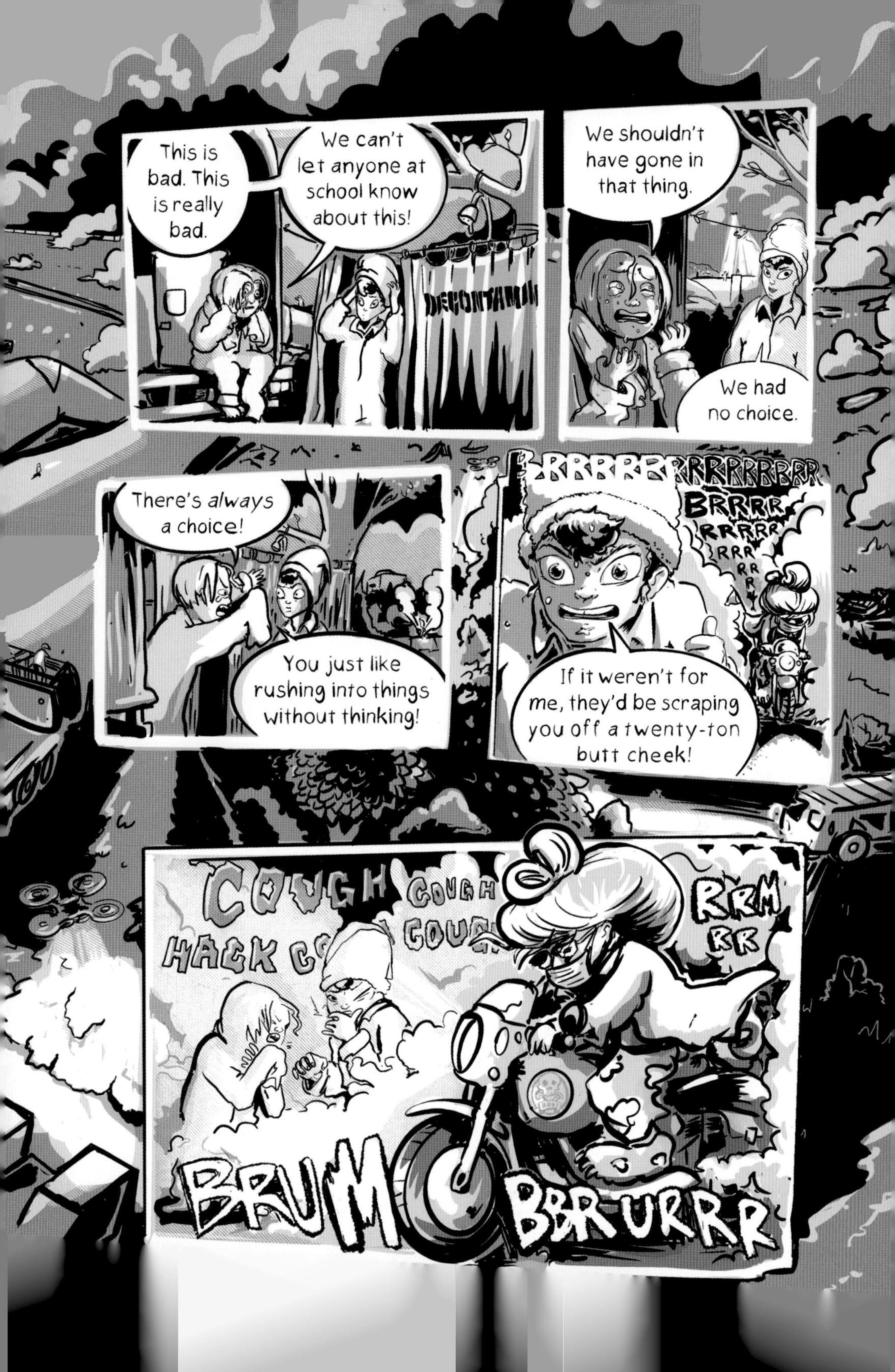
This is bad. This is really bad.
We can't let anyone at school know about this!
DECONTAMIN
We shouldn't have gone in that thing.
We had no choice.
There's always a choice!
You just like rushing into things without thinking!
BRRRRRRRRRRRRRR
BRRRR RRRRR RRR RR R
If it weren't for me, they'd be scraping you off a twenty-ton butt cheek!
COUGH COUGH
HACK CO COUG
RRM RR
BRUM BBRURRR

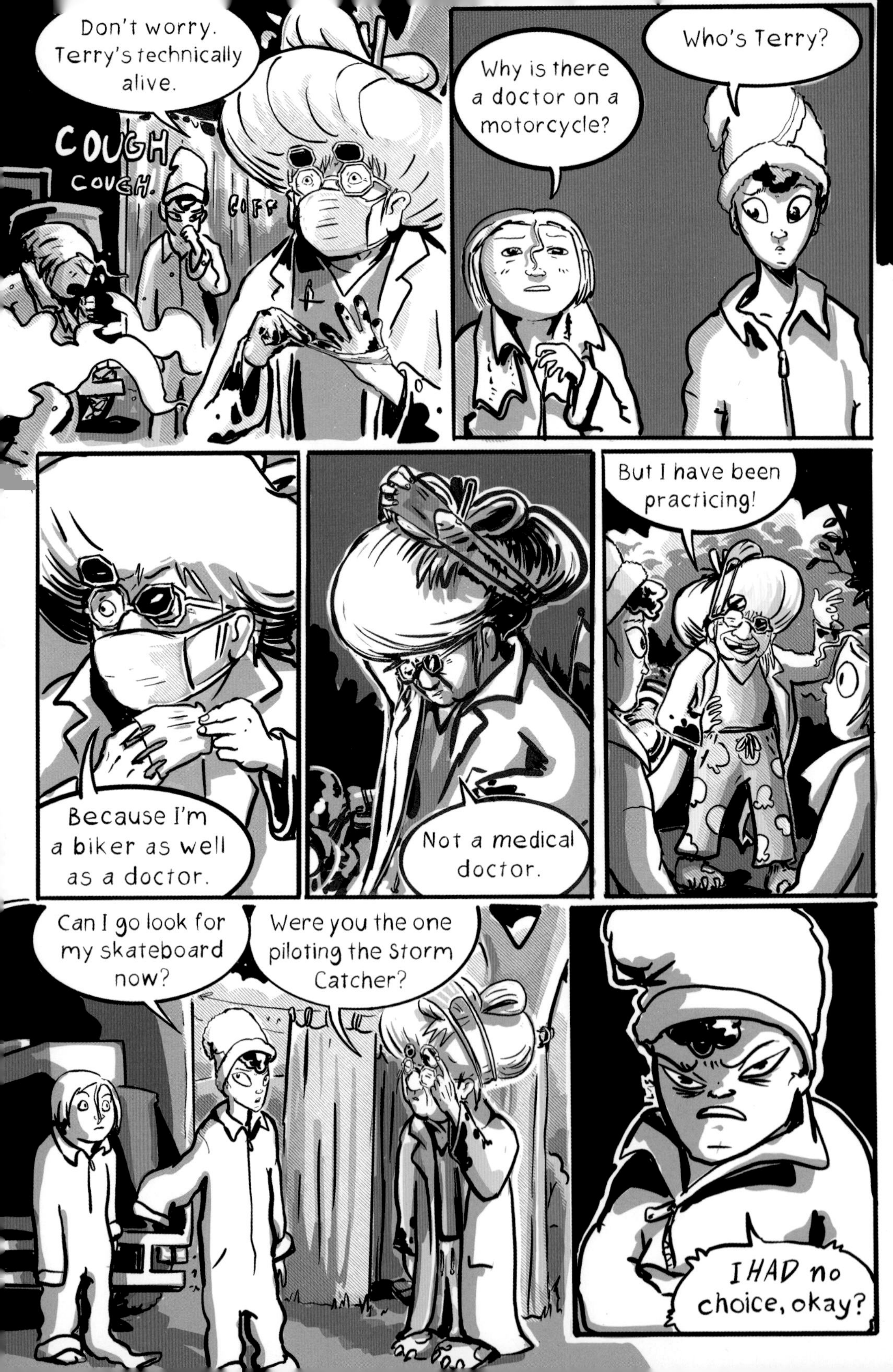
Don't worry. Terry's technically alive.
COUGH
COUGH.
COFF
Why is there a doctor on a motorcycle?
Who's Terry?
Because I'm a biker as well as a doctor.
Not a medical doctor.
But I have been practicing!
Can I go look for my skateboard now?
Were you the one piloting the Storm Catcher?
I HAD no choice, okay?

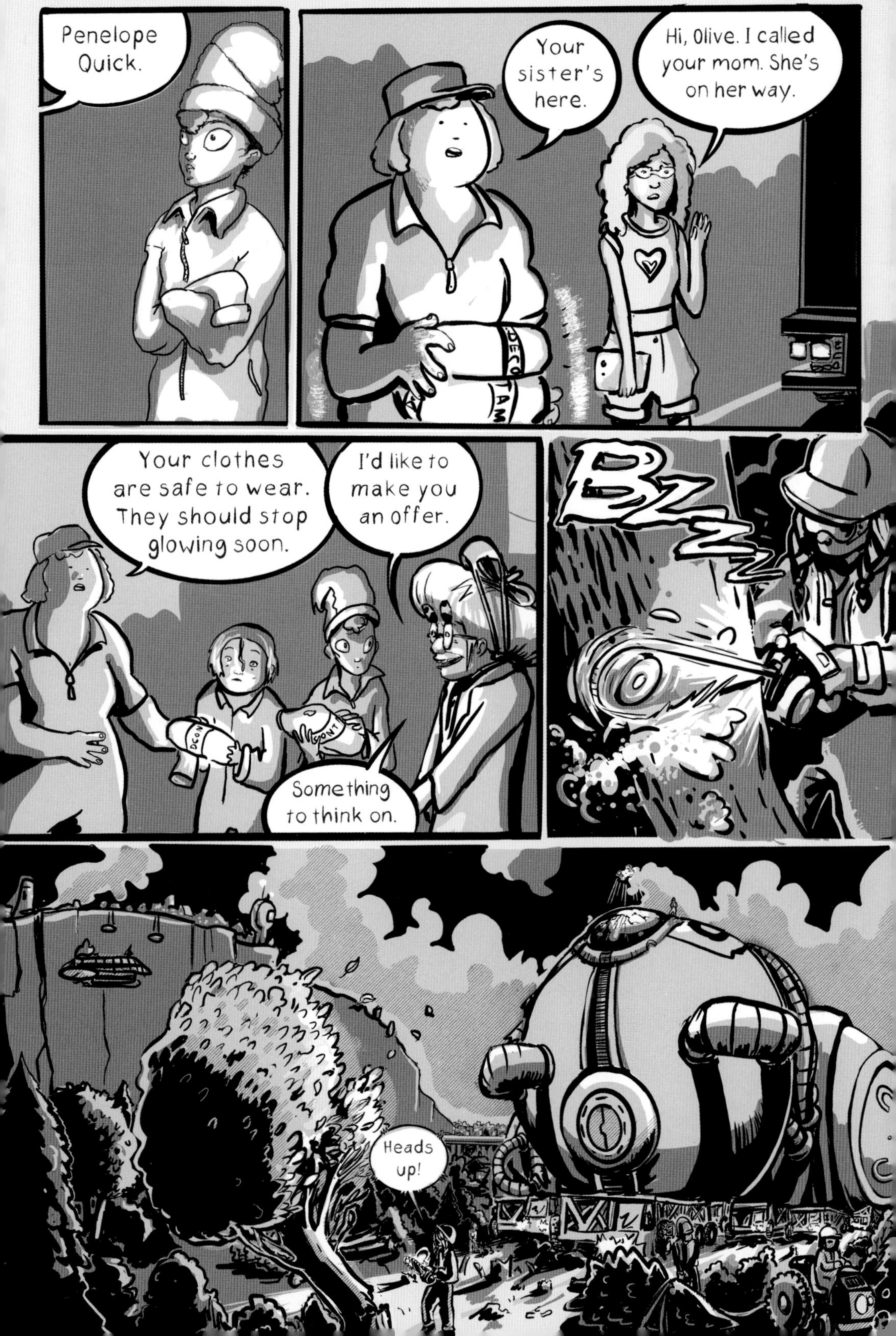
Penelope Quick.
Your sister's here.
Hi, Olive. I called your mom. She's on her way.
Your clothes are safe to wear. They should stop glowing soon.
I'd like to make you an offer.
Something to think on.
BZZZZ
Heads up!

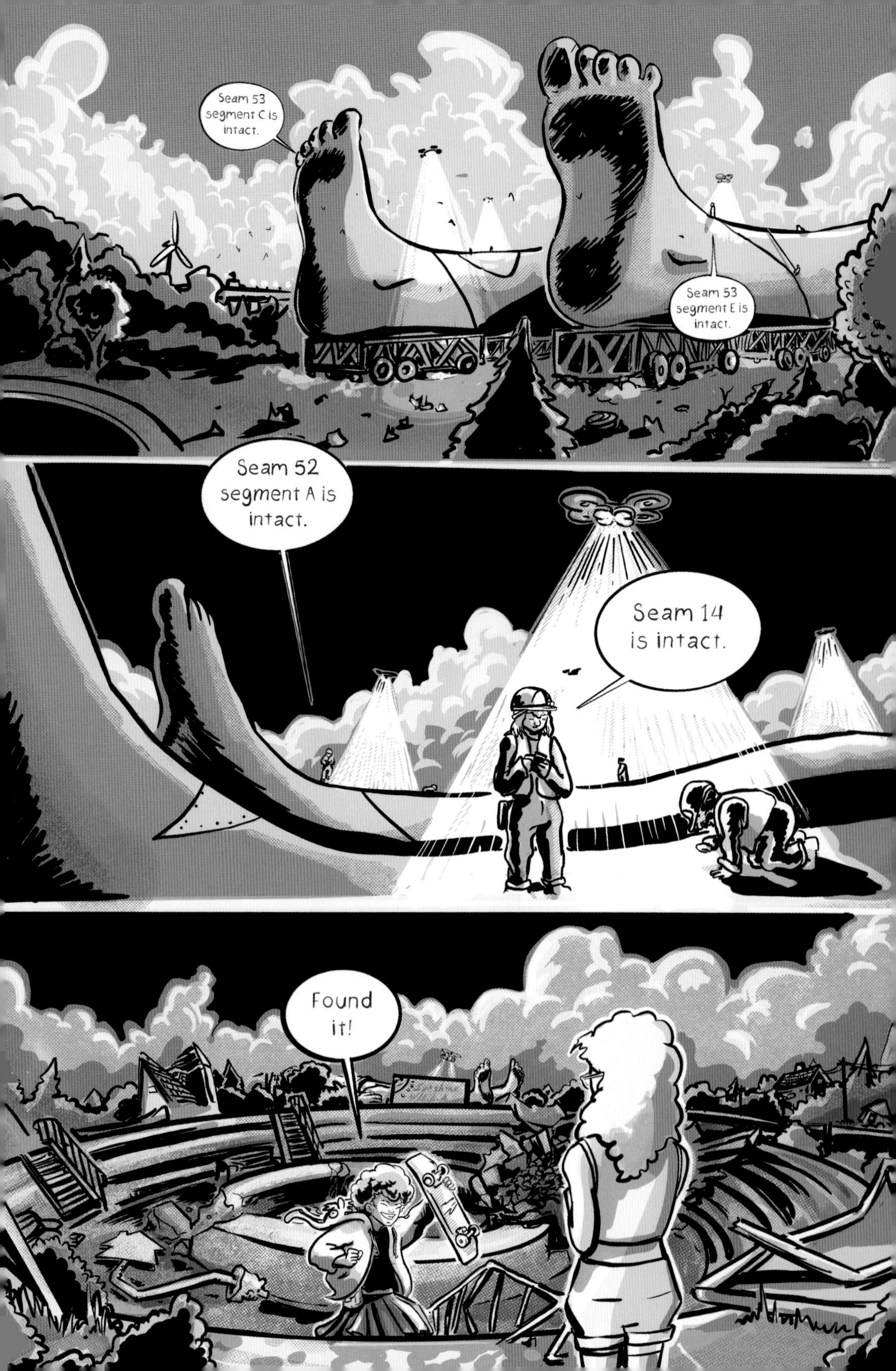
Seam 53 segment C is intact.
Seam 53 segment E is intact.
Seam 52 segment A is intact.
Seam 14 is intact.
Found it!

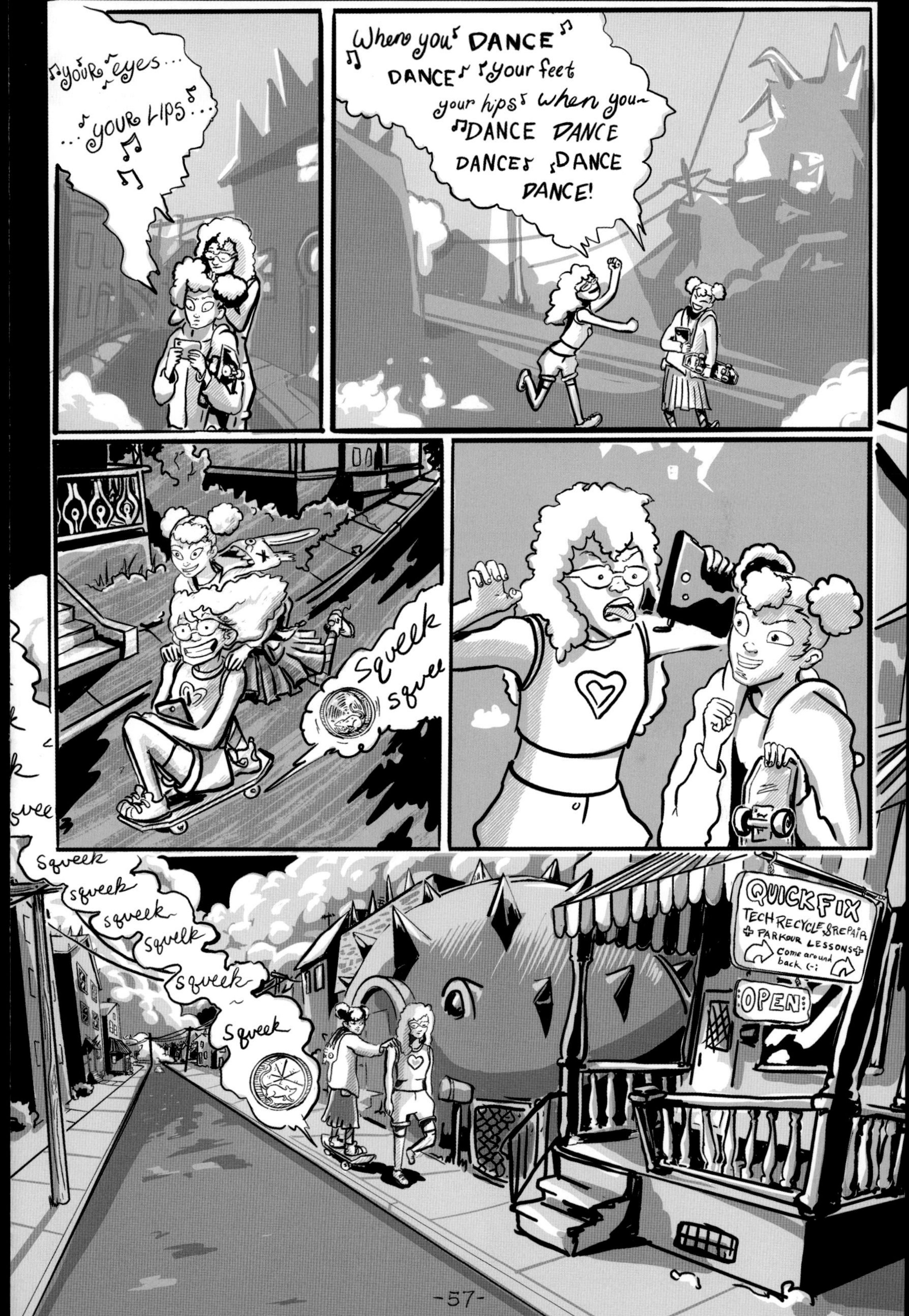

♪ your ♪ eyes...
...♪ your lips ♪...
When you ♪ DANCE ♪ DANCE ♪ ♪ your feet your hips ♪ when you ♪ DANCE DANCE DANCE ♪ ♪ DANCE DANCE!
Sqveek sqvee
sqveek sqveek sqveek sqvelk sqveek ~ sqveek
QUICK FIX
TECH RECYCLE & REPAIR
+ PARKOUR LESSONS +
Come around back (-:
OPEN

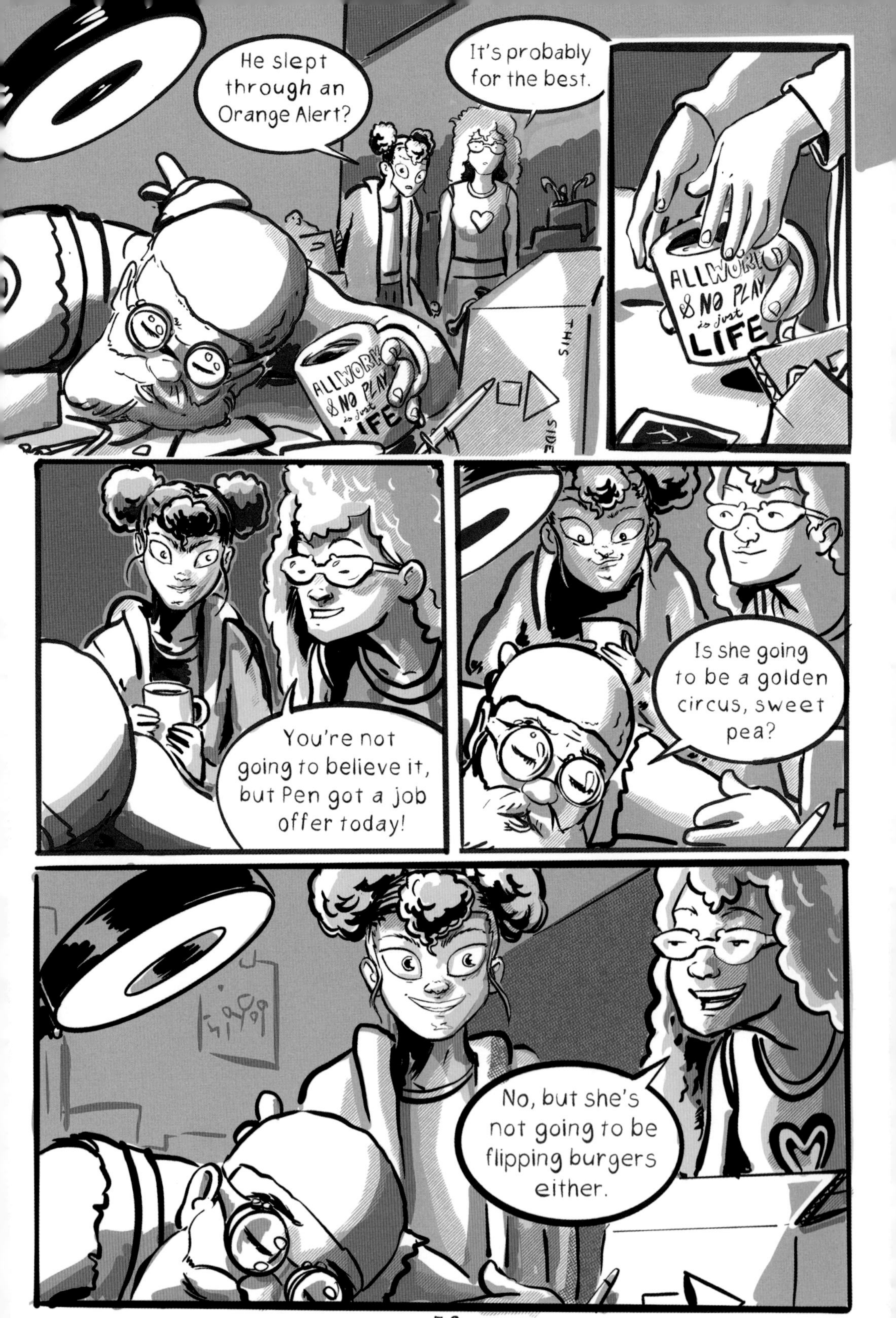
He slept through an Orange Alert?
It's probably for the best.
THIS SIDE
ALLWORK & NO PLAY is just LIFE
ALLWORK & NO PLAY is just LIFE
You're not going to believe it, but Pen got a job offer today!
Is she going to be a golden circus, sweet pea?
No, but she's not going to be flipping burgers either.

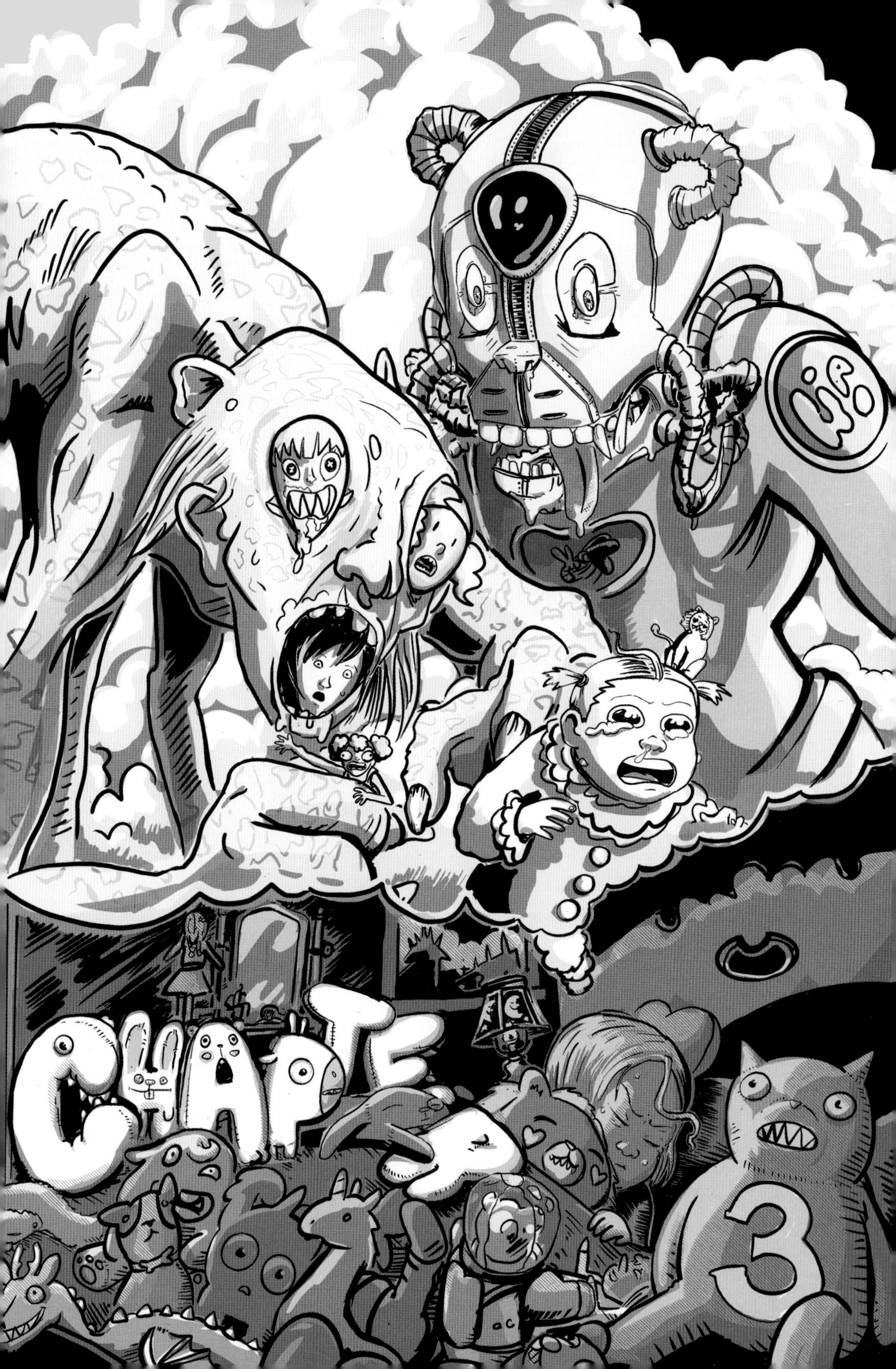
CHAPTER
3

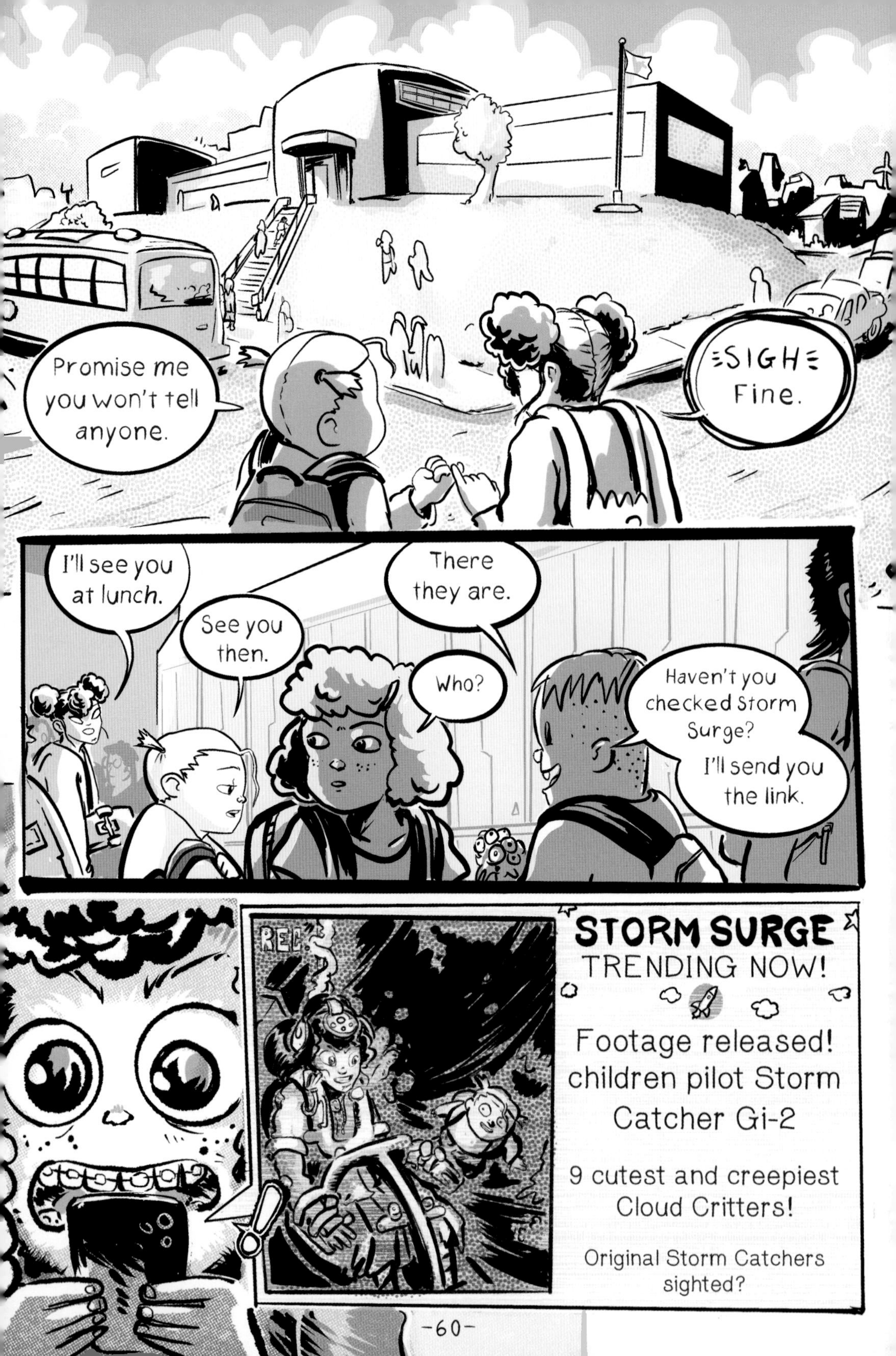
Promise me you won't tell anyone.
SIGH Fine.
I'll see you at lunch.
See you then.
There they are.
Who?
Haven't you checked Storm Surge?
I'll send you the link.
REC.
STORM SURGE
TRENDING NOW!
Footage released! children pilot Storm Catcher Gi-2
9 cutest and creepiest Cloud Critters!
Original Storm Catchers sighted?

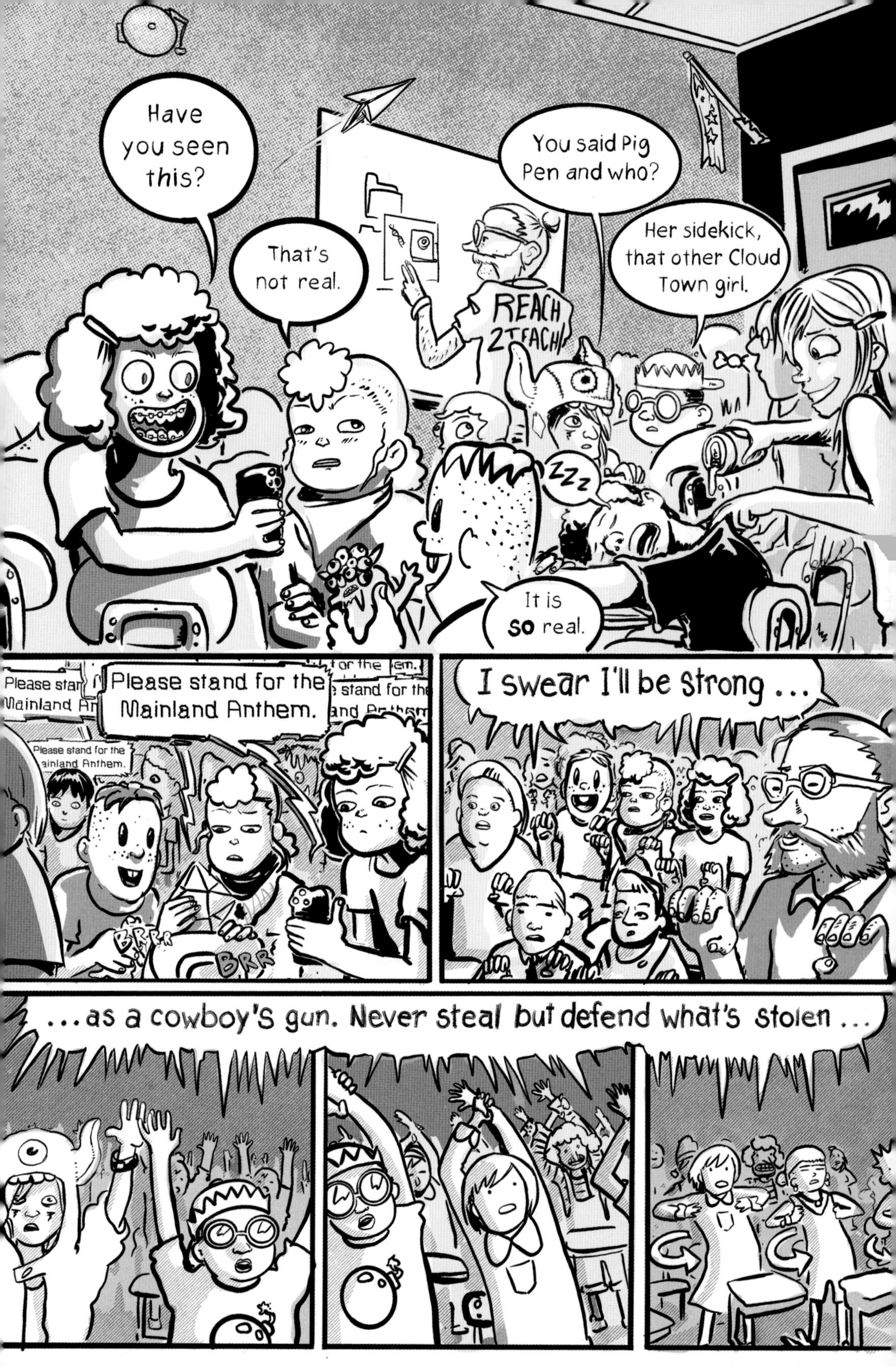
Have you seen this?
That's not real.
You said Pig Pen and who?
Her sidekick, that other Cloud Town girl.
REACH 2 TEACH
ZZZ
It is **so** real.
Please stand for the Mainland Anthem.
BRRR
BRR
I swear I'll be strong . . .
. . . as a cowboy's gun. Never steal but defend what's stolen . . .

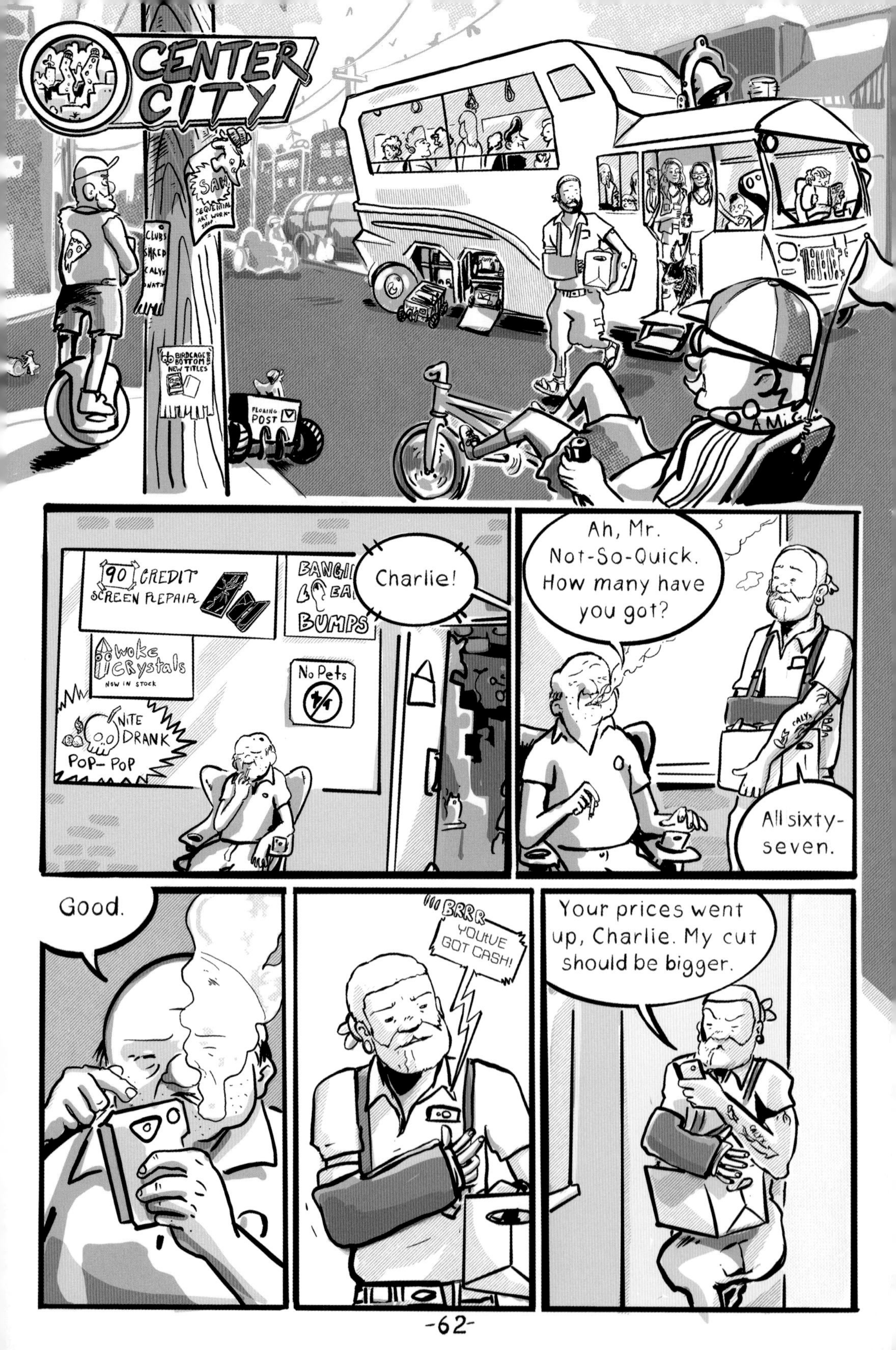
CENTER CITY
SAW SEQUENTIAL ART WORKSHOP
CLUBS
SHRED
CALYX
BIRDCAGE BOTTOM NEW TITLES
POST
90 CREDIT SCREEN REPAIR
BUMPS
woke CRYstals NOW IN STOCK
NITE DRANK POP-POP
No Pets
Charlie!
Ah, Mr. Not-So-Quick. How many have you got?
All sixty-seven.
Good.
BRRR
YOU'VE GOT CASH!
Your prices went up, Charlie. My cut should be bigger.

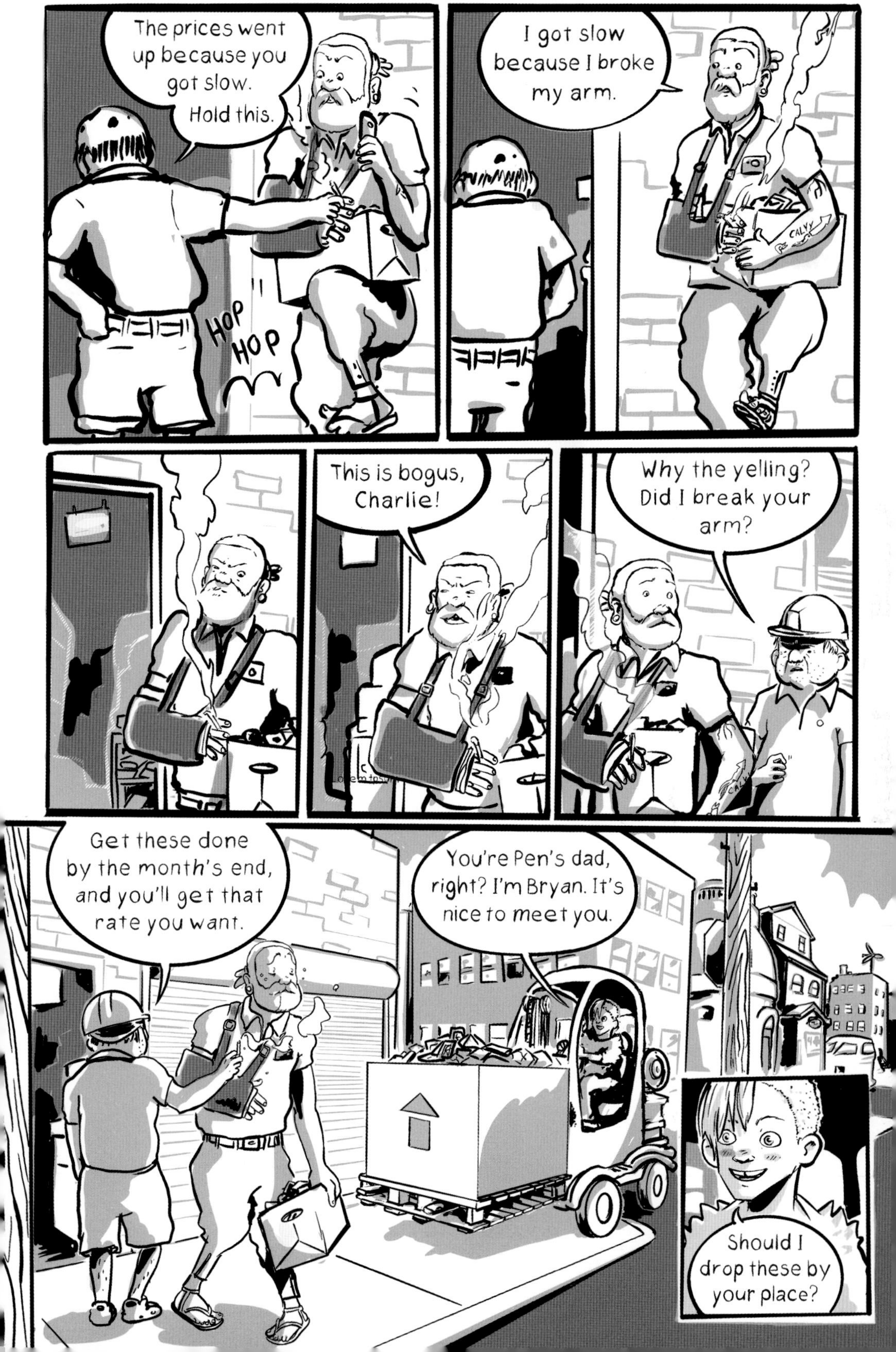
The prices went up because you got slow.
Hold this.
HOP HOP
I got slow because I broke my arm.
CALVY
This is bogus, Charlie!
Why the yelling? Did I break your arm?
Get these done by the month's end, and you'll get that rate you want.
You're Pen's dad, right? I'm Bryan. It's nice to meet you.
Should I drop these by your place?

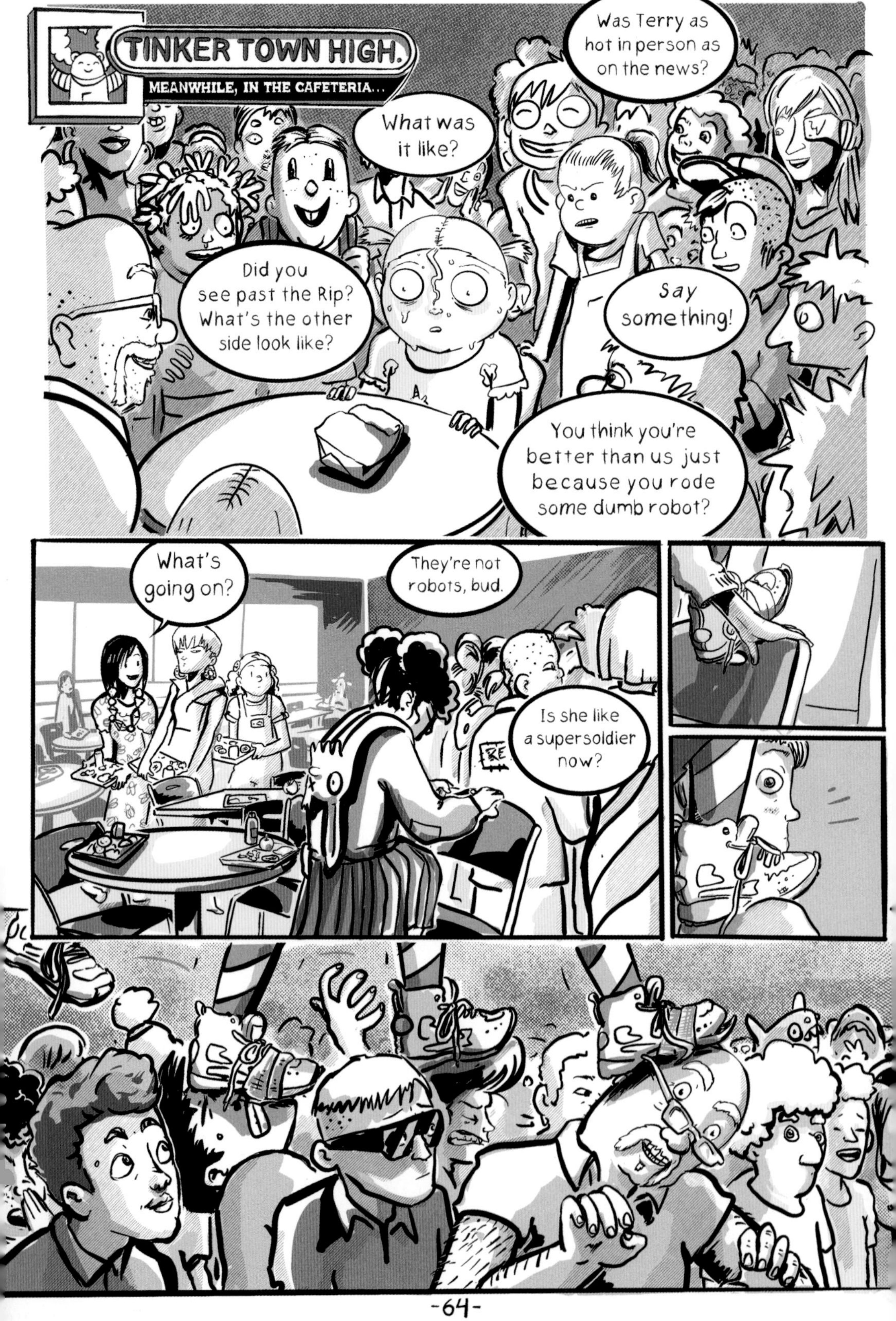
TINKER TOWN HIGH.
MEANWHILE, IN THE CAFETERIA...
Was Terry as hot in person as on the news?
What was it like?
Did you see past the Rip? What's the other side look like?
Say something!
You think you're better than us just because you rode some dumb robot?
What's going on?
They're not robots, bud.
Is she like a supersoldier now?

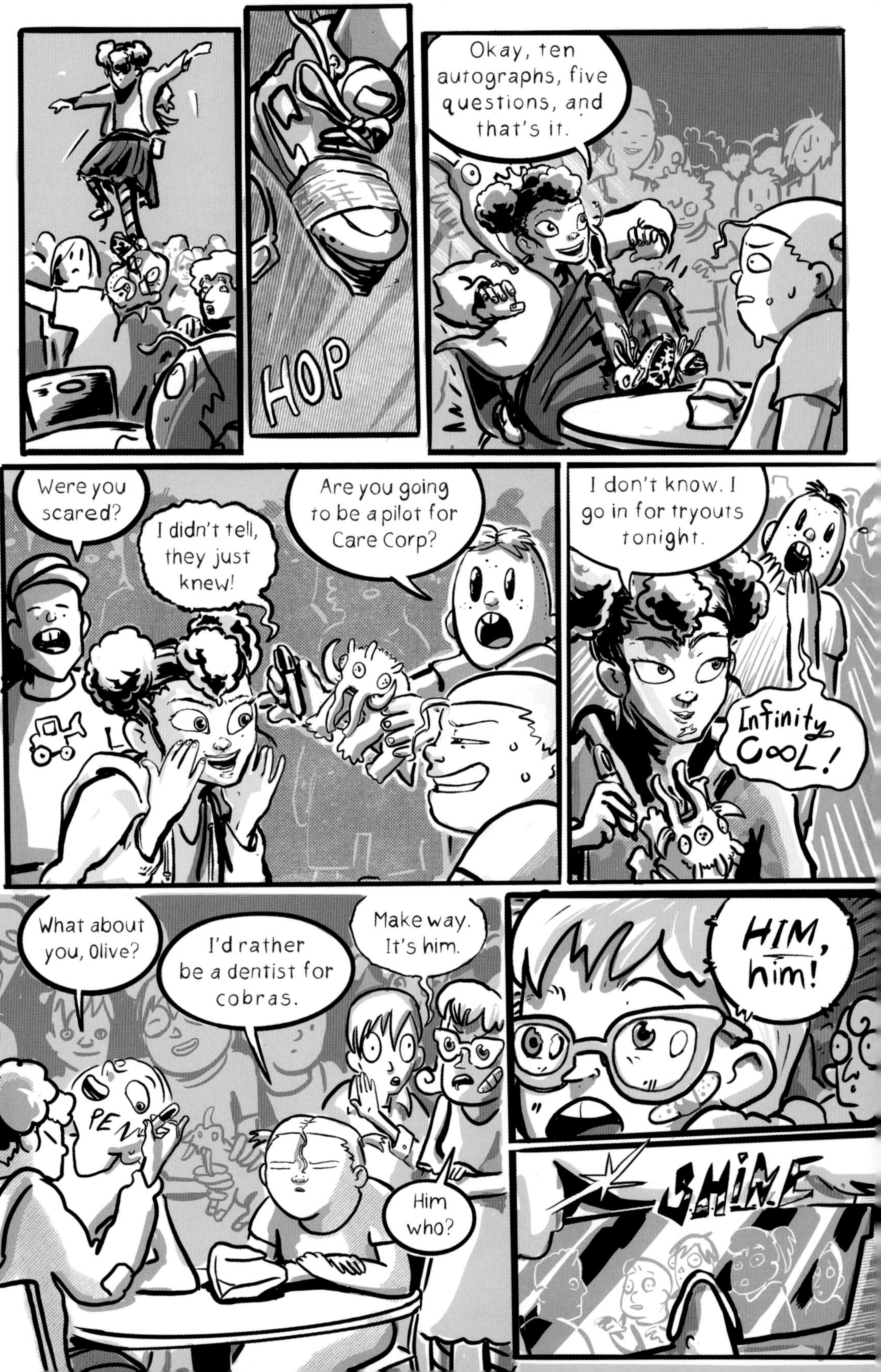
HOP
Okay, ten autographs, five questions, and that's it.
Were you scared?
I didn't tell, they just knew!
Are you going to be a pilot for Care Corp?
I don't know. I go in for tryouts tonight.
Infinity COOL!
What about you, Olive?
I'd rather be a dentist for cobras.
Make way. It's him.
Him who?
PEN
HIM, him!
SHINE

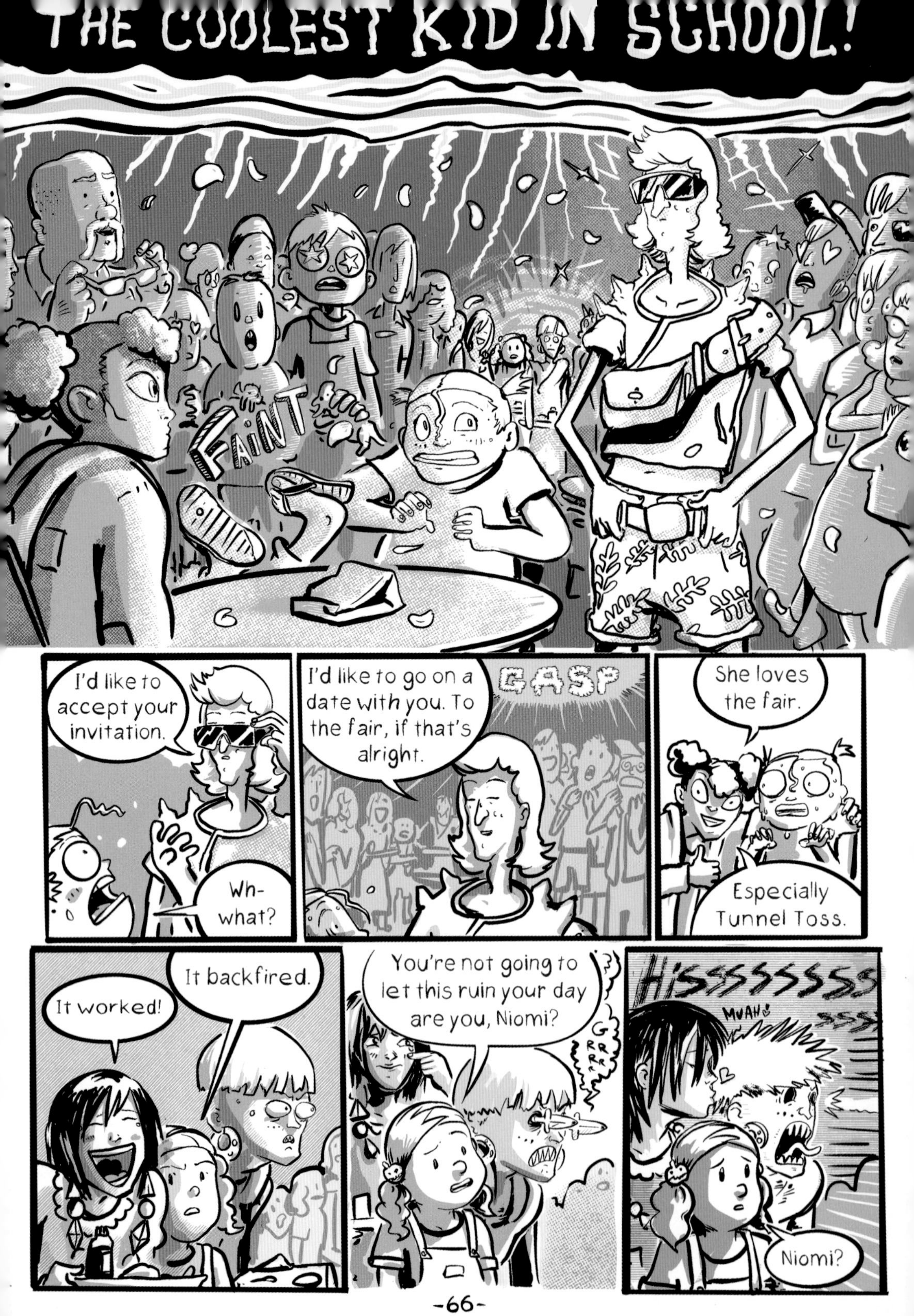
THE COOLEST KID IN SCHOOL!
FAINT
I'd like to accept your invitation.
Wh- what?
I'd like to go on a date with you. To the fair, if that's alright.
GASP
She loves the fair.
Especially Tunnel Toss.
It worked!
It backfired.
You're not going to let this ruin your day are you, Niomi?
GRRRR
HISSSSSSSSS
MUAH
Niomi?

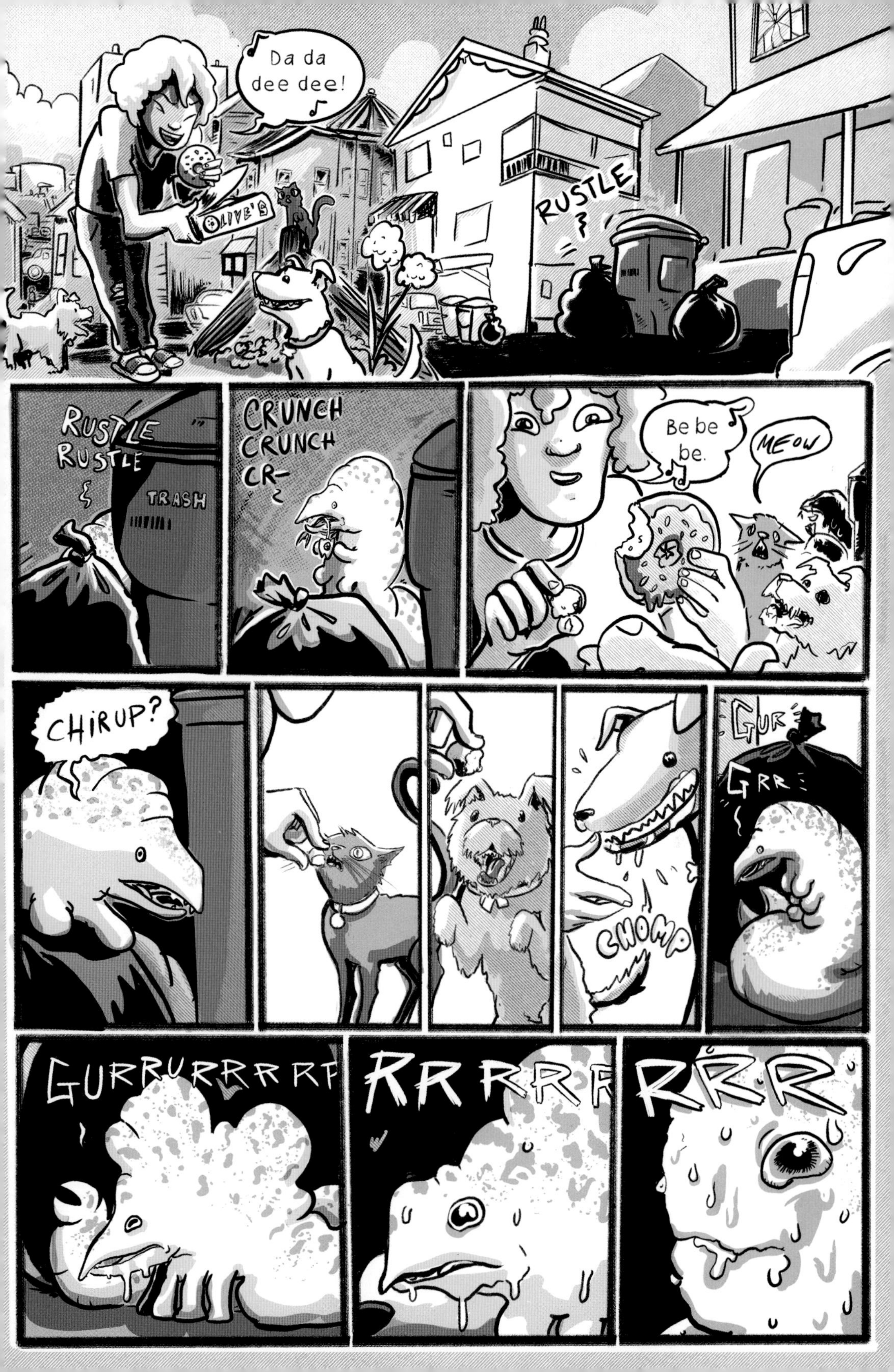
Da da dee dee!
OLIVE'S
RUSTLE
RUSTLE RUSTLE
TRASH
CRUNCH CRUNCH CR-
Be be be.
MEOW
CHIRUP?
CHOMP
GUR
GRR
GURRURRRRRR
RRRRRR
RRR

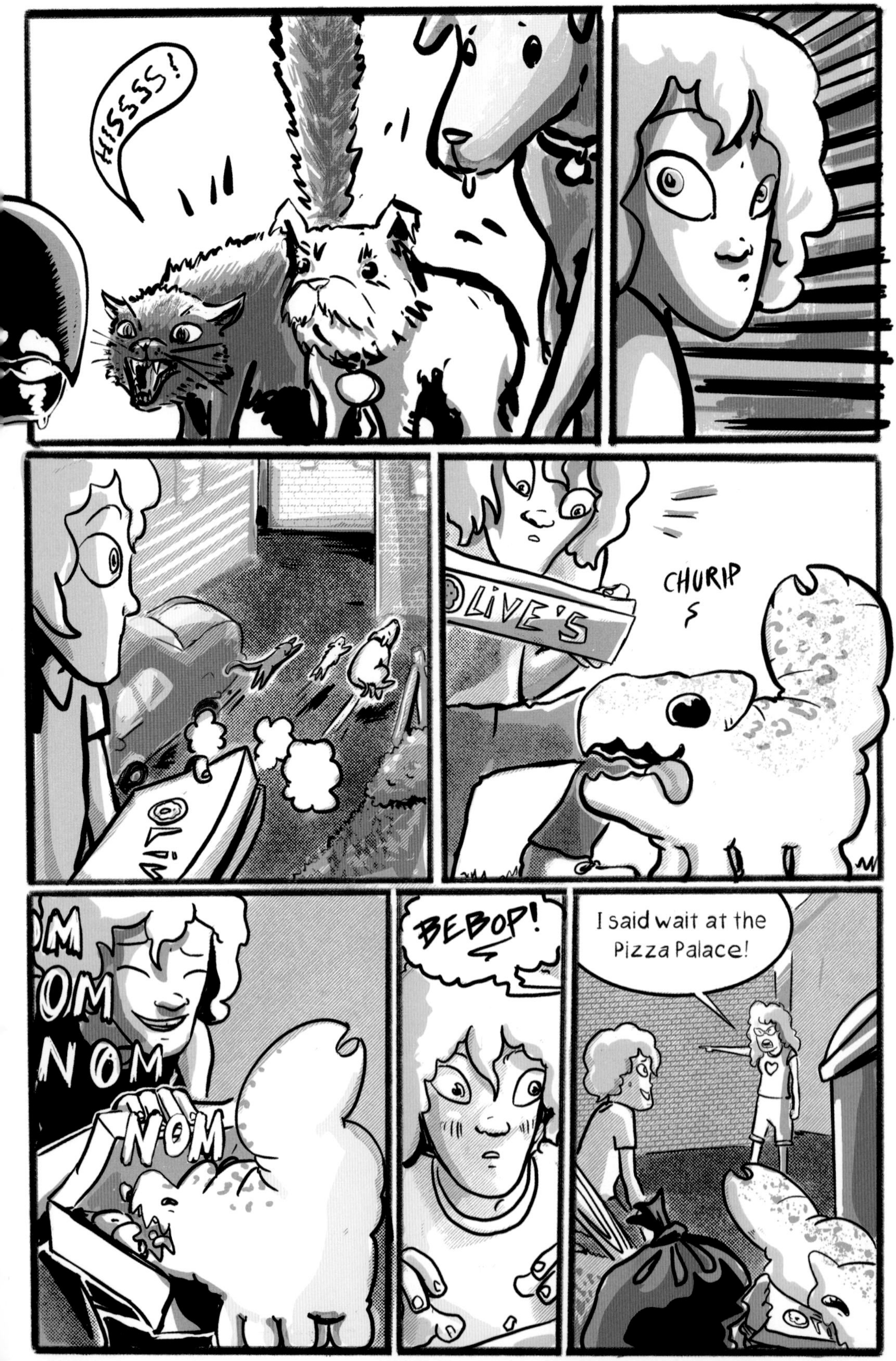
HISSSS!
CHURIP
OLIVE'S
OM
OM
NOM
NOM
BEBOP!
I said wait at the Pizza Palace!

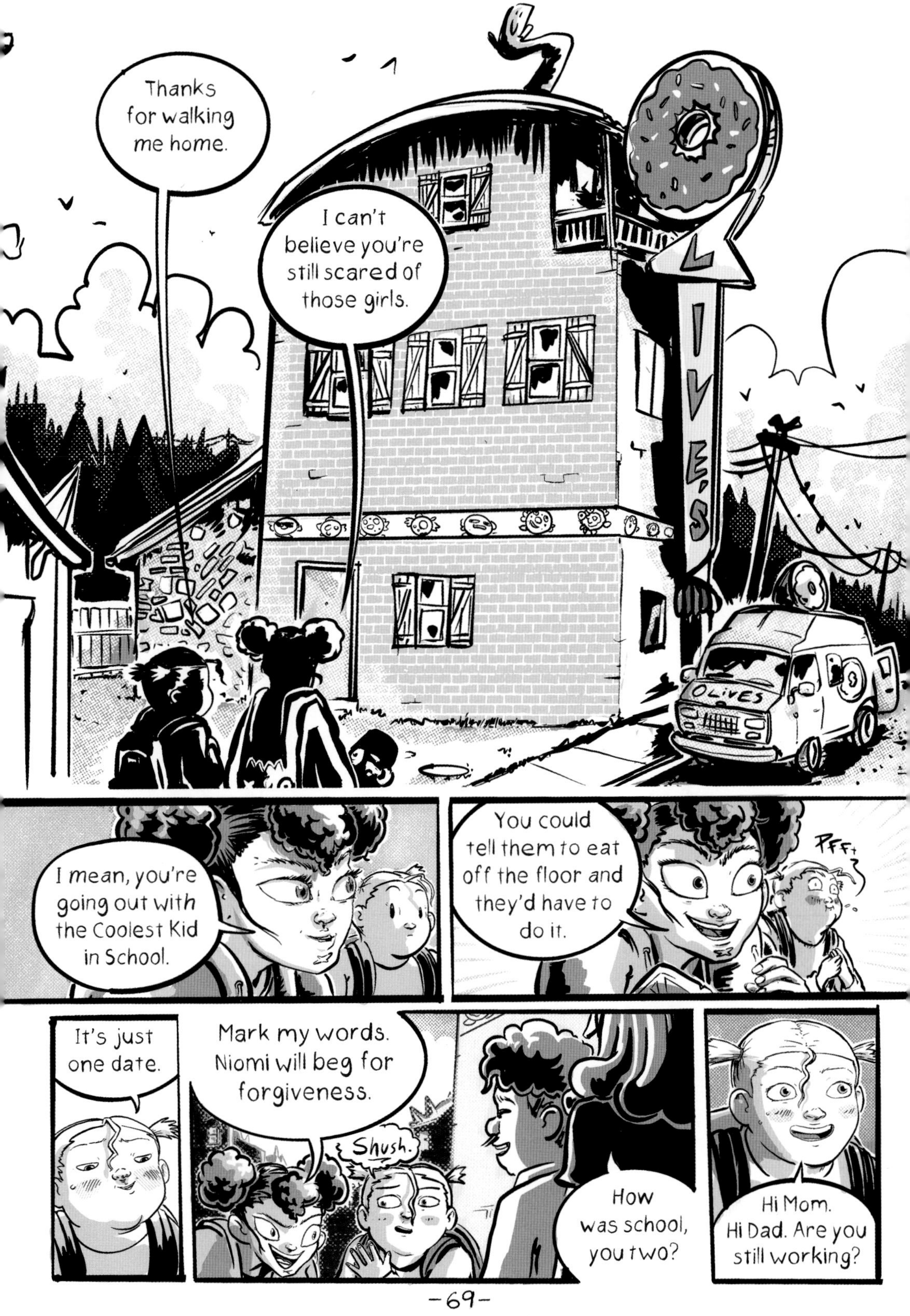
Thanks for walking me home.
I can't believe you're still scared of those girls.
OLIVE'S
OLIVES
I mean, you're going out with the Coolest Kid in School.
You could tell them to eat off the floor and they'd have to do it.
PFFT
It's just one date.
Mark my words. Niomi will beg for forgiveness.
Shush.
How was school, you two?
Hi Mom. Hi Dad. Are you still working?

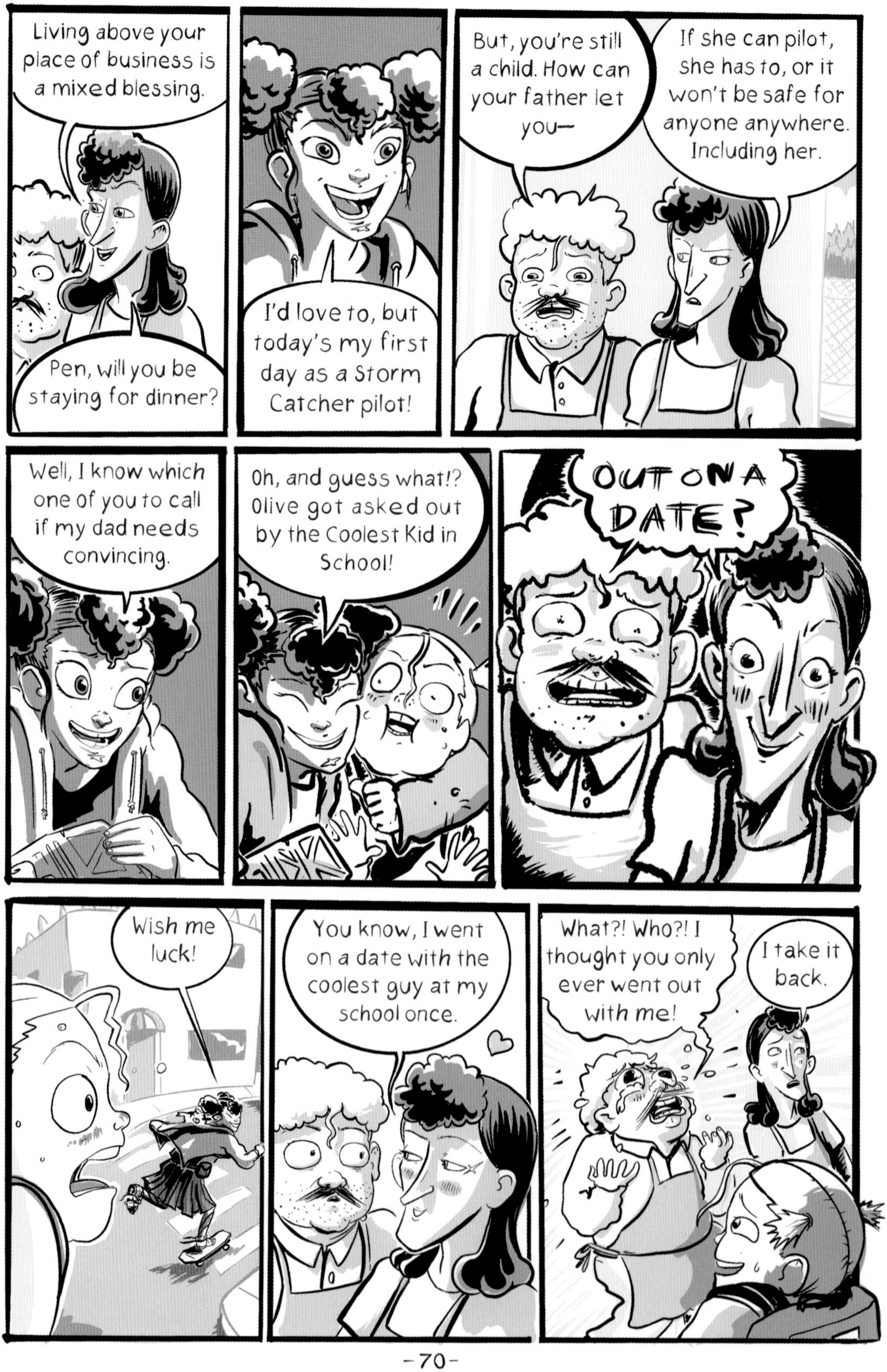
Living above your place of business is a mixed blessing.
Pen, will you be staying for dinner?
I'd love to, but today's my first day as a Storm Catcher pilot!
But, you're still a child. How can your father let you—
If she can pilot, she has to, or it won't be safe for anyone anywhere. Including her.
Well, I know which one of you to call if my dad needs convincing.
Oh, and guess what!? Olive got asked out by the Coolest Kid in School!
OUT ON A DATE?
Wish me luck!
You know, I went on a date with the coolest guy at my school once.
What?! Who?! I thought you only ever went out with me!
I take it back.

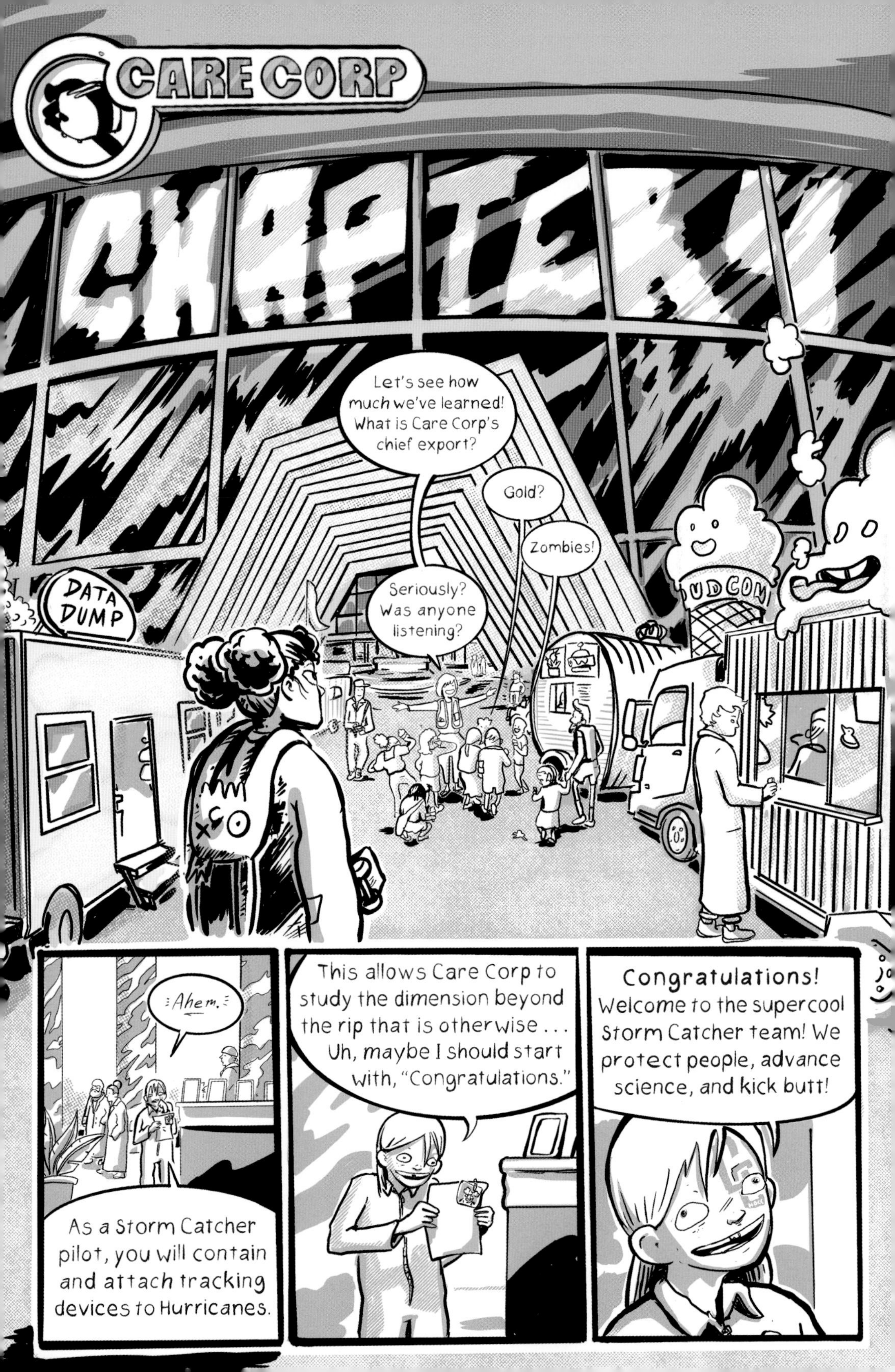
CARE CORP
CHAPTER
DATA DUMP
Let's see how much we've learned! What is Care Corp's chief export?
Gold?
Zombies!
Seriously? Was anyone listening?
Ahem.
As a Storm Catcher pilot, you will contain and attach tracking devices to Hurricanes.
This allows Care Corp to study the dimension beyond the rip that is otherwise . . . Uh, maybe I should start with, "Congratulations."
Congratulations! Welcome to the supercool Storm Catcher team! We protect people, advance science, and kick butt!

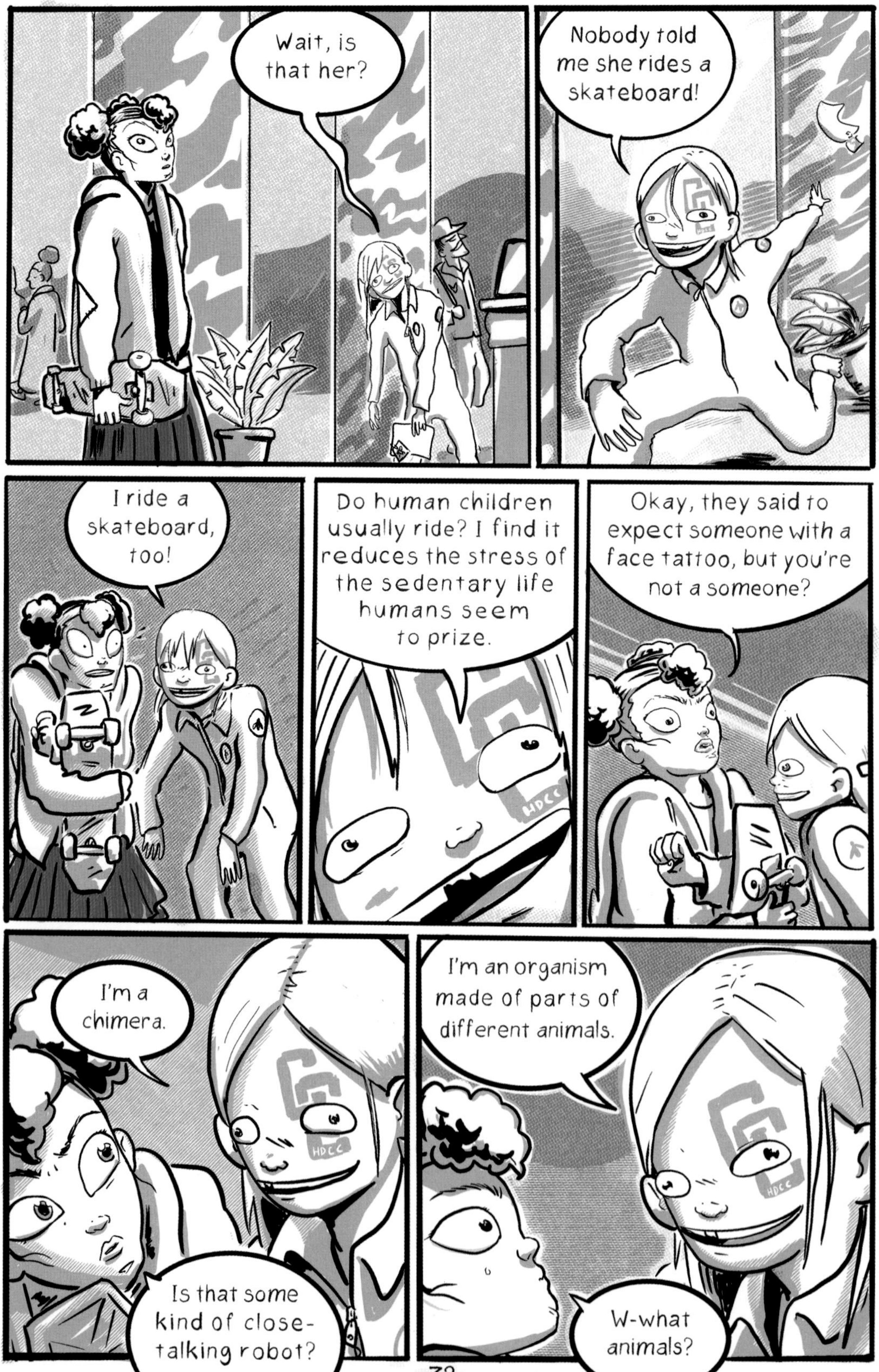
Wait, is that her?
Nobody told me she rides a skateboard!
I ride a skateboard, too!
Do human children usually ride? I find it reduces the stress of the sedentary life humans seem to prize.
Okay, they said to expect someone with a face tattoo, but you're not a someone?
I'm a chimera.
Is that some kind of close-talking robot?
I'm an organism made of parts of different animals.
W-what animals?

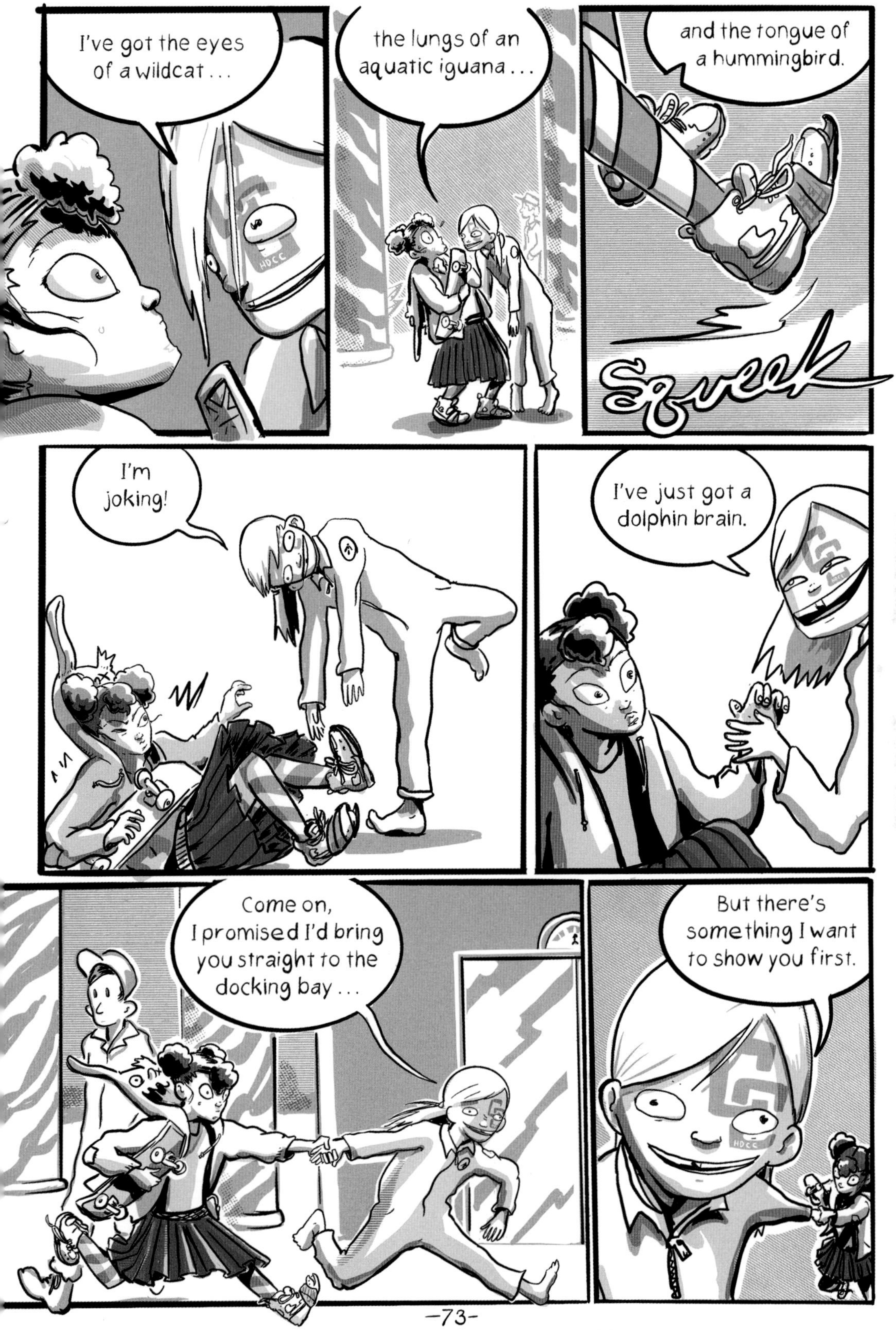
I've got the eyes of a wildcat . . .
HDCC
the lungs of an aquatic iguana . . .
and the tongue of a hummingbird.
Squeek
I'm joking!
I've just got a dolphin brain.
Come on, I promised I'd bring you straight to the docking bay . . .
But there's something I want to show you first.
HDCC

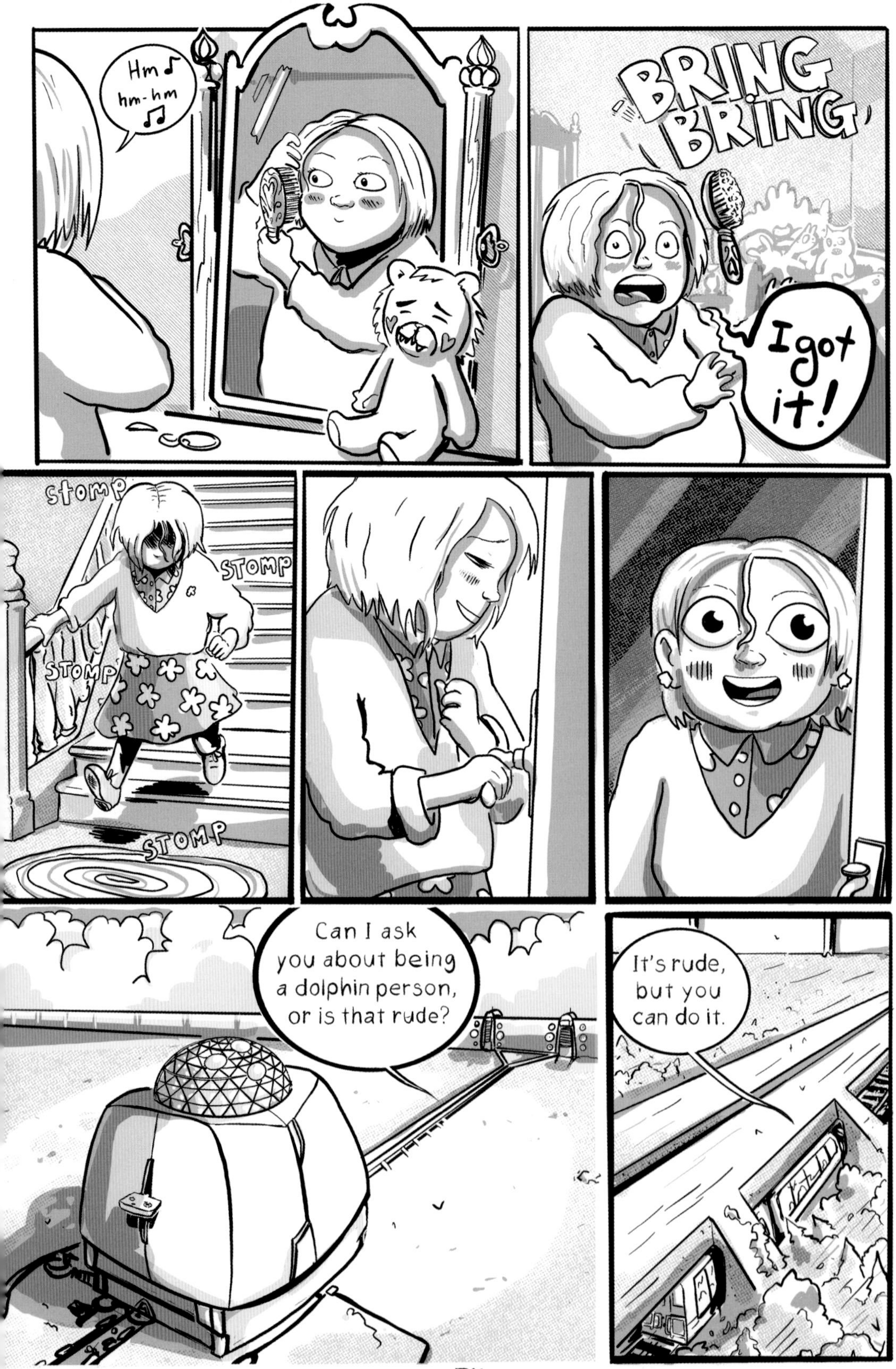
Hm ♪ hm-hm ♫
BRING BRING
I got it!
STOMP
STOMP
STOMP
STOMP
Can I ask you about being a dolphin person, or is that rude?
It's rude, but you can do it.

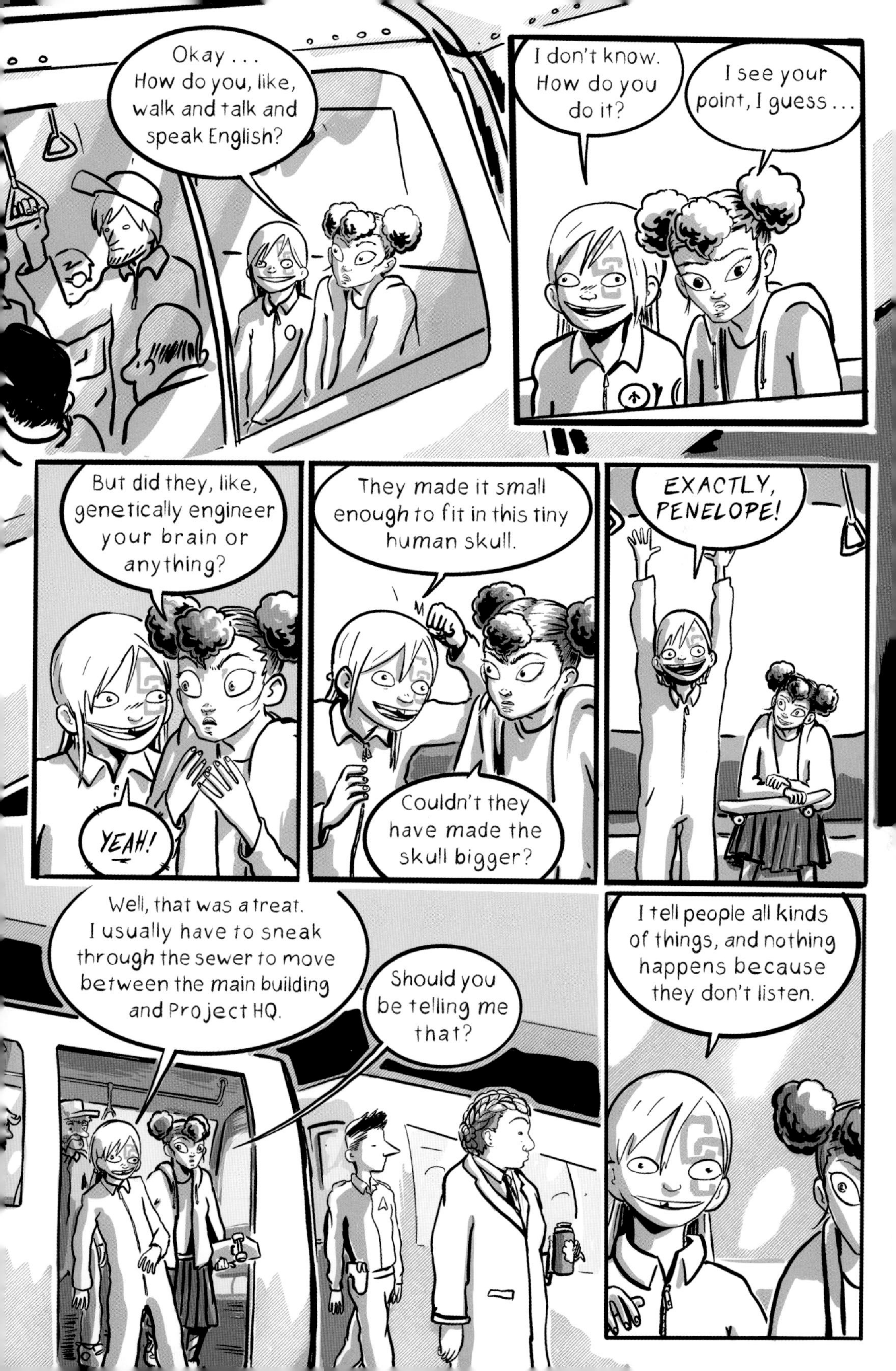

Okay . . .
How do you, like, walk and talk and speak English?
I don't know. How do you do it?
I see your point, I guess . . .
But did they, like, genetically engineer your brain or anything?
YEAH!
They made it small enough to fit in this tiny human skull.
Couldn't they have made the skull bigger?
EXACTLY, PENELOPE!
Well, that was a treat. I usually have to sneak through the sewer to move between the main building and Project HQ.
Should you be telling me that?
I tell people all kinds of things, and nothing happens because they don't listen.

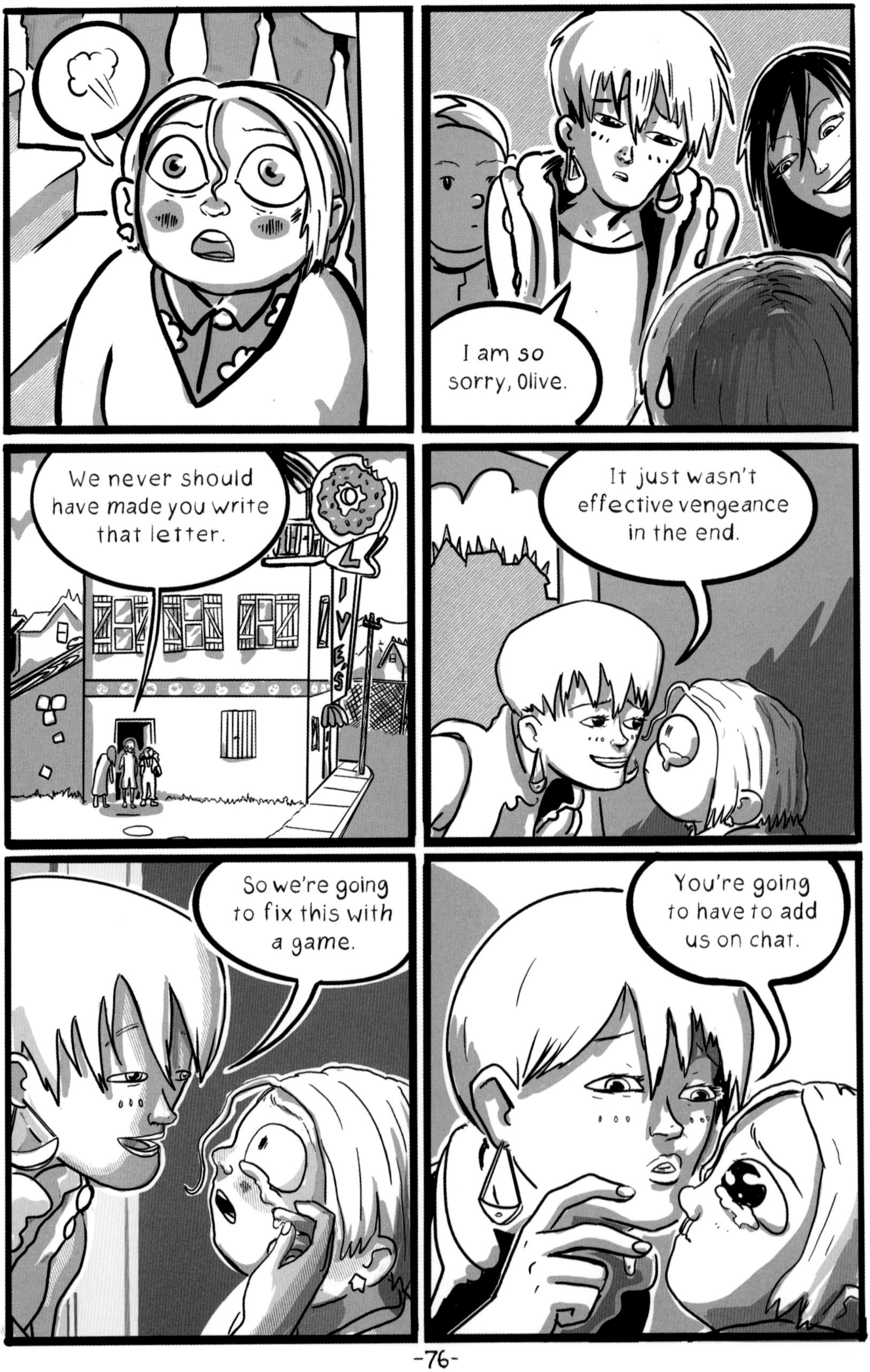
I am so sorry, Olive.
We never should have made you write that letter.
It just wasn't effective vengeance in the end.
So we're going to fix this with a game.
You're going to have to add us on chat.

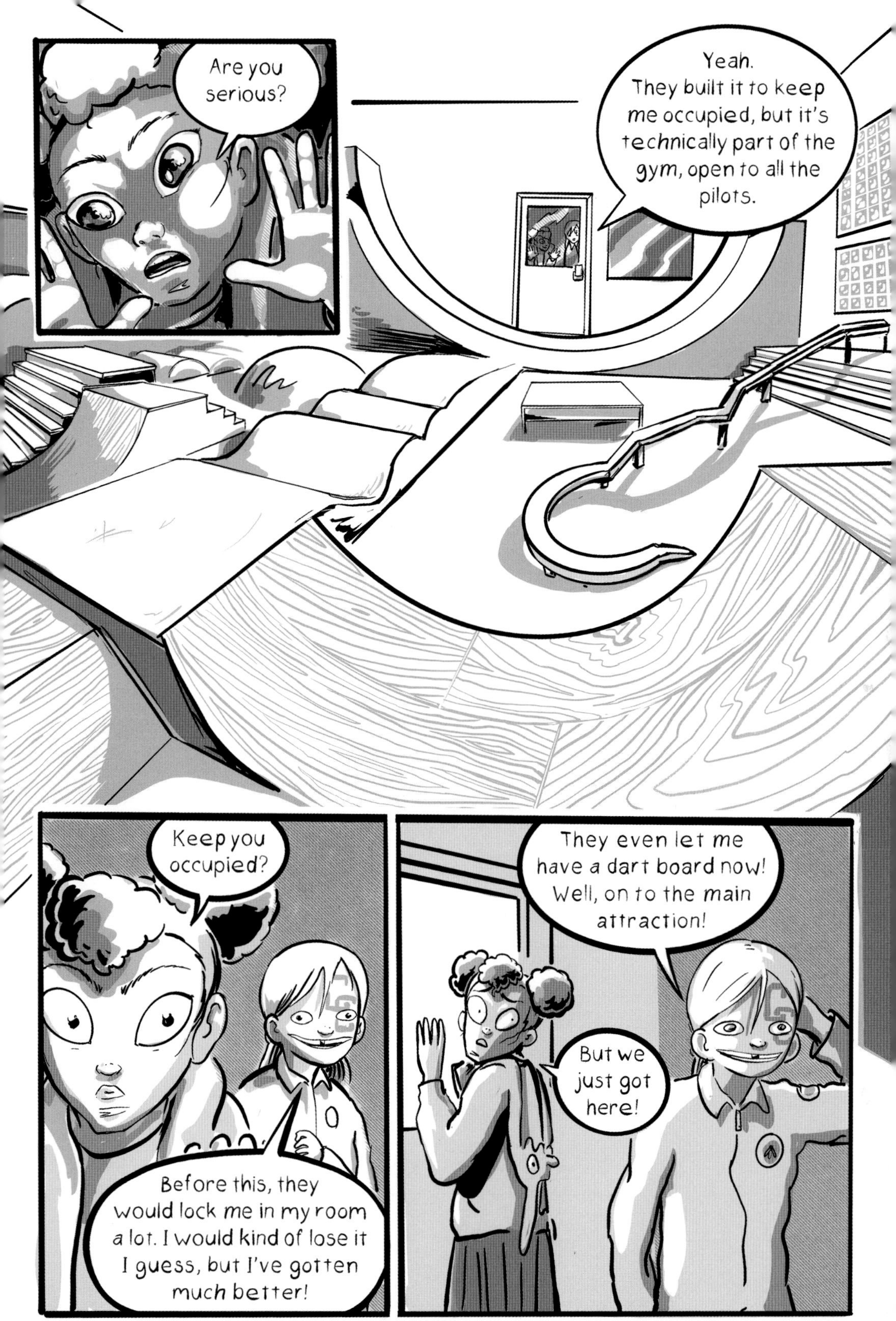
Are you serious?
Yeah. They built it to keep me occupied, but it's technically part of the gym, open to all the pilots.
Keep you occupied?
Before this, they would lock me in my room a lot. I would kind of lose it I guess, but I've gotten much better!
They even let me have a dart board now! Well, on to the main attraction!
But we just got here!

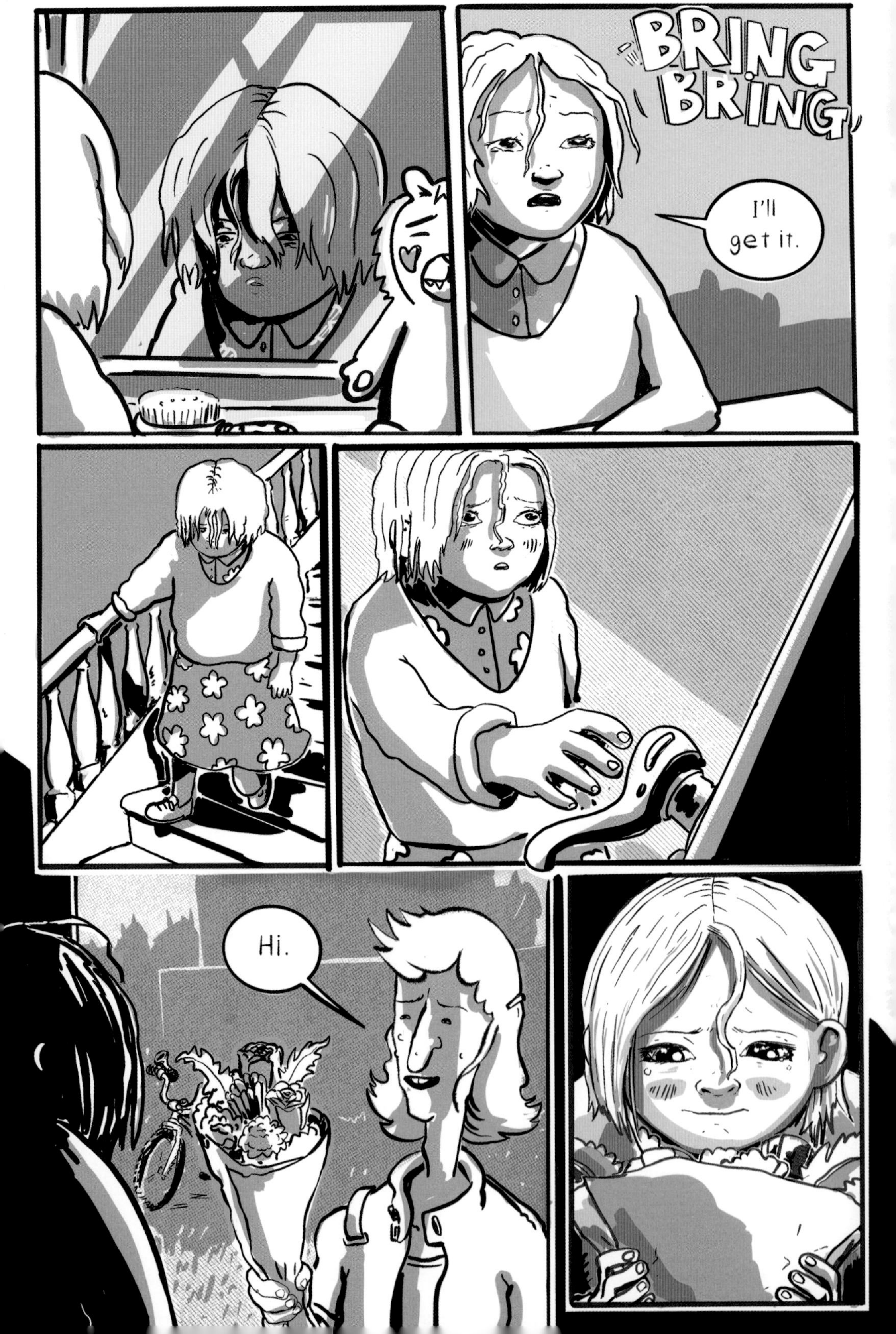
BRING
BRING
I'll get it.
Hi.

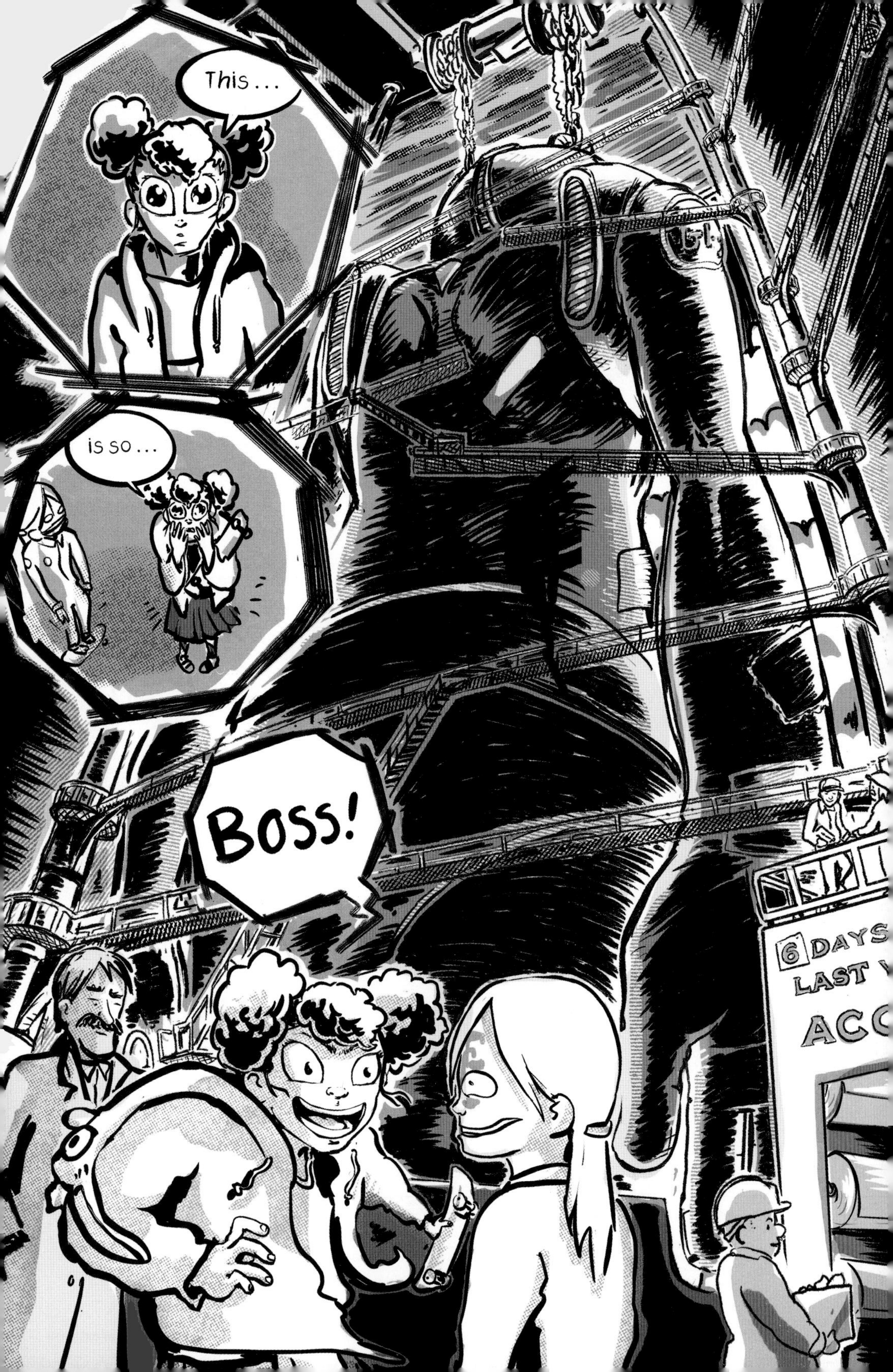
This...
is so...
Boss!
6 DAYS
LAST
ACC

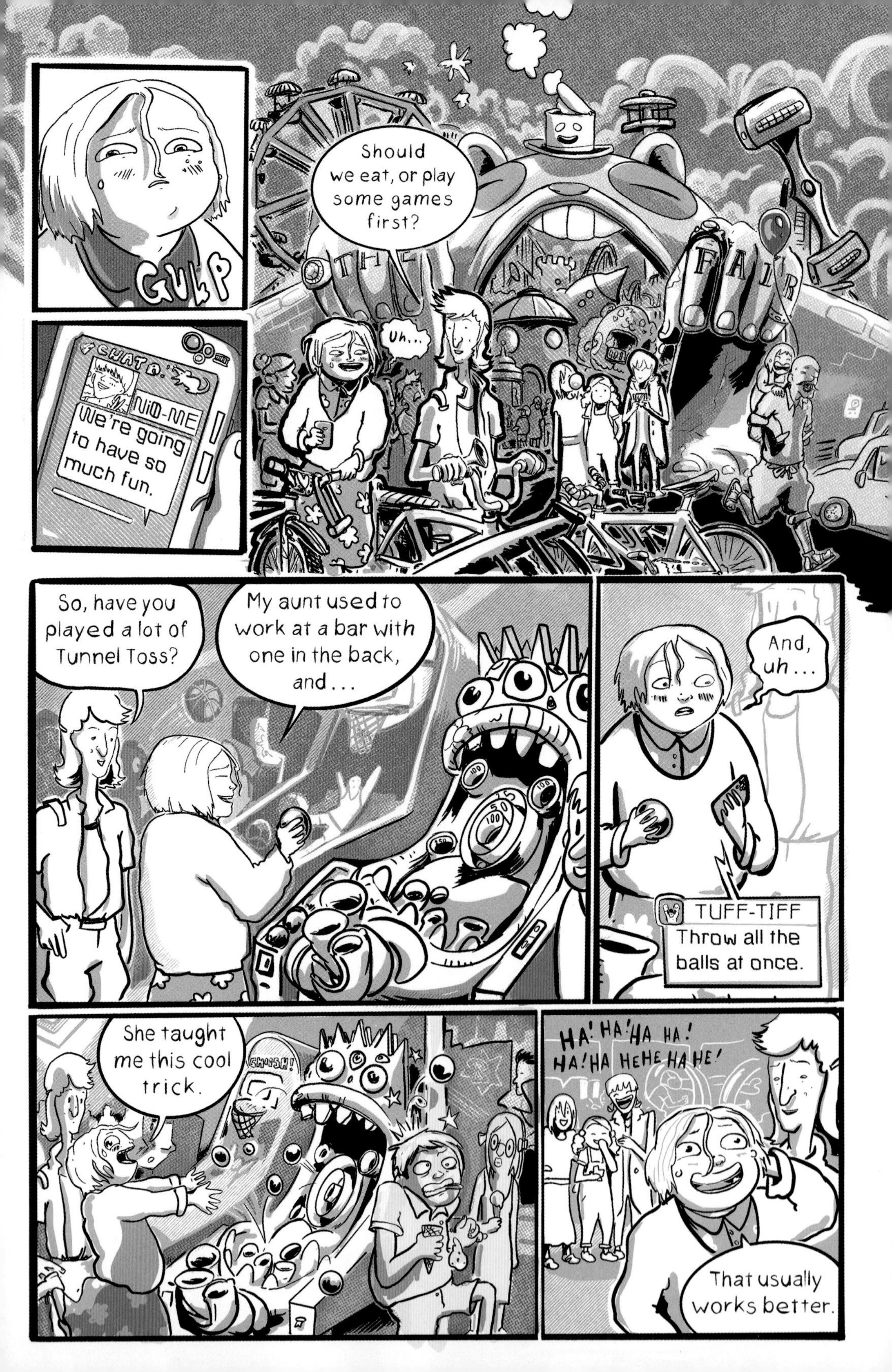
GULP
CHATd
NiO-ME
We're going to have so much fun.
Should we eat, or play some games first?
Uh...
THE
FAIR
So, have you played a lot of Tunnel Toss?
My aunt used to work at a bar with one in the back, and...
And, uh...
TUFF-TIFF
Throw all the balls at once.
She taught me this cool trick.
SWISH!
HA! HA HA HA HA!
HA! HA HEHE HA HE!
That usually works better.

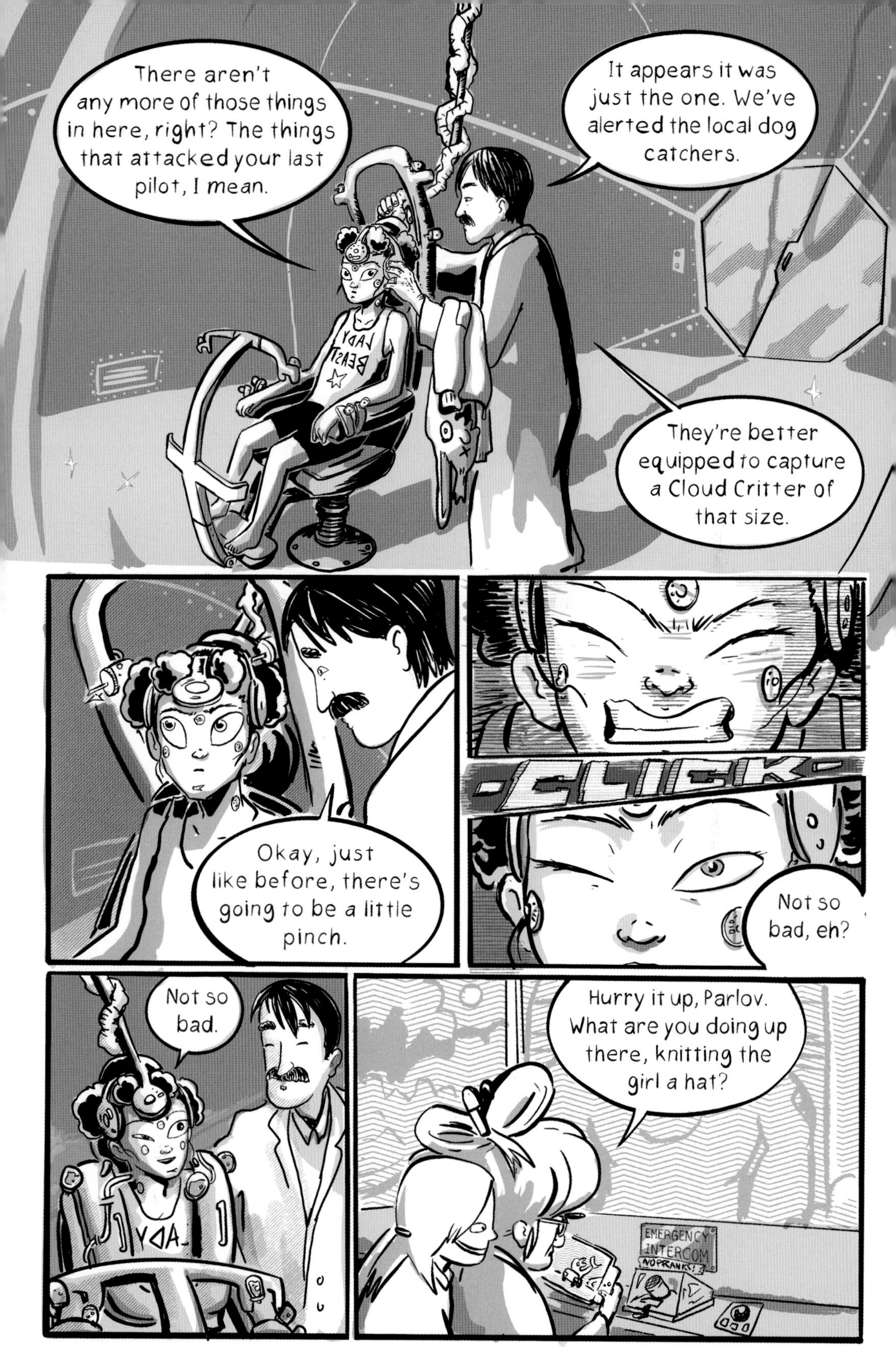
There aren't any more of those things in here, right? The things that attacked your last pilot, I mean.
It appears it was just the one. We've alerted the local dog catchers.
They're better equipped to capture a Cloud Critter of that size.
LADY BEAST
Okay, just like before, there's going to be a little pinch.
-CLICK-
Not so bad, eh?
Not so bad.
Hurry it up, Parlov. What are you doing up there, knitting the girl a hat?
EMERGENCY INTERCOM
NO PRANKS!

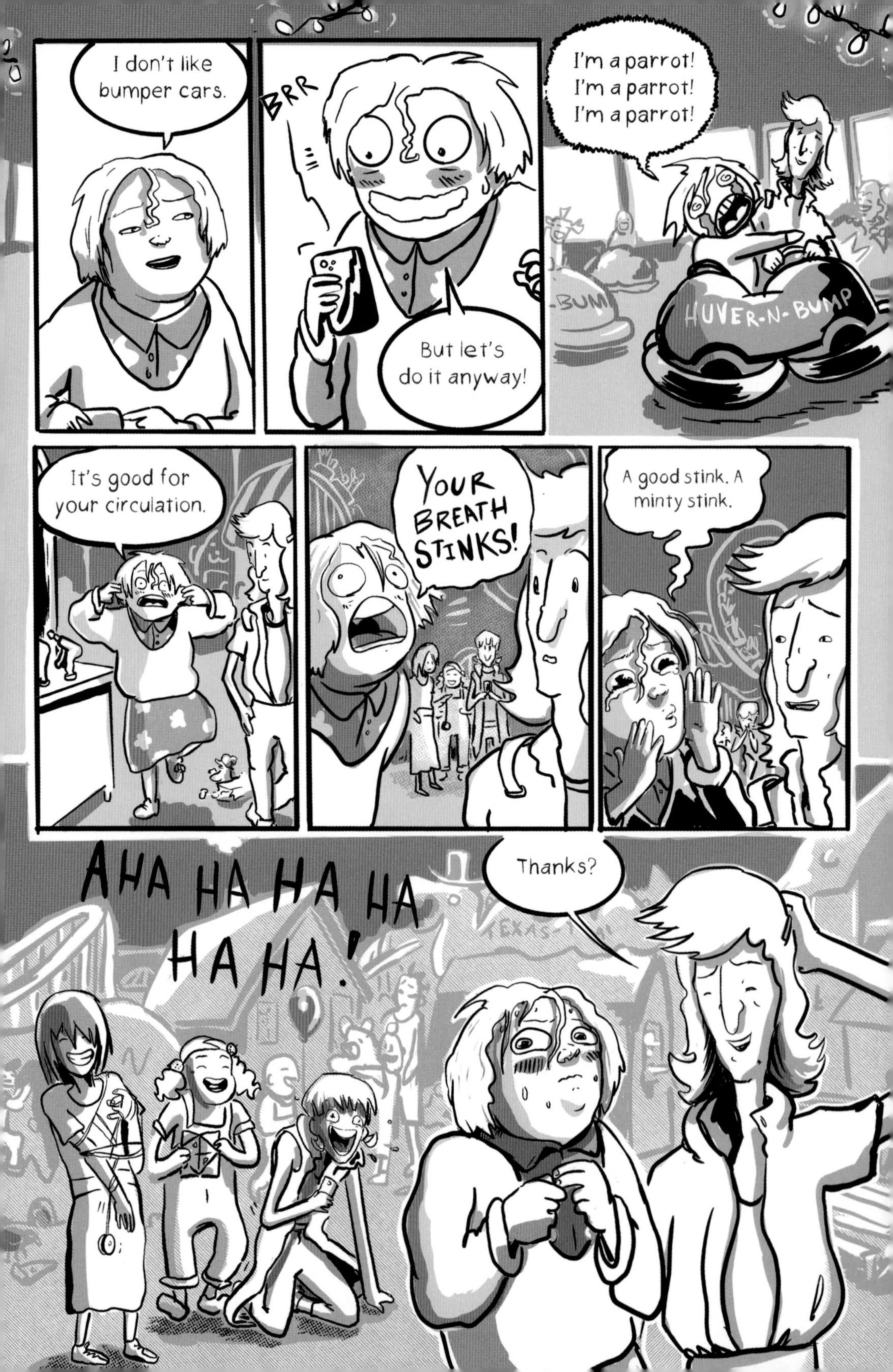
I don't like bumper cars.
BRR
But let's do it anyway!
I'm a parrot! I'm a parrot! I'm a parrot!
HUVER-N-BUMP
It's good for your circulation.
YOUR BREATH STINKS!
A good stink. A minty stink.
AHA HA HA HA HA HA HA!
Thanks?

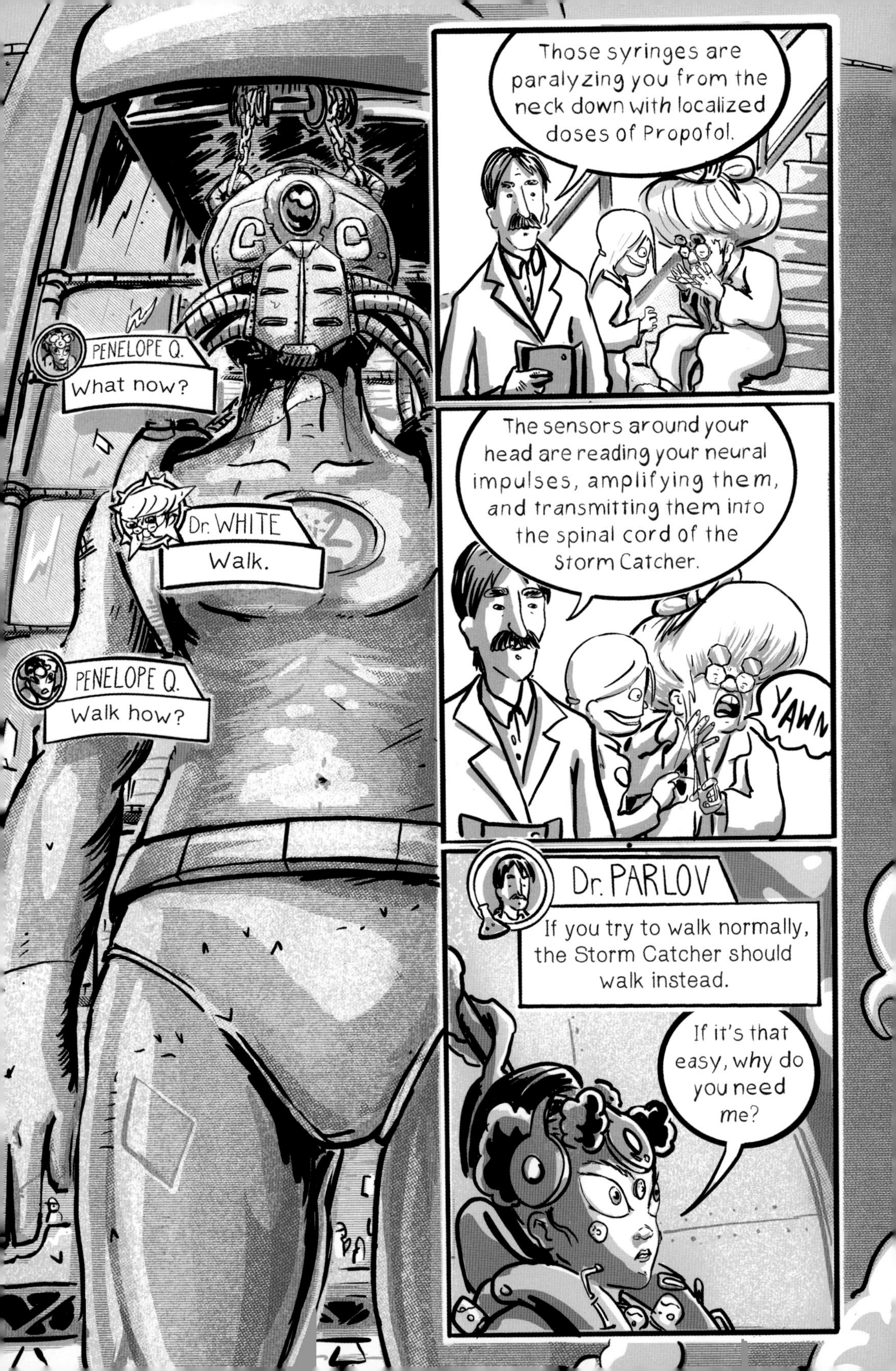

PENELOPE Q.
What now?
Dr. WHITE
Walk.
PENELOPE Q.
Walk how?
Those syringes are paralyzing you from the neck down with localized doses of Propofol.
The sensors around your head are reading your neural impulses, amplifying them, and transmitting them into the spinal cord of the Storm Catcher.
YAWN
Dr. PARLOV
If you try to walk normally, the Storm Catcher should walk instead.
If it's that easy, why do you need me?

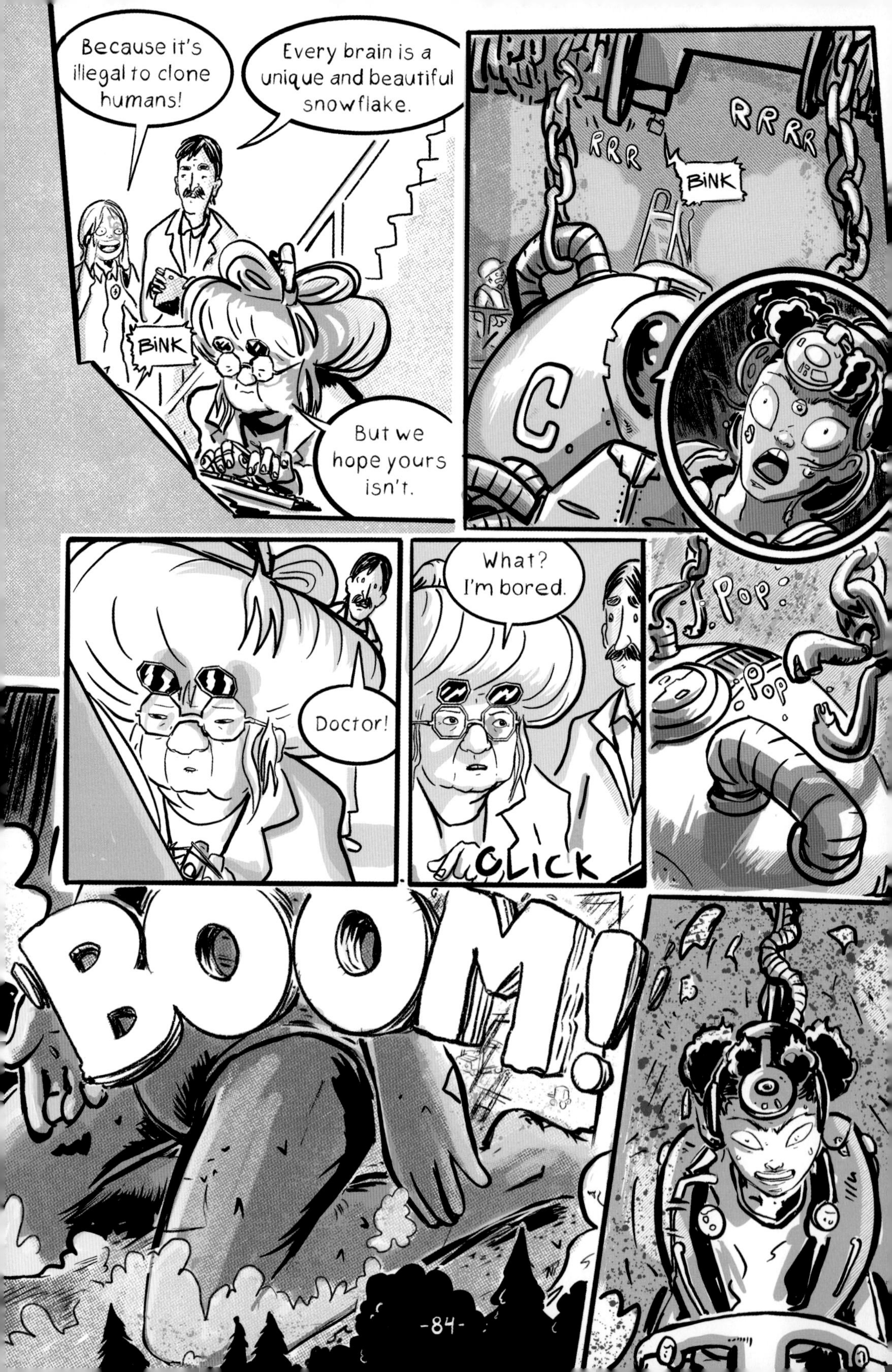
Because it's illegal to clone humans!
Every brain is a unique and beautiful snowflake.
BINK
But we hope yours isn't.
RRR
RRRRR
BINK
Doctor!
What? I'm bored.
CLICK
POP
POP
BOOM!

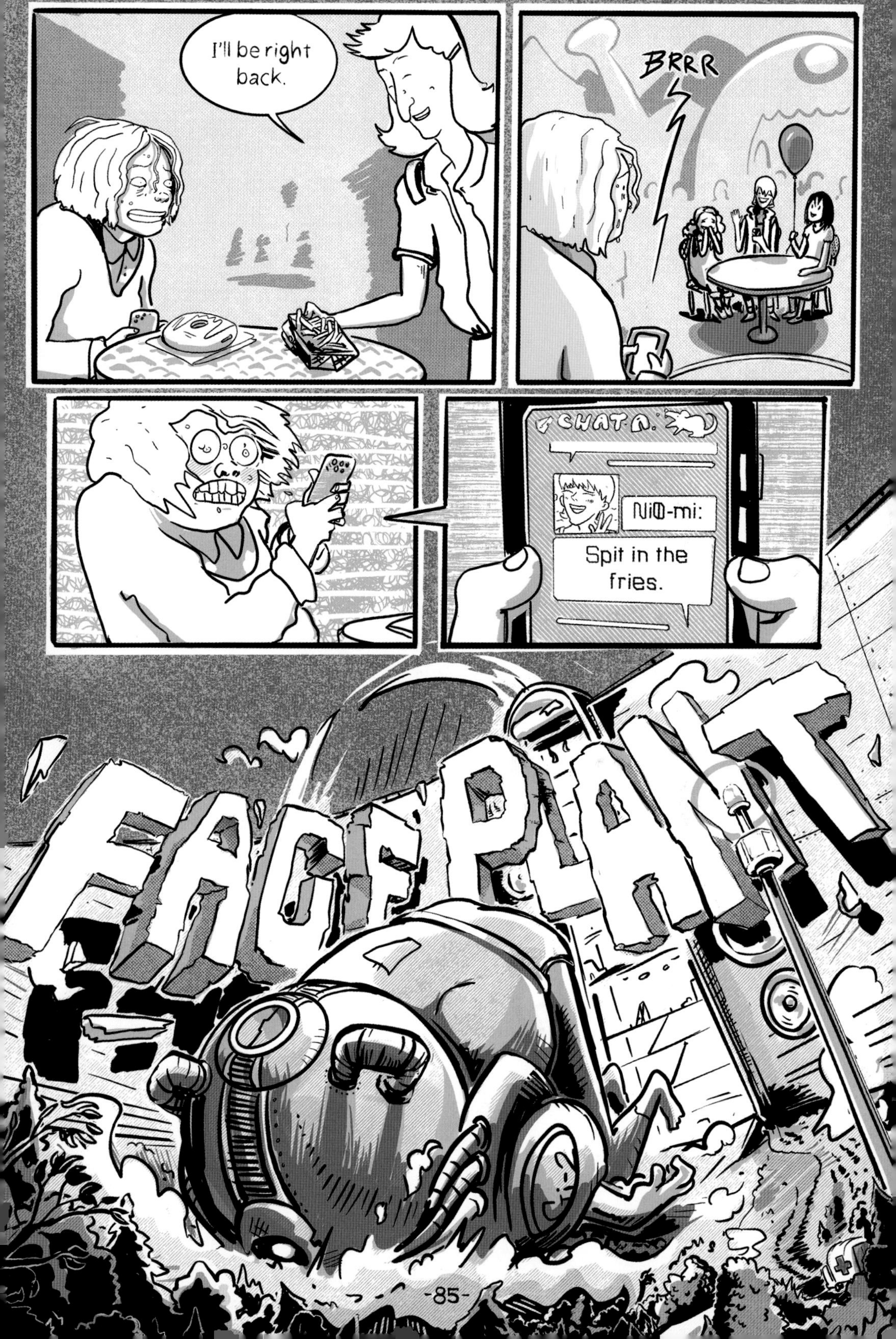
I'll be right back.
BRRR
CHAT-A.
NIO-mi:
Spit in the fries.
FACEPLANT

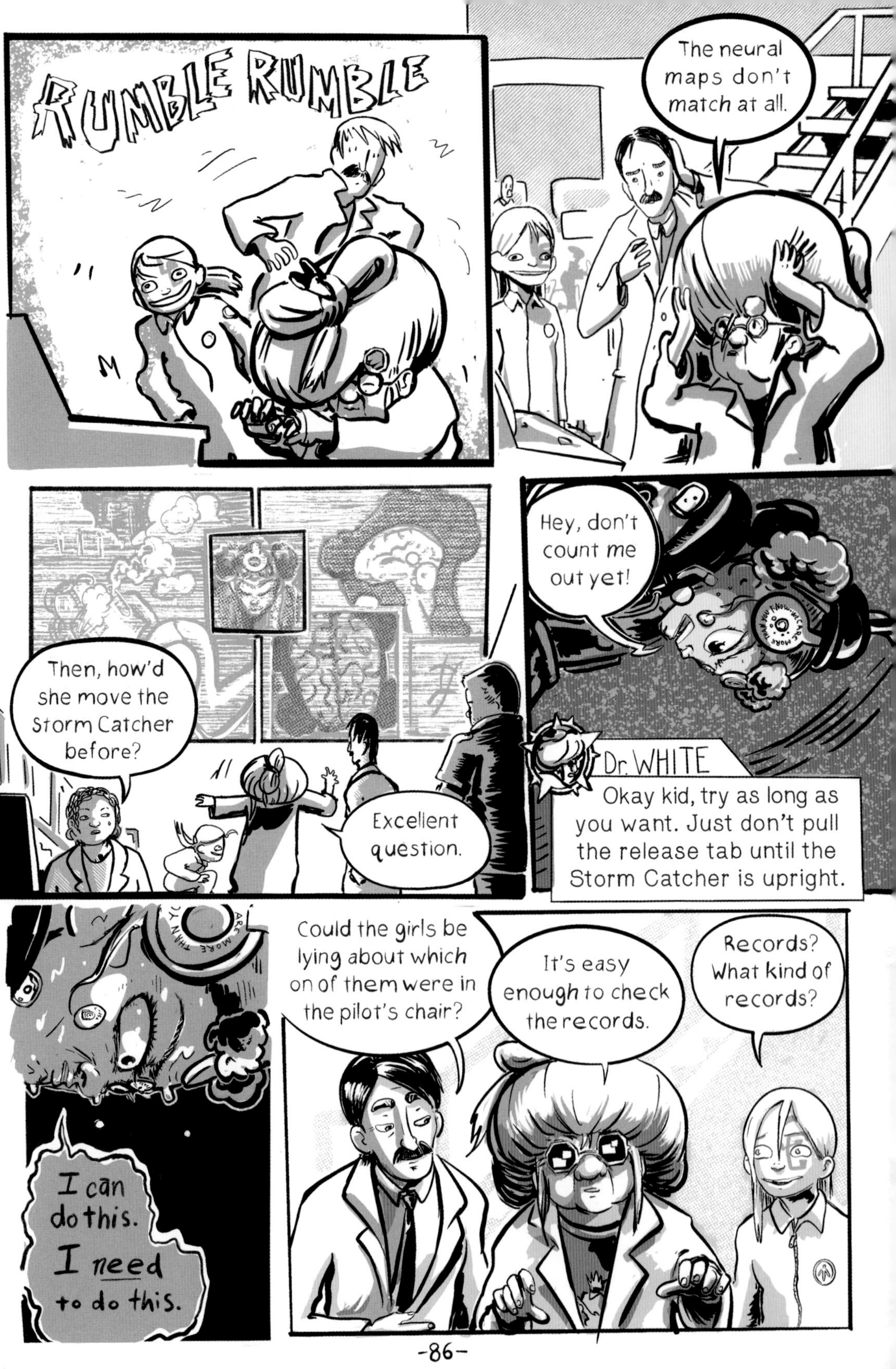
RUMBLE RUMBLE
The neural maps don't match at all.
Then, how'd she move the Storm Catcher before?
Excellent question.
Hey, don't count me out yet!
Dr. WHITE
Okay kid, try as long as you want. Just don't pull the release tab until the Storm Catcher is upright.
I can do this. I need to do this.
Could the girls be lying about which on of them were in the pilot's chair?
It's easy enough to check the records.
Records? What kind of records?

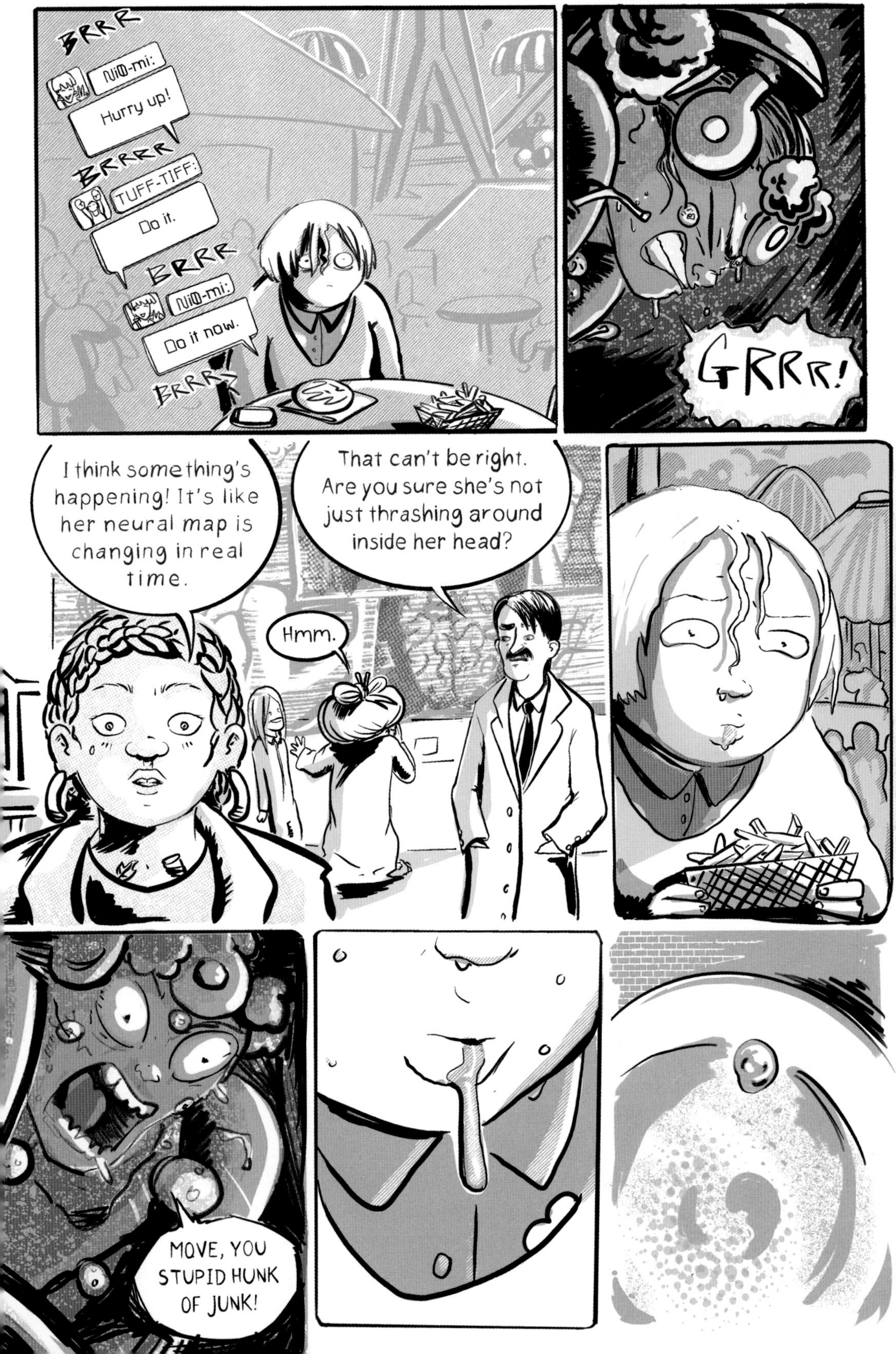
BRRR
NIDI-mi:
Hurry up!
BRRRR
TUFF-TIFF:
Do it.
BRRR
NIDI-mi:
Do it now.
BRRR
GRRR!
I think something's happening! It's like her neural map is changing in real time.
That can't be right. Are you sure she's not just thrashing around inside her head?
Hmm.
MOVE, YOU STUPID HUNK OF JUNK!

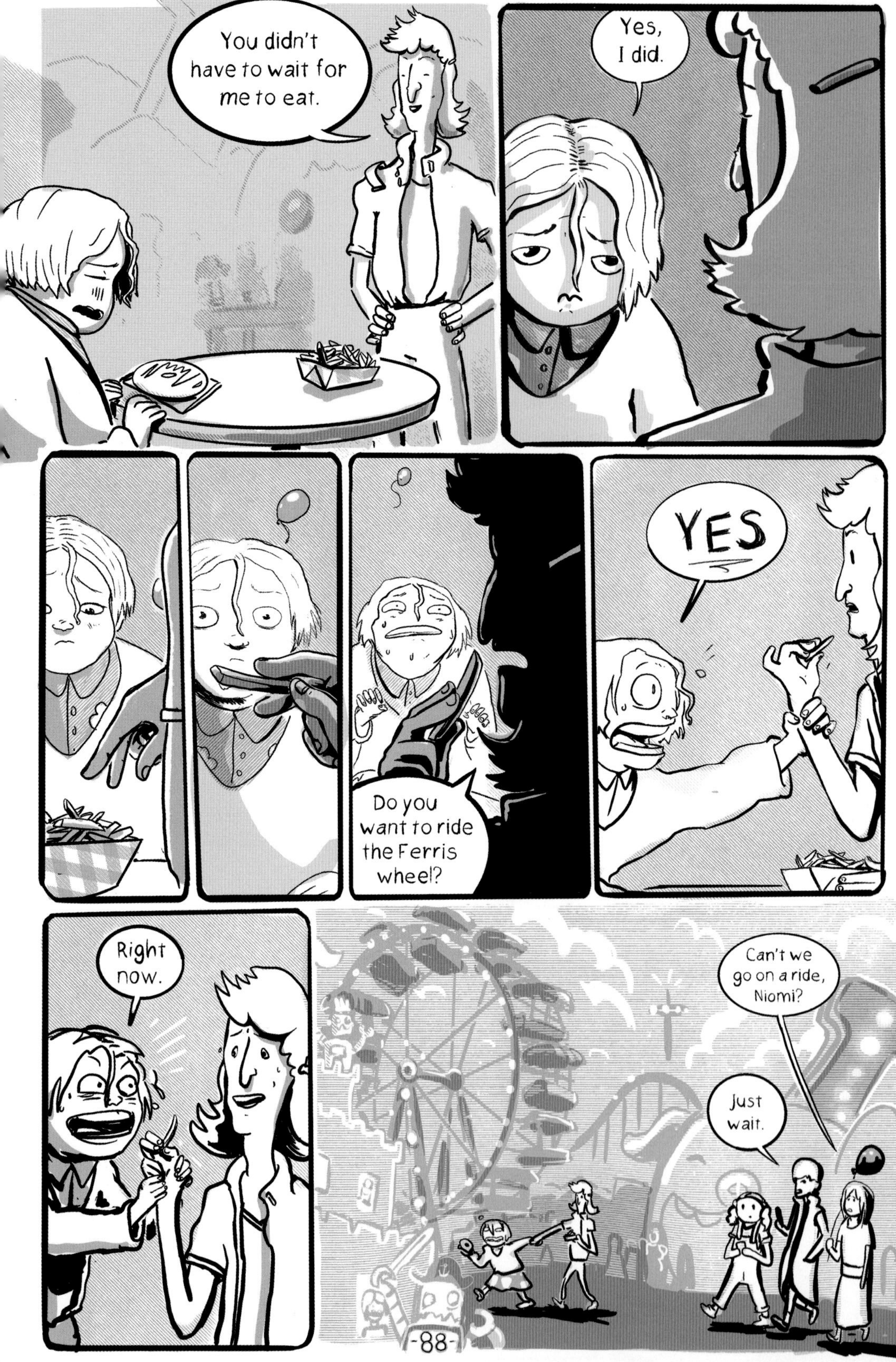
You didn't have to wait for me to eat.
Yes, I did.
Do you want to ride the Ferris wheel!?
YES
Right now.
Can't we go on a ride, Niomi?
Just wait.

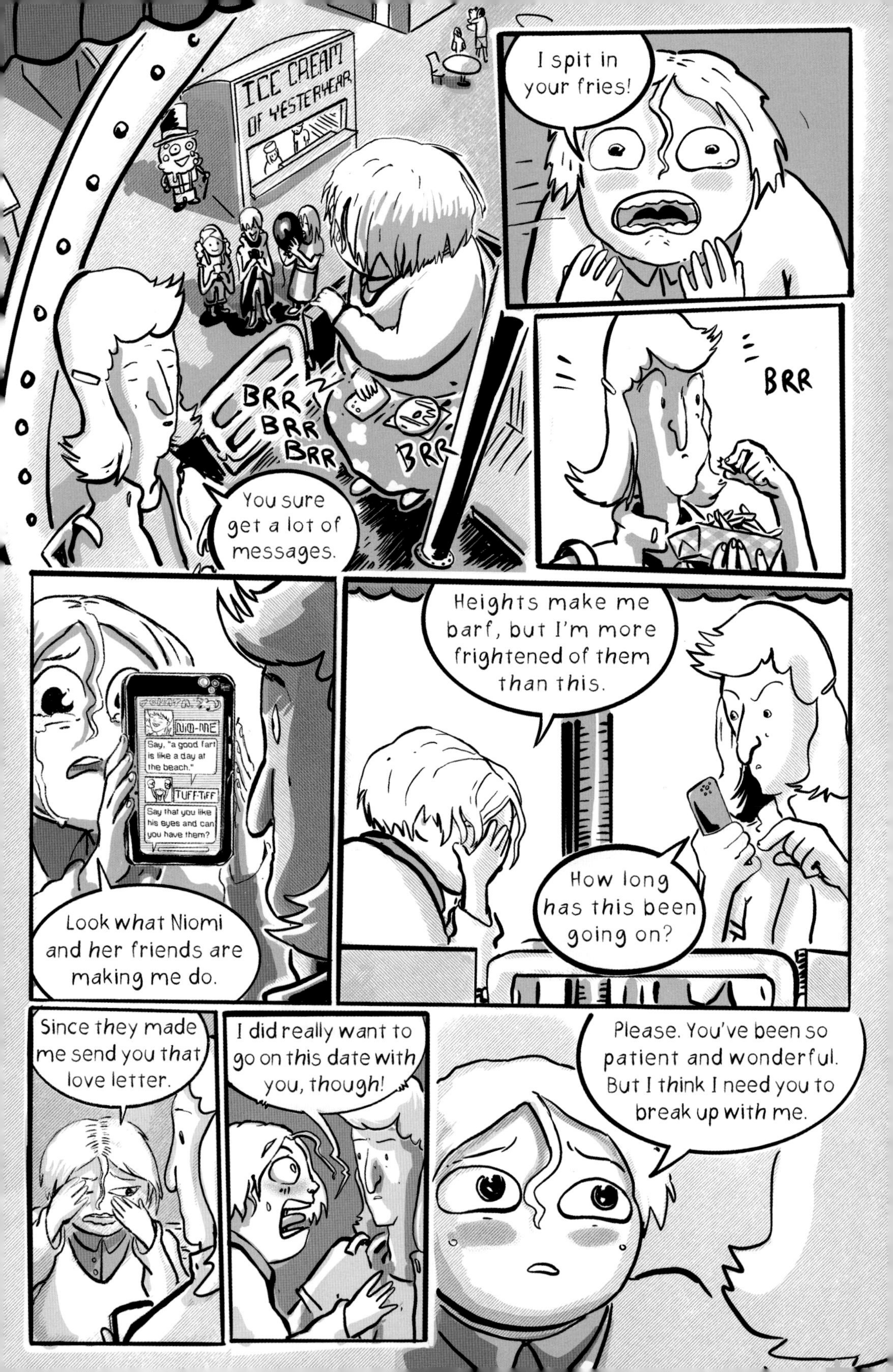
ICE CREAM OF YESTERYEAR
BRR BRR BRR
BRR
You sure get a lot of messages.
I spit in your fries!
BRR
NIO-ME
Say, "a good fart is like a day at the beach."
TUFF-TIFF
Say that you like his eyes and can you have them?
Look what Niomi and her friends are making me do.
Heights make me barf, but I'm more frightened of them than this.
How long has this been going on?
Since they made me send you that love letter.
I did really want to go on this date with you, though!
Please. You've been so patient and wonderful. But I think I need you to break up with me.

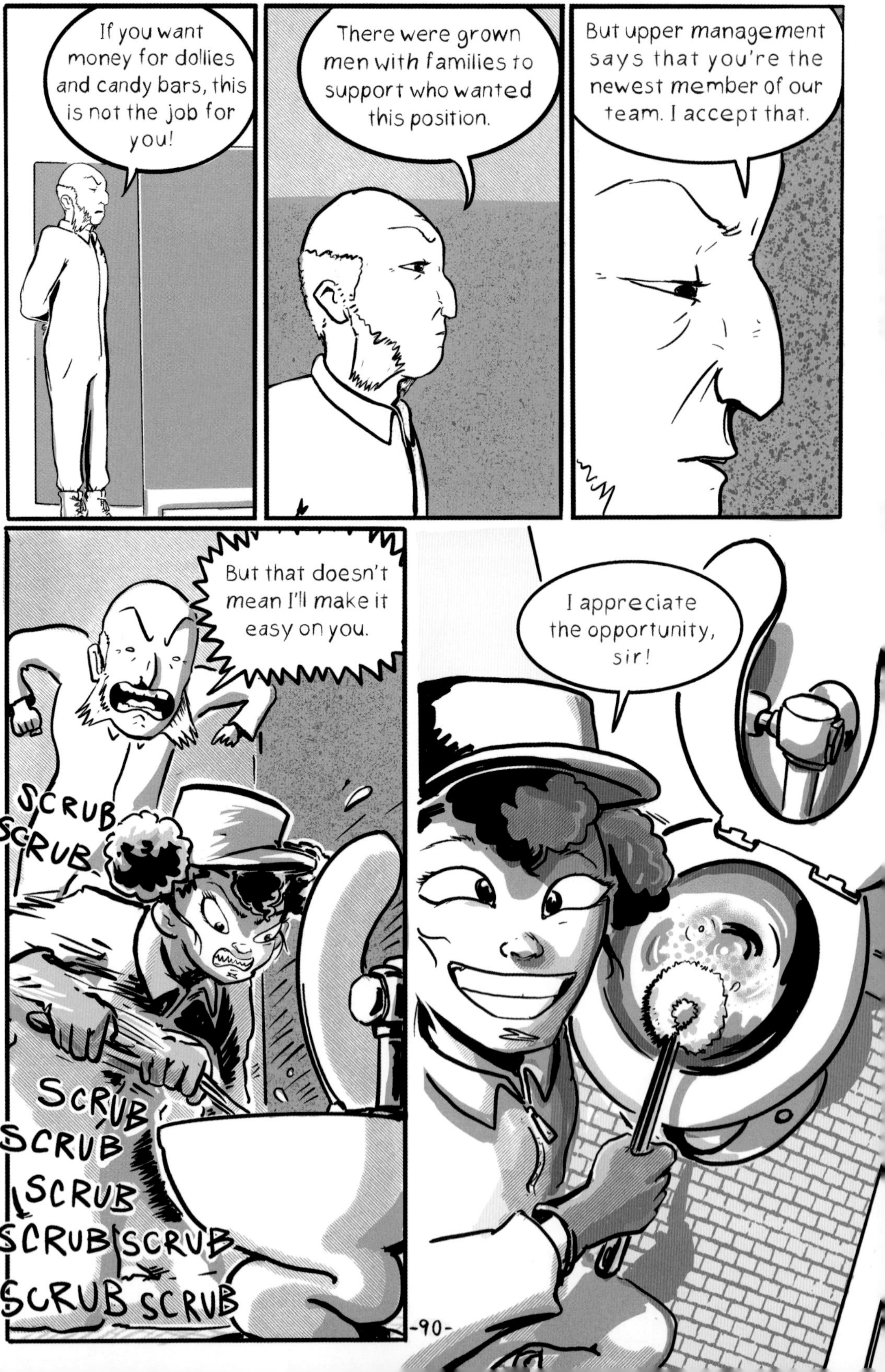
If you want money for dollies and candy bars, this is not the job for you!
There were grown men with families to support who wanted this position.
But upper management says that you're the newest member of our team. I accept that.
But that doesn't mean I'll make it easy on you.
SCRUB
SCRUB
SCRUB
SCRUB
SCRUB
SCRUB
SCRUB
SCRUB
SCRUB
I appreciate the opportunity, sir!

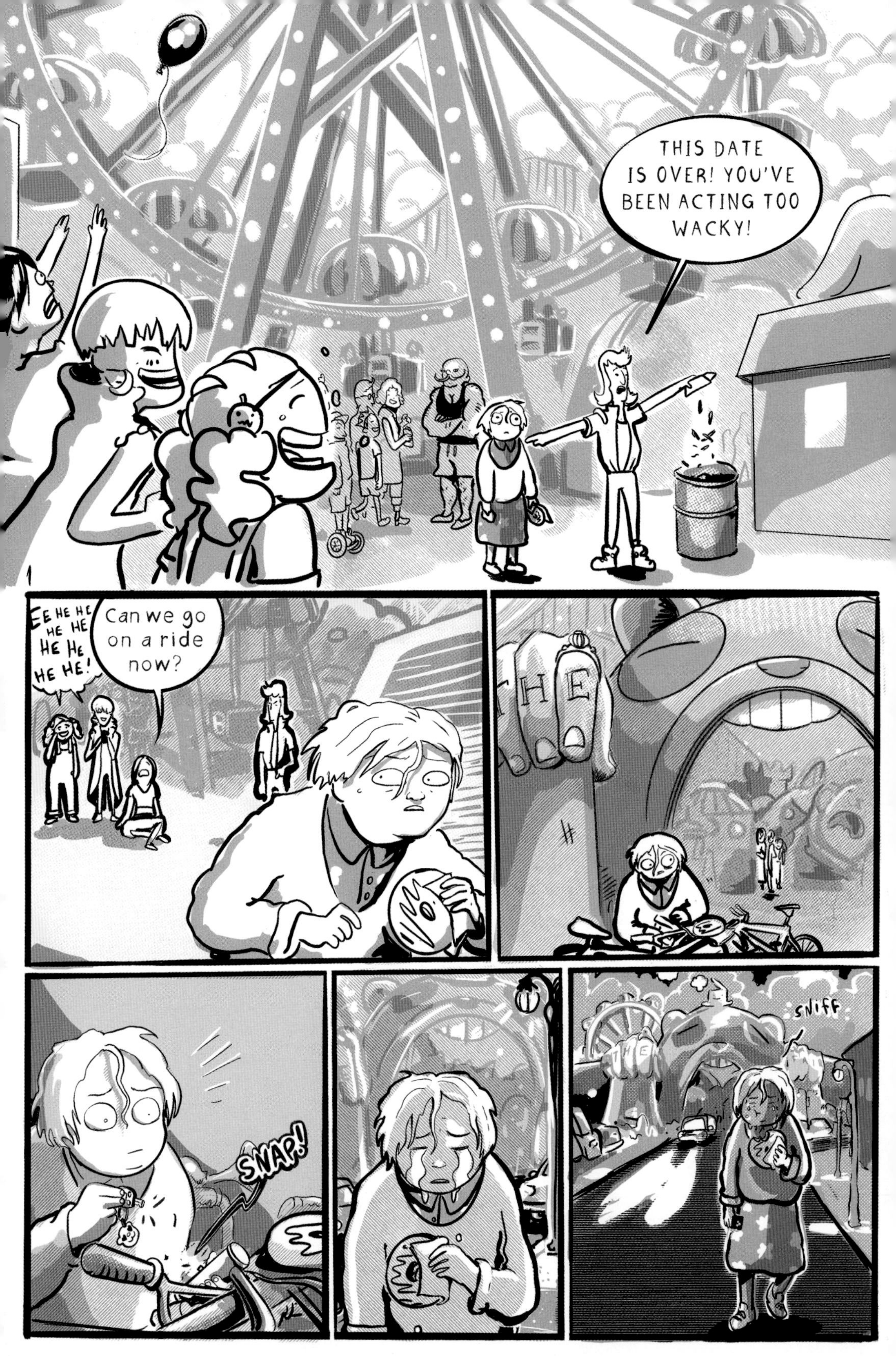
THIS DATE IS OVER! YOU'VE BEEN ACTING TOO WACKY!
EE HE HE HE HE HE HE HE HE!
Can we go on a ride now?
THE
SNAP!
SNIFF

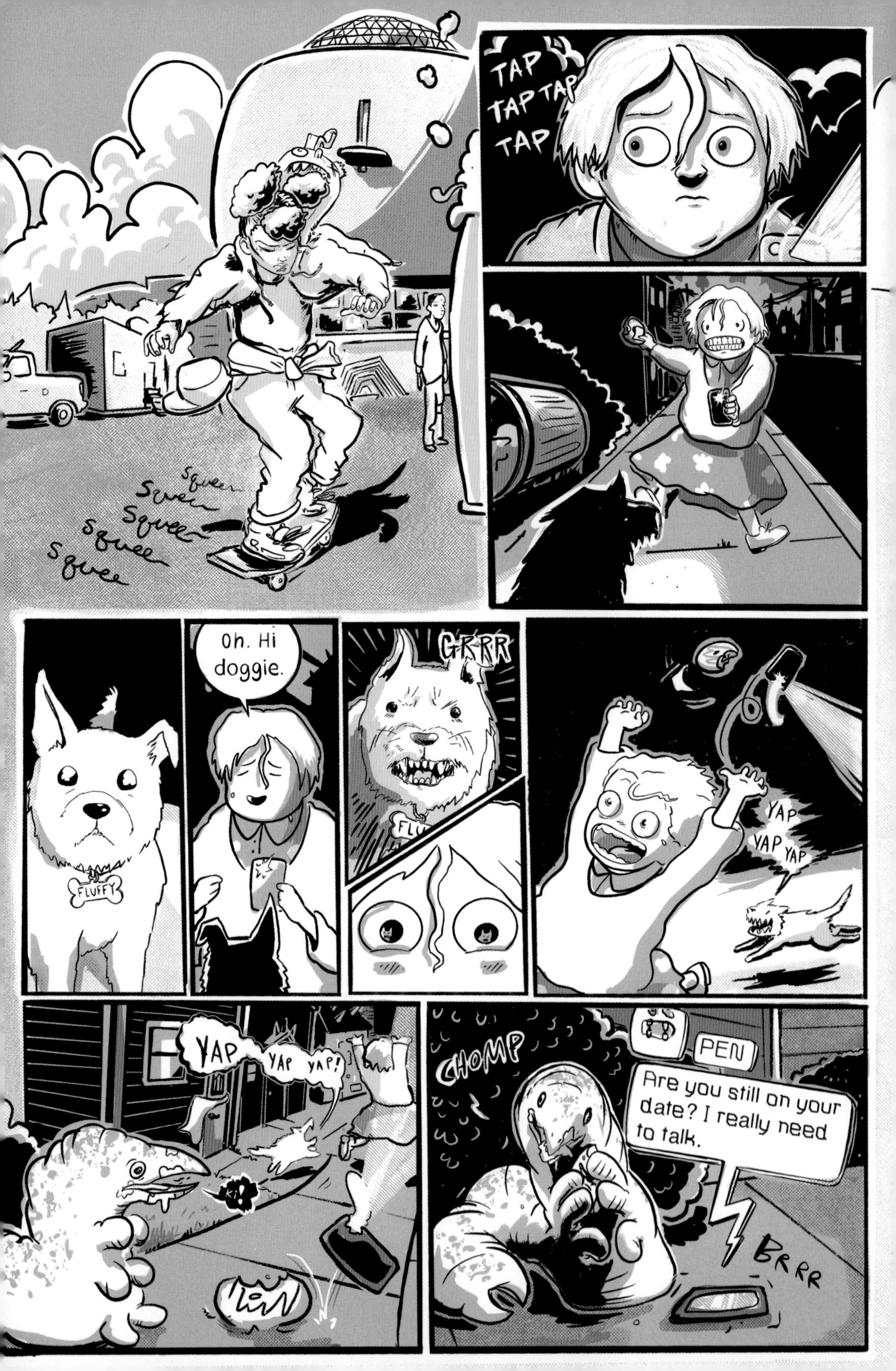

Squee
Squee
Squee
Squee
Squee
TAP
TAP TAP
TAP
Oh. Hi doggie.
GRRR
FLUFFY
YAP
YAP YAP
YAP
YAP YAP!
CHOMP
PEN
Are you still on your date? I really need to talk.
BRRR

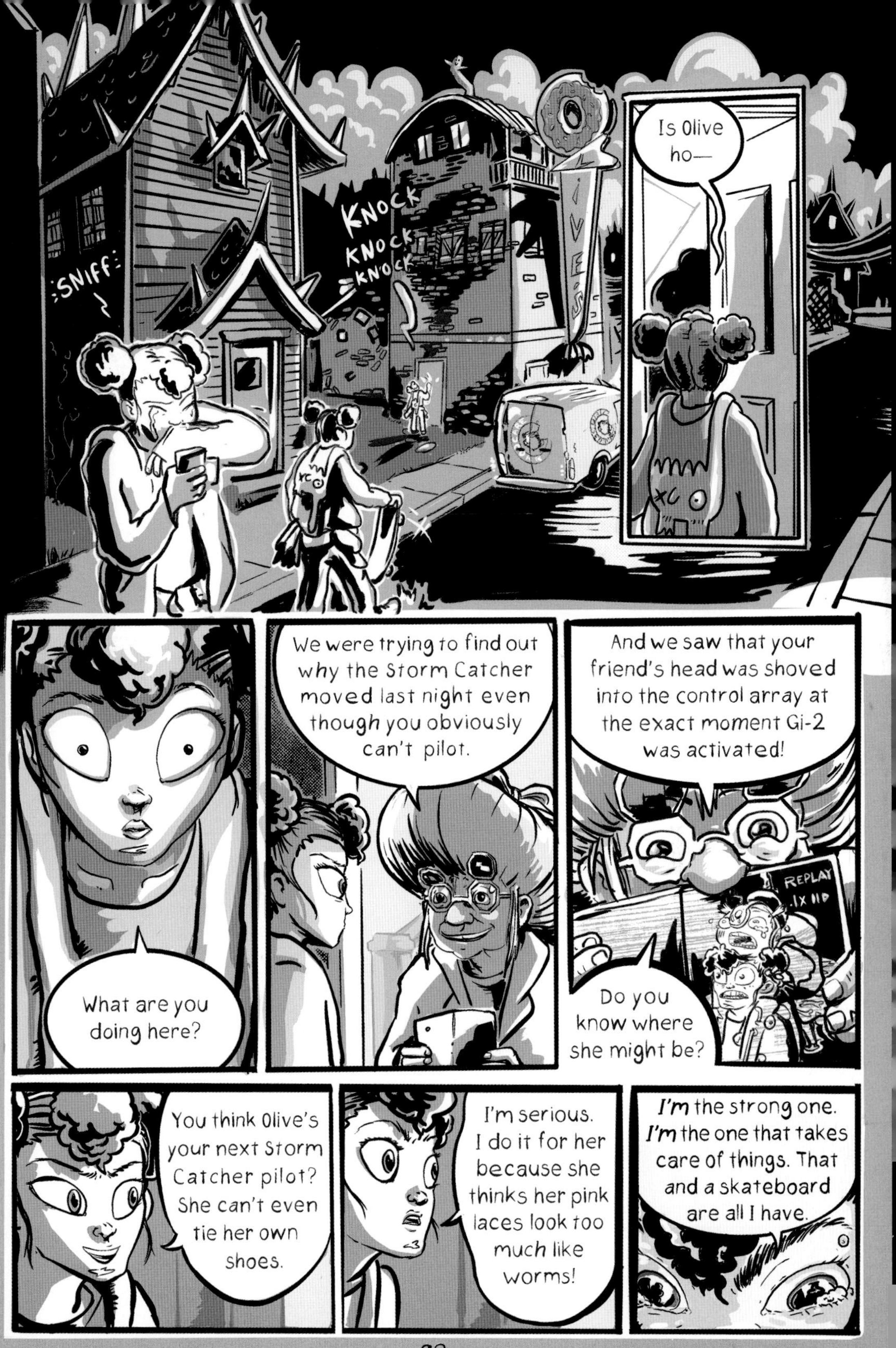
SNIFF
KNOCK
KNOCK
KNOCK
Is Olive ho—
What are you doing here?
We were trying to find out why the Storm Catcher moved last night even though you obviously can't pilot.
And we saw that your friend's head was shoved into the control array at the exact moment Gi-2 was activated!
REPLAY
Do you know where she might be?
You think Olive's your next Storm Catcher pilot? She can't even tie her own shoes.
I'm serious. I do it for her because she thinks her pink laces look too much like worms!
I'm the strong one. *I'm* the one that takes care of things. That and a skateboard are all I have.

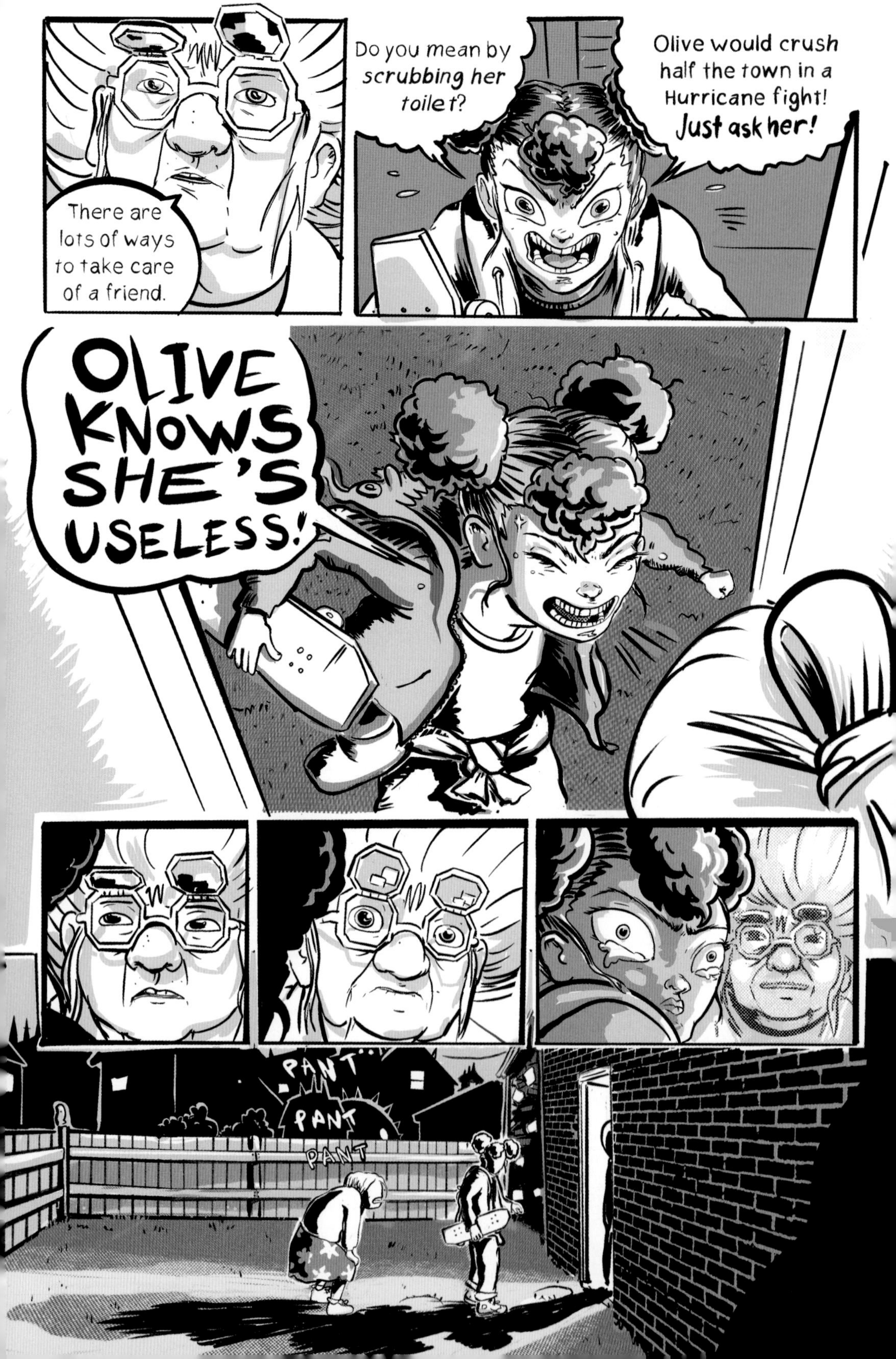
There are lots of ways to take care of a friend.
Do you mean by scrubbing her toilet?
Olive would crush half the town in a Hurricane fight! Just ask her!
OLIVE KNOWS SHE'S USELESS!
PANT...
PANT
PANT

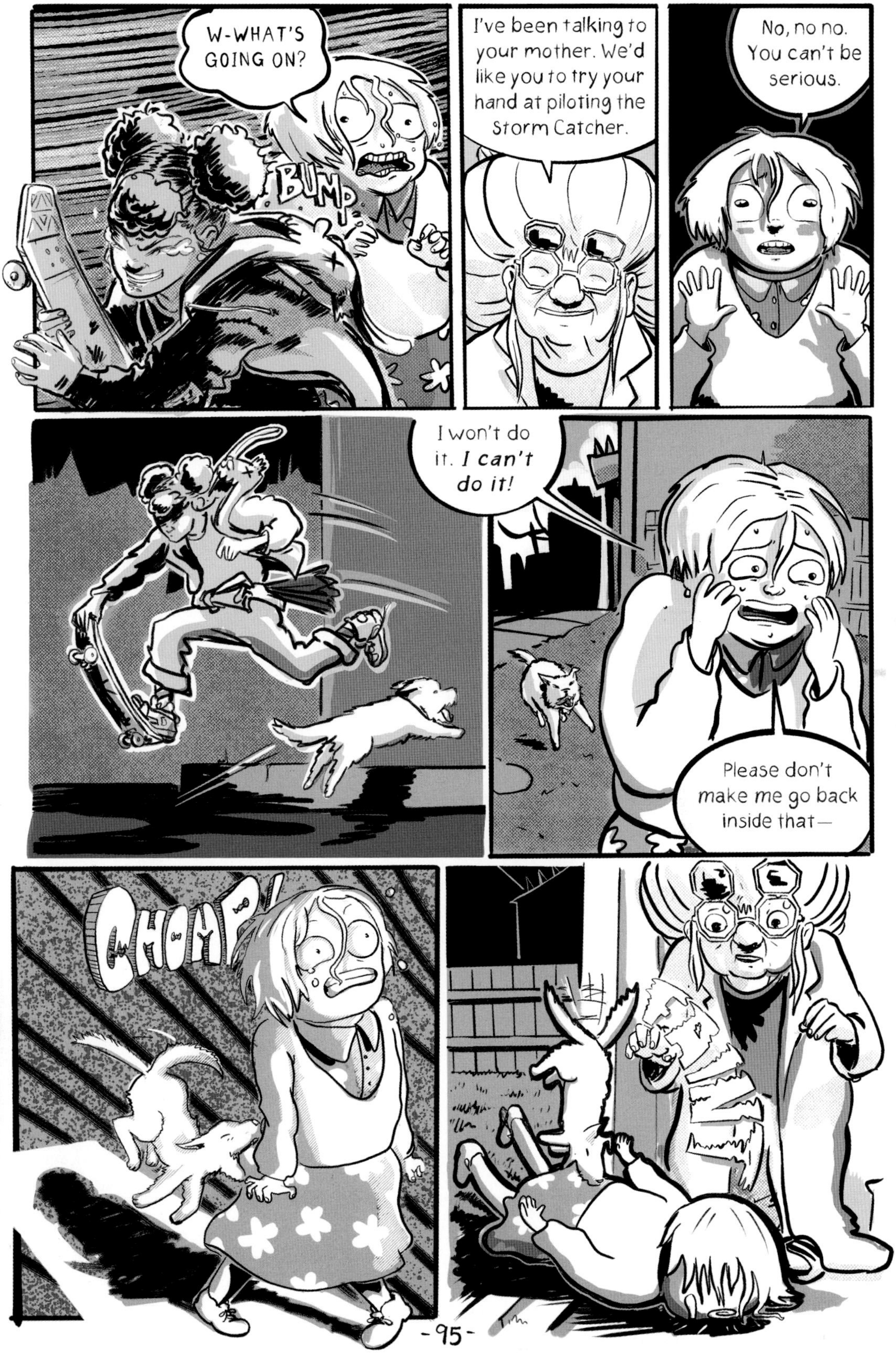
W-WHAT'S GOING ON?
BUMP
I've been talking to your mother. We'd like you to try your hand at piloting the Storm Catcher.
No, no no. You can't be serious.
I won't do it. *I can't do it!*
Please don't make me go back inside that—
CHOMP!

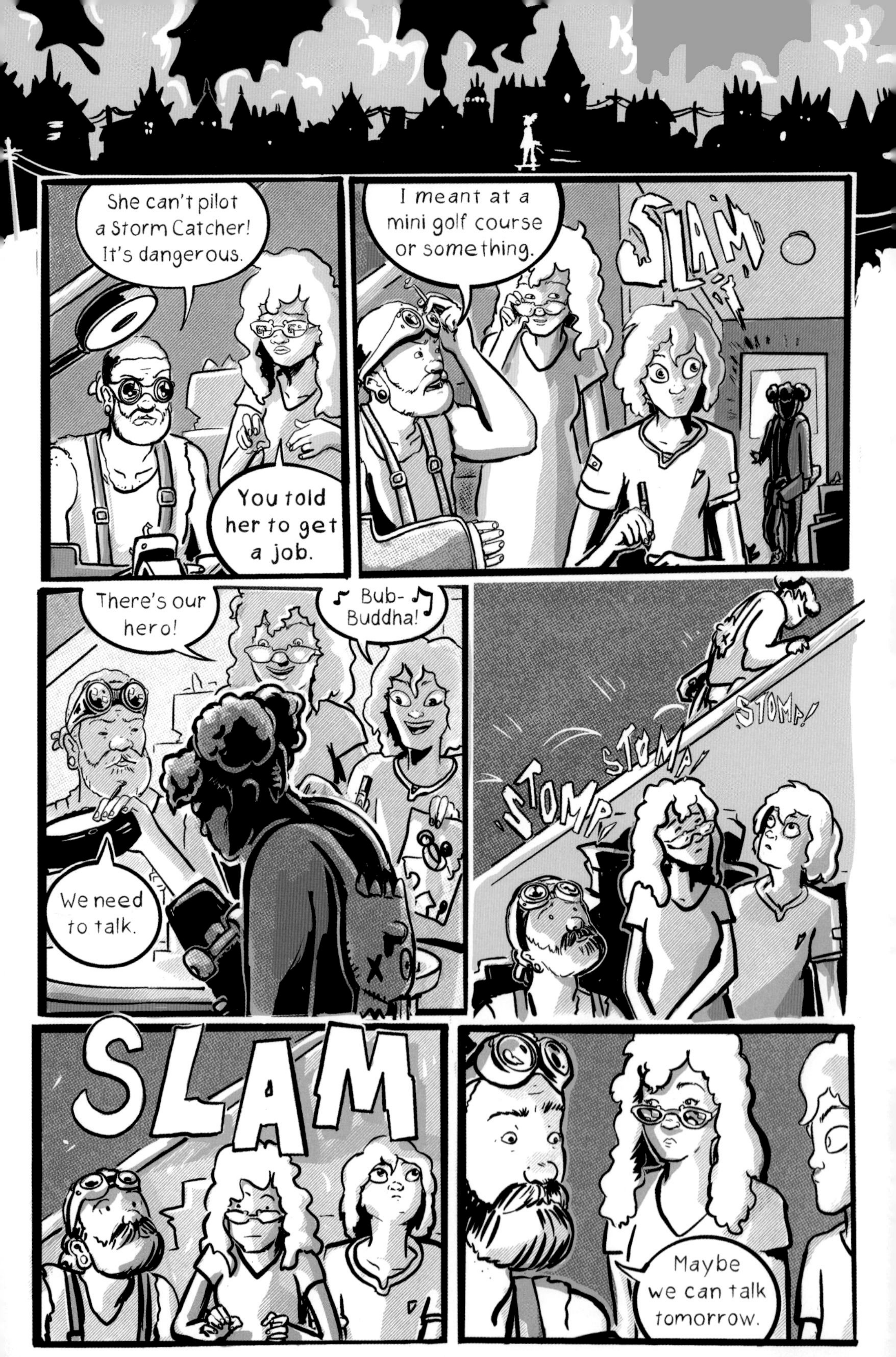
She can't pilot a Storm Catcher! It's dangerous.
You told her to get a job.
I meant at a mini golf course or something.
SLAM
There's our hero!
Bub-Buddha!
We need to talk.
STOMP
STOMP
STOMP!
SLAM
Maybe we can talk tomorrow.

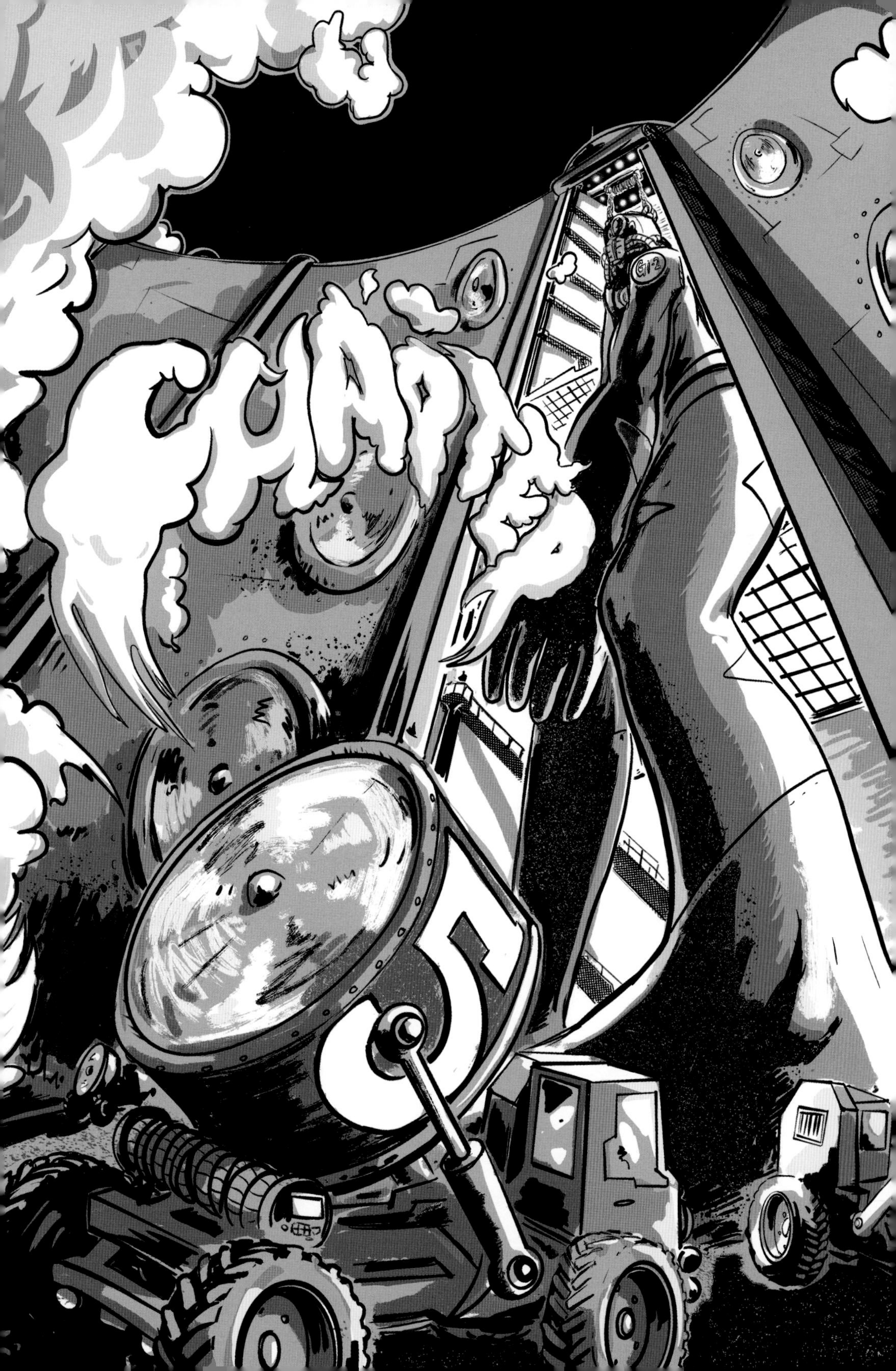

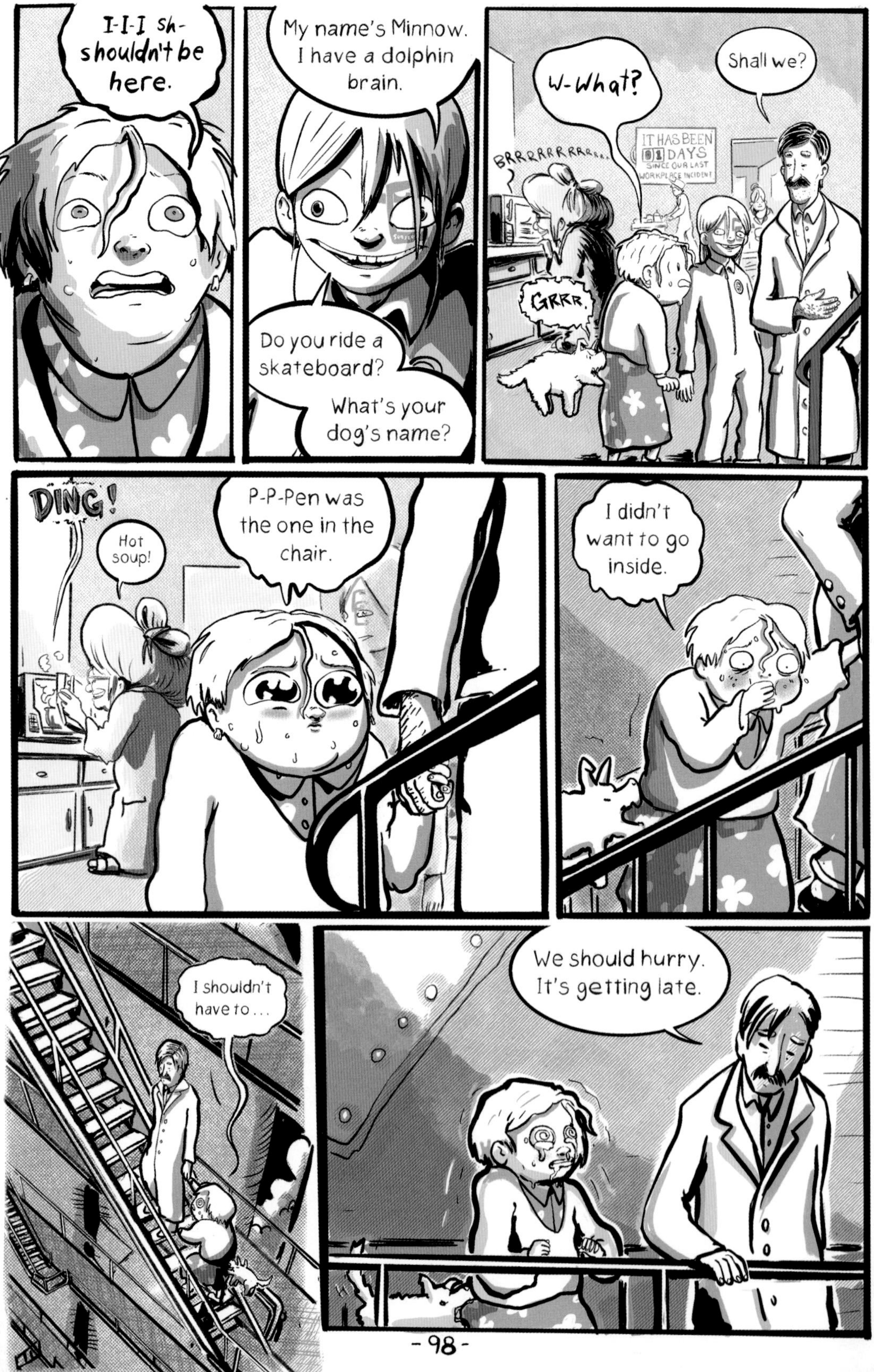
I-I-I sh- shouldn't be here.
My name's Minnow. I have a dolphin brain.
Do you ride a skateboard?
What's your dog's name?
W-What?
Shall we?
BRRRRRRRRRR...
IT HAS BEEN 01 DAYS SINCE OUR LAST WORKPLACE INCIDENT
GRRR.
DING!
Hot soup!
P-P-Pen was the one in the chair.
I didn't want to go inside.
I shouldn't have to...
We should hurry. It's getting late.

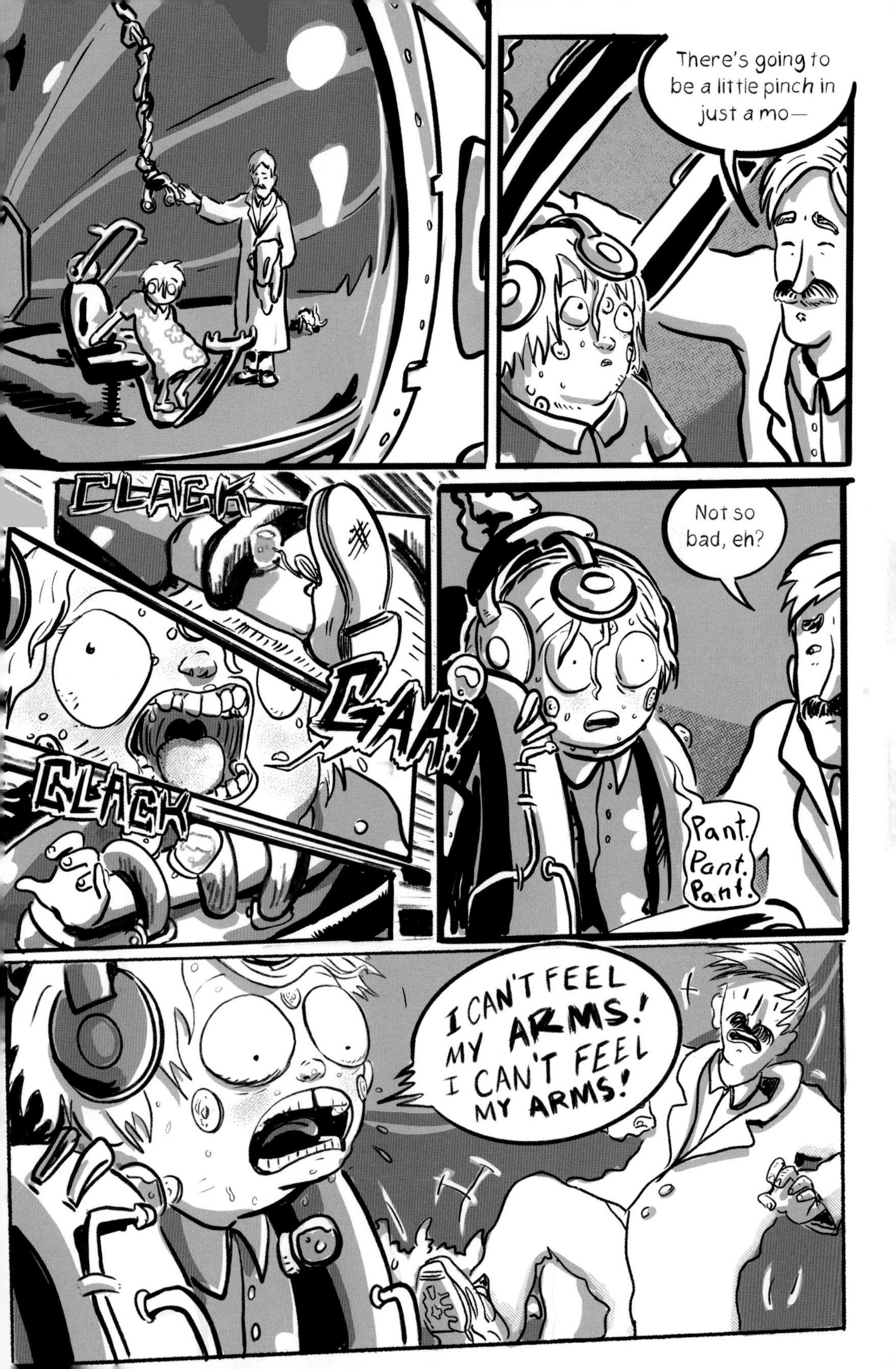
There's going to be a little pinch in just a mo—
CLACK
GAA!
CLACK
Not so bad, eh?
Pant. Pant. Pant.
I CAN'T FEEL MY ARMS! I CAN'T FEEL MY ARMS!

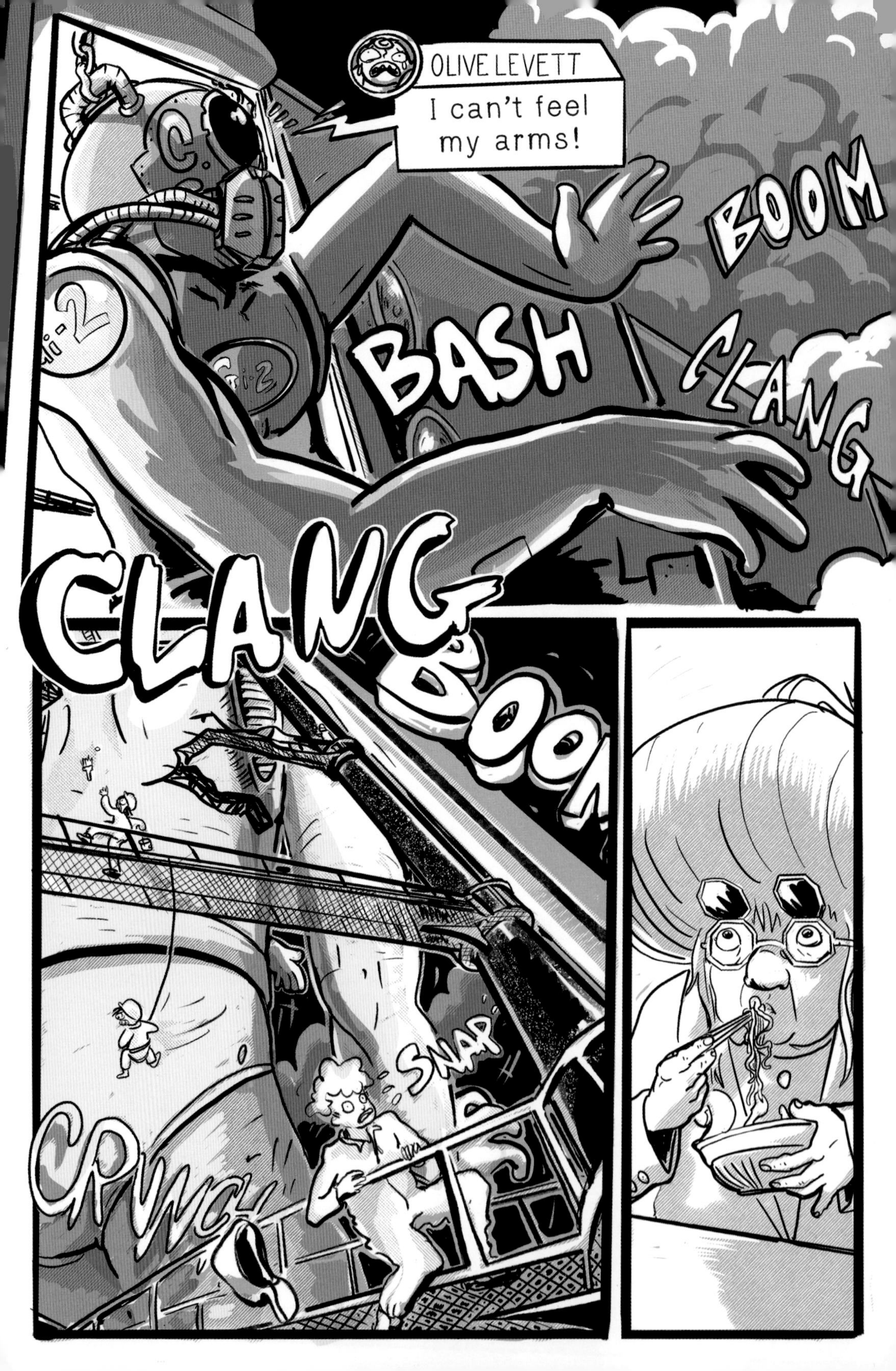
OLIVE LEVETT
I can't feel my arms!
BOOM
BASH
CLANG
CLANG
BOOM
SNAP
CRUNCH

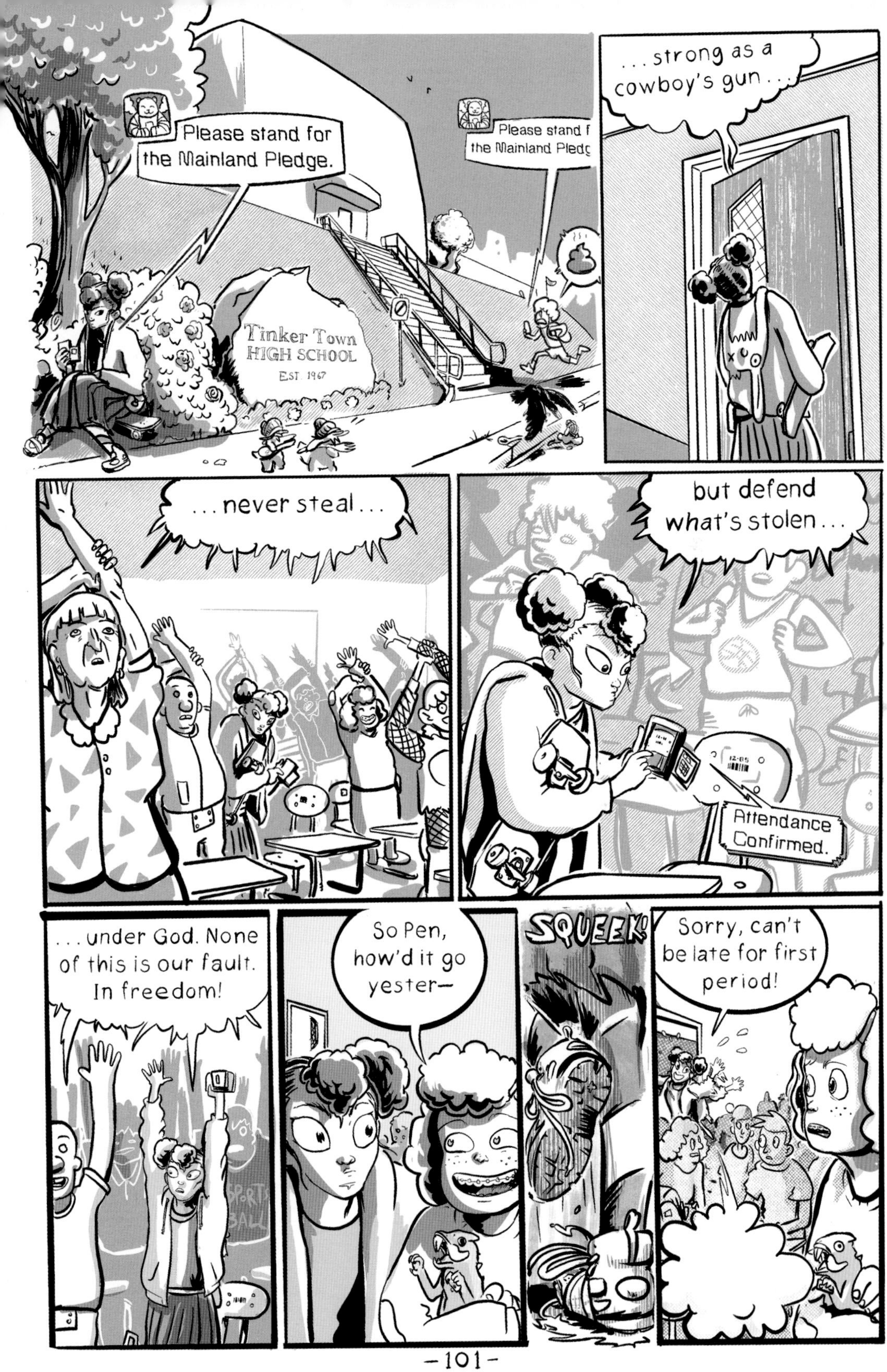
Please stand for the Mainland Pledge.
Tinker Town HIGH SCHOOL EST. 1967
Please stand f the Mainland Pledg
. . . strong as a cowboy's gun . . .
. . . never steal . . .
but defend what's stolen . . .
Attendance Confirmed.
. . . under God. None of this is our fault. In freedom!
So Pen, how'd it go yester—
SQUEEK!
Sorry, can't be late for first period!

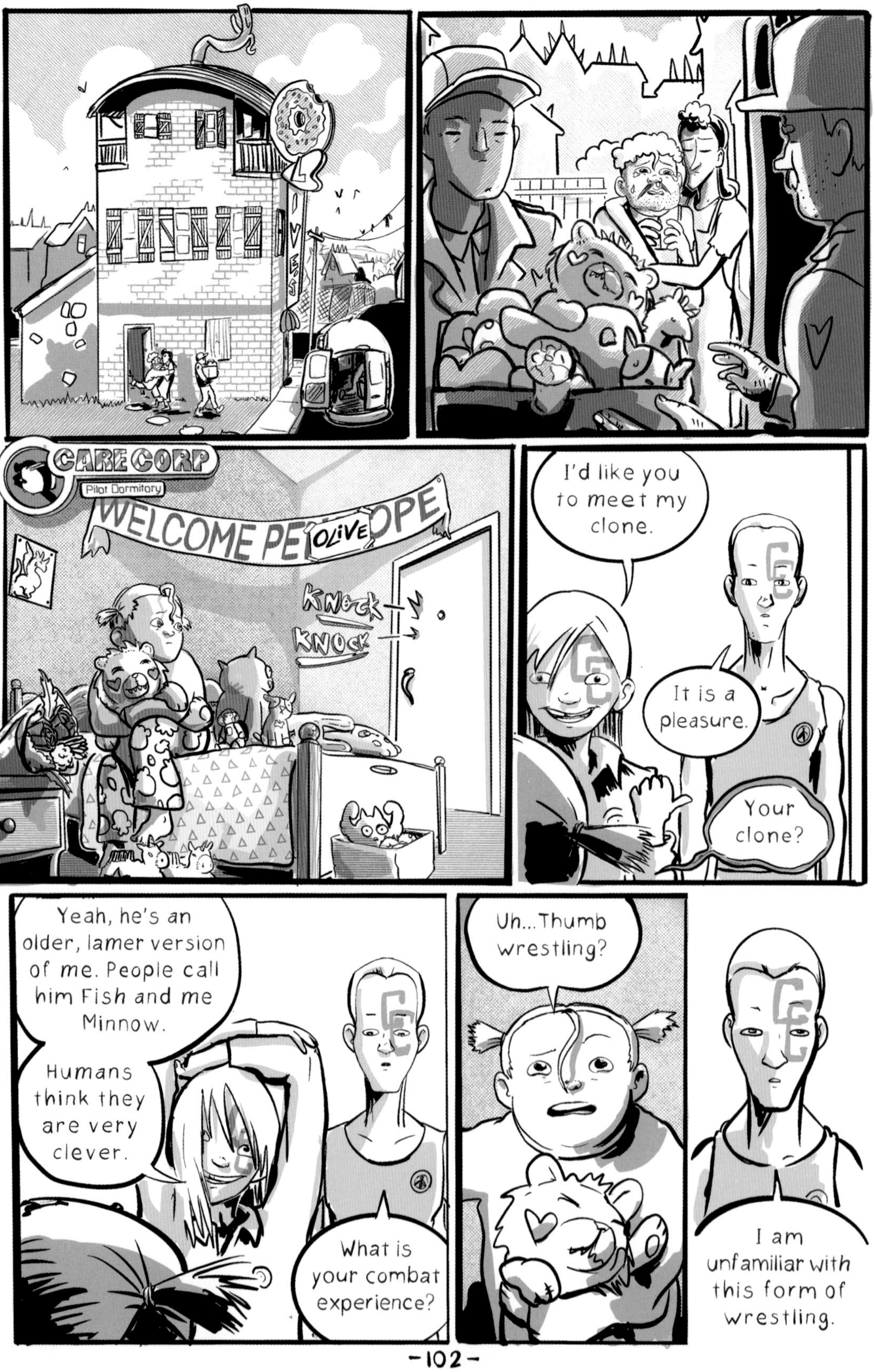
CARE CORP
Pilot Dormitory
WELCOME PE OLIVE OPE
KNOCK
KNOCK
I'd like you to meet my clone.
It is a pleasure.
Your clone?
Yeah, he's an older, lamer version of me. People call him Fish and me Minnow.
Humans think they are very clever.
What is your combat experience?
Uh... Thumb wrestling?
I am unfamiliar with this form of wrestling.

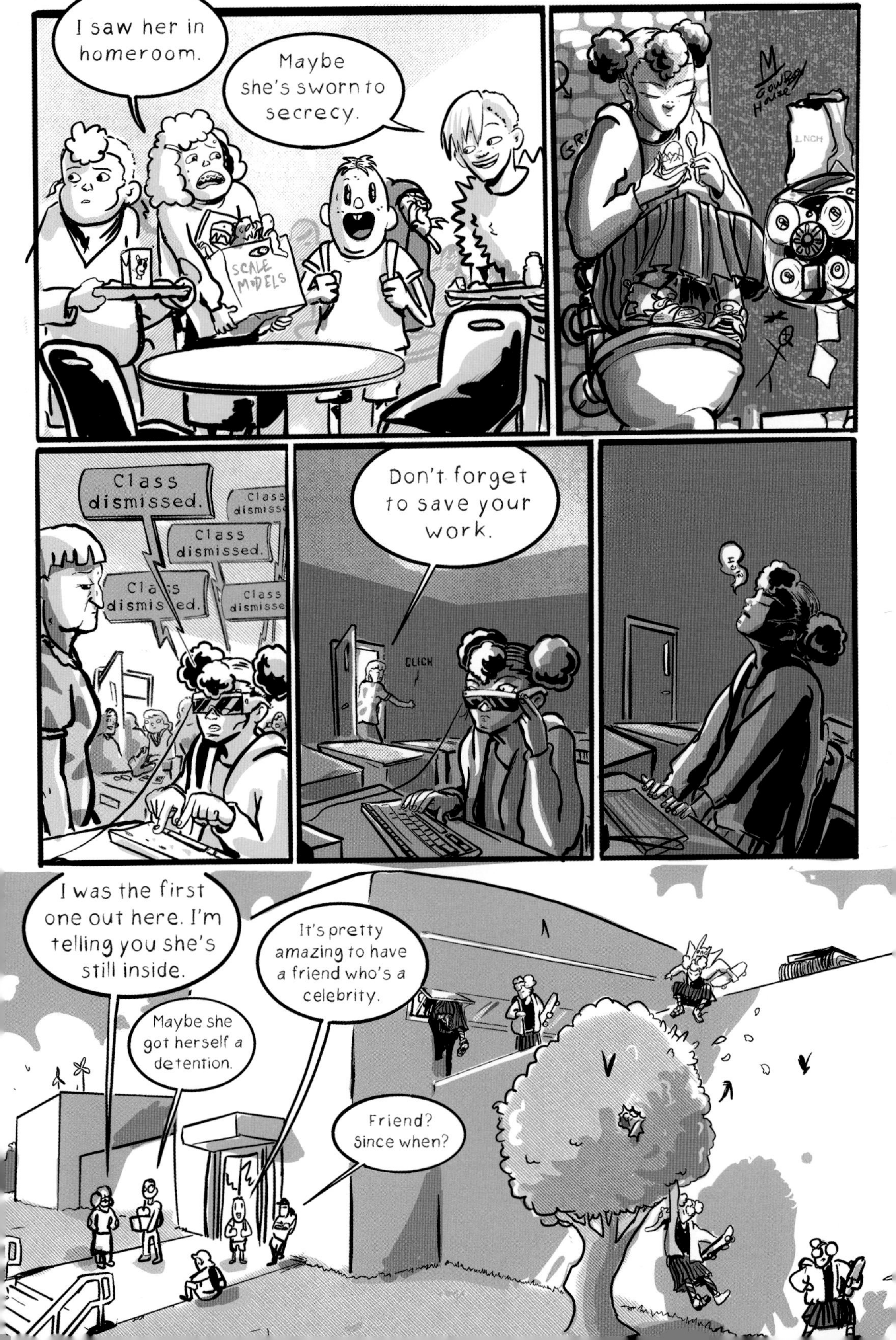
I saw her in homeroom.
Maybe she's sworn to secrecy.
SCALE MODELS
LNCH
Class dismissed.
Class dismissed.
Class dismissed.
Don't forget to save your work.
CLICK
I was the first one out here. I'm telling you she's still inside.
Maybe she got herself a detention.
It's pretty amazing to have a friend who's a celebrity.
Friend? Since when?

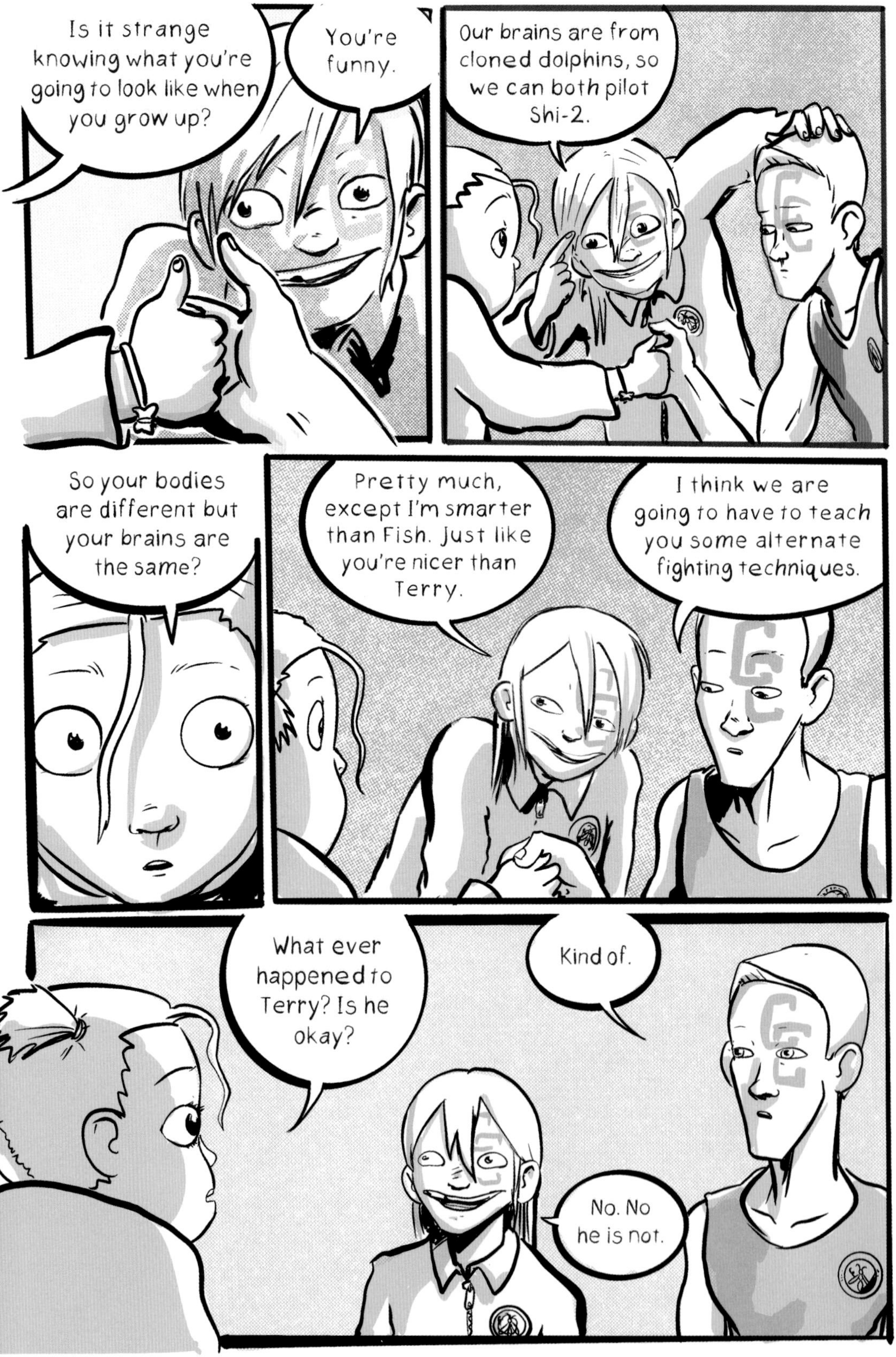
Is it strange knowing what you're going to look like when you grow up?
You're funny.
Our brains are from cloned dolphins, so we can both pilot Shi-2.
So your bodies are different but your brains are the same?
Pretty much, except I'm smarter than Fish. Just like you're nicer than Terry.
I think we are going to have to teach you some alternate fighting techniques.
What ever happened to Terry? Is he okay?
Kind of.
No. No he is not.

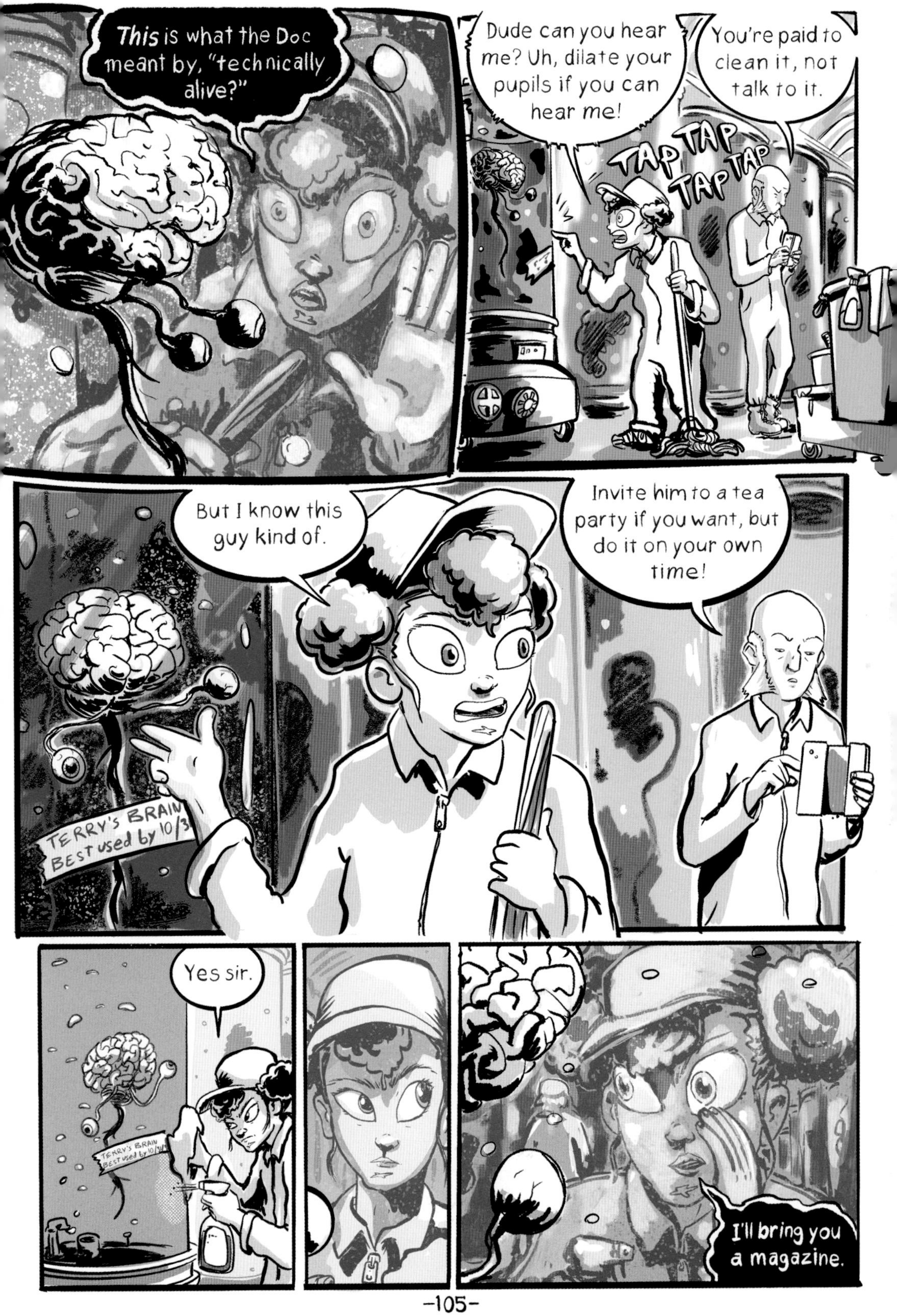

This is what the Doc meant by, "technically alive?"
Dude can you hear me? Uh, dilate your pupils if you can hear me!
TAP TAP TAP TAP
You're paid to clean it, not talk to it.
But I know this guy kind of.
TERRY'S BRAIN BEST used by 10/3
Invite him to a tea party if you want, but do it on your own time!
Yes sir.
I'll bring you a magazine.

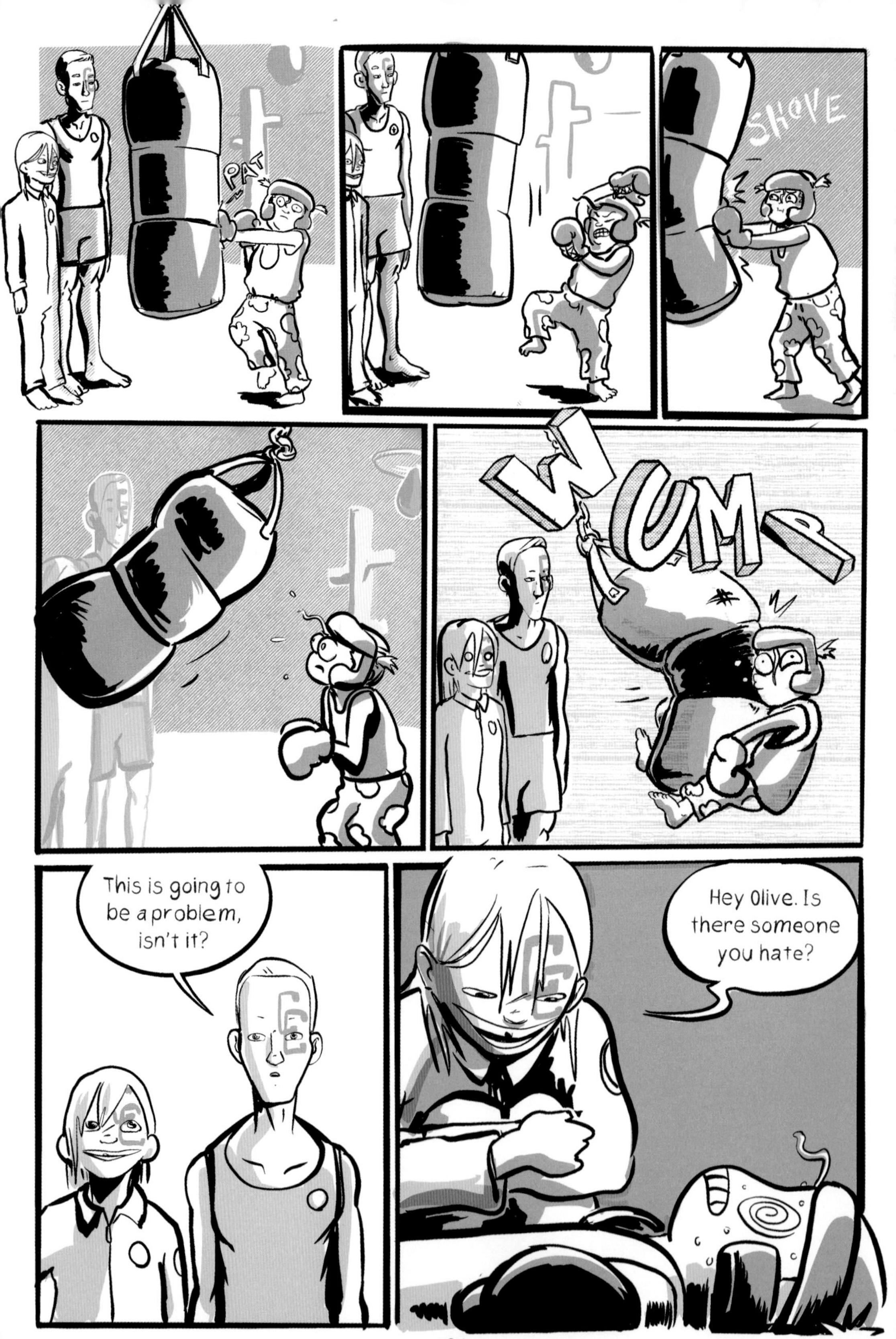
PAT
SHOVE
WUMP
This is going to be a problem, isn't it?
Hey Olive. Is there someone you hate?

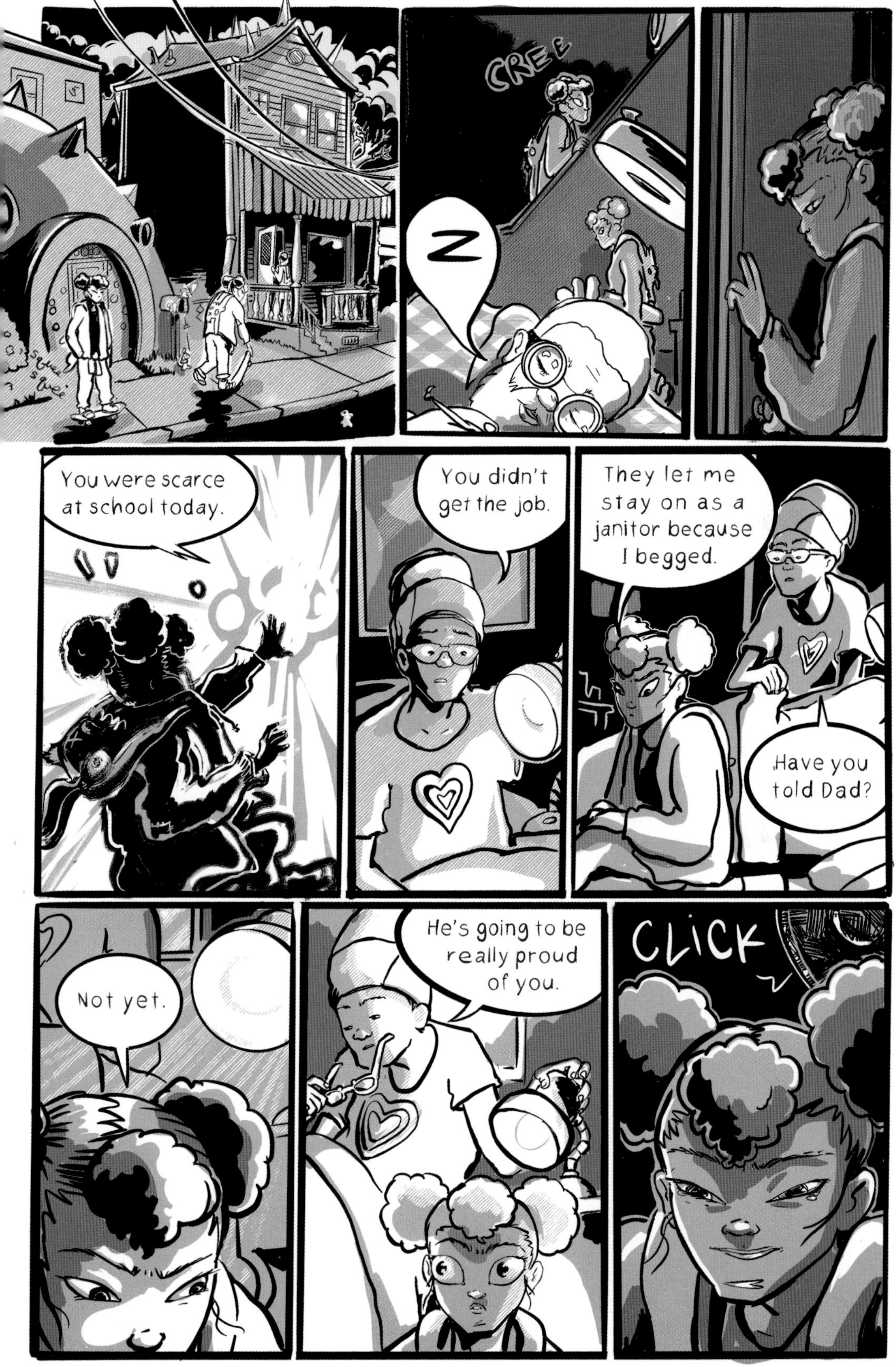
CREE
Z
You were scarce at school today.
You didn't get the job.
They let me stay on as a janitor because I begged.
Have you told Dad?
Not yet.
He's going to be really proud of you.
CLICK

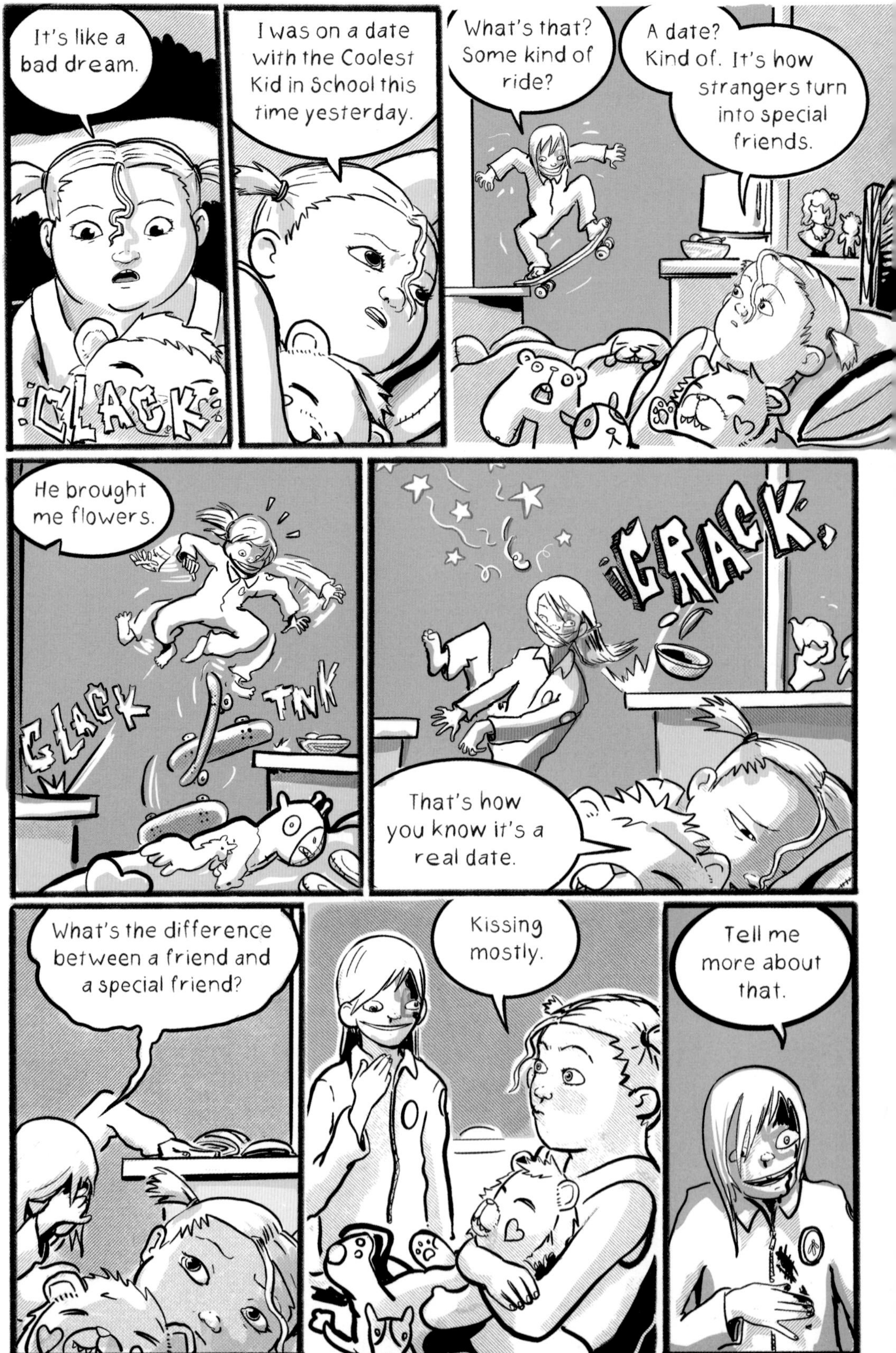
It's like a bad dream.
CLACK
I was on a date with the Coolest Kid in School this time yesterday.
What's that? Some kind of ride?
A date? Kind of. It's how strangers turn into special friends.
He brought me flowers.
CLACK
TNK
CRACK
That's how you know it's a real date.
What's the difference between a friend and a special friend?
Kissing mostly.
Tell me more about that.

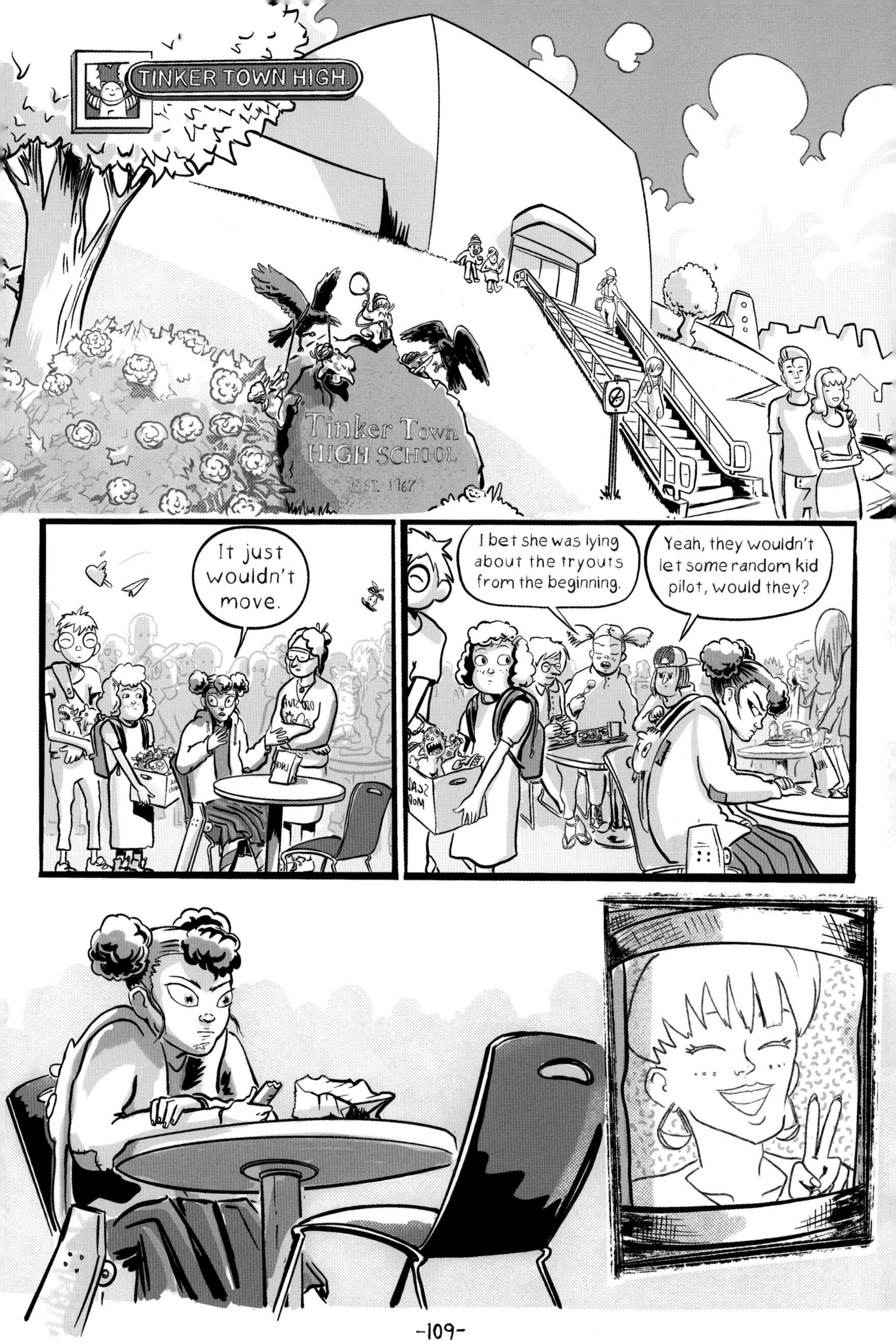
TINKER TOWN HIGH.
Tinker Town
HIGH SCHOOL
EST. 1967
It just wouldn't move.
I bet she was lying about the tryouts from the beginning.
Yeah, they wouldn't let some random kid pilot, would they?

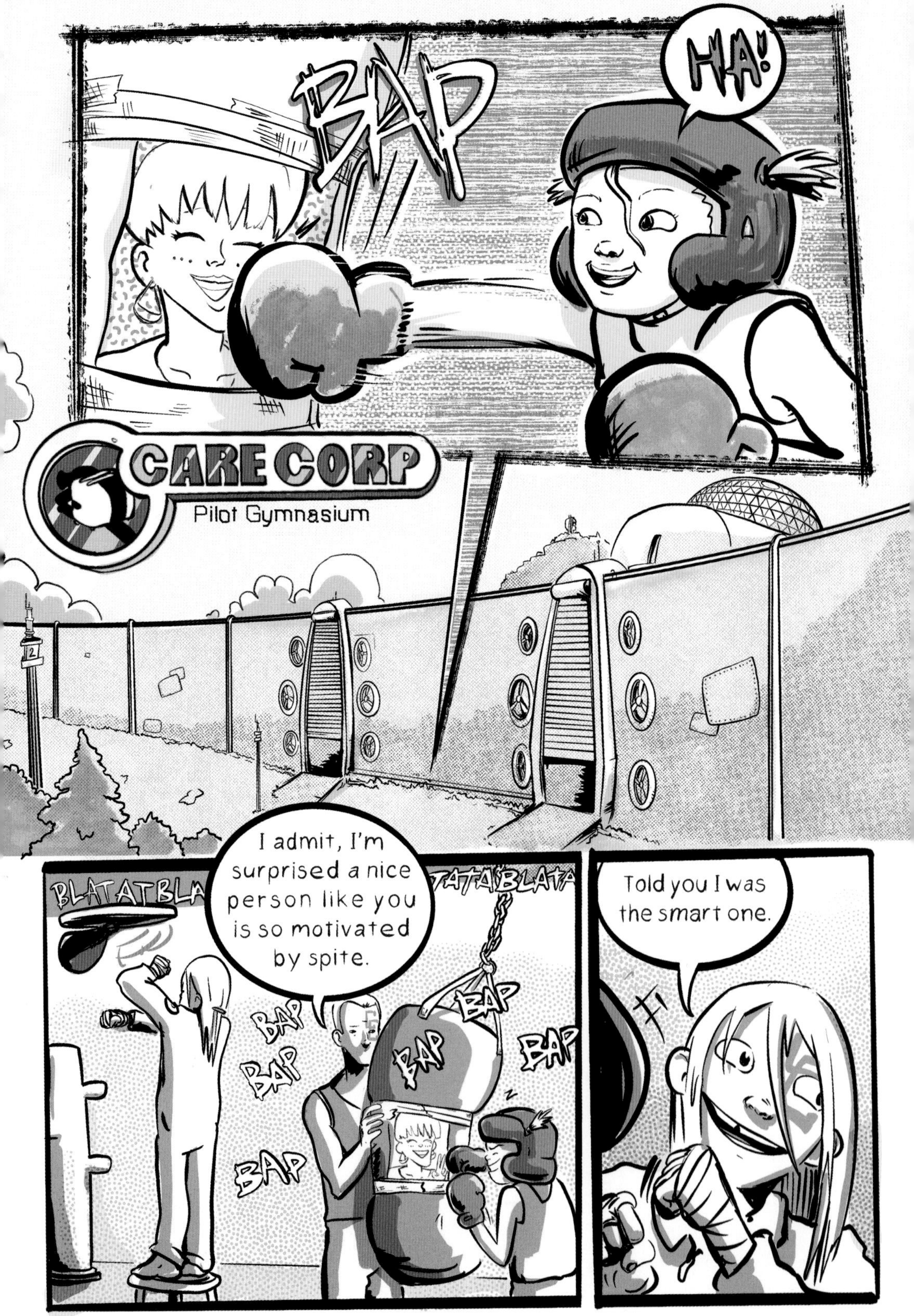
BAP
HA!
CARE CORP
Pilot Gymnasium
BLATATBLA
TATABLATA
I admit, I'm surprised a nice person like you is so motivated by spite.
BAP
BAP
BAP
BAP
BAP
BAP
Told you I was the smart one.

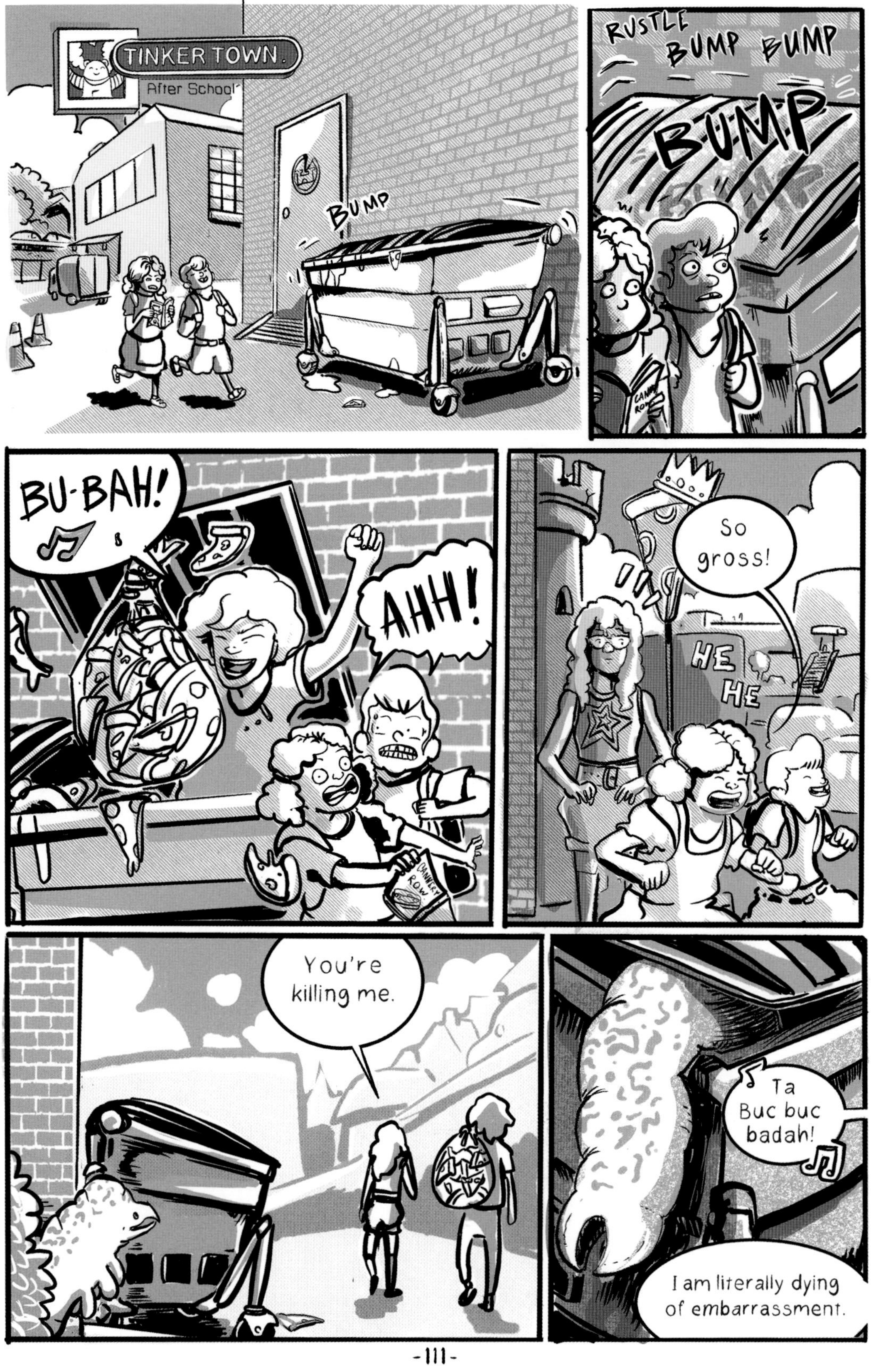
TINKER TOWN.
After School
BUMP
RUSTLE
BUMP BUMP
BUMP
BU-BAH!
AHH!
CANNERY ROW
So gross!
HE HE
You're killing me.
Ta Buc buc badah!
I am literally dying of embarrassment.

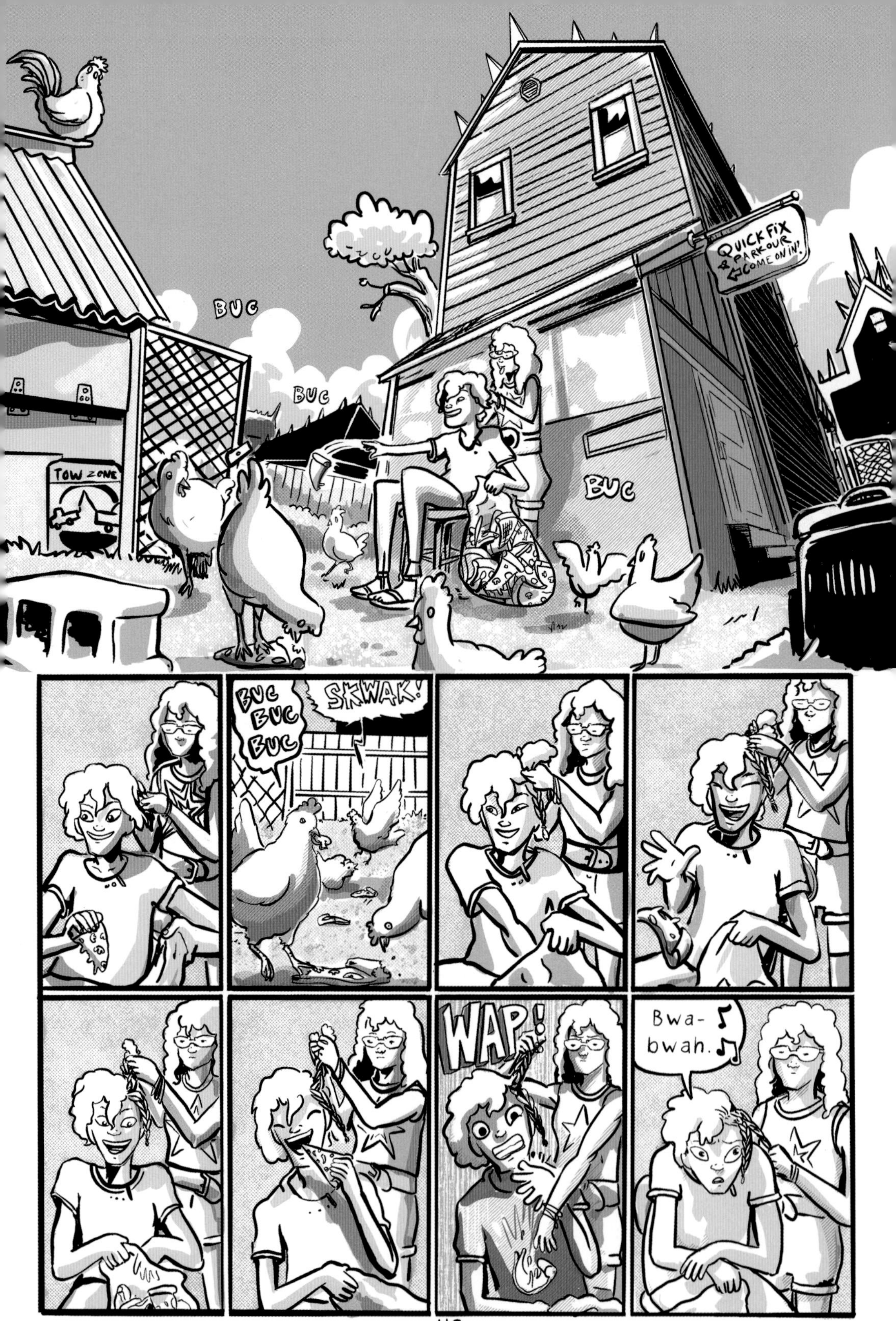
BUC
BUC
QUICK FIX & PARKOUR ⇦COME ON IN!
TOW ZONE
BUC
BUC BUC BUC
SKWAK!
WAP!
Bwa-bwah.

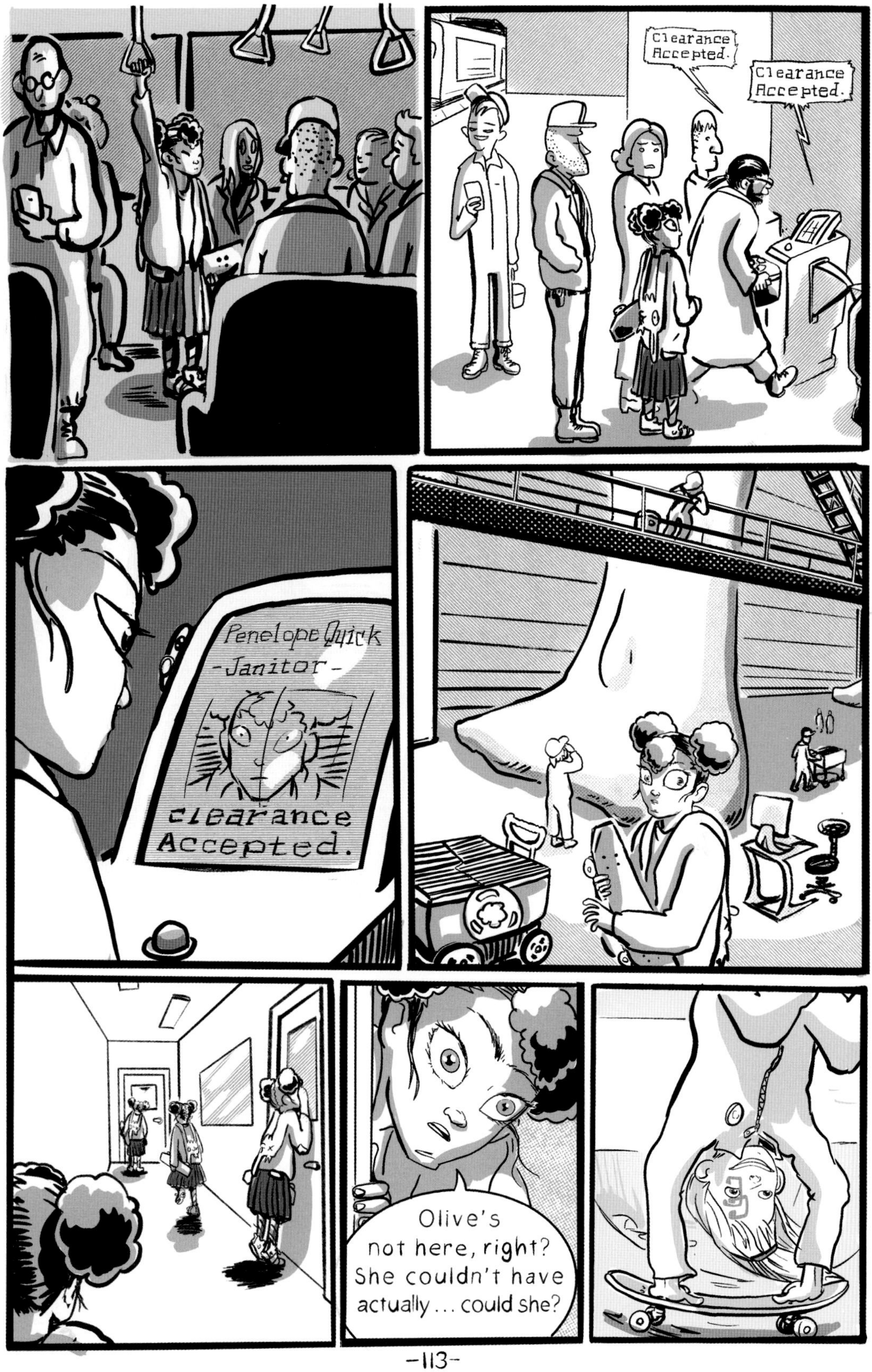
Clearance Accepted.
Clearance Accepted.
Penelope Quick
-Janitor-
clearance Accepted.
Olive's not here, right? She couldn't have actually... could she?

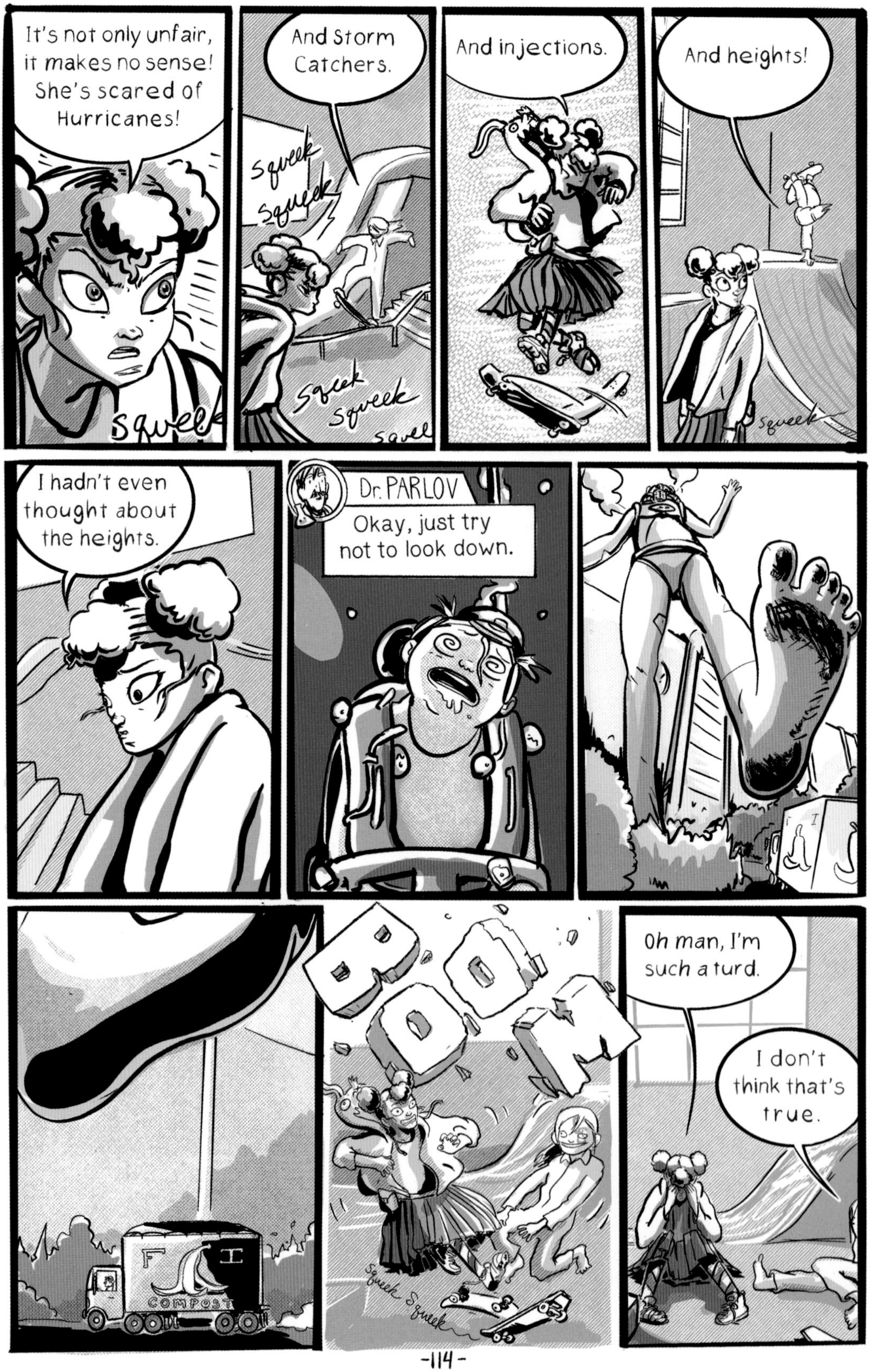
It's not only unfair, it makes no sense! She's scared of Hurricanes!
Squeek
And Storm Catchers.
Squeek Squeek
Sqeek Squeek
Squek
And injections.
And heights!
Squeek
I hadn't even thought about the heights.
Dr. PARLOV
Okay, just try not to look down.
F I
COMPOST
BOOM
Squeek Squeek
Oh man, I'm such a turd.
I don't think that's true.

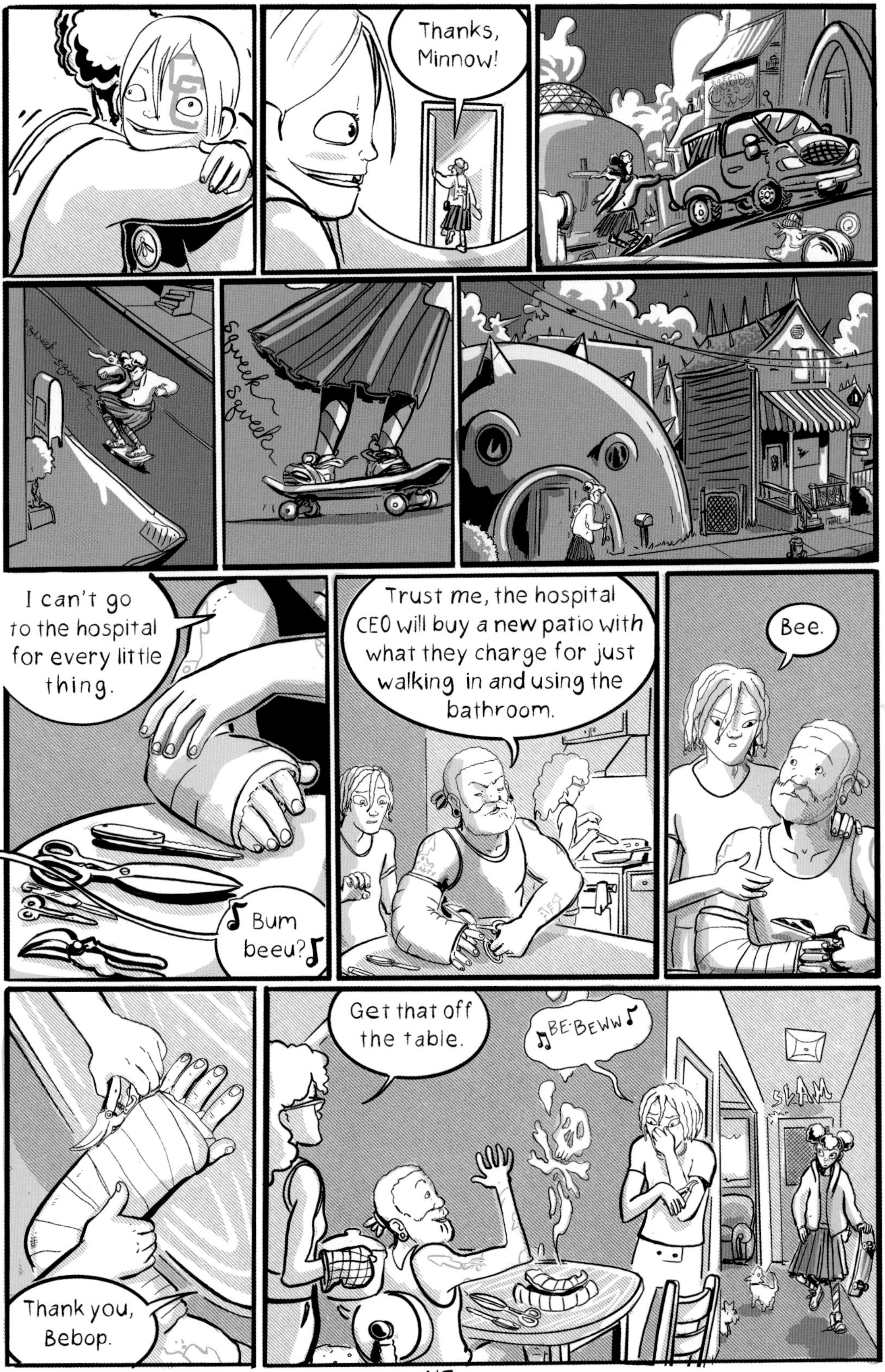

Thanks, Minnow!
squeek squeek
squeek squeek
I can't go to the hospital for every little thing.
Bum beeu?
Trust me, the hospital CEO will buy a new patio with what they charge for just walking in and using the bathroom.
Bee.
Thank you, Bebop.
Get that off the table.
BE-BEWW
SLAM

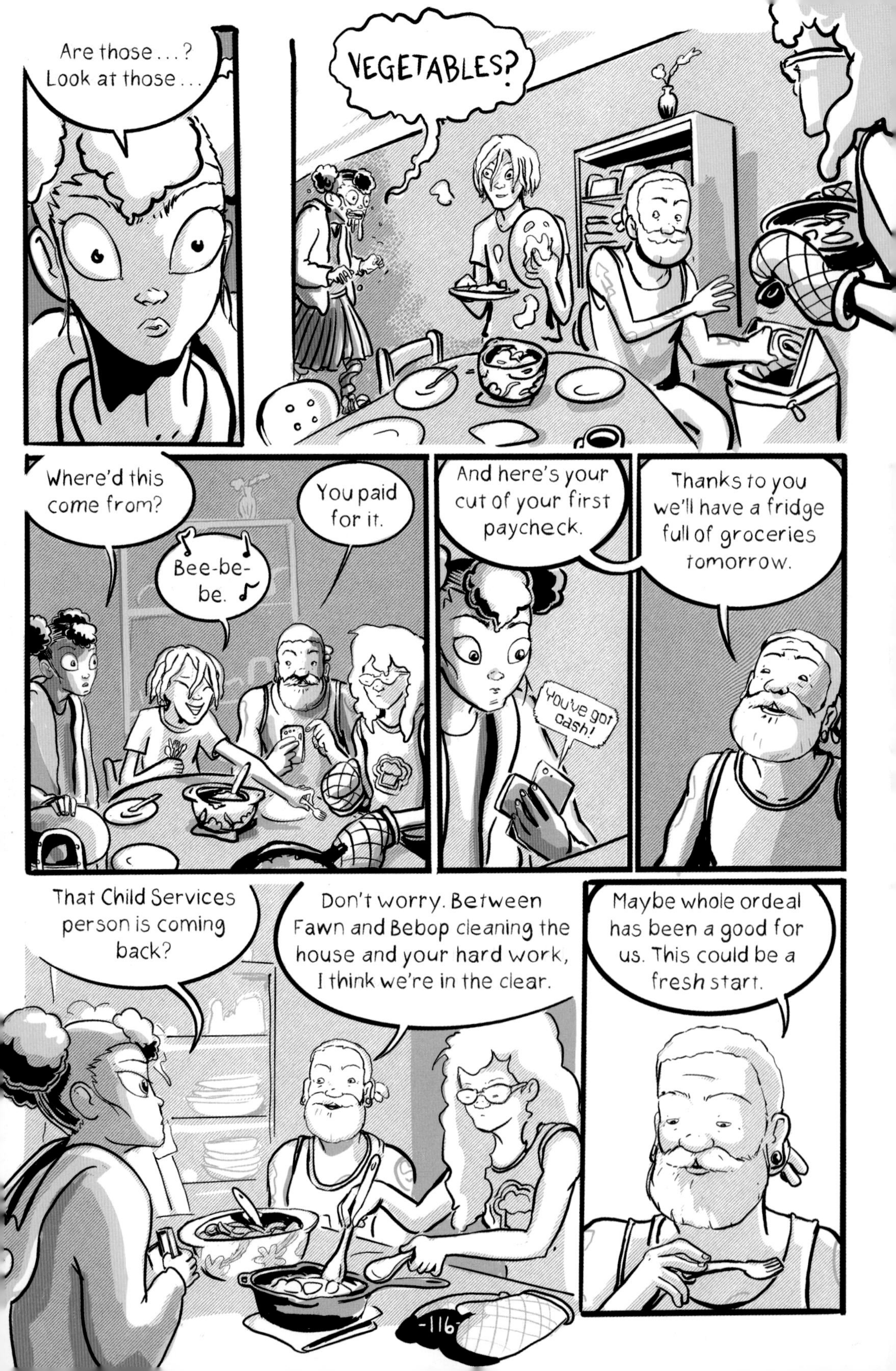

Are those . . . ? Look at those . . .
VEGETABLES?
Where'd this come from?
Bee-be-be.
You paid for it.
And here's your cut of your first paycheck.
You've got cash!
Thanks to you we'll have a fridge full of groceries tomorrow.
That Child Services person is coming back?
Don't worry. Between Fawn and Bebop cleaning the house and your hard work, I think we're in the clear.
Maybe whole ordeal has been a good for us. This could be a fresh start.

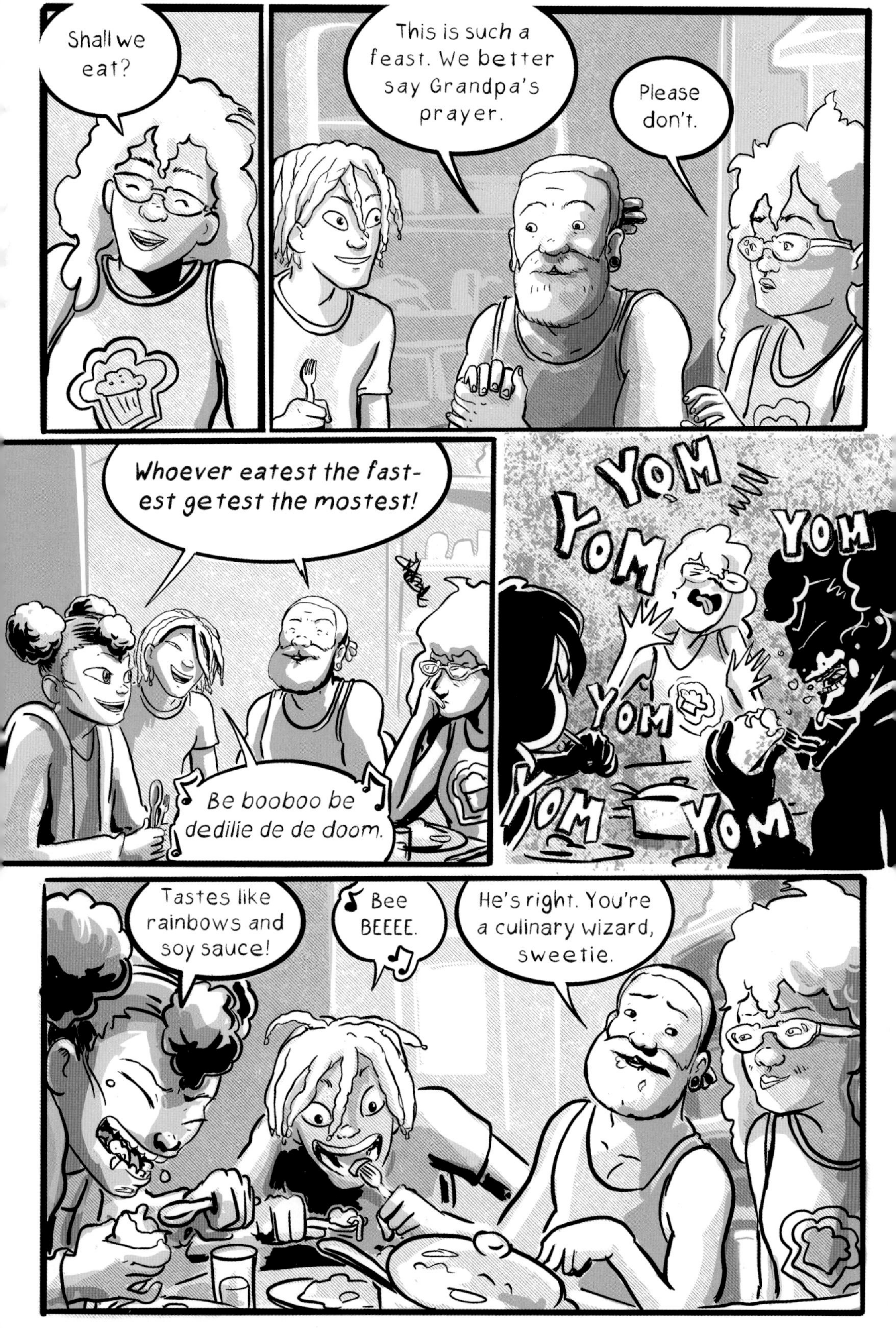
Shall we eat?
This is such a feast. We better say Grandpa's prayer.
Please don't.
Whoever eatest the fastest getest the mostest!
Be booboo be dedilie de de doom.
YOM
YOM
YOM
YOM
YOM
YOM
Tastes like rainbows and soy sauce!
Bee BEEEE.
He's right. You're a culinary wizard, sweetie.

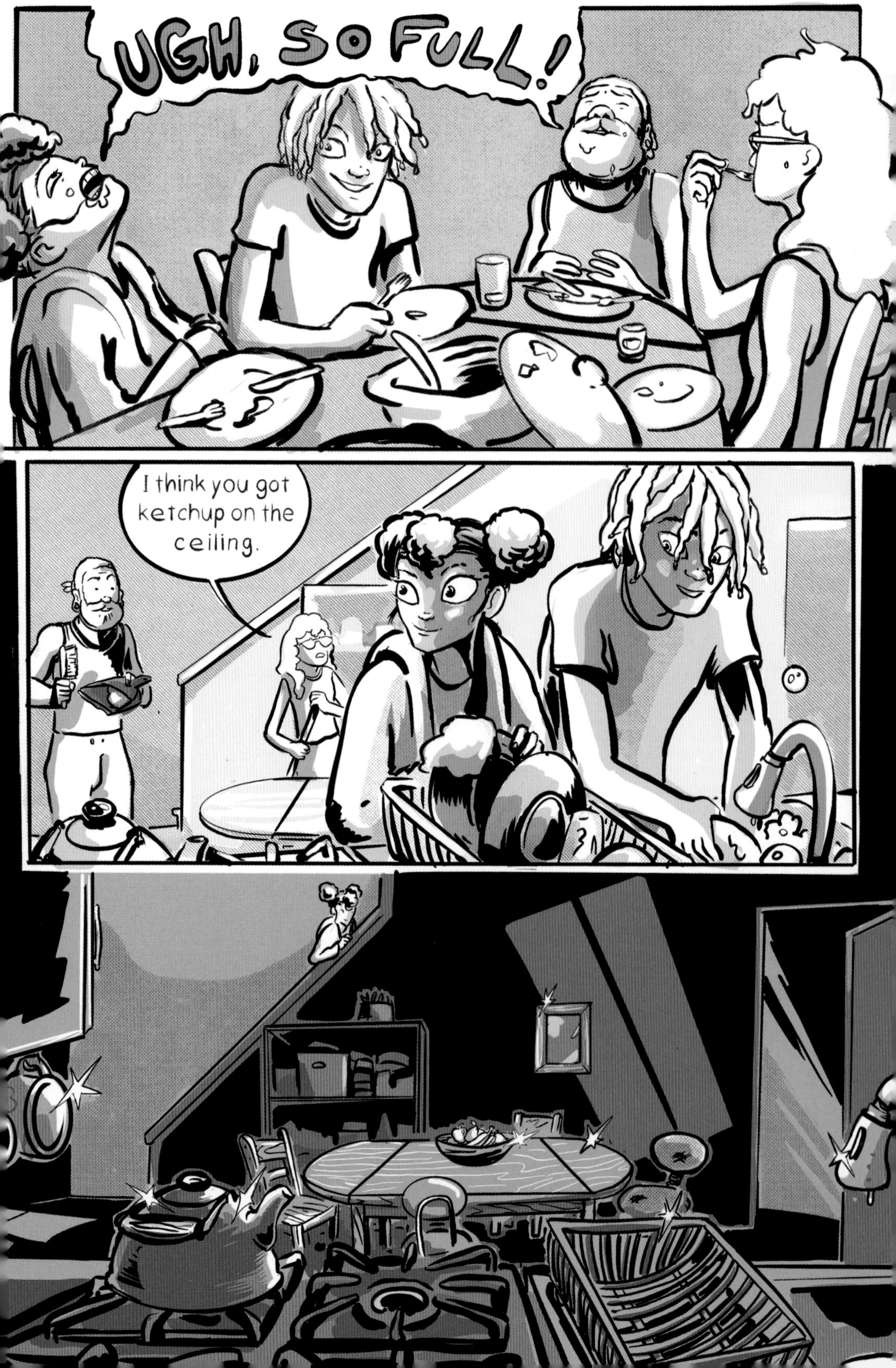
UGH, SO FULL!
I think you got ketchup on the ceiling.

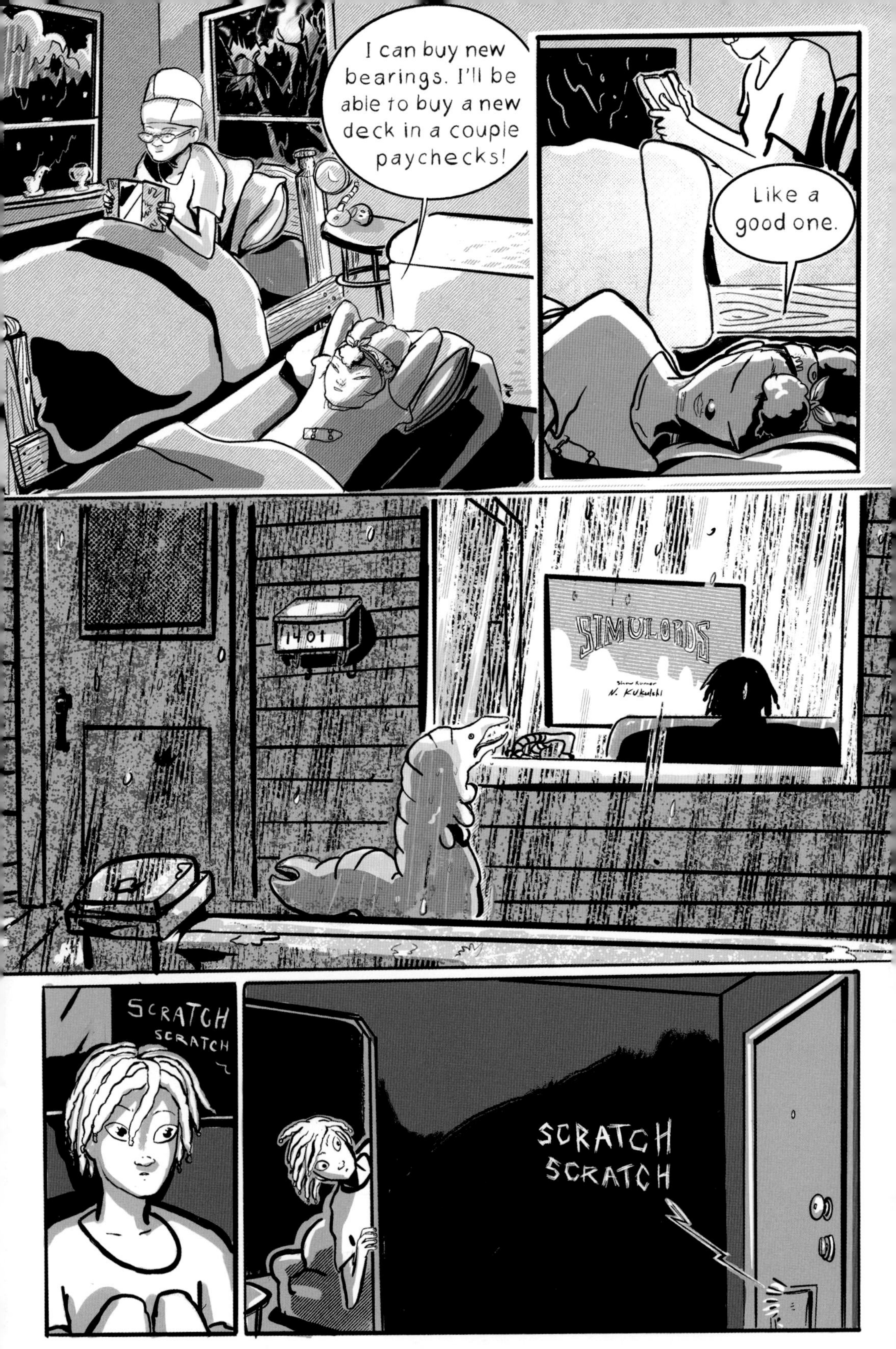
I can buy new bearings. I'll be able to buy a new deck in a couple paychecks!
Like a good one.
1401
SIMULORDS
Show Runner
N. Kukulski
SCRATCH
SCRATCH
SCRATCH
SCRATCH

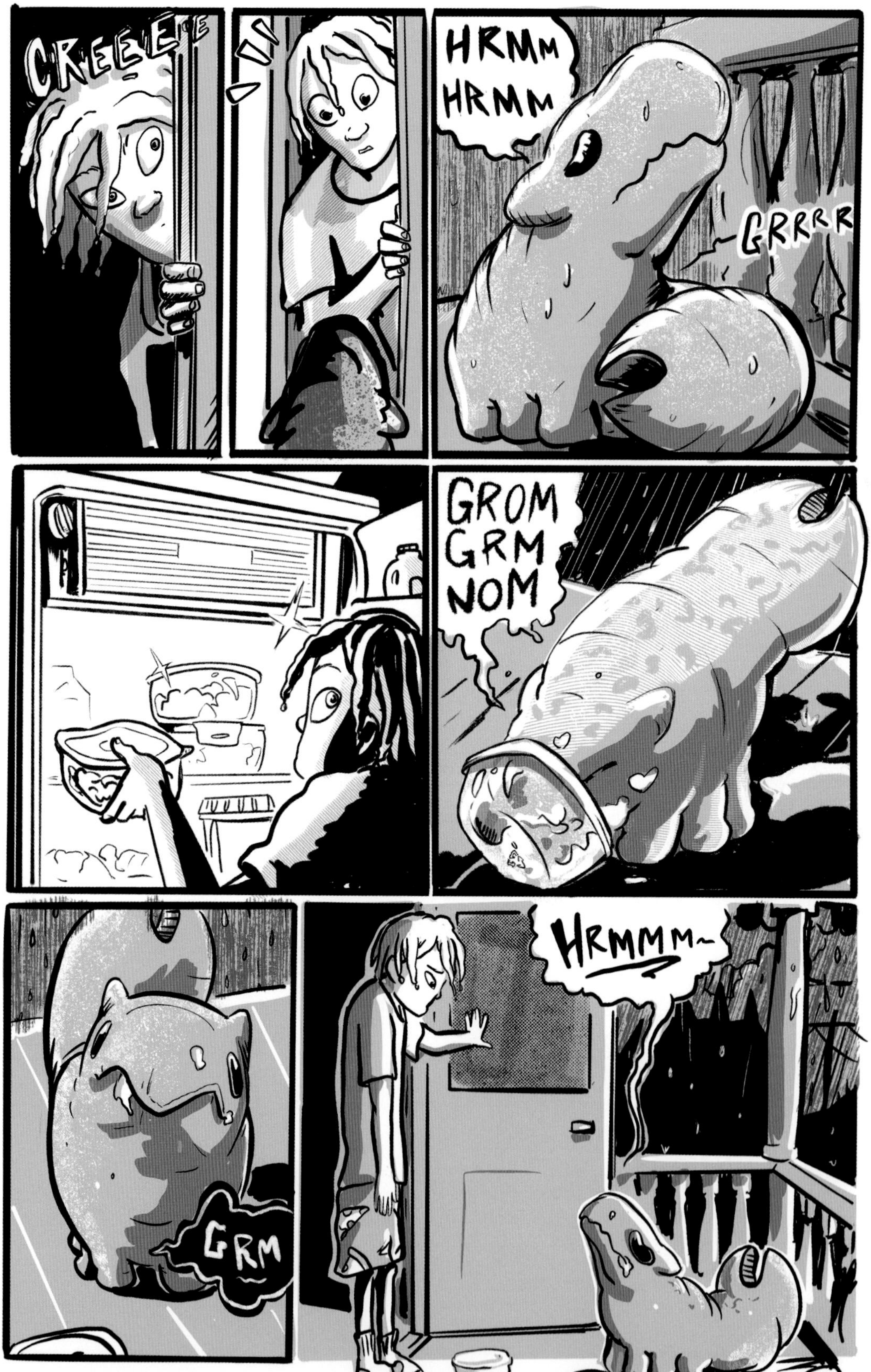
CREEEE
HRMM HRMM
GRRRR
GROM GRM NOM
GRM
HRMMM~

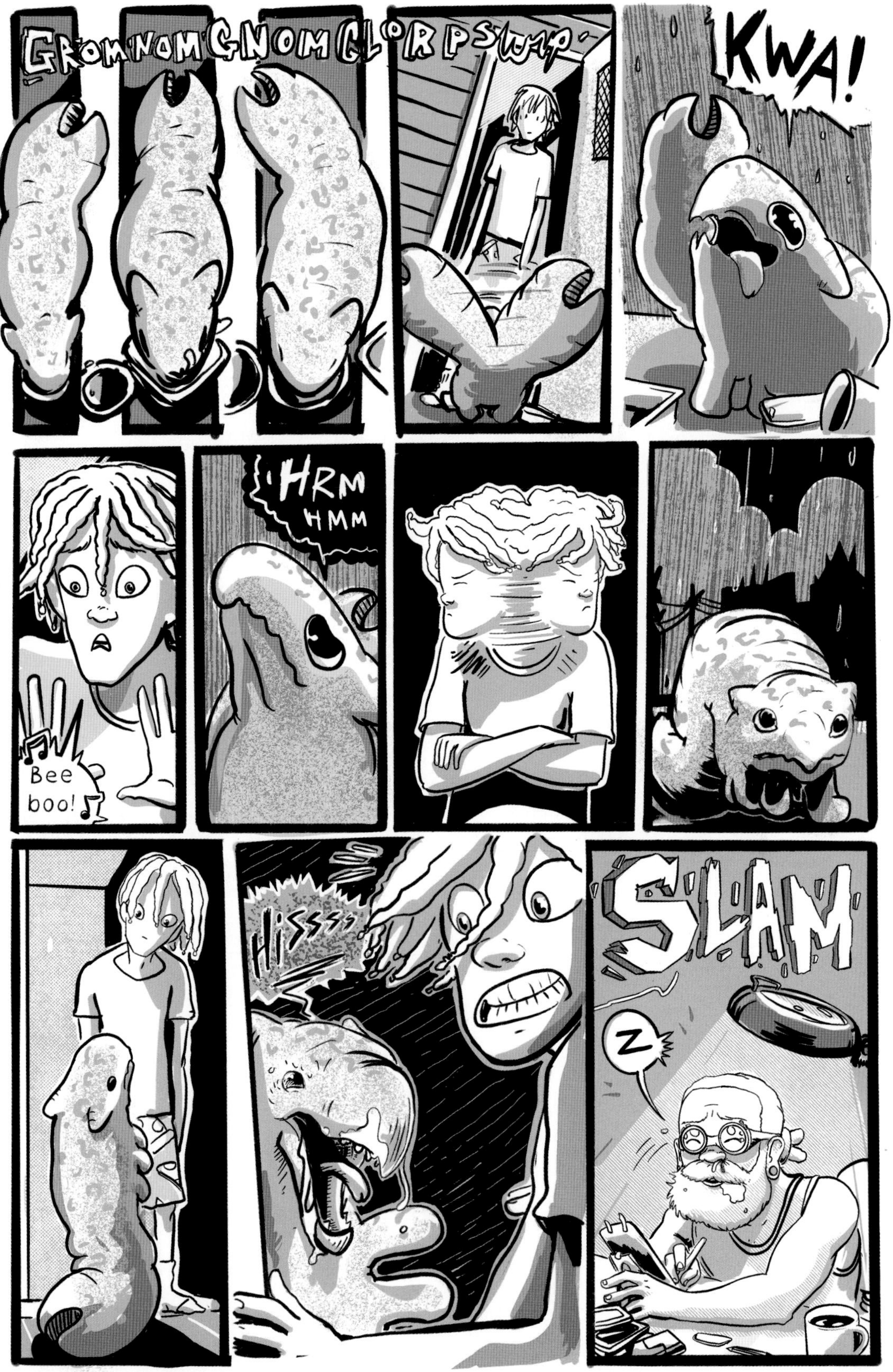
GROMNOMGNOMGLORPSWAP
KWA!
Bee boo!
HRM HMM
HISSSS
SLAM
Z

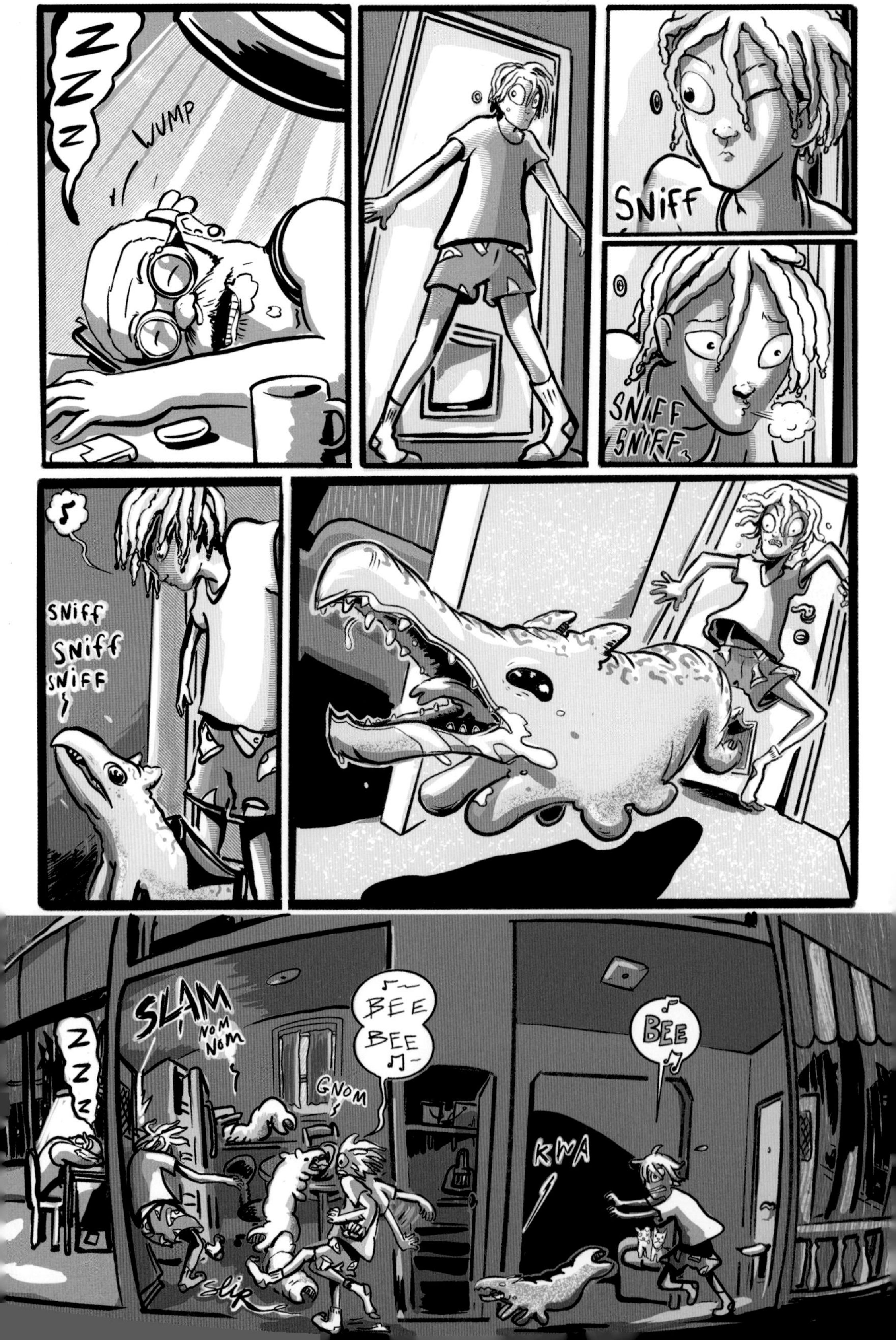
ZZZZ
WUMP
SNIFF
SNIFF
SNIFF
SNIFF
SNIFF
SNIFF
SNIFF
SLAM
NOM NOM
ZZZ
GNOM
BEE BEE
BEE
KWA
SLIP

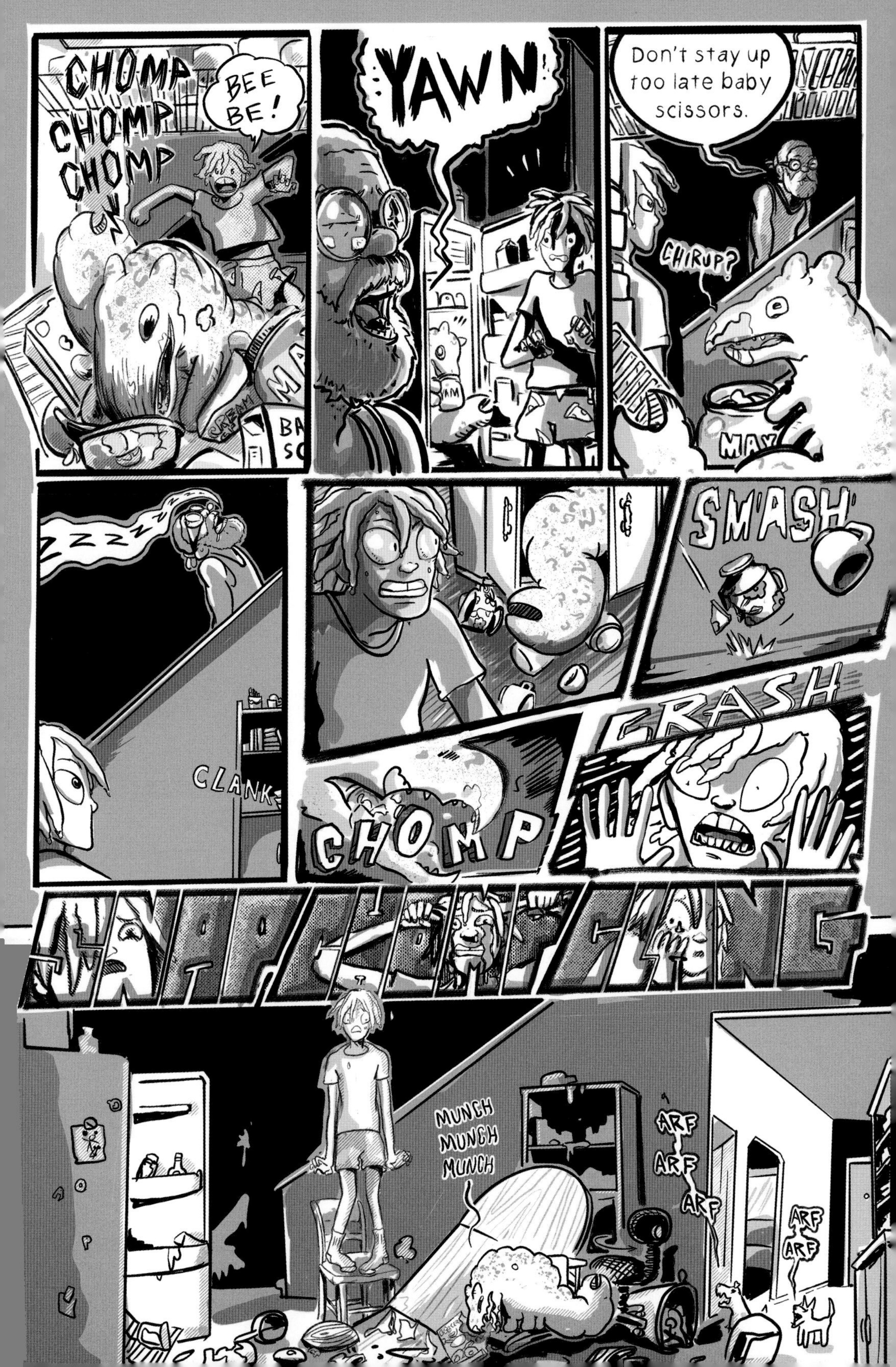
CHOMP CHOMP CHOMP
BEE BE!
YAWN
Don't stay up too late baby scissors.
CHIRUP?
ZZZZZ
CLANK
SMASH
CRASH
CHOMP
MUNCH MUNCH MUNCH
ARF ARF ARF
ARF ARF

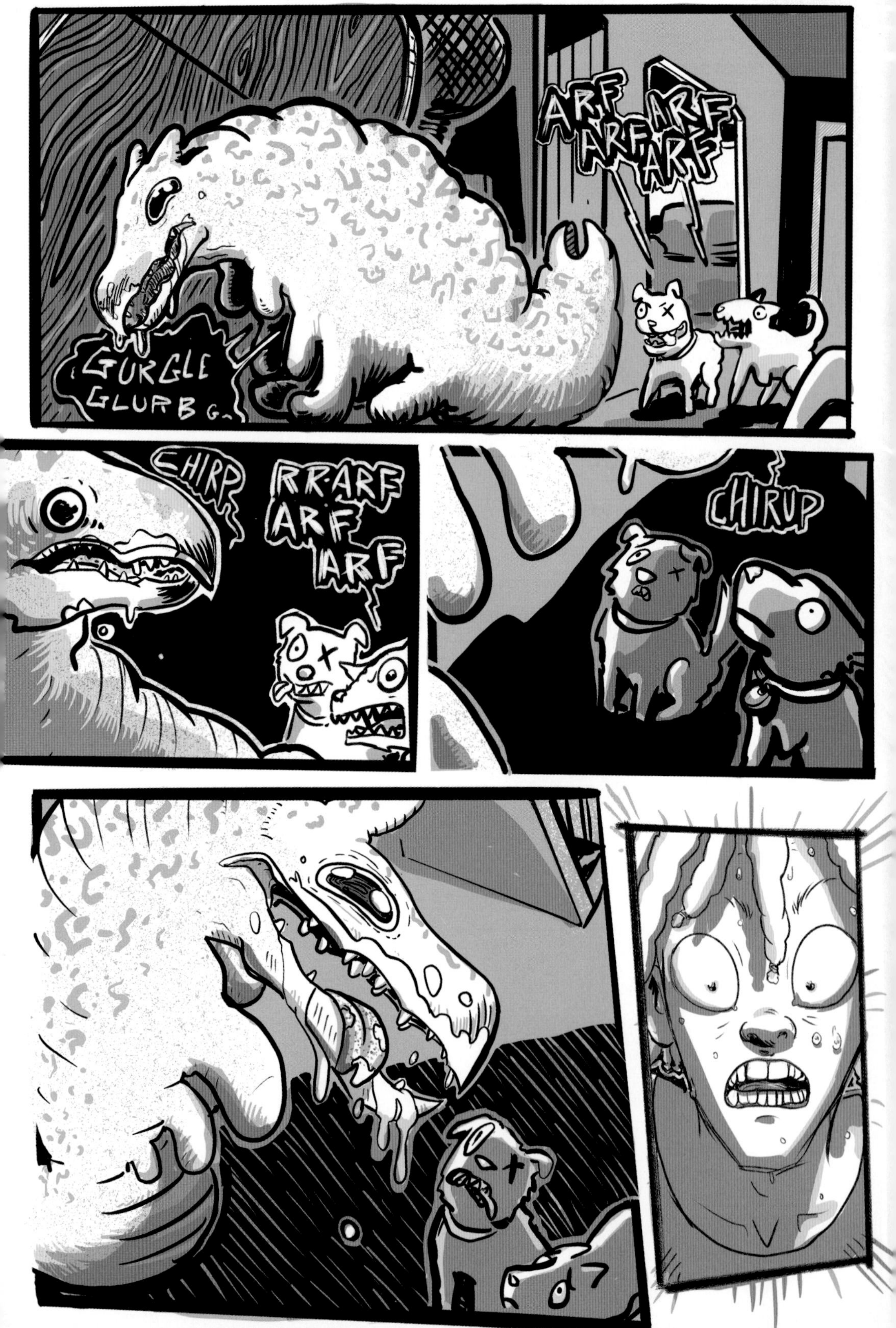
GURGLE GLURB G~
ARF ARF ARF ARF ARF
CHIRP
RR-ARF ARF ARF
CHIRUP

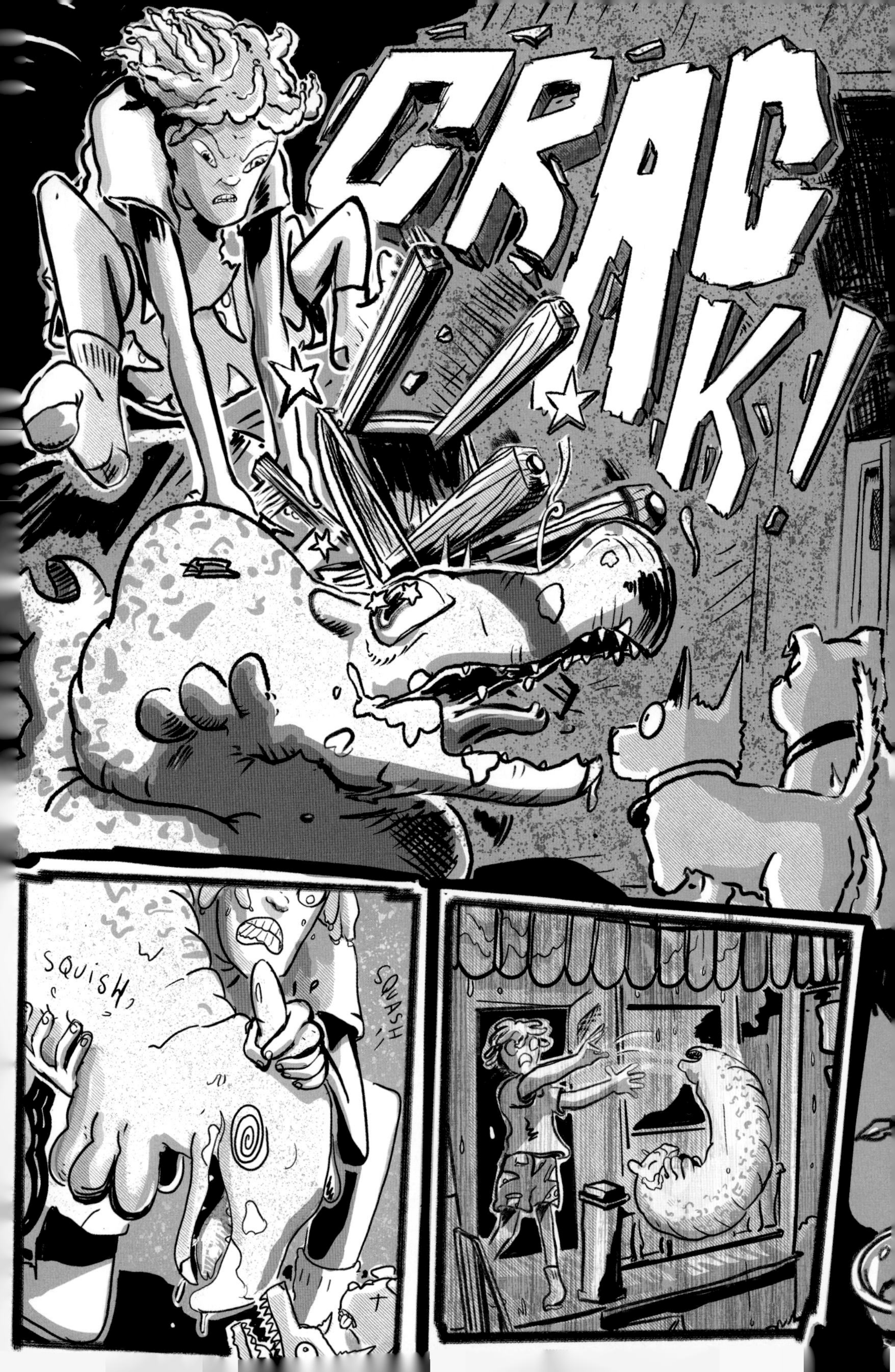
CRACK!
SQUISH
SQUASH

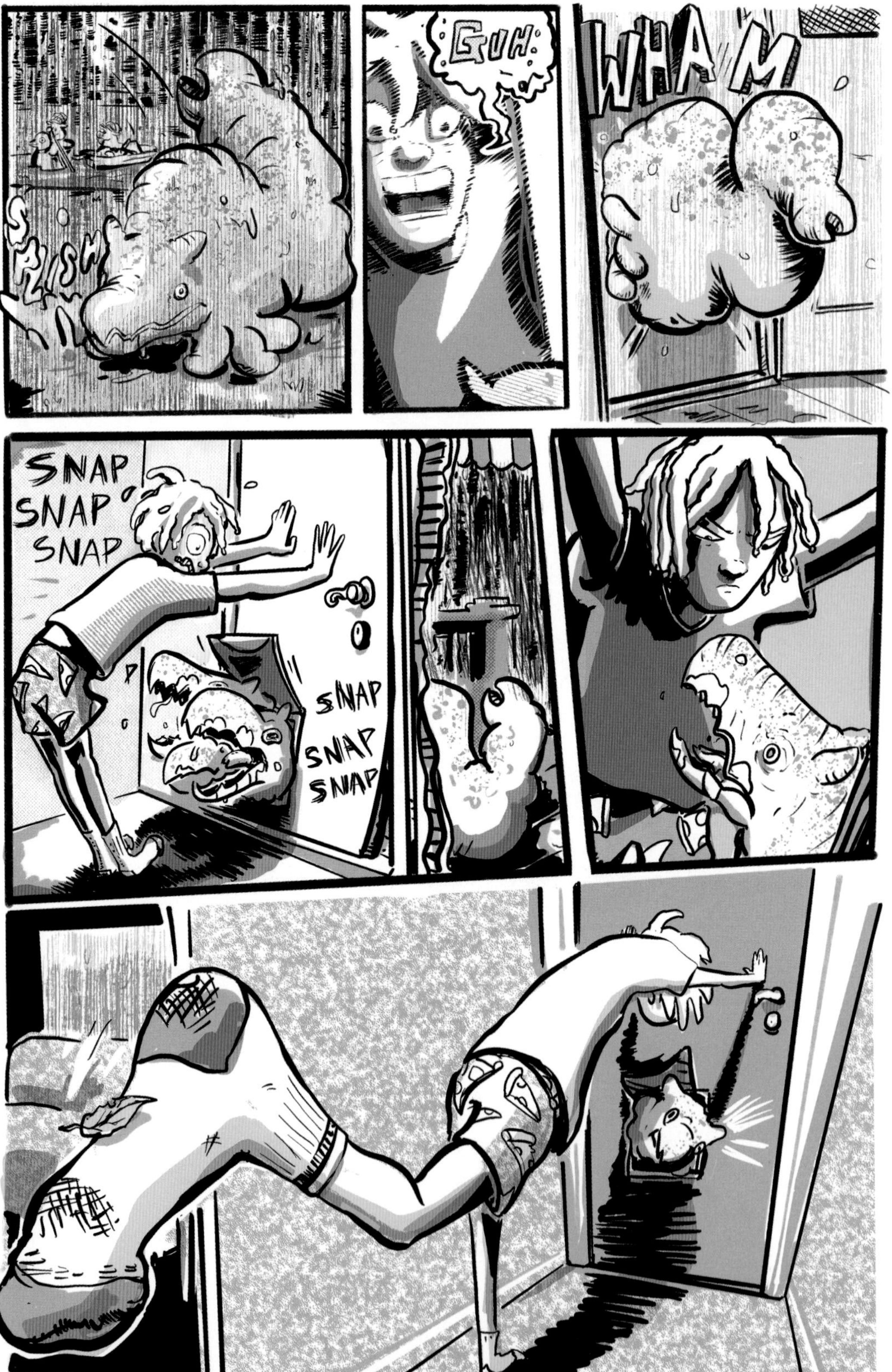
SPLOSH
GUH
WHAM
SNAP
SNAP
SNAP
SNAP
SNAP
SNAP

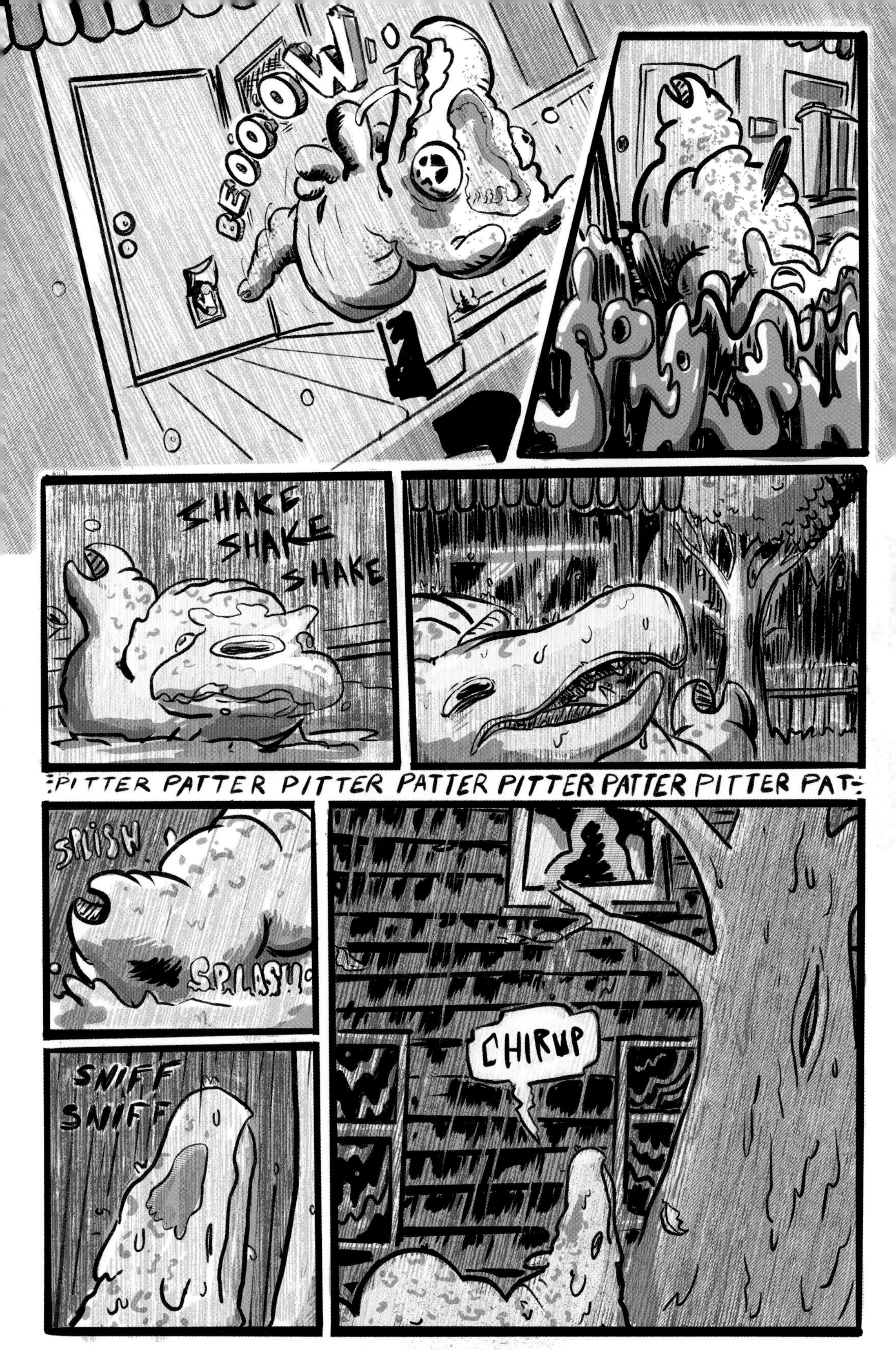
BEOOOOW
SPLASH
SHAKE
SHAKE
SHAKE
PITTER PATTER PITTER PATTER PITTER PATTER PITTER PAT
SPLISH
SPLASH
SNIFF
SNIFF
CHIRUP

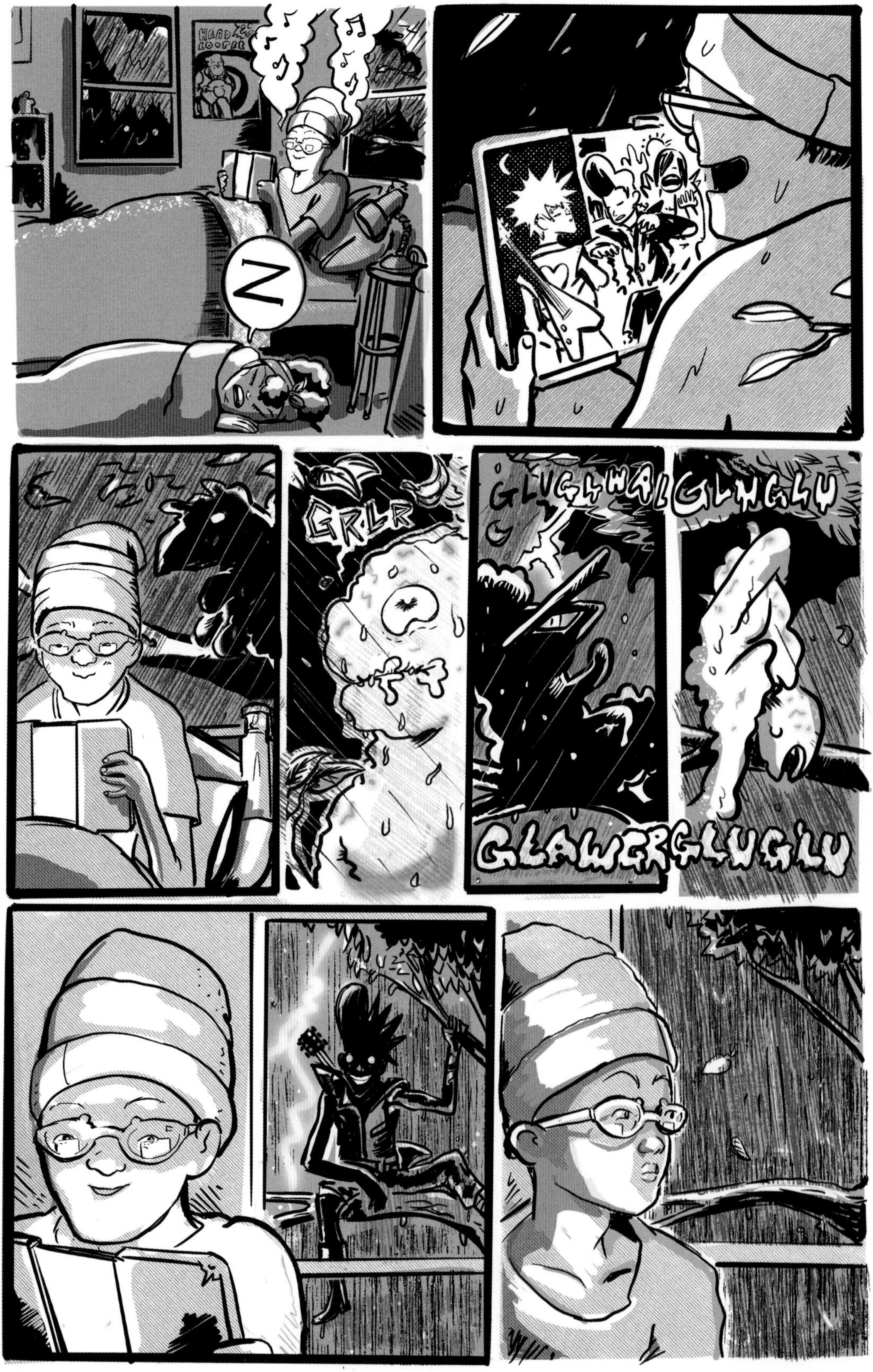

Z
GRLR
GLUGLWALGLWGLU
GLAWERGLUGLU

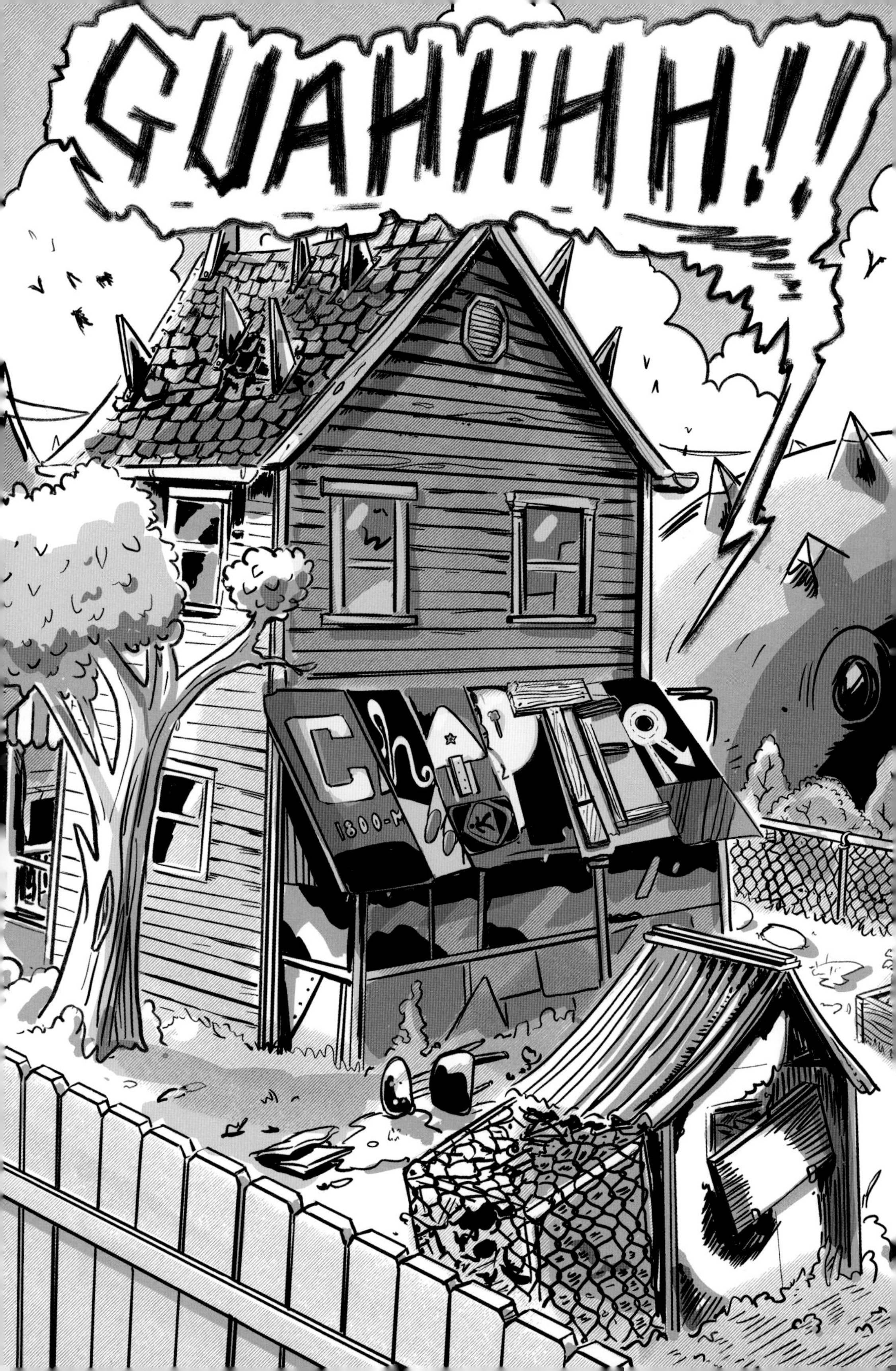
GUAHHHH!!
1800-M

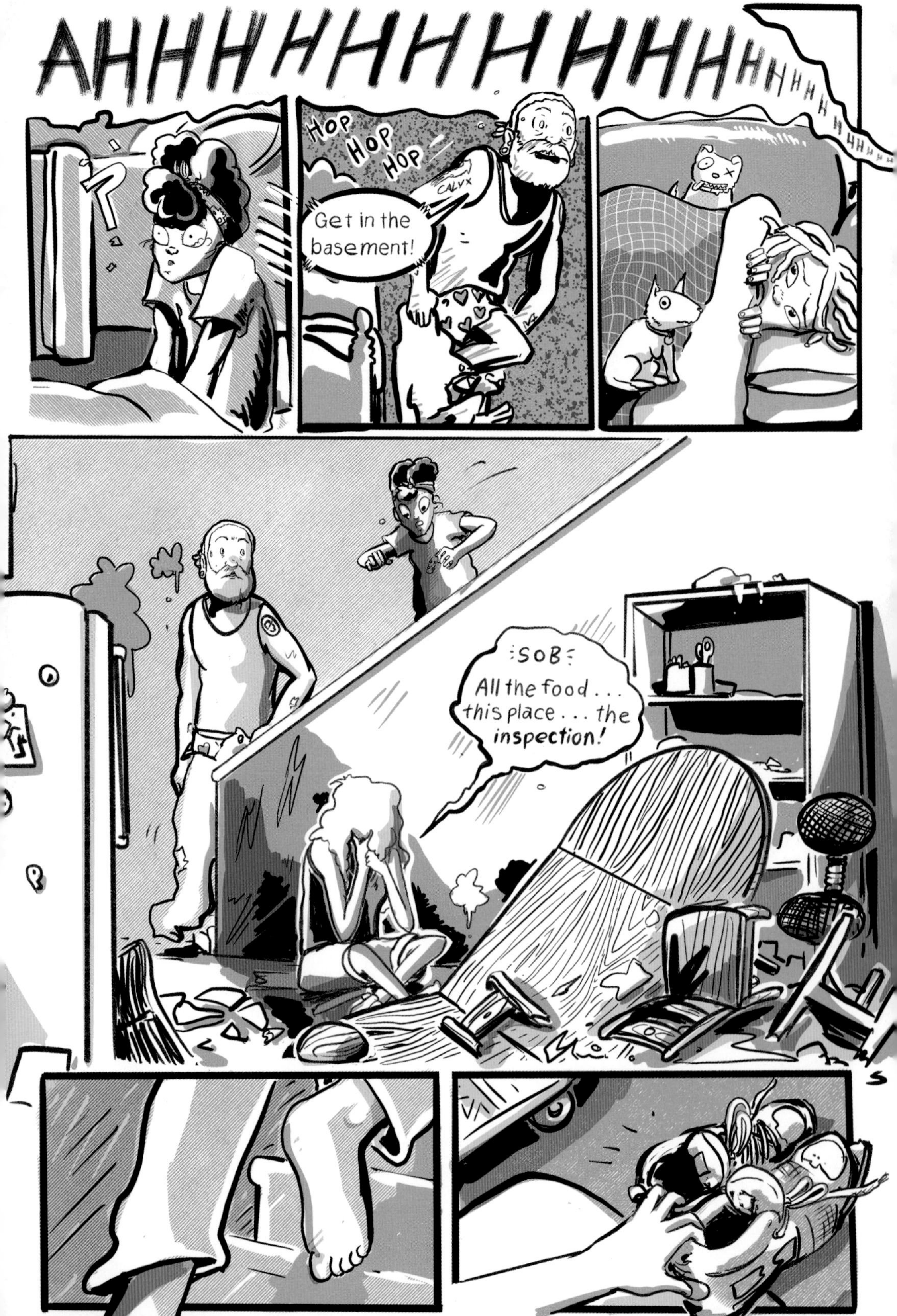
AHHHHHHHHHHHHHHHHHHHHH
HOP HOP HOP
Get in the basement!
CALYX
:SOB:
All the food . . . this place . . . the *inspection!*
5

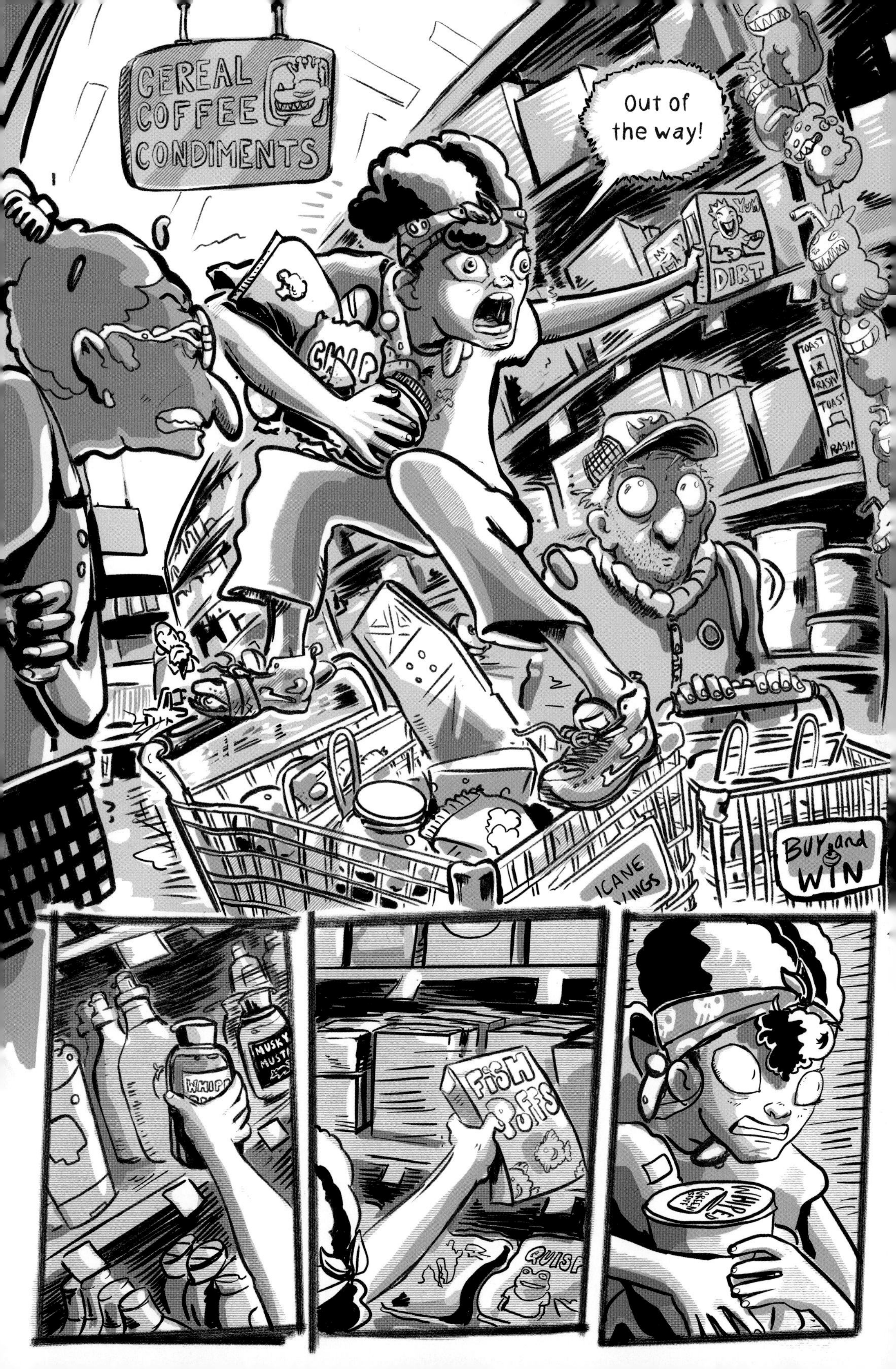
CEREAL
COFFEE
CONDIMENTS
Out of the way!
YUM
DIRT
TOAST
RASIN
TOAST
RASIN
BUY and WIN
WHIPP
FISH PUFFS

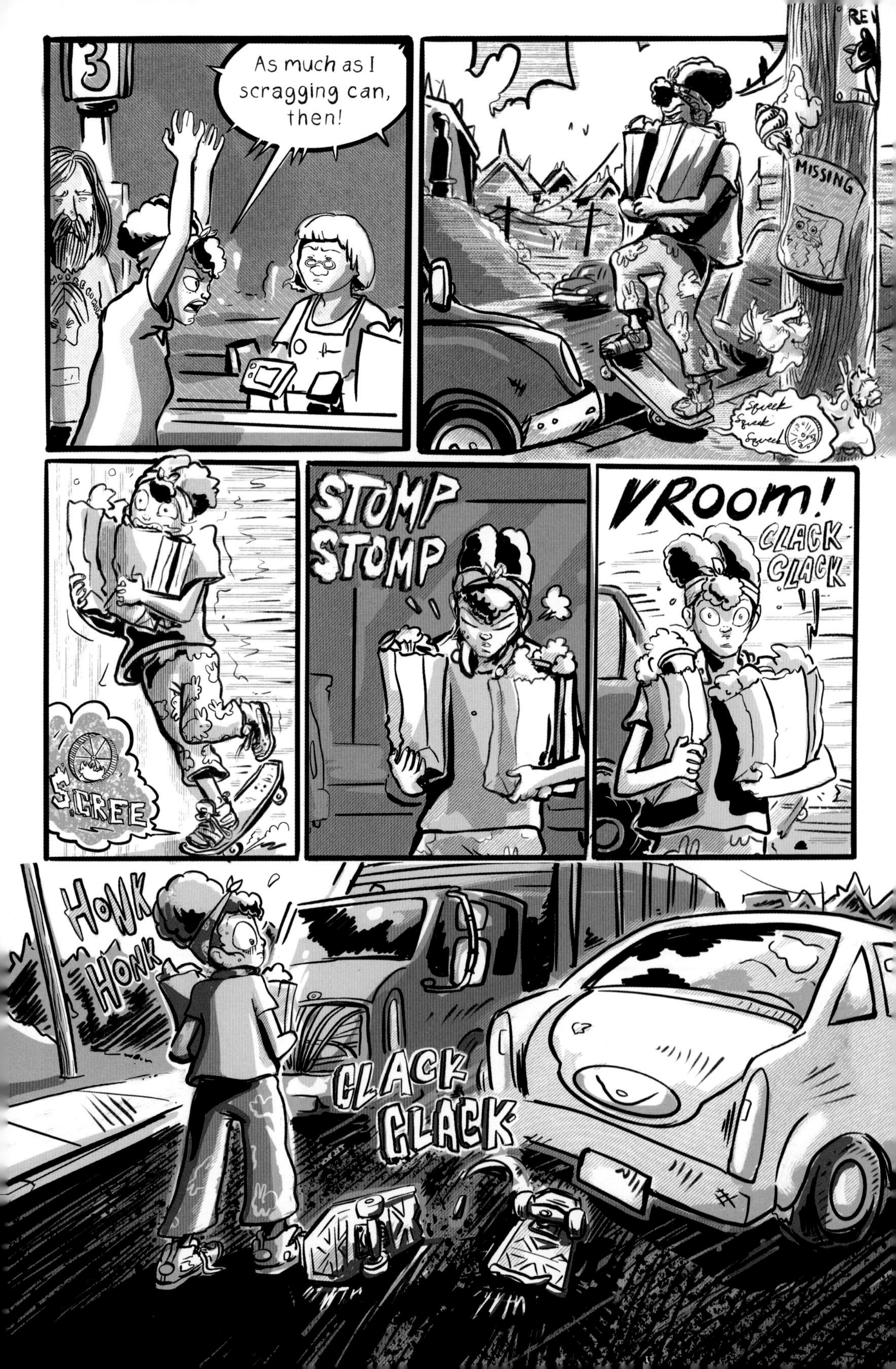
3
As much as I scragging can, then!
MISSING
Squeek Squeek Squeek
SCREE
STOMP STOMP
VRoom!
CLACK CLACK
HONK HONK
CLACK CLACK

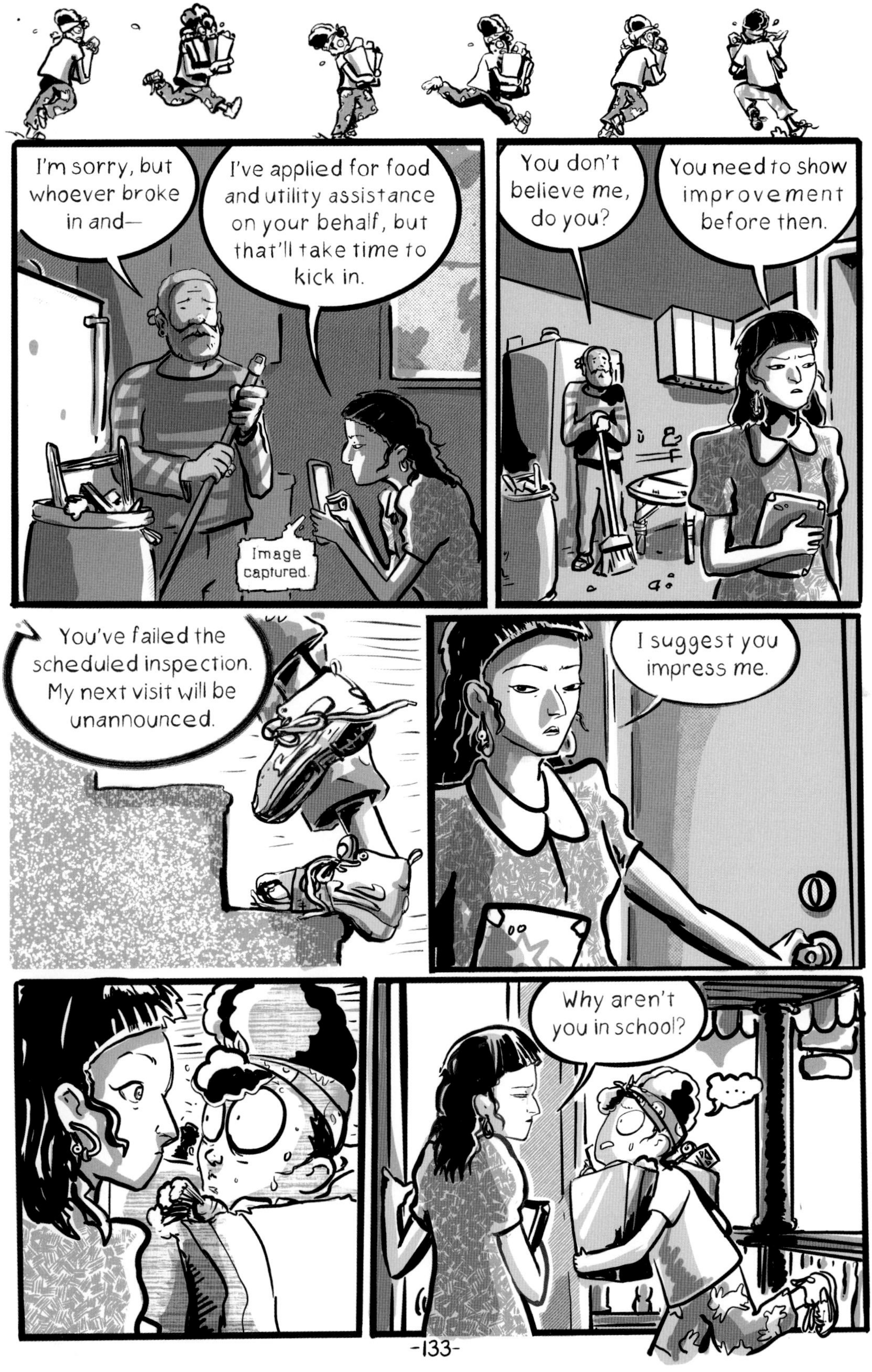
I'm sorry, but whoever broke in and—
I've applied for food and utility assistance on your behalf, but that'll take time to kick in.
Image captured.
You don't believe me, do you?
You need to show improvement before then.
You've failed the scheduled inspection. My next visit will be unannounced.
I suggest you impress me.
Why aren't you in school?
...

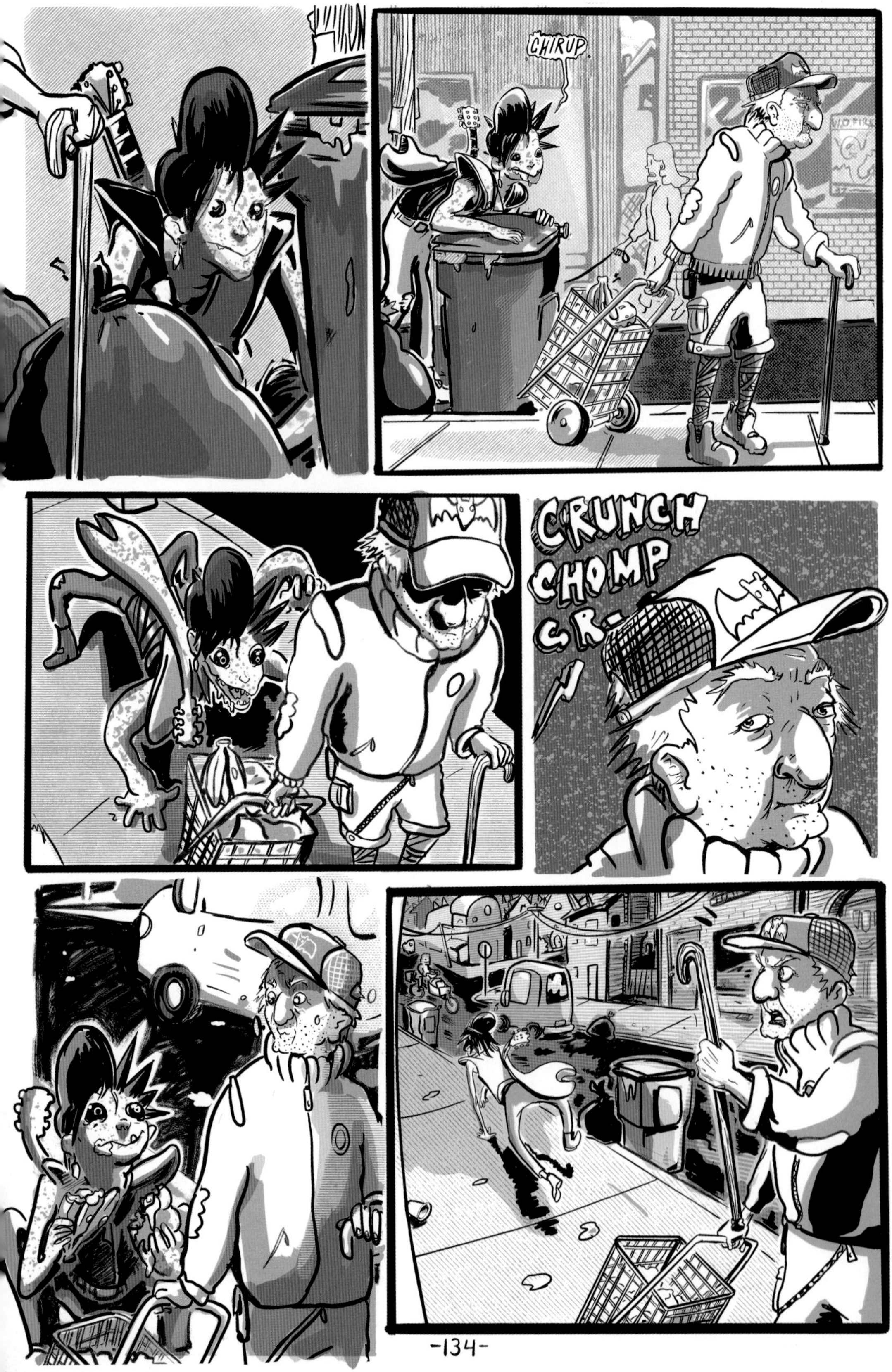
CHIRUP
CRUNCH
CHOMP
CR-

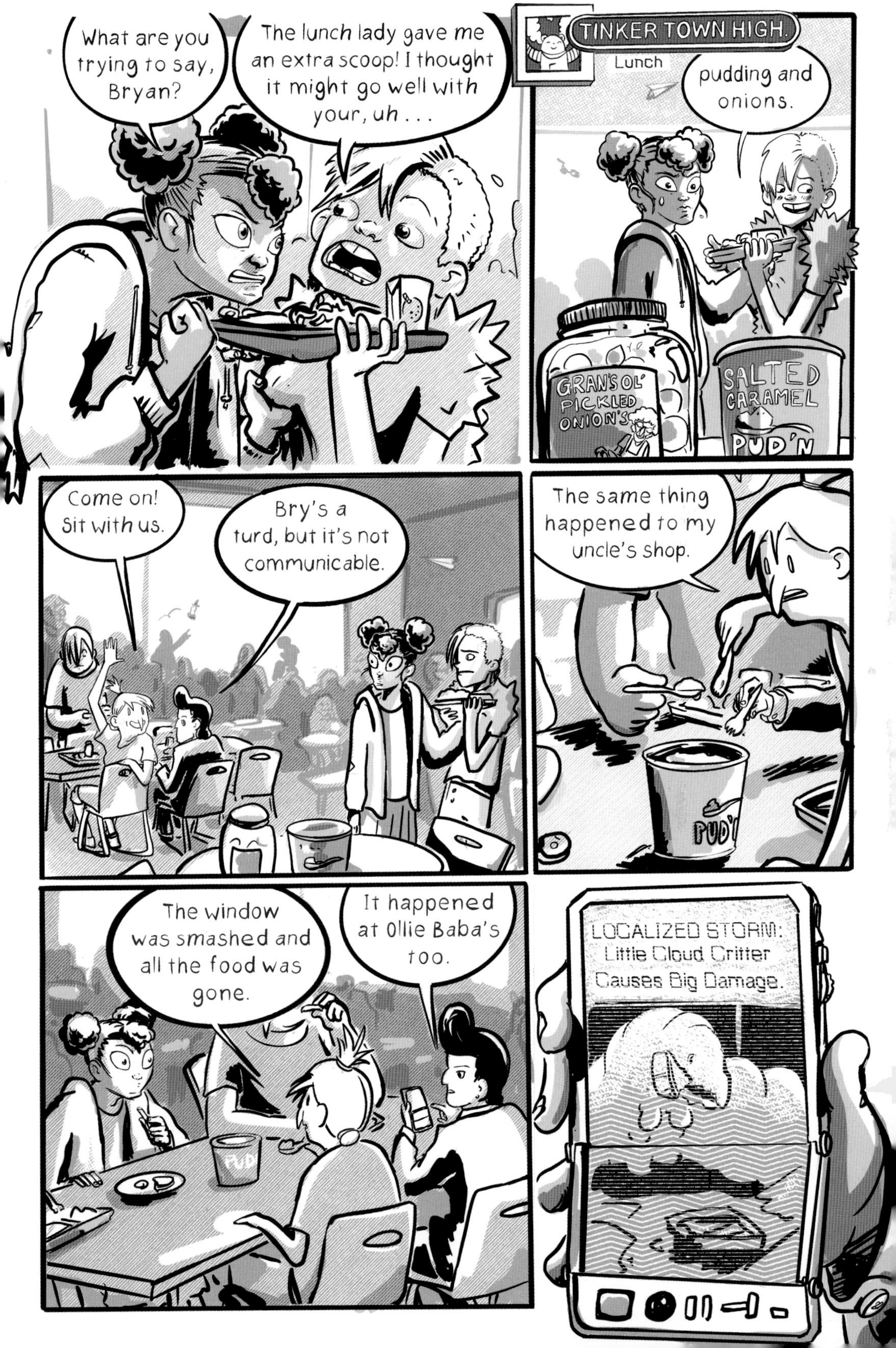
What are you trying to say, Bryan?
The lunch lady gave me an extra scoop! I thought it might go well with your, uh . . .
TINKER TOWN HIGH.
Lunch
pudding and onions.
GRAN'S OL' PICKLED ONION'S
SALTED CARAMEL PUD'N
Come on! Sit with us.
Bry's a turd, but it's not communicable.
The same thing happened to my uncle's shop.
PUD'
The window was smashed and all the food was gone.
It happened at Ollie Baba's too.
LOCALIZED STORM: Little Cloud Critter Causes Big Damage.

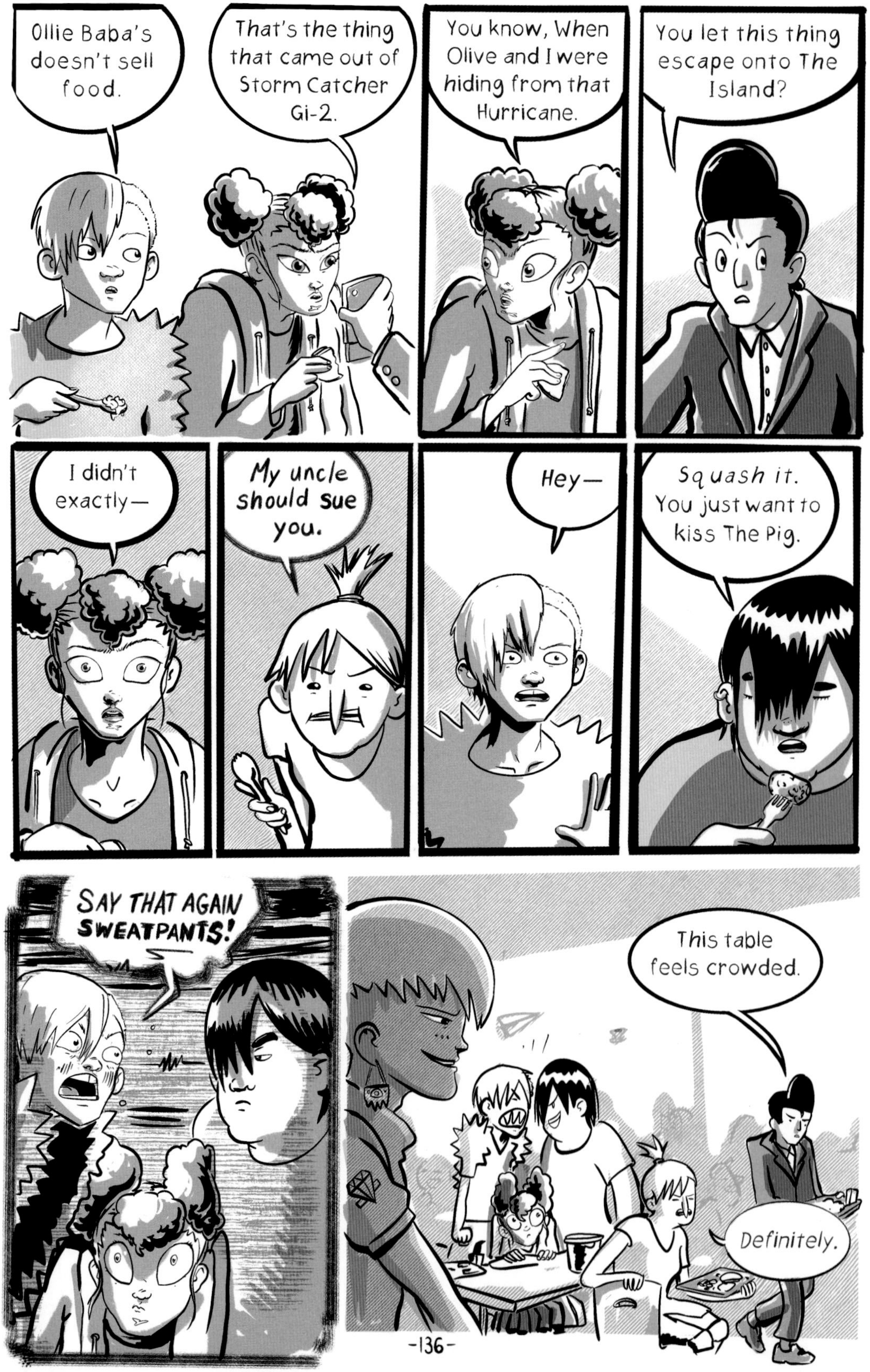

Ollie Baba's doesn't sell food.
That's the thing that came out of Storm Catcher Gi-2.
You know, When Olive and I were hiding from that Hurricane.
You let this thing escape onto The Island?
I didn't exactly—
My uncle should sue you.
Hey—
Squash it. You just want to kiss The Pig.
SAY THAT AGAIN SWEATPANTS!
This table feels crowded.
Definitely.

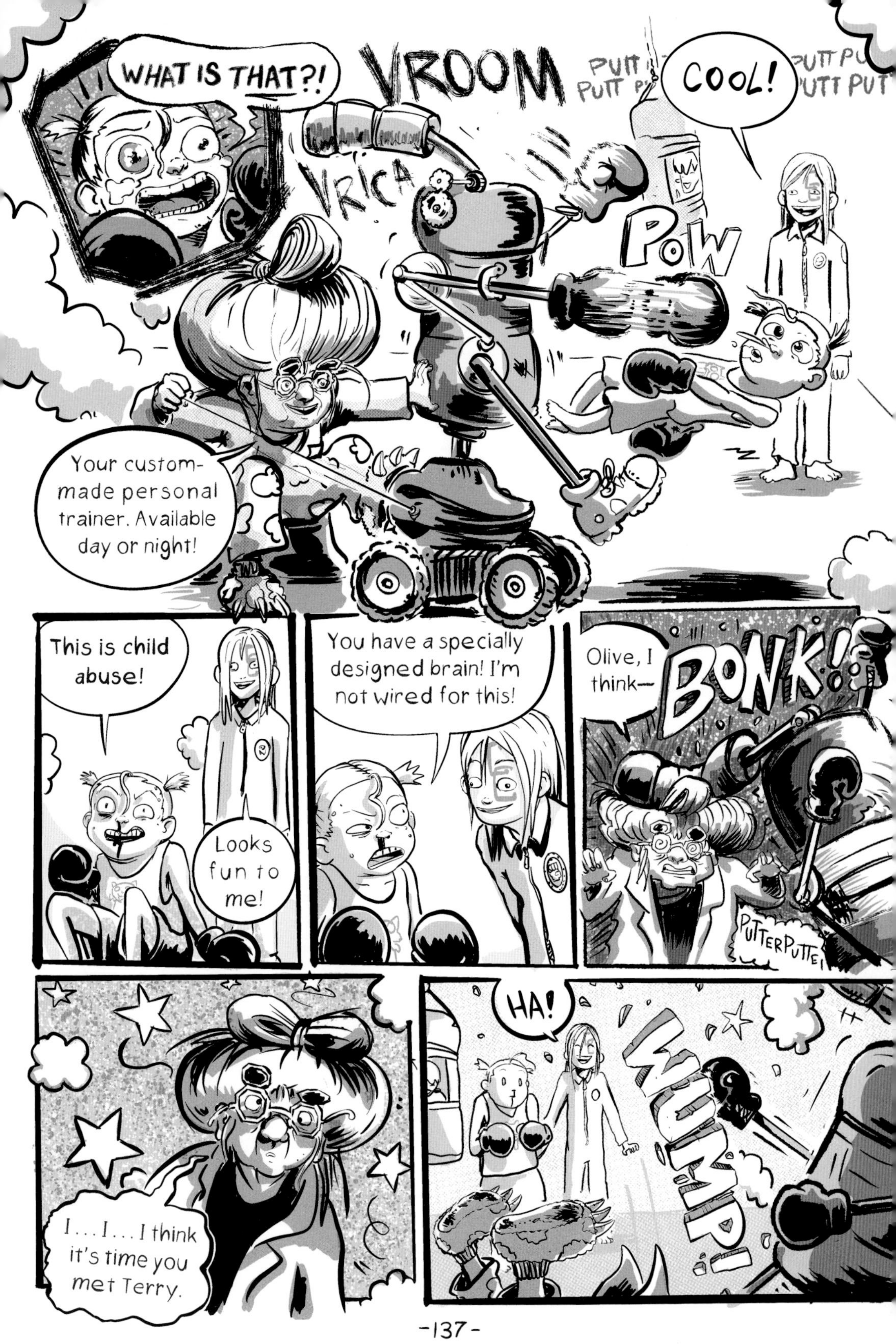
WHAT IS THAT?!
VROOM
PUTT PUTT
COOL!
PUTT PUTT PUTT
VRICA
POW
Your custom-made personal trainer. Available day or night!
This is child abuse!
Looks fun to me!
You have a specially designed brain! I'm not wired for this!
Olive, I think—
BONK!!
PUTTERPUTTE
HA!
WUMP!
I . . . I . . . I think it's time you met Terry.

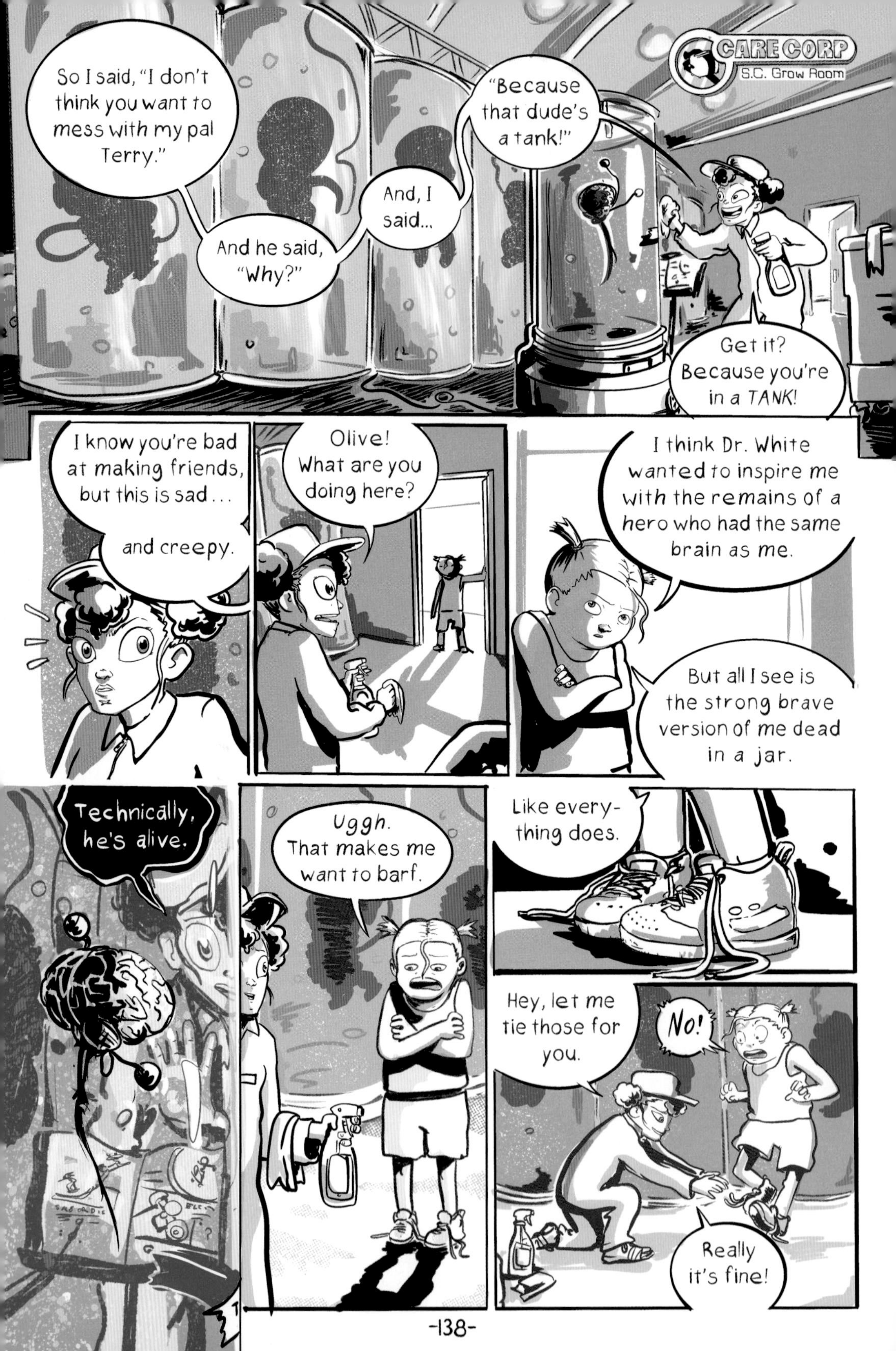
CARE CORP
S.C. Grow Room
So I said, "I don't think you want to mess with my pal Terry."
And he said, "Why?"
And, I said...
"Because that dude's a tank!"
Get it? Because you're in a TANK!
I know you're bad at making friends, but this is sad . . .
and creepy.
Olive! What are you doing here?
I think Dr. White wanted to inspire me with the remains of a hero who had the same brain as me.
But all I see is the strong brave version of me dead in a jar.
Technically, he's alive.
Uggh. That makes me want to barf.
Like every-thing does.
Hey, let me tie those for you.
No!
Really it's fine!

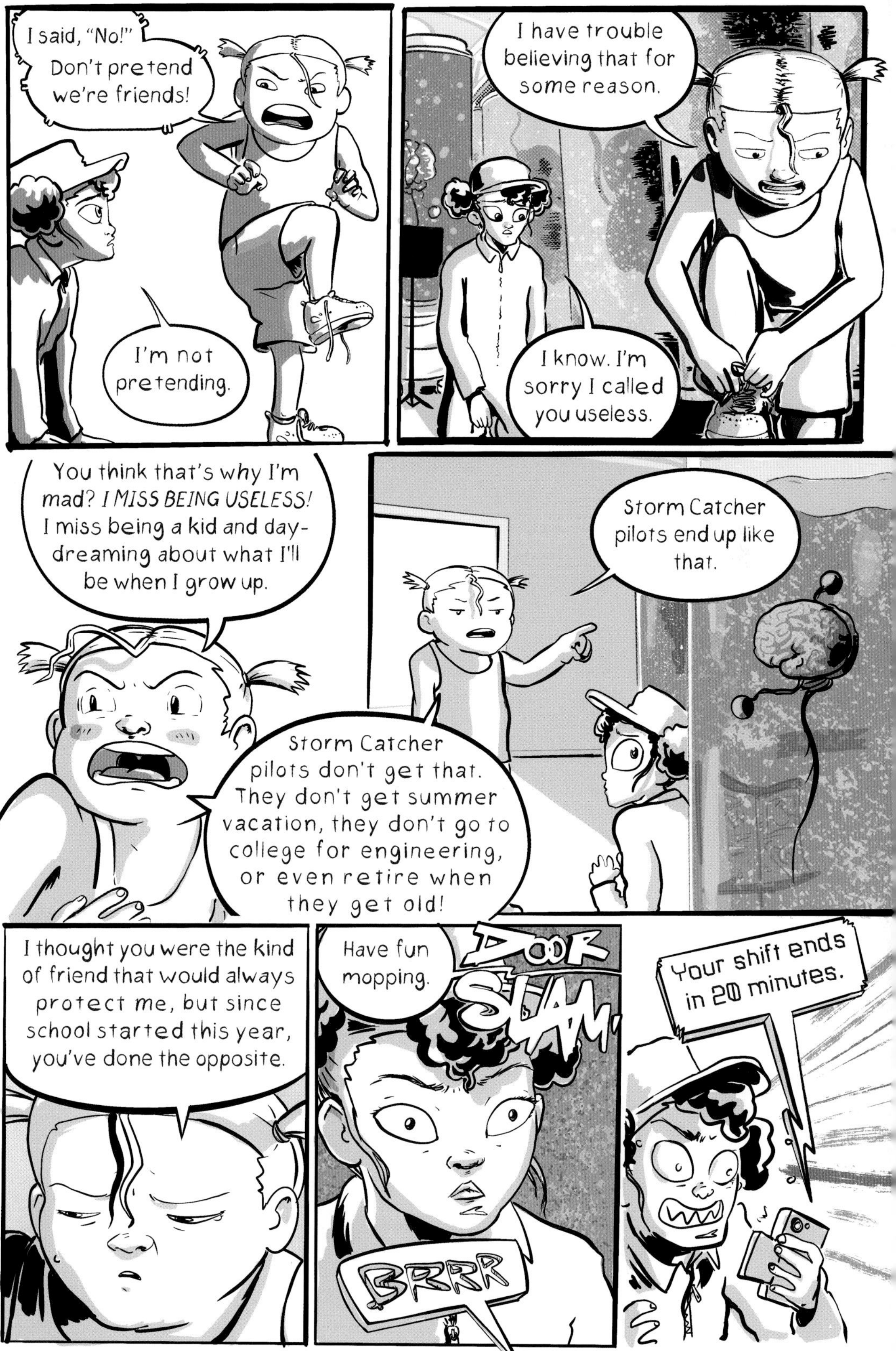
I said, "No!" Don't pretend we're friends!
I'm not pretending.
I have trouble believing that for some reason.
I know. I'm sorry I called you useless.
You think that's why I'm mad? *I MISS BEING USELESS!* I miss being a kid and day-dreaming about what I'll be when I grow up.
Storm Catcher pilots don't get that. They don't get summer vacation, they don't go to college for engineering, or even retire when they get old!
Storm Catcher pilots end up like that.
I thought you were the kind of friend that would always protect me, but since school started this year, you've done the opposite.
Have fun mopping.
DOOR SLAM
BRRR
Your shift ends in 20 minutes.

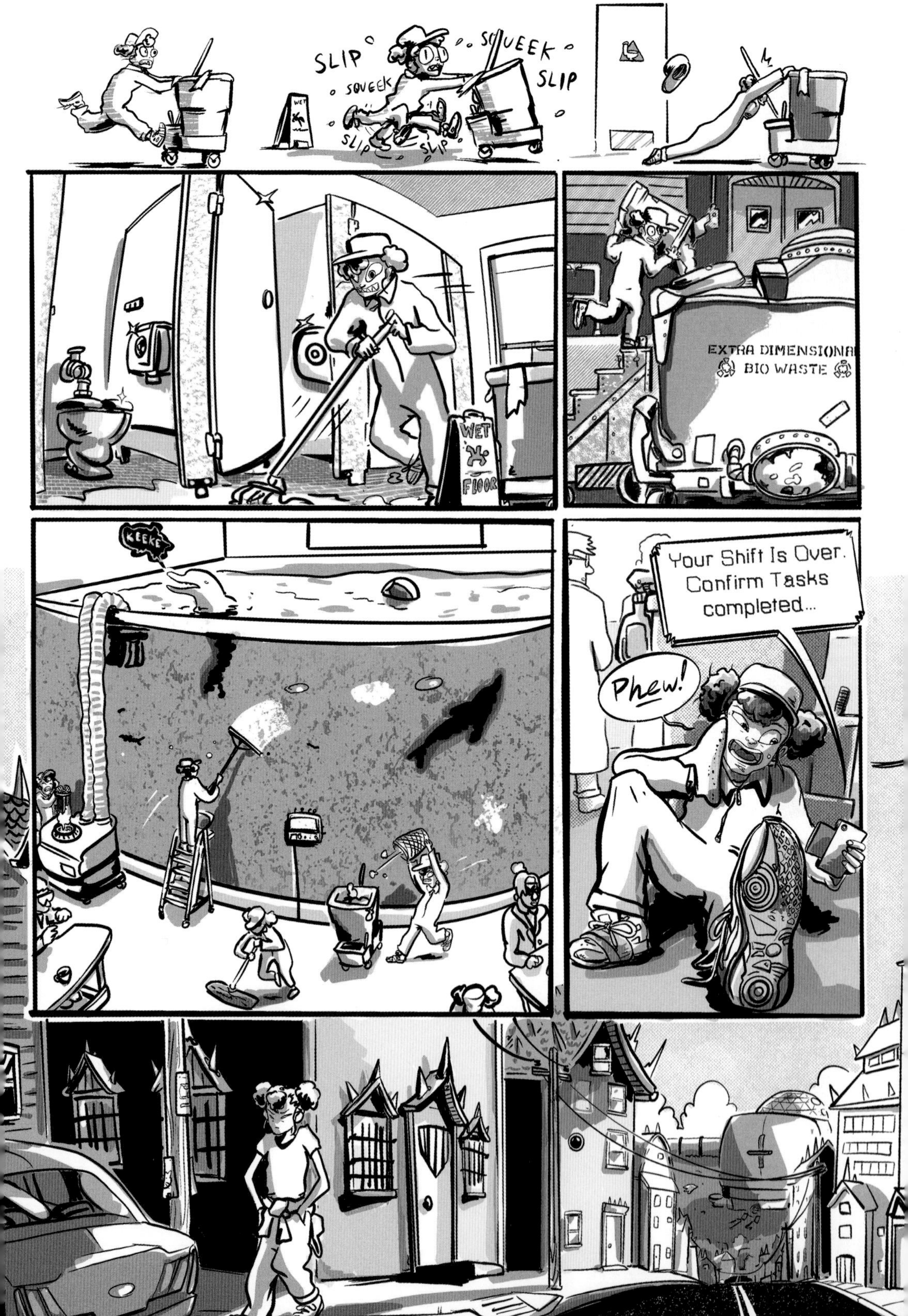
SLIP
SQUEEK
SQUEEK
SLIP
SLIP
SLIP
SLIP
WET
WET FLOOR
EXTRA DIMENSIONAL BIO WASTE
KEEKE
Your Shift Is Over. Confirm Tasks completed...
Phew!

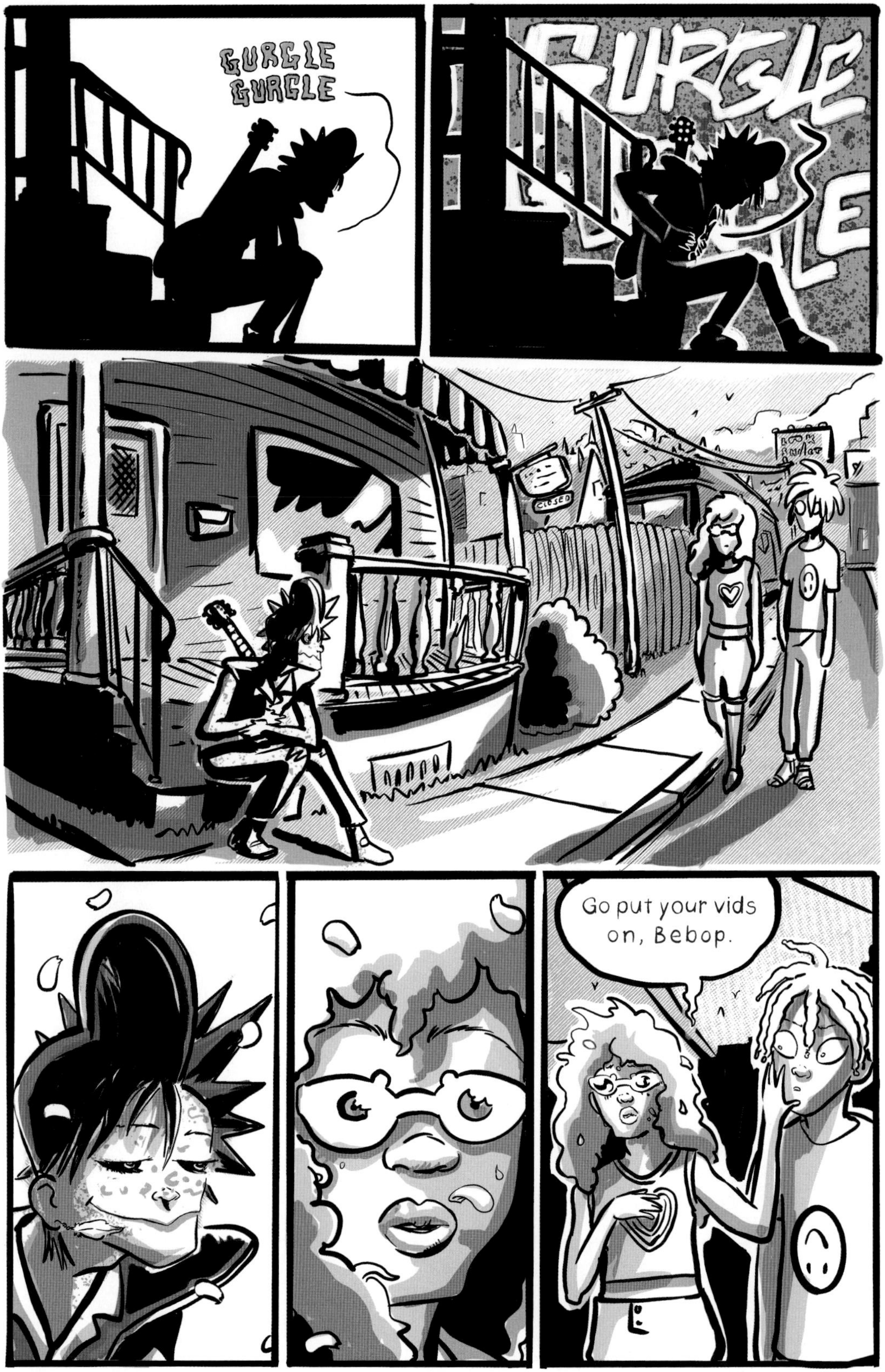
GURGLE
GURGLE
CLOSED
Go put your vids on, Bebop.

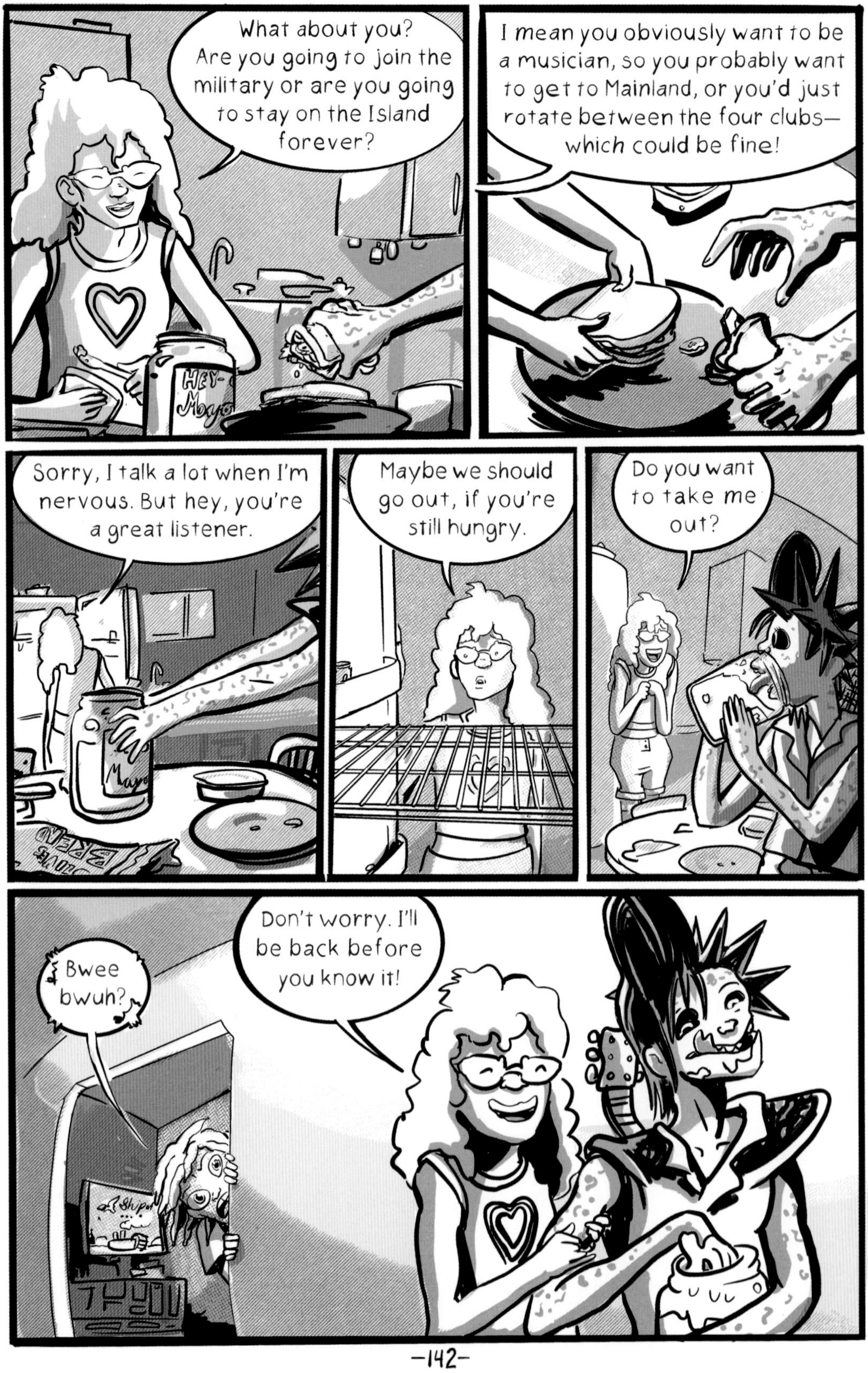
What about you? Are you going to join the military or are you going to stay on the Island forever?
I mean you obviously want to be a musician, so you probably want to get to Mainland, or you'd just rotate between the four clubs—which could be fine!
Sorry, I talk a lot when I'm nervous. But hey, you're a great listener.
Maybe we should go out, if you're still hungry.
Do you want to take me out?
Bwee bwuh?
Don't worry. I'll be back before you know it!

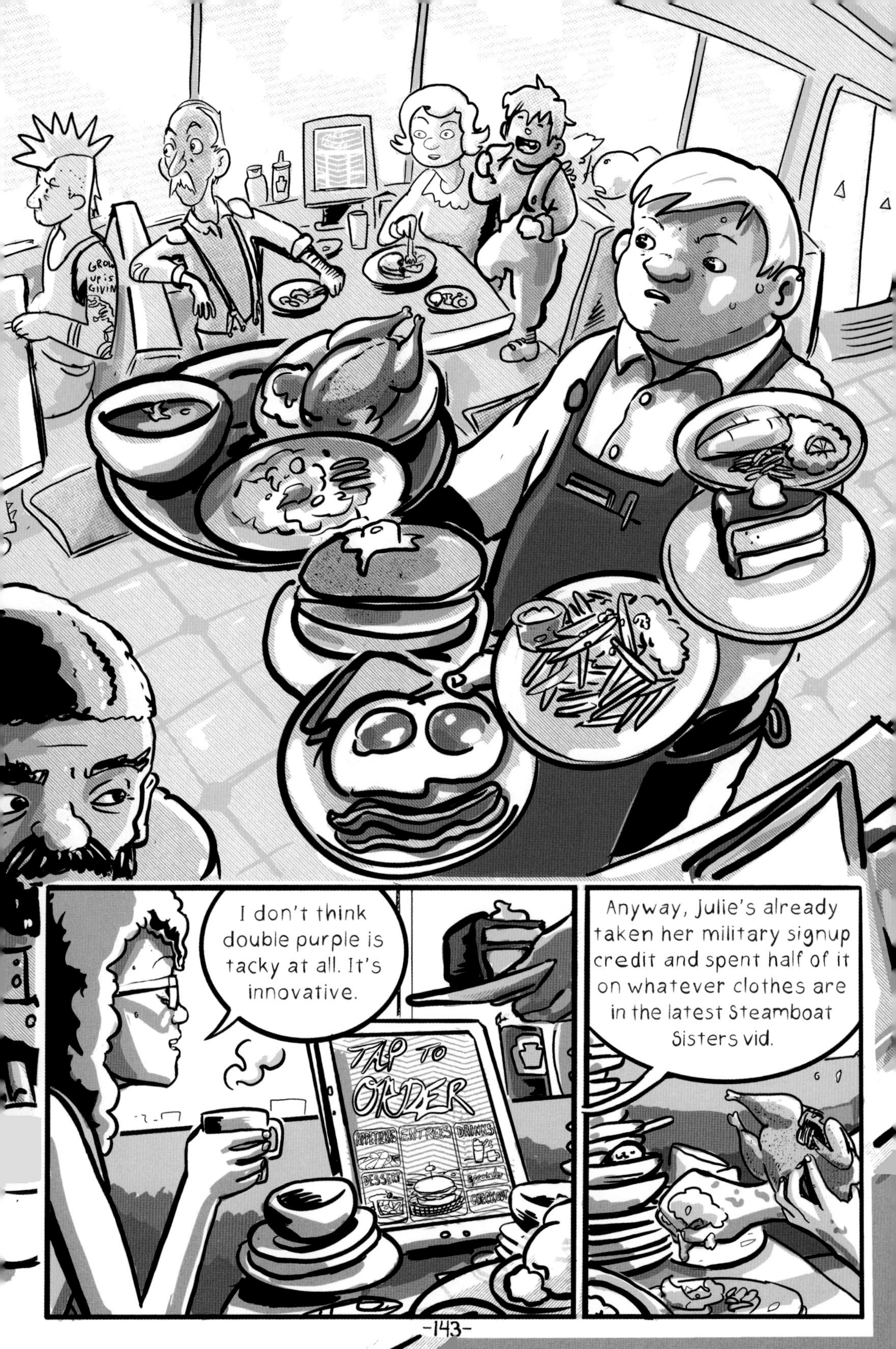
I don't think double purple is tacky at all. It's innovative.
TAP TO ORDER
APPETIZERS
ENTREES
DRINKS
DESSERT
specials
CHECKOUT
Anyway, Julie's already taken her military signup credit and spent half of it on whatever clothes are in the latest Steamboat Sisters vid.

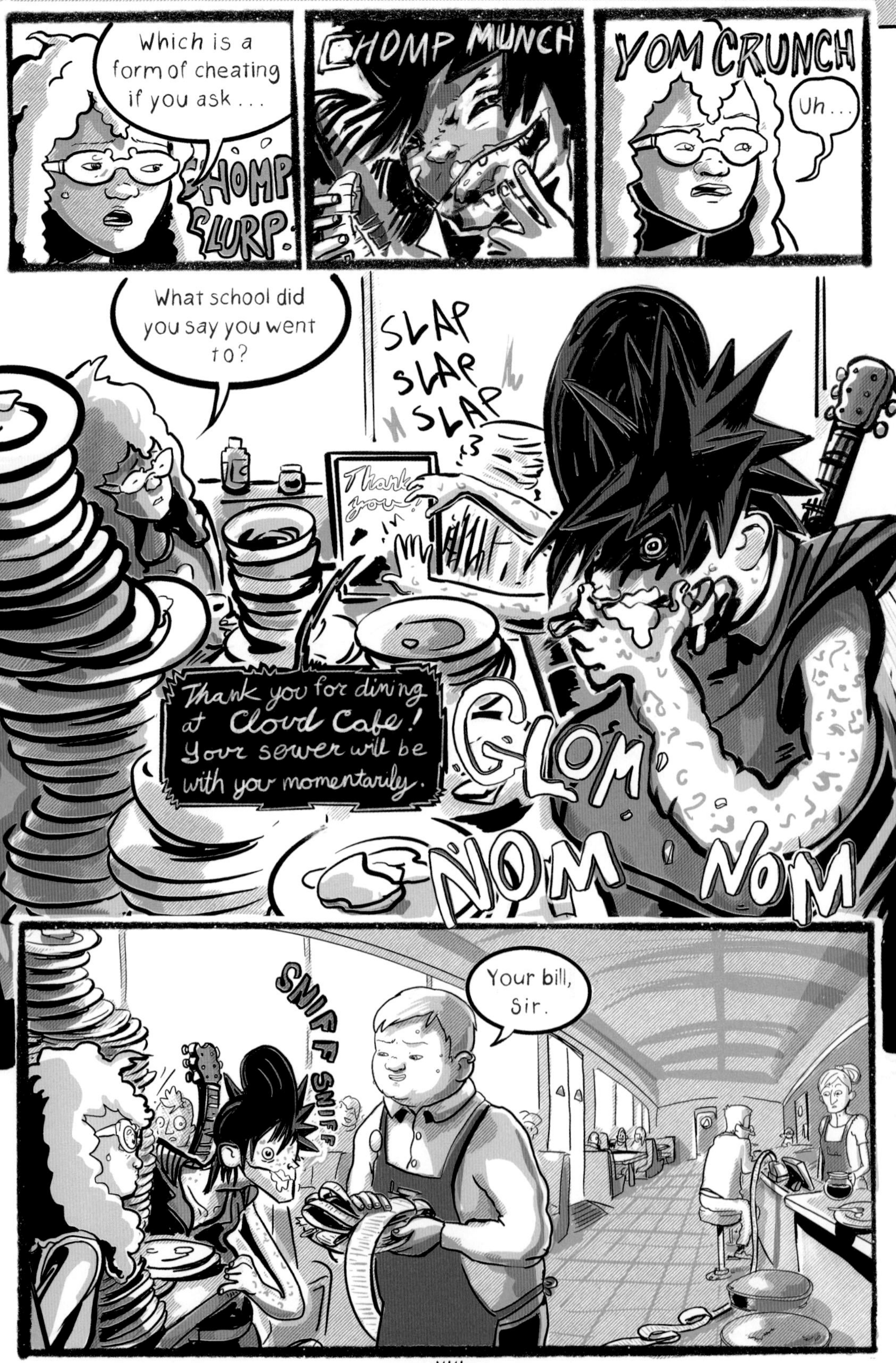
Which is a form of cheating if you ask . . .
CHOMP SLURP.
CHOMP MUNCH
YOM CRUNCH
Uh . . .
What school did you say you went to?
SLAP SLAP SLAP
Thank you!
Thank you for dining at Cloud Cafe! Your sewer will be with you momentarily.
GLOM
NOM NOM
SNIFF SNIFF SNIFF
Your bill, Sir.

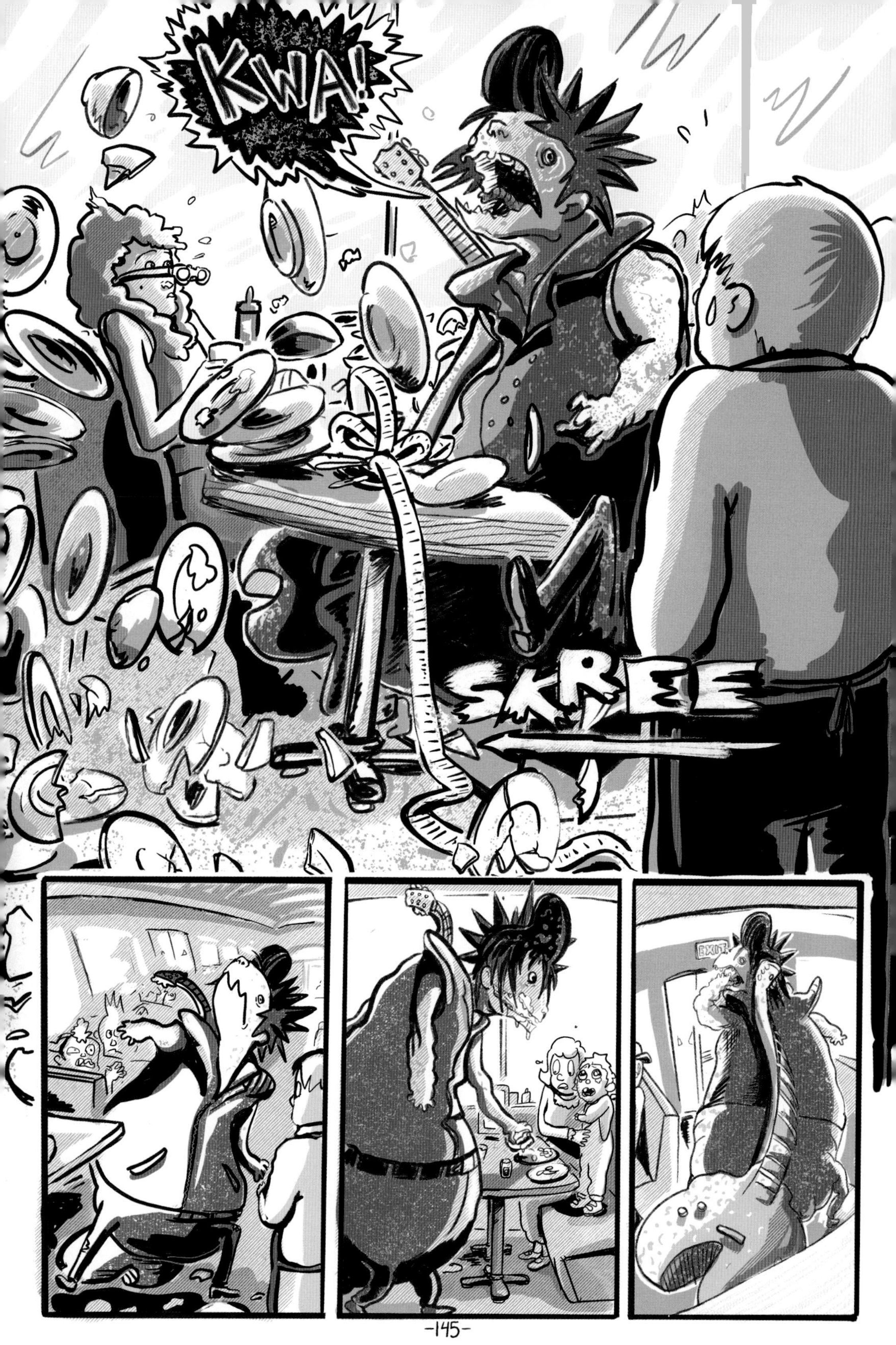
KWA!
SKREE
EXIT

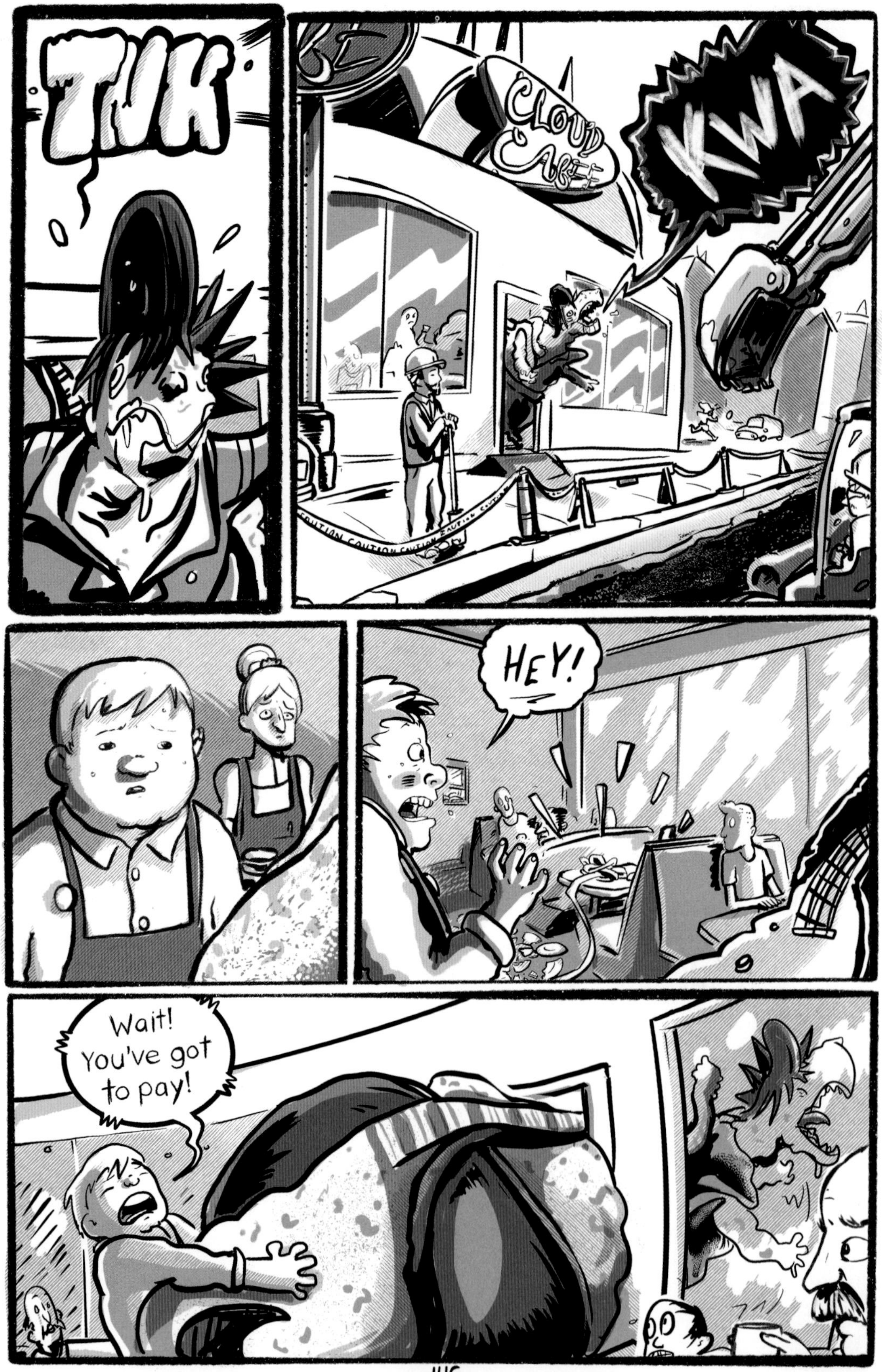
TUK
CLOUD CAFE
KWA
CAUTION CAUTION CAUTION
HEY!
Wait! You've got to pay!

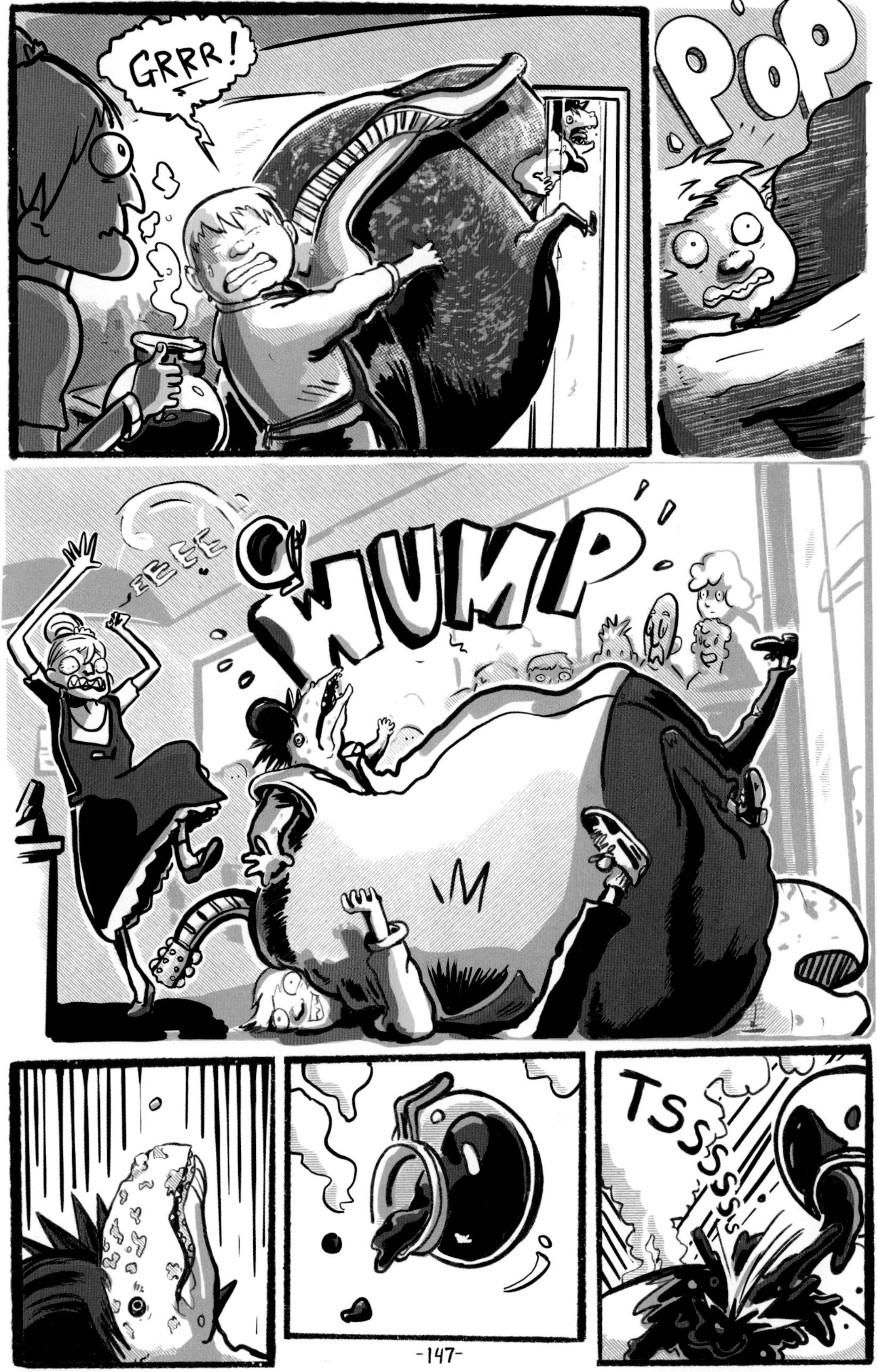
GRRR!
POP
EEEE
WUMP
TSSSSSS

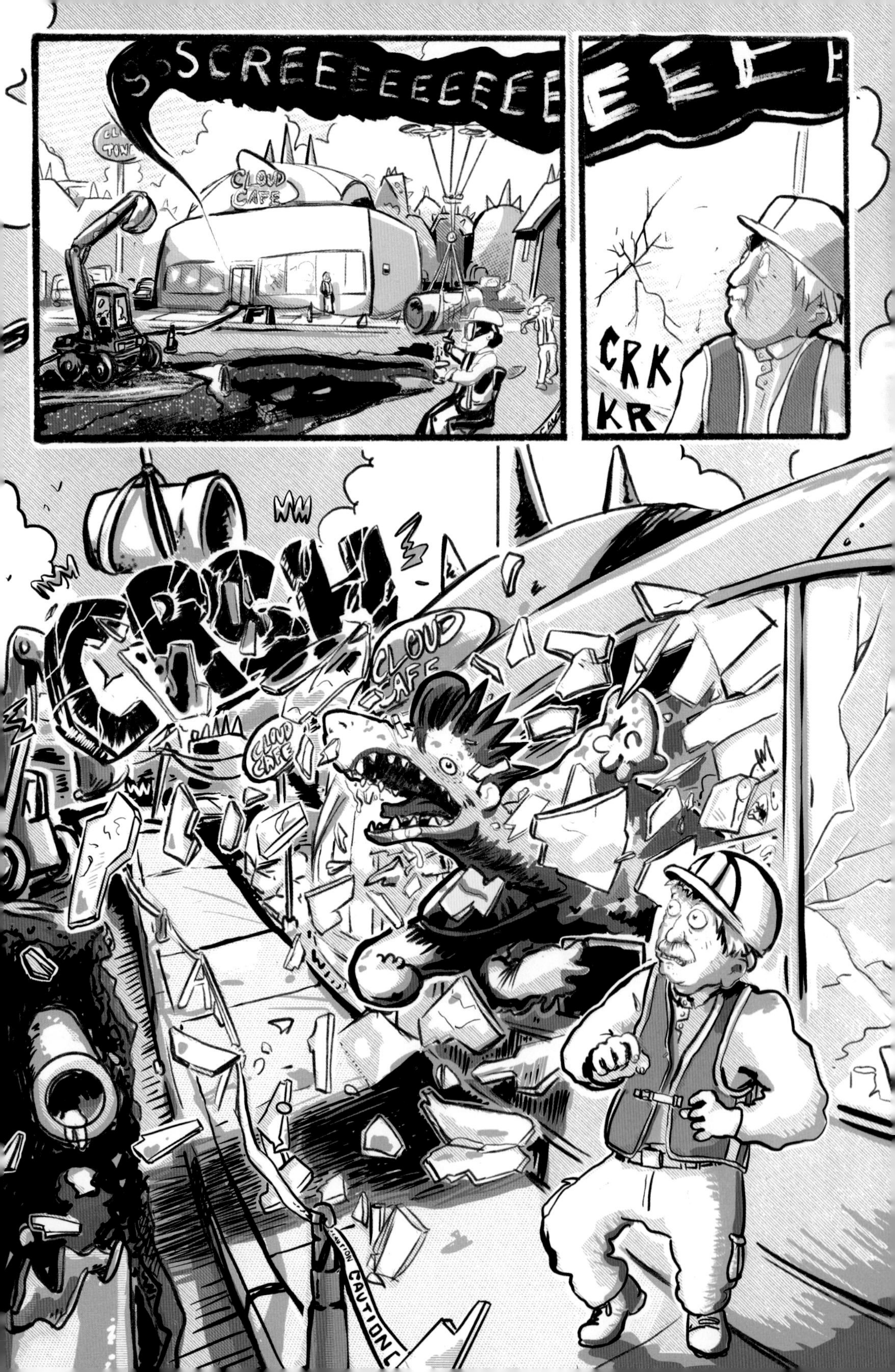
SSCREEEEEEEEEEEEEE
CLOUD CAFE
CRK KR
CRASH!
CLOUD CAFE
CLOUD CAFE
CAUTION

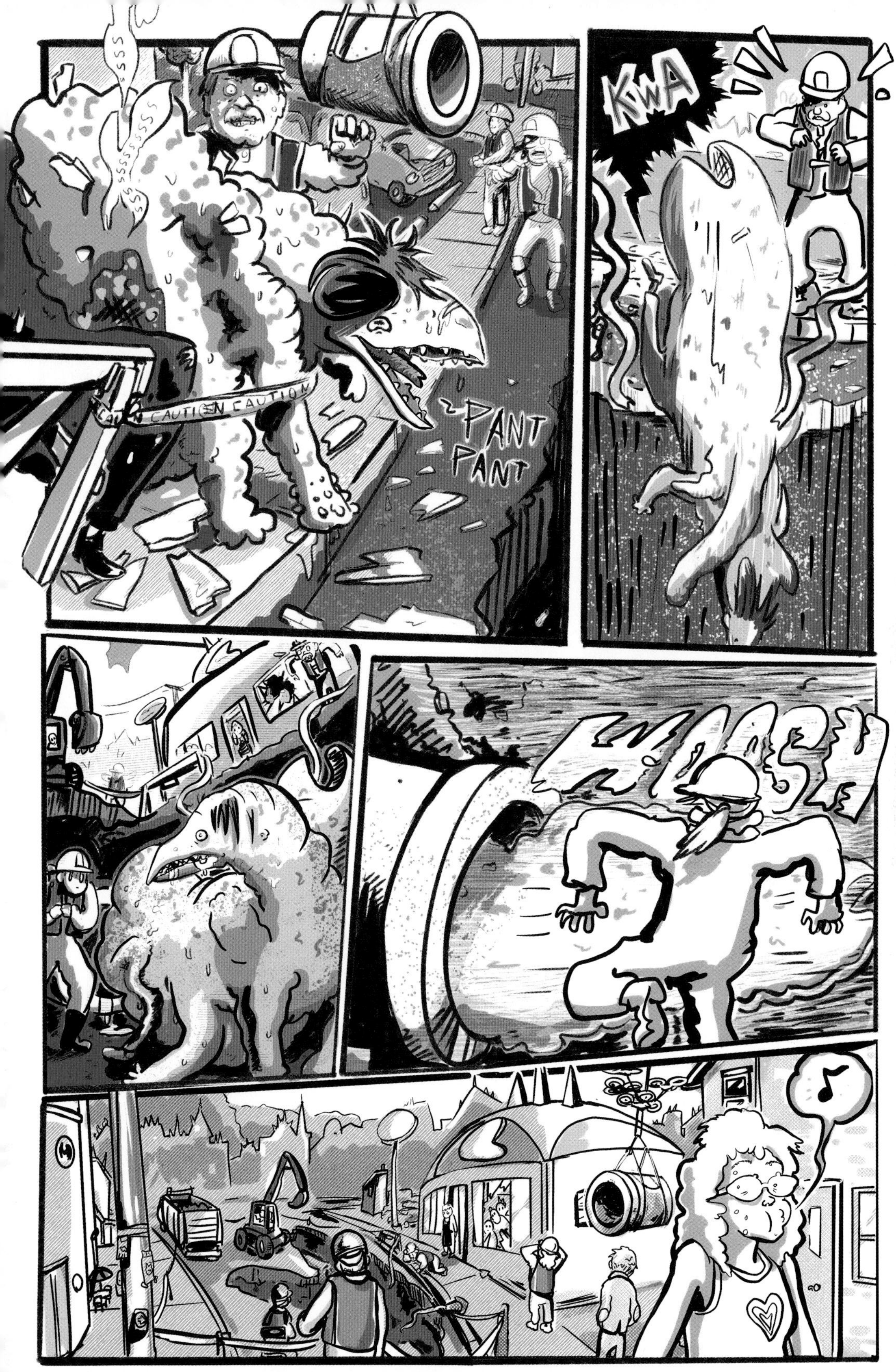
CAUTION CAUTION
PANT PANT
KWA
KWOOSH

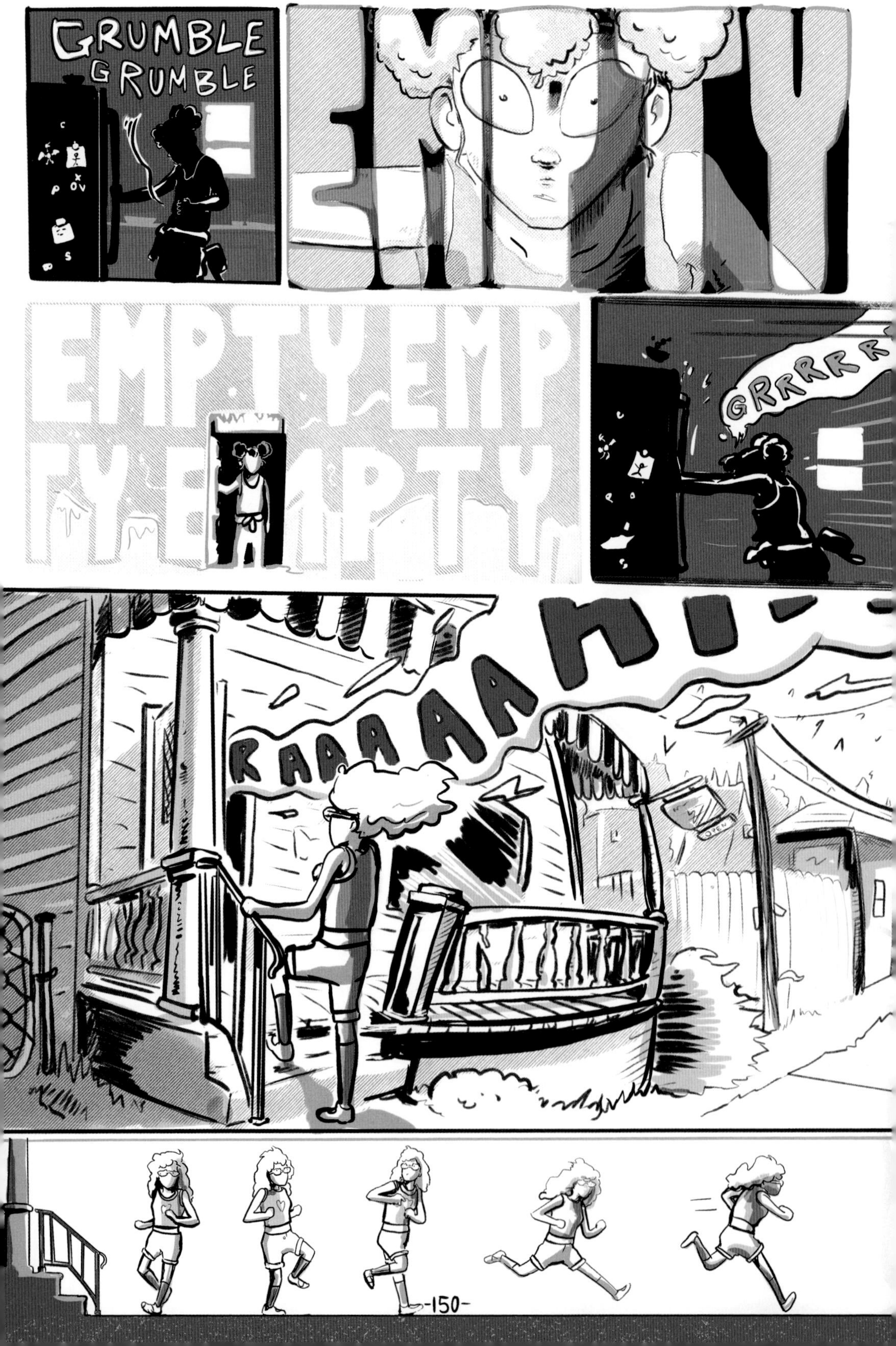
GRUMBLE
GRUMBLE
EMPTYEMP
TY EMPTY
GRRRRRR
RAAAAAH
OPEN

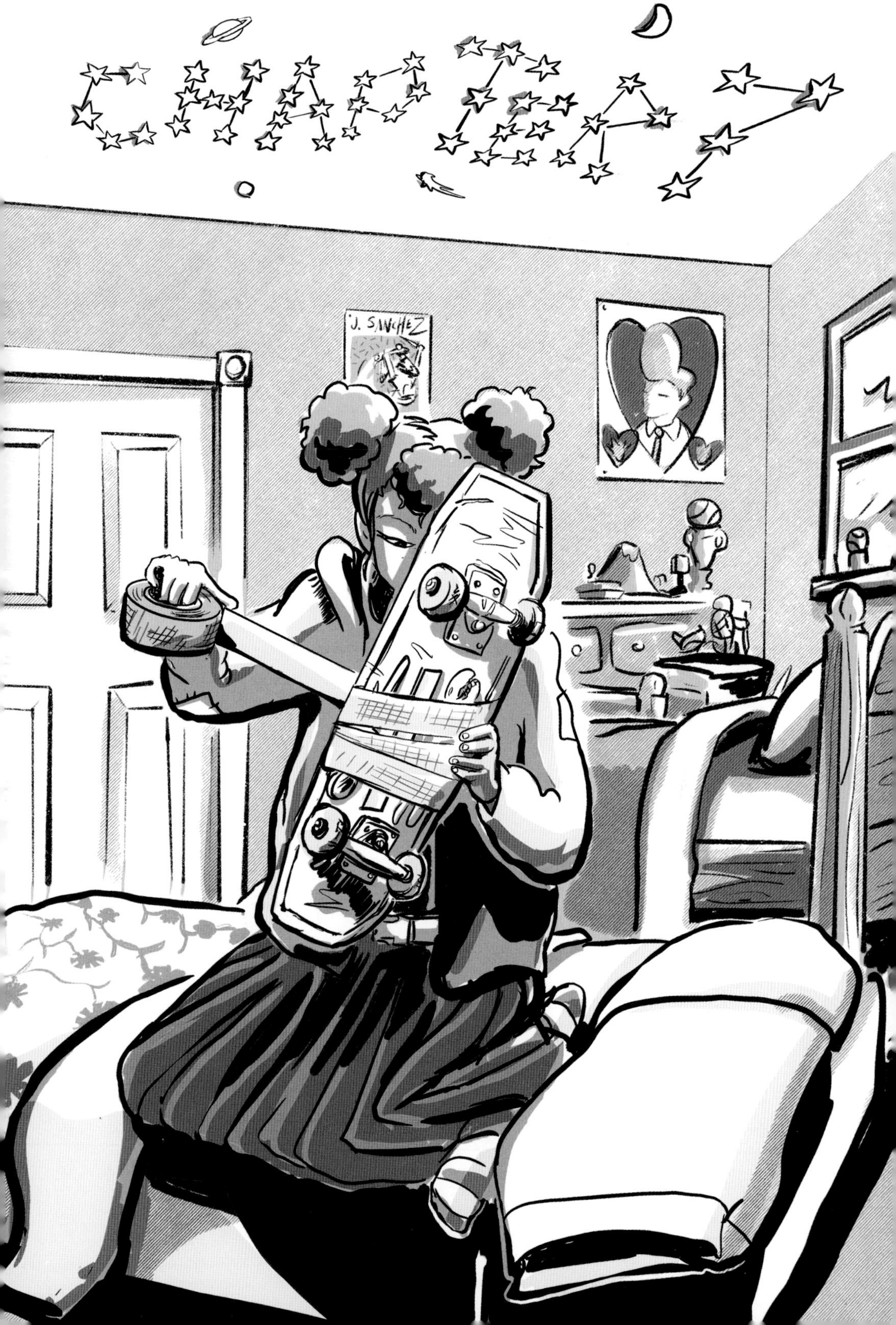
CHAPTER 7
J. SANCHEZ

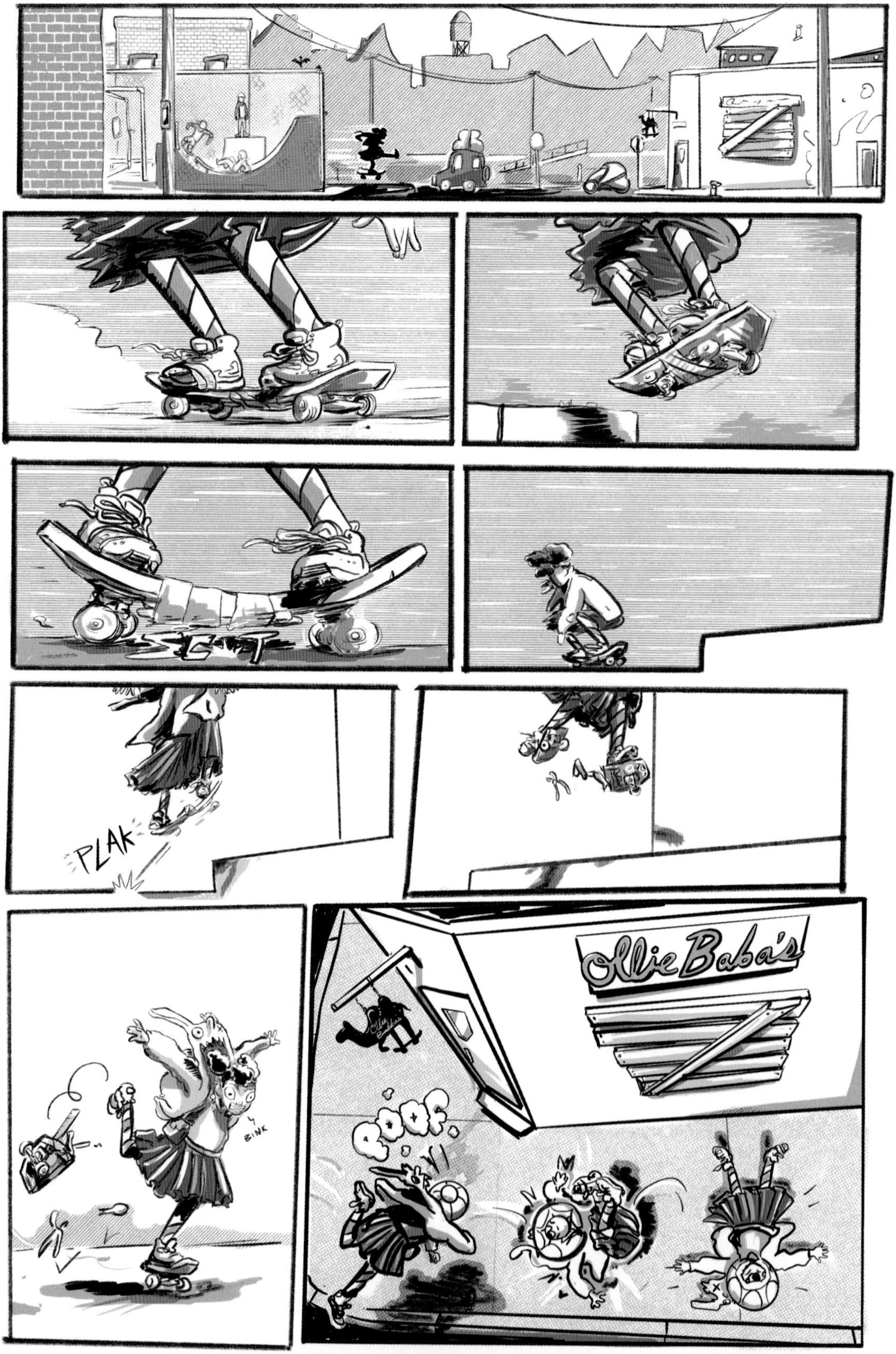
PLAK
BINK
Ollie Baba's
POOF

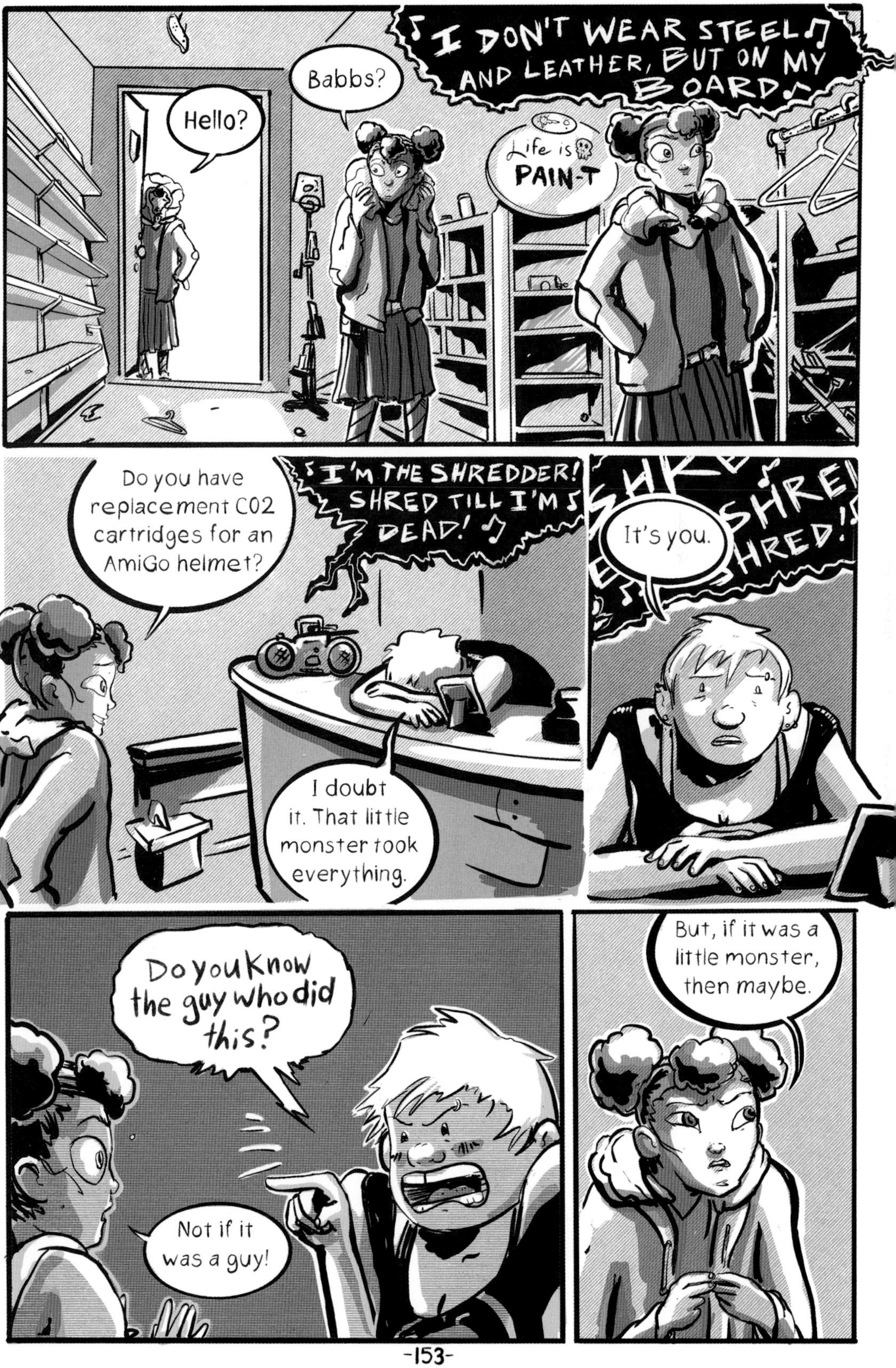
♪ I DON'T WEAR STEEL ♫ AND LEATHER, BUT ON MY BOARD ♪
Hello?
Babbs?
Life is PAIN-T
Do you have replacement C02 cartridges for an AmiGo helmet?
♪ I'M THE SHREDDER! SHRED TILL I'M ♪ DEAD! ♪
I doubt it. That little monster took everything.
It's you.
SHRED!
Do you know the guy who did this?
Not if it was a guy!
But, if it was a little monster, then maybe.

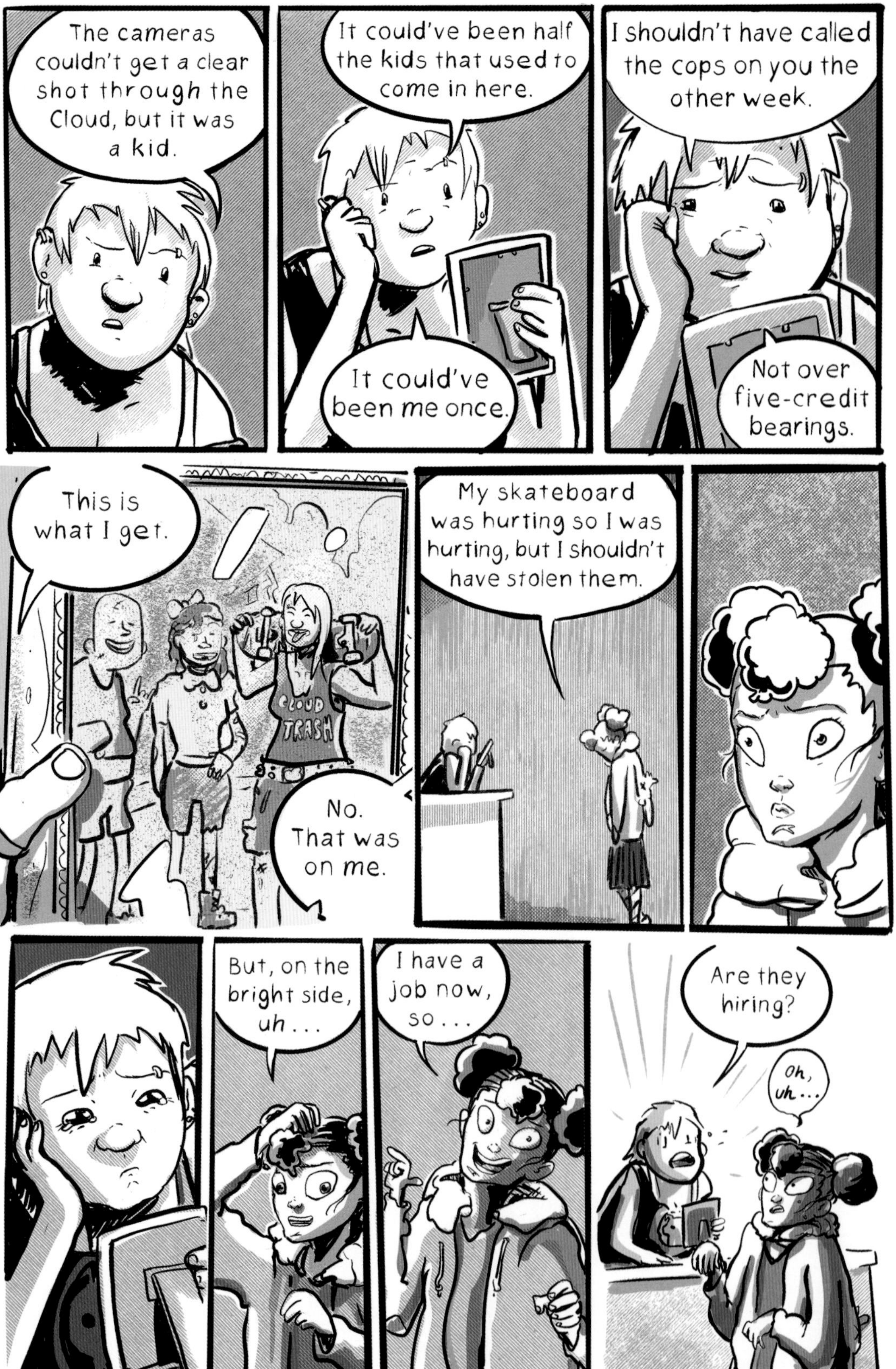

The cameras couldn't get a clear shot through the Cloud, but it was a kid.
It could've been half the kids that used to come in here.
It could've been me once.
I shouldn't have called the cops on you the other week.
Not over five-credit bearings.
This is what I get.
CLOUD TRASH
No. That was on me.
My skateboard was hurting so I was hurting, but I shouldn't have stolen them.
But, on the bright side, uh . . .
I have a job now, so . . .
Are they hiring?
Oh, uh . . .

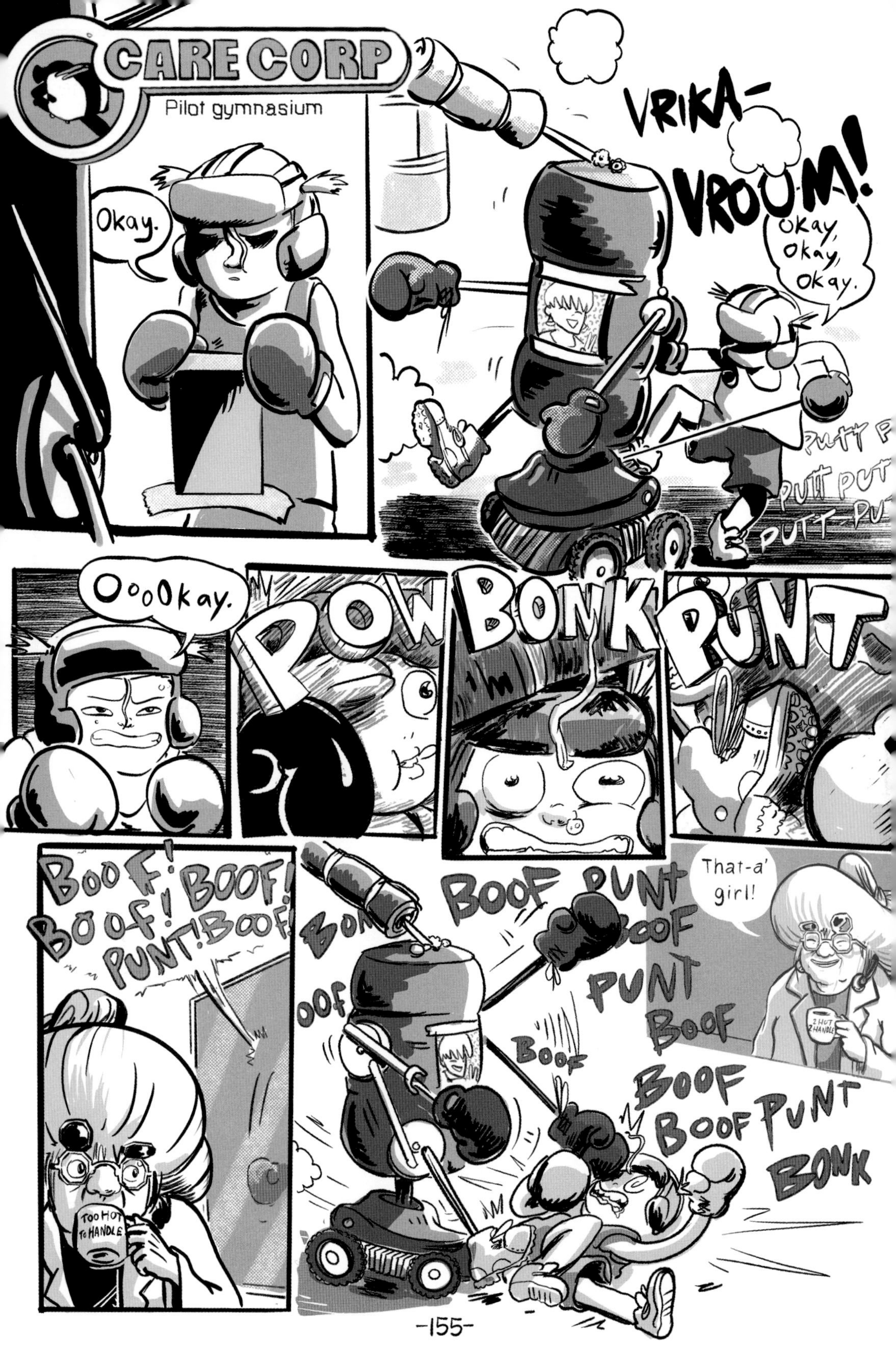
CARE CORP
Pilot gymnasium
Okay.
VRIKA-VROOM!
Okay, Okay, Okay.
PUTT PUTT PUTT PUTT-PUT
OooOkay.
POW
BONK
PUNT
BOOF! BOOF! BOOF! PUNT! BOOF!
TOO HOT TO HANDLE
BOOF PUNT BOOF PUNT BOOF
BOOF
BOOF BOOF PUNT
BONK
That-a' girl!

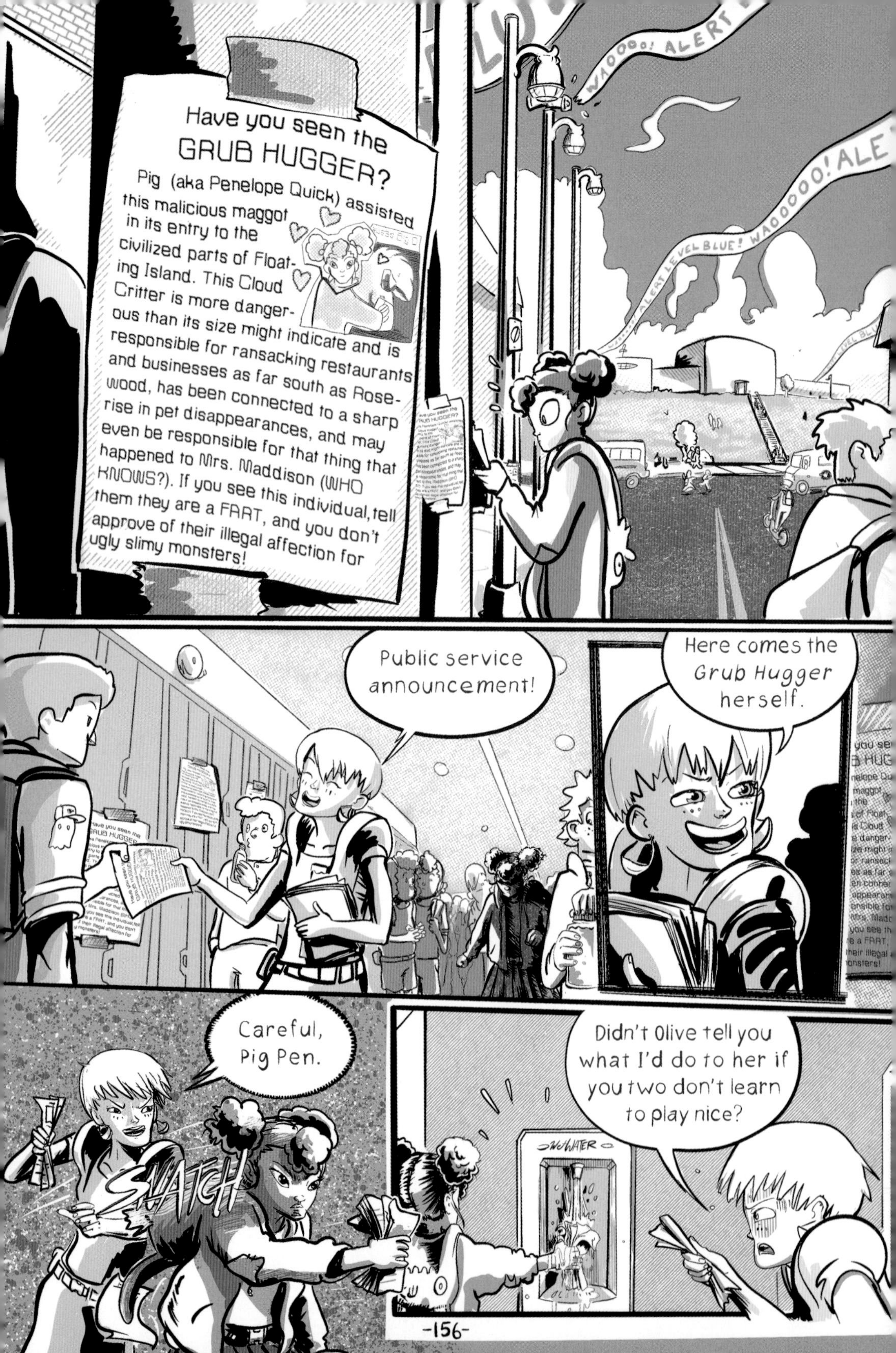
Have you seen the GRUB HUGGER?
Pig (aka Penelope Quick) assisted this malicious maggot in its entry to the civilized parts of Floating Island. This Cloud Critter is more dangerous than its size might indicate and is responsible for ransacking restaurants and businesses as far south as Rosewood, has been connected to a sharp rise in pet disappearances, and may even be responsible for that thing that happened to Mrs. Maddison (WHO KNOWS?). If you see this individual, tell them they are a FART, and you don't approve of their illegal affection for ugly slimy monsters!
WAOOOO! ALERT
WAOOOOO! ALE
ALERT LEVEL BLUE! WAOOOO!
Public service announcement!
Here comes the Grub Hugger herself.
Careful, Pig Pen.
SNATCH
Didn't Olive tell you what I'd do to her if you two don't learn to play nice?
WATER

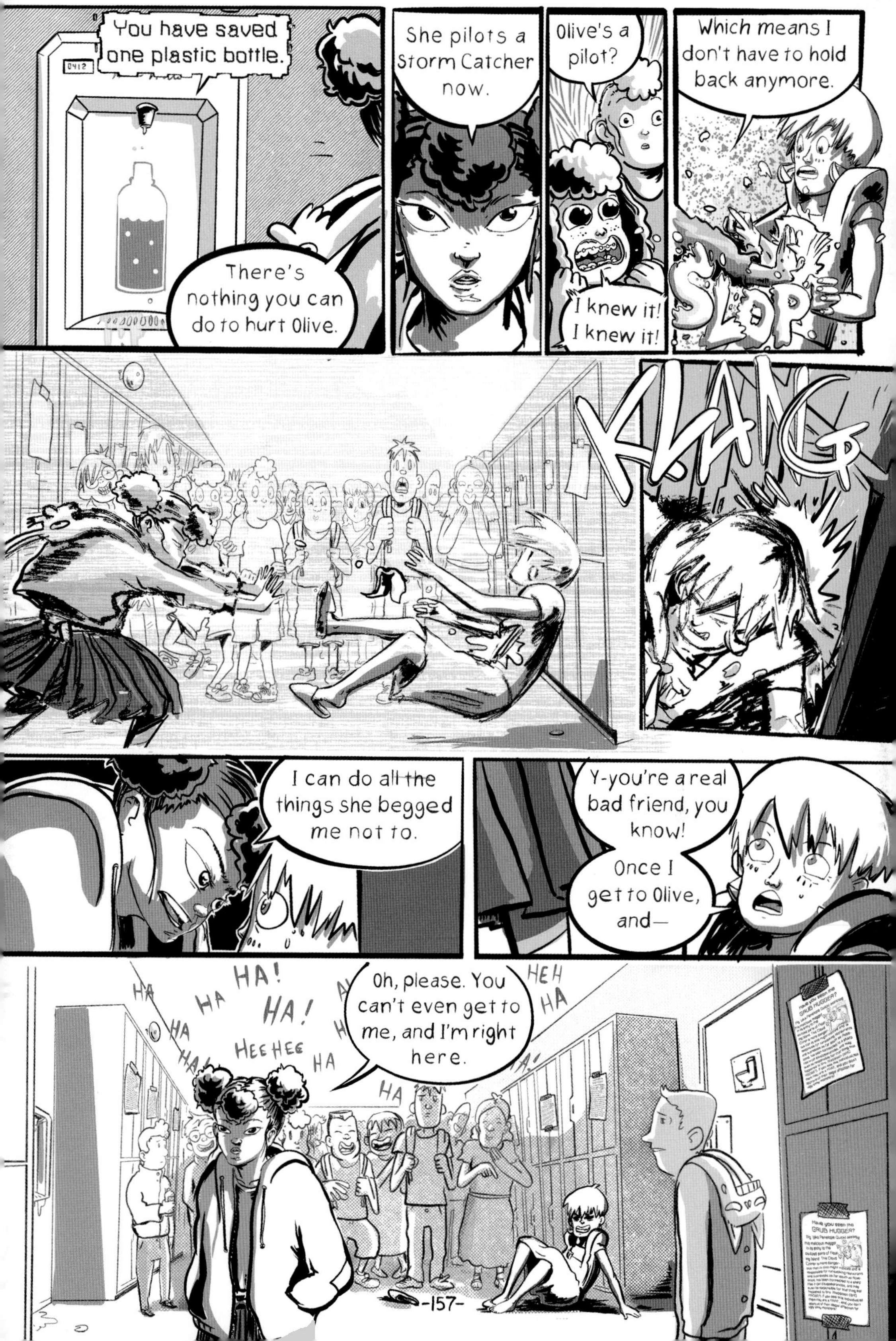
0412
You have saved one plastic bottle.
There's nothing you can do to hurt Olive.
She pilots a Storm Catcher now.
Olive's a pilot?
I knew it! I knew it!
Which means I don't have to hold back anymore.
SLOP
KLANG
I can do all the things she begged me not to.
Y-you're a real bad friend, you know!
Once I get to Olive, and—
HA HA! HA HA! HA HA HA! HEE HEE HA HA
Oh, please. You can't even get to me, and I'm right here.
HEH HA

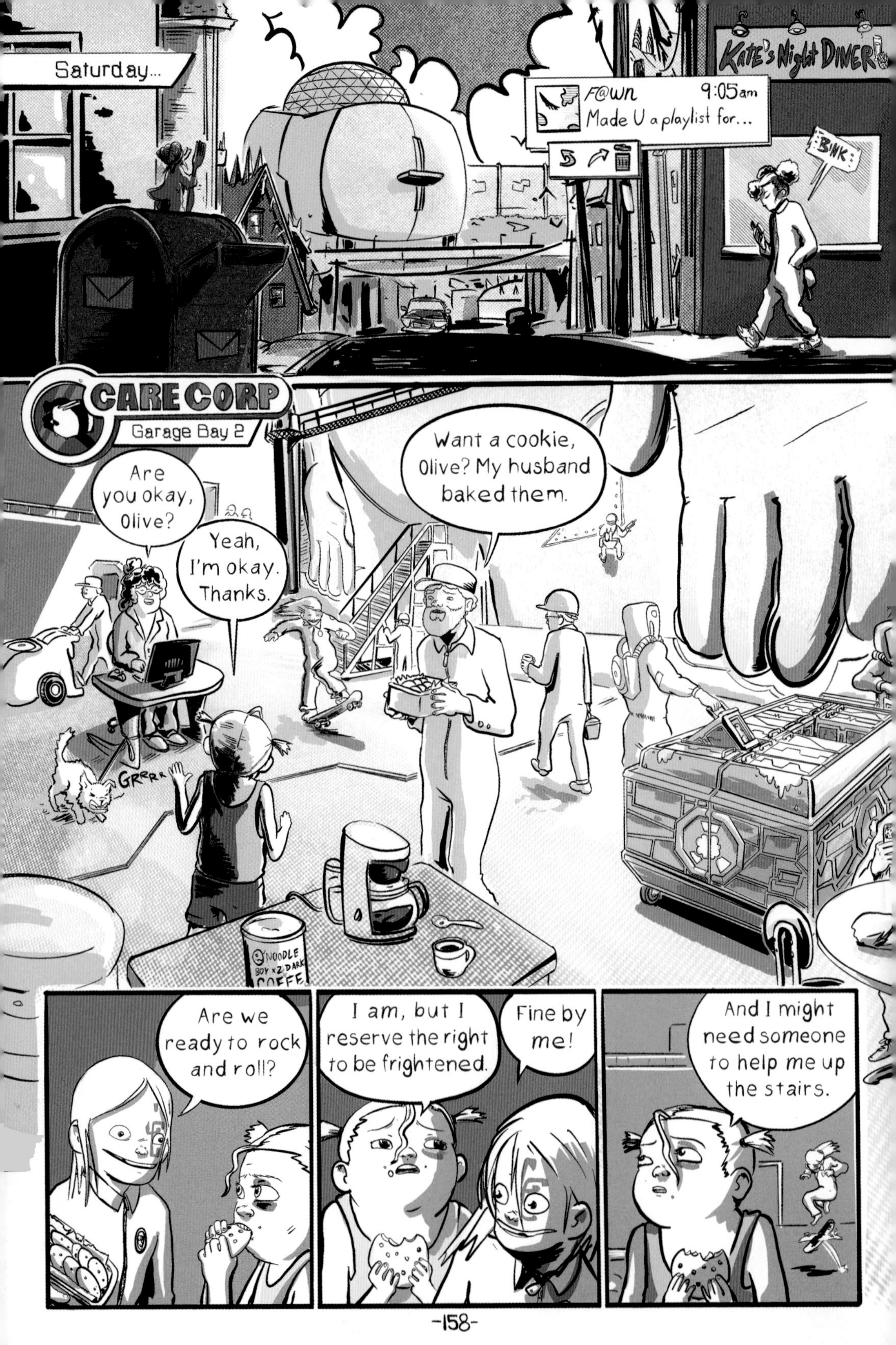
Saturday...
KATE'S Night DINER
F@wn 9:05am
Made U a playlist for...
BINK
CARE CORP
Garage Bay 2
Are you okay, Olive?
Yeah, I'm okay. Thanks.
Want a cookie, Olive? My husband baked them.
GRrrr
NOODLE BOY x2 DARK COFFE
Are we ready to rock and roll?
I am, but I reserve the right to be frightened.
Fine by me!
And I might need someone to help me up the stairs.

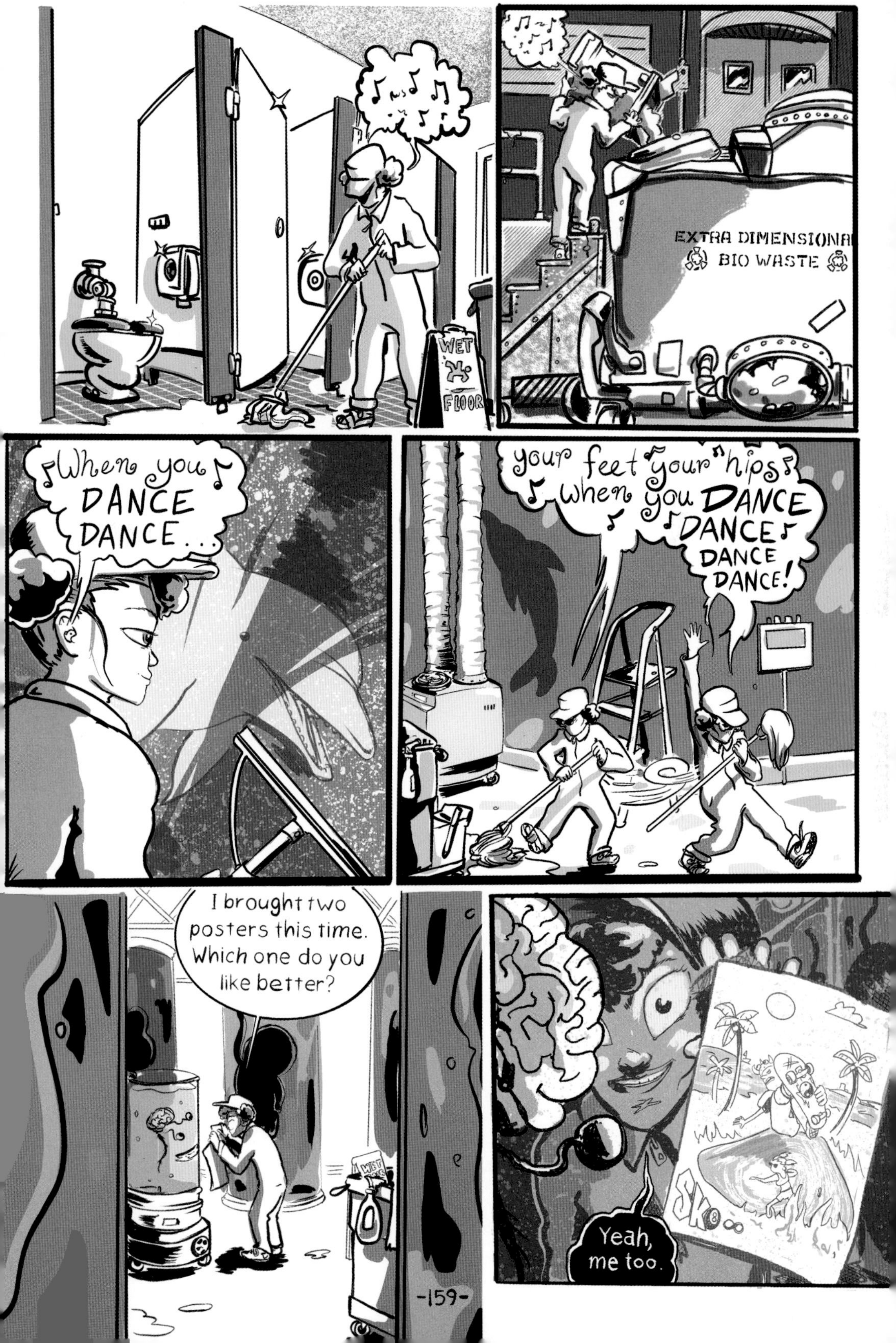
WET FLOOR
EXTRA DIMENSIONAL BIO WASTE
When you DANCE DANCE...
your feet your hips when you DANCE DANCE DANCE DANCE!
I brought two posters this time. Which one do you like better?
Yeah, me too.

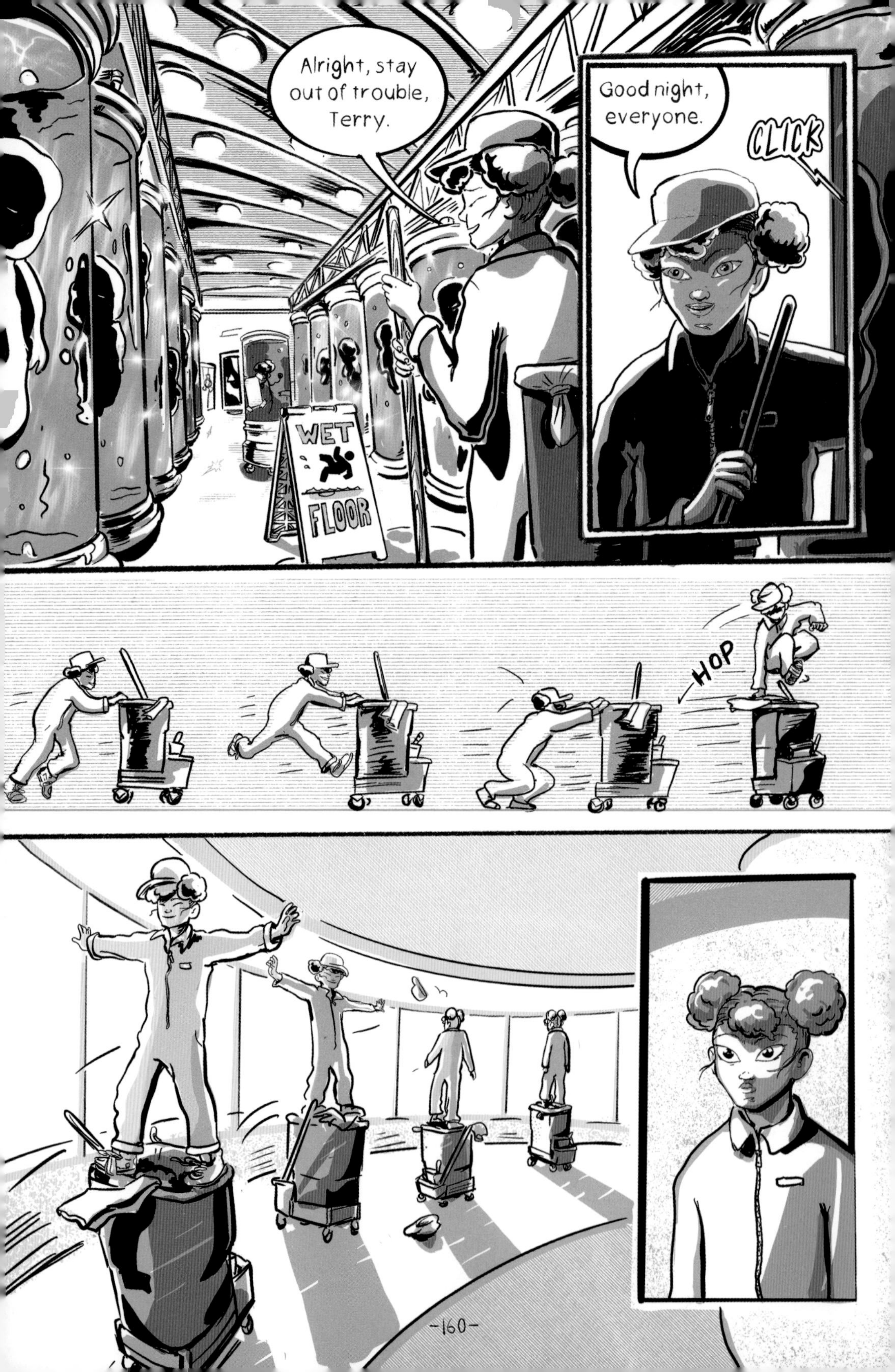
Alright, stay out of trouble, Terry.
Good night, everyone.
CLICK
WET FLOOR
HOP

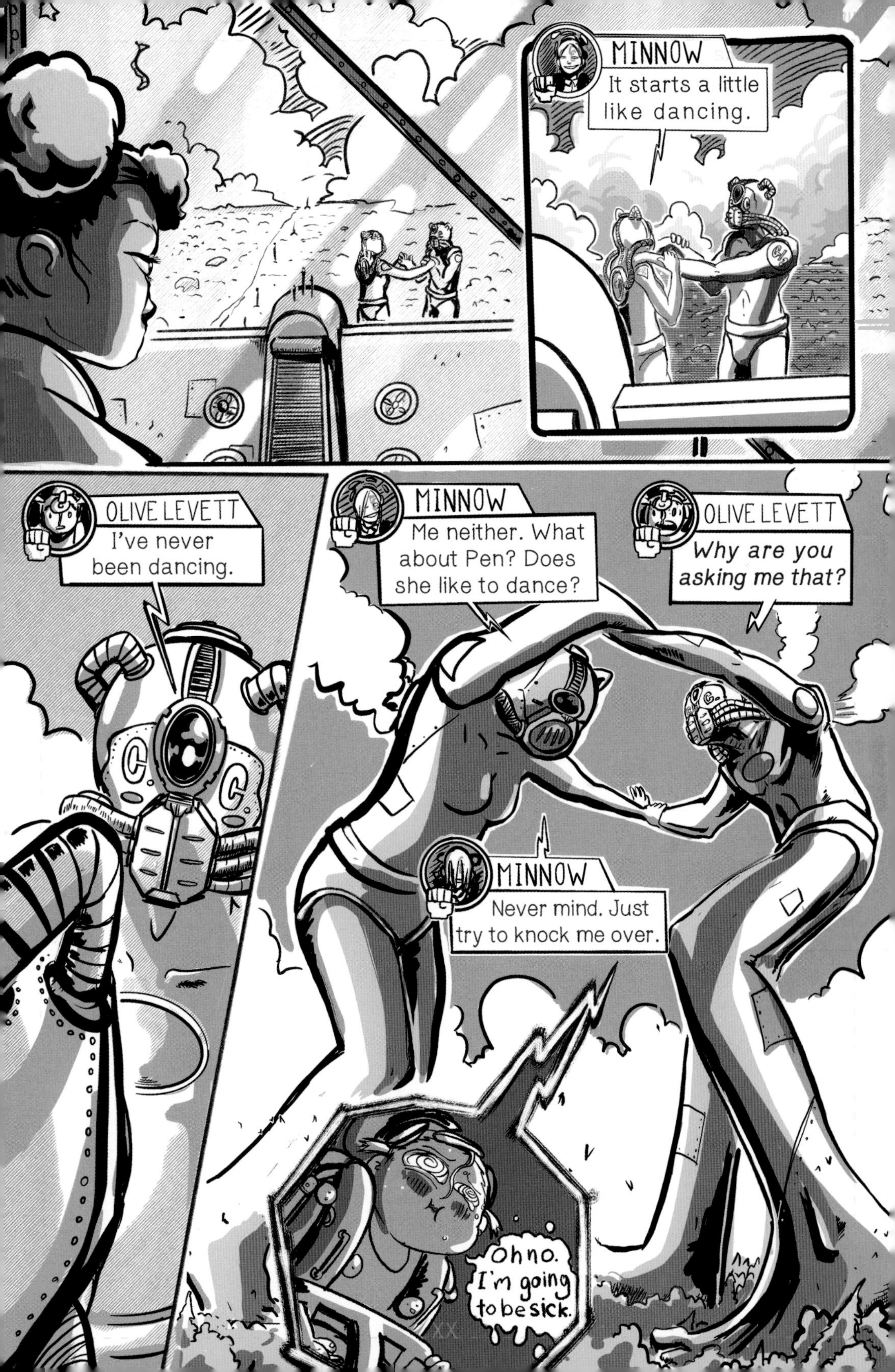
MINNOW
It starts a little like dancing.
OLIVE LEVETT
I've never been dancing.
MINNOW
Me neither. What about Pen? Does she like to dance?
OLIVE LEVETT
Why are you asking me that?
MINNOW
Never mind. Just try to knock me over.
Oh no. I'm going to be sick.

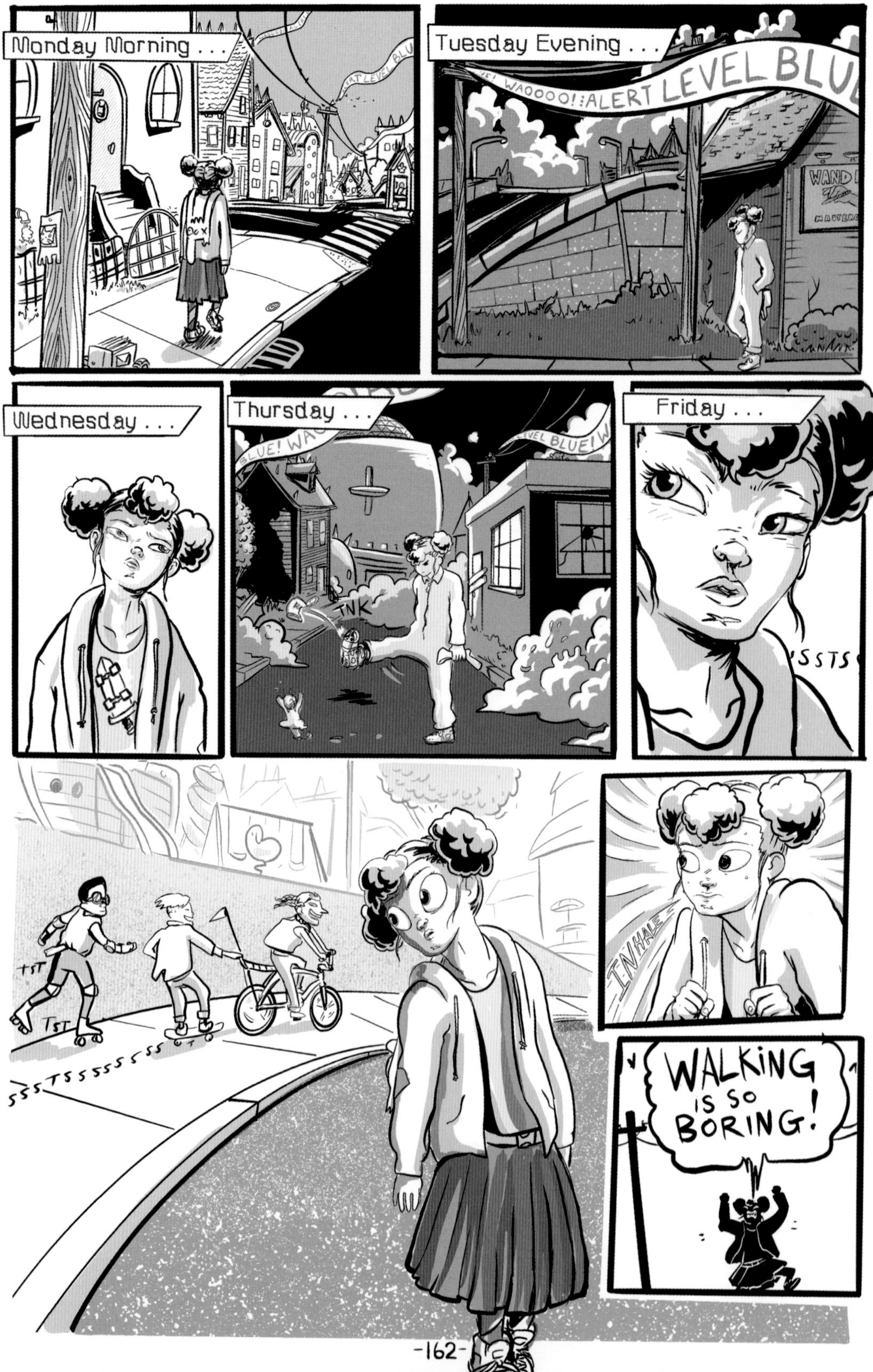
Monday Morning . . .
Tuesday Evening . . .
WAOOOO!!ALERT LEVEL BLU
Wednesday . . .
Thursday . . .
TNK
Friday . . .
SSTS
TST
TST
SSSTSSSSSSSS
INHALE
WALKING IS SO BORING!

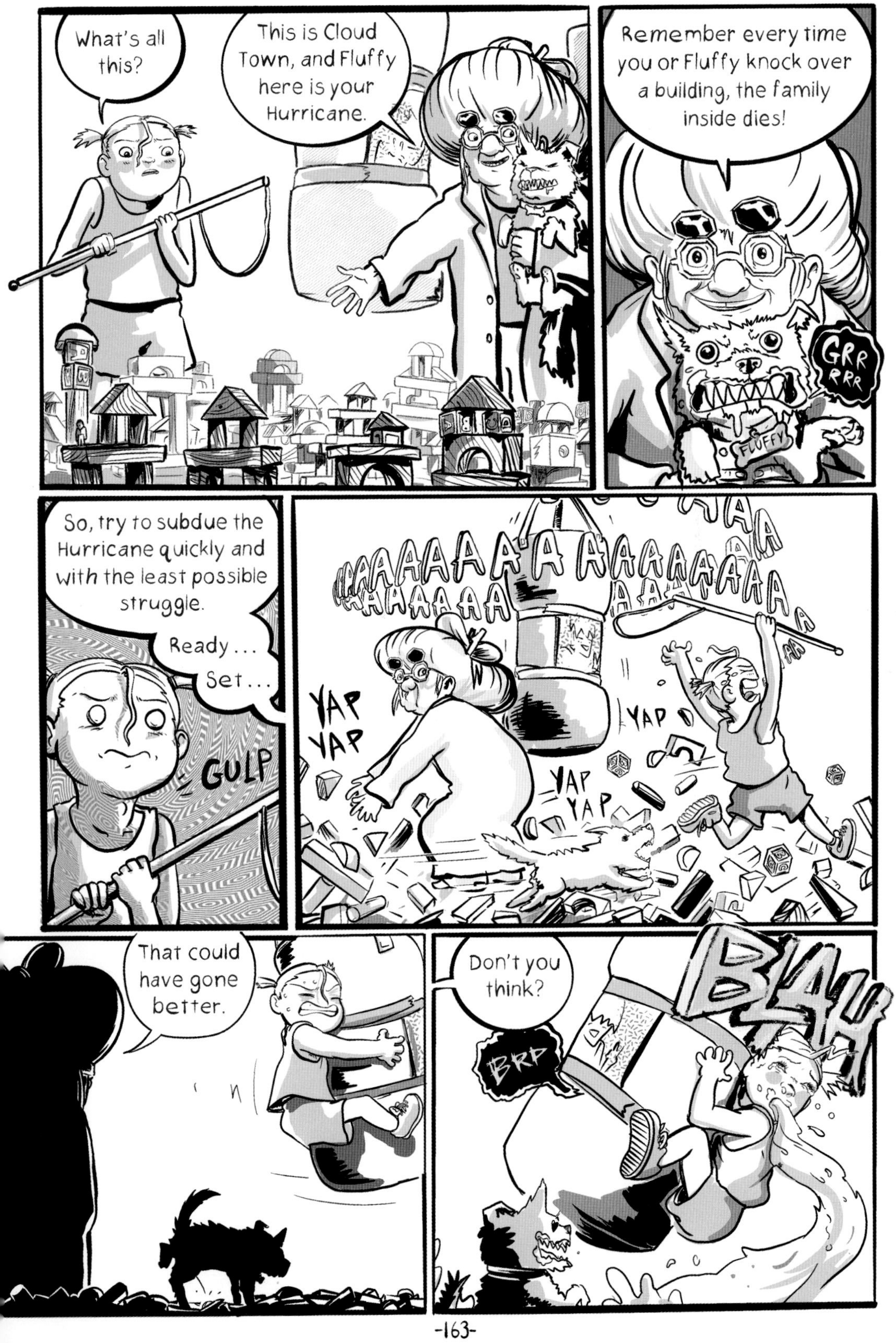
What's all this?
This is Cloud Town, and Fluffy here is your Hurricane.
Remember every time you or Fluffy knock over a building, the family inside dies!
GRR RRR
FLUFFY
So, try to subdue the Hurricane quickly and with the least possible struggle.
Ready...
Set...
GULP
AAAAAAAAAAAAAAAAAAA
YAP YAP
YAP
YAP YAP
That could have gone better.
Don't you think?
BRP
BLAH

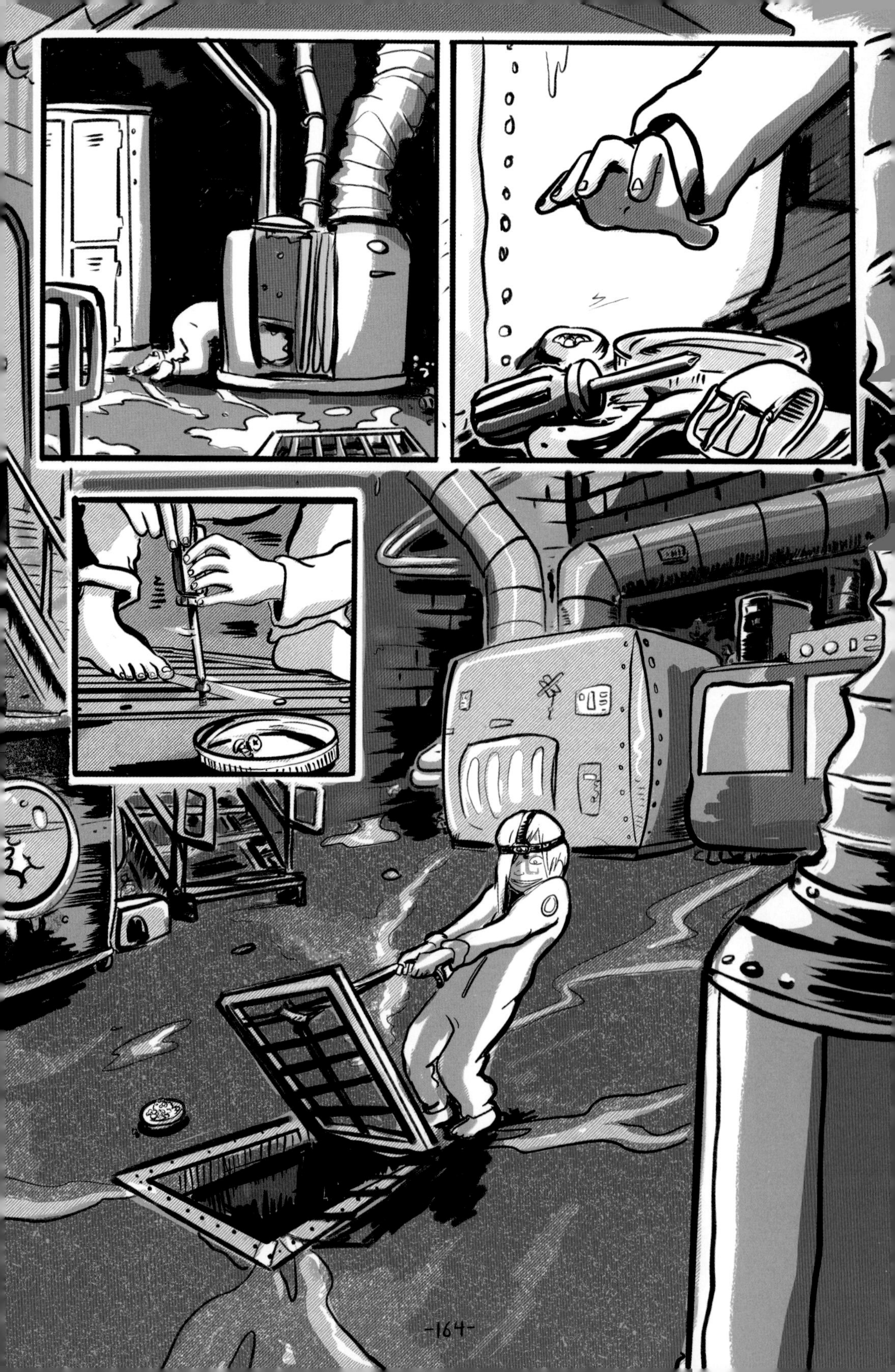

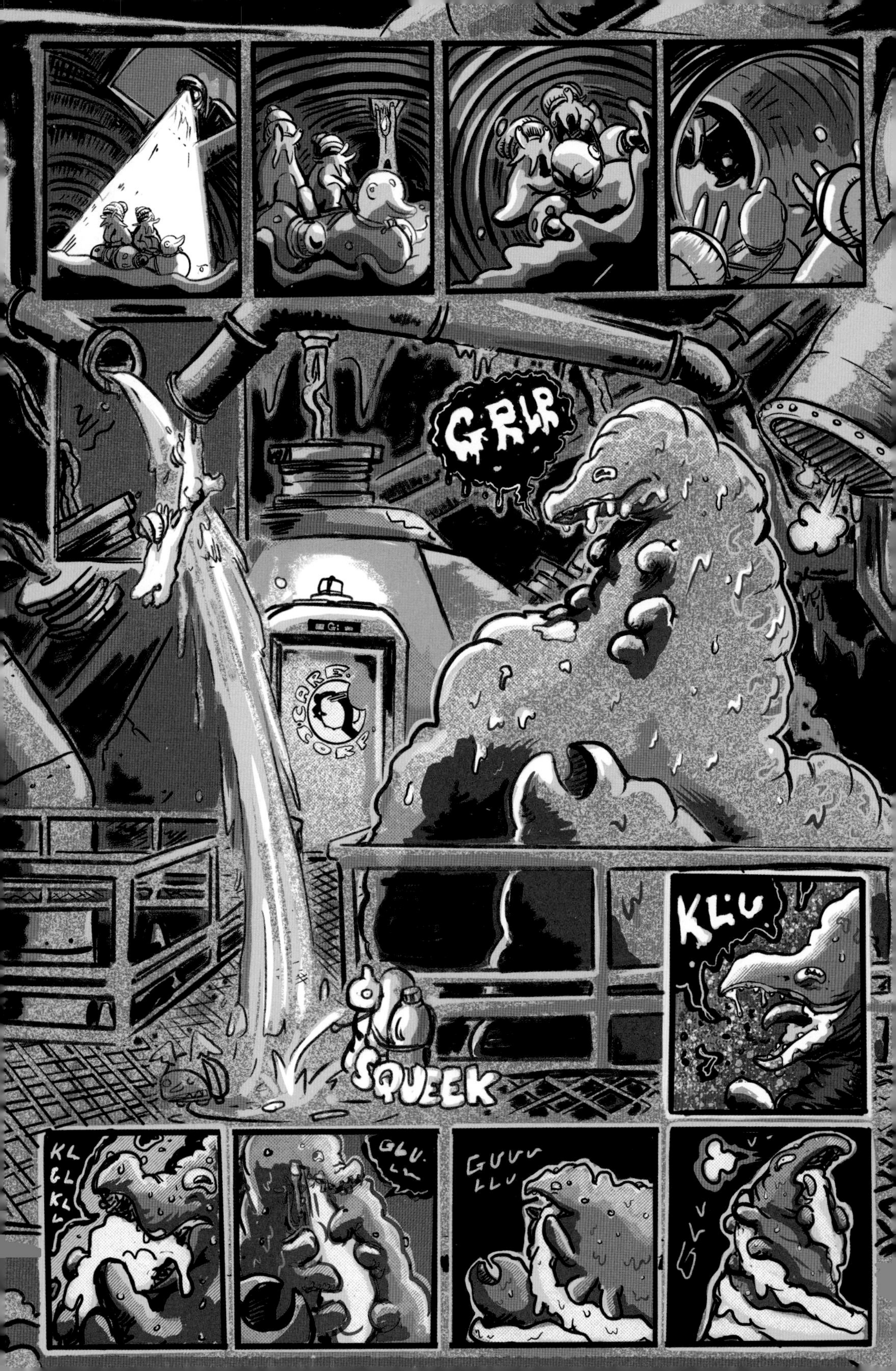
GRLR
SQUEEK
KLU
KL GL KL
GLU.
GUUV LLU

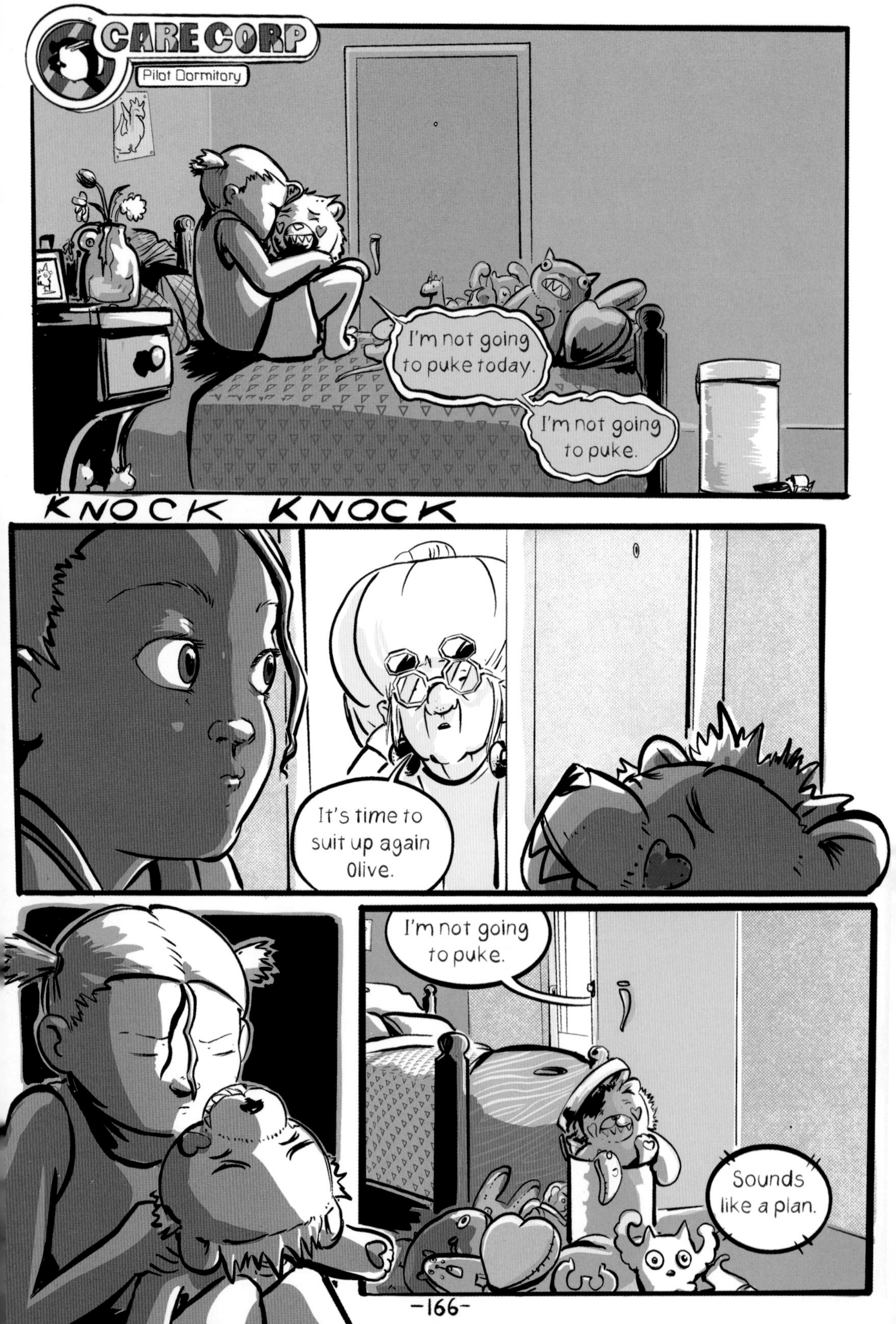
CARE CORP
Pilot Dormitory
I'm not going to puke today.
I'm not going to puke.
KNOCK KNOCK
It's time to suit up again Olive.
I'm not going to puke.
Sounds like a plan.

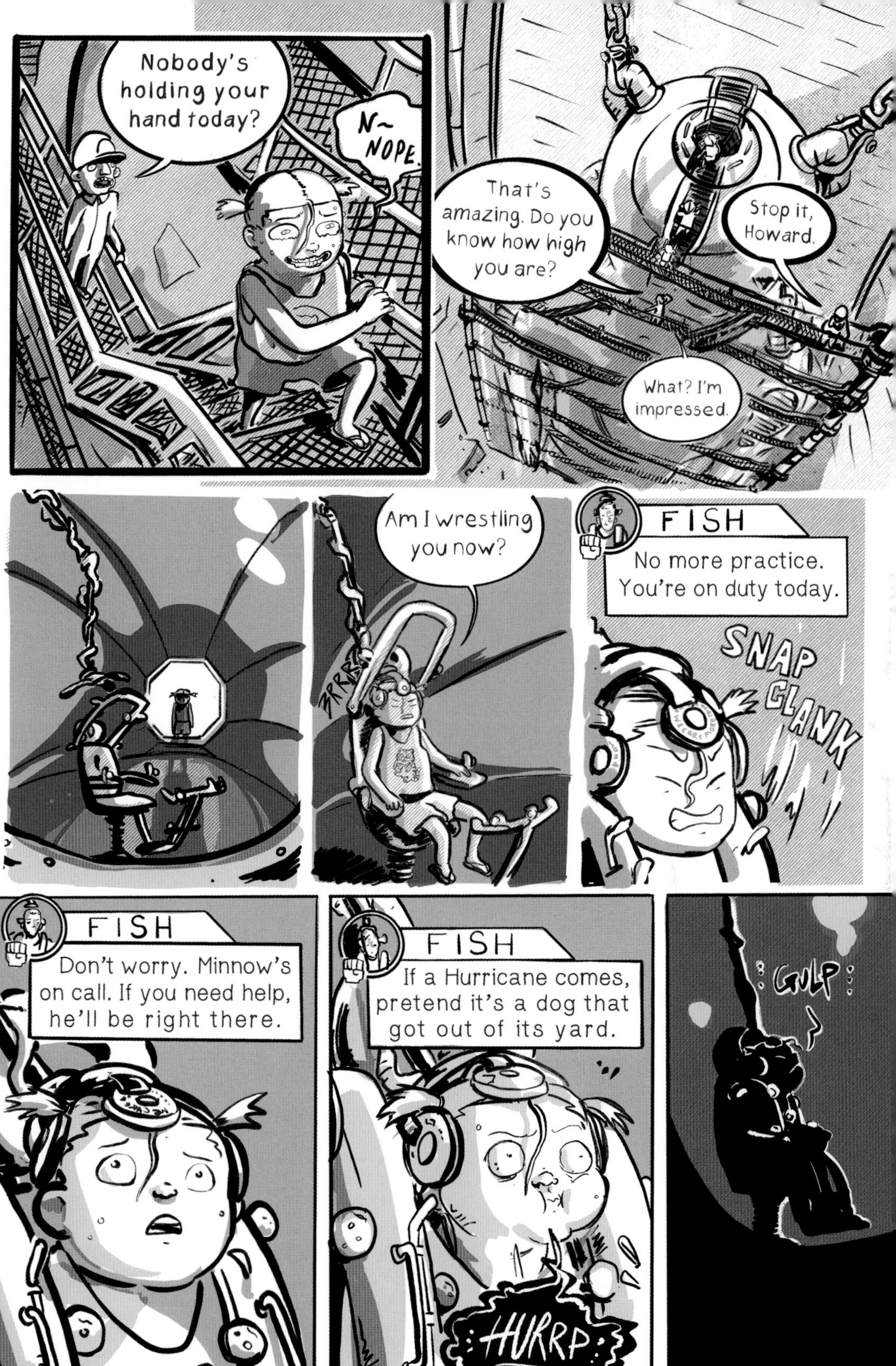
Nobody's holding your hand today?
N~ NOPE.
That's amazing. Do you know how high you are?
Stop it, Howard.
What? I'm impressed.
Am I wrestling you now?
BZRRR
FISH
No more practice. You're on duty today.
SNAP
CLANK
FISH
Don't worry. Minnow's on call. If you need help, he'll be right there.
FISH
If a Hurricane comes, pretend it's a dog that got out of its yard.
HURRP
GULP

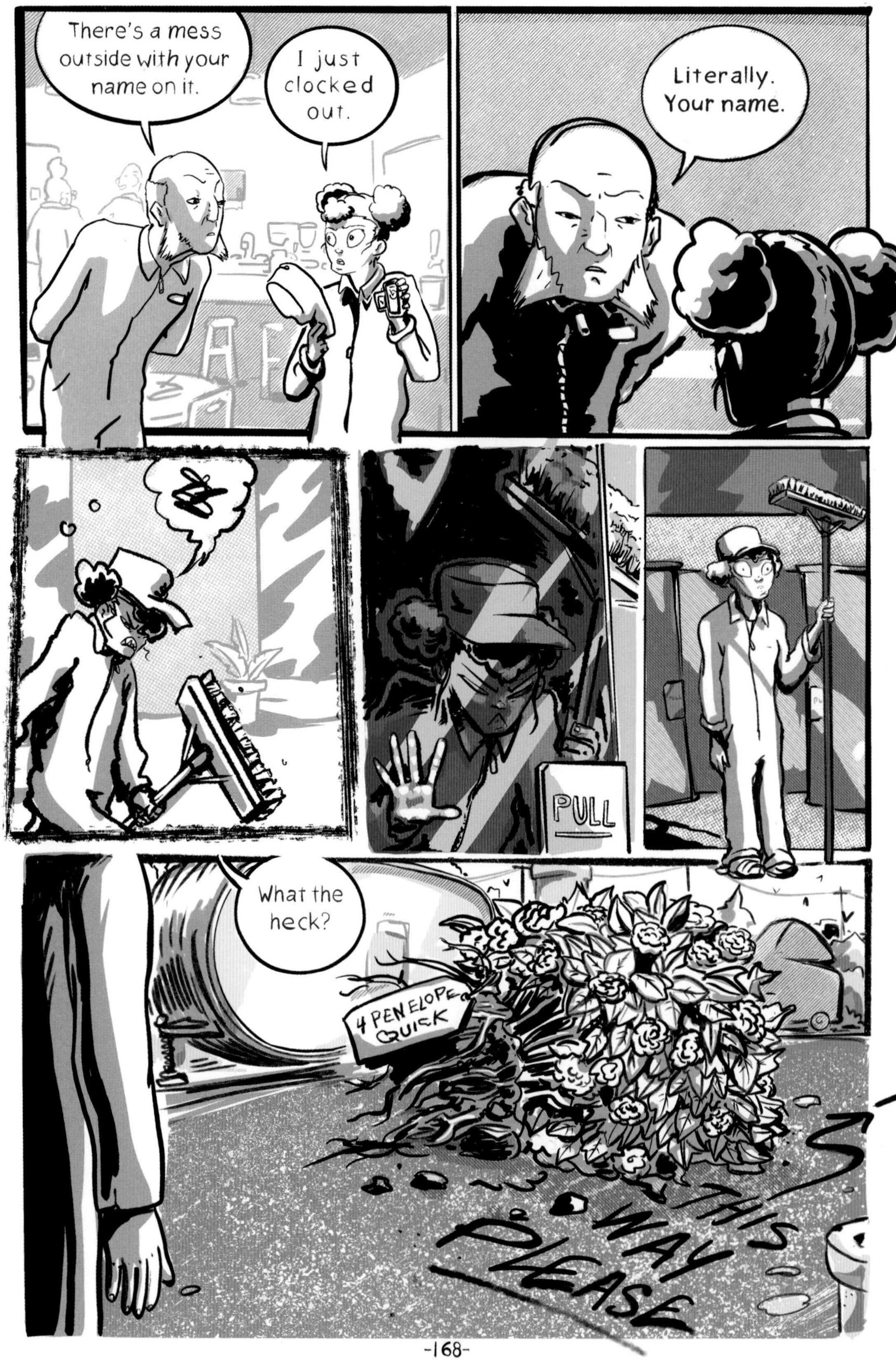
There's a mess outside with your name on it.
I just clocked out.
Literally. Your name.
PULL
What the heck?
4 PENELOPE QUICK
THIS WAY PLEASE

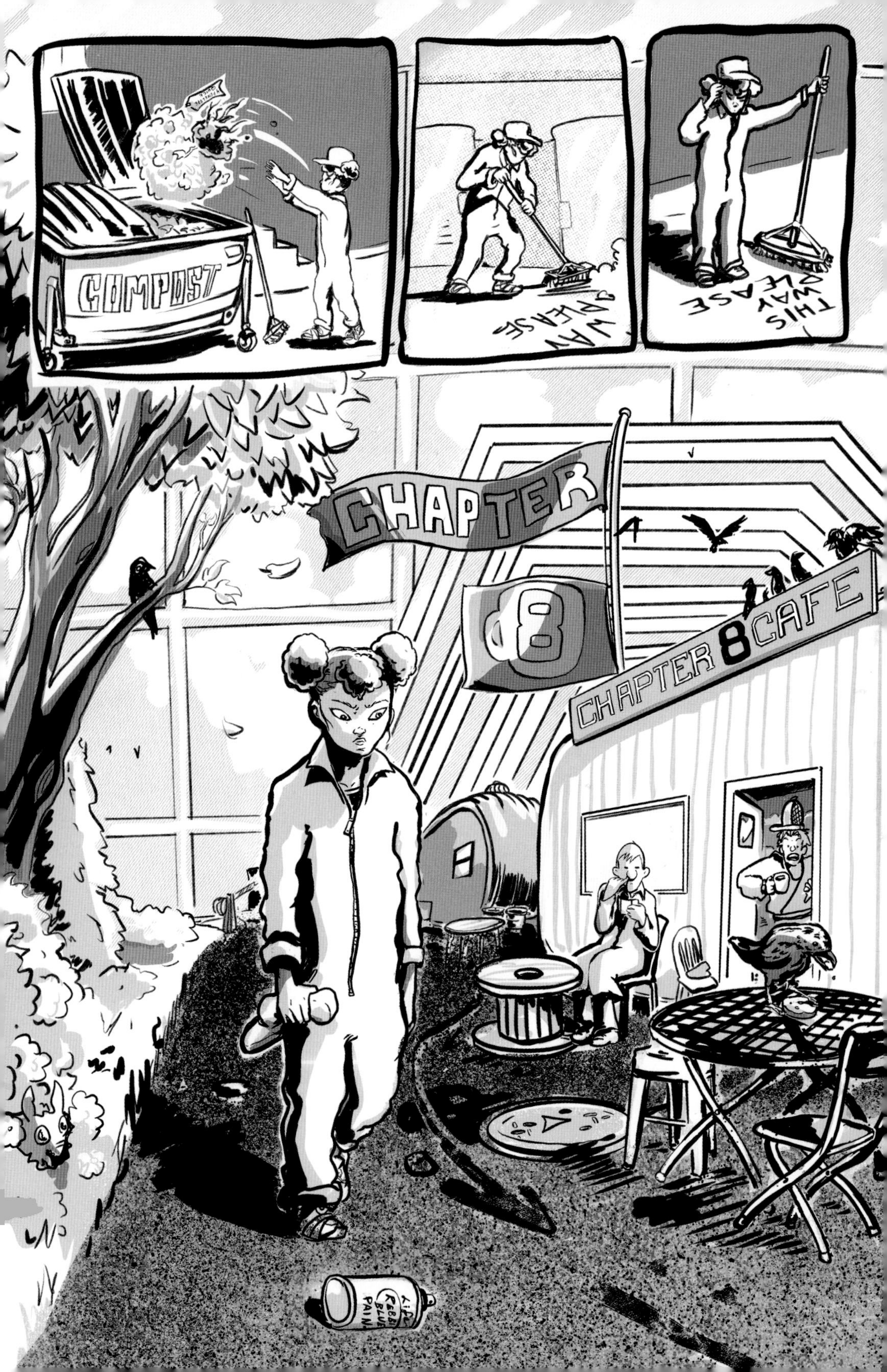
COMPOST
CHAPTER
8
CHAPTER 8 CAFE

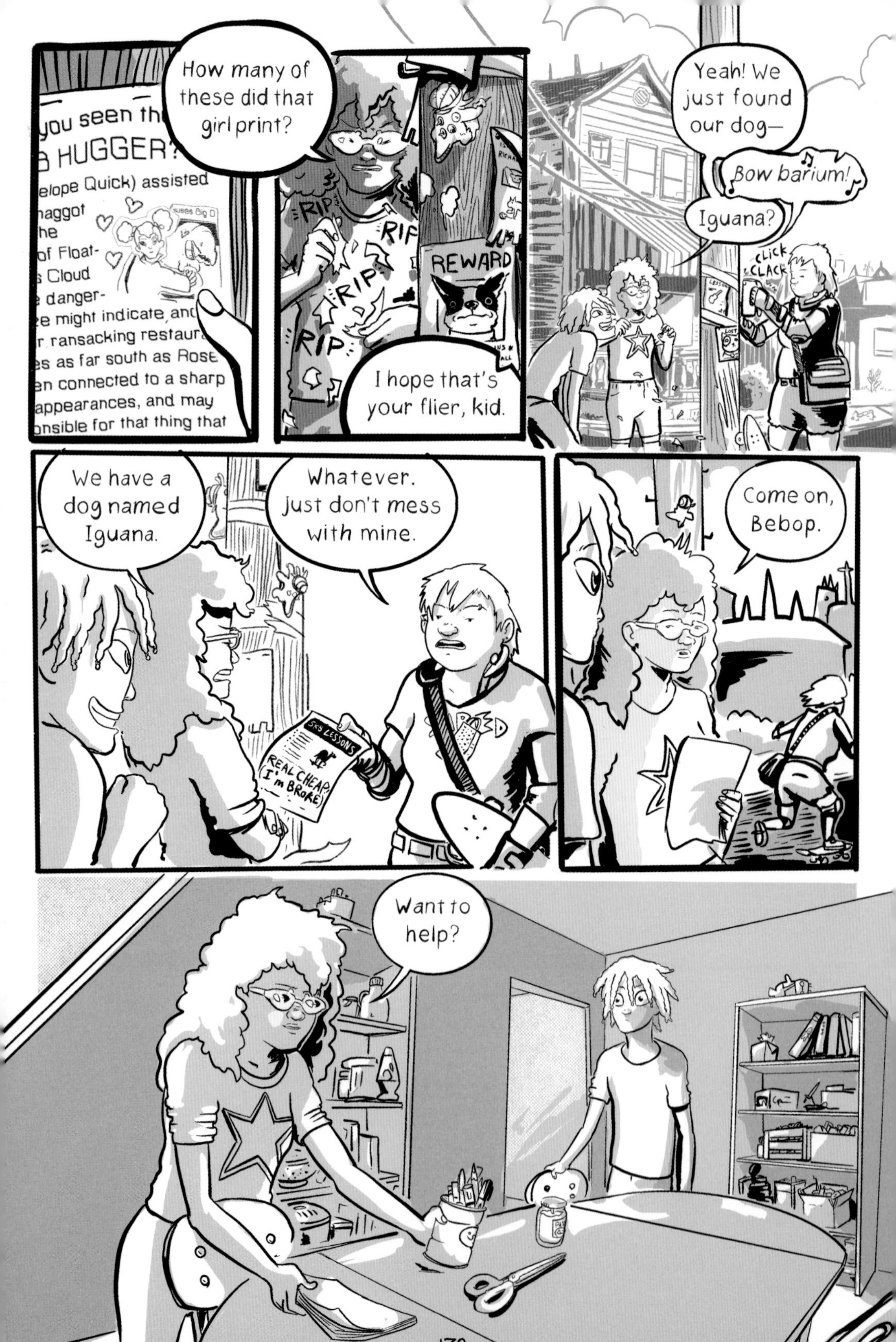
you seen th
B HUGGER?
elope Quick) assisted
haggot
he
of Float-
s Cloud
e danger-
ze might indicate, and
r ransacking restaura
es as far south as Rose
en connected to a sharp
appearances, and may
onsible for that thing that
How many of these did that girl print?
RIP
RIP
RIP
RIP
REWARD
I hope that's your flier, kid.
Yeah! We just found our dog—
Bow barium!
Iguana?
CLICK CLACK
We have a dog named Iguana.
Whatever. Just don't mess with mine.
SK8 LESSONS
REAL CHEAP! (I'm BROKE)
Come on, Bebop.
Want to help?

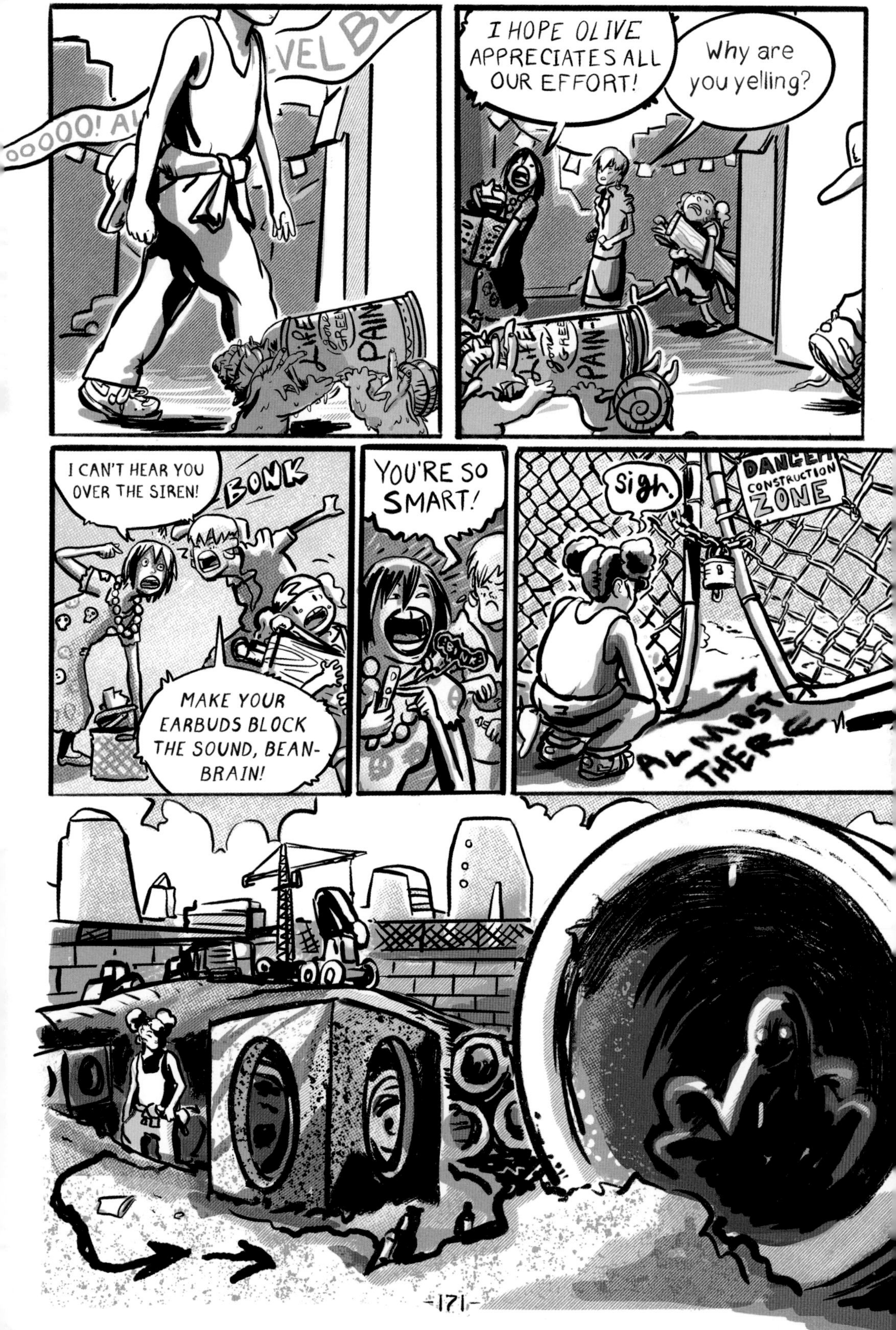
OOOOO! AL
EVEL B
I HOPE OLIVE APPRECIATES ALL OUR EFFORT!
Why are you yelling?
I CAN'T HEAR YOU OVER THE SIREN!
BONK
MAKE YOUR EARBUDS BLOCK THE SOUND, BEAN-BRAIN!
YOU'RE SO SMART!
Sigh.
CONSTRUCTION ZONE
ALMOST THERE

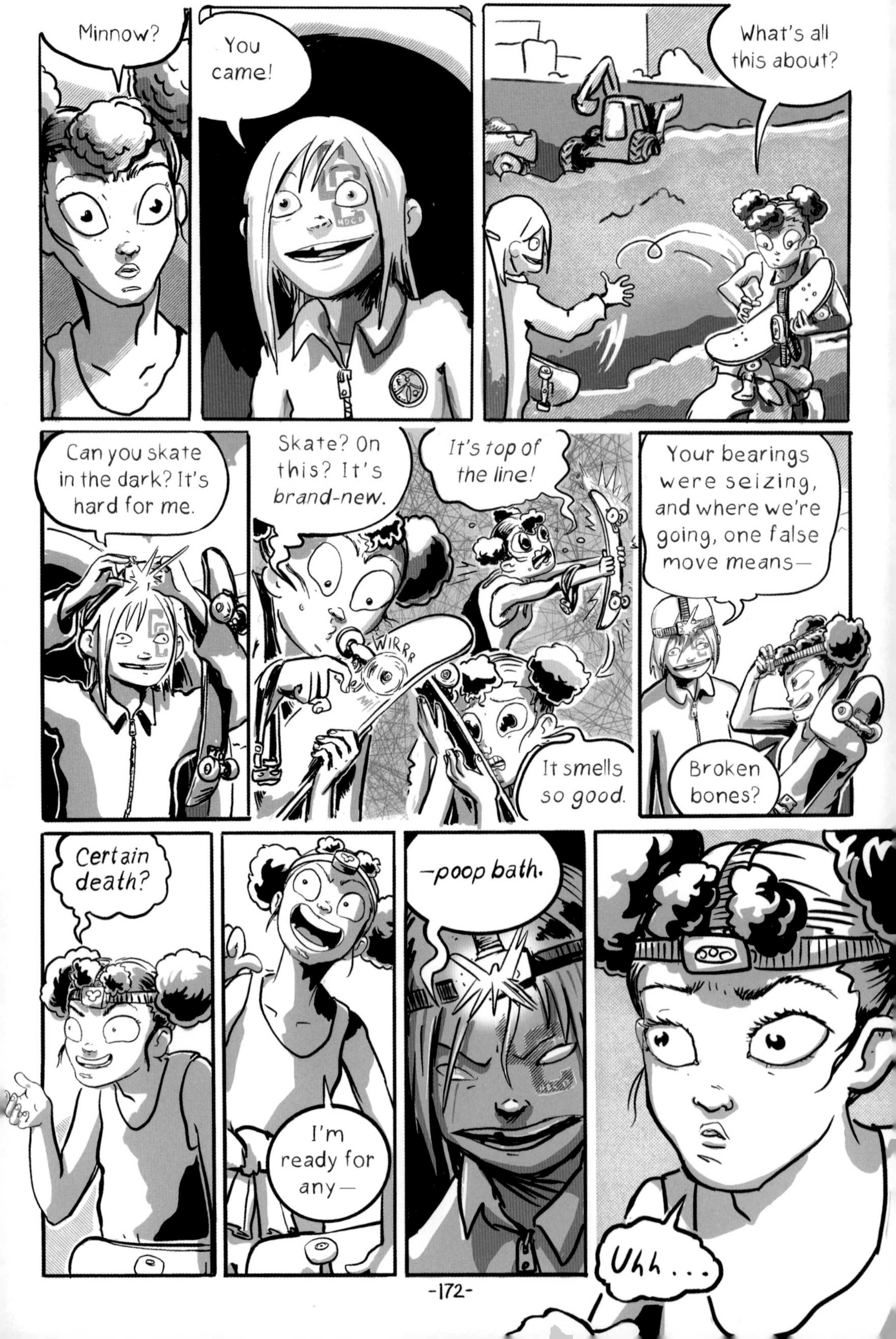
Minnow?
You came!
What's all this about?
Can you skate in the dark? It's hard for me.
Skate? On this? It's brand-new.
WIRRR
It's top of the line!
It smells so good.
Your bearings were seizing, and where we're going, one false move means—
Broken bones?
Certain death?
I'm ready for any—
—poop bath.
Uhh . . .

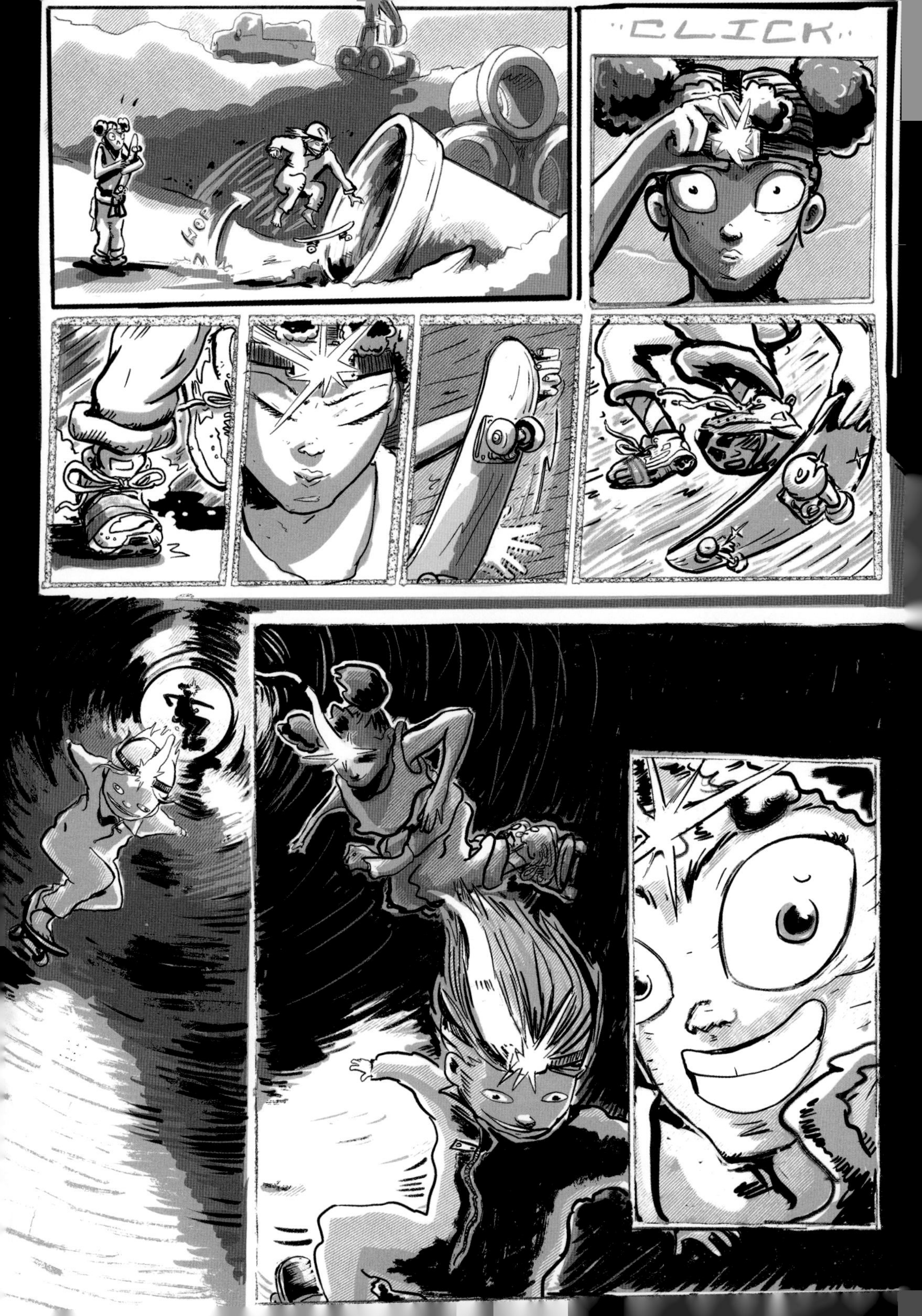
HOP
CLICK

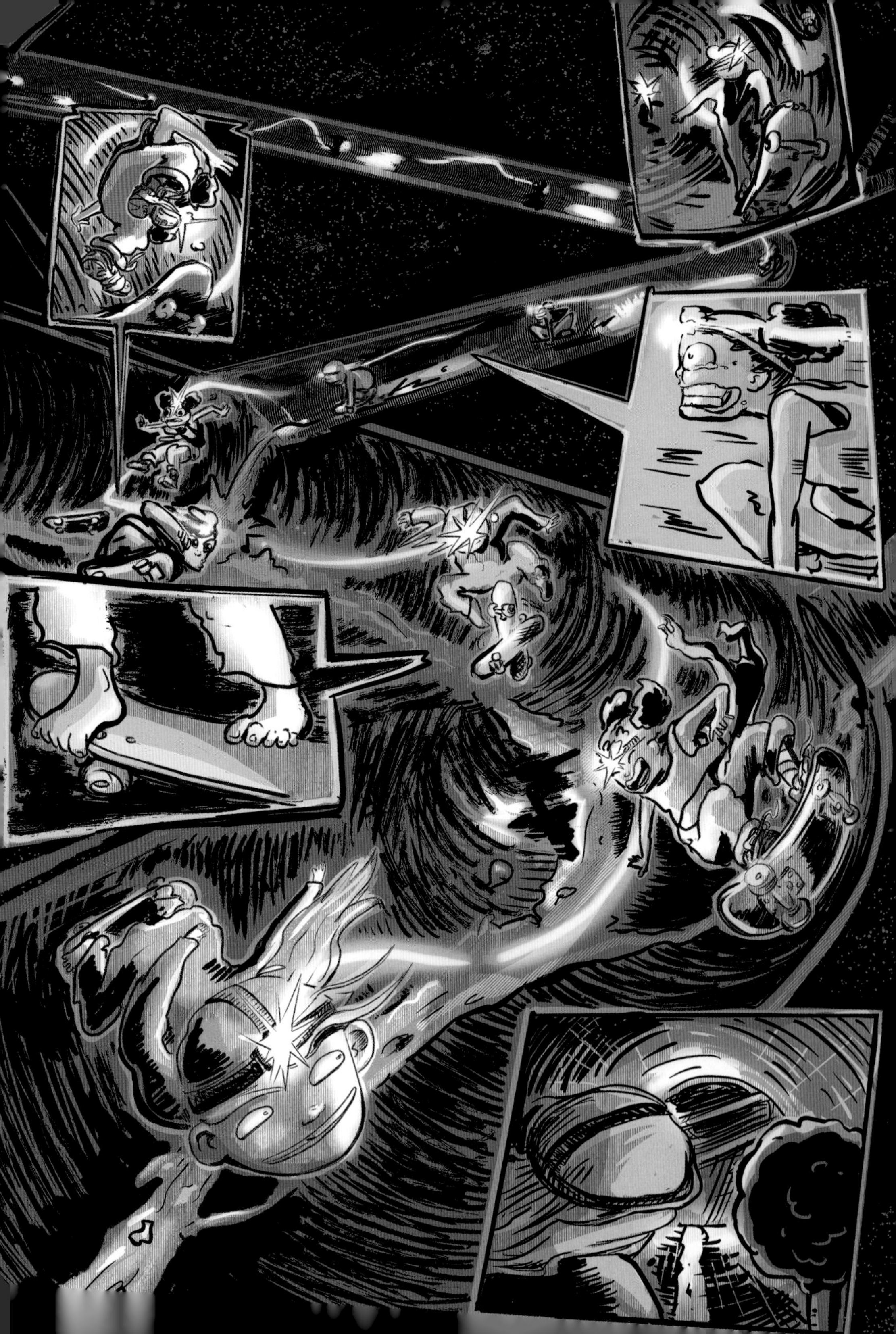

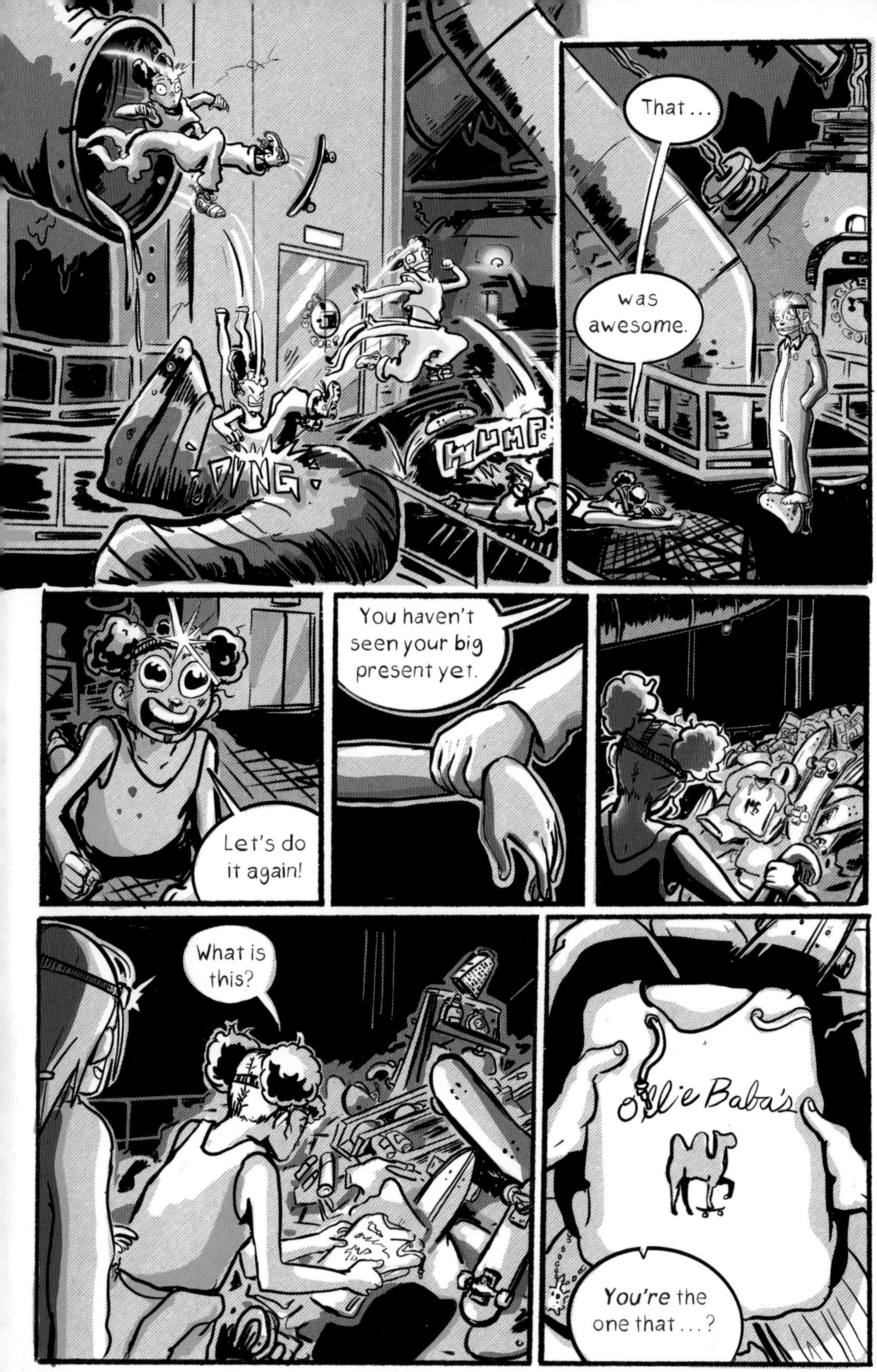
DING
WUMP
That . . .
was awesome.
Let's do it again!
You haven't seen your big present yet.
What is this?
Ollie Baba's
You're the one that . . . ?

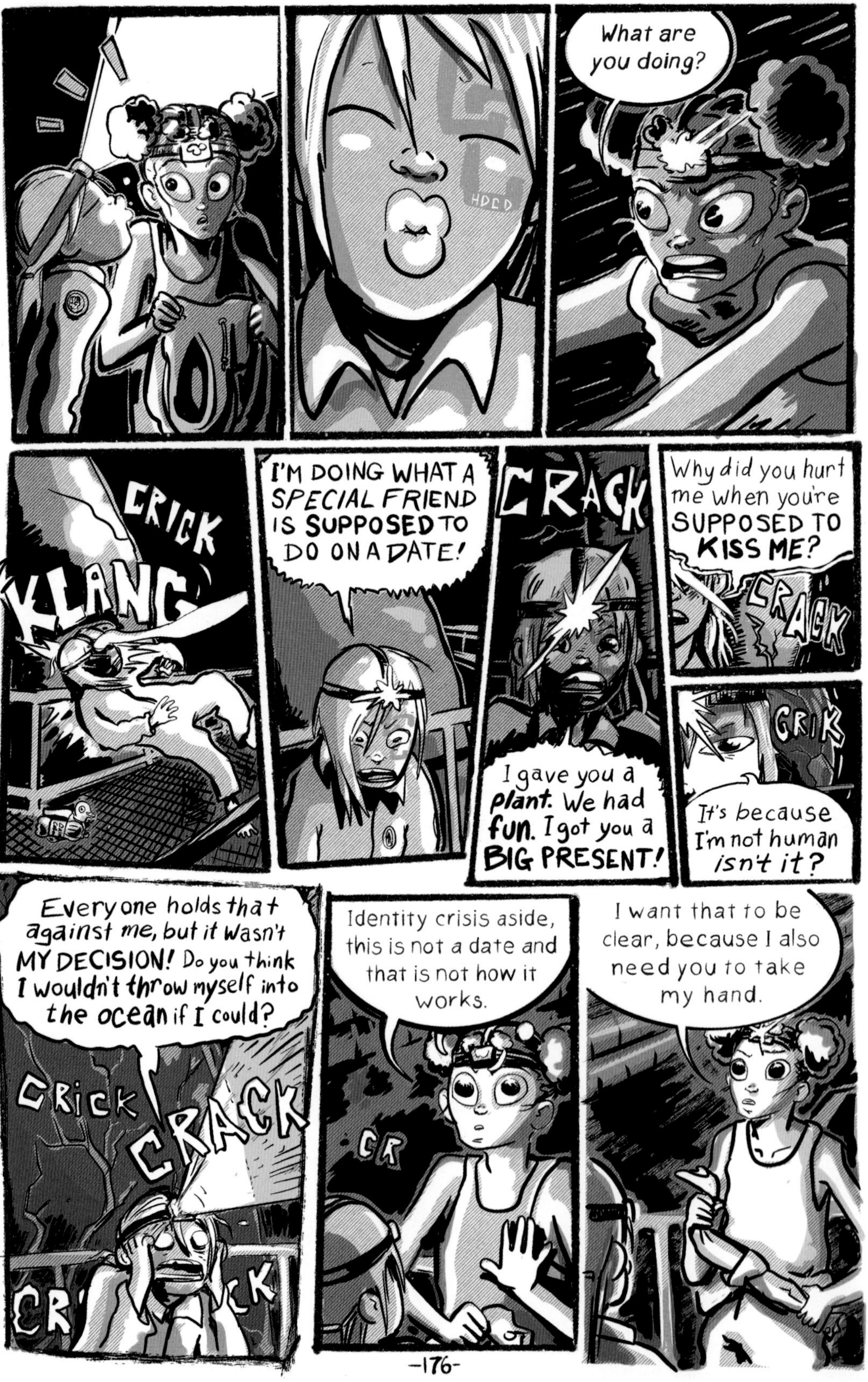

What are you doing?
CRICK
KLANG
I'M DOING WHAT A SPECIAL FRIEND IS SUPPOSED TO DO ON A DATE!
CRACK
I gave you a plant. We had fun. I got you a BIG PRESENT!
Why did you hurt me when you're SUPPOSED TO KISS ME?
CRACK
GRIK
It's because I'm not human isn't it?
Everyone holds that against me, but it wasn't MY DECISION! Do you think I wouldn't throw myself into the ocean if I could?
CRICK
CRACK
CR
CK
Identity crisis aside, this is not a date and that is not how it works.
CR
I want that to be clear, because I also need you to take my hand.

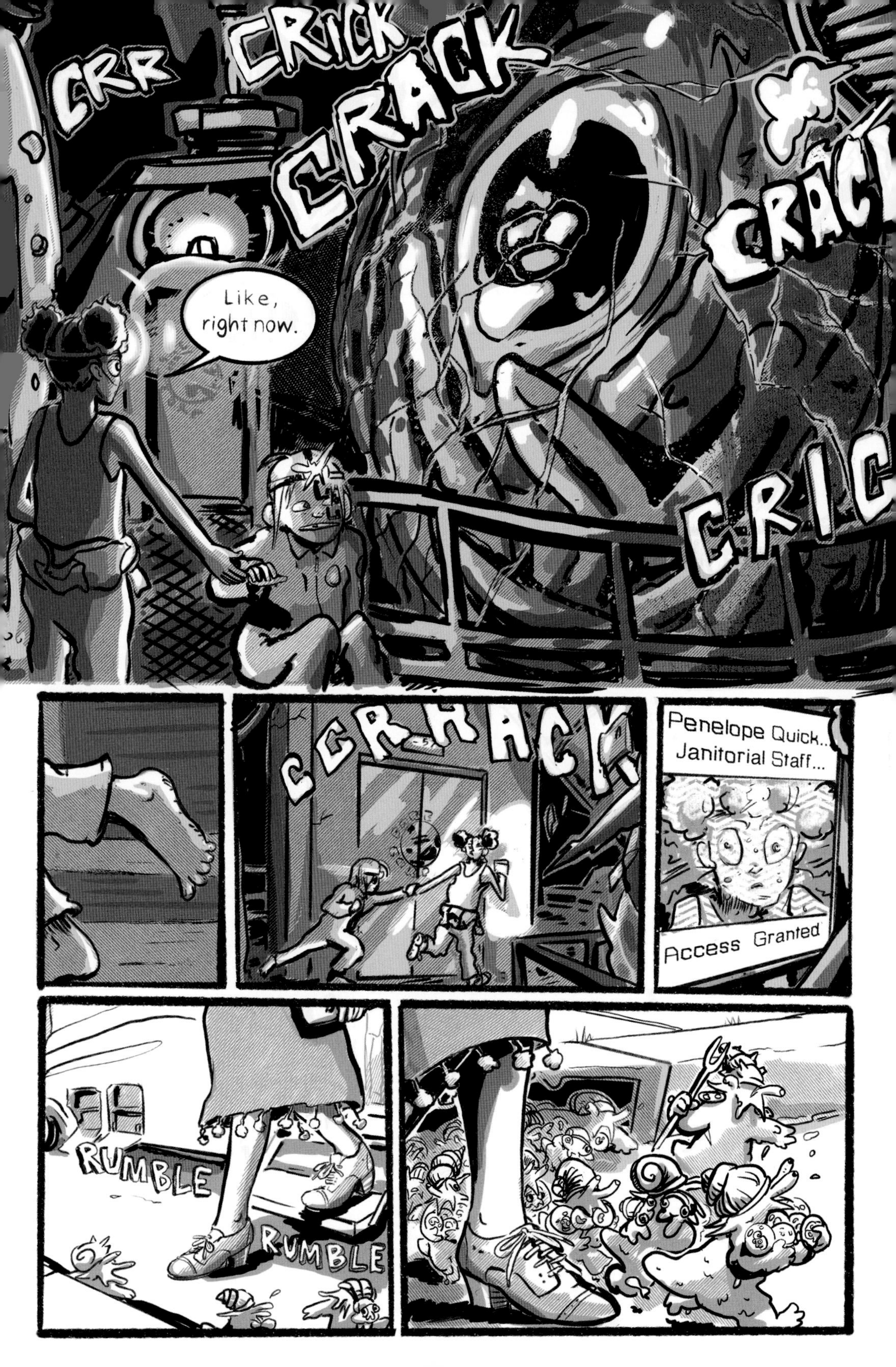
CRR
CRICK
CRACK
CRACK
Like, right now.
CRIC
CCRRACK
Penelope Quick...
Janitorial Staff...
Access Granted
RUMBLE
RUMBLE

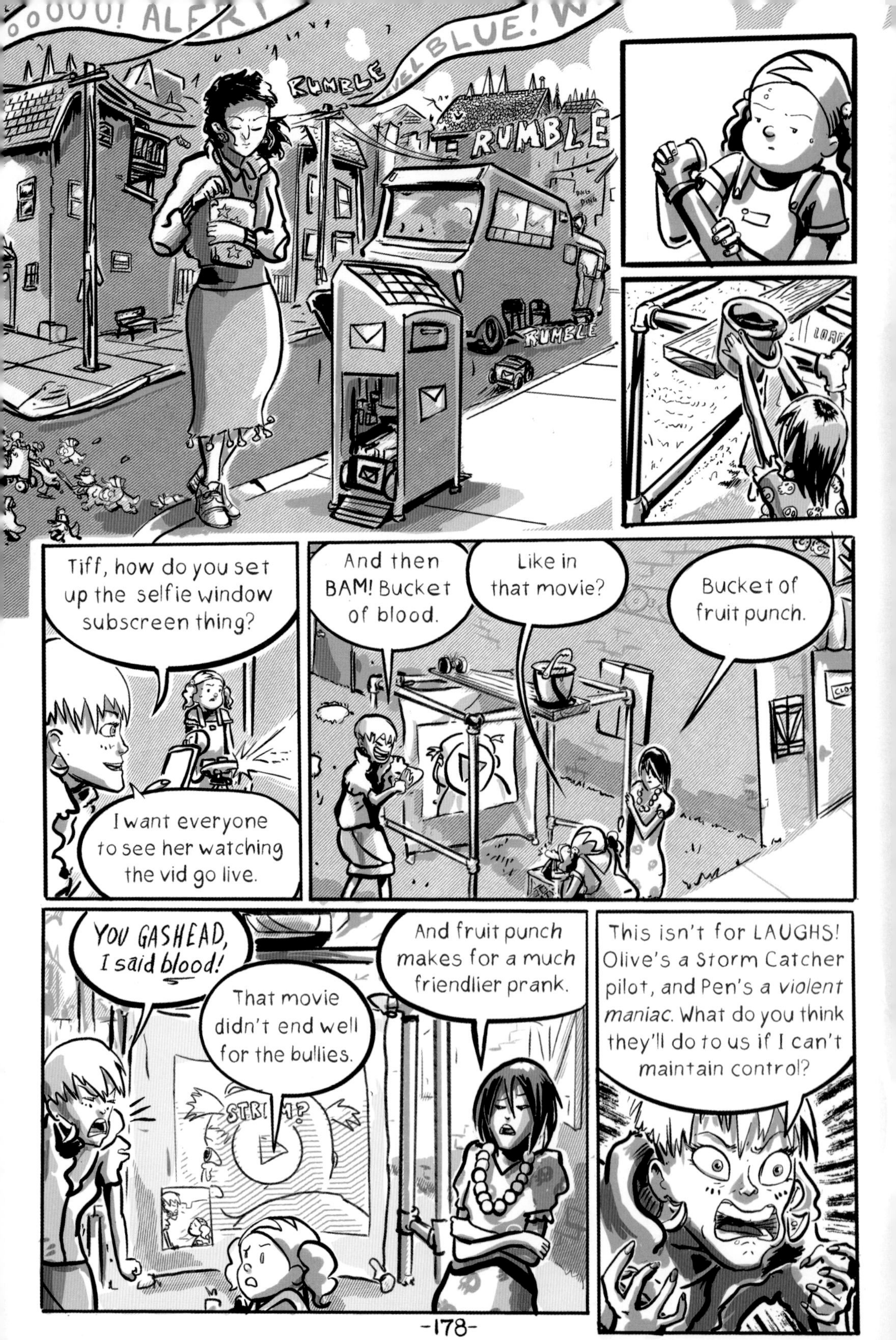
OOOOU! ALER
BLUE! W
RUMBLE
RUMBLE
RUMBLE
Tiff, how do you set up the selfie window subscreen thing?
I want everyone to see her watching the vid go live.
And then BAM! Bucket of blood.
Like in that movie?
Bucket of fruit punch.
YOU GASHEAD, I said blood!
That movie didn't end well for the bullies.
And fruit punch makes for a much friendlier prank.
This isn't for LAUGHS! Olive's a Storm Catcher pilot, and Pen's a violent maniac. What do you think they'll do to us if I can't maintain control!?

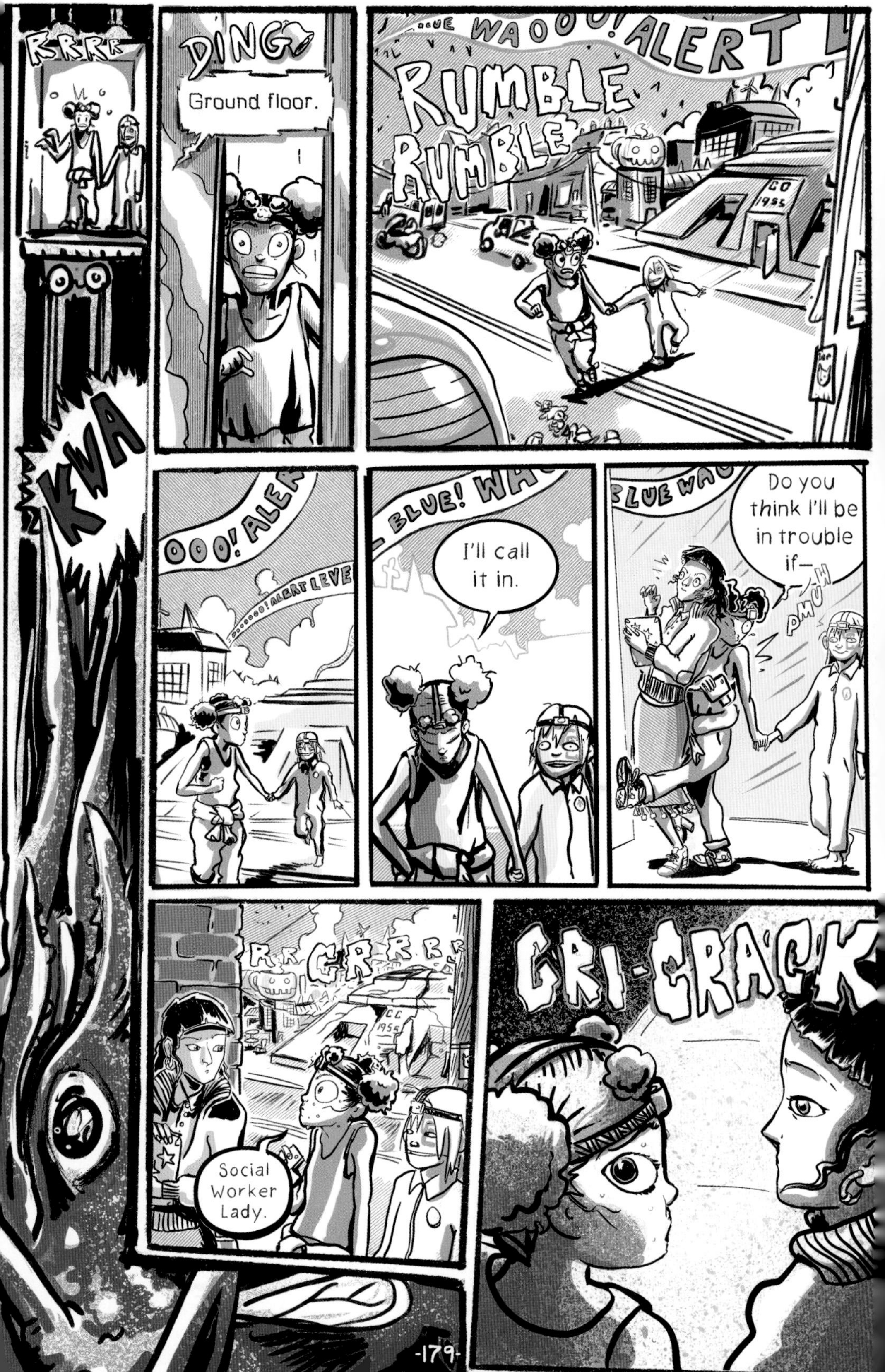
RRRR
DING
Ground floor.
BLUE WAOOO! ALERT
RUMBLE
RUMBLE
KWA
OOO! ALER
BLUE! WA
I'll call it in.
BLUE WA
Do you think I'll be in trouble if—
GRRRR
Social Worker Lady.
GRI-CRACK

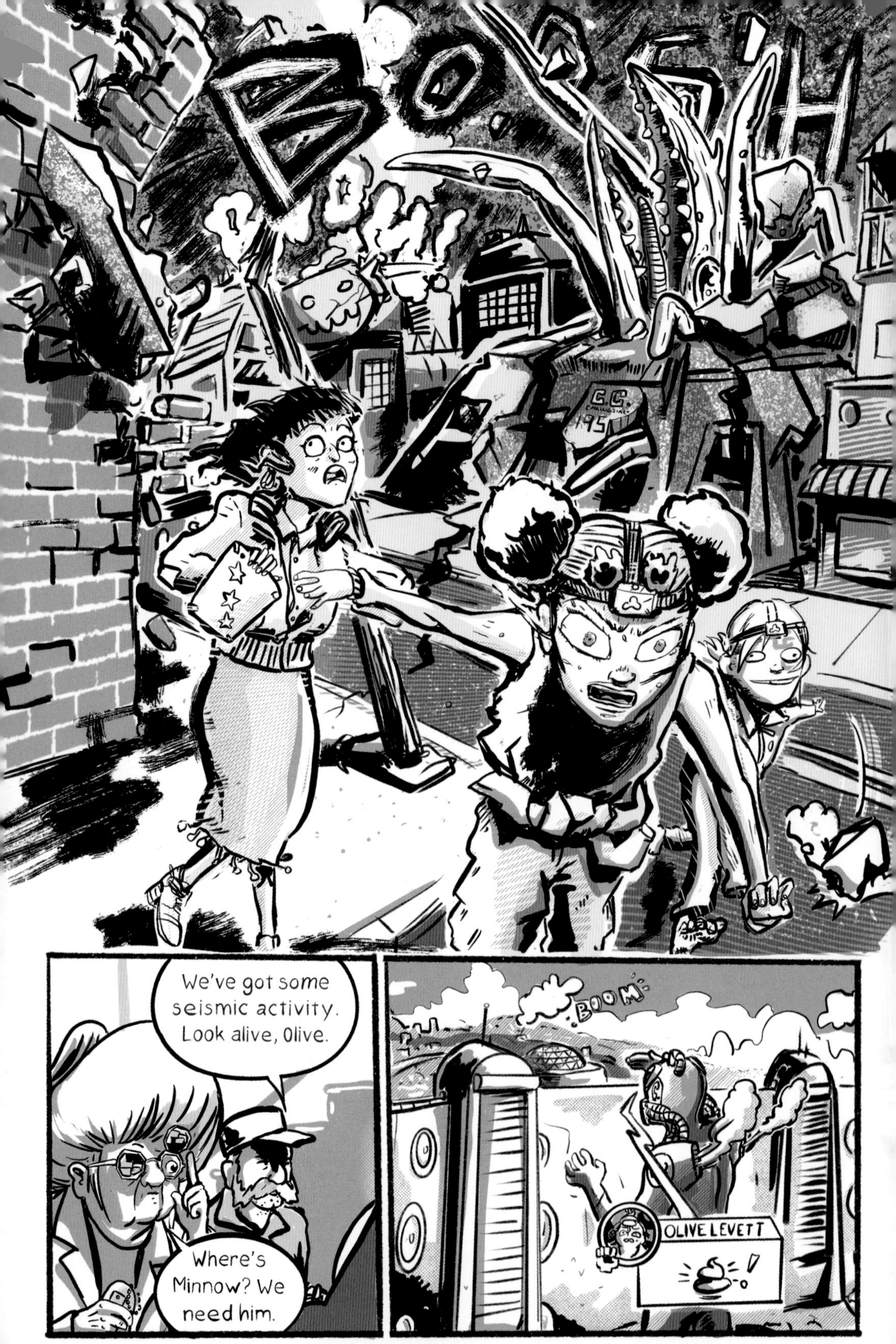

We've got some seismic activity. Look alive, Olive.
Where's Minnow? We need him.
BOOM
OLIVE LEVETT

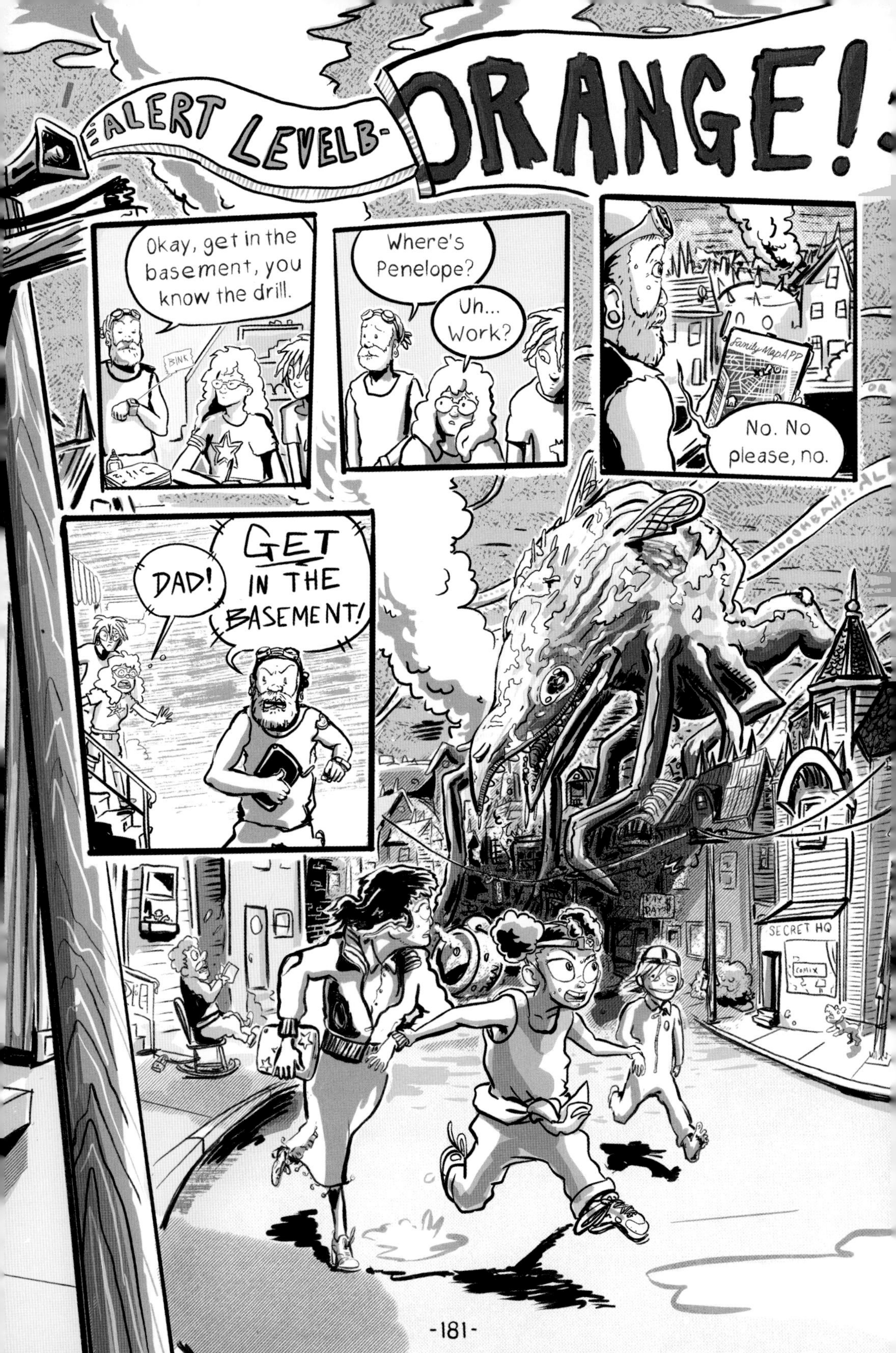
ALERT LEVELB-
ORANGE!
Okay, get in the basement, you know the drill.
BINK
Where's Penelope?
Uh... Work?
Family MapAPP
No. No please, no.
DAD!
GET IN THE BASEMENT!
RAHOOOMBAH!
SECRET HQ
COMIX

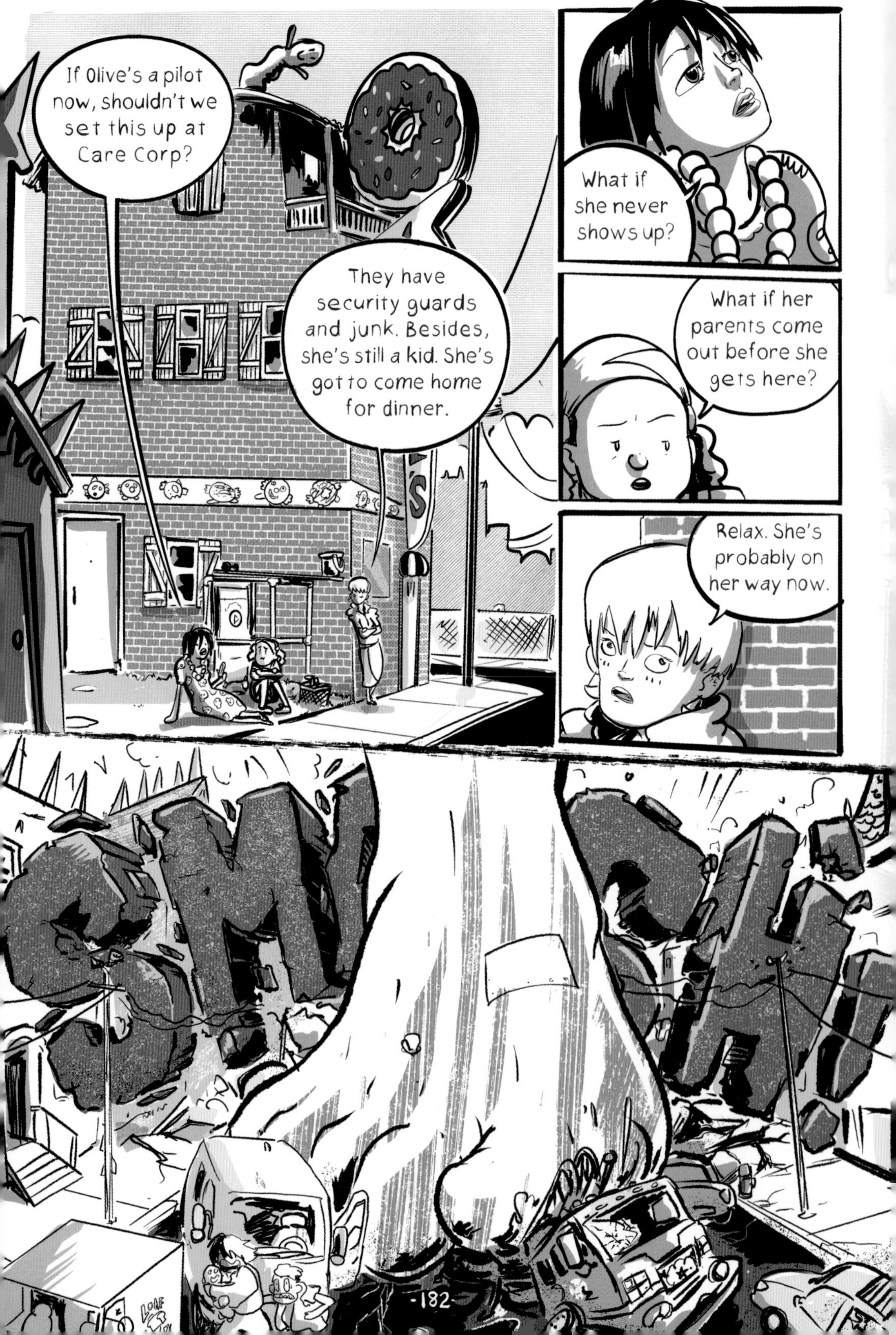
If Olive's a pilot now, shouldn't we set this up at Care Corp?
They have security guards and junk. Besides, she's still a kid. She's got to come home for dinner.
What if she never shows up?
What if her parents come out before she gets here?
Relax. She's probably on her way now.

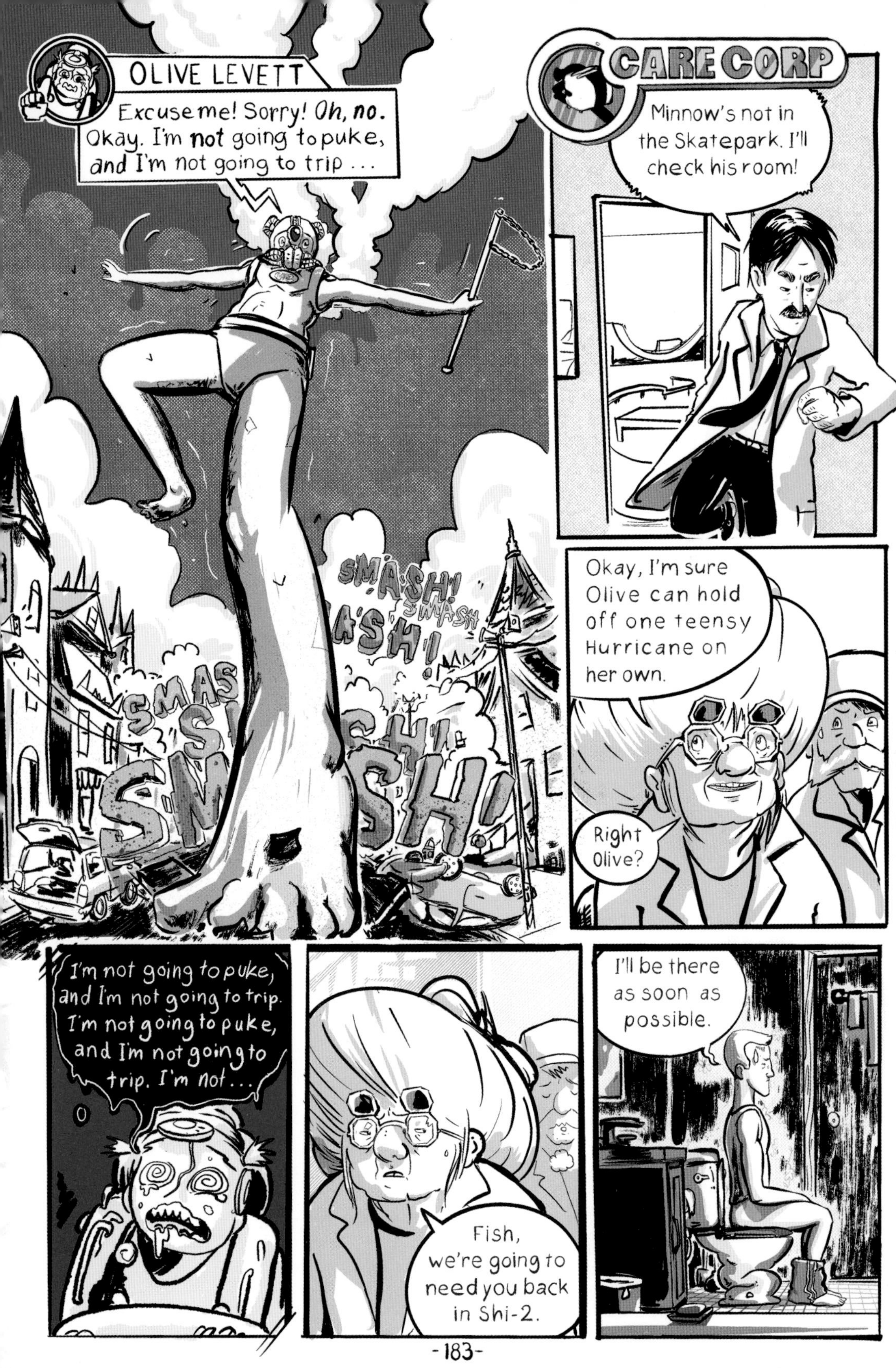
OLIVE LEVETT
Excuse me! Sorry! Oh, no. Okay. I'm not going to puke, and I'm not going to trip . . .
SMASH! SMASH SMASH! SMASH! SMASH!
CARE CORP
Minnow's not in the Skatepark. I'll check his room!
Okay, I'm sure Olive can hold off one teensy Hurricane on her own.
Right Olive?
I'm not going to puke, and I'm not going to trip. I'm not going to puke, and I'm not going to trip. I'm not . . .
Fish, we're going to need you back in Shi-2.
I'll be there as soon as possible.

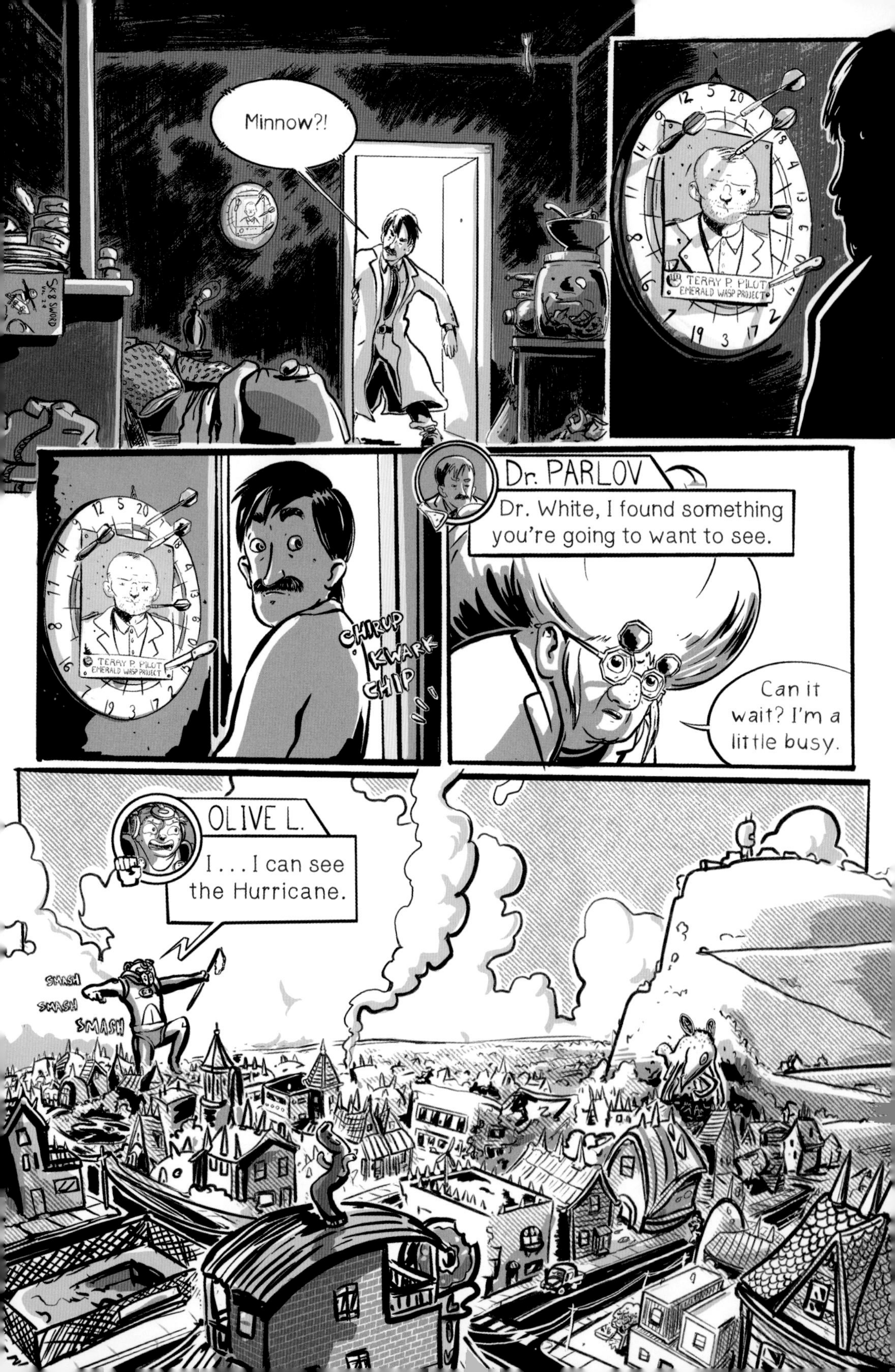
Minnow?!
TERRY P. PILOT
EMERALD WASP PROJECT
TERRY P. PILOT
EMERALD WASP PROJECT
CHIRUP
KWARK
CHIP
Dr. PARLOV
Dr. White, I found something you're going to want to see.
Can it wait? I'm a little busy.
OLIVE L.
I . . . I can see the Hurricane.
SMASH
SMASH
SMASH

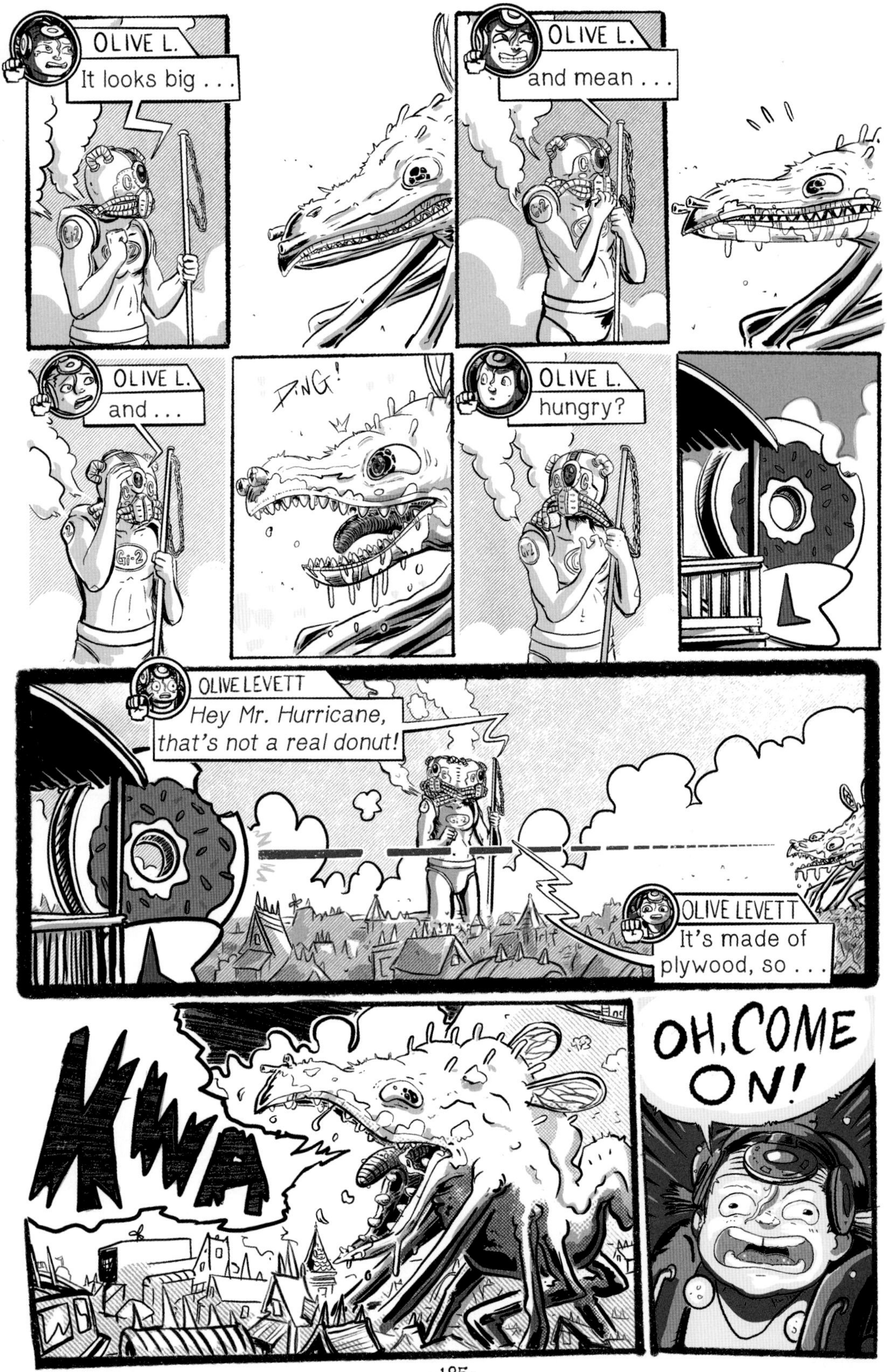
OLIVE L.
It looks big . . .
OLIVE L.
and mean . . .
OLIVE L.
and . . .
DING!
OLIVE L.
hungry?
OLIVE LEVETT
Hey Mr. Hurricane, that's not a real donut!
OLIVE LEVETT
It's made of plywood, so . . .
KWA
OH, COME ON!

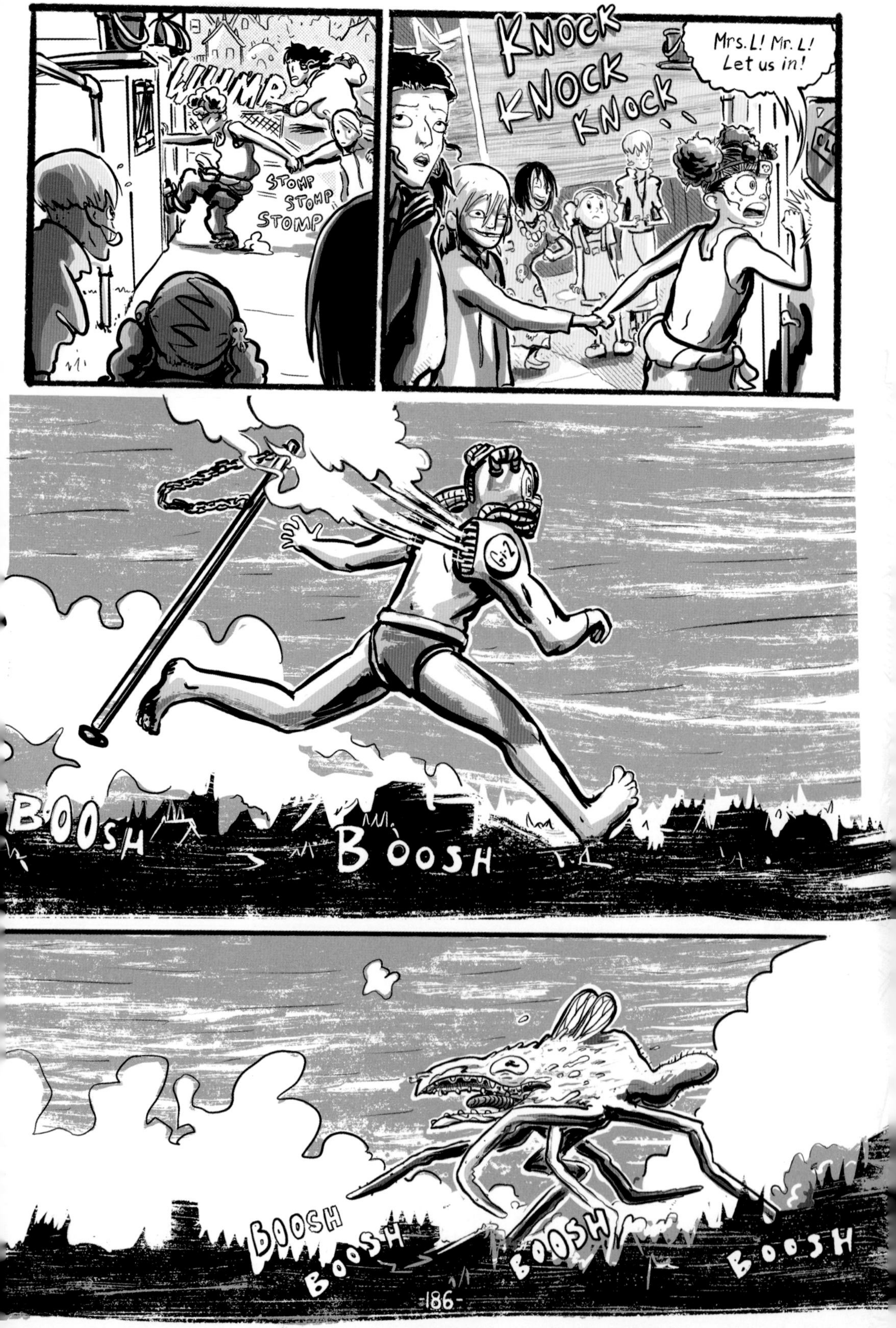
WHUMP
STOMP
STOMP
STOMP
KNOCK
KNOCK
KNOCK
Mrs. L! Mr. L! Let us in!
BOOSH
BOOSH
BOOSH
BOOSH
BOOSH
BOOSH

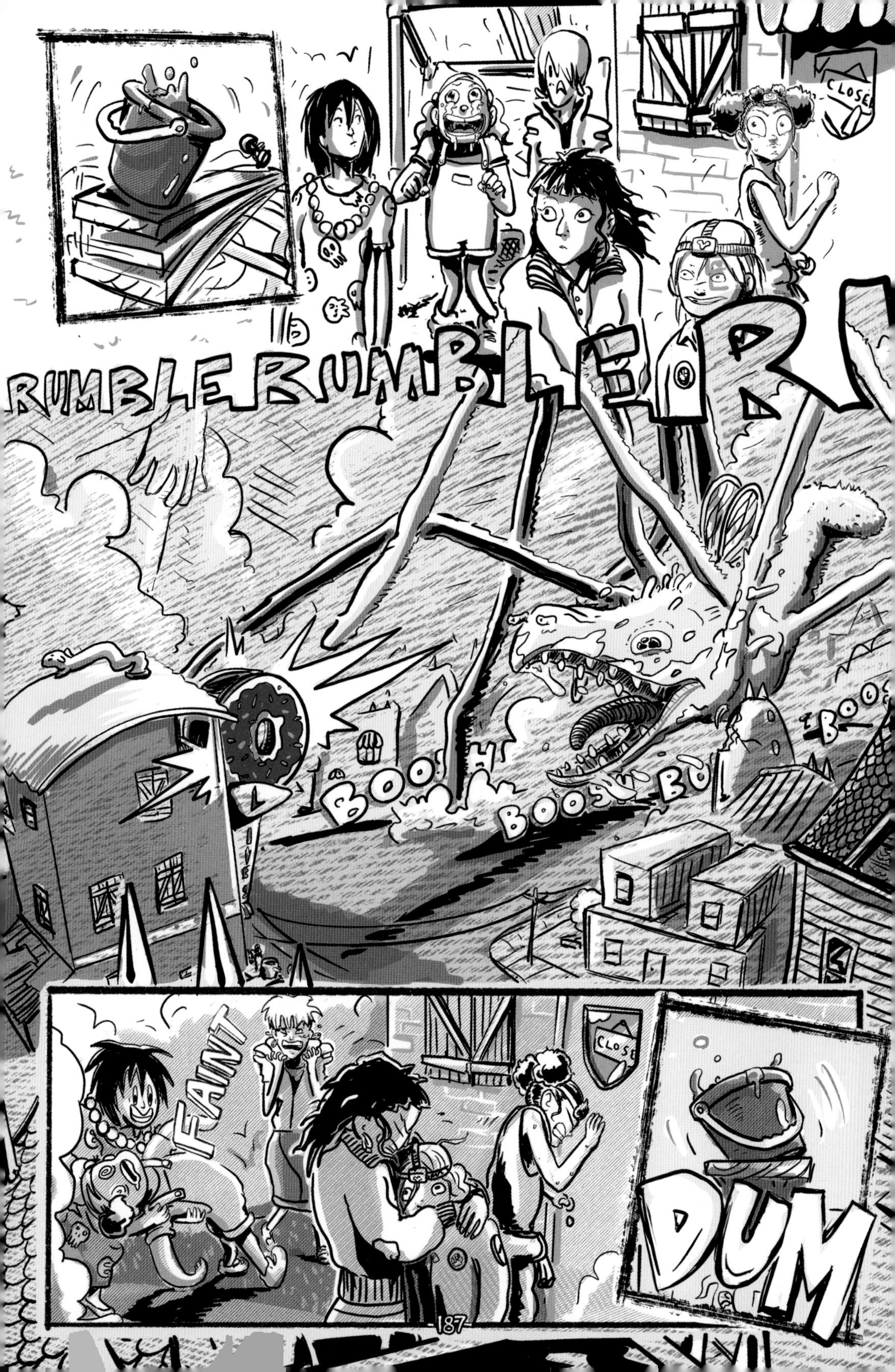

CLOSE
RUMBLERUMBLERU
BOOSH
BOOSH
BOOSH
BOO
FAINT
CLOSE
DUM

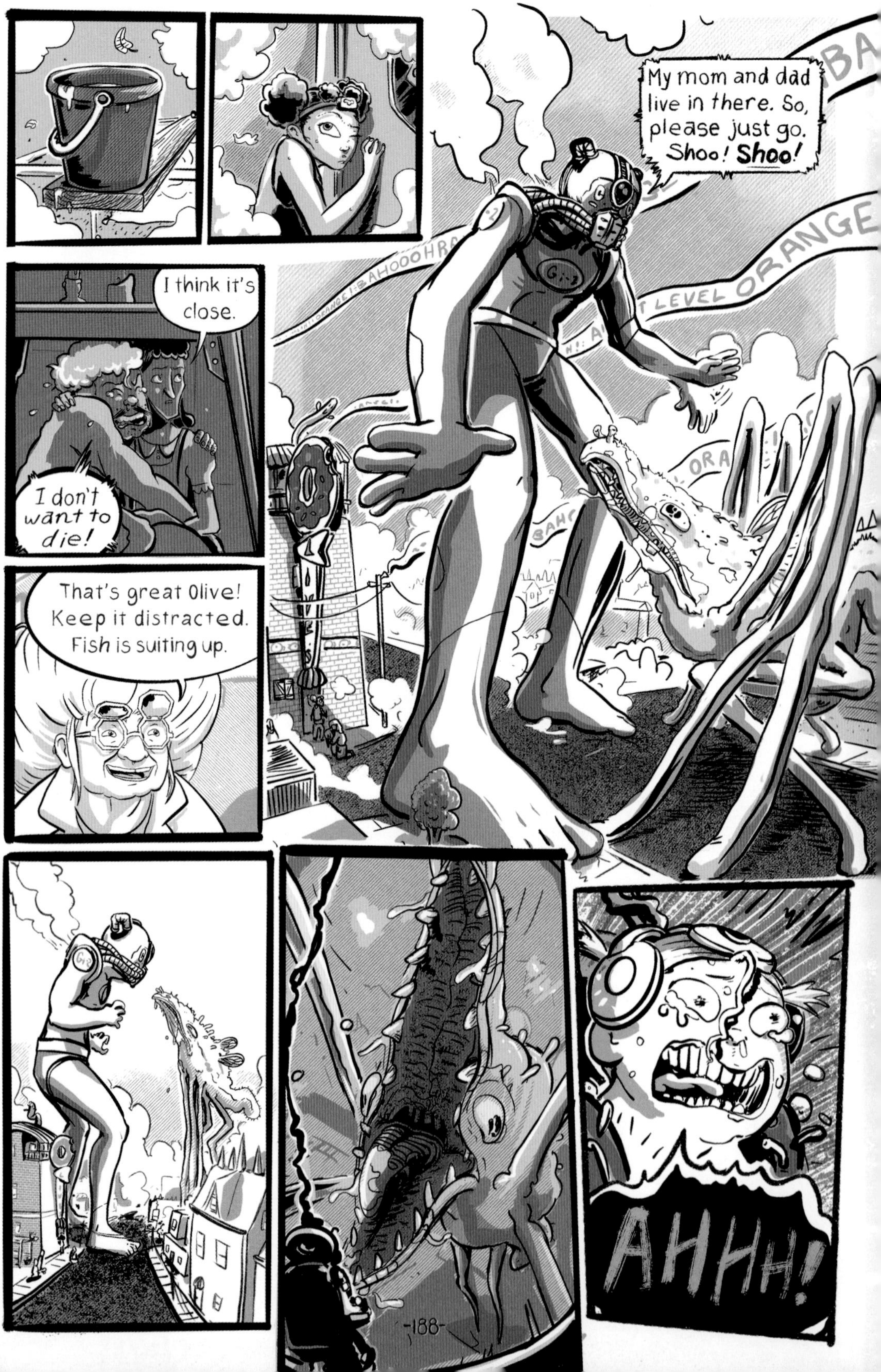
My mom and dad live in there. So, please just go. Shoo! **Shoo**!
I think it's close.
I don't want to die!
That's great Olive! Keep it distracted. Fish is suiting up.
AHHH!

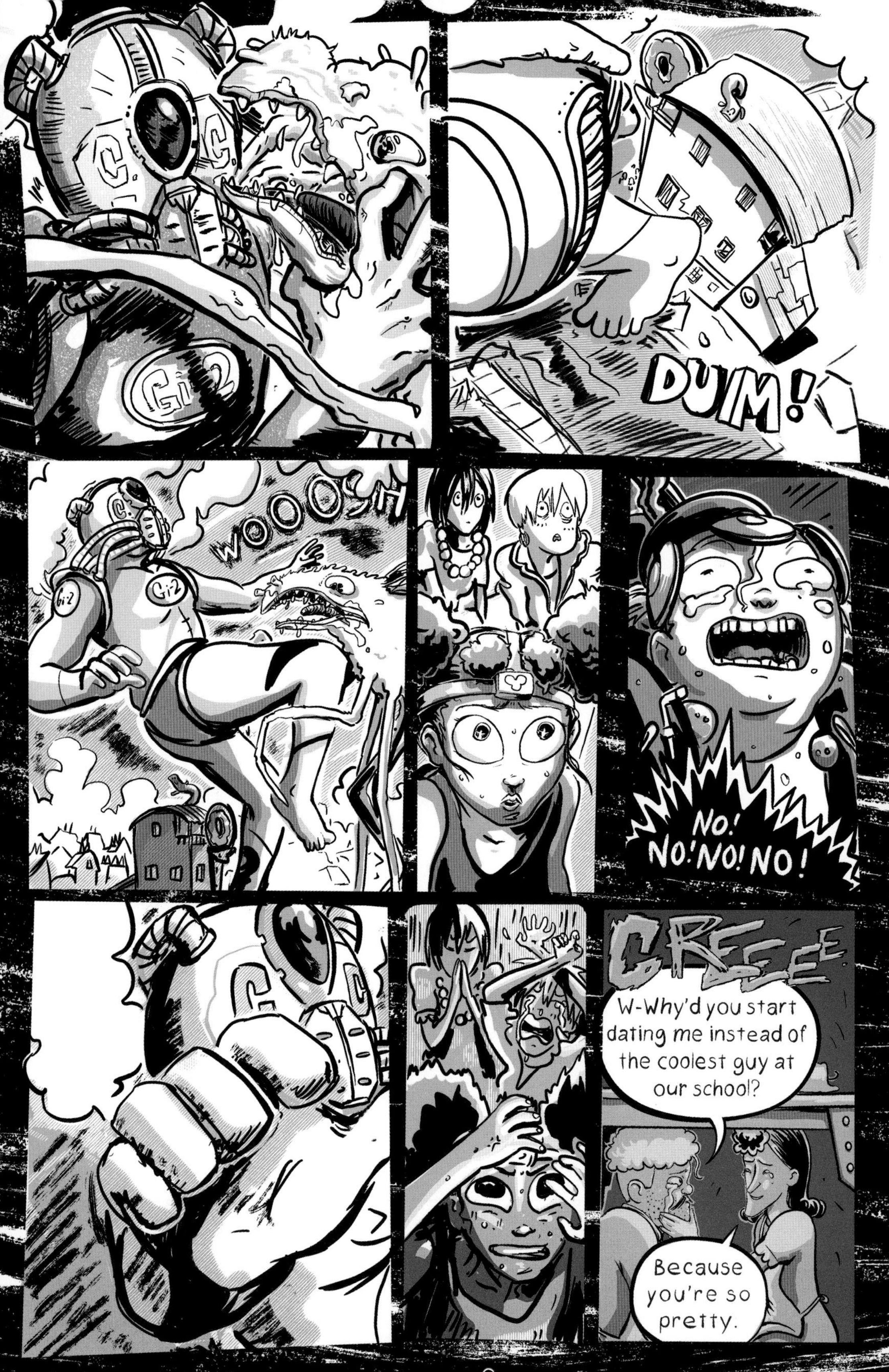
DUM!
WOOOOSH
NO!
NO! NO! NO!
CREEEE
W-Why'd you start dating me instead of the coolest guy at our school?
Because you're so pretty.

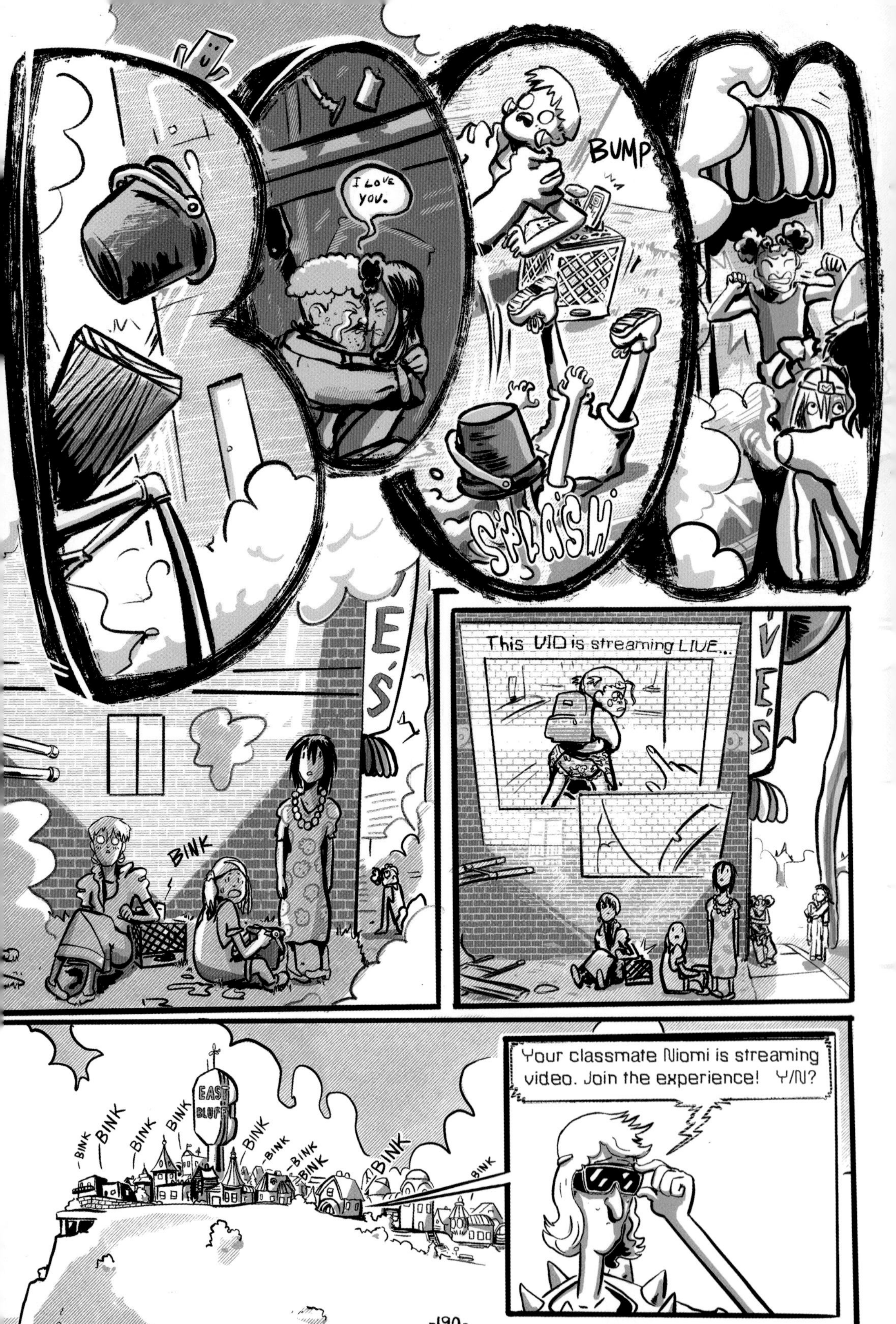
I LOVE YOU.
BUMP
SPLASH
This VID is streaming LIVE...
E'S
VE'S
BINK
EAST BLUFF
BINK
BINK
BINK
BINK
BINK
BINK
BINK
BINK
BINK
BINK
Your classmate Niomi is streaming video. Join the experience! Y/N?

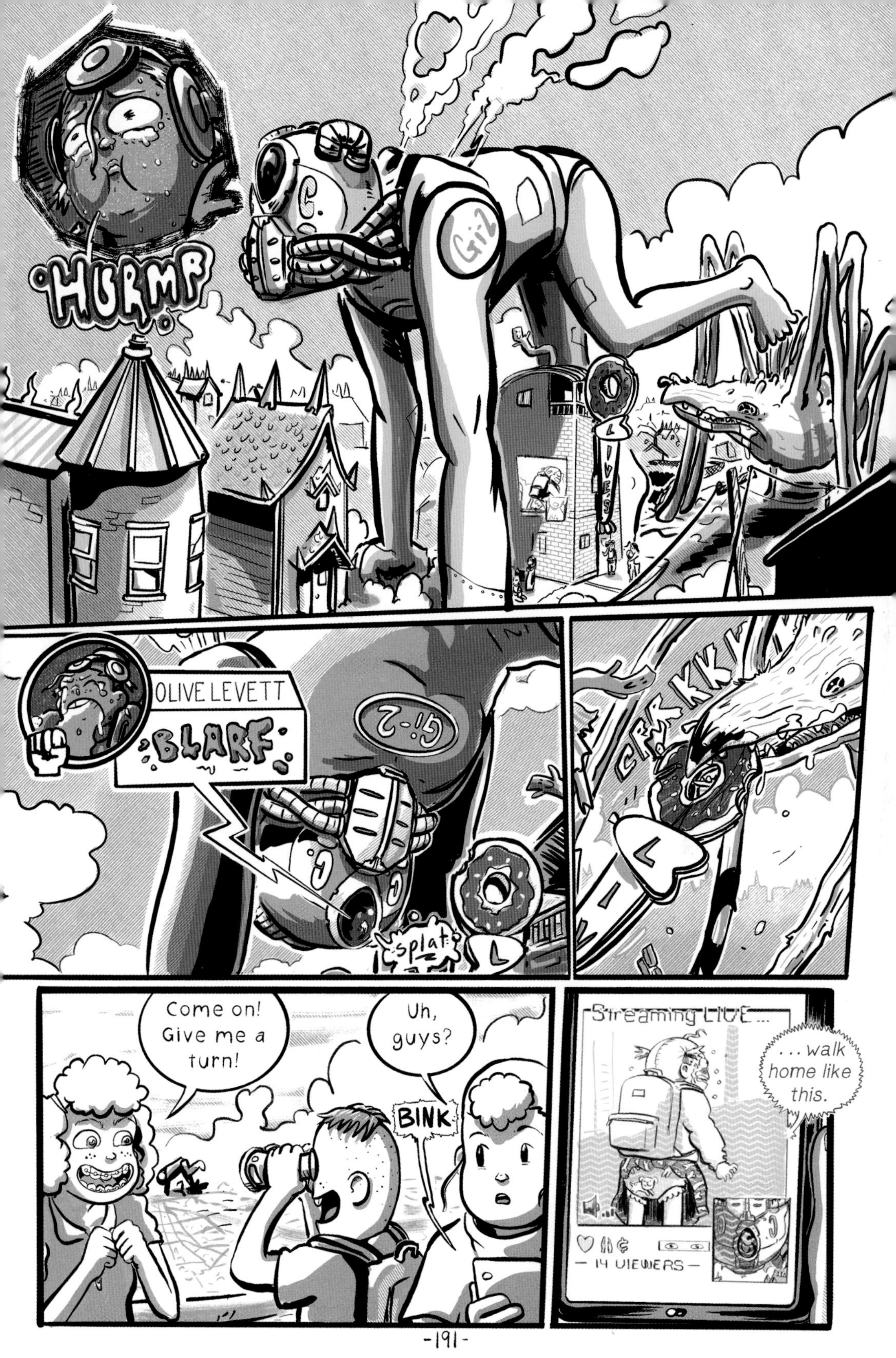

HURMP
OLIVE LEVETT
BLARF
splat
CRKKK
Come on! Give me a turn!
Uh, guys?
BINK
Streaming LIVE...
...walk home like this.
14 VIEWERS

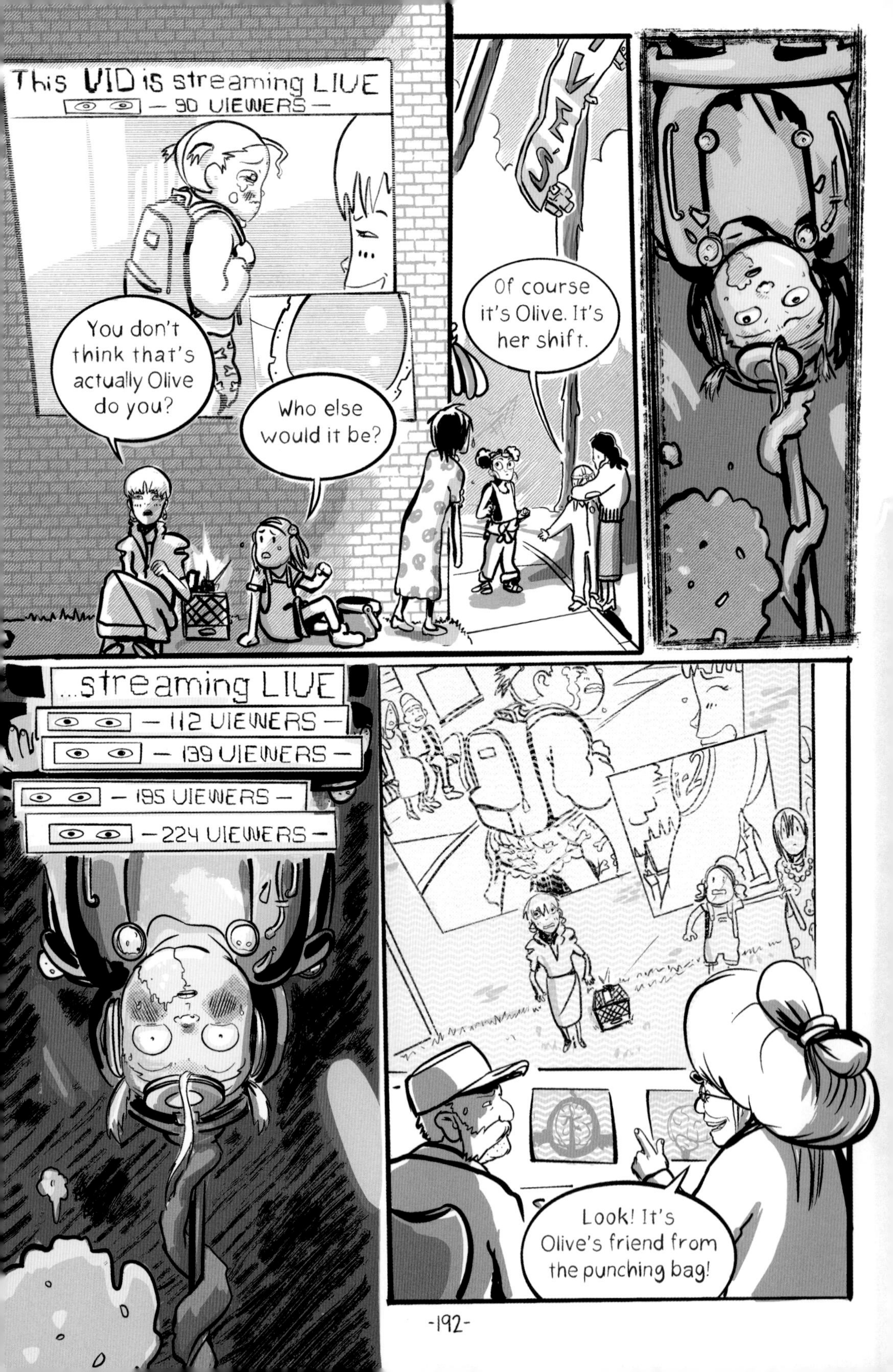
This VID is streaming LIVE
— 90 VIEWERS —
You don't think that's actually Olive do you?
Who else would it be?
Of course it's Olive. It's her shift.
...streaming LIVE
— 112 VIEWERS —
— 139 VIEWERS —
— 195 VIEWERS —
— 224 VIEWERS —
Look! It's Olive's friend from the punching bag!

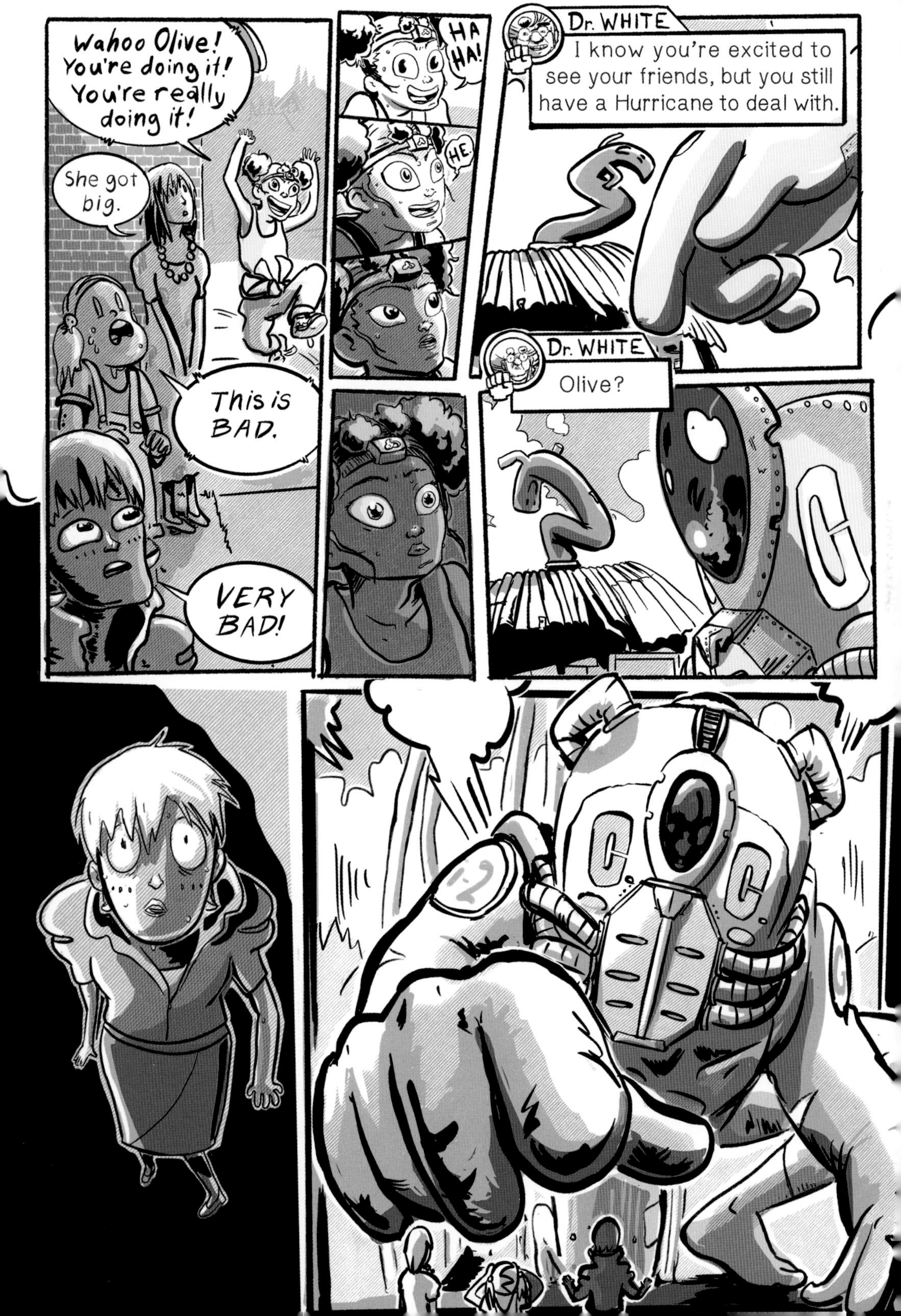

Wahoo Olive! You're doing it! You're really doing it!
She got big.
This is BAD.
VERY BAD!
HA HA!
HE.
Dr. WHITE
I know you're excited to see your friends, but you still have a Hurricane to deal with.
Dr. WHITE
Olive?

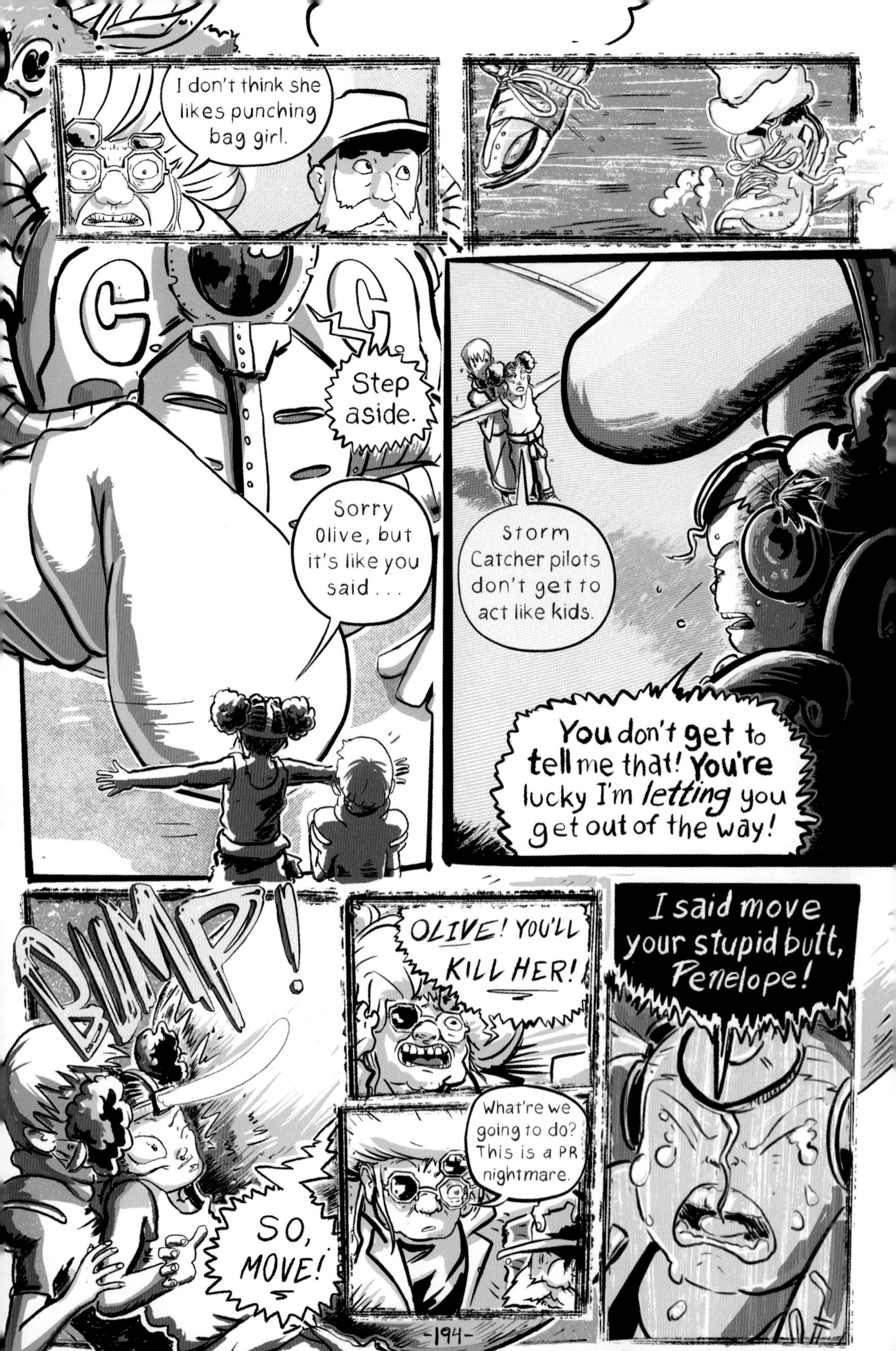
I don't think she likes punching bag girl.
Step aside.
Sorry Olive, but it's like you said . . .
Storm Catcher pilots don't get to act like kids.
You don't get to tell me that! You're lucky I'm *letting* you get out of the way!
BUMP!
SO, MOVE!
OLIVE! YOU'LL KILL HER!
What're we going to do? This is a PR nightmare.
I said move your stupid butt, Penelope!

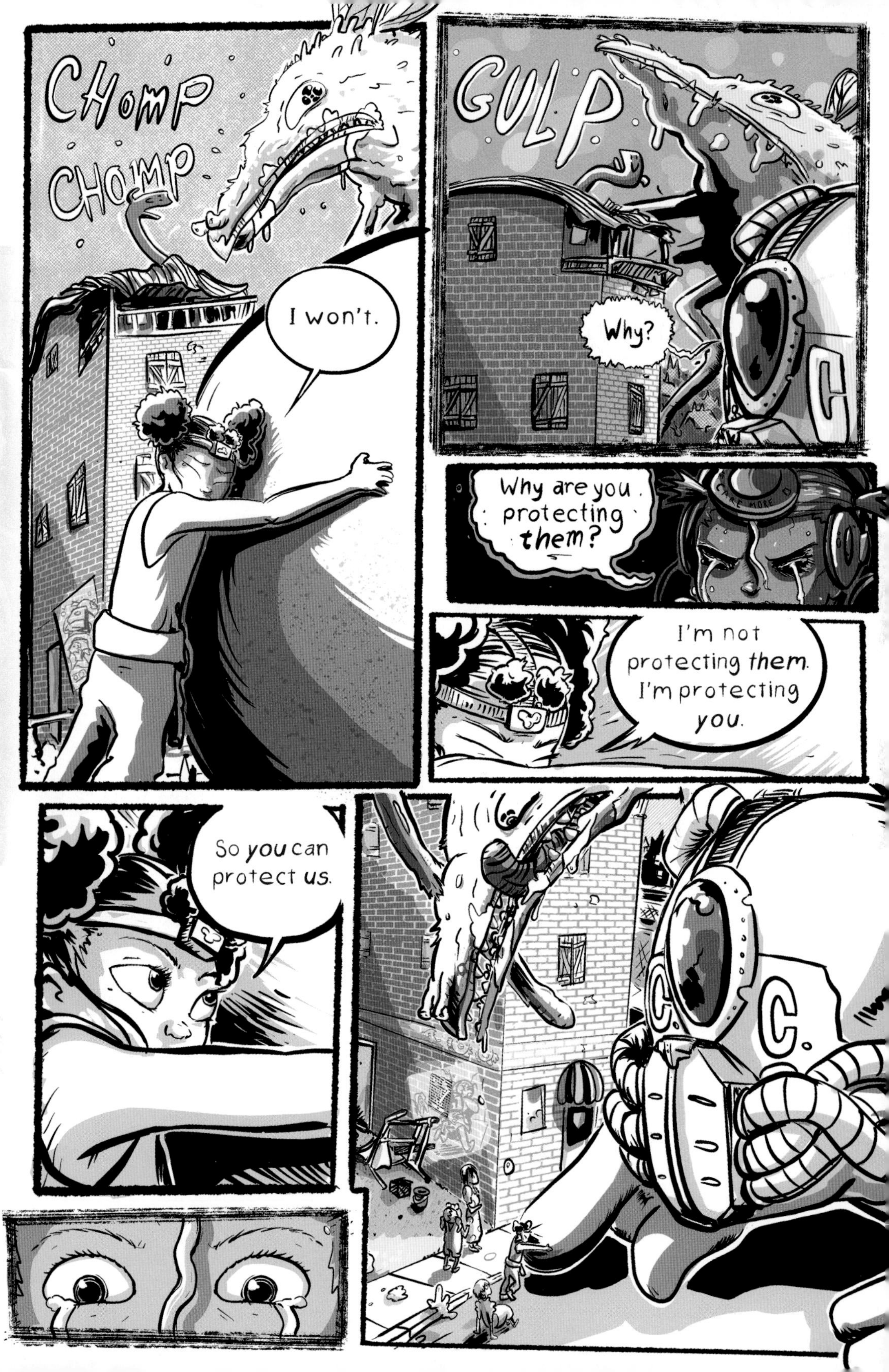
CHOMP
CHOMP
I won't.
GULP
Why?
Why are you protecting them?
CARE MORE
I'm not protecting them. I'm protecting you.
So you can protect us.
C
C.

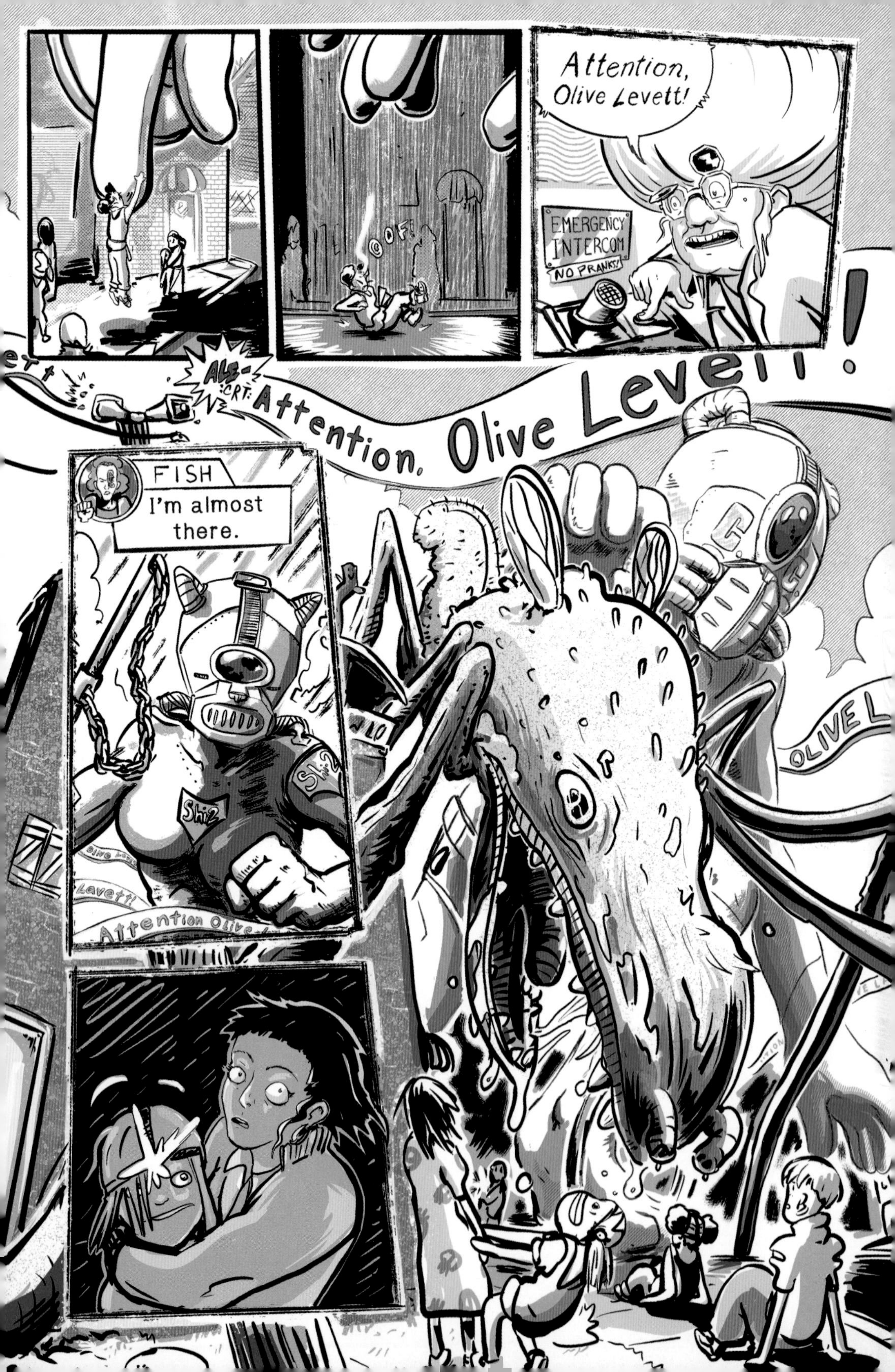

OOF!
Attention, Olive Levett!
EMERGENCY INTERCOM
NO PRANKS!
ALE- CRT: Attention, Olive Leve
FISH
I'm almost there.
Shi2
Shi2
Lavett!
Attention Olive
OLIVE L

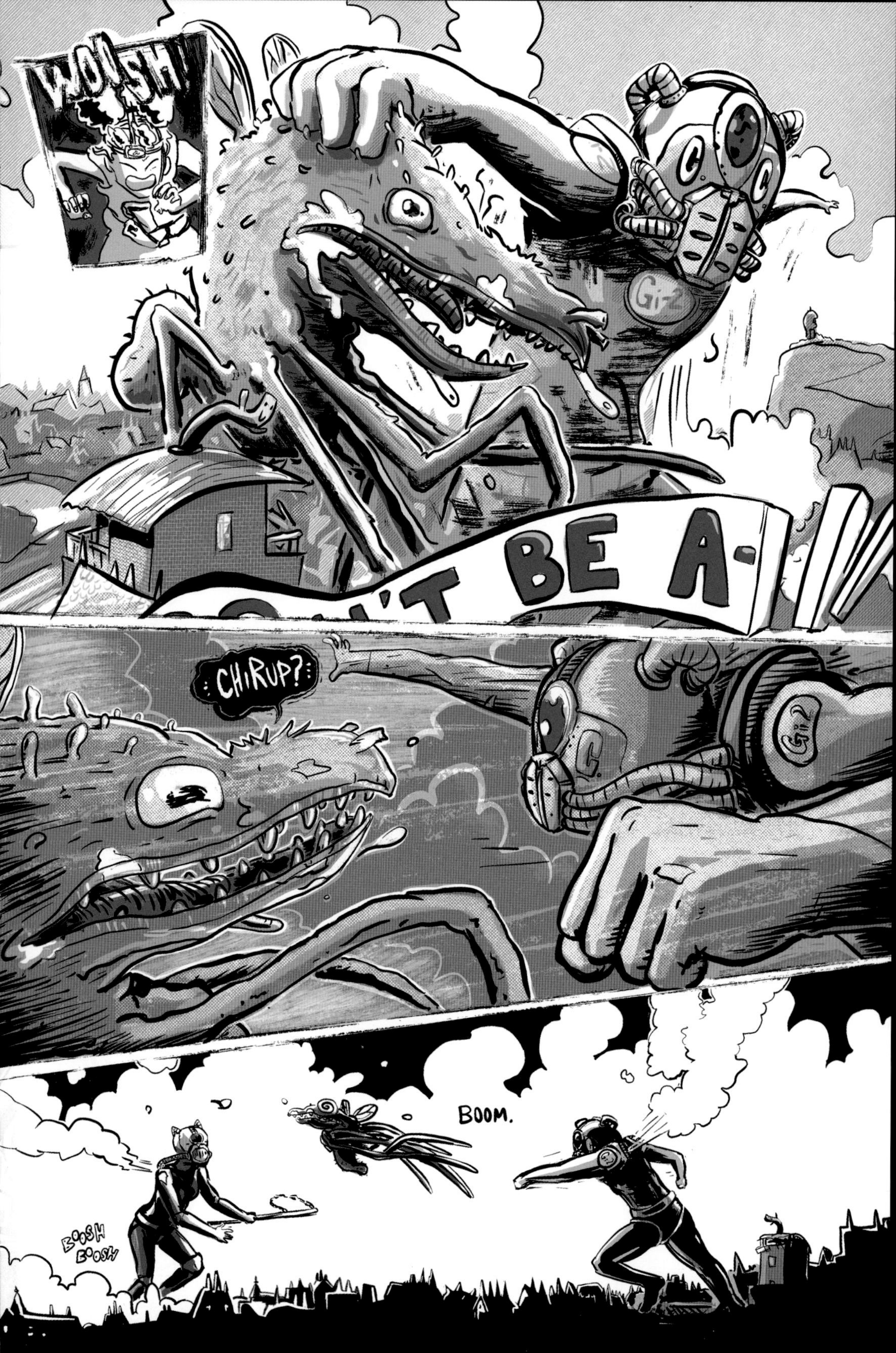
WOOSH!
'T BE A-
CHIRUP?
BOOM.
BOOSH BOOSH

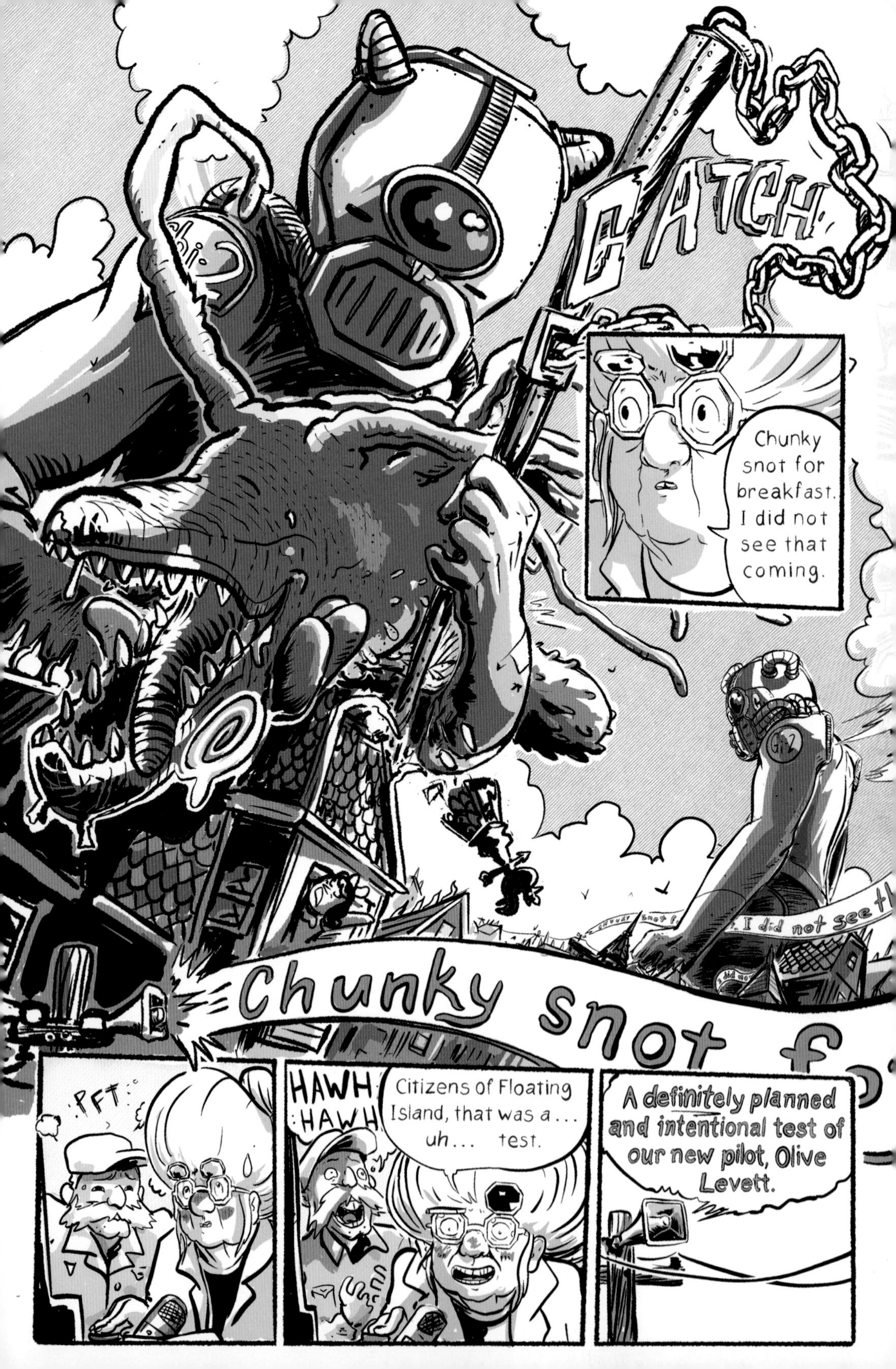
CATCH
Chunky snot for breakfast. I did not see that coming.
Chunky snot f
PFT
HAWH HAWH
Citizens of Floating Island, that was a . . . uh . . . test.
A definitely planned and intentional test of our new pilot, Olive Levett.

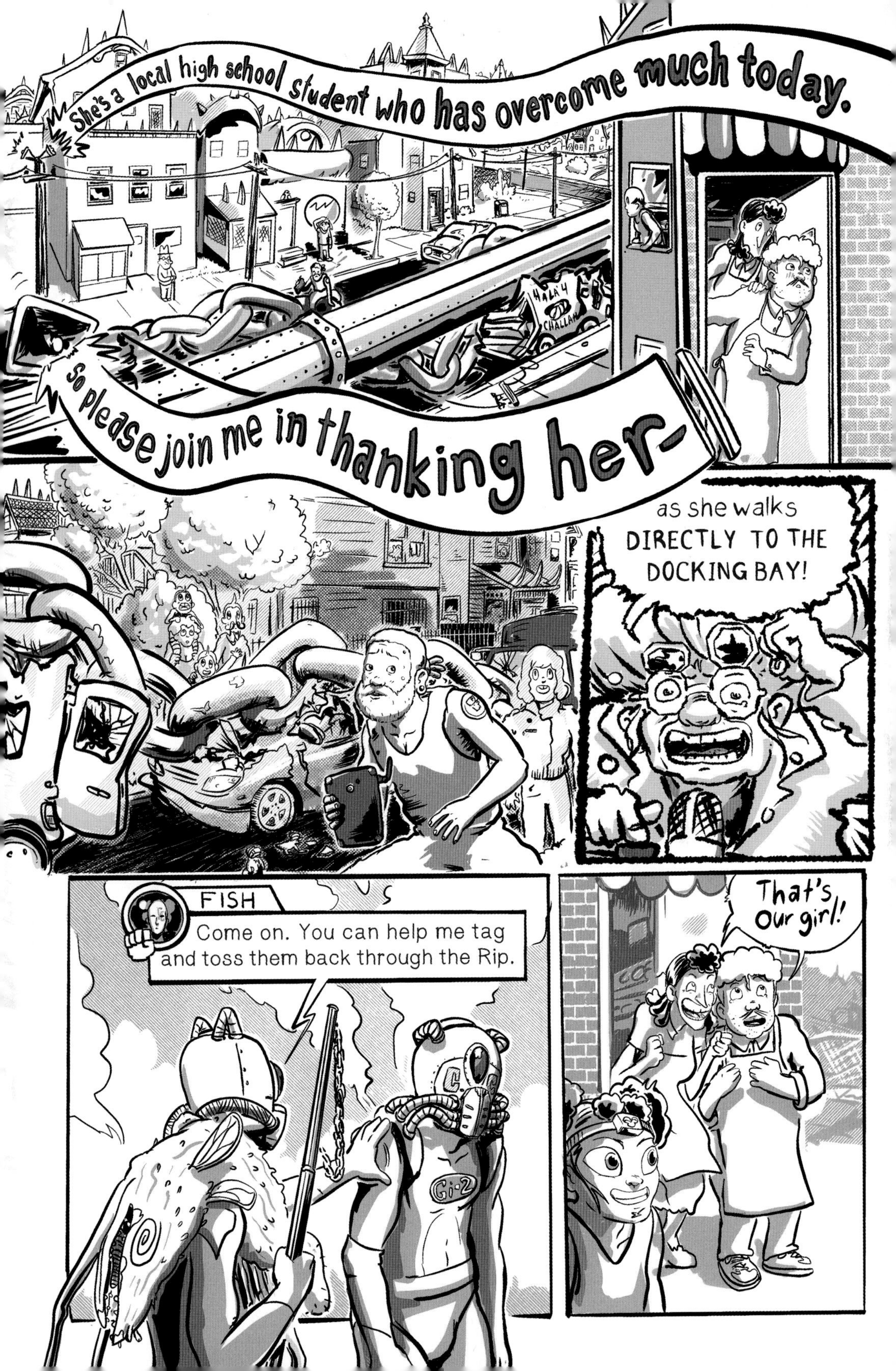

She's a local high school student who has overcome much today.
So please join me in thanking her-
as she walks DIRECTLY TO THE DOCKING BAY!
FISH
Come on. You can help me tag and toss them back through the Rip.
That's our girl!

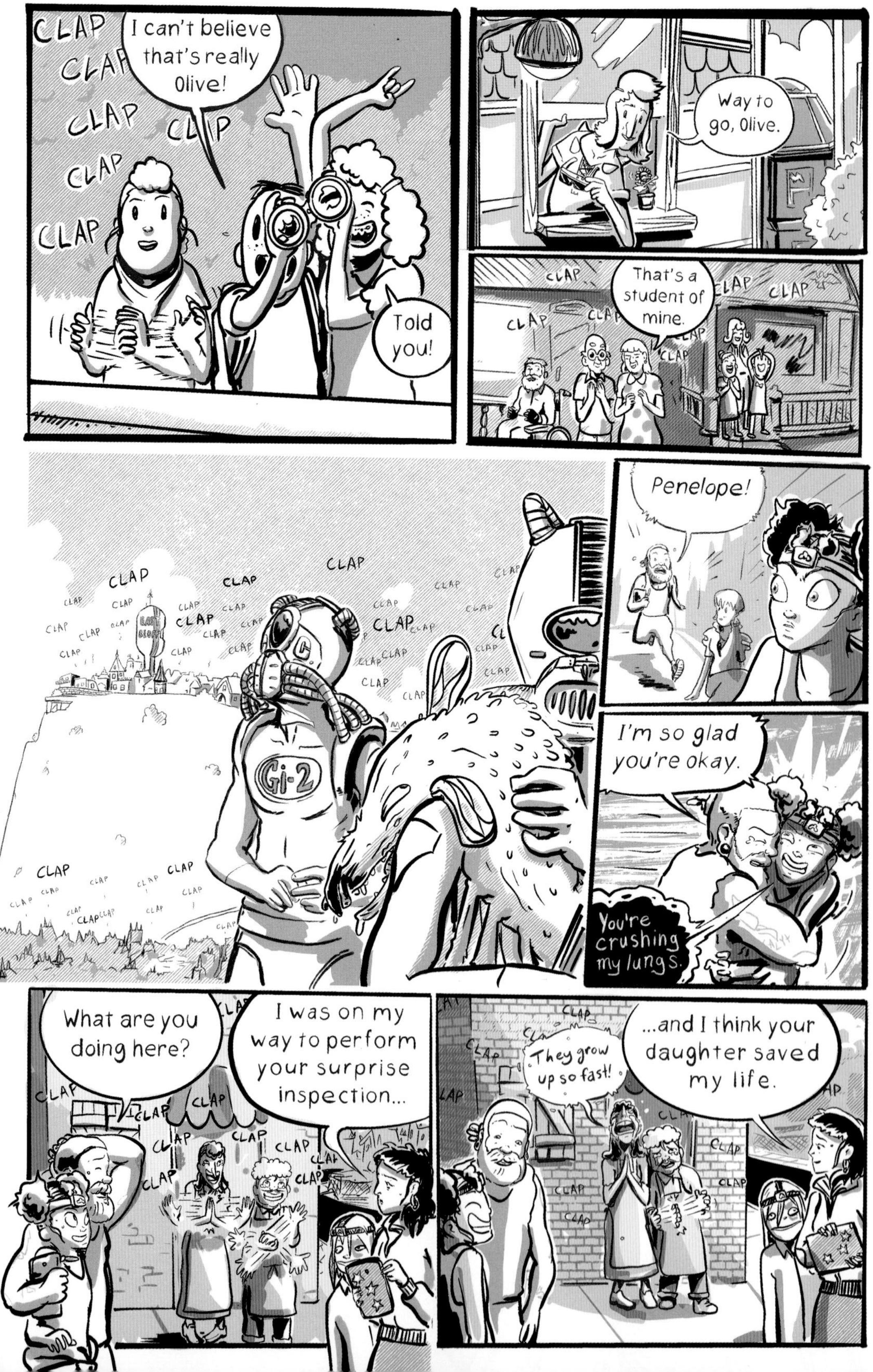

CLAP CLAP CLAP CLAP CLAP CLAP
I can't believe that's really Olive!
Told you!
Way to go, Olive.
CLAP CLAP CLAP CLAP CLAP
That's a student of mine.
CLAP
Gi-2
Penelope!
I'm so glad you're okay.
You're crushing my lungs.
What are you doing here?
I was on my way to perform your surprise inspection...
CLAP CLAP CLAP CLAP
They grow up so fast!
...and I think your daughter saved my life.

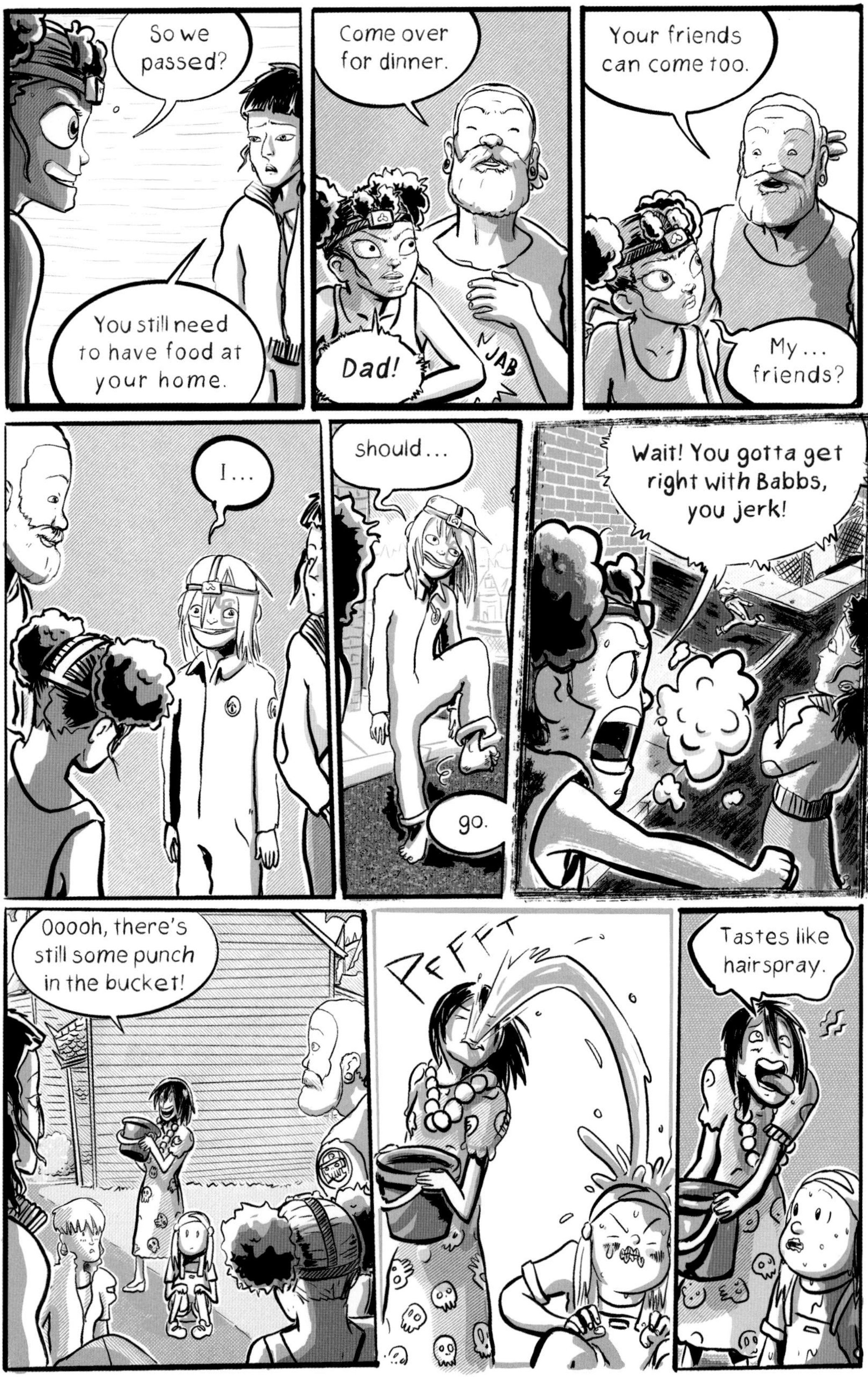
So we passed?
You still need to have food at your home.
Come over for dinner.
Dad!
JAB
Your friends can come too.
My... friends?
I...
should...
go.
Wait! You gotta get right with Babbs, you jerk!
Ooooh, there's still some punch in the bucket!
PFFFT
Tastes like hairspray.

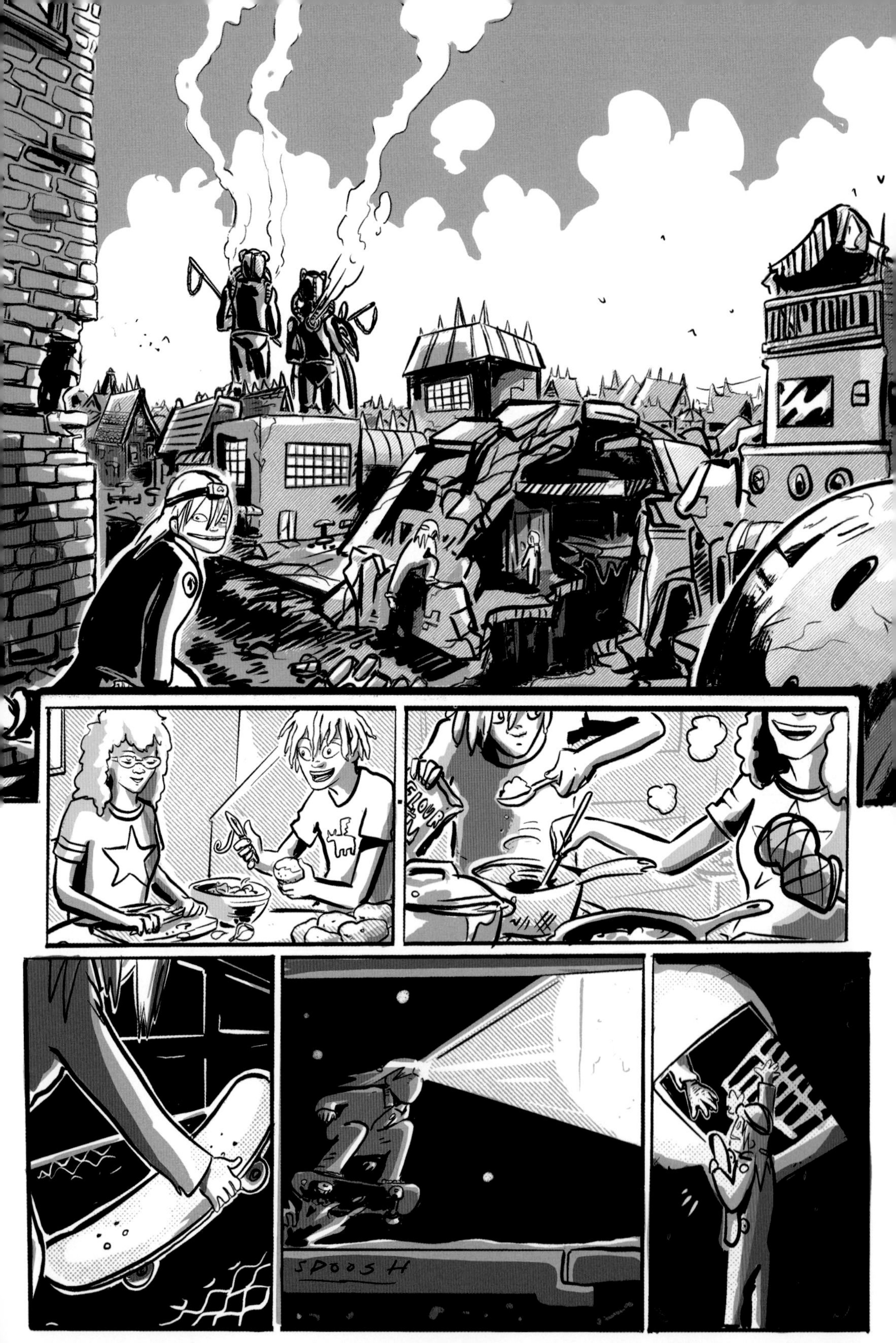
FLOUR
SPOOSH

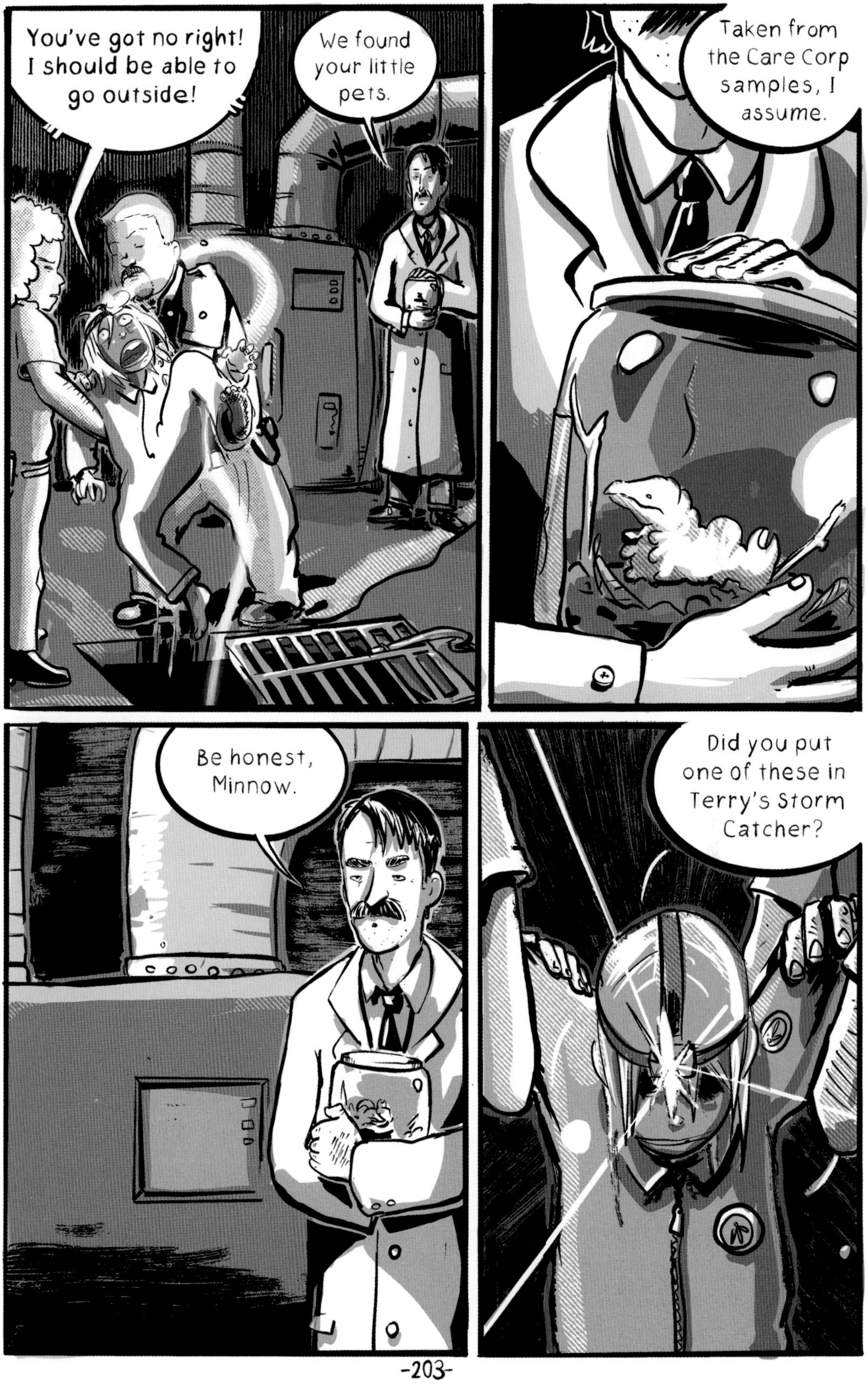
You've got no right! I should be able to go outside!
We found your little pets.
Taken from the Care Corp samples, I assume.
Be honest, Minnow.
Did you put one of these in Terry's Storm Catcher?

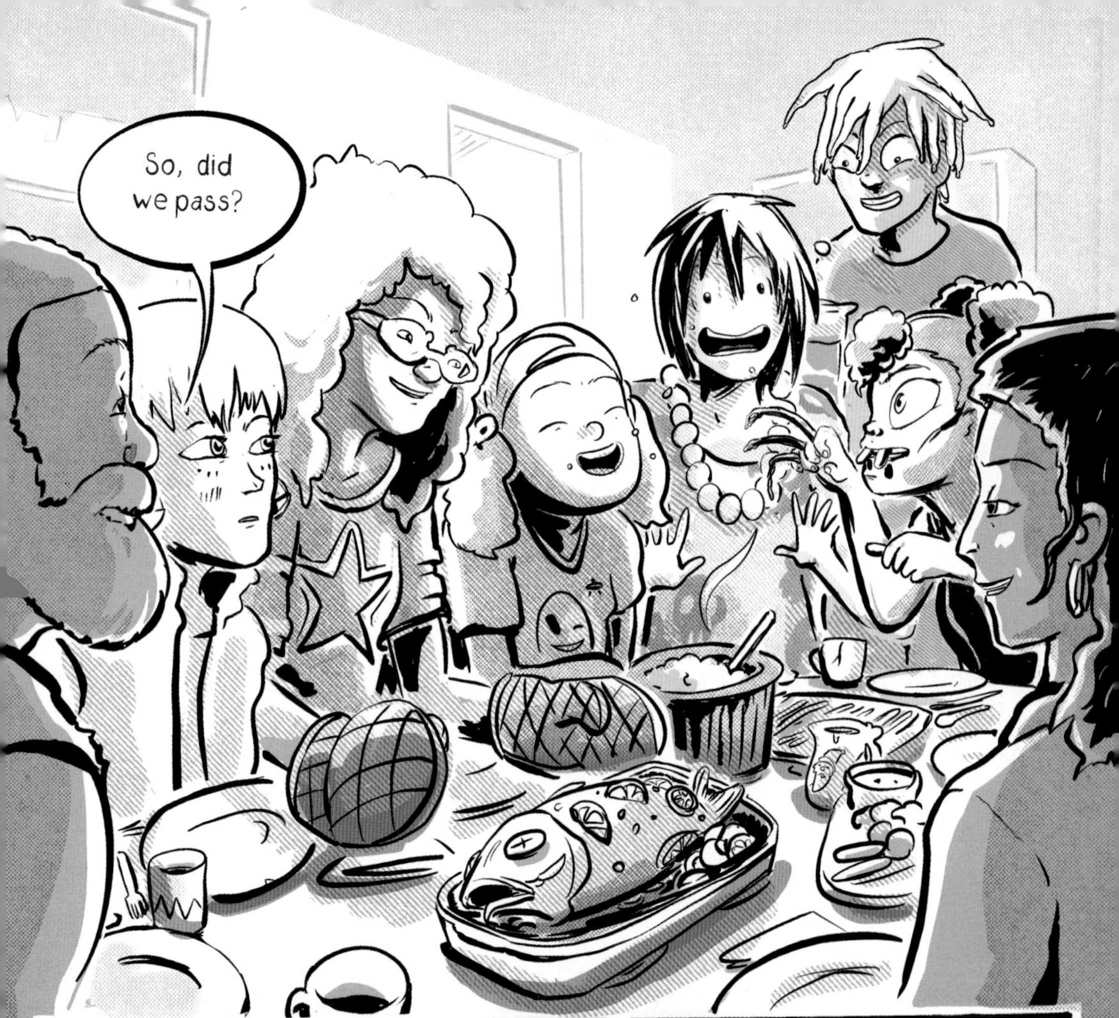
So, did we pass?

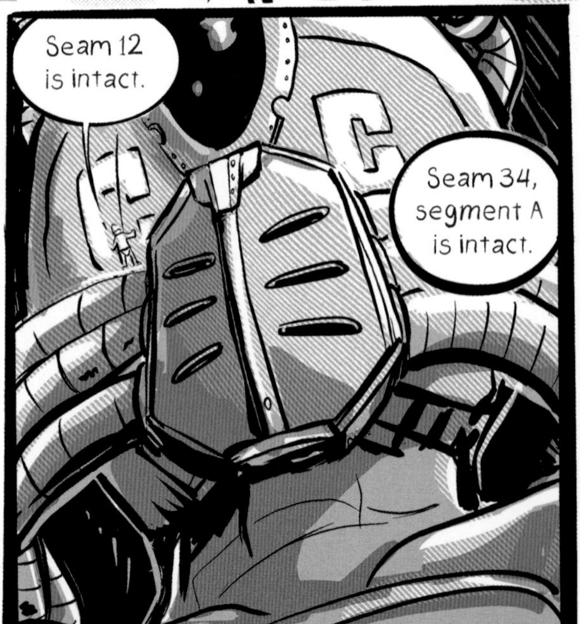
Seam 12 is intact.
Seam 34, segment A is intact.

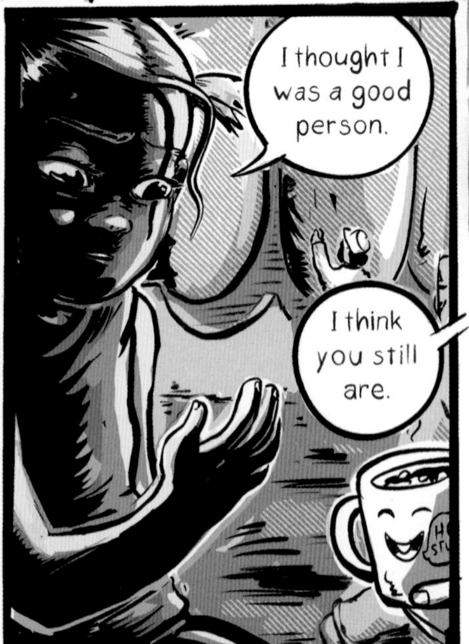
I thought I was a good person.
I think you still are.

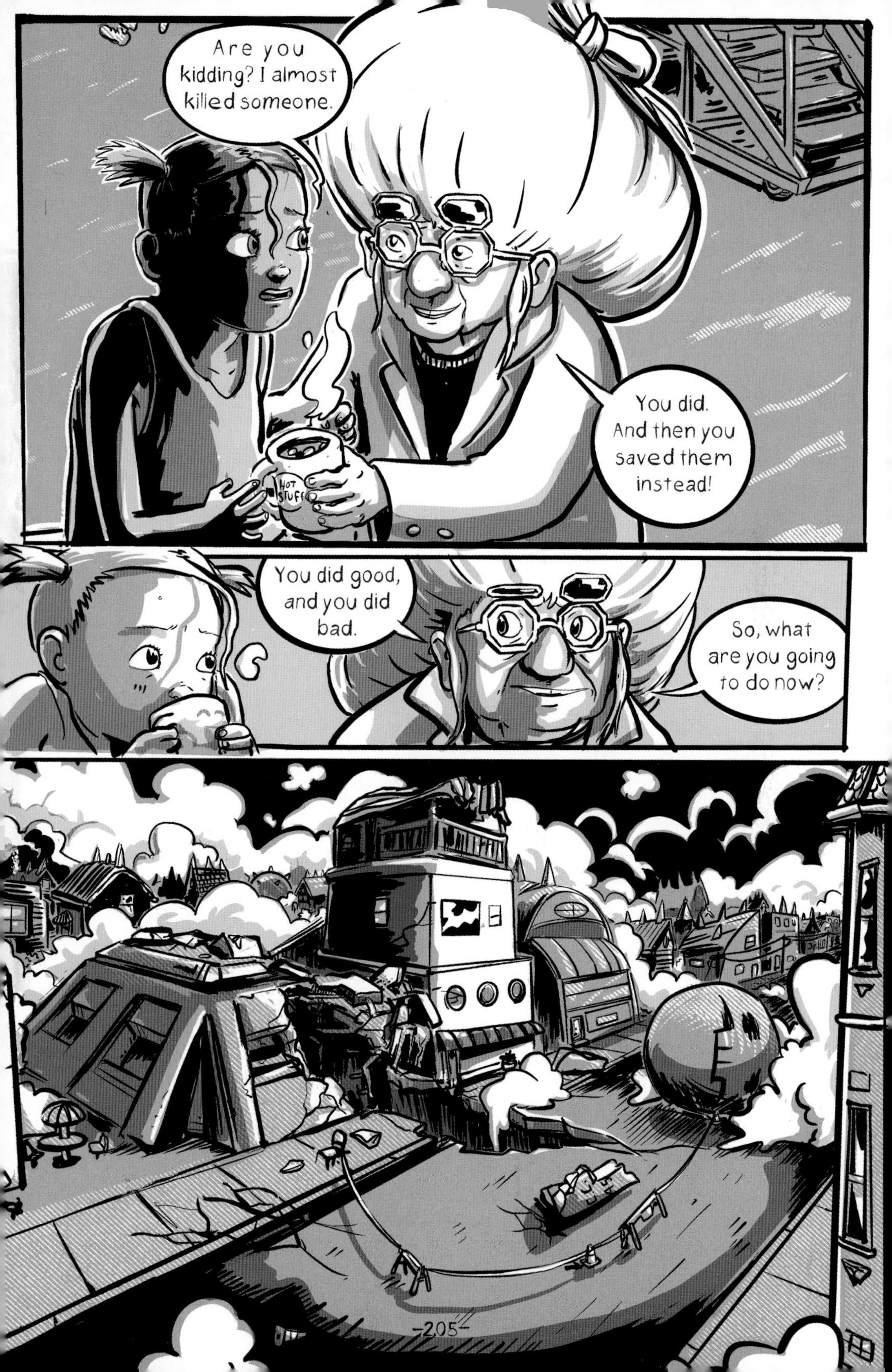
Are you kidding? I almost killed someone.
You did. And then you saved them instead!
HOT STUFF
You did good, and you did bad.
So, what are you going to do now?

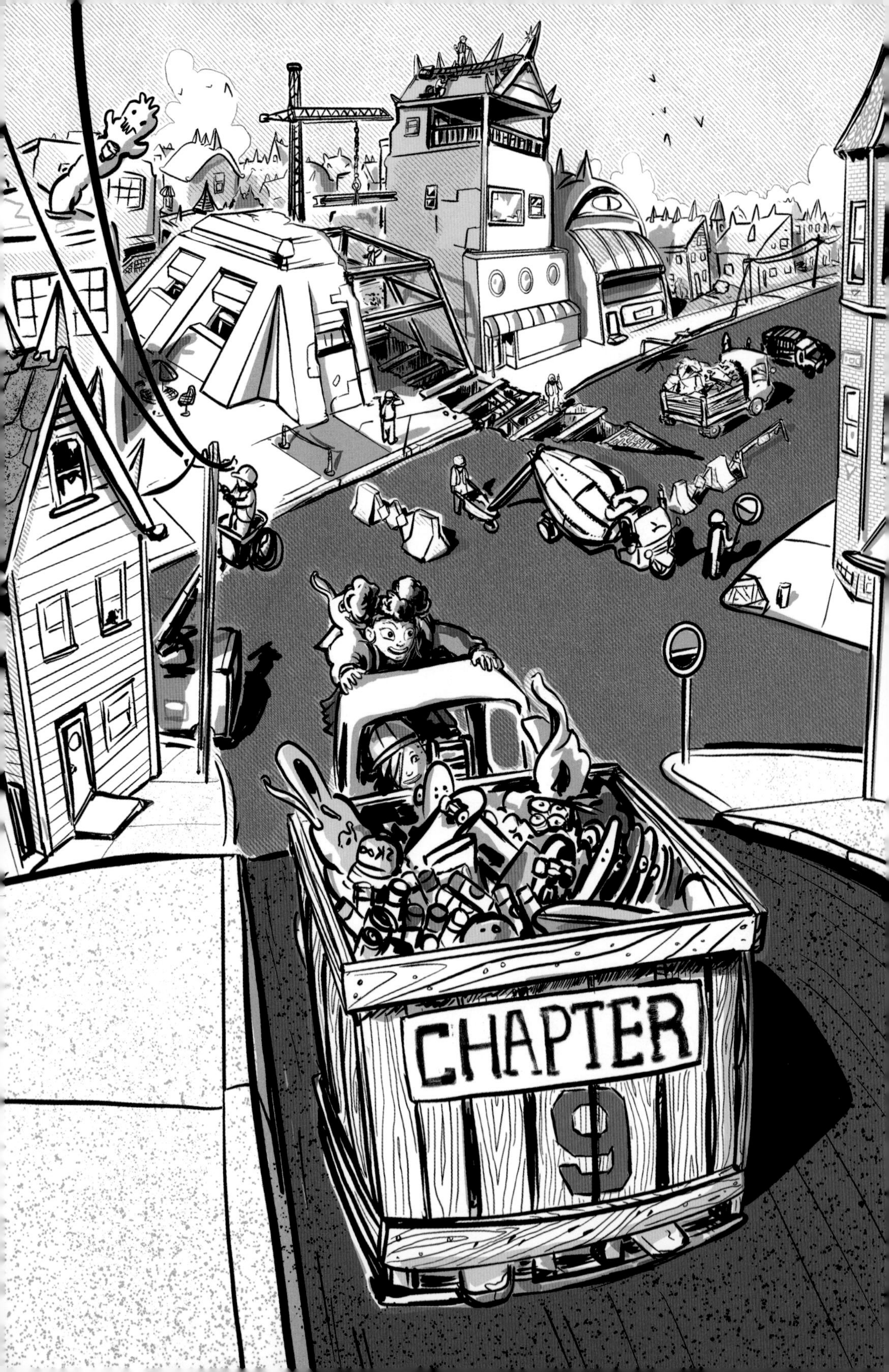
CHAPTER
9

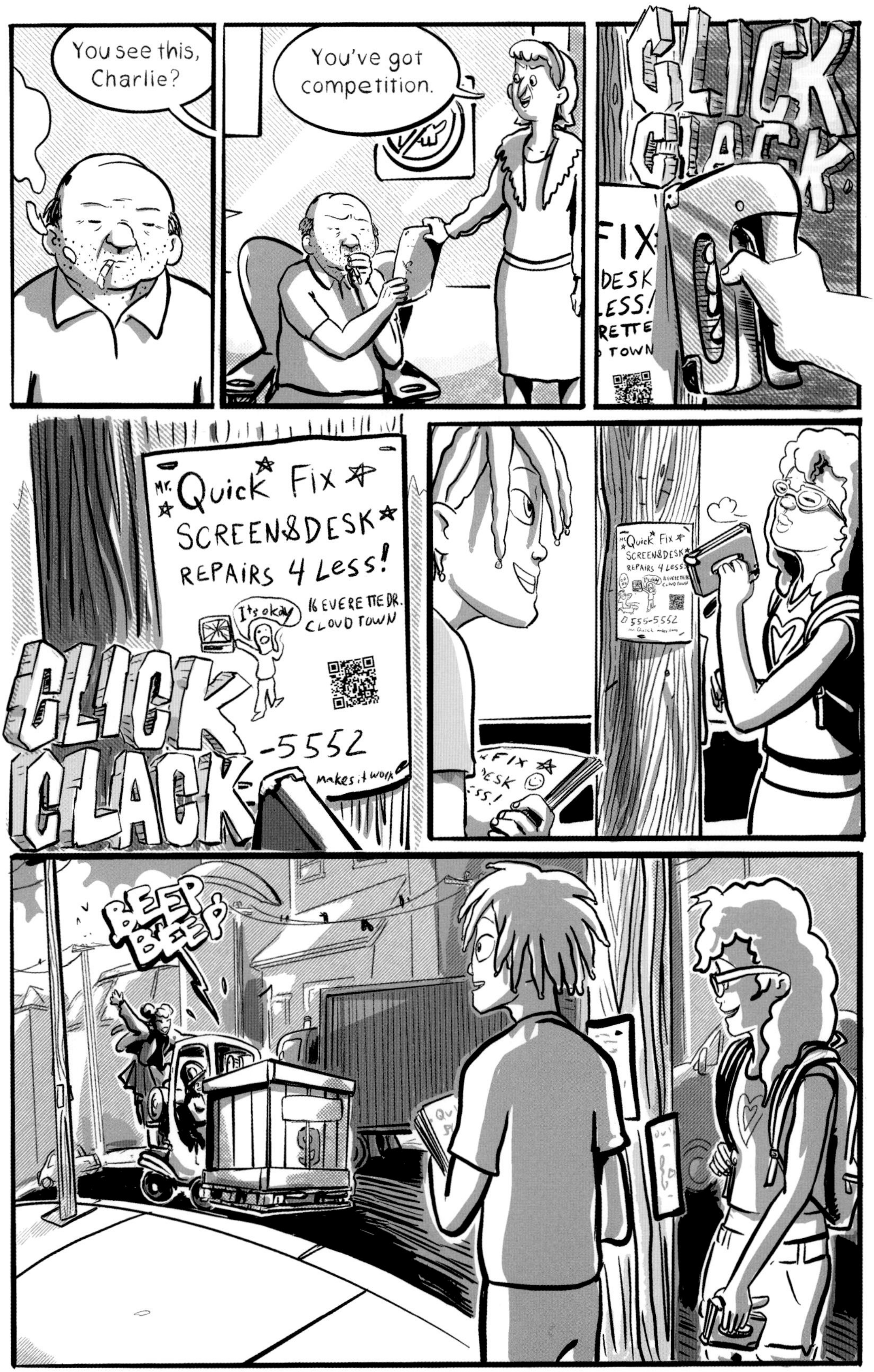
You see this, Charlie?
You've got competition.
CLICK CLACK
Mr. Quick Fix
SCREEN&DESK
REPAIRS 4 Less!
It's okay
16 EVERETTE DR.
CLOUD TOWN
-5552
makes it work
CLICK CLACK
555-5552
BEEP BEEP

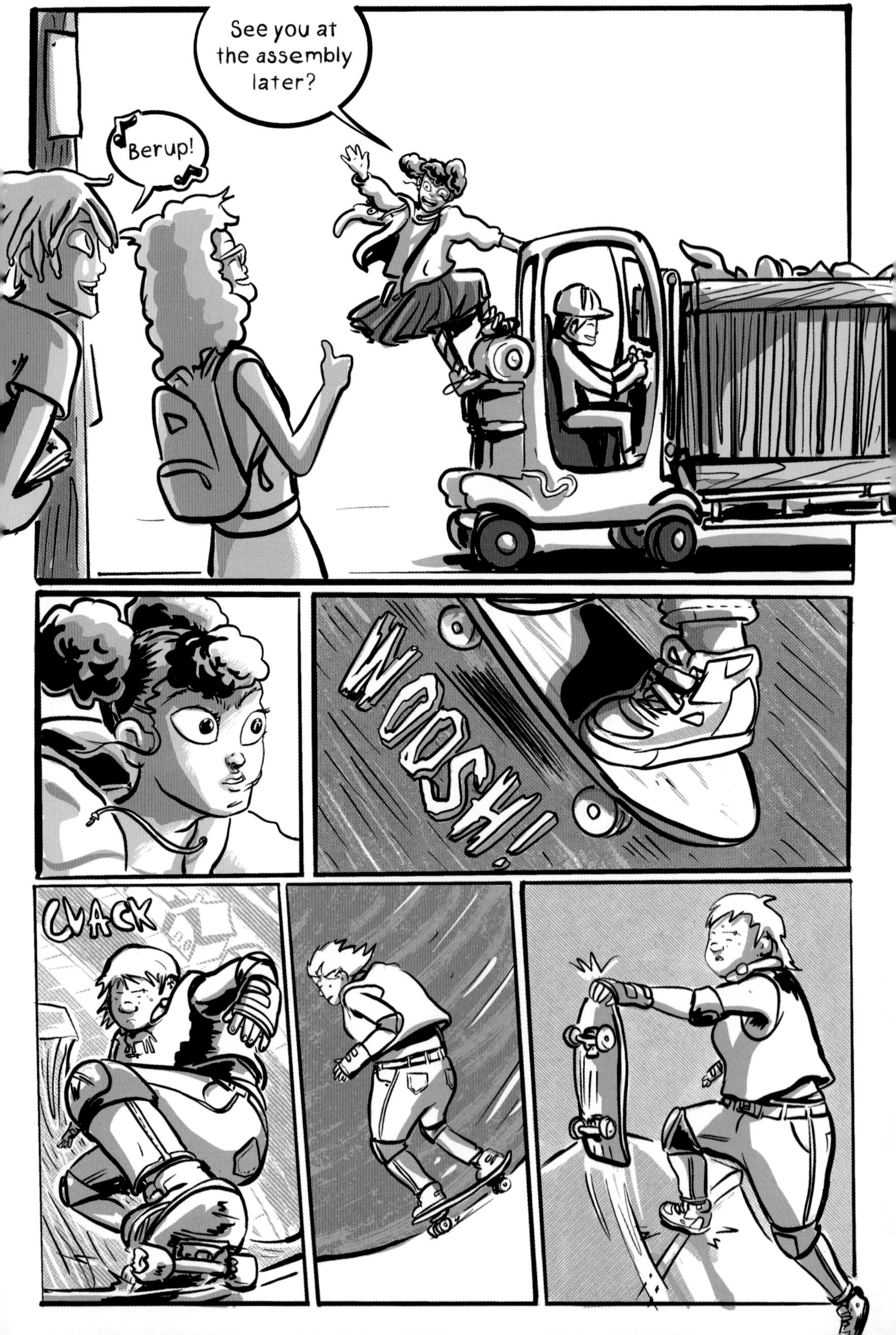
See you at the assembly later?
Berup!
WOOSH!
CLACK

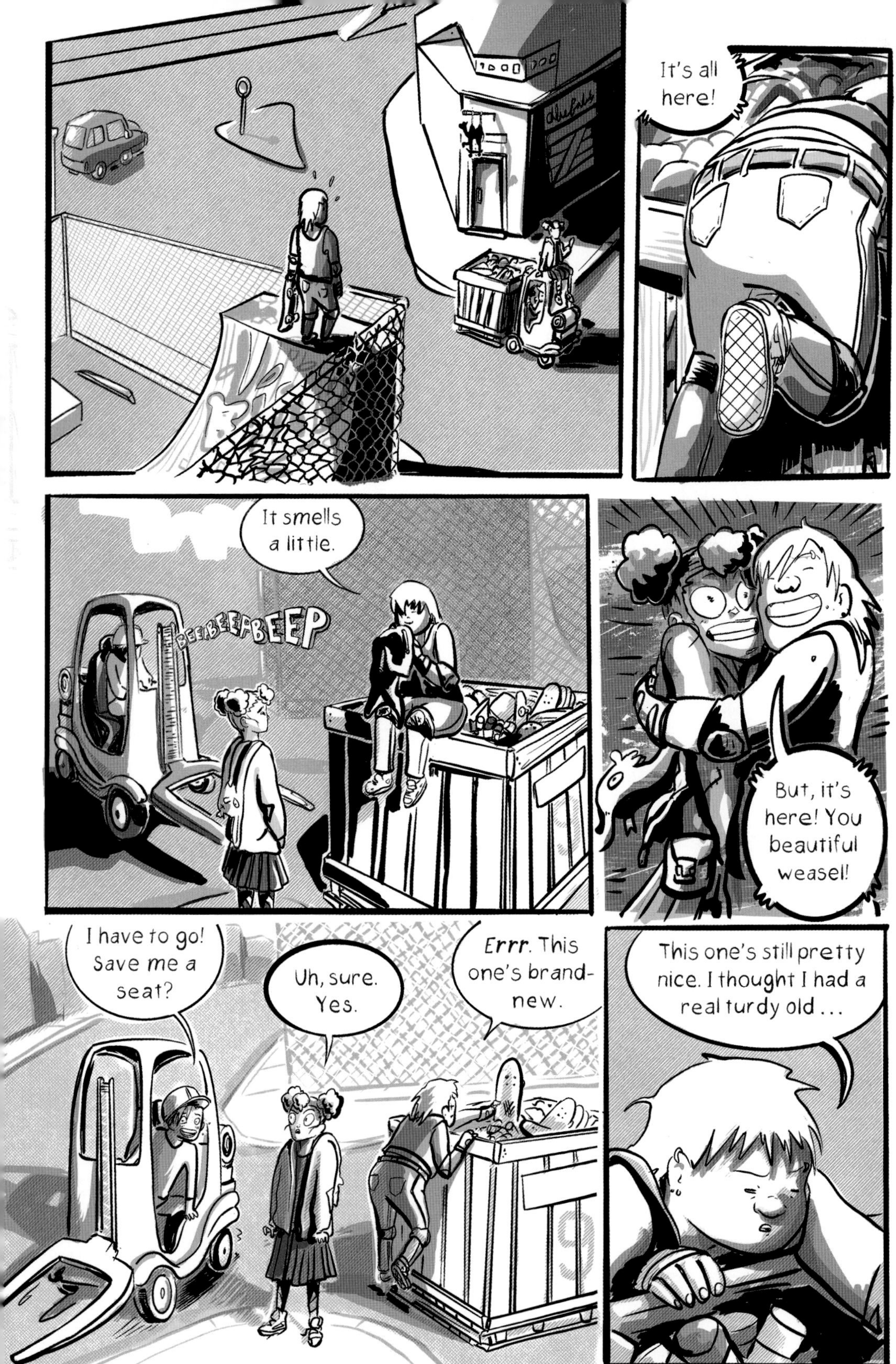
It's all here!
It smells a little.
BEEPBEEPBEEP
But, it's here! You beautiful weasel!
I have to go! Save me a seat?
Uh, sure. Yes.
Errr. This one's brand-new.
This one's still pretty nice. I thought I had a real turdy old . . .

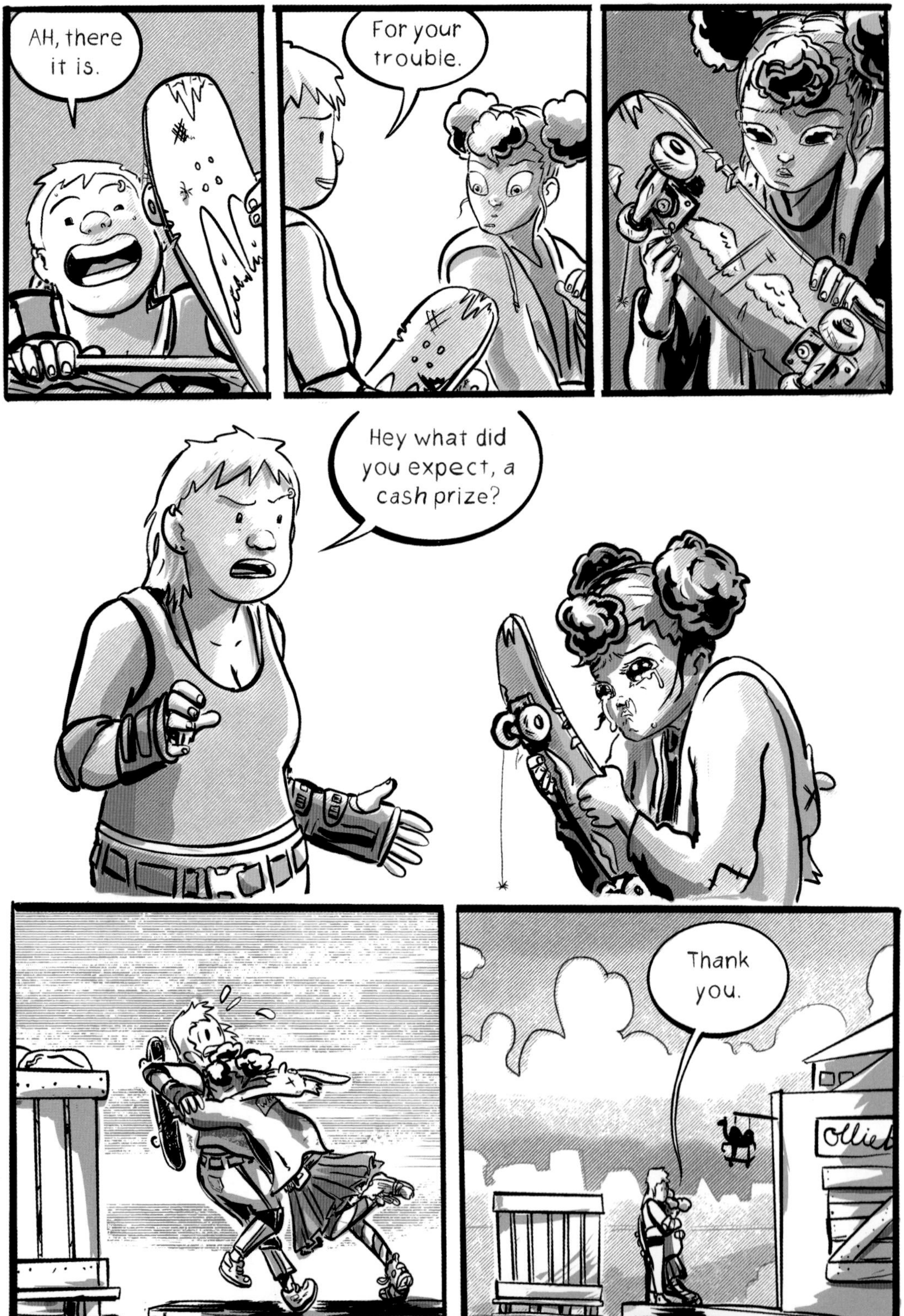
AH, there it is.
For your trouble.
Hey what did you expect, a cash prize?
Thank you.
Ollie

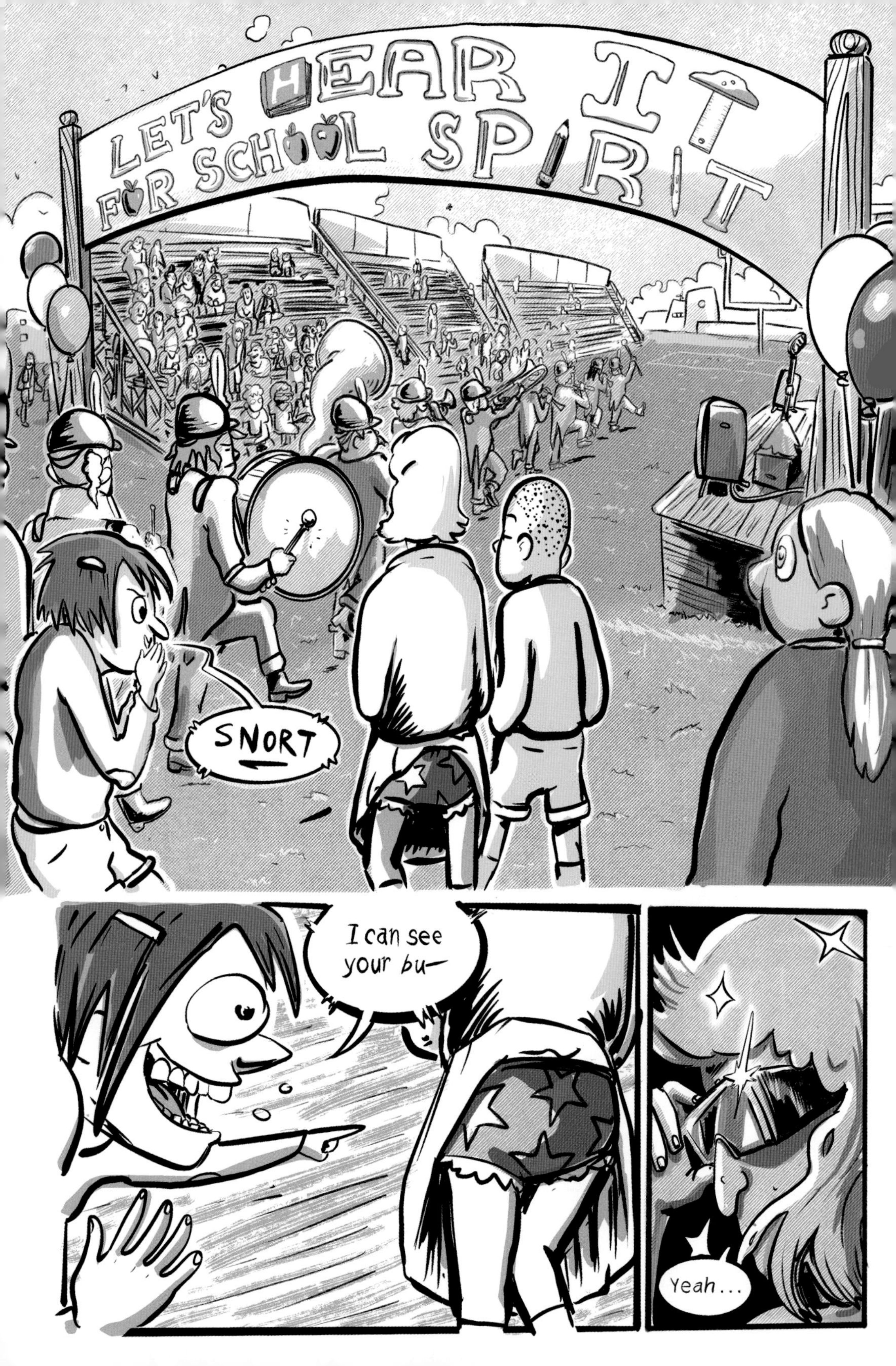
LET'S HEAR IT FOR SCHOOL SPIRIT
SNORT
I can see your bu—
Yeah...

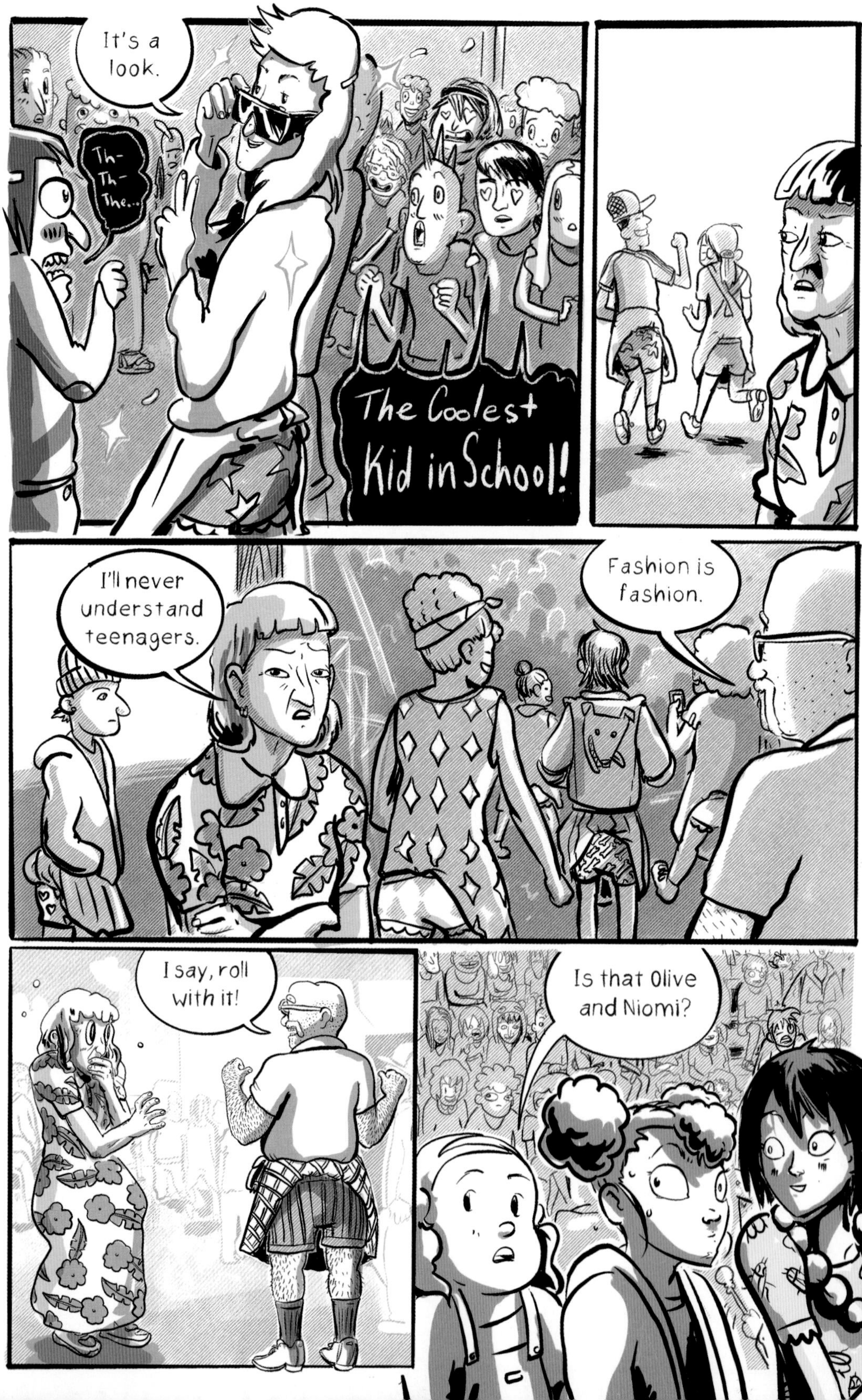
It's a look.
Th- Th- The...
The Coolest Kid in School!
I'll never understand teenagers.
Fashion is fashion.
I say, roll with it!
Is that Olive and Niomi?

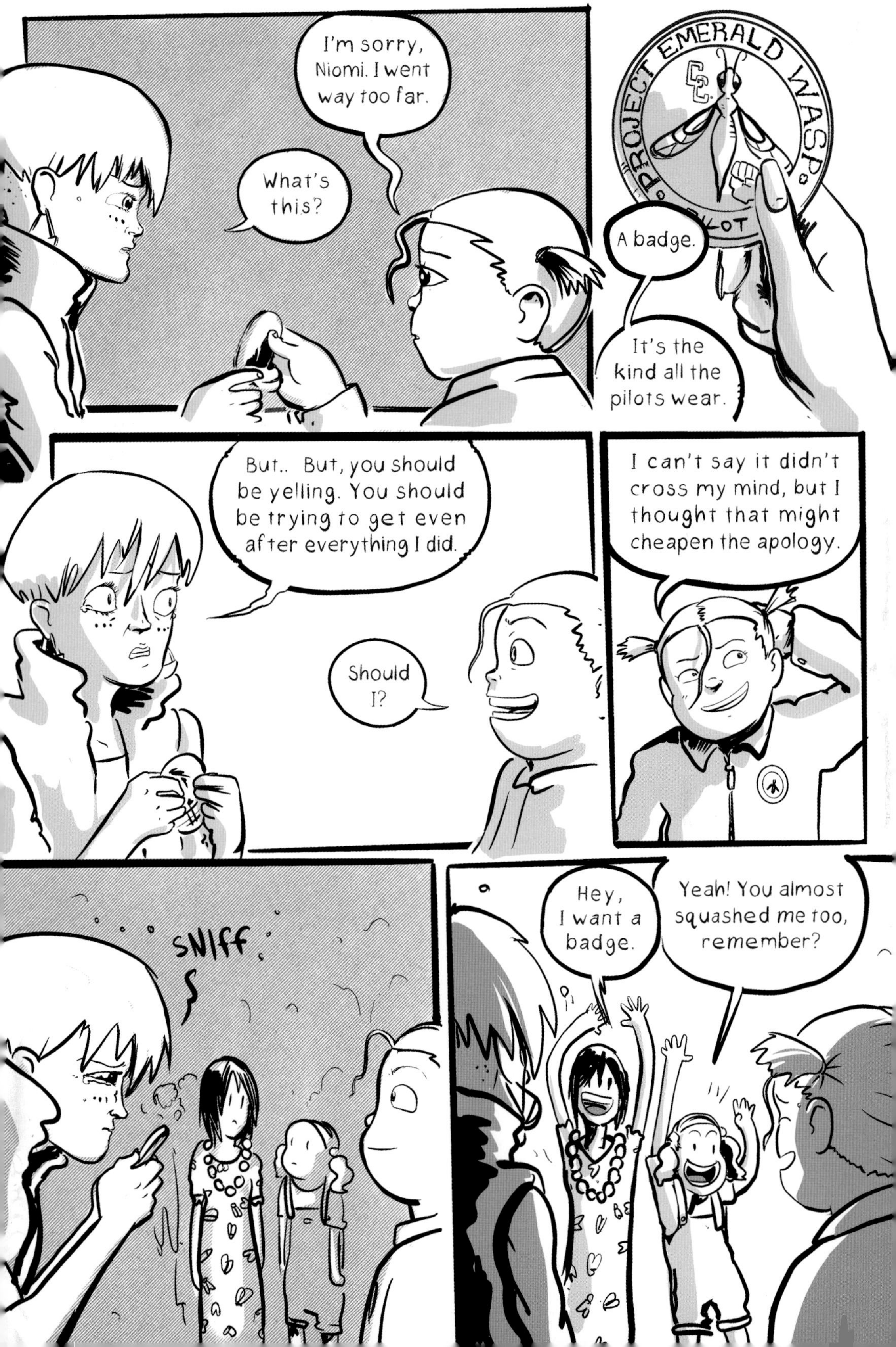
I'm sorry, Niomi. I went way too far.
What's this?
PROJECT EMERALD WASP PILOT
A badge.
It's the kind all the pilots wear.
But.. But, you should be yelling. You should be trying to get even after everything I did.
Should I?
I can't say it didn't cross my mind, but I thought that might cheapen the apology.
SNIFF
Hey, I want a badge.
Yeah! You almost squashed me too, remember?

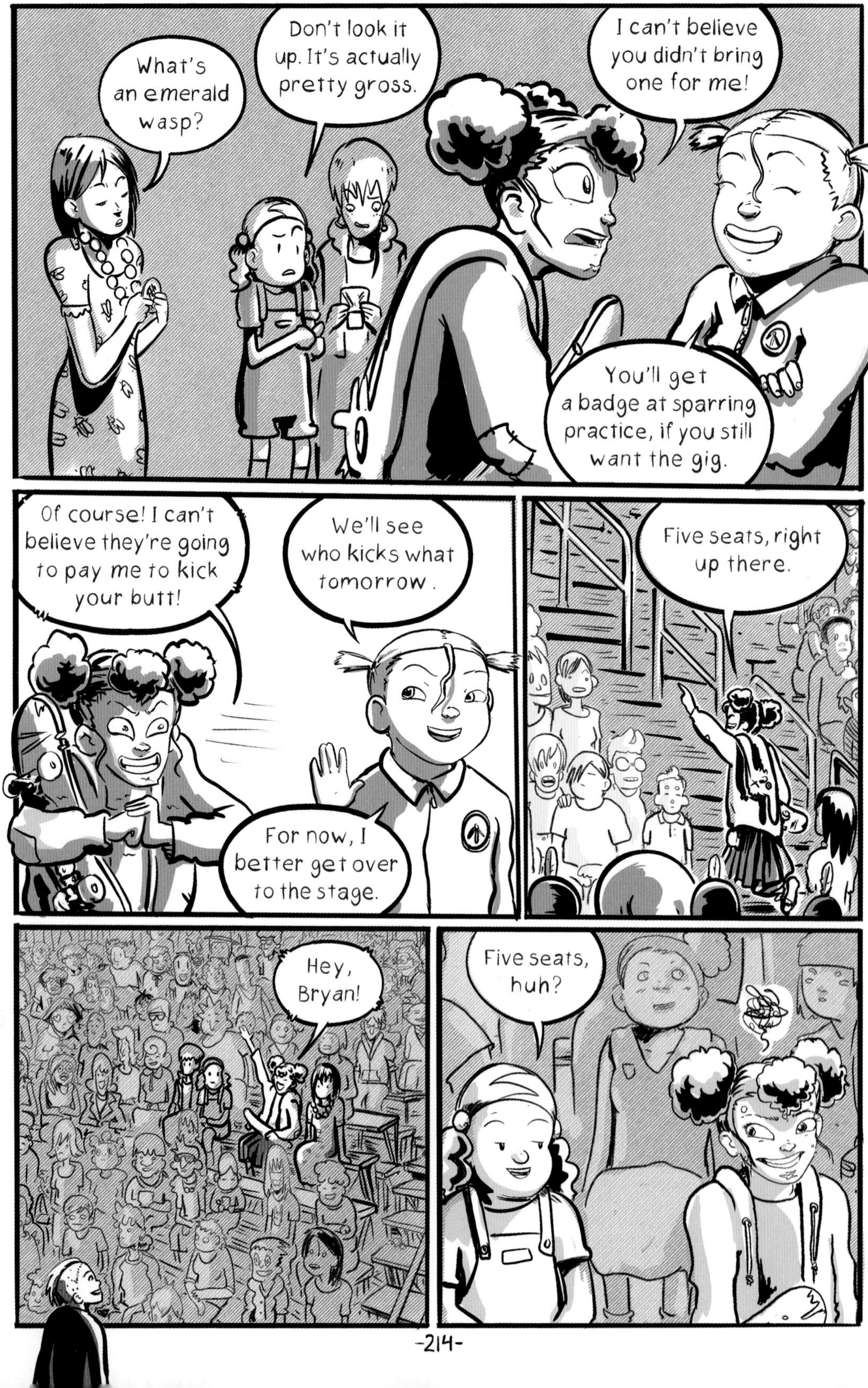
What's an emerald wasp?
Don't look it up. It's actually pretty gross.
I can't believe you didn't bring one for me!
You'll get a badge at sparring practice, if you still want the gig.
Of course! I can't believe they're going to pay me to kick your butt!
We'll see who kicks what tomorrow.
For now, I better get over to the stage.
Five seats, right up there.
Hey, Bryan!
Five seats, huh?

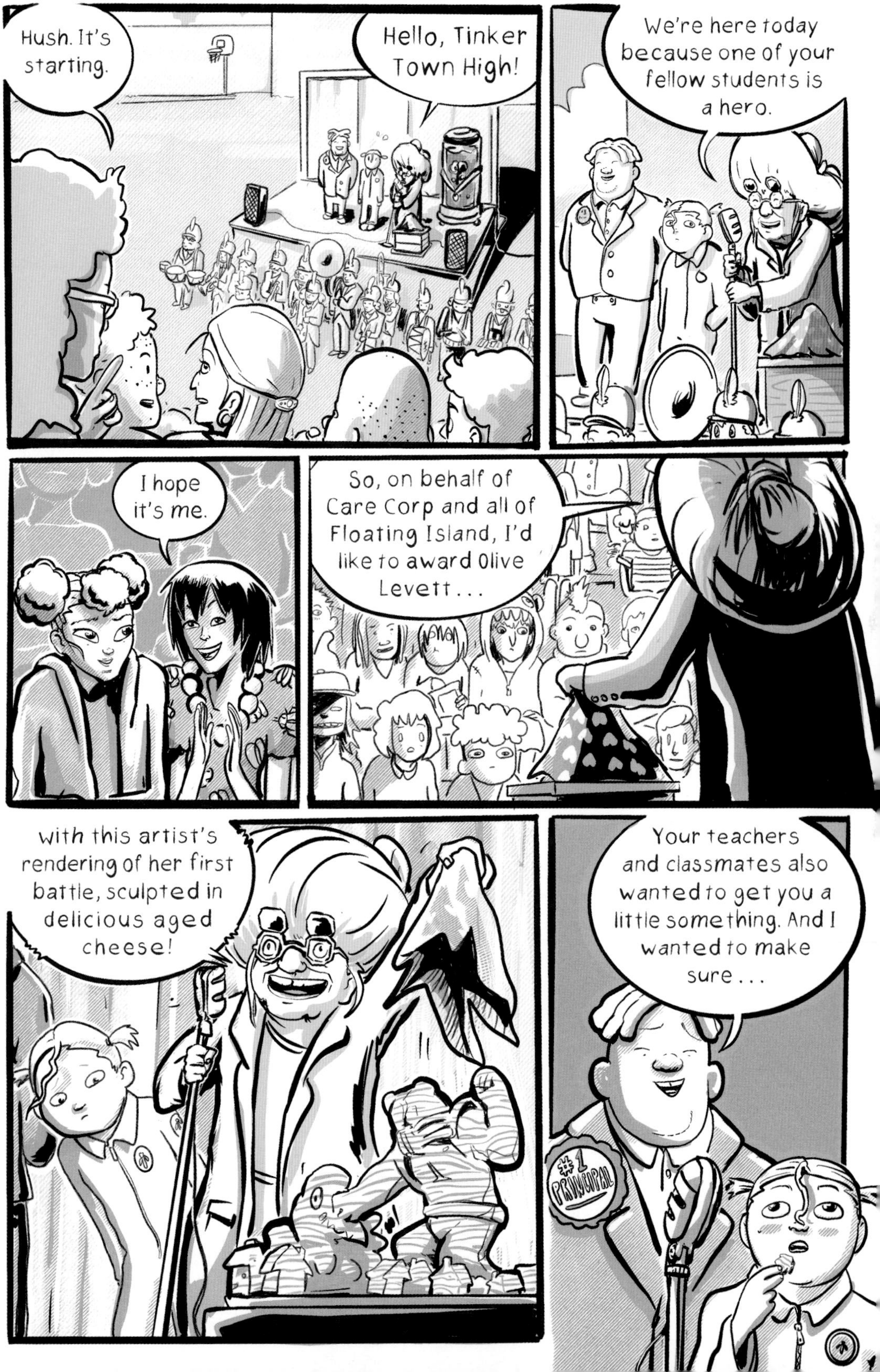
Hush. It's starting.
Hello, Tinker Town High!
We're here today because one of your fellow students is a hero.
I hope it's me.
So, on behalf of Care Corp and all of Floating Island, I'd like to award Olive Levett . . .
with this artist's rendering of her first battle, sculpted in delicious aged cheese!
Your teachers and classmates also wanted to get you a little something. And I wanted to make sure . . .
#1 PRINCIPAL

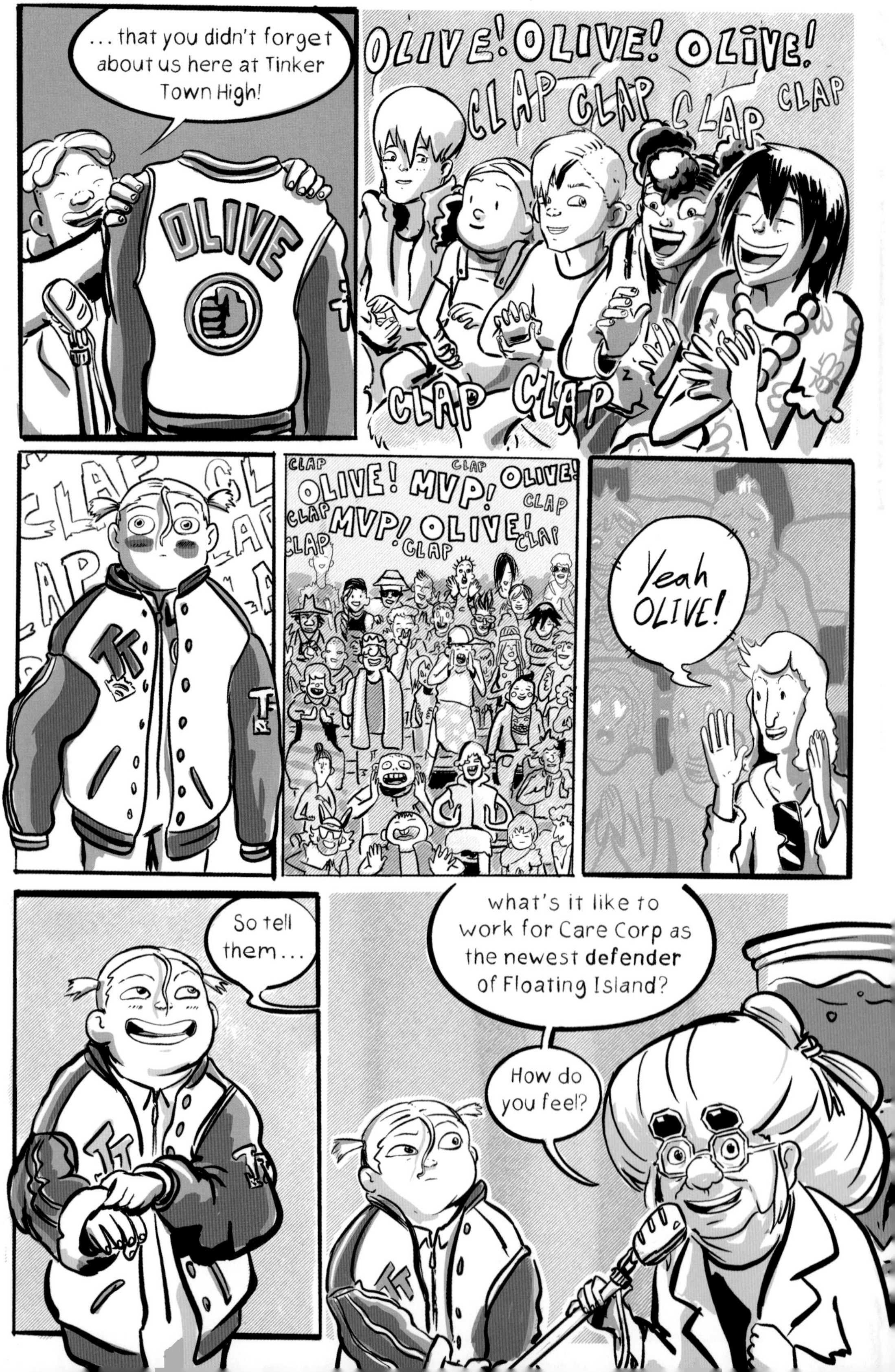

... that you didn't forget about us here at Tinker Town High!
OLIVE
OLIVE! OLIVE! OLIVE!
CLAP CLAP CLAP CLAP
CLAP CLAP
CLAP
OLIVE! MVP! OLIVE!
CLAP
MVP! OLIVE!
CLAP CLAP CLAP CLAP
Yeah OLIVE!
So tell them...
what's it like to work for Care Corp as the newest **defender** of Floating Island?
How do you feel?

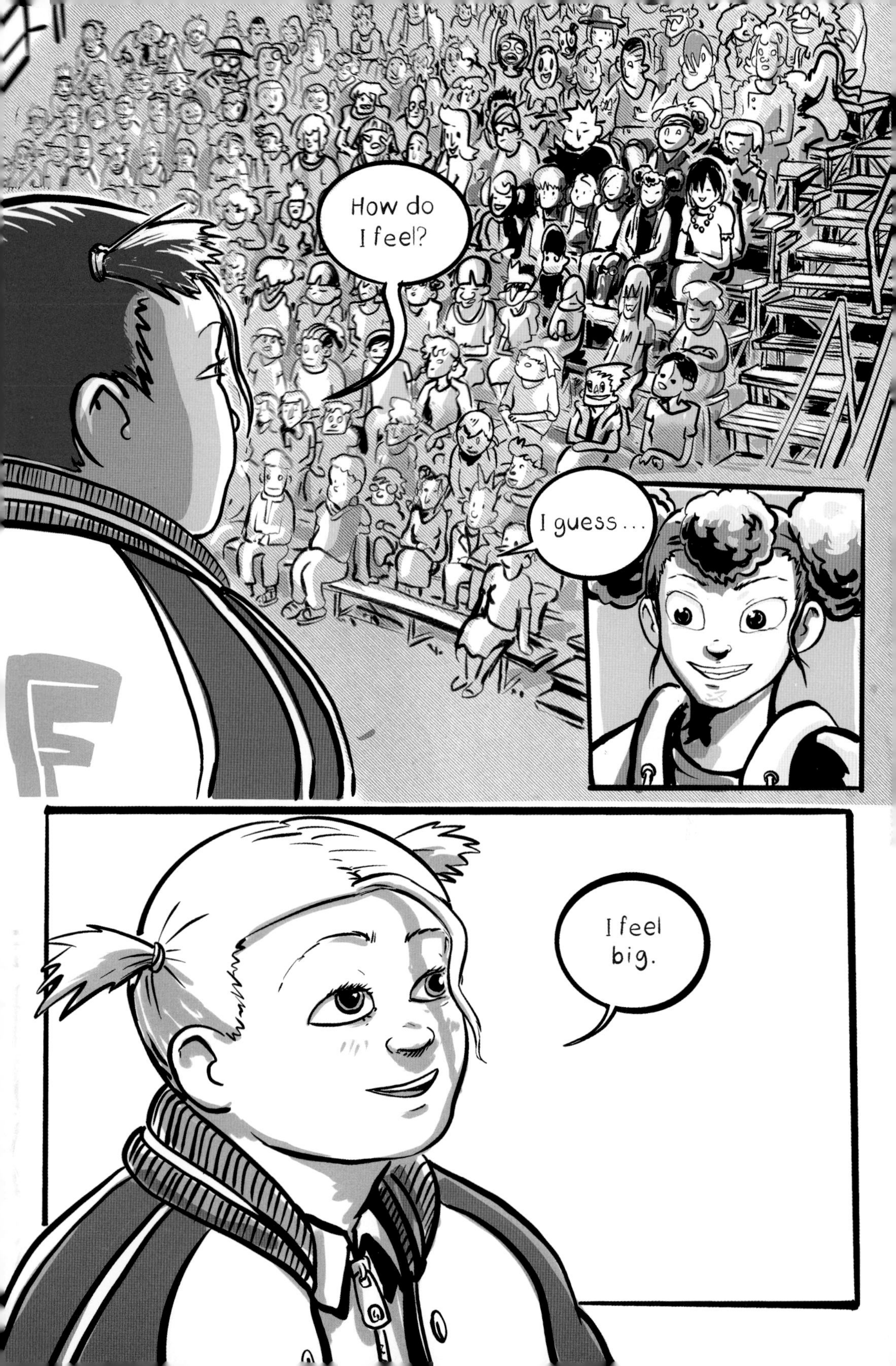
How do I feel?
I guess . . .
I feel big.

Dear Reader,

Thank you for reading comics when you could be watching videos, riding bikes, or hunting hobgoblins with your friends. If you enjoyed this one, consider writing a short honest online review—it helps people like you find out about our friends, the Cloud Townies, Pen and Olive.

I wrote this book as I traveled the United States living in a van and drew it in Oakland, California. Thank you to Kate Horsting, my travel and life partner, for always making room for me, my dog, and my drawing desk. Thanks to everyone who gave us a place to park and use the bathroom on our travels. A special shout-out to FreeCampsites.net and LittleXLittle Farms! Thank you to Brennan Robinson, who gave us a place to work in Oakland before we even had a place to live.

Thank you to my agent, Ed Maxwell, and editor, Charlotte Greenbaum, who both fought for this book to become a reality. Thank you to the Pittsburgh Foundation and Heinz Endowment for supporting artists like me and helping me begin the exploration of this story along with the Imagine Butte Resource Center. Thanks to everyone who gave me feedback as I tinkered with the basic elements of this book, especially Jim Rugg—if you liked the skateboarding segments of this book, look up his comic *Street Angel*. Thank you, Nathan Kukulski, my great friend and much-needed first-round copy editor. Thank you to my family—Zoe, Patt, and Kevin McCloskey—all of whom are talented artists and storytellers in their own right.

Thank you to all of my writer/comix friends who helped me get better and work harder by sharing their opinions and energy. Special shouts to Dr. Tameka Cage Conley, Nate McDonough, Nilz Hanczar, Laura Brun, Tyler McAndrew, and Yona Harvey. Thank you to all the wonderful comic shops and bookstores that carry indie books and zines, especially Bill Boichel of the Copacetic Comics Company, who has been watering the garden of Pittsburgh comics creation for decades.

So many people have helped me get where I am that I couldn't possibly name them all, and you are one of them.

Thank you.

Daniel McCloskey